"SUPERB . . . I enjoyed *Bard* enormously. Not only about a bard, it is also written by a bard."
—ANDREW M. GREELEY

"Superb characterization and fascinating descriptions of ancient Celtic civilization. *Bard* will appeal to fantasy buffs as well as to readers of historical fiction."
—SCHOOL LIBRARY JOURNAL

"A stunning novel that brilliantly evokes the times and the people . . . a full-bodied historical novel sure to be savored by many."
—BOOKLIST

"The most intriguing of [Llywelyn's] warrior/mystic/romance concoctions."
—KIRKUS

"She brings the legends of Ireland to life and presents us with characters who are living, breathing individuals, with all the strengths and weaknesses of the humans who walk the earth today."
—IRISH ECHO

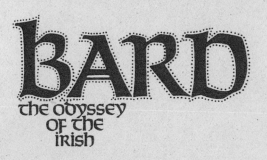

BARD
the odyssey of the irish

MORGAN LLYWELYN

BARD

THE ODYSSEY OF THE IRISH

TOR

A TOM DOHERTY ASSOCIATES BOOK

BARD

The Robert Graves quotation on page 459 is reprinted by permission of Farrar, Straus & Giroux, Inc. Excerpt from *The White Goddess* by Robert Graves. Copyright © 1948 by International Authors N.V. Renewed © 1975 by Robert Graves.

Reprinted by arrangement with Houghton Mifflin Company

First Tor printing: March 1987

A TOR Book

Published by Tom Doherty Associates, Inc.
49 West 24 Street
New York, N.Y. 10010

Cover art by Don Maitz

ISBN: 0-812-58515-1
CAN. ED.: 0-812-58516-X

Library of Congress Catalog Card Number: 84-6645

Printed in the United States of America

0 9 8 7 6 5 4 3 2 1

For
CHARLES
my hero
and
in loving memory of my mother
HENRI LLYWELYN PRICE
a bard who has gone adventuring

He was a harp; all life that he had known and that was his consciousness was the strings; and the flood of music was a wind that poured against those strings and set them vibrating with memories and dreams ... Past, present, and future mingled; and he went on oscillating across the broad, warm world, through high adventure and noble deeds to Her—ay, and with her, winning her, his arm about her, and carrying her on in flight across the empery of his mind.

—Jack London, *Martin Eden*

NOTES ON PRONUNCIATION

The author is indebted to Kenneth E. Nilsen, Ph.D. in Celtic Studies, Harvard University, and instructor in Irish in both the United States and Ireland, for his invaluable contribution in providing the archaic Celtic pronunciations for this book.

The Irish language apparently underwent a series of major changes between the fifth and seventh centuries A.D., evolving from an ancient derivative of the continental Celtic mother-tongue into the language scholars today call Old Irish. But that earlier form of the language is nearest the one spoken by the Celtic tribes in this book and is also easier for non-Irish speakers to pronounce. Therefore, I have used this primitive precursor of Irish with modified phonetic spellings for the names of Gaelic characters throughout *Bard*.

In the archaic tongue, stress usually falls on the first syllable. *C* is always pronounced like the letter *k*. *G* is always hard. *Ch* is pronounced as in the German *ach*. *Gh* is a soft guttural. Unstressed vowels generally have a sound similar to the *a* in sofa.

Amergin is pronounced almost as spelled, Ah´-mer-gĭn. An accented É is pronounced "ay," so *Éremón* is Āy´-rā-mōn, showing also the accented long *ó*. An accented Í is pronounced "ee"; thus *Míl* is Meel, *Ír* is Eer, *Ítos* is Eetos.

Other Gaelic names are pronounced as follows: *Éber Finn*—Āy-ber Finn; *Donn*—Dŭnn; *Colptha*—Kolp´-thăh; *Irial*—Irr´-ee-ăl; *Nial*—Neel; *Breoghan*—Bray´-o-ghăn; *Conmael*—Kon´-mĭle; *Ferdinón*—Fer´-di-nōn; *Odba*—Od´-bă; *Lugaid*—Loog´-id.

For the names of the *Túatha Dé Danann* (Too´-a-hah Day Dăn´-ănn), I have used the customary spellings from Irish legend. *Greine* would be pronounced Gray´-neh in the archaic Celtic tongue, however; *Eriu* would be Ayr´-yoo before time transmuted her name to *Erin;* *Cuill* was probably called Koo´-l, and *Cet* was pronounced Kāyt. As for *Ierne*, that fabled name from the maps of Greek geographers more than two thousand years ago, I suggest the pronunciation of I-yearn. It seems singularly appropriate.

IERNE

ALBION

FIR MORCA

the odyssey of the irish

GAUL

GALICIANS

ASTURIANS

IBERIA

TARTESSIANS

CARTAGENA

MEDITERRANEAN SEA

PILLARS
OF HERAKLES

CARTHAC

NOTE: ALL OF AFRICA WAS CALLED - LIBYA

◇ **1** ◇

SEE A TALL MAN pacing alone on the twilight beach, caught between the dying day and the incoming tide. Smell the moist air, heavy with salt. Hear the lapping of waves slapping the shore, the hiss of their withdrawal, their rushing return. Tide flirting with sand, seducing, inviting, whispering tales from beyond the dark sea.

Dark sea, fading light, and an old familiar restlessness combined to haunt Amergin the bard. All his life he had suffered an itch in his soul, a formless yearning that blew toward him on the north wind. The green wind, he named it to himself, for to Amergin it seemed laden with verdant aromas from some fair otherworld existing only in his imagination. Yet the north wind persisted in torturing him with hints of that achingly beautiful and unreal land, his heart's home.

Amergin had never felt truly at home anywhere, even inside his own skin. Tonight the mood was particularly strong, driving him to stalk the beach and endure his melancholy with gritted teeth.

For once Clarsah did not ride his shoulder. Evening wind off the sea could damage the voice of a harp. But in a way Clarsah was always with him, for she was an intimate part of the man, her music constantly in his thoughts. In the gradually deepening twilight he began trying to capture the essence of the songs he heard on the wind and shape them to fit the harp's capabilities.

But tonight the ocean seemed to be a sentient presence, willfully intruding on his efforts at composition. He found himself gazing toward the horizon again and again, as if he expected to see . . . what? Some goddess shaped from waves and foam to dispel his loneliness?

Lust flickered through Amergin, random as heat lightning. He shook his head, wryly amused at himself. Even a

1

druid's vision could not see a goddess where none existed, or summon the spirit of the ocean herself and clothe her in flesh for his pleasure. Druid vision, like druid talent, was a sometime thing, not under a man's control. Its occurrence and usage were chosen by the spirits for their own communication. Amergin, bard and druid, understood this all too well.

Yet Amergin the man still longed to grasp his elusive gift firmly and use it, somehow, to shape something better . . .

He paused and bent to strip off his sandals, knotting their thongs together so he could sling them over his shoulder. He had an urge to walk barefoot and let the damp, sunwarmed sand ooze between his toes.

He watched a lace of foam run up the beach and skitter back, glowing with hoarded luminosity. What was the source of such light and how was it held? he wondered. The tide painted serpentines on the sand and he bent to study them, curious to know what artisan had designed such graceful patterns and taught the sea to reproduce them. Amergin felt the glamour of a mystery beyond even druid knowledge and wished there were someone to whom he could express his thoughts. But he was singularly alone.

When he was a small child, enthusiasm had bubbled up in him like a wellspring and he reached out to everyone, trying to touch, eager to share. Each new discovery of beauty or wonder delighted the young Amergin almost beyond bearing. But when he tugged at the nearest arm—"Look, oh, *look!*"— his clanspeople pulled away impatiently, or offered him the polite patronization adults substitute for interest. They assumed the little boy's excitement would fade when the spirit newly housed in his body grew accustomed to the world around it.

But for Amergin that never happened. The rebuff of busy adults drove him back behind a shield of shyness, hiding his vulnerability. He learned the lesson early: if you cared too much, if you opened yourself too far, you got hurt.

Among the garrulous Gaelicians he became notable for his quietness. His brothers teased him unmercifully for a time, accusing him of having been born with his jaws locked together. When he endured their taunts with unfailing good humor they at last quit teasing the little boy and went in search of more responsive targets.

Many seasons would pass before the great spirit demanded that Amergin fight free of self-consciousness and speak up boldly, risking rejection and misunderstanding. Life forces weakness to give way to strength; it is the Law.

Now, as a trained bard, he still recalled the intensity of those early emotions and longed to communicate them to others, to bring to life with his poetry radiant realms transcending mere survival. His soul was nourished by beauty; his spirit was drawn to mystery. A bard's art must somehow harness both.

The task was not easy. There were dark days when he sweated and struggled and swore over one slippery phrase that would not come right; sleepless nights when he feared his skill would never equal his desire. Last night had been sleepless and today had seemed dark, though the summer sun shone. Still Amergin sensed the brooding weight of a storm beyond the rim of the world, heightening his restlessness, driving him to prowl the beach and . . .

"What?" he cried aloud, startled. He froze in midstride, staring northward beyond the sea, beyond the rim of the world. An urgent summons came winging to him on the green wind, shocking him like a lightning bolt. A powerful presence . . . not imagined but unbearably real! . . . was calling to him, reaching out to him from beyond the farthest horizon.

He could not move except to lift his arms in reply, stretching them wordlessly as he stared transfixed beyond limits of human vision. No seafoam goddess, this, created from restlessness and the body's fever-dreams; whatever called Amergin was irresistibly alive and as compelling as the tide.

His soul rose into his throat, aching to answer.

The bard was so intent on whatever beckoned from beyond the ninth wave that he was blind to the sea before him. Yet at last his brain forced him to recognize objects his eyes had been ignoring. Ships.

A fleet!

Their intruding reality shattered the spell and he found himself staring in disbelief at a line of merchant galleys, battered and beaten, limping toward the harbor beyond the headland.

Amergin could hardly believe he was seeing traders arriving again after so many seasons. He rubbed his eyes but when he looked again the ships were still there, struggling closer. The oars swam through air and water in a ragged rhythm betraying the weariness of the oarsmen. The vessels seemed close to foundering in increasingly heavy surf.

3

The bard gasped and began to run. He must reach a point where he could wade into the sea and pull out survivors if the galleys went onto the rocks; failing that, he would have to get to his clan's stronghold on the headland as quickly as possible and summon help. There was suddenly so much to do and so little time!

Yet even as he ran, anger ran with him. The traders were coming at the most inopportune time for him. Their arrival had broken a vital connection between Amergin and whatever it was that called him on the green wind, and it hurt.

It hurt terribly.

The source of the green wind was far to the north. The current of living air lay like a broad band across the sea, stretching from Amergin's coast all the way to a large island of mountains and meadows and sweetwatered rivers.

Water, water, running water. Shinann was always drawn to the sound of running water, water going somewhere. Somewhere in the past or the future, perhaps, and time a stream you could wade into and then step out of on any curve of the bank you chose.

So the teachers had taught.

The sun had dropped below the rim of the world but the sky was still as filled with light as a plum with juice. The woman loitered along the riverbank, lifting her skirts to her thighs and wading into the shallows, kicking the water playfully to make it pronounce her name, "Shi-*nahn*, Shi-*nahn*," for the golden gorse on the opposite bank.

The small woman paused and cocked her head, listening. She thought she heard an echo of something other than the voice of the river, a sound like that of a stringed instrument. The wind harping through the trees, perhaps. Yet the music it made was like none she knew, with a compelling quality that drew her to seek its source, calling out to the unseen musician. Looking southward, she waded deeper into the water, stepping confidently, very much in her element. Water, water, running water.

And sudden sharp pain! Something hidden in the riverbottom ooze slashed her bare foot and Shinann jerked back, shocked that a river would attack her without provocation.

She clambered onto the nearest bank, dragging her skirts through a mass of reeds. Settling down crosslegged, she

4

examined her injury in the fading light. Along her instep was a raggedly deep cut, welling blood.

Shinann frowned in concentration. The bleeding stopped.

She was a small woman, slender, with pale coppery hair streaming over her shoulders. Her eyes were the color of clear water. She was dressed in a soft robe caught around the waist with a twisted rope that glittered. Perhaps the rope was woven gold. Perhaps not.

A little woman with a curiosity out of all proportion to her size, Shinann had a questing nature that sent her back into the water in search of her attacker. She crouched down until only her head was above the surface, hair floating around her face like the petals of some fantastic flower. Then she took a deep breath and ducked to grope in the mud.

Her fingers closed on a shape alien to the natural debris of a watercourse. She worried the thing free and carried it to the riverbank. The last daylight revealed a bronze dagger nearly long enough to be called a shortsword, nicked and pitted but still radiating a palpable viciousness. The blade had been rippled in the forging to make an ugly wound going in, and an uglier wound coming out.

Shinann flung the thing aside while she wrung the water out of her gown. Then she picked it up again and examined it with interest, turning it over and over in her hands. Looking around, she caught sight of a lichen-covered boulder and struck the dagger a sharp blow against the stone, deftly calculating the exact point at which the blade could be snapped from the hilt.

The weapon broke apart with a loud crack and Shinann grinned like a mischievous child.

Holding the rippled blade balanced between her thumb and forefinger, she tipped her head back and sighted along an invisible arc, then hurled the weapon with all her strength. She watched it tumble through the air, silhouetted against the evening sky for a long distance until at last it fell and was lost in a tangle of briars.

Shinann then turned her attention to the dagger hilt. The bronze had been shaped to fit a man's grasp and decorated with an elaborate inlay of wide brass wire. Using her fingernails, she worked the wire free. The metal curled itself into a gleaming tendril in the palm of her hand. Shinann patiently rebent the wire into a flowerlike form and thrust its stem through her bodice. Beauty made her smile.

The wind was blowing harder now. She stood on the riverbank, listening again, but heard no trace of the mysterious music. Its absence filled her with longing. She held out both her arms, reaching across empty space. Then she shrugged, feeling a little foolish.

Tossing her hair out of her eyes, Shinann headed away from the river, toward the Gathering Place.

◇ **2** ◇

FROM HIS VANTAGE POINT on the northernmost tip of land Amergin was first of the Gaelicians to see the incoming fleet, yet his mind could scarcely accept the reality of their arrival. Merchants had once been an exciting element of his world but they had not played a part in it for many seasons now, and they never entered his dreams, where Amergin truly lived.

He was running as hard as he could along the narrow, sandy beach, trying to intersect the ships. The vessels were in a precarious situation. The square, painted sails identifying them as Phoenician galleys had already been lowered, due to a rising gale from the north, and the forty oarsmen propelling each cargo ship were struggling to hold to deep water. The wind threatened to drive them onto the rocks of the jutting Iberian headland. If they got safely past that point, a fine sandy harbor awaited them, but white crests were beginning to curl the waves and Amergin's green wind was howling hungrily.

The bard ran even faster, digging his toes into the sand for purchase. He scrambled over a tumble of boulders and onto another crescent of beach, waving his arms to try to get the attention of someone on board the ships. His trained voice shouted a great cry of encouragement no one could possibly hear.

On board the flagship of his merchant fleet, Commander Age-Nor noticed the man running along the beach and felt a small relief. If they broke up in this terrible place at the end of the world, at least their passing would be noticed.

From the shore, Amergin recognized the basic Phoenician design of the vessels, but he was also aware of details setting these newcomers apart from the Carthaginian galleys that once had sailed into these waters, in the seasons of his youth. Then he had spent long days at the harbor, wandering among foreign ships beached stern-first while cargoes were unloaded and loaded and trade arrangements were argued and re-argued. The air in those days had rung with the crude comments and lewd jests of the seamen, mixed crews drawn from Utica and Joppa and Sidra and all the points between. Short, swarthy men, typical of the peoples rimming the distant Mediterranean basin. Bitter men who had been recruited or bound or enslaved by the mighty trading empire that was Carthage of the Phoenicians.

As a boy, Amergin had listened openmouthed to their babble, struggling to understand their language so he could learn about the wondrous places from which they came.

Then the merchants started losing interest in trading with his tribe, and the big wooden galleys came less and less often to the harbor. Finally they stopped coming altogether. Fleets were still glimpsed from the headland, making the long voyage up the west coast of Iberia from southern seas, but they never stopped. And their loss was felt more deeply with every passing season . . . until this evening, and their miraculous return.

The last of the battered galleys rounded the point safely and the harbor opened out in front of them, allowing them to move into calmer waters, sheltered by the headland.

The tall man on the beach slowed to a walk and watched them pass by him. In the lingering summer twilight, he and the commander in the prow of the flagship gazed at each other across the water, but neither saw the other clearly.

Amergin moved with the swinging stride of a rangy man, lean as a racing hound. A long-jawed man with a gaunt and roughly hewn face. Vividly blue eyes, fringed by coarse black lashes, provided a startling note of color against his fair skin. The wind tousled his black hair and billowed his summerweight cloak to reveal a sinewy body clad only in a brief tunic, with faded knotwork embroidery around its hem.

He was not considered handsome by the standards of his people, but the passage of the seasons had blended the homely,

7

outsized features of his youth into a grave intensity more compelling than beauty. Now, like a solitary pine on a hilltop, he dominated the space around him. No one could ignore the presence of Amergin the bard.

The big galleys passed the curve of the headland and out of his vision, yet eddies of turbulence remained. Amergin was disturbed not only by the interruption of his mood, but by the momentous importance of the event itself. The arrival of the Sea People could mean a rebirth of prosperity or a final crushing loss of hope, if trade could not be reestablished. And Amergin, as a bard and therefore entrusted with knowing the history of his people, was very much aware that the position of the Gaelician tribe in the northwestern corner of the Iberian peninsula was, in its own way, as precarious as the situation of the storm-threatened fleet had been.

He turned and began searching for the nearest path leading up the cliff face from the beach. He must get to his clan's stronghold and spread the news so a delegation could be sent to welcome the Phoenicians, and the women could start roasting festival meats.

A stone turned under his naked foot. He raised one hand to his shoulder, but instead of knotted sandal thongs his fingers found only the bronze brooch fastening his cloak. The sandals were gone, then; slipped off somewhere as he ran after the ships. And there was no time to look for them now; the urgency of the moment was an irresistible force. Yet even so he paused briefly and looked back, though his eyes did not scan the dark beach for lost sandals. Instead, they sought the horizon, and a sweet ache rose in him, calling, beckoning . . .

He shook his head ruefully and plunged up the pathway toward the headland. Then he heard the sound of hooves.

Pounding, pounding, pounding! The young team pulling the chariot was green-broken and had not learned to spare themselves. They attacked the Earth as if she were an enemy instead of the Mother, and they would tire themselves out when more experienced horses were still unsweated. But Éremón was pleased with them. They were dark brown and glossy, a pleasing contrast to the crimson and saffron leather medallions affixed to the sides of his wicker war cart. They were a headstrong pair of young stallions who enjoyed a contest as much as Éremón enjoyed pitting his strength against theirs. The sons of the Míl generally scorned the use of a driver. Milesios had no charioteer, preferring to show off his horsemanship as yet another of his many skills, and those who would emulate him did likewise. Particularly his favorite, Ércmón, who strove to be the mirror of the great chieftain's mind.

Éremón leaned back, wrapping the reins around his brawny forearms and yelling for the joy of yelling, calling the colts by profane endearments that would have goaded a man to fighting frenzy.

"I'll eat you alive if you don't run faster, you lopeared drinkers of asses' milk! Run, you smallheaded wreckage picked out of the afterbirth!"

The horses, understanding that such phrases were not meant personally, pinned their ears against their heads and ran. They galloped with all their young strength, eager to be home after a long trip; and Éremón rode behind them, shouting, exulting, lashing them along the rising road.

The chariot leaped and jolted, and Éremón shifted his weight with it, adjusting without thought to the bucking of the vehicle. The wooden flooring was splintery beneath his feet but it gave secure footing; the cloud of dust raised by the horses filled his mouth with grit but made him feel alive. The world flashed by and he possessed it. He flung back his head and yelled, full-throated, a great tribal warcry born of lust for life.

Éremón began sawing on the reins reluctantly, fighting to slow his team. If they were still steaming when they reached the stronghold, someone—Colptha, undoubtedly, who always told—would run to Milesios about it, and the chieftain would not hesitate to accuse his favorite son of being a poor horseman. Would say it aloud in the Heroes' Hall where everyone could hear, and Éremón's brothers would snicker over their wine bowls and enjoy a victory over him. Particularly Éber Finn, who bragged endlessly of his skill with animals.

The roadway was empty. The fields above the sea were deserted in the gathering dusk. In the distance Éremón heard the clank of bronze cowbells and the hoarse cries of a youthful herder, sauntering home with his charges. The chariot horses trotted along an old pathway worn through yellow furze, amid a scattering of boulders. They passed narrow fields divided by rock walls sheltering patches of Celtic beans from the sea wind. Beside these plots, round stone cottages chinked with clay sent the welcoming gleam of firelight from their open doorways. Freemen called out in friendly voices and Éremón answered back cheerfully.

His stomach was growling, excited by the smells of cooking food in the cottages. The trestle tables in the Heroes' Hall would already be heaped with the evening meal, and the hounds of the Míl would be quarreling over scraps before he, Éremón, arrived and took his first bite. By the time he got there the women would probably be carrying away the remnants of the honeycakes.

Thinking of women reminded him of Odba. Odba, waiting for him, her tongue writhing with questions, her ears closed to answers. "Why did you stay away so long?" she would demand to know. "Why do you avoid me, Éremón? Answer me, Éremón!"

He reined the horses to a very slow walk. The young stallions jigged and pranced, snatching at their bits. They did not dread returning to a woman called Odba. To give them plenty of time to cool off he walked them well past the stronghold and out toward the headland—until he saw the traders' fleet arriving. Then he let out a great whoop of joy and whirled the team around, eager to race to the Heroes' Hall and deliver the news.

A figure suddenly materialized before him, rising up from the cliff path. The chariot horses shied and Éremón fought them to a snorting standstill. Then he recognized his brother.

"Ai, Amergin!" he cried. "Were you down on the beach? Did you see the fleet coming in?" He quickly wrapped the reins and jumped from the chariot to give the bard an exuberant punch on the shoulder. Éremón was as tall as Amergin, with eyes as blue, but he had inherited the ruddy gold hair and massive torso of their sire, Milesios. Éremón's shoulders bulged with muscle. Strong, blunt fingers habitually stroked his drooping mustache to call attention to its virile fullness. Only warriors flaunted such mustaches; other men of the Gaelician tribe were generally clean-shaven, like Amergin.

Éremón wore his powerful body with easy arrogance and enjoyed his occupation of it. He was an arm-waver and foot-stamper, a man who filled up space and cheerfully overflowed it. His voice was a merry bellow. "I always thought the traders would come back," he now claimed on a rising tide of optimism, pounding on his brother's arm again. "Are you on your way to the Heroes' Hall to tell them? I'll go with you and help you shout the news, and then I want to be sure they have some good cooked meat and fresh bread to take down to the ships in the harbor. The best of everything . . . plenty of drinking water, the sailors will be glad to see that . . . and wine . . . or do you suppose they'll be bringing us wine?'' He grinned.

"I hope they're bringing some brass wire for harp strings," Amergin replied. "My harp is growing desperate."

Éremón laughed. "We're all growing desperate for something, but the traders will fix that. Just think of it. No more making do with local substitutes—soon we'll have new metals for the craftsmen and new fabrics for the women to sew, eh?''

He peered at his brother through the growing darkness. "Are you afoot, Amergin?" he wanted to know. "Then get into my chariot and let's hurry to the hall. That storm will be blowing right in on us and I'll feel better when I know our visitors are well fed and have safe shelter."

Just at that moment a scream of wild laughter, out of control and devoid of mirth, rang across the headland like the shriek of some malignant spirit. Even the rising wind was not sufficient to drown out the chilling sound.

Amergin and Éremón exchanged glances.

"That was Ír," Éremón said unnecessarily.

Amergin nodded. "He's been . . . difficult . . . all day. You know Letis, wife of Merdith the herder?''

"I know her," Éremón said with a chuckle. "A spirited woman with bold hands. Once, while I was trying to harness break a colt, Letis sneaked up behind me and ran her hands under my tunic. We had a wonderful romp on the grass, but my horse ran away and broke his harness. Now there's a woman for you, Amergin. But go on, what were you saying about Ír?''

"Shortly after midday Ír intercepted Letis at one of the wells and upset her so badly her husband won't let her serve in the hall anymore. He may ask the brehons for a judgment against our clan."

Éremón whistled. "Merdith must be offended if he's willing to forgo a share of leavings from the Heroes' Hall. What does Milesios say about this?''

"He passed it off as a joke. Whatever Ír did left the woman shuddering and almost speechless, but Milesios just clapped our brother on the shoulder and said he was a great man for the women. If the brehons award Meredith an eric the Míl will no doubt pay it and forget the whole matter."

"I swear by the wind! Amergin, has the chief gone blind? Ír's become as unpredictable as a mountain flood, and he's likely to cost us more than one eric if something isn't done about him."

"What would you suggest doing? Milesios will never admit anything is wrong with him," the bard said. "No child of his can be less than perfect."

"Ír's no child; he's a blooded warrior with children of his own and a wife who's begun to watch him out of the corners of her eyes. When he has one of his spells he might kill us all in our beds—and that wife of mine would hold me down for him so he could take my head."

"Nonsense," Amergin said briskly. "Ír would never harm one of his own clan, and you misjudge Odba."

"I live with her; I know her better than anybody. She's one trouble and Ír is another. If he keeps on as he's going, someone will suggest the Míl's entire bloodline is tainted. A tribal chieftain has to be unblemished, and his blood free of such flaws as . . . as madness. When the time comes to elect a successor to the Míl his sons could be disregarded altogether and the new leader chosen from another clan entirely, Amergin. The next man to sit on our father's bench could be Ferdinón, or Brego. And it should be me!"

Éremón heard the ring of vehemence in his own words, threw back his head, and laughed. "Listen to me, I sound as greedy as a rutting boar. Hold—do you hear that? A pipe on the headland?"

Amergin listened. "It's the summons for the clan," he said. "Someone else must have carried news of the traders' arrival to the stronghold. We had better hurry to the Heroes' Hall. I am needed to sing of the ships and the sea and let those who were not on the headland tonight see this event through my eyes."

"Get in my chariot, then," Éremón urged. "It's been many seasons since I've taken my brother the bard for a ride."

Éremón's whip sang out and the horses leaped forward. Amergin grabbed for the rim of the cart and held on. Éremón drove hard and fast, as he did most things, and the cart swayed and jounced violently.

They followed the cliffside road until it veered into an

12

arrangement of standing stones positioned like soldiers on guard, unevenly spaced to break up any potential attack force. Showing off for Amergin, Éremón wheeled his team back and forth between the stones, which were only faint glimmers in the darkness. An iron wheel-hub struck one, sending out a shower of sparks and rocking the chariot violently, but, roaring with laughter, Éremón never drew rein. Then they were thundering through a narrow gateway in a stone wall atop an earthwork embankment, and the sights and sounds of a Celtic stronghold welcomed them.

"I have to get my harp before I go to the hall," Amergin shouted in his brother's ear. Without slowing the team, Éremón shoved the bard from the chariot at the doorway to his dwelling and whirled away, still laughing.

Amergin's house was one of a cluster of stone buildings lining the inner perimeter of the protective embankment. At the center loomed the granite bulk of the Heroes' Hall, proclaiming this as the fortress of a tribal chieftain rather than the simple ring-fort of a minor cattle lord.

One brief spattering of raindrops slanted ahead of the wind, forming tiny cups in the dust. Normally a coast of mist and rain, the place was now thoroughly dried out by seasons remarkable for their drought. The rain stopped almost as soon as it began, leaving only a tantalizing scent of damp earth.

Amergin ducked inside his doorway and called the harp's name, the secret soul name that every harp possesses and no man tells another, for the secrets of the spirit are private.

"Clarsah," Amergin murmured, with love.

When he emerged from his house a short time later, the harp rode his shoulder. She was tucked safely in her protective leather satchel, which was carved and gilded in her honor. Supple thongs held the instrument in place, for a harp accompanied her bard almost everywhere and must be assured of safe travel. Yet even through the leather Amergin could feel her, and as always, that touch reassured him.

As the bard walked toward the Heroes' Hall his clansmen ran past him, shouting happily to one another of the ships in the harbor. "Traders!" someone cried. "New goods from the south, and iron, and grain . . ."

"What do we have to trade for them?" a more practical voice asked. "The tin mines are almost exhausted; we get hardly enough for our own needs now. That's why the Carthaginians quit coming seasons ago."

13

"Milesios will have an answer," a third Gaelician said. "He is the head of the tribe; he always knows what to do."

The bard entered the Heroes' Hall between monolithic doorposts carved with Celtic knotwork. A high peaked roof soared above him, surfaced with wooden shingles instead of the less prestigious thatch used elsewhere as roofing material. The trunks of entire pine trees, elaborately carved and inlaid with copper and brass and silver, supported this roof, and between these pillars openfronted waist-high stalls served as personal compartments for the sons of the Míl and the clan-chiefs of the tribe.

Wooden benches assigned to warriors of lesser rank filled the remaining floor space around the central hearth. Against the walls were seats provided for prominent celsine, or clients, the clan-chiefs of subjugated neighboring tribes. These celsine had placed themselves under the Míl's protection and rendered in turn agreed payments, such as the tin they mined. The chieftains of Celtic tribes like the Gaelicians cultivated numbers of celsine, thus adding to their own wealth and prestige without forcing any sacrifice of either liberty or dignity on the part of their clients. Celsine remained free men and were able to terminate the agreement whenever they wished, though few did so. Protection by a warlord as powerful as the Míl was a valued asset.

The interior walls of the hall were blackened and shiny with smoke. Pine-knot torches thrust into iron holders provided pools of amber light at intervals; passing through these pools of light Amergin moved from shadow to shadow, as if between worlds.

He sniffed the familiar smells of pine pitch and human sweat and roasted meat. He stepped aside to make way for attendants carrying a tray laden with food prepared in the cooking house beyond the hall. The freemen of the tribe considered it a high honor to serve the warrior aristocracy, and the wives and daughters of carpenters and stonemasons and metalsmiths, herders and carters and shepherds, vied with one another in serving with grace and vivacity. Even the daughter of the most skilled craftsman, a rank only slightly below that of warrior, might be seen carrying a slab of roast ox to some acclaimed hero and gladly claiming the leavings for her mother's cooking pot.

All were aware that the reputation of the warriors kept their tribal holdings secure. It had been many seasons since one of the other Celtic tribes in the region had dared a major invasion of Gaelician territory.

At the center of the hall, facing the entrance, was the bronze-sheathed bench of the leader of the tribe, the indomitable Milesios. The great chieftain had answered to another name once, but he had been the Míl, the term for undisputed tribal champion, for so long now that everyone simply referred to him as Milesios. In his prime, no man in the entire region had been able to defeat him in single combat. His prowess had not only earned him the leadership of his people, but the Gaelicians had also voted to award him the belt of the champion for life, an unprecedented gesture of respect. For the rest of his days Milesios would wear at his waist the heavy golden ornament with its Celtic interlace, and other men would regard him with envy and awe, knowing his reputation was so far beyond challenge he no longer had to defend it.

As Amergin entered, Milesios had just taken his seat. Although the usual evening meal would be served, on this night food was secondary to the urgency of the situation. The tribe must be quickly organized and plans made to deal with the unexpected windfall of traders—yet Milesios secretly wished it had happened some other time. Some other night, when the ache in his bones was not so relentless. He sat slumped on his bench and gazed across his hall with weary eyes. "This will be a long night," he said to no one in particular.

A weighty gold torc encircled a scrawny neck that had once been as thick as a bull's, and more rings of gold and electrum and bronze were clustered on the chieftain's fingers. Milesios was past the age when a man proudly displayed naked muscular legs; his thinning shanks were hidden by woolen leggings bound with thongs. Over an embroidered tunic of cloth-of-Egypt the Míl wore a heavy red-and-green checkered cloak more suitable to the chill of Imbolc than a summer night, but even so he sometimes shivered.

No bodyguard was allowed to embarrass Milesios by hovering near him, for was he not the champion? Yet a night's feasting was invariably interrupted by quarrels as quick and hot as fires in dry grass. For this reason, Milesios had long ago ordered that weapons be left stacked outside the hall, and men and women entered armed only with tongue and fists, and a plain knife for cutting meat.

The Míl looked up as Amergin shouldered his way through

his clansmen toward the place of honor traditionally reserved for bards. Milesios squinted at his son through the haze of smoke and gave him a brief ceremonial nod, but offered no gesture of personal recognition or fatherly affection.

Amergin had long ago quit expecting either.

The bard's brothers, with one exception, were already in their compartments, their voices adding to the general roar of excitement. "Where is Ír?" Donn was asking Éber Finn. "I heard him shriek out a while ago, but he hasn't come to the hall yet."

"If he doesn't come, so much the better," Éremón called out to them. "We have enough to handle without him."

Milesios forced himself to sit erect. "Be quiet, all of you," he ordered, but his voice was thready and did not carry. He glanced impatiently toward the bard and Amergin immediately took Clarsah from her case and strummed her strings. At the harp's command, silence descended on the hall. The assembled throng of the Míl's family—blood, marriage, and foster-kin, comprising the largest single clan in the tribe— grew quiet and waited respectfully for the words of their patriarch.

Milesios thought about standing up to address them, but was not very enthusiastic about the idea. "Our sentries bring word of a fleet of traders from some Phoenician city called Tyre," he announced, "and their emissaries will visit us here tomorrow to discuss trade. As clan of the chieftain, those of you here tonight will have the responsibility for dealing with the Sea People and seeing that all goes well."

"Aren't you going to conduct the trading negotiations yourself?" called an alarmed voice from the women's balcony, a separate timbered compartment running the length of the hall above the seats of the celsine. The Míl's wife leaned down from the balcony, her forehead furrowed.

"Of course, of course;" Milesios said wearily, waving his hand with a rather vague gesture that his wife did not find reassuring. "But I think my sons should start playing a larger part in tribal affairs. One of them will undoubtedly succeed me one day, not only as chief of this clan but perhaps even as chief of the tribe. It's time they started getting experience in acting on behalf of all the Gaelicians, so they will be ready."

His wife, Scotta, sat back down at this, finding his logic inarguable, but Donn just as quickly stood up. "I was first born," he reminded his father.

Éremón was on his feet at once. "Leadership has nothing to do with order of birth. Leadership goes to the strongest!"

Éber Finn immediately tried to outshout both of them, making his own claims, and even Colptha joined in, demanding recognition. Scotta in her balcony and Milesios on his bench exchanged amused glances, acknowledging the choleric but basically good-natured wrangling that had become second nature to their sons since early childhood.

Only Amergin kept silent, lounging on his bench with the harp in his hands. Scotta, who had promised herself she would never make her husband's mistake and show favoritism, nevertheless found herself looking at him rather than at his quarreling brothers. When everyone else was yelling the bard seemed most eloquent in his silence.

Eventually Milesios tired of the commotion and signaled another chord on the harp. As the shouting reluctantly ceased, he ordered, "Donn, by sunrise I want you in your chariot, on your way to question our celsine about the availability of tin for trade. Colptha, you will go to the sacred groves and offer a sacrifice to win the favor of the spirits. A sumptuous sacrifice, perhaps even a bull. Ír . . . ? Ah, yes, Ír is not with us." He did not allow himself to sound relieved. "Éber Finn, you will go to the harbor with a formal delegation to extend my greeting to the Sea People and offer them the hospitality of my hall for a feast tomorrow . . ."

"Don't send him without me!" Éremón protested. "Éber will claim all the best merchandise before anyone else even gets a look at it!"

Éber snorted. "You already sent freemen running down there in your name, carrying food and fresh water. I suppose you didn't ask them to try to find out what the Phoenicians brought so you could make your claim early?"

The two men were on their feet, facing each other, with heated air between them and four doubled fists. Milesios pushed himself off his bench with a deep sigh and went to stand between them, a hand against each heaving chest. "Éremón, I know you were just being generous, that is your nature and I'm certain it made a favorable impression on the traders. A man who aspires to be chieftain must always be openhanded. And Éber Finn, I know full well you would never try to cheat your brothers out of their rightful share, so you need not act so indignant. A man does not insult you who accuses you of the impossible."

17

He turned away from them and made his way back to his bench, sitting down a little too quickly. "A feast tomorrow," he repeated in a voice that lacked strength. "We will summon the clan-chiefs and heroes, we will impress these traders with all the symbols of strength and prosperity we can manage . . ." He seemed to lose the thread of his thought, staring with vacant eyes across the smoky hall. Amergin looked toward his father with concern, sensing a loosening of the Míl's strong hands on the reins at a crucial moment for the tribe. When he glanced up into the women's balcony he saw the same worry mirrored on his mother's face.

◇ **3** ◇

EVEN BEFORE the next dawn, the clan of Milesios was feverishly busy. Signal fires summoned chiefs from the other Gaelician clans to attend the feast in the Phoenician commander's honor. The women planned a sumptuous banquet of ox-meat and mutton, freshly caught sardines furnished by celsine of a fisher tribe, hake and conger eels and baskets of plump oysters, stewed Celtic beans and chewy emmer bread and pungent cheeses. Warriors scattered in all directions, loaded with hunting gear and eager to bring back game to add to the feast. All would be washed down with the pressings from sweet native grapes. Not for these folk the sour Greek vintages the Hellenes brought into Iberia farther south.

A whole roast boar, the customary offering to the champion, would be carried into the Heroes' Hall on a bronze shield. The acquisition of that boar had been Éremón's predawn challenge. Wild boar had grown very scarce in the territory of the Gaelicians.

Donn was having problems as well. He had gone very early to call upon the celsine of the nearest tin-mining tribe and discuss the availability of merchandise for trade, but had received a chilly reception. The miners had grown poor since their vein of ore, near the surface and easily worked, had begun to fail them, and they were already resentful of the continuing Gaelician demands for more tin to be used in bronze-making. Their leader told Donn rather icily that no tin whatsoever was available for trade. "In fact," he added, glad to have the opportunity to bring up the subject, "by the end of this summer we may not have enough left for our own most urgent needs. Then we will be coming to the Míl's stronghold and asking his assistance, for we will be impoverished and we rely on the strength and generosity of your tribe. You are honor bound to help us."

The Gaelicians were indeed honor bound to help their celsine, and it was known throughout northern Iberia that the Míl never went back on his word. Other tribes, lesser tribes, still thought the Gaelicians prosperous and all-powerful; they did not see the tarnish, only the gleam.

Milesios expected the traders to restore that gleam, but traders wanted tin and, as Donn sadly reported to his father, "There is no tin for trading. I was told they can let us have none at all, not even any worked pieces."

Milesios frowned. "I expected as much, but you must not always believe what you are told, Donn. You must ask little sideways questions and listen hard to what the miners do not say in reply. They must have a hoard stashed somewhere, they are not foolish people. Go back to them and be persuasive, be intimidating, but get us enough tin for the Phoenicians or this will surely be the last fleet we ever see here!"

Donn had grown up in the shadow of the Míl's nimble tongue and crafty leadership, but now he felt he must have dozed when he should have been learning. He was not certain what Milesios would say, how he would handle the matter. Donn knew only that the responsibility had come to him unexpectedly and he must live up to it; could live up to it, if he could just organize his thoughts and take it all step by step.

He got back into his chariot and set off again, anxious and uncertain.

Great galleys waited in the harbor, loaded with badly needed raw materials and highly prized luxury goods from the mercantile empires of the Mediterranean, and every member of the Míl's clan felt the tugging need to secure those goods for their people; to return to a prosperity that had gradually slipped away from them with the diminution of the tin supply. Without that visible prosperity and the stature and respect it afforded them among the other tribes, the Gaelicians could look forward to a long, slow fading until they too became a subjugated and secondary people, dominated by a better-equipped tribe.

No one felt the responsibility more keenly than the sons of Milesios.

Since their earliest childhood the Míl had pitted them against each other in every possible way, demanding they test and retest themselves in contest and combat. "We are warriors," he never ceased to remind his sons. "Our ancestors fought their way successfully across all the northern broadlands and hold the entire region in their sway now, as we hold the coast of this land. But we must always be vigilant, for what the sword won can be lost. Keep yourselves strong against the day we are attacked again; keep yourselves strong to defend what we have won!"

Every night, beside their father's hearth, young Donn had wrestled with Ír, or Éremón and Éber Finn had come to blows while Milesios watched them approvingly, roaring with laughter and offering a bowl of wine to the winner. Only if they lashed at one another in real anger did he separate them, pulling Amergin and Colptha apart at the height of a wrestling match that had become too vicious, perhaps, with Colptha shouting and swearing and his face contorted by tears of rage. Colptha, who always lost, could not bear to lose.

"You are brothers," Milesios would remind them then. "You are members of the same clan, in the same tribe, and though you may fight each other for pleasure you must never forget how to stand together. All members of a family are one unit; that is the Law."

But he continued to encourage their rivalries in order to toughen them, and in time the natural playfulness of boys became the battle lust of men.

Yet once the games were over and a victor decided, the warrior sons of Milesios draped their arms around each other's shoulders and laughed together over both winning and losing, praising one another with the characteristic openheartedness of their race. It was often said of the sons of the Míl, in those days, that they were as close as the fingers on a hand, and when they closed together into a fist they were invincible. Any outsider who attacked one of them would have to fight them all.

But not every brother fitted comfortably into that fraternal knot. Colptha suspected he was included only because he gave his brothers an opponent they could be certain of defeating. As seasons passed he became more confirmed in this conviction, simply because he never caught them openly making fun of his weaknesses. Secrecy and malice were peculiarly natural to Colptha, so he attributed them to everyone else as well.

Amergin, who won often and easily, began to be bored with the battles. They did not seem to accomplish anything; they just had to be fought again and again. Something in him urged him to seek other satisfactions, and a faraway look was seen in his eyes.

"Amergin is the one dark leopard in my litter of golden lion cubs," Scotta often said of him, setting him apart from his ruddy brothers. He had become her secret favorite the day he entered the world with a full crop of dark hair like hers, a harkening back to an ancient infusion of Scythian blood commemorated by Scotta's very name. "The Skythai were the fierce horse-warriors of the eastern plains, the great plunderers," she was fond of boasting when anyone commented on her coloring.

As Amergin grew older and demonstrated the grace of the born warrior, he was the one his mother's eyes most frequently followed. Milesios, too, began to speak of him in the way a man speaks of the son he expects to emulate and surpass him.

"Take my children to the training ground and make warriors of them, Scotta," Milesios said to his wife. "No one has prepared more champions than you."

Scotta gladly complied. Like all women of the Celtic race, she had trained in childhood as a warrior so she could fight at her future husband's side if he needed her. Some girls were content just to learn the skills; others showed reflexes quicker than a boy's, and the best of these eventually would train warriors herself, a valuable asset to her husband's clan. Scotta had proved the best of the best. She was lightning-quick with a casting spear and as unflinching as a stone.

"My Scotta has a face like a sword blade," Milesios had boasted not long after her prowess first caught his eye and he welcomed her into his clan as his wife and ally.

Now she trained his sons together with other youngsters who showed a gift for fighting fury. She drilled them all hard, repeatedly demonstrating the style and grace mandatory in a

21

Celtic warrior and scolding them mercilessly when they fell short.

At her summons, the clan's bard came to recite the heroic epics for the Míl's sons and inspire them to strive harder. "Listen to him," Scotta commanded. "You will never be remembered as heroes unless you, too, rise to such heights of splendor and courage that bards sing your praises."

The family bard of Amergin's youth was an old man, filled with the dignity of his calling, and he made an impressive picture standing on the trampled earth of the training ground. His white hair streamed over the shoulders of his multicolored cloak, one of the entitlements due a bard. With the skill of polished oratory he brought to life dead champions. With detailed, vivid recountings of ancient battles he demonstrated the stylized rules of Celtic warfare to a huddle of openmouthed, snotnosed children who imagined themselves striding off to glory.

Dark and wiry Amergin listened, dazzled; surrounded by sturdy and fair-haired brothers. When the bard spoke Amergin saw the battlefield, felt the rising excitement, heard the galloping hooves and the shouted warcries. His youthful imagination was captured by the poetry as it never was by the actual practice of combat, and when the bard left the training ground Amergin's eyes followed him until he was out of sight.

"Listen to me!" Scotta commanded, summoning her son's attention back to the practical arena of thrust and hurl and jab. She stood tall, her body oiled to make it hard to grasp, bare-breasted above a brief battle apron, with a wooden shield strapped to her arm. ("She's beautiful, isn't she?" young Éber Finn murmured to Éremón.)

"The bard has whetted your taste for battle; now you must acquire the style needed for victory. Warriors owe their allegiance to one leader and they follow him without question, trusting in his courage. Chariots are the first line, a broad band capable of sweeping like a scythe through the mass of the enemy. Chariot warriors must be able to hurl javelins at the gallop from a small, jouncing platform, so they must have great balance, and we will do exercises to help you perfect that balance.

"Foot soldiers will follow you, but as the sons of Milesios you are members of the dominant clan and will always have horses." ("Yes!" shouted Éber Finn, who loved the horses.)

22

"You must learn to do feats of strength and skill which will intimidate your opponents," she went on, "for that is the essence of battle art. Combat is won in the head, the sacred head. A truly great warrior need not soak a battlefield with blood. Warriors of our race are valuable and take a long time to train; it is wasteful to slaughter them needlessly if they can be overawed and made to retire from the field. That is the reason for having battles decided by conflict between single champions." ("Like Milesios, my father!" shouted Éremón.)

"Yes," Scotta agreed. "When both tribes consent, the war is decided between two men and no one else is lost that day." ("Then there are no trophy heads to take," lamented Colptha to Ír.)

"Formal battles begin with boasts and demonstrations of skill on both sides," Scotta said sternly, raising her voice to enforce their attention. But she did not have the ringing power the bard possessed, Amergin thought. "After the opening phase, the two sides either send out their champions or charge each other in a broad line. If you have the greater courage, if you refuse to turn aside no matter what the enemy does, you will win. You will be heroes.

"But if tempers run very hot between two Celtic tribes and there is danger too many good men will be lost, then the bards who are there to commemorate the battle can always intervene. Remember that the bard is sacred on the field of battle and no weapon must touch him; that is the Law."

"What if our opponents are not members of a Celtic tribe and do not obey our rules of warfare?" Donn asked.

Scotta looked grim. "Then you defend yourselves to the death," she said. "And you will prove yourselves deathless in your courage, for the bards will sing of you ever after, naming you among the heroes."

It seemed to Amergin that the bards had the greatest challenge of all, for they must go forward in the front line with the chariots but carry no weapons, other than their harps. The sword could win a quick victory, but it was the bard's recounting of the battle that won the permanent glory. The poem, not the deed, survived the battlefield.

"What does it take to become a bard?" Amergin asked Scotta.

Ír hooted at him. "Ha, brother, you have to be born with wings!" the beautiful blond boy cried fancifully, waving a

23

battered practice-sword in the air with a frantic gaiety that was beginning to color many of his actions.

"You have to be born with a gift from the spirits," Scotta said, intending to discourage pursuit of this byway. "It's very difficult to become a bard, Amergin; many seasons of training, even as an apprentice, and then a man may be only one of the lesser bardagh and never become a true poet. That's why there are so few of them. Many clans have none at all and must rely on use of the chief bard, whose talents belong to the entire tribe."

This topic did not interest her and she did not like the way it was making Amergin's eyes shine. "Here, forget about bards and let's see you handle the sword again," she ordered, tossing him her own weapon.

Even though he was not yet old enough to have hair between his legs, Amergin caught the shortsword and rolled it backward over his wrist with such dexterity that even Éremón called out in admiration. Amergin caught the weapon by its hilt, brandished it, then set it slashing across the nearest straw target.

Scotta nodded, pleased. "You will make a daunting warrior," she assured him.

"I think it would be more challenging to be a bard," Amergin replied, surprising himself with his unexpected boldness in speaking up. "When I try to imagine all the things bards must carry in their heads . . ." His eyes were dreamy.

In that moment Scotta felt her son begin to grow away from her.

Amergin continued to train with the other youngsters, but his attention wandered. In the evenings, when his brothers gathered in a bruised and sweaty huddle to relive the day's victories, Amergin often slipped away to seek out the bard. And when the old man died of the weight of his seasons Amergin made frequent journeys to the bards of other clans, so he could sit, enthralled, drinking in the craftsmanship of phrases and the vivid rhythms of poetry. The hero-frenzy so admired and cultivated by young warriors fitted his spirit no better than an ill-made tunic. He was as brave as any of them, but he was a gentle boy. He would become a gentle man.

Milesios summoned the chief bard of the tribe, a member of Gosten's clan named Nial, to fill the poet's place of honor in the Heroes' Hall. When Amergin heard Nial recite a brilliant satire condemning a distant chieftain for a personal dishonor, he realized what a sharp edge polished words could carry and how cruel laughter could be. No weapon in the Míl's armory was capable of inflicting so savage a wound as the mockery of a great bard.

Amergin began to dog Nial's footsteps, soaking up eulogies and battle epics as boiled wool soaks up dye.

I could never learn all that, Amergin told himself. I could never make myself stand up in front of everyone and recite. I could not make them listen.

Or . . . perhaps I could. If I just thought about the poem, and not about myself, not about the people listening . . . maybe I could. I could make the words ring like bells . . .

The dream gripped him, demanding.

I have to find out if I can do it, he thought. I have to *try*.

Other Celtic tribes in the region challenged the supremacy of the Gaelicians, and the sons of the Míl went bravely out to their first battles on radiant sunny afternoons, bedecked in jewelry, jouncing in chariots that were no more than small platforms on wheels, easily overturned and dangerous. They went out to parade in front of one another, to boast and impress and return home laughing, having watched the other side back down in the face of so much splendor.

And Amergin tried to shape in his head, secretly, the words that would bring it all to life and outlive the day.

He spent less and less time on the training field, though he was scarcely aware of it. He was always being lured away by the changing light on the distant hills, or the song of some bird he had never heard before. It was incredible to the others that he should find these things interesting, and incredible to him that they did not. He tried to tell them about his discoveries and when he could not, he began putting the words into private poems of his own, for safekeeping.

Scotta and Milesios hurled their children like casting spears into the future, but Amergin followed his own path, never knowing where it might lead. Seeing things differently.

That was when the druids began watching him, sensing a kinship in him.

When there were no formal conflicts between tribes, there were always contests and battle games to keep the warriors' skills sharp. As trade decreased and the tribe became increasingly aware of a paucity of the imported goods which heightened its intimidating martial display, those skills became less showy and more savage. An unspoken desperation stalked onto the training field. Iron was harder to come by; swords had to be cherished like sons. And sons must summon the splendid ferocity of their ancestors if they were to continue to defend and hold their place in the world.

Young Amergin could not find that splendid ferocity inside himself, though he looked for it. Lying awake nights, he stared into the darkness, wondering why he did not feel the same lust Donn or Éremón enjoyed when they postured and pranced and attacked.

"There must be something wrong with me," he whispered to Donn one night beside the Míl's hearthfire.

"Are you sick?"

"No. Not in my body—just my thoughts. I'm sick of spending all my time thinking about war and talking about war and preparing for war. There must be something better to do with a life than that."

"You *are* sick," Donn said with conviction, shaking his head.

Colptha overheard the conversation and repeated it to his other brothers. "Amergin thinks he's too good for us, he turns his back on our traditions."

They chose to think he was deliberately insulting them, for an insult was as good an excuse as any to have a lovely battle. "Maybe he's losing his courage," Éber Finn suggested. "Perhaps we should test him."

Donn disagreed. "I've never seen Amergin show fear of anything," he reminded them.

"If he's not afraid, then let him prove it to us!" Ír cried eagerly. "Let's all attack him at once and see how he reacts!"

"Let's sneak up on him through the bushes," Colptha said, "so he won't see us until it's too late."

"I don't want to hide in the bushes," Éremón said. "*I'm* not afraid of anything. We should meet him out in the open and challenge him as champions challenge each other. If he shows either fear or contempt, we will know what he is made of."

They decided to confront Amergin when he returned from one of his increasingly frequent rambles away from the stronghold on the headland. Without Scotta's zealous eye fixed on them, demanding formal style and grace, they would give their brother a sound thrashing and force him to match their aggression or be beaten. A man could not call himself a

26

warrior until he had collected scars of honor, and Amergin had none.

The sons of the Míl laughed and joked about it, telling one another just how they would make Amergin yell for mercy.

They waited beside a clump of scrub pine on the cliffside road, chortling to themselves and elbowing one another, until Amergin came sauntering along dreamy-eyed, his thoughts otherwhere. Then they leaped at him, yelling.

But that particular day was an unfortunate choice for such an attack, because young Amergin had his practice-sword with him. He had taken it down to the beach to investigate a peculiar beauty he had recently discovered in a flashing sword carving patterns through the air, with sunlight on its blue iron blade. He had been practicing alone on the sand, whirling the weapon into shapes of light and trying to think of words with which to describe what he saw, to capture its essence as bards captured the essence of all that was important in life. He was coming home from this experiment in a mellow frame of mind, pleased with himself for having found art where others only found violence.

Then his screaming brothers came running at him, with Éremón in the forefront and Colptha in the rear, keeping someone else's back between himself and danger. None of Scotta's training had been wasted—Amergin's reflexes were deadly keen, and before his eyes had recognized his brothers his sword had slashed the first of them.

"Aaaiii!" cried the startled Éremón, staggering backward and clutching at a bleeding arm. Éber Finn, who had learned well the lesson of standing up for one's brothers, stepped in quickly to take his place, feinting at Amergin with a pine branch.

Amergin's sword knocked the wood from his hand.

There was a brief moment of confusion while everyone scrambled for a weapon. A stick, a stone, and then the forgotten meat knives tucked in their belts. Amergin's brothers could not let one boy with a sword outface them all so easily. Soon they were launched at him again, truly angry now.

From the moment he realized he had wounded Éremón Amergin wanted to end the confrontation, but they would not let him. They crowded around him, shouting insults, and forced him to fight.

So he fought. Fought with a dazzling skill he summoned

from his inborn talent and Scotta's training and threw into their teeth, defying them. He held them all off, though one after the other they tried to dart beneath his guard. Colptha, on hands and knees, crept up behind him and tried to signal Éremón to knock Amergin against him so he would fall, but Éremón shook his head disdainfully and refused to take such an advantage. "Only Colptha would have thought of it," he said to Éber Finn, later.

Amergin's sword sang around him, creating a deadly perimeter. His muscles were freshly warmed from the exercise he had been doing on his own with the sword, and his agility was considerable. He held them all off successfully, dancing on the balls of his feet, until he caught a glimpse of a granite outcropping out of the corner of his eye and leaped up onto it, just out of their immediate reach.

Standing above them, Amergin looked down at their contorted faces and suddenly surprised them all—himself included —by bursting into laughter. He did not mean to mock; he just found the whole performance silly and was amused that his brothers should prize so highly a skill he scarcely valued at all.

He tossed the sword right at them, throwing away the weapon with a careless gesture that denied all its power.

The sword hit Donn squarely in the chest. "Oof!" he gasped, losing his balance and sitting down hard on his tailbone, meeting the beaten earth of the road with a force that made him blink in pain. Éremón immediately stooped and seized the weapon and ran forward with it. Amergin stood unarmed on his rock, waiting, letting his brothers see his relaxed arms and empty hands, his blue eyes laughing at them.

Éremón lifted the sword. He paused, then slowly lowered it again. If Amergin refused the weapon, so would he. He felt that his brother had somehow gained an obscure advantage over him and he wanted to balance the scales. "I won't hit you when you have no weapon," he said. "A champion never attacks a weaker opponent." Then his stern face dissolved into a laugh mirroring Amergin's own. "Not that you're weaker—you may be better than all of us, Amergin! Come down here and let's go to the Heroes' Hall and share a bowl of wine together."

"Are you saying he's *won?*" Colptha hissed through his teeth. "I'm not surrendering to Amergin!"

"Nobody won," Donn said. "But nobody lost. That's a good idea about the wine, I could drink a bowl right now in one gulp." He stood up, ruefully rubbing his backside with solicitous hands.

Éremón had already forgotten his bloodied arm, and Éber Finn was laughing too, his face almost a replica of Éremón's, line for line and bone for bone. Two good-natured and exuberant youngsters, loving life . . . Éber Finn draped his arm across Éremón's shoulder in a habitual fond gesture. Donn and Ír stood beside them, equally willing to forgive and forget.

But Colptha, sallow and sour Colptha, did not join the brothers. He stood to one side, still red-faced and nursing a grievance. There was an air of unresolved tension about him that Amergin suddenly, startlingly, perceived as a dirty yellow shimmer on the air.

"I don't think I want any wine right now," Amergin said, reluctant to add that he had no taste for Colptha's company. Besides, he wanted to think about the fight and try to work out its pattern in his own mind. Find words to describe it, to capture the joy of battle and the flush of exhilaration a man felt when he knew he could win.

Bards sang songs like that in the front row of war, exhorting the heroes to valor.

Only after he had left his brothers, going his own way, did he realize they might have misinterpreted his actions. He had made a mistake, he should have gone with them . . . he spun around and started after them, but they were striding along in a tightly bunched pack, all those golden heads together, and he felt like a dark outsider. Different, somehow . . . perhaps he really did not belong with them at all.

If he were Éremón or Éber Finn, never abashed by anything, he could have yelled, "Wait for me!" and run to join them without hesitation. But he was Amergin, sensitive to a whole layer of colorings and emotions his brothers did not seem to perceive. He stared at them as if he stood on the other side of a wall of Phoenician glass, and he was suddenly, terribly afraid he could never break through and find himself where he longed to be at that moment, in the heart of that golden pack.

He stood alone on the headland and heard the north wind croon softly at his back as his brothers moved inexorably away from him.

Colptha was saying to the others, "We could have made him surrender to us if we'd fought for blood. We were playing with him, we were too gentle. You can't be gentle with the enemy."

"He's not an enemy," Donn said reasonably. "We only meant to teach him a lesson, not do him any real harm."

"Amergin taught us a lesson instead," Ír laughed, his eyes almost too bright, his cheeks too flushed. "Next time we face a man with a sword we'll have to be faster, bigger, better! But that man won't be Amergin—I think he's taught us to leave him alone."

From that day forward his brothers did, indeed, leave Amergin alone, though it was neither conscious nor deliberate. They merely felt the difference in him more acutely than before and responded to it. Amergin became aware of a real and growing sense of isolation, but he did not know how to break free of it, to plunge back through that invisible wall. He hurt in silence, Scotta's son—too proud to give voice to pain.

His brothers spoke a martial language that grated on his inner ear, though he longed to be one with them; to be a companion to Éremón, a friend to Ír; to share Éber Finn's fondness for animals and the flashes of wry humor that occasionally burst from stolid, thoughtful Donn. But he could not fit into their circle. He had to learn to find comfort in solitude and compatible conversation in the voices of pinewind and seawave. He grew up with a certain sadness in his eyes, though he himself was unaware of it.

It was inevitable that someday the druids would claim him as one of their own.

Now an adult man, Amergin belonged to that division of the druid order known as bardagh, and he still found himself set apart. At his initiation the chief bard Nial had warned him, "Druids are separated from the rest of the tribe by the very natures of their professions, though those professions are indispensable to the tribe's survival. A bard must stand in the center of the tribe, observing and remembering, letting the existence of his people flow through him like a river. But he must also stand outside, so his own involvement does not dye his perception of the truth.

"Only by achieving such duality can you be a poet who will give voice to the true soul of your people, Amergin."

Duality was a druid word, often heard in the sacred groves

30

but rarely uttered beyond them, where the Gaelicians had become preoccupied with ships and swords and tangibles.

On this hot summer morning Amergin was observing the scurrying of his clanspeople and an influx of arriving tribesmen drawn by news of traders. Within a few nights even the warriors standing watch at the far reaches of Gaelician territory, prepared for the occasional skirmishes to be expected at a distance from the Míl's sword arm, would be abandoning their posts and hurrying to the headland. Anxious for the distribution of goods at the generous hands of Milesios, chief of the tribe.

The atmosphere was as effervescent as fermented fruit juices. Amergin's druid senses tingled with the invisible excitement, which ran unseen along his arms and sparked from his fingertips. He walked bemused, searching for words and phrases that would interpret today's hope for tomorrow's children. He was so preoccupied he did not notice Taya until she stood right in front of him.

"Amergin, I'm talking to you!" cried an indignant voice, demanding his attention.

Taya had a round face and a neat economy of feature; a horizontal span of brows like a line drawn with a sooty finger. At first glance her hair seemed as black as Amergin's, but the strong Iberian sunlight found brown glints in its springy curls.

Taya was a daughter of Lugaid, the son of the patriarch Ítos, who had the clanhold adjacent to the Míl's. Since childhood Taya had been a frequent visitor to the stronghold on the headland. She seemed a peripheral member of the family, and when Amergin began attempting to master a storyteller's skills it was often little Taya who sat patiently at his feet through half a long morning, hugging her knees and listening with parted lips and shining eyes to tales he spun out. She laughed at his first awkward satires, embarrassing him because he knew they had not yet earned cruel laughter. She wept at his eulogies.

Taya, nine winters younger than Amergin, had always been his best audience.

"Are you busy?" she asked him now, and whatever thread of concentration the bard had been following was cut by the shear of her words. But he only smiled at her fondly—for who could be angry with Taya?—and replied, in truth, "Not now."

"Good! No one else seems to have time for me, but you always do. Amergin, tell me at once, for I need to know—did the traders bring any silver?"

The bard shrugged. "We don't know what they've brought, not yet. Milesios won't open negotiations with them until after the banquet this evening; he needs to buy all the time he can to accumulate enough trading goods to offer them in exchange."

"Do you think they might *not* have silver? Or they wouldn't give it to us?" She sounded deeply distressed. Everything was urgent with Taya of late—at her age women grew tired of their fathers' houses and sought more interesting company.

"Why are you so concerned about silver in particular?" the bard asked her, curious to follow the workings of a young woman's mind.

"A polished silver mirror is the proper possession of a woman of marriageable age, and I don't have one, Amergin! You know the Law, you're one of the bardagh. A woman must bring her own property into a man's house, so she can stand with him in equal dignity, and the Law sets down all those things which are appropriate for me to possess as the granddaughter of a clan-chief. But I don't have a silver mirror, and the craftsmen have had no silver to make me one for seasons and seasons. I was no higher than my mother's waist the last time the traders came with silver, Amergin!" Her soft voice came in a breathless rush, tumbling over her dreadful woes.

Amergin's fond smile broadened. "If we do any business at all with the Sea People, surely we'll get enough silver for your mirror, Taya."

"I hope so," she sighed. "I am a woman, after all . . . even if *you* never notice, Amergin," she added with a certain annoyance. "Just look at me."

He had automatically shortened his long stride to match hers as they walked together, and when he bent nearer to hear her voice he caught a whiff of pinesmoke and the sweet fragrance of pearwood in her hair. A blind man could tell the seasons from the smell of cooking smoke in a woman's hair. Greenwood after Imbolc, when the ewes were lactating; oak deadfall for the ritual relighting of the fires at Samhain; driftwood and dung in winter, when the Mother seemed cold and dead.

"Summersmoke," Amergin murmured, sniffing Taya's hair.

"You would notice that," she replied indignantly. But she did not pull away from him. She stepped closer, letting her warm breast press against his arm.

Amergin was suddenly and painfully aware of just how long it had been since he shared pleasure with a woman. Days and nights galloped by, filled with the duties of his profession: singing the young into life and the old into transition, inspiring warriors, satirizing those who overstepped themselves, eulogizing those who had lived and died brilliantly. When had he last taken time for himself away from the harp?

On the beach the night before he had envisioned a goddess from seafoam and green wind, reaching out to him . . .

He shook his head, fracturing the image, and looked down at Taya. *Saw* Taya as she just demanded he see her—but with the vision that marked him as a druid, the sight sinking down through layers of flesh and blood to the luminous bone of the spirit.

In Taya, Amergin discovered an immature spirit, though her body had rounded and she was anxious to test her womanly skills. It was not the bard she desired, but some affirmation of adulthood, and he was the nearest man. A familiar man, too well-known to be threatening, too kind to hurt her with rejection. She looked up at him and offered her most inviting smile, and the bard saw, with amused regret, that she was not smiling at him at all. Taya's charm was being tentatively tried on like a new gown.

No matter how eagerly his body responded, the man within held back. Not this one, his spirit told him with regret.

His brothers would have laughed at him. How could they be expected to understand something he did not understand himself, a personal integrity which demanded that mating be a harmony involving the totality of both people—body, mind, and soul? Amergin needed a woman to fit his inner being the way Clarsah fitted into his hands, and when he got a glimpse of the spirit within Taya he saw that she was not that woman at all. Never could be; would not be happy if she were.

She leaned toward him, bobbling like a fledgling on the rim of the nest, eager to try its wings.

At that moment he bitterly resented the druid gift.

"Taya," he said carefully; tightly; holding himself back. "Under the Law, you can express your desire to any man who attracts you, but you must use that freedom wisely. Do not waste yourself on anyone less than the best . . ."

33

"Who stands higher than a son of Milesios?" she inquired. "Your status is far above mine, I am only the younger daughter of a clan-chief's younger son. You are also a druid, a bard. You are so many splendid things!"

He shook his head, stopping the admiring rush of words, breathless and childish, feeding on their own enthusiasm. "You don't know what I am," he told her. "You don't even know yourself very well yet.

"Find a man who will teach you the joys of the body, Taya. But be careful. I think you are not one who will ever take pleasuremaking lightly, so be certain the man you choose is one you can marry and bear children for. You are a soft and yielding woman, and that is a lovely thing, but you need a firm and resolute man to provide a balance for you. You are half of something . . . but I am not the other half."

Taya put one hand to her mouth and gnawed unconsciously on the knuckles. She could not make herself argue with him; that was not her way. But her eyes brimmed with unshed tears and Amergin was angry at himself for being in this position at all. Eber Finn would just have reached out and grabbed her and had a wonderful time.

"Listen to me, Taya," he said as kindly as he could. "I am still struggling to master the bardic arts; it is enough challenge to fill a lifetime. Sometimes I feel I am a foolish youth overmounted on a colt too strong for me. I don't have enough of myself left over to share with a woman, at least not yet. Before I am ready for that I have to know if I will ever be able to weave the words and dreams in my mind into a truly great poem."

"I'm not asking you to share anything with me, Amergin. I just want to be close to you."

"Ah, but I would need to share with you, Taya—don't you understand? That's how I am. I know I'm strange; all my life I've been aware of how different I am from the others, but there's nothing I can do about it."

His druid vision saw the complete bafflement within her and knew he had made the right decision, but that did not relieve the discomfort of the moment. He tried to explain further, driven by his passion for communication. "I have to spend myself on my work, Taya. Since Nial died the title of chief druid of all the Gaelicians goes unclaimed; it will only be given to a poet whose compositions are certain to live for many generations. He bequeathed me his harp but I have yet

34

to earn the right to have her. Until I do that, I cannot reward myself with anything more. Please try to understand. I am not comfortable with myself and you would not be comfortable with me!''

Her eyebrows rushed together, forming one perturbed line across her forehead. ''Are you saying that you're unhappy? A bard . . . with all your gifts . . .''

''There is no fire in the phrases I compose and I know it,'' he told her, bravely touching the central tragedy of his life.

And Taya did not even see that it was a tragedy. She just looked at him imploringly, trying to return the conversation to things that really mattered.

''Please, Amergin. We've known each other all my life. I trust you. I'm tired of waiting for the rites of womanhood and I don't want to celebrate them for the first time with a stranger. It's just a little thing to ask. Amergin?''

◇ **4** ◇

THE SEASON OF LEAF-SPRING-OUT had ended and summer was a lusty newborn, vibrant with life. The high hot Iberian sun beat down on Amergin and Taya. Their people swirled around them, radiating a contagious excitement. Tension built with every beat of the heart, filling the throat, heating, pounding . . .

Amergin the bard was a sensual man in the floodtide of his strength, with a great pool of tenderness concealed inside him, carefully hidden from his warrior clan. With a mighty effort he took one step backward from Taya, and it seemed that he had, for one brief flash, achieved that longed-for duality. He could actually watch himself putting her aside for both their sakes, passionate and dispassionate at once. Torn.

''Your season will come soon, Taya, I promise you,'' he told her—and saw the power of the poet's promise demonstrated at once, shockingly.

Éremón's chariot came wheeling through the gate, the big

ruddy warrior lashing his horses and yelling. Sun glinted on his hair; the necks of his horses were elegant curves and foamy froth frosted their hides.

Éremón bellowed a bold laugh, a man's laugh. He was the youngest of the Míl's sons, but no one could guess it from looking at him. The boyish brashness he had never outgrown emboldened the planes of his face. His confidence in his own power was so total no one else questioned it.

Taya turned toward him as naturally as a flower turns toward the sun.

"Not Éremón . . ." Amergin said quickly, reaching out to catch her arm and hold her back, but she was already walking briskly away from him, eager to get on with her living.

Éremón yanked his horses onto their haunches in front of the Heroes' Hall. An admiring crowd formed around the rearing, snorting animals as Éremón recounted the adventure of the boar hunt, making it sound as if he had fought the animal alone at first—then reddening and laughing and heaping credit upon his comrades.

Taya wriggled through his audience until she was close to the chariot and the golden hero within, and he looked down and saw a full-grown woman smiling up at him.

When the season comes, do not resist it. So says the Law.

Someone snickered with malicious pleasure. Amergin turned to see his brother Colptha approaching, his lank yellow hair clinging damply to his temples and his thin lips drawn back from his teeth in an almost feral grin. A druid like Amergin, Colptha the sacrificer was clean-shaven. Unfortunately. A warrior's luxuriant mustache might have disguised the weasel shape of his head atop its narrow neck.

"I see that women do not fall into your hands like ripe fruit, Amergin," Colptha remarked.

"What Taya and I do is no business of yours," Amergin replied.

"Suppose I told you I had already bedded Lugaid's daughter," Colptha said, watching closely for Amergin's reaction.

"I wouldn't believe you."

"Ha! You accuse me of *lying?* That's a bloodletting accusation, bard; are you prepared to prove it?"

It was typical of Colptha to offer combat in arenas where he was sure no one would bother to meet him, so Amergin did not bother answering.

But Colptha decided to press his advantage. "Women al-

36

ways pursue druids of whatever rank, Amergin," he said. "You know that. Being born with the special talents which predispose one to be a sacrificer or a judge or a musician or a healer . . . or even a bard, I suppose . . . creates desirability in women's eyes. They pursue us in hopes of bearing children who will carry our gift. And Taya is no different from the others. Except that she must have better taste than some, since she rejects you."

Colptha's voice had an insinuating quality that could grate on the nerves after a time, like flints raked together. Amergin bore it as long as he could and then he struck back. "She has never approached *you*, Colptha, and everyone knows it. What woman has ever managed to stomach you? Your hands reek with the blood of sacrifice more often than not, and for some reason known only to yourself you seem disinclined to wash it off."

"Blood is the emblem of my rank," Colptha said with hauteur. "And let me remind you: in the druidic order I am senior to you. The druids recognized my gifts first and came for me when you were still sprouting teeth."

"*You* went to *them*," Amergin corrected him, with a bard's determination to be precise. "You were hopelessly awkward with sword and spear but you had to win somehow, at something. I've always suspected you deliberately chose the order as an area in which you thought you could stand on equal footing with warriors, and you somehow arranged that occasion when you predicted the future from the entrails left after the butchering, just so the druids would take an interest in you and accept you as an acolyte."

Colptha contrived to look very injured. "I arranged nothing," he said. "I saw the future then as clearly as I see your face now."

"You saw that Donn would break his arm, and announced it so loudly everyone could hear you. Then several nights later he tripped over something he never saw in the darkness, on his way to the night-trench, and did break a bone. Except it was only a fingerbone. But that was still enough to get you attention, wasn't it?"

"The druids are always eager to learn of someone who has special sensitivities," Colptha said. "And they were not mistaken in me. I have proved my worth as sacrificer many times over. As a diviner I belong to the priestly class, after all, and you are merely one of the bardagh."

Amergin's eyes were the dark of blue thunder. "A bard has a greater honor price than a clan-chief—or a sacrificer," he reminded his brother. "The priestly class are revered, but the bardagh are a necessary part of daily life; poetry and music are the soul of our people. Why else do chief bards merit six-colored cloaks and sit in seats of honor beside their chieftains? Never try to insult one of the bardagh again, Colptha, or I warn you . . ."

He did not need to finish. "Beware the curse of the poet!" mothers warned their children from infancy onward. "Sword death is quickly over, but a bard's mockery will follow you down all the generations and bring shame to your children's children."

Colptha bit back the retort he longed to make. He glared silently at Amergin, who turned away with distaste, anxious to smell the sea wind and have a look at the ships in the harbor. When he was gone, Colptha murmured softly to himself, "You may command a higher honor price, but mine is the greater gift, bard. Someday you will all acknowledge it."

The sons of the Míl had been driven to excel since childhood, and Colptha was the most driven of all.

He stared with burning eyes at the bard's receding back, but Amergin was unaware of his brother's animosity. He was thinking with regret of Taya, and preparing himself for an onslaught of that loneliness which gnaws a man's spirit.

If not Taya, who? When?

Or would Clarsah claim the rest of his life, to the exclusion of everything else?

When Shinann arrived at the Gathering Place they were all waiting for her: the great queen Eriu the ardent; Eriu's husband Greine, Son of the Sun; her sisters, brave Banba and wise Fodla, and their husbands; all the nobility of the Túatha Dé Danann. The people of the goddess Danu had gathered on the most sacred high ground in Ierne for the periodic Being Together, and Shinann's attendance was expected.

They had been concerned about her tardiness but tried to conceal it—as if anything could be hidden from Shinann. She felt the shimmer of their relief as she joined them. "You were the firstborn of a special new generation," they often reminded her. "You are the repository of our future; your talents will exceed ours and make many new things possible. Take care of yourself, Shinann.''

They were so sober and serious about her welfare, these people who wove their lives from laughter, that Shinann could not resist teasing them. She had deliberately loitered, coming here, until she was certain they would be anxious, and then she sauntered into their midst with the greatest nonchalance, tossing back a lock of hair that habitually fell across her eyes, grinning mischievously. Shinann is here! every line of her body announced.

She laughed into their faces and wrinkled her nose and they had to smile back at her. Only Greine made an effort to chastise her. Imagine Greine, trying to look stern!

He faced her with his hands on his hips and his features drawn into a scowl that did not fit very well, Shinann thought. It kept trying to slide off the side of his face. She mimicked his expression and his eyes betrayed him by twinkling beneath his lowered brows.

''We were all to be here by sundown, Shinann,'' he reminded her. ''The moon is high and we have heard wolves singing, yet you are just now joining us.''

She bowed her head in negligible contrition. After all, Greine was one of the kings. But how foolish of them to be concerned—had she not sat on the earth in the wolves' circle, a gray beast on either side of her, their clear minds open to hers?

Her people loved her but they could not contain her, any more than they could contain a bubble in a net, and both she and they knew it. Still, it was nice to know they worried about her.

Greine held out his hands and she took them, melting into his hug for the Joining. He handed her on to Eriu and she moved down the line of her kinspeople, enjoying the warmth of the familiar ceremony.

An outsider might have noticed a similarity among the Dananns, a brightness of hair, a lightness of movement possessed by all. Some were thinner, some older, some more comely than others, but every one had a clarity of complexion that shone, even through lined faces, like the glow from an inner lamp. Each face was stamped with its own individuality but built on a common bone structure: a round skull, broad through brow and cheekbone, with wideset eyes of unusual size and luster, and a narrow jaw tapering to a pointed, resolute chin. They were faces with a contradictory blend of strength and delicacy; faces to haunt the mind.

They surrounded Shinann now, laughing and chattering, and she flung herself into each pair of arms in turn with the perfect faith of one assured of welcome. Though some scolded, all hugged.

"Shame on you for worrying us, you wicked woman," Cian the Son of the Healer said to her, clucking his tongue reprovingly. Cian had asked for her as wife more than once, and complained bitterly when she put him off, as she put them all off; but he would forgive Shinann everything. Who could not? She rubbed her cheek against his shoulder and smiled up at him as radiantly as if he had paid her a compliment. Her eyes sparkled with fun; she tweaked his nose. Cian shook his graying head helplessly, his dignity in shards around him, and gave her one more hug before passing her on.

"Shinann will marry someday," Eriu often said. "She just has to do it in her own way and time. Remember, she is not quite like us."

Then Cuill of the Hazel, husband of Banba, noticed the brass ornament glinting on Shinann's bosom. Cuill had lived long and seen much, and the crosshatched surface of that wire was the characteristic design of a tribe he knew.

"Where did you get that, Shinann?" he demanded to know, pointing but not touching. "Wire like that is found only on Iverni weapons!"

The others crowded around to look, the light and laughter gone from their voices. Simple charm would not restore them. Shinann must recount the entire incident of the bronze knife in the river and recall for them its destruction, pleased that she had turned the ugliness of a Bodykiller into something beautiful. But the others did not see it from her point of view.

"That river is too close to our heartland," said Cet of the Plow, husband of Fodla. "If a Fir Bolg tribe has gotten brave enough to bring weapons so near us, they may mean to force a battle."

"I would hate to think it has come to that," said Greine. "For three generations they have seldom challenged us; most seemed to accept our dominion over Ierne."

"In three generations they have forgotten, perhaps," suggested Tuan, Keeper of the Legend. "Their poets may no longer tell them stories of the Sword of Light and the Irresistible Spear. For whatever reason, they grow bold again and venture into our territory carrying weapons. Shinann's wound is the proof of it. Show us again, Shinann."

She held up her foot and there was no wound on it, not even a faint white line to show that only the night before there had been pain and blood. But they did not doubt her; her recollection of the injury had been too vivid.

"Look at that," said Cet. "No scar left. Even your father could not heal that way, Cian."

"He was not like our young people," Cian agreed.

"Children are born to us now who have never seen the wounds left by shortsword and battle-axe," Fodla said. "Even the scars left by the Earthkillers are healed and overgrown with woods and wild roses. But . . . last night there was an uncommonly strong wind blowing, did you notice it? It made me anxious for some reason. A wind of change, our teachers would have called it."

"Perhaps we need a thorough drilling in the use of Bodykillers if there is to be an outbreak of battles with the Fir Bolg," Cian suggested.

"It might be better if we teach our young people to use the Earthkillers," said practical Cet of the Plow, folding his arms.

"No!" Eriu leaped to her feet and held out her hands as if she would draw down the lightning to her fingertips. "The new generation must never touch the Sword and the Spear. They are meant for better things, our children. In all the years since we took control of this island we have been trying to convince our cousins the Fir Bolg to give up their warlike habits and learn their way into the future with us. So far we have not succeeded; they still take great pleasure in attacking one another and now seem determined to test us again, as well. But with the special gifts of Shinann and the men and women like her we may at last be able to free the sacred island from the cycles of battle. The strength of mind, not the strength of weapons, is theirs."

Shinann stood up abruptly and tore the brass remnant of a dagger hilt from her bodice, dropping it to the floor with disdain.

The rest of the Being Together was spent in serious discussion, as befitted the heirs to ancient wisdoms, and in enjoyment of the musicians and poets, as was appropriate for the Children of Light. Yet the remnant of a weapon lay at the periphery of their community consciousness like a bad odor they could not escape, and from time to time each of the Dananns sneaked a speculative glance in its direction.

No matter the fine talk, no matter the great plans and shining dreams. The piece of yellow metal spoke of other plans and different ambitions, and was eloquent enough in its silence to enter every conversation.

The great queen Eriu felt its presence like a brand, burning her skin. At last she left the circle of conversation and went to crouch beside Shinann's discarded ornament, sweeping the skirts of her gown backwards with her hands so they did not touch the gleaming wire. She lifted it gingerly, as one would touch offal, and carried it away to be buried in the earth, a prayer murmured over and the wind sighing above.

The others watched her leave the assemblage.

"Eriu wants to pretend there is no danger," Greine said, his fond eyes following her.

"There is always danger," Cet reminded him. "We had better be prepared. We may not have time for Shinann's generation to develop to its full strength and persuade our enemies out of war."

◇ **5** ◇

MEANWHILE, across the sea on the Iberian peninsula, the bard Amergin moved through the heart of his clan, observing their frantic activity as they prepared for a banquet to impress the Phoenician commander. The undercurrent of their anxieties swirled around him, troubling him. Words were his gift, and there must be words to hearten his people at such a time.

Such a potentially dangerous time, a quicksand time. Druid vision could foresee the possibilities. Amergin had not received the specific talent for prophecy, but he had been given a heightened sensitivity, an inescapable awareness of tomorrow's skeleton beneath today's rounded flesh. He could imagine all too clearly his tribe's descent into increasing poverty and the apathy that would follow, shape-changing them from victors into victims, while rival tribes crowded ever closer, eager to pick their bones.

And other unseen dangers hovered in the bright air. The day must come when the struggle for power within the tribe would begin again, and one Gaelician would challenge another for the chieftain's bronze bench. The interlocked clans could be torn apart as warring factions pulled this way and that . . . and waiting enemies grew bolder . . .

Twin ravens of worry and doubt sat hunched on Amergin's shoulders, invisible but painfully heavy, and he heard the dry rattle of their wings as their claws bit into his flesh. They were waiting to tear out his eyes that saw too much, that envisioned great changes coming.

The bard drew a deep breath and prepared to fight back in the best way he knew how. He paused close to the gateway of the stronghold and recited an old and well-loved saga of the great trading days, recalling the inflow of wealth and the busy bustle of prosperity. People gathered around him to listen, hoping the images he invoked from the past would become truth for the future.

"Sing of bales of linen, bard," someone requested. "Remind the listening spirits that we used to welcome great sledges of ore through this gateway, and crates of tools and utensils."

Amergin quickened the pace of Clarsah's accompaniment and the heartbeats of his listeners quickened in response. He sang as the bards used to sing when the arrival of ships in the harbor was an everyday occurrence, and those who heard him began to believe such arrivals would become frequent again. They went away with new confidence in their steps, ready to make the saga a reality.

Donn, the Míl's oldest son, did not hear Amergin's recitation. He was being told, for the final terrible time by the very poorest of the miners, that there was no tin. None. "You must offer your merchant other goods," was the suggestion.

Donn set his jaw stubbornly. "My task was to arrange for tin," he insisted. Tin was a step on a ladder, clear in his mind. He was not the sort of man who could skip that step or invent a new one in a different place. "What do I say to Milesios?"

Éremón, driven by the same concern, had found and managed to slay a half-grown wild boar and had come rushing back at the head of his hunting party, nearly killing a good chariot team in his hurry to get the boar to the roasting pit. The meat would be served almost too raw even for Celtic stomachs, but at least Éremón had not failed in his responsibility.

Éremón refused failure as other men refused moldy bread.

Éber Finn was with the clan-chiefs, trying to arrange for other trading goods, while his bright bevy of wives piled fruits on platters and cracked nuts and arranged their hair and set out their very best garments for the evening's festivities. Throughout the clanhold, women were preparing even more busily than their men, eager to be partners in the vital restoration of trade.

But Amergin the bard walked alone. The life of the tribe flowed through him but did not fill him, and when the north wind sang he felt a curious hollowness that tormented him, distracting him.

I should have responded to Taya, he thought. How can I compose poems about the people if I do not know what it is like to wake in the morning with a woman's face next to mine and her belly mounding with my child?

I have not achieved duality at all, only the part about being outside. And I do not want to watch from outside, he thought.

But you cannot argue with the spirits or send back the gift they have given you because you are not content. A gift is a garment you must grow to fill; that is the Law.

Amergin had lived only nine summers when the druids, who noticed everything, remarked the differences between himself and the other youths of his clan. In three more summers they came for him, though Milesios objected.

Colptha had recently been initiated into the druid order as an acolyte, training to be a sacrificer. A second child being credited with invisible gifts was a great honor, but Milesios and Scotta had other plans for their dark leopard.

"Amergin is already considered a man, and skilled with weapons," Milesios protested. "He will be a fine warrior with the eye of an eagle and sinews like boiled leather."

"You have many warriors," replied Irial, the chief druid. "Perhaps too many for the number of druids; I sense an imbalance growing. The tribe will lose touch with the spirit world and become too dependent on things it can touch and taste. That is a great danger, Milesios. Hear me! We need your son Amergin, and any others like him who can truly see and really hear. Once the spirit world was perceived and experienced by all, but you are drifting away—have been drifting away for generations. You are cutting off parts of yourself and you do not even realize it."

Milesios made an impatient gesture. "Druids and warriors do not understand each other," he said. "But I know my sons, Irial, and I know the black-haired one is meant to be a warrior. Tell him, Scotta."

He turned to his wife but she looked off into the distance and said nothing.

"Scotta?" Milesios asked again, with an edge in his voice.

She met his eyes then; she who had trained many heroes of sword and spear. As Milesios read her face the light in his own faded.

"Take Amergin if you want him," the Míl said at last, in a tone dulled by disinterest. "I have more promising sons."

So Amergin went to the druid groves, where all those unseen talents a man may possess, gifts of the spirits, were tried on him as iron is tried in fire. The testers reported to Irial that he had a passion for words and symbols, an instinctive feeling for the rhythms of language, but dreamed no prophetic dreams, saw no visions.

"Ai, he is meant to be bardagh, then, not a diviner," the chief of the order decreed. "Keep him apart from his clanhold for the first two seasons while he undergoes the waking and sleeping rituals. When his rebirth from clan life to the life of the spirit world is complete, we will begin to see just what sort of bardagh he may become, this quiet fellow."

The two seasons passed quickly and Amergin was kept too busy to be lonely in the echoing shade of the forest. The druids took the place of his family; they extended a formal welcome, banishing some of his shyness. But they kept a hard school, filling Amergin's head with lessons and hammering his character with discipline.

"You will not sleep!" Irial thundered at him when his eyelids drooped at the end of an endless day of studies. "Sleep is a reward you allow yourself when you have done your work well. You have accomplished nothing of importance today, Amergin, so you have not earned sleep. Sit on that log—sit straight as a sapling tree, remember you are a druid—and recite again for me the genealogy of your family

45

for ten generations. And let me hear a change of voice for each name, so I can see different faces!"

When he was allowed to return to his clanhold at the close of the first two seasons, Scotta noticed that his eyes were older and his voice was stronger, more assured. His brothers sensed the change in him, too, and sniffed around it as hounds sniff at a stranger, uncertain, ready to bristle or befriend.

Éremón was the first to grin at him and punch him on the arm. Ír sidled up to him later, and whispered, "Will you become a samodhi, a reader of patterns in the sky?"

"I don't think my gift lies in that direction," Amergin told him honestly.

Ír looked disappointed. "I was hoping . . . you could find my pattern and tell me what I am. Why I am." The flesh around his eyes crinkled with pain, startling Amergin.

Amergin returned to the groves and his work began in earnest. During the long course of his training he heard the Law sung by those bardagh who had become brehons, and heard the entire history of his people pieced together by the various poets, who came in turn to recount their family stories and genealogies. Under the tutelage of the samodhii he did indeed study the courses of the stars in the sky—though he never found a pattern he recognized as shaping Ír's destiny— and learned to measure distances on the Earth Mother. Diviners familiarized him with the rituals of prophecy and propitiation; healers lectured on the curative arts.

And he sat in the shade of a great oak at the feet of Irial himself and heard the immortality of spirits explained, saw his essence demonstrated as being one with the great spirit which animated all living things.

"There is no mistaking your gift," Irial told him at last. "You will be trained as a member of the bardagh, but I suspect you will be neither a brehon judge nor an instrumental musician. You have poet's eyes, Amergin. If you show skill at composition, someday you may aspire to become a full bard."

The young man's heart thudded heavily at the base of his throat when he heard those words. The challenge he yearned for was being offered to him, then, and he had spent enough time in the groves to realize what a daunting undertaking it was to become a bard, what enormous expenditures of physical and mental energy were required to memorize all the

46

collected knowledge of the tribe and distill it into new compositions, new sources of pride and inspiration for the people.

Bard. Bard.

Nial undertook the arduous task of giving muscle to Amergin's memory, reciting histories and sagas and then having the young man recite them back, again and again, correcting him sternly if even one word was altered or one shading changed. "Nothing must be mis-said when bards hand on the past to the future," Nial warned an exhausted Amergin for the twentieth time that day. "Yours is a sacred trust—if you become a bard at all. The great ones who precede you leave truth in your hands and you must not tarnish it."

Tense, tired, sweating, wishing he were anywhere else, Amergin recited the slippery words again. And again and again. And when he had them right, Nial summoned the other druids to listen and requested them to talk loudly to one another throughout Amergin's recitation, forcing the young bard to stand his ground and learn to project his voice until he could command their attention.

The exercise was torture for a shy young man, but Nial was without mercy. I cannot do this, Amergin told himself. I cannot.

But he kept on trying. And the day came when his voice rang out clear and strong, full-bodied and resonant with power. A manly, mighty voice, flawlessly clear.

And the others stopped talking. They listened.

They heard only the splendor of the old tales, the vivid phrases, the musical alliterations. It was not a man but a living poem, a living history, who stood before them, and when Amergin realized this the last of his self-consciousness fell away. With the bardic gift, he could be bold.

"Now you must learn the harp," Nial told him, not bothering to hide the pride he felt in this most gifted of his students. "Music can provide a framework to support memory and give color to the emotions of others. If you would be a bard, you must master the harp. Instrumental music to provide a background for the music of your words."

Nial positioned Amergin's fingers on the strings for the first time. The harp he gave the boy was an old one that had not been sufficiently cherished by the other apprentice bards who had learned on her. Her wood had dried out and her temper was uncertain. She resented being placed in yet another pair of clumsy hands and by the end of their first day together she made Amergin's fingertips bloody.

Scotta noticed his wounds that night when she gave him his evening meal, but she said nothing. Scotta did not acknowledge wounds.

The next day Amergin's hands were so sore he could hardly hold the instrument, much less strum her wire strings. The druids ignored him; this was a battle he must fight and win on his own.

Birds must break their own eggshells before they can grow and fly; so says the Law.

Amergin carried the harp everywhere with him, hating it. Hating the blurred and ugly sounds his too-cautious fingers made on the strings. Looking closely at the hands of other harpers, he saw that they had callus pads that protected them from the bite of the brass, and his mind moved backward through time to understand how that callus had been formed, unraveling a mystery. Every bard he saw had gone through pain.

When he knew it was not his alone, the pain began to shrink, and he forced his hands back on the strings.

But still mastery of the instrument eluded him. "A harp is alive and aware," Nial told him. "She is part of any composition you may create, she is your friend and comrade and sometimes your enemy. When the brehons recite the Law, they define the shape of our people and begin molding lawless little boys into men of honor. So it is with you and the harp—the harp will be your law. She will help shape you into what you must become if you are to be a bard, the voice of your people."

While his brothers raced their chariots over sunbaked earth and pursued full-fleshed young women, exploring the first joys of pleasuremaking, Amergin and the harp sat on a bench in the Heroes' Hall and tried to establish a relationship. The harp's temper had not improved, and Amergin's own Celtic temper was rising to a boil. The fire seemed to glow sullenly on the hearth. The stone walls sent back dissonant echoes of sound, ugly and discouraging. His world seemed to be conspiring against Amergin to deny his dream.

Scotta had been larding a tough ox-haunch with boar-fat, crouching over her task by the light of a bronze Hellene oil lamp. She heard the plinks and plunks of the harp, and if they were off-key she did not mind, for she was not sensitive to music. But then she heard them cease, and as a warrior she was sensitive to unexpected silences.

She got up and crossed the hall in silent strides until she stood behind Amergin. He was slumped on his bench, the harp propped against his knee. His broad shoulders—ai, they might have been a swordsman's shoulders!—sagged with weariness. Firelight and torchlight were lost in the blackness of his hair. She heard him draw a deep, ragged breath, as a warrior breathes when he must raise his weapon once more time and there is no strength left in his arm.

Scotta's strong hand clamped hard on Amergin's shoulder. "I learned all I know of pride from hearing the bard of my own clan recite our history," Scotta said, somewhere over his head. "Pride will carry a Celt when all else fails him. You will be a bard, Amergin. You will play the harp." The fingers bit deep into his skin; iron fingers, demanding. Amergin felt Scotta's will flowing through his body, down to his own sore fingers, and he picked up the harp and began to play again.

When he looked up with a grateful smile Scotta was already back at her task, bending close to the bronze lamp, patiently poking slivers of tender fat through tough meat.

The next morning Amergin ran to find Nial. "I can play her!" he cried. "Listen!" And with fingers and palm he summoned sounds of beauty from the harp, a soft voice that tinkled and a strong voice that commanded.

"You have begun to play her," Nial corrected him, obedient to the law of words. "But you have a long way to travel. And once you master the harp, you must begin to think about creating compositions of your own. Beyond that is the step of creating something that will outlive you, a permanent gift for your people."

"But when do I know that I have succeeded? When do I stop needing to learn more?"

"Never," Nial told him, stern with reality. "You are going to be a bard."

He learned to care for and repair his instrument and cherish the strings of brass wire, which were even then becoming scarce as the ships in the harbor became scarce. He saw first Donn, then Ír and Éremón and Éber Finn leave the Míl's roof to build houses of their own and welcome wives into them, and he stood with the wedding parties and recited the genealogies of his clan to the new clanswomen, so they would be

49

proud. He watched his brothers and their wives go through doors that they shut firmly behind them, leaving him outside.

He began seeking women himself, finding each one beautiful in her own way, submerging himself joyously in the poetry of womanflesh—but other poetry always summoned him back, and no woman could permanently displace the harp in his thoughts. When he held a woman most tightly the north wind sang to him and he found himself anxious to go and listen, to interpret the music no one else heard as clearly as he.

Nial sent for him. The messenger said the chief bard had a saga he wanted to teach Amergin, and the young man drove his chariot at an eager gallop to the clanhold of Nial's family. But when he arrived, great Nial was dying. The bard lay in his carved wooden bedbox, heaped high with furs and fine fabrics. His lips were blue, his eyes closed. A druid healer, standing by the bed, indicating with a shake of his head to Amergin that there was nothing more to be done. "His spirit insists on seeking a different life and prepares to leave us," he said.

Sensing Amergin's presence, Nial opened his eyes. "The Míl's son . . ." He sighed, fighting for breath. "Bend to me, lad."

Amergin stooped over him, straining to hear each of the whispered words as Nial told him, "You will take my own harp, Amergin." The dying bard spoke one slow word at a time, forcing them from the last residue of stamina a poet must possess. "She was carried . . . in famous battles, by legendary . . . heroes. She was taught to . . . inflame warriors to splendor or . . . lull enemies to sleep. In the forests of Gaul, generations ago . . ." He stopped, coughed, was silent. Amergin waited.

"She has turned aside mortal foes and the . . . ravening spirits of the unmourned dead," Nial said suddenly, with surprising clarity. "But she is . . . jealous, Amergin. You must always . . ." He paused again, and then his eyes flared wide. "Take her, take Clarsah, Amergin!" he commanded, telling the harp's secret soul name to her new partner with the final exhalation of his lungs.

In the suddenly silent house, the only voice was that of the fire crackling on the hearth.

Clarsah, whose name Amergin must never repeat to a human until he passed her on to his successor, was more than a harp. She was a presence beyond gleaming wood and gilded carving and rows of brass strings. She had a soul of Celtic complexity. The first time Amergin held her in his hands he forgot his envy of easygoing, contented Donn and his plump young wife, or Éber Finn who attracted women like mares to a lush meadow.

The first time he chanted a poem to her accompaniment, people leaned forward breathlessly to listen. Trained to venerate bards, the Celtic tribes were excellent listeners, enjoying each hint and allusion, sensitive to patterns, appreciative of style as much as story. When they heard Amergin recite with Clarsah, their faces fired with admiration.

"I am a bard," Amergin said to himself in the darkness of the night. Alone, savoring. "I am a bard."

But within a very few days he realized it was not enough. When he held Clarsah the words flowed easily, as if they came from her alone and not as a result of his gift. He always felt he could do better, if only . . . if only it all came together at once, if he could somehow reach beyond the traditional forms and grasp the very souls of his listeners in strong fingers, dragging understanding out of them, making them obedient to the message of the words, filling them with awe at the beauty of poetry he himself composed.

But such rarefied heights of creativity eluded him, although his clan admired and honored him by naming him bard for all his family. Still there were nights when he sat alone, embracing Clarsah, and felt like a fraud, wishing he had more to give.

He saw the baffled looks his father occasionally shot his way and suspected Milesios had the same opinion. The Míl openly praised his warrior sons, but he could think of nothing to say for druids, for bards; for men whose superiority lay in areas where the Míl could not compete and had no shining reputation to brandish. The warrior existed in the daylight world, the druid dealt with shadows and the shadowy regions of mind and spirit.

Both men sensed some subtle shift in the balance between them, and Milesios quit consciously naming Amergin among the sons of his siring.

Sons were an extension of oneself.

The clan had always looked to Milesios for leadership and moved in the directions he moved. He was the head, his clan was his body. When he replaced family intimacy with distance and respect, the clan did likewise, edging away from Amergin in ways he saw and felt but could not name. He made himself continue to reach out with offerings of story and song, but simultaneously he, too, drew back a little, watching a chasm widening. That inward and invisible isolation was his own emblem of office, regrettable but seemingly unavoidable.

When he tried to strengthen a relationship with the one brother similarly affected by druidry, Colptha responded with an icy rebuff. "I am diviner and you are bardagh," Colptha reminded him, choosing to accent the differences between them.

Colptha had resented from the first the admiration Amergin attracted in the groves. Irial liked Amergin, but no one liked Colptha. Colptha thought that favoritism must surely smooth Amergin's way and give him rewards he, Colptha, had to claw and fight for.

That was how the world, the real world, worked. Rewards and accolades were heaped on those who already had them; Colptha had seen it all his life. Tribute to Milesios, gift after gift to the most outstanding druids in return for the sharing of their talents. But who handed out largesse to those with empty hands?

The sacrificer nursed his jealousy and dreamed of a day when all the admiration would come to him, pulled into the vortex of his spirit by the sheer ravening magnetism of his hunger.

The seasons passed—four, eight, sixteen—and the two druid sons of Milesios rose through the ranks of the order. And still Colptha's resentment grew, like fungus in a dark place.

For the banquet in honor of the trader Age-Nor, Colptha dressed himself in his best linen tunic and belted his waist with an intricately carved leather belt inset with imported carnelian. It would be a pity to cover such attire with the hooded and symbol-embroidered cloak of a sacrificer, so Colptha decided to put that into the hands of an attendant to carry for him. The apparel of his station would go with him, demanding attention—as would the possession of that attendant.

Amergin had no attendant.

In eager, chattering groups, the family of Milesios and the most important members of the other clans approached the Heroes' Hall, anticipating the feast.

52

Amergin arrived early. The seat of honor reserved for chief bard of the tribe at the Míl's side was empty since the death of Nial, but Milesios would require the formal services of a bard this night. "You will sit behind Nial's bench," Milesios had requested, "and play your harp to create a jovial mood. When the time is right I want you to recite my genealogy and the most recent victories in our tribal history—and be certain you go into some detail about past trading successes, Amergin. I want that Phoenician to know what he's dealing with and feel honored that we're willing to see him at all."

"What if he does not understand our tongue?" Amergin had asked.

"Commanders used to make a substantial effort to understand the language of those they dealt with, and I'm sure this Age-Nor is no different. But if there is a problem, do you remember any of that babble you learned from the Sea People when you were a boy?"

Amergin's mind raced over the impossible task of translating complex Gaelician poetic structure into half-remembered Phoenician, but before he could answer Milesios was already talking to someone else about something else, leaving the problem in his lap.

Amergin came to the hall early to take his place and get a feel for the atmosphere while he worried over this latest problem in a growing pile of problems. When he made his entrance the Míl's eyes flicked casually over him, but no warmth animated that glance. Milesios was waiting for his other sons, for Éremón and Éber Finn, for Ír and Donn—the ones who had tried to model themselves on him.

Other interested eyes followed Amergin's progress, however, as he paced the length of the hall with Clarsah on his shoulder. The wives and daughters of the clan-chiefs were already waiting in the women's balcony, and many of them leaned forward when Amergin entered. "The Milesian bard has a presence about him!" one murmured to another. "See what a long stride he has."

"Look at his hands," replied the other. "Are they not gracefully shaped for so bony a man? Do you suppose he is as skilled with them on a woman's body as on harpstrings?"

A ripple of laughter ran along the balcony.

Díl, Donn's wife, remarked to Scéna Dullsaine, daughter of the clan-chief Ferdinón, "Amergin has been given a poet's house, but there is no wife in it."

53

"A bard has many entitlements," Scéna replied, measuring Amergin with her eyes. "All that—and such an *interesting*-looking man, too! He does not much resemble his brothers, does he?"

Scéna was considered the beauty of the tribe, a lively creature with a splendid white neck and the grace of a seabird. In a race where women sought pleasure as freely as men, Scéna had already sampled her share of blond Celtic warriors. It occurred to her that perhaps she would enjoy something different. "Has the bard much experience of women?" she asked Díl.

Donn's wife was a buxom, red-cheeked woman who found any discussion of pleasuremaking intensely interesting. Her eyes danced as she told Scéna, "I have heard around the well-curb that he is exceedingly virile, as full of heat as a warrior before battle but also quite tender, very solicitous of his partner's pleasure. He does not share a bed with every woman who arches her back for him, however—and it is said he likes to take a long time about his pleasuremaking."

Scéna Dullsaine caught her lower lip between her teeth. "I would not hold that against him," she said, her eyes on Amergin. "And he has no wife yet? Not one? A son of Milesios, an honored bard—I would be willing to go to a man like that as a second wife or even a third. Of course, Ferdinón is a clan-chief so that is unthinkable; I must be a senior wife or not a wife at all. Still . . ." She leaned out over the balcony railing, her eyes on the tall man with the gilded harp case. "The bard is a riddle I would dearly love to solve," she said.

Díl laughed. "You and many other women."

A commotion at the portal signaled the arrival of Éremón. He entered as always amid a crowd of admirers, men who shared hunting and wine bowls and battle stories with him. Unblooded youngsters who longed to emulate him elbowed one another aside to be close to the Míl's favorite son, and grown warriors pushed them back, reserving that honor for men who had fought shoulder to shoulder with him and shared the brotherhood of battle.

You could recognize them in any crowd. No matter how amiable they seemed, there was something behind their eyes that waited and watched. Their faces were lean, the flesh tight to the bone. Theirs was the inner stillness of energy tightly leashed. Meant for battle, shaped and defined by it, they lived in a state of readiness that gleamed from the caverns of their eyes. Taut, intense men, protectors and predators.

The warriors.

Donn was among them, and Éber Finn, who was just growling at the clan-chief Gosten, "Here, don't rub your shoulder against that lion-skin! It came from Libya many seasons ago and the Míl traded a fortune in ore for it. I'm going to drape it over the side of my compartment tonight."

"You'll never get it in that box of yours," Donn told him. "You have the place so jammed now with cushions and blankets and jars of mead—and how do you manage to get honey-wine from the Celtiberians, anyway? They won't trade it to me for anything."

Éber Finn looked smug. "You don't know how to approach them. I get the mead for my wives; they like it and I like to keep them happy. I have a gift for keeping females happy. Even the cows in my share of our clan's herd have twins to show me their favor. Bull twins," he added gratuitously, digging at Donn.

In the seasons that had passed since Amergin received Clarsah, Éber Finn had taken three wives to Donn's one, and like Éremón and Ír he had sired several sons already. Donn's Díl had thus far borne only daughters, but her husband sought no second wife. "Too many women under one roof cause confusion," he claimed.

Éber Finn, who thought there was no such thing as too many women, liked to argue the point.

Ír squeezed past the cheerful squabble and made his way almost unobserved to his own compartment. Only Scotta, sitting in the women's balcony, marked his progress and frowned to herself. Ír had been conspicuous by his absence all day, and she had hoped he would be somewhere—anywhere—else tonight.

Magnificent Ír, the perfectly proportioned, possessed of a flowing golden mustache heavier than the Míl's own and a face of incomparable beauty. Of disconcerting purity, but as unknowable as a demon or a god.

Ír did not see his mother watching him. He sat immobile in his compartment, gazing vacantly into space, tense and unaware as a pot coming slowly to the boil.

Milesios looked up then and saw him, too. Recognizing the dreaded glassy stare in his son's eyes, the Míl sighed and looked away. He was sick and he was tired; his spirit was worn too thin for this. Donn had already reported failure in arranging for tin, and the eager expression on Colptha's face showed that the sacrificer obviously meant to harangue his father about the spirits as soon as he could—as if even the good will of the spirits could keep the traders here, or fill the holds of their ships.

Whatever happened would happen, Milesios thought. He had raised strong sons; perhaps it was time to leave it all in their hands. Perhaps it was time to think of leaving altogether.

For the first time in a long and valiant life the old chieftain gave in to a pleasant sense of helplessness. He let his eyes drift closed. His aching body hurt him less; conversation flowed around him but he felt no obligation to join in. He would rest a bit, until the Phoenician arrived. He would . . .

His head began to bob in jerky little nods.

As life pulsed around him, Milesios slumped lower on his bench and half-remembered, half-dreamed the days of his youth, when he cut down every opponent who faced him and the cheers of the tribe were like wind in pine trees. His fingers closed convulsively as if they once more held the great iron slashing sword with the jeweled hilt in the shape of a horse's head.

In dreams, as in name, he was still the champion.

Ír stirred on his bench and then sank back into simmering. His hands clenched into fists, relaxed, and clenched again. He pulled his feet under him, like a lion about to pounce.

◇ **6** ◇

AIRLESS, MUGGY HEAT enveloped the Heroes' Hall. Dusky golden torchlight within the hall seemed equally oppressive, weighted with smoke and the aromas of roast meat, tense with anticipation as the Gaelicians watched the doorway, waiting for the arrival of the foreign trading ambassador.

The bard on his bench was sensitive to the massed anxieties

around him. The atmosphere seemed strangely bitter, reminding him of the chords he would play to introduce a tragic tale. He shifted on his seat and held Clarsah more tightly, as if she shielded him from the sudden stab of doubt he felt about the future.

Something was wrong. Or something was about to go wrong. Amergin could feel it as he waited with the others for the commander of the fleet in the harbor.

"Why isn't he here already?" Gosten asked Éber Finn. "Are you certain he's coming? Did you say something down at the harbor to offend him?"

"Of course not! He'll be here, he's as hot for trade as we are. He'll be here, I tell you."

"He had better be," commented the ancient patriarch Ítos. "Every member of my clan has come to me today, reminding me of this or that imported item they need desperately. I am exhausted just from fending them off."

They looked eagerly toward the portal, but the next arrival was not Age-Nor.

Colptha the sacrificer, having waited until the rest of the nobles had entered, swept through the doorway, drawing all eyes as he intended. He wore his customary expression of calculated superiority; a man of privilege and secrets. A young attendant trotted at his heels.

"Who's that with Colptha?" Brego asked Éremón.

"My son, Conmael," Gosten told them, leaning forward across the low wooden wall of his compartment. "A nimble boy not yet of swordbearing age, and biddable. I heard Colptha was looking for a bodyservant, so I proposed Conmael as bedwarmer for him. He has no wife to serve that function; every woman he looks at refuses his bride gifts."

"I wouldn't send a son of mine to Colptha," remarked Étan, another clan-chief. "To one of the other druids, certainly—to Amergin, for example."

"The bard has never taken a bedwarmer," Éremón interjected. "He refuses bodyservants of any kind; he says it distracts him too much to have someone in his house when he's composing."

"But you must agree that a storyteller is more desirable company for a child than a sacrificer."

"Colptha performs a very necessary service for the tribe," Gosten reminded them, beginning to feel defensive. "Reading the entrails and divining the future . . . Besides, if Conmael

57

pleases him he may take the boy as a foster son and strengthen my family's ties to the clan of Milesios. With a resumption of trade, the Míl will have more wealth to distribute throughout the tribe, and he's always been generous to foster kin.''

Colptha and Conmael were nearing the sacrificer's compartment. The boy's head swiveled from side to side as he recognized the heroes assembled in the hall, but Colptha whispered to him, ''Cling to me, boy, as an echo clings to sound, and pay no attention to anyone else.''

Conmael obediently scuttled closer, and felt the druid's hand briefly smooth his sandy hair in approbation.

Conmael gulped. Proximity to one of the mysterious and powerful priestly class left him weak-kneed with awe—and very mindful of his father's stern injunction to please.

They entered the druid's compartment and Colptha beckoned to the boy to sit beside him on his bench. ''We will be friends, you and I,'' Colptha said. ''I was a boy like you once, with an unfillable belly and a skinny neck.'' His fingers cupped the base of the boy's skull, feeling the shape of the bone. Colptha rarely touched a living human being; this was almost a voyage of exploration for him. How fragile was the joining where head met neck! How eager for acceptance was the young face turned up to his! A knot of old anger seemed to loosen inside the sacrificer as Conmael's natural warmth reached out to him, offering a bonding.

Conmael was just noticing that the druid had a peculiar habit. Colptha continually moved his head back and forth on his neck as he spoke to his new attendant, reminding the boy of a snake weaving in tall grass to freeze a fieldmouse for capture. He met Colptha's eyes and their glances locked. Conmael sat helpless, frightened but also excited and flattered, until Colptha jerked his head to one side and gazed off across the hall, breaking the link between them. He was smiling faintly, and Conmael had the impression of having passed some obscure but very important test.

The buzz of conversation was reaching a feverish pitch in the Heroes' Hall. Warriors and clan-chiefs were shouting to one another or to the women in the balcony, servitors were weaving among the nobles and their women with great trays of food, firelight gleamed on gold and silver, copper and iron. Every Gaelician was decked in jewelry, clanking with splendor to impress the traders. Éber Finn wore a pectoral of lapis lazuli, and Scotta's long gown of pleated and imported linen, worn thin now by the seasons, was held to her thickening waist by a girdle inset with gold and carnelian. Celtic folk loved ostentation, particularly massive jewelry and bright tartans woven in their clan colors, and on this most important occasion everyone present was arrayed as splendidly as possible.

The older wives of the clan-chiefs had threadbare silk mantles from the days when traders still frequented the harbor. Younger women competed with such luxury goods in various ways, such as arranging their hair in constructions as complex as the interlace characterizing Celtic jewelry.

Last season Éremón's wife Odba had adopted a pattern of parallel rows of waxed curls spaced across her forehead, and drawn the rest of her tawny mane into a high twist held in place with amber-headed pins. The first night she had worn it this way she waited tensely, but when Éremón made no comment she was not surprised. In a perverse way she was even pleased; he acted as she expected. "Nothing I do satisfies that man," she complained with practiced petulance at the well-curb.

She would not humiliate herself by openly calling Éremón's attention to her new hairstyle, and he, who would have noticed the smallest addition to his horses' harness ornaments, never thought to comment on the waxed curls or the high twist. Odba retaliated by serving him badly cooked food and neglecting to mend his tunics.

Since she frequently used such reprisals for real or imagined injury, Éremón was not even aware that a new crime had been added to his list. He only knew he liked her less each day, and avoided her more.

Now Odba sat with the other noblewomen in the balcony, watching resentfully as Éremón laughed and gestured below, immersed in companions, oblivious to her.

Díl was watching her own husband, and at last she remarked, "Donn seems so glum, don't you think? And this should be a festive occasion. Why does he look worried, Scotta—do you know?"

Scotta leaned forward, sweeping her eyes over her sons. Donn was indeed sitting low on his bench, with a downturned mouth. Éremón and Éber Finn were having a wonderful time. Amergin had taken Clarsah into his lap and begun playing her very gently, stroking sleepy music from her strings to lull the dozing Míl and shield his ears from the sea of noise around them.

And Ír was sitting very still, not moving. Suddenly his presence filled Scotta's vision and she felt the chill of premonition, just as a new figure entered the Heroes' Hall.

Ír had been sitting alone for a long time, unaware of his surroundings, only dimly perceiving light; sound. Laughter. The harp music Amergin directed to the Míl's ears alone could not reach and soothe him, but he did begin to hear shards of laughter. Men laughing. A new swirl of excitement nearby.

Bile flooded his mouth. They were laughing over some conspiracy against him—see how they had all clotted together there, near the portal? They were pointing at him, whispering about him, only pretending to be interested in someone else. But they could not deceive Ír. He knew he had enemies everywhere and must be on constant guard. He was superior to them all and they hated him for it.

Like the play of sun and shadow in changeable weather, his mood altered. The laughter sounded different as it beat against him, and he understood that he was inferior to them and they despised him for it. They slashed him with the whip of satire. They would destroy him if they could, taking his beautiful head as a trophy and tying it to the neck of a horse; galloping with the trophy swinging and Ír's blood dripping onto the Earth Mother.

He must not let that happen. Beware. Beware!

They were all around him now, a mass of men moving slowly through the hall toward Milesios. Enemies. Take that one, for example, in the purple robes. Who was he? He was dressed in the conspicuous style of the Phoenicians, the far-flung race of Sea People referred to as the Purple Empire because of their passion for dye of that color.

But the stranger looked like none of the Carthaginians Ír remembered from his youth. This man's nose was too beaky, his complexion too olive. Ír watched him covertly. The stranger laughed too often and his laugh had a false ring. He was trying to ingratiate himself with the Gaelicians, to blend in among them, but Ír recognized him as an impostor. Yes! An impostor who was only pretending to be a Phoenician trader in order to gain entry to the Heroes' Hall.

He must have been sent by Ír's enemies. Why? What were they plotting?

Ír's senses were honed to a sharp edge. He muttered a swift invocation to Goibniu, spirit of the iron, summoning the

60

strength of metal to his hands. He was keen and indomitable, let them come after him. All those who despised him, let them try him in battle!

And the sights and the sounds swirling and the colors pulsing and the pounding in his head demanding release . . .

Threads of scarlet and yellow lashed across his brain. Heat lightning scorched the backs of his eyeballs.

The man in purple turned and met his eyes, staring back at him with beady black orbs. He must poke those eyes back into that spying skull!

Screaming defiance, Ír vaulted over the side of his compartment and seized the astonished Phoenician by the throat.

Scotta jumped to her feet and yelled at him, but it was useless. She gazed down at the scene with an infuriating feeling of frustration. She had carried Ír in her womb, had heard him acclaimed as the most beautiful man in the tribe. Once, women had envied her his motherhood, had envied the women he bedded. But no longer.

She threw a supplicating glance toward Milesios, but the aging chieftain, eased by Clarsah's sleepy music, had fallen into an oblivious darkness. Amergin had meant to wake him when Age-Nor arrived but everything had happened too fast. Now the bard forgot the chieftain snoring beside him and stared helplessly, like everyone else, at his screaming brother.

Scotta looked frantically for someone to take control of the situation. She shouted to Milesios but her voice vanished in the general pandemonium. Milesios, resigned from it all, slept on.

Ír's bright blue eyes rolled wildly as he shifted his hold, jerking the Phoenician's head back by the hair. A knife flashed in Ír's hand. He thrust it beneath the forked black beard of the hapless merchant Age-Nor of Tyre, whose ships were newly arrived in the harbor below the headland.

Feeling the blade press against his windpipe, Age-Nor gasped and struggled to control his flailing hands, afraid he might jostle his attacker into cutting his throat. "I will wash your robe with your blood," Ír panted to him. "Then I will poke out those staring eyes of yours so you can no longer spy on me."

Ír's voice rose to a shriek. "This man has lurked around the walls of my house season after season, trying to learn my secrets! He has come to kill me and steal my strength for himself. You are all my witnesses and can testify to the brehons. I have a right to kill this man to protect myself!''

No one moved. The incident had happened too suddenly and Ír's volatility was well known. If anyone tried to reach the weapons stacked beyond the door, Ír might well complete what he had begun and leave an important trading ambassador from the Sea People cooling on the floor like butchered meat.

The aquiline features of the Phoenician supported ashen skin. His eyes bulged from his head. Éremón, alarmed, had risen from his bench, aware that he was the nearest warrior to Ír and his victim, but he froze when he got a good look at his brother's face. Ír's eyes were wild and emptied of reason.

For many seasons, Éremón had been dreaming of replacing his sire as champion of the tribe. He was always the first to take on a challenge or rush into danger. His tribesmen might well expect Éremón to dispatch Ír with a quick thrust of his own meat knife in order to save the Gaelicians the loss of desperately needed trade.

When the joy of battle bubbled in his veins, Éremón had willingly sent men to their tombs. He had no compunction about killing, for the druids taught that death was merely a transition, a directional change between lives. Death was not to be feared like the shuddering of the Earth Mother, or the sea bursting from its bounds.

But Éremón was reluctant to attack Ír, even for the sake of the tribe. A man who killed a brother burdened his immortal spirit with a debt that would take many lives to repay.

Besides, a mere meat knife might not be sufficient against Ír's raging strength.

Age-Nor, who lacked the comforting belief that death was transitory, closed his eyes and whispered desperate prayers to his own gods, though the dagger at his throat warned him he was out of favor with Baal-Shamim, the Terrible Lord; with Melqart, God of Tyre; with Asherat-Yam, She Who Devours the Sea. They had put their hands over their ears and turned their faces from him, though he had spent his fortune in frantic propitiation of them. Now he would fall into the blackness that had no bottom. He would die at the end of the world with savages who might not even give him the decency of a funeral pyre. His ships would be sold for scrap. It was a hard fate.

No one dared make a grab for Ír or his knife, but there was

62

one formidable weapon within easy reach in the hall—in the hands of Amergin the bard.

Rising slowly to his feet so no sudden movement would alarm Ír, the bard ran his fingers over the strings of the harp Clarsah and she answered him in her liquid golden voice.

Sacred to all Celtic tribes were the oak tree, the stones of the Mother, and the sound of the harp. When Clarsah commanded, human voices fell silent. Even Ír stood immobile, his eyes a shade less wild, his knife ready but not yet stained with blood.

Amergin played softly at first, to make his audience lean into the hush and listen. Then with rising volume he plucked from the strings the music of the incoming tide and the wind in the twisted pines along the cliffs. The voice of the harp was as soothing as the lowing of cattle in the evening; it was the song a mother sang to a fretful child; it was the calming touch of a druid healer's hands on a fevered body.

The Phoenician, slumping against Ír's heaving chest, surrendered to despair. Age-Nor thought he was hearing his funeral dirge.

Amergin had risen to his full height, his multicolored cloak flung back from his shoulders to give freedom to his sinewy arms as his fingers moved across Clarsah, palm and pad and fingernail summoning sound. The harp knew that touch and held nothing back.

Clarsah was the most ancient Gaelician in the hall, and the most powerful.

As Amergin held Clarsah a poem came to him from some uncharted deep, welling up strongly, born complete. Its incantatory structure was determined by generations of bardic tradition, but the composition was his alone, summoned from the extravagant passions locked within Amergin himself. He had never been able to draw on them, to free them, until this moment.

Looking across the hall at his mad and beautiful brother, Amergin recognized an outburst of that elemental energy which fueled all creative fires. The bard had never let himself surrender to the unfettered wildness Ír represented, yet, seeing it embodied, he understood. And soared.

The pure curve of a gull's wing had the power to move Amergin to tears; the comic absurdity spattered across human nature had occasionally bent him double with laughter. There were times when he longed to stand on a cliff as Ír did, shrieking into the storm. Longed to fly with the birds or leap heedless into the dark sea. Wild impulses surged through the bard—joy and melancholy, savagery and tenderness warred within him. His blood, his heritage.

And from all those passionate threads the poem wove itself.

Looking into Ír's glazed eyes Amergin saw, at first, only red chaos. Then the deeper druid vision gripped him, and he saw through chaos to the small boy crouched somewhere inside. A bright little fellow who had been afraid of the dark until Scotta thrashed it out of him. An overly energetic youth who had fought harder and danced longer than any of his brothers, as if he were afraid to stop. A grown man helpless as a child, pinioned between overweening sadness and frenzied gaiety.

Amergin locked Ír's gaze with his own so the words could be driven into that tormented skull. The poem filled the bard's mouth. A druid poem, shrouded in mystery to distract Ír and force him to contemplation; a Celtic poem, containing hidden in its phrases an homage to the Earth Mother and the many aspects of her annual face.

Clarsah thundered a compelling, repetitive rhythm, lifting Amergin's voice like the crest of a wave until it filled the hall. The assembled Gaelicians felt the hairs begin to bristle on the backs of their necks as the Heroes' Hall rang with a mighty bardic chant, perfectly attuned to the night and the need.

> I am the wind upon the sea,

. . . and they could hear the high keening of the stormvoice; they could feel the wind on their faces! Men glanced at one another, startled.

> I am the flood across the plain,

And their visions were filled with a tremendous wall of water bearing down upon them as the rivers burst periodically from their banks, surging across the land.

> I am the hawk above the cliff,
> I am the thorn beneath the rose,

Sharp stab of pain making beauty more poignant, as death does life, as winter does summer.

> I am the stag of seven tines,
> I am the salmon in a pool,
> I am wisdom; who but I
> cools the head aflame with smoke?

A soft curling of sound surrounding a pulsing center, soothing and easing.

> I am the hill where poets walk,

The stately tread of revered feet from a height above them; an awareness of remote creation.

> I am the lure from beyond world's end,

A haunting call of irresistible beauty. The bard's voice ached with longing and they were all forced to share it, suddenly hungry for they knew not what, or where.

> I am the spear that rears for blood,
> I am the tear the sun lets fall,
> I am the breaker, threatening doom,
> I am an infant; who but I
> peeps from the unknown dolmen arch?

The implacable power of granite stones, bones of the Mother, arranged in a portal linking worlds. The earth's womb with a newborn face emerging from the archway, its eyes already ancient with wisdom.

The harp's voice ceased; the bard was silent. Still the crowd in the Heroes' Hall vibrated as one being, one string that Amergin's powerful fingers had seized and plucked and possessed, obedient to the magic of the bard.

The Gaelicians threw off the spell slowly. They had been buffeted by too many vivid impressions, too much sensual assault. Flood had rolled over them and bloody spears flashed before their eyes. They fought their way back into the reality of the hall while Amergin's poem was being absorbed into the stone walls around them, already immortal.

Ír's knife slipped from nerveless fingers. The men nearest him saw it. Though their own eyes were still glazed, they closed in on Ír and gently extricated the Phoenician, who fled at once to the far side of the hall.

Ír did not notice. He stood alone in the center of a cleared space, hugging himself as if he were cold. His lips silently shaped the words of the poem.

"Amergin," he said in a faroff voice. "That hawk . . . I was that hawk. I flew as you sang. I never felt so free . . . And the rose and the thorn . . ." His voice trailed away. He lifted his chin and stared up at the smoked underside of the roof. "The sea for depth, the flood for horror, the stag for strength," he mused aloud.

Then he laughed. Not the uncontrolled shriek his clan had come to dread, but the easy mirth of an ordinary man. His eyes were clear and lucid. Forgetting his meat knife lying on the packed earthen floor, he turned and looked for the Phoenician.

"Ai, sea trader!" Ír called cheerfully. "I had you worried, didn't I? Don't stand there gaping. We always insist that ambassadors come unarmed and without bodyguards to the Heroes' Hall to show good faith, but your courage must be tested, for Milesios welcomes only the brave here. Come, bring a bowl and I'll pour you some wine myself. I feel a thirst, for some reason."

Ír sauntered to the nearest big terra-cotta wine jar, but the Phoenician made no effort to join him. Ír quickly forgot he had even extended the invitation and was soon chatting to those around him in a casual, if one-sided, conversation.

Like blood returning to a damaged limb, life flowed back into the hall.

Scotta came down the steps from the women's balcony. As she approached the Míl's bench her eyes met those of Amergin and she gave her head a small, worried shake. The bard knew the same thought was in them both. While castastrophe hovered over the tribe, Milesios had slumped on his bench, asleep. And if the head was disengaged, what—who—would take its place?

His wife's furious whisper summoned Milesios to cobwebbed wakefulness. "What? Wife?" he said blankly. "Has the trader arrived?" he mumbled, making an effort to sit straighter in spite of a sudden stab of pain through his bones.

Scotta stepped in front of his bench, effectively hiding him

66

from the eyes of his tribespeople until he could recover himself.

Amergin slowly sat down, feeling both exultant and drained. He propped the harp against his leg with reverent tenderness. Clarsah had known; she had guided and supported him, lending him her power. But the words! Where did the inspired words come from? Had the spirits put them in their entirety into his mouth?

He did not believe that. The phrases of his composition were a distillation of his own flashes of vision and awareness, his unique view. His seeing.

That, then, was the essence of the gift, and the obligation was to return it to the tribe in ways that would answer their need.

He wanted desperately to be alone in some quiet, undistracting place and think on these things. A powerful seduction came over him; a desire to relive that awesome moment when he felt his audience bound to him, one with him, a great interchange of beauty and energy flowing between them and uplifting them all. Self-doubt had washed away then, leaving him on a pinnacle only a bard—a great, true bard—could ever hope to describe.

His brothers might know ecstasy on the battlefield or at the climax of the hunt, but tonight Amergin had touched the flaming heart of poetry, and was forever changed.

But what about tomorrow? And the day after? Would that moment ever come again, and if not, how could he live without it?

The bard brooded on his bench, his dangling fingers touching the harp.

Someone cleared his throat very loudly. Amergin glanced up to find Age-Nor of Tyre standing before him, surrounded by solicitous Gaelicians trying to outshout each other in an effort to make amends. But Age-Nor ignored them. He was still trembling with fear, yet he had a pressing obligation before he could flee this barbaric place.

Folding his hands beneath his chin, the commander bowed low to the bard. "I owe my life to the sweet singer," he said. His command of the Celtic mother-tongue was limited and when he tried to add a Gaelician accent the results were atrocious. "Come to my ships as soon as there is light in the morning and choose whatever reward you want," he urged.

Amergin shook his head. Fumbling among his own memories of the Phoenician language to make things easier for both of them, he said, "You owe me no reward. I am of the order of druids, and one of our responsibilities is separating combatants when necessary. My tribe rewards me for my gifts, but an outsider has no obligation to me."

Age-Nor stared at him in disbelief. The Hellenes of Athens referred to the Keltoi tribes of Gaul and Iberia as barbarians, a derogatory epithet that, in their conceit, they applied to anyone who did not share their mother-tongue. But more than a difference of language separated the Celts from the world Age-Nor knew. Their thought processes were beyond his comprehension, and the Gaelician branch of the race had just terrified and now baffled him.

Did this man not realize he could ask for wealth and have it heaped in his arms like bales of cloth? Or, at least, such wealth as Age-Nor still possessed, which was not what it had been at the beginning of this disastrous voyage. But if Amergin operated under peculiar constraints, Age-Nor had laws circumscribing his life as well. The gods must be appeased. A life had been spared and something must be exchanged for it.

"When you saved me a debt was incurred," Age-Nor tried to explain, his speech a confusion of Phoenician and Gaelician. "In my birthplace, the city of Tyre, I am reckoned a prince. Many children fill my villas. Fairest of them is a girl child called U-ropa, lovely as a full wind in the sails. If you will not accept merchandise, sweet singer, upon my return to Tyre I will offer U-ropa as a sacrifice to Melqart in your name, that the city god of Tyre may look upon you with favor."

Amergin remembered hearing of the moloch, the Phoenician passion for excessive human sacrifice that swallowed up countless children from each generation in an attempt to mollify man-made idols. The druids were appalled at such senseless wastage of new life, and considered the priests of the Sea People cruel and greedy, exponents of destruction with no real idea of the way to win favor from the spirits.

The idea of a beautiful child in a distant land being casually slaughtered to appease such demons dismayed Amergin.

"I beg of you, Age-Nor, spare your daughter!" he pleaded hastily. "If I can ask anything I want of you, grant me this: preserve her life and give her special honor in your house."

Age-Nor's shiny black eyes were blank, uncomprehending. These barbarians made no sense to him at all, and such a request seemed ludicrous in a company where someone had just tried to murder him for no apparent gain.

All these Keltoi tribes from the far fringes of the known world seemed to be fearsome giants, two heads taller than a normal man. White-skinned, pale-eyed, wearing brilliant colors and flaunting enough jewelry to dazzle any professional thief in Tyre, they appeared bizarre in Age-Nor's eyes. Even the smallest of their women looked as if she could break him across her knee. Yet this man pleaded for one inconsequential child's life as if that life by itself had any meaning.

Age-Nor was swept by sudden longing for the plastered villas of sea-girt Tyre, for white southern light and the rattle of palm trees. For people who understood that life was both cheap and expendable and only property had lasting value.

He did not understand any of these Keltoi savages reputed to hold all the northern lands in their sway by virtue of iron weapons and skilled horsemanship, and he did not want to understand them. His only immediate desire was to get out of the hall alive.

"I will do as you request, of course," he assured Amergin, bowing from the waist. "But I must remind you, I am a prince and the commander of a fine fleet. So trivial a thing as the child's life does not balance the life you have saved. I will have to see that you are repaid, somehow. Sweet singer."

Amergin longed for the conversation to end. The effusive little man made him uncomfortable. Age-Nor carried the stench of cities in the pores of his skin; payments and manipulations shifted constantly behind his eyes, clearly visible to the vision of a druid.

"We will talk again," Age-Nor promised. "But for now I am very tired, and I have no taste left for this banquet of yours. The behavior of your chieftain in allowing me to be assaulted beneath his roof contradicts all I was told about the hospitality of Keltoi tribes, and I will not forget it. I never forget anything," he added, turning away. "Now I go to my ship."

Hands reached out, voices protested in desperation, but Age-Nor was determined. He had only the smallest reservoir of courage left, courage given him by terrible fear, and he must use it to carry him safely out of these walls as quickly as possible.

Ignoring the Gaelicians' pleas, he pushed his way through

them toward the door, showing them all the stiff back of a mighty indignation.

A wail arose before he was out the door. "What will we do now?"

"*What about the trade?!!*"

◇ **7** ◇

THE HEROES' HALL SEETHED with confusion. No one seemed certain of anything except that great damage had been done to a potential trading relationship—and that they had heard the bard Amergin recite one of those rare and inspired poems which many lesser bards would live and die without ever producing.

Milesios was genuinely surprised to find his wife was angry with him. "I tell you I was merely tired and didn't realize what was happening," he insisted. "I have never breached the sacred laws of hospitality; you know that, Scotta!"

"I thought I did," his wife said in a tight voice.

Clan-chiefs crowded around the Míl's bench, bemoaning the anticipated loss of imported goods they had already promised to their families. "We need iron!" shouted Gosten. "We need dyes," complained Un, chief of a clan with many skilled weavers. "My wives are clamoring for beakers of Phoenician glass," said Éber Finn, elbowing through the others. "What will we do if Age-Nor refuses to trade now?"

"Our own ores are exhausted, where will we get more?"

"Where will we get jewels and spices?"

"How will we satisfy the demands of our followers?" worried clan-chiefs wanted to know.

Everyone expected Milesios to retrieve the situation. His own forefathers had first established trade with the Sea People; surely he knew the secret. Surely he could bring it all back again, no matter what mad thing his son did.

Surely . . .

But Milesios felt a curious disinclination to grapple with

70

the problem, serious though it was. So many things had been serious in his life . . . he had faced so many challenges . . . Nothing seemed to matter so intensely anymore.

He gestured to Donn. "I sent you for tin and you came back without. I expected more of you."

Donn's shoulders sagged. Only pride kept him from offering a babble of excuses.

Milesios sighed. He could drag himself into his own chariot and go to the celsine, use all the arts of persuasion and intimidation he had once polished . . . and still, he knew with irrefutable belly-knowledge, coming from the center of the body and not the brain—still, there would be no tin.

His back ached cruelly and he seemed to have a toothache throughout his ribs. Pain he would admit to no one was sapping his strength, day by day.

Let it go, he thought. Just let it go.

His sons crowded around him, each dreaming of finding some way to fill the sudden hollowness where leadership had been.

The bard was not exempt from that desire, but a bard's duties did not impinge upon a chieftain's. And yet . . . Amergin squinted his eyes, looking through memory. Seeing the galleys as he had besung them for his people: battered, exhausted ships, with the unmistakable aura of disintegration about them, more clear to his druid vision than Age-Nor would have liked.

"We have something the Sea People have to have," Amergin said aloud. "They would like tin, and if we could provide it they might come back. But they will never be able to leave at all without a sizable amount of timber to repair their ships. Those vessels are badly damaged, though they would deny it if you asked, for the truth isn't in them."

"Are you sure of this?" Milesios asked, suddenly more alert.

"I am."

The Míl stroked his mustache. "Even if we have no way to lure them back again, at least we can force them to trade us the goods they carry. Our backs are not against the wall, but the Tyrian's is. I wonder what he meant to do? Make us an offer to take some of our worthless timber off our hands, just to create a token trade, and give us his cheapest goods in return? Ai, I remember the old days . . ." The Míl grinned, fierce and wise for one more brief moment. "Age-Nor will empty his ships in return for our timber," he vowed.

"A druid would think of timber, of trees," Donn remarked, pleased to have the emphasis shift from his own failure.

"I am also of the order of druids," Colptha reminded them loudly, thrusting white-lipped through the crowd. He was furious to see Amergin coming to the forefront for a second time in this most surprising evening. "If the Phoenicians will buy timber, I will consult with the samodhii so we may determine which trees are willing to be sacrificed and sold to the Sea People. Such determinations are the functions of diviners, not bardagh," he added, looking at Amergin with cold eyes. "It may be that I can make up in full for Donn's failing."

"You're a bigger braggart than I am, Colptha." Éremón laughed suddenly, his hearty voice booming out in a hall now emptied of laughter. "And with less reason!"

The two brothers glared at each other, but Milesios made himself get to his feet and step between them. "Very well, Colptha, do what you can," he said. "And Éremón, Éber Finn . . . one of you, go to the harbor in the morning, take gifts, make promises, do whatever is necessary to mollify the Phoenicians, if you can. You're my sons, surely you can manage that much."

"What about you?" Donn asked in obvious alarm.

"I'm going to bed. It is in the hands of my sons, so prove yourselves."

They stared at each other, disconcerted, as Milesios left the hall. Scotta mirrored their surprised expressions before hurrying after him.

"I never thought I would hear that," Éremón remarked. Then his teeth flashed white through his flowing mustache. "But I have an idea. Listening to Amergin, I felt the hair stand up on my head, and I thought to myself, How can any of us ever surpass his achievement? Then it came to me . . ."

"What?" Eber demanded to know, but Éremón shook his head.

"Why should I tell you and give you a chance to claim the credit? Find your own way to impress the tribe. You'll know my plan soon enough; everyone will, and then they'll sing my praises as loudly as they'll be singing the bard's tomorrow."

He went back to his compartment, whistling jauntily, to

work out his scheme in the privacy of his head and with a little help from his wine bowl.

The crowd remaining in the hall was still too awed by Amergin's performance; they dared not presume to request any more recitations from him that night. Magnificence should stand alone. Gratefully, Amergin took Clarsah and went back to his own house, to savor in private this unexpected summit to his life.

In the morning a delegation set out for the harbor to attempt repair of the fractured relationship with Age-Nor. They took him gifts of jewelry from the collection belonging to the Míl himself—a gift Éber did not approve. "I wanted that gold torc to be mine someday," he complained. But he put the torc into Age-Nor's hands when the time came, and smiled, and put a good face on it.

Ír did not accompany the delegation. He did not even offer to, to everyone's relief, for who could refuse the chieftain's son? He spent most of the day snoring in his bed in his own house, a common occurrence after one of his outbursts.

Colptha had risen long before dawnlight to consult with the nearest samodhi about the cutting of timber, but then he too had joined Donn and Éremón and Éber Finn at the harbor. The sons of Milesios, trying to rescue a bad situation.

Amergin had not gone with them. Only Donn thought of requesting a bard to come and witness the event—but feared the outcome might be less than satisfactory and decided it was better not to have a bard's infallible memory record unfortunate mistakes.

Others were thinking of Amergin, however; an undertone of admiration for him rang across the clanholds like an eagle's cry. "The bard of the Milesians recited a remarkable poem last night," those who had been there rushed to tell those who had not. "The words still ring in our heads. It is possible that a new chief bard will soon bring prestige to the entire tribe!"

Amergin had not let himself dwell on such a possibility, badly though he desired the honor. The bardagh would name a chief bard only when they were sure of a man with enough extraordinary gifts; they would not hurry. Druids never hurried. Still, it would be so . . .

The best way to quit worrying about oneself was to think of others. That decided, Amergin found an overturned basket to sit on and took Clarsah from her case, and within a few

73

heartbeats he had a circle of children around him, eager to hear him recite. The bard loved the little folk and they knew it.

Scéna Dullsaine noticed him there, and made her way toward him.

Ferdinón and his party had spent the night in the guesting house of Milesios, for their own clanhold lay a long way distant. They would linger in the region until the trade was settled and distribution began—a golden opportunity, Scéna thought, to take a better look at that bard.

Bold, beautiful Scéna Dullsaine tucked up her skirt in both hands and sat down at the edge of the circle of children, surprising Amergin. She was a very great prize, born to be a chieftain's woman, and she had never paid any attention to him before.

Scéna arched her spine so he could see the grace of her bearing, even as she sat crosslegged in the dust, and smiled at the bard.

Amergin slipped the tough horn of his fingernails among Clarsah's strings and began telling the story of his tribe, strumming the harp to give an effect of galloping hooves and swinging iron swords. He tried to avoid looking at Scéna Dullsaine. Surely he would make a dreadful fool of himself if he mistook her interest in his recitation for something more personal. He willed himself to think only of the history he was about to relate, but it was not easy.

Generations ago, ancestral Celtic chieftains had turned their backs on the gloomy forests and diseased riverlands of Gaul and headed south, searching for warmer pastures and more room for their expanding clans. Wagons loaded with children and possessions had ventured into the torturous mountain passes and thence to the broad Iberian peninsula, while fearless warriors pitted their superior iron weapons against the weaker bronze of the indigenous natives.

Amergin sang of it all, throwing in the lowing of cattle and the bleating of the herds of goats the Gauls brought with them; the listening children laughed in delight at that part. Responding to their pleasure, Amergin brought to life the valor of a race fighting for land and existence every step of the way because the pulsing energy of Celtic folk unflinchingly accepted challenge.

Challenge was growth. Movement was growth. Growth was life.

The foremost tribe of colonizers, who had come to be known as the Gallaeci or Gaelicians, had moved across the lands of the Iberians, conquering and intermarrying, until they were stopped at last by the western sea. They had settled there and forced weaker tribes to mine the metal ores that would give the region fame.

The story seemed as inevitable as the turning wheel of the seasons. A druid affirmation of recurrent life and growth and success, meant to hearten people in a dark and dangerous world. The small people loved it, and when the harp fell silent and Amergin's story telling ended they stamped their feet on Gaelician earth and yelled their approval.

The bard put Clarsah in her case and stood up. Scéna Dullsaine remained where she was. She looked up as Amergin came toward her and watched his long legs scissor beneath his brief tunic. Sinewy legs, well formed, capable of wrapping around a woman's body as easily as she could clamp hers around his.

She tipped her head back and beamed her generous smile up at him. She had raised and flexed her knees, propping her forearms on them so her fingers could angle gracefully between her slightly parted legs. Lush and languid and inviting as summer was Scéna Dullsaine, and there was no mistaking her intention.

Anything might happen, Amergin thought. Then, with a rising certainty: anything I *want* to happen.

He saw too much glisten of healthy pink gums when Scéna smiled, and the skin of her throat had a grainy texture. Small and human flaws could be endearing if he chose to see them that way. Amergin willed his vision to go no deeper, limiting itself to externals. He did not want to be forced to look deeply into this exciting and accessible woman. He wanted his reward; his season.

Where the sleeves of her linen gown fell back from her arms he saw firm white flesh, well-rounded. The iris of her gray eyes was warmly flecked with brown. If he looked at the flecks and not the pupils he did not have to see into her soul.

"That sun is too hot to sit in for so long," he remarked. "You would be more comfortable in a shady place, Scéna Dullsaine."

"I am warm," she agreed. "Too warm, perhaps. Where can I go? Is it cooler in your house?"

75

Amergin hesitated. Anything I want, he thought again, with the residual confidence of last night's triumph.

He did not have to take her to his house, his inner preserve. He never took a woman there. And the Míl's guesting house was already filled with Scéna's kin and other visitors. But Amergin was a private man and knew many private places.

"There is a cove on the beach," he told her, "where a rock outcropping cuts off the wind, but it is always cool, even on the hottest days. You would enjoy it, I think."

Scéna stood up in one easy motion, not one muscle disturbing her smile. "Show it to me, bard," she said. "We may be here many nights and days, until the trade arrangements are made and Ferdinón has collected his share. In the meantime I would like to enjoy . . . whatever there is to offer, here."

He did not drive her out to the headland in his chariot. They walked, and he enjoyed the way she moved, long-limbed and sinuous. It occurred to Amergin that a song might be sung about the way a woman walked, though no such songs were part of his people's bardic tradition.

Not yet, he thought, watching Scéna out of the corner of his eye.

He led the way down the path to the beach and she came close behind him, chatting easily of her family and his, of the ships and the weather. Amergin felt the hard knot of his effort and ambition loosen a little. He no longer had to concentrate so fiercely on such things; there seemed more room in his life today than there had been yesterday.

And Scéna Dullsaine filled that room with summer.

Scéna was not tentative about her pleasuremaking as Taya would have been. The use of her body for joy was but one of its many purposes and she took pride in doing everything she did very well. She sat on the beach with Amergin and they talked of familiar topics and common interests as Donn must talk with Díl, or Milesios with Scotta. When the silences became longer than the speaking they turned to each other at the same moment. Scéna met Amergin fully and confidently, pressing into his arms as if she had been there before and knew all his body's geography.

Her breasts cushioned him; she adjusted her body easily so he could move their clothing aside. Looking down into her eyes from a mere hand's-width above her, Amergin thought that they were very beautiful.

Looking up into his, Scéna thought she had never seen blue

eyes so hot, so intense and hungry and . . . then she was not thinking at all. To Scéna Dullsaine, thinking was a function of the body and her body was now otherwise occupied.

She groaned once, fitting her hips to his. Amergin was lapped in her heat, listening only to her panting breath and the roaring of his blood in his ears. At the last moment he was even stronger than Scéna had expected, gripping her fiercely as if he would bend her into some new shape of his own creation. She strained upward to meet him. They were the only people alive anywhere, their joined existence was the only existence.

Yes, Amergin thought for one blinding flashing moment of pleasure. This was no child but a woman, a possible partner, a possible completion.

And then the world revolved slowly away from them and they were aware of it again, receptive to its sights and sounds. Their sweat-locked bodies began separating because they could not do otherwise; flesh could not permanently fuse with flesh.

Separateness. Amergin perceived it as pain. In a moment Scéna would stir beneath him, sit up, wade into the sea to wash herself, retwist the hair atop her head and smile at him with those bold and dappled eyes.

Before she could initiate the first gesture of separation the bard made it himself for his own protection. But he did not pull away completely, or turn over and fall into snorting sleep like the warriors she had known before him. He remained close to her, tender and interested in her, complimenting her in phrases like jewels that made her more beautiful.

He lifted the harp he had carefully set aside before their pleasuremaking, and locking Scéna's eyes with his own he played music for her. The strings seemed strangely stiff, at first, and Amergin had to pluck them hard to get Clarsah to sing for this woman; this other woman. But he was master of the harp and she must obey. He sat relaxed on the white sand, smiling at Scéna from time to time as he drew rainbows of sound from Clarsah, and Scéna watched him with growing admiration.

He was the first of the complex class of gifted professionals known as druids she had ever welcomed into her body, and he was a revelation to her. Was this what the druidic talent brought: this enveloping intensity, this savage tenderness?

"I am beginning to regret the time I have wasted on warriors," Scéna Dullsaine murmured drowsily to Amergin the bard.

When they returned to the Míl's stronghold together, the old women were the first to take note of their arrival. The old women noticed everything first; their eyes had had the most practice. They nodded and cackled to each other, clucking over choice grains of gossip. "Amergin will take Ferdinón's daughter into his house in the next marrying season," they assured one another. "When the leaves spring out again three seasons from now and we light the Bealtaine fire, Amergin will add a new wife's name to the genealogy of the Milesian clan."

"More than leaves spring out in the season of Bealtaine," the old women told one another with bawdy laughter. They grinned their yellow-toothed grins and their eyes glittered with their personal recollections of the marrying season.

Amergin had taken his own moment from the day, but the day had not paused in its hurrying to wait for him. He watched Scéna walk away from him toward the guest house and his mind was briefly flooded with a pictured memory of her sunlit back, straight and well-muscled. The back of a proud Celtic woman, a Gaelician . . .

Clarsah hung heavy on his shoulder, reminding him of his duty and his dreams. And the green wind began singing again, insistent.

In the dark time when only the stars watched the world last night, Amergin had dared a very large dream. Flushed with the exhilaration of his poem in the Heroes' Hall, he had begun to imagine that he might be able to do that which had eluded bards for generations.

The spirits had willed that the bards be repositories of history and chroniclers of change, but no poet had yet woven the diverse strands of Celtic history into one cohesive epic, following the entire flow of the Celtic river from the past to the future; following the Gaelicians and their kindred tribes as they came out of distant, ancient darkness and headed toward . . . toward what?

No such epic existed, studded with the many facets of Celtic passion and brilliance, the inborn love of beauty and learning and craftsmanship, the melancholy and the gaiety, the hero-frenzy and generosity and the sheer zest for living. No such epic existed, other than that embodied by the people themselves. And if a bard was to be the voice of his race, should he not be able to sing them all together into history?

In the dark quietude of his house, the poet Amergin had

begun to dream a great dream—one that came back to him now while the memory of Scéna's body was still imprinted on his flesh and the north wind circled around him, promising, urging.

Dreams can be relentless tyrants.

The commander of the merchant fleet in the harbor understood the tyranny of dreams very well indeed. A dream he now saw as incredibly foolish had led Age-Nor of Tyre to this desolate place at the end of the world. If the Gaelician clans were anxious about their future and desperate to recapture their fading prosperity, the Tyrian merchant was even more anxious and desperate as he prowled the harbor examining ships that might be irreparably damaged and felt the last grains of his fortune slip through his fingers like so much sand.

On a golden day that now seemed impossibly distant, Age-Nor had begun this voyage with high hopes. While Amergin dreamed on the headland of composing a mighty epic, Age-Nor stood on the beach below and cast his mind back through a series of epic misadventures, trying to remember the exact moment when everything started to go wrong for him. Was it the day the voyage began?

The future had seemed full of promise, then. He had been wealthy and respected, and his life had seemed as secure as life could on the eastern shores of the Mediterranean. Almost unique among the merchant princes of Tyre, Age-Nor had still sailed on his own vessels and made his own deals, for he could not bear to delegate authority. He was known from Ugarit and Salamis to Berytus—Bay*root,* the caravan drivers called it—and even as far west as Carthage. He had thought himself a reasonably happy man.

Before this voyage began.

No, the trouble must lie still farther back in time. Carthage; that was the true beginning of disaster, he thought as he remembered.

Was it only six years ago that he had offered burnt sacrifices in the ocher-stained temple of Baal-Hammon in Carthage and listened for the first time to a ritual reading of Hanno's voyage of discovery down the west coast of Libya? Giant birds and giant gemstones and a race of hairy people whose women the Carthaginians had captured and ultimately stuffed for exhibition.

That was where the trouble began, Age-Nor decided: the first time he heard of the wondrous voyages being made beyond the Pillars of Herakles—by the admirals of Carthage.

Age-Nor paced the beach, surveying the wreckage of his dreams, and remembered. Remembered his excitement and then his horror as he heard concomitant accounts of demons and cannibals and sea monsters that the Carthaginians claimed to have encountered beyond the Pillars. Such reports were sufficient to discourage other adventurers from trying to re-trace Hanno's profitable route, and no eastern Phoenician ever tried.

Would that I had followed their example, Age-Nor thought in his misery.

But the stories he had heard stayed with him, teasing him.

On his very next voyage to Carthage he had found himself the houseguest of a fellow shipowner who also owned a partnership in a thriving glassworks. Abhiram was one of that network of Phoenicians Age-Nor assiduously cultivated through the Mediterranean basin, for the alliance of trade was a wide net and must have many strongpoints.

Abhiram had been in an ebullient mood; Age-Nor recalled that very clearly. Not only was his fleet doing well at the time, but he had just learned that his share of the profits from the glassworks was double that of the preceding year. At such times a man's tongue may slip its moorings a little. Cartha-ginians were excessively circumspect about discussing the extent of their sea routes with citizens of rival cities, but on that long-ago evening Abhiram lost control. Well into their third amphora of wine he had begun telling Age-Nor of the exploits of one Himilco, commander of another fabled fleet.

One generation before Hanno, Himilco was known to have sailed through the Pillars of Herakles and then north, rather than south, but what happened afterward was veiled in mys-tery, whispered as a tale of terror to scare young sailors out of their appetites. As far as he knew, Age-Nor was one of the first to hear the true story from the inside, for Abhiram belonged to a family that had helped fund Himilco's expedition.

". . . and makes me proud to be a citizen of Carthage," Abhiram was saying once more in Age-Nor's memory. The dinner had been long and over-rich, floating on both wine and Egyptian beer. The servants could not conceal their yawning and even the entertainers hired for the evening were sprawled asleep in the corners. Only Age-Nor remained awake and alert, listening to his host's rambling discourse with growing fascination.

"Hanno and Himilco. Wonderful accomplishments. And I am not saying that just because my family wisely invested in both of them. You understand, Age-Nor, you understand trade." Abhiram belched and scratched his nose. His features were clustered in the center of his large face, leaving a broad expanse of skin around the perimeter.

"Carthage used to be just a colonial outpost, you know," he reminisced. "Tyre founded it, to give them an arm into the west like Tingus and Lixus and Utica. All Carthaginian now, of course. Not to denigrate you Tyrians. Your people were the ones who redesigned those long, narrow Egyptian coasters and made good seagoing ships out of them. Compact, manageable. I grant you that. But Carthage in turn improved on your designs. Yes. And it took a Carthaginian like Himilco to sail those ships all the way to the Pretanic Islands and . . ."

Some blurred instinct warned him and he hesitated. Age-Nor quickly refilled his host's wine glass himself, and waited, smiling encouragement. At last Abhiram's tongue, warmed by wine, came to life again. "What were we saying, old friend?"

"We were discussing the improved shipbuilding techniques of Carthage," Age-Nor said smoothly. "There is a rumor that you have been able to sail with some frequency very far north, though of course no one really believes it."

"You had better believe it," Abhiram boasted. "Best ships in the world, right out there in the harbor. Forty oars to a galley; fifty, some of them. What power, eh? Sail anywhere we want to.

"You know what Himilco did, for example? He took a great fleet up the west coast of Iberia and . . . that was not such a feat in itself, of course, for we of Carthage know Iberia very well. You Tyrians have spent little time there since we gained the ascendancy in the region, but we began just the way you did, selling cheap trinkets to natives who had no civilized standards to judge them by. And we took enough raw materials in return to make Carthage wealthy.

"Tartessos, in the southwest quarter of the peninsula, had mountains of copper and rivers of tin. That is all a man needs to make bronze, and where would any of us be without bronze, eh? Eh? Did you know that Tartessos once had a fleet of its own on the ocean-river, as long ago as the early days of

Tyre? And a city, Tarshish, of such splendor and vice . . . we reduced it all to rubble, that foul, magnificent city, and we took so much treasure out of it even the Persians would have been dazzled. Then the time came to enlarge our sphere still more. No limit to trade, eh, Age-Nor?"

He had momentum now, his words ran on of their own accord. They tumbled out of him like vomit, and Age-Nor wore his ears thin, listening.

"Tarshish. You could buy any kind of sex with human or animal in Tarshish, and someone else would pay to watch. But we moved on. Our Himilco went northward to the shores of the Gaulish territory and opened new trade routes for us with the Keltoi. While Tyre and Sidon sat in the sun, growing fat and lazy from Persian commerce, Himilco sailed in cold waters and . . ."

"But everyone knows there are terrible sea monsters beyond the Pillars of Herakles," Age-Nor interrupted, unable to contain himself.

Abhiram chuckled, an oily laugh. "Monsters. You believed those stories, you gullible fools. Your supposedly bold captains decided to stay safe in the Mediterranean because we gave them reports of demons in the ocean-river, and horrors no ship could survive. But I tell you this in strictest confidence, my friend. Himilco survived them easily, because those were just tales to frighten children. And see how well it worked!" His laughter was bubbling and obscene, pleasure taken in a giant hoax that had discouraged the eastern Phoenicians for generations, while Carthage looted the west.

Age-Nor held his face carefully impassive. "So Himilco made it to the west coast of Gaul. And what was that you said? The islands the Greek geographers call the Pretanic Isles?"

Abhiram was nodding, his mind befogged by fumes. "Ah, yes. Pretanic. The two great islands which lie west of Gaul in the ocean-river. Albion, the natives call the first. And Ierne beyond that. Himilco sailed to Albion and found the natives mining vast quantities of tin. He made very profitable arrangements with those natives—arrangements in the name of Carthage, not of Tyre or Sidon or any other eastern city. The natives of Albion speak a tongue not unlike that of the Gauls; they are Keltoi, too. Our northern business partners . . ." His head drooped but Age-Nor could not let the conversation end now.

"What of the other place your mentioned, Ierne?"

Abhiram cocked a bleary eye. "What do you know of Ierne?"

"Very little. I seem to remember hearing, when I was a child, that the most prized red-gold of the Egyptian pharaohs originally came from some place known as Ierne."

"True enough," Abhiram verified, poking with greasy fingers into the wreckage of a stuffed and roasted peacock. "Various of the Sea People have visited Ierne as far back as anyone can remember. Plenty of gold there, nuggets shining in the rivers just waiting to be picked up. Copper, too, enough to make a fine quality of bronze. Natives who resisted foreigners, but all it took was a few warships and a little bloodletting . . ." He waved a be-ringed hand and Age-Nor promptly refilled his thin glass goblet.

"Did Himilco arrange trade with Ierne as well as Albion?" the Tyrian asked.

"He meant to, I suppose. But then he heard of . . . or saw, the story is unclear . . . a new race of people who seemed to have come out of nowhere and infested Ierne. A race of sorcerers who had mastered such dark arts that even those on Albion whispered dreadful tales about them.

"When Himilco came back to Carthage he advised those who would take up the Albion trade route to leave Ierne alone. We concentrate on tin from the north, not gold now, and we have no fear of rivals, as you know. Oh, a few Greeks venture timidly through the Pillars of Herakles from time to time, to supply their dwindling colony on the west coast of Iberia, but you easterners stay in safe familiar seas and avoid the terrors of the ocean-river. The terrors. Ha! Carthage grows ever more prosperous while other Phoenician cities start to stink of their own decay . . ." Abhiram bellowed a gurgling laugh that subsided into a snore. He slumped lower on his gilded and upholstered stool, leaning forward slowly until his drunken snorts were muffled by the gnawed carcass of a heron glazed with apricots.

The next morning the Carthaginian had a blinding headache and no memory of the night's conversation. Age-Nor did not enlighten him. He felt like a man who had discovered hidden treasure as he wandered through the city, surveying the wealth the western trade routes had brought to Carthage. Sprawling villas in the suburbs possessed gardens of Persian opulence, and in the teeming city crowded shops snuggled between massive public buildings of fine marble and colorful sand-stone. Even the enormous necropolis housing Carthaginian dead boasted tombs far-famed for their splendor, and statuary of higher quality than anything in the collection of the kings of Tyre and Sidon.

Wealth from trade in the ocean-river, beyond the Pillars of Herakles.

All a man had to do was be brave enough to go get it.

He had tried; he had done everything a man could do. But Age-Nor of Tyre had somehow earned the enmity of the cruel gods. There was no other explanation for the series of disasters that had culminated with his arrival on the coast of the Gaelicians.

◇ **8** ◇

DAWN ROSE over Ierne.
The great queen Eriu lay on her stomach with the upper part of her body supported by her elbows so she could watch Greine's sleeping face. Every line in that face was dear to her. She smiled to herself, and as if a smile were audible, Greine opened his eyes.

"What amuses you?"

"I was just enjoying you."

"You enjoy everything."

"I do, but not so intensely as Shinann." Eriu laughed. "She enjoys rain for its wetness, winter for its cold, summer for its heat. She loves rainbows as much for fading as for their brilliance. It is easy for her, she opens her heart and accepts everything."

"Except suitors," Greine commented. "All these years, and still she has not accepted a man and begun raising children. Why is that? Is it something only another woman can understand?"

"Being different is hard," Eriu told him. "Because Shinann was the first one born as she is, she feels that more keenly than the others, I think. And she does not look at things quite as the rest of us do, you must admit that. So it may be that she has never seen, in any of the men who desire her, the qualities a woman like Shinann needs.''

"If she keeps on being so particular she may spend her life childless, and that would be a great pity for us all.''

Eriu could not bear to hear any of the Dananns criticized; it was like hearing one of her own offspring rebuked. She quickly changed the direction of his thoughts. "I was very particular—until you came along,'' she said. She stretched out one hand and traced the line of his brow with her forefinger. "When I first saw you I thought you were the most beautiful man in the world.''

"I probably was," Greine responded very seriously.

Eriu chuckled. "Perhaps. But I was only seeing your flesh. Now I have lived with you long enough to see your spirit, and it shines so strongly through skin and bone I no longer remember what you looked like in those days. Now I know how beautiful you really are.''

"Woman, woman.'' Greine shook his head. "What have I done to deserve you?''

"Many wicked things, no doubt," she teased him. "Are you hungry? Shall I set a pot to simmering before we go to the stones?''

"You want to feed everyone," he said. "Which brings me back to Shinann . . . ah, you thought you had led me off that road, didn't you? She is looking a little thinner than usual, don't you agree? And there are circles under her eyes. A good man would fatten her up, Eriu; happy women get softer and rounder.''

"Shinann is not sleeping well, she admitted as much to me.''

"There, you see? All she needs is . . .''

"She is having disturbing dreams," Eriu interrupted. "Many of the younger people are. They awaken to tell of assaults, attacks. They are troubled.''

"They are getting ready in their minds to fight the Fir Bolg," Greine explained. "Dreaming of battles is normal at such a time.''

Eriu looked dubious. "The conflict they dream of does not sound like a skirmish with the Fir Bolg. We know we can subdue the Fir Bolg, if it comes to that, with bronze blades and misdirection. They are easily dazzled. But the atmosphere of the dreams Shinann and the others are having sounds very . . . ominous. They relate their impressions almost fearfully. Except for Shinann, of course."

Greine snorted. "Shinann is never afraid of anything. That's why we must worry for her."

"I worry for all our people," Eriu told him. "It is as if I carry every living thing—every one of the Túatha Dé Danann, every deer and bird and flower on Ierne—under my own heart. Infinitely dear to me.

"And I worry about this beautiful, sacred land as well. Perhaps even more, Greine, for all who live here should consider themselves blessed, and yet again and again the soil is watered with blood and tears. Anger and hostility seem to be embedded in our very bones and they come to the surface when we least expect them, disfiguring us. I hate to see the young ones practicing with weapons. If only we could all be clean and clear and Unbodied *now* . . . !"

Greine felt a stab of fear at her words, but he would not let her see it; would not let his woman know that the concept frightened him. He grabbed her and pulled her hard against his chest, silencing her. "Woman, I awoke in a rare good mood and I want no more of this sad talk. We are here together, safe and content, and our lives will continue as they always have. Show me that smile of yours, Eriu; more sunshine and less clouds, please?" He put his fingers beneath her chin and tilted her face up, warming her with his smile until she grew one to match it.

How dear his face was to her! She knew every angle of the bone, every pore, every curl of hair; yet even as she looked at him she could imagine herself saying good-bye to that face. Good-bye to those warm eyes and that sunny smile.

Eriu swallowed hard. That which was mortal in her was possessed by its own nature. That which was immortal knew too well that the flesh must eventually be put aside as an outgrown garment, and this devotion to it was one last hug to a loved friend before parting.

They rose together, being particularly tender with each other. Greine's arms were walls shielding Eriu, yet he knew in his heart there were many things for which strong arms were no defense.

The gray mist of early morning had given way to a nacreous dawn, the sacred time.

Arm in arm Eriu and Greine went together to the hill where

86

a group of Dananns was already awaiting them within the circle of standing stones. Apple trees, heavy with fruit, drew warmth and strength from those stones and began to rustle in the breeze. The moist air seemed to glow from within in response to the coming of the Light.

Within the stone circle the chanting began.

Age-Nor had not fully recovered from the maniac's attack, but the exigencies of trade would not wait. A deputation of Gaelicians descended on him the next morning before he could even sort out his thoughts. They all talked at once and very quickly, so he could hardly understand anything they said.

"Is the sweet singer with you?" he asked several times. "He and I are able to talk to each other."

Colptha, who had come to the harbor with Éremón and Éber Finn to assess the Phoenician's timber requirements, stepped forward hastily. "I am a druid, if you require one," he said.

Age-Nor disliked him on sight. The cloaked figure with rapacious eyes was obviously a priest, and the priests represented the gods, who had turned their faces from Age-Nor. Colptha had the same hungry, ambitious look about him the priests of Melqart had, always demanding more . . .

"I do not need . . . a druid . . . ," Age-Nor said in his broken Gaelician. "Whatever that may be."

"I represent the trees," Colptha told him haughtily.

Age-Nor stared, uncertain he had heard correctly. There were people who referred to themselves as lions or their enemies as jackals, but never before had he heard a tribe identify itself as trees.

Barbarians. He would have to be very careful, the air was heavy with potential misunderstandings.

They had met on the sand beside Age-Nor's beached flagship. If this were the Mediterranean, the commander might have invited them on board and offered them refreshments, but he felt a curious reluctance to have the Gaelicians on his ship at all. The first negotiation was probably best conducted on neutral ground. He did not want them to see how damaged and shabby his fleet was.

But as he looked at the barbarians closely, he saw something he had not had time to realize the night before, in the dimly lit and smoky hall. They were weighted down with clanking jewelry, but their bronze had the patina of age. Their woolen cloaks were dyed with native materials, the colors recognizably different from fine southern dyes. They wore all the trappings of prosperity and yet it was a faded prosperity, a little worn and out of date.

Age-Nor understood all too well.

He muttered over his shoulder to his flagship captain, Bomilcar, whom he had instructed to stand close at all times, "I have a suspicion this tribe is not sitting on a mountain of tin."

He tried to force the conversation around to the availability of metals, either ore or worked, but the Gaelicians pretended not to understand him.

"He keeps saying tin," Éber Finn whispered to his own retinue. "What am I supposed to offer him, granite and furze? That's the only excess we have!"

Donn, his eyes downcast, stood at the edge of the deputation. This should have been his moment of glory, when he spread out the wealth of the tribe for inspection and directed an examination of the materials offered in turn. That was the way Milesios used to do it, in the good days.

He felt useless and empty-handed and wished he were home with Díl, who could always think of something comforting to say.

Éber Finn, remembering Amergin's words, remarked casually to Age-Nor, "Your ships seem to need many repairs."

The Tyrian turned and looked blankly, refusing to see splintered timbers and patched prows. "Do you think so? You do not understand Tyrian shipbuilding. These vessels could sail all the way around the world on the ocean-river, just as they are."

He knew how to sound convincing, but Amergin had been more convincing; Amergin had seen with druid eyes. Even Colptha reluctantly acknowledged the confidence this gave the Gaelician deputation.

The sacrificer crowded close to Éber Finn's shoulder. "Speak to him of softwoods," Colptha murmured. "Talk to him of pine trees. The samodhii are very reluctant to let these foreigners have any of our sacred oak, but try to make a deal with lesser lumber. They have to accept it; I can smell it on them."

"You have a keener nose for blood than I do," Éber

commented. But he kept dragging the issue of ship repair into the conversation and playing deaf to Age-Nor's frequent allusions to tin, until at last the negotiations broke up for the day leaving neither side satisfied.

And each side increasingly suspicious.

"Why haven't they shown us any of their merchandise yet, if only to encourage things along?" Éber wondered.

The sons of the Míl returned to the stronghold determined to look as if they had accomplished something. They swept in through the gateway with bluff heartiness, feeling the eyes of their tribespeople fix on them in hope. They grinned, they waved, they drove their horses with a flourish of the whip, but they said nothing to anyone until they reached the Heroes' Hall and had a chance to speak with Milesios in private.

Scotta waited at the Míl's side, her gaze more intense and demanding than his.

Old Irial, the chief druid of the Gaelicians, was also there, for a matter of such importance to the entire tribe could not be ignored by the chief representative of the spirit world. Irial had just been scolding Milesios—who else would dare?—when Éremón and the others arrived.

"The balance between the invisible and the visible worlds has been disturbed, or you would not be having these problems," Irial was saying. "For too many seasons the tribe has concentrated its energies on things it could see. Attendance at the rituals is not what it once was; the sacrifices you offer are often less than your best. So trouble comes, things begin to go wrong. I have warned you of this before, Milesios."

"Many times." The Míl sighed. "Must I hear it again? I am not feeling sunny today, Irial."

The chief druid nodded. "Of course not. You have neglected to keep both the visible and invisible parts of yourself in their proper alignment with the forces of nature; you have concentrated on your body and let your spirit grow ill. You are the head of the tribe, it follows your lead. You will bring a sickness to all your people if . . ."

At that moment the Míl's sons burst into the hall and Milesios leaned eagerly forward, thankful for the interruption.

"What news of trade? Is the Tyrian willing to overlook our little misunderstanding of last night?"

Éremón and Éber Finn exchanged glances. "Amergin was right about the timber," Donn spoke up. "The Phoenicians need it, all right, though they won't admit it."

"*I* saw that," Colptha said through stiff lips.

"So—we have a tool for bargaining." Milesios sat back on his bench, resisting the temptation to throw a smug look at the chief druid.

Éber Finn shuffled his feet. "Ai . . . yes. We have something to trade, but not very much. Timber has never been our strong point. But the Sea People don't have much to offer, either."

"What do you mean?" Scotta asked sharply.

"We have not yet reached the stage of seeing their merchandise—not until we can show them some of ours. But the commander was talking in very obscure ways about pots and rugs and beads. He never mentioned iron. He was deaf when we asked about linen, or even silver from Tartessos."

Irial arched his brows in silence.

Milesios would not meet his eyes.

"So we are to trade our scarce woods for rubbish?" Scotta asked scornfully, glaring at her sons. "The tribe will hold such a failure against their chieftain and our clan, and it will reflect poorly upon all of you. You must do better than this."

She could shame them into anything, knowing their pride. The pride they had inherited from their ancestors, the pride of conquerors who would never accept defeat.

Amergin entered the hall, the harp case on his shoulder. Just behind him came Ír, rubbing sleep from his eyes.

Milesios looked at each of his sons in turn; even at Ír. "One of you must grow enough to fill this bench," he said slowly. "Or the head of some other clan will someday sit upon it and lead the Gaelicians, and our family will lose a standing generations old. My father sat here, and his father before him. Which one of my sons will be able to lead when I am gone?"

He did not include the druids in that question, for theirs was a calling apart from physical leadership. Yet both Amergin and Colptha heard the challenge in his voice and felt the blood in their veins answer.

Éremón, youngest and brashest, heard it too.

"Trade is not the only answer for our people," he said. "Let my brothers continue to go to the harbor and wipe their noses on the hem of the Tyrian's robe. I have another plan for bringing wealth back to our people."

"What?"

"Tell us!"

But he would not. He grinned and winked broadly, enjoying himself. "When it is all worked out in my head," he said. Then he turned his back on his brothers and swaggered from the hall.

"Worked out in his head," Milesios snorted. "Éremón does very little work in his head; what he does he does boldly and without thought. I was much like him at that age."

"Until the spirits bestowed upon you the wisdom you would need for the good of the tribe," said Irial.

Milesios absent-mindedly rubbed his belly with the heel of his hand. His latest ache was situated there, and moving. "Wisdom," he murmured. "Wisdom takes strength . . ." His voice faded.

His sons looked at one another uneasily.

Age-Nor the Tyrian was equally uneasy. Days passed, and it became obvious there was no tin. The Gaelicians kept talking of lumber, and they certainly had tools of magnificent, elaborate craftsmanship that would always bring a good price elsewhere on his trade route, but the sale of such worked goods would not pay for this voyage. He needed ore and there was none left here. He learned there had once been large quantities of it, near the surface and eagerly mined, but the Carthaginians had stripped it and moved on, just as they had picked Tartessos clean. Nothing remained here that would be worth the risk of continuing to run the Carthaginian blockade. No great commercial triumph awaited him unless he followed the Carthaginians north, further risking their anger, and dared the misty terrors of the Pretanic Islands.

The fabled gold of Ierne.

Age-Nor felt physically sick.

His men set up a portable shrine to Baal and Age-Nor visited it daily, in despair rather than supplication. "I have come so far," he complained to the indifferent god, "and achieved so little."

With Colptha acting as liaison, an arrangement was finally concluded allowing Age-Nor to have the materials he needed for repairing his vessels. His shipwrights complained about the ratio of softwoods to hardwood, but the druids seemed adamant about not selling "sacred trees." Colptha defended them with the zeal of a fanatic, acting as if his own lifeblood were being demanded whenever Age-Nor mentioned oak.

In return, the Tyrian spread his merchandise on the beach and the Gaelicians came down to look.

Their disappointment was obvious—and the sons of the Míl could not help hearing the complaints rained down on their father's head. For too long, his tribe had been in the habit of expecting superlatives from him. Inferior trade goods came as a nasty shock.

"Even old Ítos has better things than these in his clanhold, and he's the poorest of us all," Éber Finn commented, kicking over a pile of third-rate Euboian pottery with his soft leather boot. "What am I going to tell my wives?"

The galleys were hauled well clear of the water and repairs began which promised to take the remainder of the summer. Age-Nor spent his time nominally supervising them, but actually gazing moodily at the sea and drinking the last of his private stock of wine. In spite of repeated invitations, he did not again visit the Heroes' Hall.

Milesios chose to be insulted. "That peculiar man offers us a pitiful array of merchandise my father would have pitched into the sea, and then he refuses even the hospitality of my hall. In spite of his short legs and his terrible accent he seems to think he is better than we are. He refuses to grease his knife with my meat."

"His tongue may be trained to different tastes," Scotta replied, not looking up from her task. Éber Finn had brought her a dried and cracking embossed leather panel from his favorite chariot and asked her to grease and restore it for him. A warrior usually entrusted such a task to a wife of his own, but Éber was very sensitive about the appearance of his equipment and liked to have no one but Scotta work on it. "Do you think I have nothing better to do?" she had asked. But she was flattered.

"When we still had traders from Carthage," Milesios grumbled, "they sat at my tables and shared my salt. This Tyrian— and where is Tyre, anyway?—has not only caused a lot of trouble, but is very rude. If only there were other merchants in the harbor I would send him away with empty hands."

"Perhaps it is he who has cause to think you rude," Scotta said. She was kneading melted wool fat into the leather, back and forth, back and forth, eyes on her work, red chapped hands sure of their skill.

"Me? Rude? What are you saying, woman? I am famed for my hospitality as far south as the Port of the Hellenes!"

"Your son almost killed a guest under your roof," Scotta reminded him, "and you did nothing to prevent it."

"I was *asleep*," Milesios insisted. It was less demeaning to admit to drowsiness than to a lapse of hospitality. "Besides, there was nothing to prevent, not really. You know how hot young warriors are when there's been no fighting for them for a while. Ír was playing with the fellow, that's all, and everyone was too tense, too quick to misunderstand. Why should I have interfered? No harm was done."

Scotta's hands slowed, then stopped. She looked at her husband with newly critical eyes. He really believes what he is saying, she thought—or is trying to make himself believe it. The great Míl of the Gaelicians, who has never lied to anyone, least of all himself. Where has my husband gone?

Watching him closely, she realized that even his voice no longer sounded familiar. Its former power had gradually faded, almost unnoticed, and been replaced by a breathy croaking. And sometime this season, or last, his normally high color had given way to a gray pallor. His skin looked thickened and greasy.

Scotta made herself see all these things, and did not try to shield herself from the shock.

"Ír's mood will improve soon," Milesios was saying. "My high opinion of Éremón was not misplaced, for he has presented a very good plan. He has grown up enough to look beyond himself, which is more than I can say for some of his brothers, and has realized how bereft the tribe will feel when this trading fleet leaves with no possibility of return. It will be like watching something die, and at last we will all have to admit that our lives are not as rich as they were.

"But Éremón's recent trip to the land of the Astures got him very excited about the prospect of a cattle raid. We haven't gone cattle raiding in quite some time, and he says the Asturians have amassed a fine herd. We could get a new seed bull for each of the larger clans, he says, and a few good breeding cows besides. The young warriors who have been chafing at their hobbles will all go, Ír among them, and have enough action to settle them down for a while."

"Are you anticipating a battle?" Scotta asked.

"Of course not, we're in a poor position to get into a war with the Asturians. What if they came marching here and realized the wealth of our tribe has shrunk to some played-out mines and a few herds of sheep, a scattering of cattle scarcely numerous enough to keep ourselves fed? No, Scotta, this will just be a small raid, some sport for the warriors and some new blood for our herds. Éremón thinks we should start building them up again, since it looks like we may have to depend on them as our only support in the future. His is the first good suggestion I've heard and I'm pleased. He is very much as I was, at his age."

"Amergin was first to realize Age-Nor would have to buy timber," Scotta said, but Milesios did not react.

She began wiping the wool fat off her hands. "If there's to be a cattle raid and you and your sons are going, then we will need to see to your own equipment," she said briskly, all business. "I must . . ."

Milesios waved his hand. "Save yourself the trouble. I'm not going."

"The head of the tribe missing a cattle raid? Such a thing has never been!"

"It will be now. My strength is not what it was."

Something about the flat acceptance in his tone frightened her. His was the posture of a beleaguered man, head hunched down into his shoulders.

"Don't say such things," Scotta told him. "Don't even think them. Haven't we been together a long time; don't you think I know you as well as I know myself? I say you are still strong, as I am. Look at me, Milesios! I've outlived all your other women and still my legs can run, my arms can cast the spear. And the same is true for you. You are the chief of the tribe, you *have* to be strong!"

"I remember how you were when you first came under my roof," Milesios mused. "How bright and hot you were, how full of fire. When I saw you I thought, there is a tough-minded woman, she will give me good sons. That fire still burns in you at least, Scotta, even if it is no more than ashes in me."

"You are talking nonsense."

"I am talking truth. I am not the man I was, not the champion you remember. I never thought about getting old, Scotta; it was not something I planned for. I always expected to die in battle as a hero should, to make my transition at the peak of glory. But I was so good a warlord I intimidated too many of my enemies, and the beautiful battles came less frequently. Our wealth made lesser tribes want to stay in our good graces in hopes we would allow them to share, and our young men and women intermarried and created alliances for us with former enemies, so first one season and then another passed in peace.

"The seasons have slipped by too quickly, Scotta, without my noticing them. The man I was remains inside this old shell, not very much changed from the youth I remember: quick, eager, as nimble as a fox. Yet when I think of something I want to do and jump up to do it, only my spirit leaps. This worn-out body sits like a lump, unable to follow. I have seen you glare at me, Scotta, and I know you lose patience with my slowness and my deafness. But what am I to do? I've grown too weak to kick snow off a rope."

He saw the horror in her face. "I've consulted with the druids already, Scotta," he informed her. "The healers can do nothing more, and Irial has traced my pattern in the smoke and the fire and the stars of the night. I have little of this life left, he informs me. You are concerned about the chiefdom and so am I, but . . ." His voice changed key, his mind wandering onto other paths.

"Do you remember the way I used to be, wife? I was always running, running . . ." His blearing eyes swept the walls around them. "I don't even remember where I was running to, but . . . oh, Scotta, this is as far as I get!" His voice rose in a thready wail of grief that chilled his wife's marrow.

"Don't you dare give up!" she demanded frantically, fighting back his fear and hers. "This is an uncertain time for the tribe, you must remain a strong head."

He shivered back from whatever abyss he had been staring into. "I'm doing my best," he said wearily. "I hoard my energy and keep up appearances well enough, I think. At least the tribe still believes me to be a man."

"You *are* a man," Scotta assured him. "But if you don't start acting more like one there will be trouble. People are already beginning to notice that now you do nothing, where once you would have led the action."

"The one power a man has that cannot be stripped from him is the power to do nothing, Scotta."

"Doing nothing can make a statement louder than a bard's chant on a high hill," his wife said. "That's what happened when you sat dozing on your bench while Ír attacked the trader. You must fight, Milesios. Fight, don't surrender!"

She longed to find a way to break through to the Milesios

they both remembered. Once they had been as close as two spokes on a chariot wheel, but now he was going off in a different direction and she would not follow him. She must force him to turn back.

She went to him and stood behind his bench, massaging the base of a raddled neck that once bulged with muscle. He relaxed gratefully beneath her hands, but he did not grunt with pleasure at her touch, nor turn to smile up at her as she bent over him.

"Are you stiff?" she asked solicitously. "Here? Or here?" Her hands searched across his back, finding bones where there should have been firm flesh.

Her hands groped lower, into his lap. "Are you stiff?" she asked again, a smile in her voice now, her breath fanning the curling edges of his beard. She meant to fondle him and warm him back to life but he pulled away. "Don't make fun of me, woman," he snapped. He thrust himself off the bench with a visible effort and an old man's groan. Without even looking at her, he left the hall.

Scotta stared after him, her hand still open from its caress. She closed her fingers very slowly.

Following Milesios to the portal, she saw Ír beyond, headed in the direction of the horse pens. Ír was nodding his big blond head from side to side and carrying on an animated conversation.

But no one was with him.

◊ **9** ◊

SCOTTA FROZE, with one hand clutching the carved doorpost. She saw Milesios walk right past his son, oblivious. The Míl's shoulders were hunched and his shadow dragged at his heels.

Scotta watched her husband as one would look across the lowered barriers of the living world on Samhain, observing the movements of the distant dead.

96

From the moment she had come to live in the Míl's house Scotta had never put her hands in happy lust on another man, or sought pleasure in another man's bed. The wordless homage she thus paid Milesios was a powerful testament to his virility; and as chieftain he was considered an embodiment of the virility of the entire tribe. The Míl's ability to satisfy such a woman so completely kept his followers in awe of him and reinforced his hold on the bronze-sheathed bench.

Through the many seasons they had been together, Scotta had worked ceaselessly to enhance her husband's prestige. Her fidelity began to be praised as a new model for marriage, as well as assuring the Gaelicians that the Míl's energies were unflagging and their dominance in the region was therefore secure.

Scotta's celebrated vitality had never failed her, but now her husband's deserted them both.

Something shifted within her. Ties were loosened and bonds severed as her self-protective instincts urged a new distance between herself and the failing Míl. Aware of the process, she made no effort to reverse it. She allowed herself one pang of savage grief, then turned on her heel and went back to rubbing wool fat into leather for Éber's chariot.

Milesios had taken no notice of Ír's peculiar behavior because the chieftain had given up looking outward and was now concentrating only on his own flesh, observing the process of its decay with angry fascination. What was happening was happening to him alone; the collapse of the body that had been his glory could not be shared or passed on to another. He was making his failing flesh the boundaries of his world, and Ír, Scotta, all who were beyond those boundaries must find their own way. He could spare nothing of himself for them.

For the first time in his life he did not even pay attention to the angle of the sun, or listen for the voice of the prevailing wind. They, too, had become unimportant.

The climate on the northwest coast of Iberia was like an elder member of the tribe, a voice that must always be taken into consideration. The north wind rode roughshod along the cliffs, gnawing away the land, turning the seas into a chop that intimidated the coracles of the fisher tribes. When the north wind blew, no celsine brought hake and sardines to the Heroes' Hall. Only Amergin would find such wind beautiful.

The west wind brought fog and rain, blurring the outlines

of the coast, hiding the possible approach of enemies. But there had been scant west wind for many seasons, and the land was drying out. Wilted leaves hung in the heat like limp hands too enervated to lift in prayer for rain.

When it swung around to the southeast the wind blew hard and bitter, creaking the branches of the distant pinewoods and staining the sky with a peculiar yellow light. At such times cattle were nervous and quick to stampede. Horses shied, dogs howled. When the yellow wind blew, people needed to keep busy to keep their thoughts from running wild.

The wind was from the southeast on this day. The women, as always, were well-occupied with tasks. The craftsmen labored and the stockmen soothed their charges, but the warriors had nothing to do. Land people, they had little interest in watching seagoing vessels being repaired. The races and contests that had amused them in leafspring had lost their savor. Boredom was as oppressive as the yellow sky, until Éremón sent word of an upcoming cattle raid, and summoned them to meet him for the details.

Now they hurried to a favorite gathering place, the horse pens, grinning with anticipation and shouting joyfully to one another. Their weapons were burnished and ready, thirsty swords thrust through broad belts, bronze-studded shields carried on muscular arms. Even in a season of peace, these were the warriors.

Pigeons strutted around their feet, unimpressed, picking seeds out of horsedung.

Éremón was arrayed as if for battle. His ruddy hair was bleached even lighter with lime paste and swept back from his forehead like the mane of a horse. The pattern left by a damp comb was clearly visible in his mustache. A battle apron, its brief skirt dyed with imported but long-faded saffron, was fastened around his waist with a belt of embossed Libyan birdskin, and his cloak was fastened together at his shoulder with a heavy brooch of bronze and Etruscan enamel. His iron-bladed sword had a gold inlay on its hilt and was embellished by a miniature trophy head, with eyes of glittering blue stones from beyond the Nile.

Brego and Fulman and Soorgeh, Gosten and Étan and Caicher and their followers were similarly attired as they crowded around him, shouting for action.

"Fellow warriors!" Éremón cried. "We are the most honored of men, entitled to the best share of everything because

98

we protect and provide with our weapons and our trade arrangements. But you cannot take water from an empty well. The tin is gone and even fear of us cannot make the celsine dig more from the Earth Mother. Foreign trade has fallen away to nothing. What will we do to maintain our position with the tribe?"

There was muttering in the crowd and some jabbing of elbows, but no one made a suggestion.

Éremón grinned. "While the few paltry ships of that Tyrian were sailing toward our harbor, I was squirming on my belly through a holly thicket in the territory of the Astures, spying on the largest, finest herd of cattle you have ever imagined. And magnificent horses with nostrils for drinking the wind and tails like war flags; these too the Asturian herders possess."

"Ai, Éremón!" yelled Caicher, waving a spear aloft.

"The Míl has given me permission to assemble a raiding party at once," Éremón continued. "I am to be its leader and go in place of the champion of the tribe." His chest swelled with pride.

"A cattle raid!" cried Éber Finn, already in love with the idea. "I should have been the one to think of it." Then, because he was Éber and not mean-spirited, he shrugged. "It doesn't matter what bull sires a calf as long as the meat is good, I suppose."

Éremón neglected to describe for the other warriors the way Milesios had stretched out his hands, their ropy veins threatening to break through the skin, and said in a tired voice, "You will go in my place because it was your idea, and I am not much interested in raiding parties anymore. But listen to me, Éremón—I know you and your impulsiveness. Do as I would do, and remember: when I put you on a horse of mine it is not for the purpose of having you steal the horse."

Now Éremón stood before his companions and promised himself he would make Milesios very proud of him indeed; he would do something so unexpectedly splendid he would never again be chided for being impulsive. Was not bold recklessness a necessary quality in a hero?

He told his listeners, "The land of the Astures is mountain country. They seem to think that is all the fortress they need. They haven't been raided in such a long time they post few guards; they need to be taught caution, I think. I need a company of the strongest warriors to go with me because I intend to capture enough animals to give fresh stock to every clan that supports me."

They were yelling wildly by then, each man demanding to be included. Ír and Éber Finn pushed their way, shoulder to shoulder, to the front of the group, calling to Éremón to remember they were his brothers; they should have as many cattle as he did.

Donn followed in their wake, holding aloft a wooden walking staff. The warriors' clamor dwindled to a buzz so his words could be heard. He who holds up wood is granted precedence; it is the Law.

A tall man stood apart, watching them, capturing the moment and trying out words in his mind to describe it.

"I agree something needs to be done," Donn began in his slow, deliberate voice, which weighed each word interminably before moving on to the next. "But why should Éremón decide our course of action? I am the eldest son of the chieftain and he asked me to take responsibility first."

"For getting trade goods," Fulman reminded him. "And you didn't."

"I . . ."

"Trying to revive trade with the Sea People is as useless as trying to teach a sheep to make pottery," Éremón interrupted. "We have to move ahead in a different direction, and I say that direction leads toward the Asturians and their cattle. We were cattle lords long before we controlled the tin supply, and we will be cattle lords again!"

"We should not rush into this," Donn continued stubbornly. "We should have more discussion involving those of us who are older and have more experience. Perhaps we do not even need more cattle. It seems to me there are enough . . ."

"Enough? What is enough?" Ír challenged. He thrust his face into his brother's. His angry eyes were like chipped flint.

Donn was shorter and stockier than Ír, with a freckled face beneath a thicket of sandy hair even lime paste could not control. His mustache resembled a tangle of briars. Donn made little attempt to burnish his surface, but the mind inside his large skull was as tidy as Ír's was chaotic.

The druids, who examined everything, had long ago taken notice of this counterbalance between brothers and interpreted it as yet another way in which the spirits strove to maintain harmony. Did not Éremón and Éber Finn look so much alike they might be mistaken for twins? And did Milesios not have two sons with druidic abilities, a pairing again? Such symmetry was symbolic of the balance that must be maintained to keep the world from tearing itself apart.

"I'll tell you about 'enough,' " cried Brego, thrusting forward. A powerfully built man with a florid face and an infinite capacity for wine, Brego was one of Éremón's most ardent supporters. "My clan doesn't have *enough* of anything anymore!" he complained, spraying spittle. "Éremón knows that action is the answer to every problem, and our problem right now is finding a way to restore the strength of the tribe before we fade into nothingness and are forgotten like so many other people who grew weak. Or perhaps . . ."

An idea fought its way into his belligerent brain. "Or perhaps it is Milesios himself who is failing."

"That's not true!" Donn protested immediately. "The Míl is still the strongest man in the tribe. If he is willing to let Éremón take his place at the head of this raid I certainly have no objections; I just thought we should have more discussion about the raid itself, be certain it's the wisest action at this time, consider all the possible outcomes . . ."

"Talk, talk, talk, you outblow the wind!" Caicher accused. "You want to gabble like an old head but Éremón wants to *do* something. I like his way better."

"But . . ." Donn began again, just as Éremón extended his sword and shoved the uplifted wooden staff aside. A small gesture gently done, but they all saw it. Éremón did not intend to insult his brother, yet a man who has taken charge cannot permit the endless objections of subordinates.

Amergin, watching beyond the circle of warriors, saw the protocol of the wood set aside and felt some vital harmony disturbed.

He strode forward uninvited, but bound to defend the rituals. "Donn had the right to speak fully; it is the Law," he said. His stern voice cut through the crowd like a galloping chariot.

Éremón glared at him. "Are you taking Donn's side? Do you agree with all this hesitating?"

Donn turned toward Amergin hopefully, seeking an ally.

"I am not taking anyone's side," the bard said honestly. "Nor am I urging caution. I agree that something must be done, some positive step must be taken before the tribe starts losing faith in Milesios and its own strength."

Donn looked hurt, but Amergin continued, "I speak up

because you ignored the protocol of the wood, Éremón, and that is a dangerous thing. You pull apart the pattern of invisible forces when you abandon the traditions established by generations of wise men.''

The other warriors exchanged glances. Some looked briefly worried.

Éremón scowled, not daring to defy the authority of a druid. ''Do you want me to let Donn finish whatever he was saying?''

Amergin considered. ''No, the harm is already done. But I warn you—beyond the Law that protects us is chaos and destruction.''

''Chaos and destruction,'' whispered Brego behind his hand to Étan. ''The druids have threatened us with too much for too long. The Míl is right to put his trust in flesh-and-blood warriors. We can accomplish anything with someone like Éremón to lead us.''

In the hot dust of the livestock pens, Amergin glimpsed the swirling shape of an unexpected future. Part of him yearned toward it, eager and ready, though part of him drew back, doubting and anxious. There was no doubt the tribe was in motion.

Someone must determine where that motion would lead.

Éremón resumed his speech to the warriors, willing them to forget their brief discomfiture. But Donn planted himself squarely in front of Amergin, complaining. ''That's just like you. I thought for a moment there you were going to take my side because you agreed that I have certain rights as firstborn, but then you turned away from me. I see now that you've always held yourself apart from us, Amergin, ever since we were boys.''

''I never chose to set myself apart from my brothers,'' Amergin protested, hurt by the accusation. But Donn did not believe him.

''You're better with words than Éremón is,'' he said. ''If you wanted to, Amergin, you could . . .''

''Usurp the power of a chieftain?'' the bard finished for him. ''No. That really would be dangerous, pulling the patterns into totally new shapes. The bard has his own functions and must abide by them, as do we all—craftsmen, judges, warriors . . .''

''I didn't need a lecture,'' Donn replied with bruised dignity. ''I should have known better than to appeal to you in the first place. Colptha has always said you think you are better than the rest of us, and now I agree with him. And I'm sorry about it, I would have had things be otherwise.''

Before Amergin could answer, Donn turned and plunged through the wall of warriors surrounding them, headed off at a trot across the clanhold in hopes of finding a more sympathetic ear.

The bard gazed after him, suffering a new sense of loss.

''Druids dwell alone in an inner winter,'' old Irial had warned Amergin before his initiation into the order. That oaken voice came back to him now from perfect bardic memory. ''Others will not understand you. You may be given challenges your simpler clanspeople could neither meet nor comprehend. But you must stand unyielding in truth as an oak tree stands, you must never sway to the prevailing wind of someone else's weakness. Prepare yourself for loneliness, Amergin, if you are to keep your inner ear open for the silent voice of the spirits.''

Amergin writhed rebelliously under the lash of that loneliness, but no sign of his struggle showed on the disciplined surface. Only someone who could step inside his skin could know the love and longing he felt.

He watched until Donn was out of sight and then he turned regretfully back toward Éremón, listening to his words and absorbing the atmosphere of the day. The building fever of the warriors.

The past seemed to shimmer and change before the bard's very eyes and he felt an eagerness building in him too. A need for motion, for action, for reaching beyond . . .

He clamped down hard on himself, trying to put the temptation of Donn's suggestion out of his mind.

Donn's desire for deliberation was dismissed by the other warriors as no more than jealousy; the raid was a foregone conclusion. It only remained for Éremón as leader to whip his followers to a pitch of irresistible readiness.

His men; his friends, his hunting partners, his companions of the wine bowl.

''You, Soorgeh!'' Éremón shouted. ''Here's your chance to get some new oxen for your sons to train—I've seen how many boys you've sired and how fast they are growing. And Étan—your clanspeople wear worn boots and shabby sandals and winter will come again. Some new hides would be welcome in your clanhold. Éber Finn wants a new team of chariot horses, I can see it in his eyes—he always craves good horses. And Caicher over there, he has many mouths to feed. Your people grow tired of mutton and wild game, do they not, Caicher? So carry the news to them, tell them things are going to be better. We do not need Hellene luxuries to make us important, we *are* important! We are the Gaelicians!''

The roar of approbation the warriors raised rang far beyond the stone walls of the Míl's stronghold.

Word spread quickly. Before the sun slept, men tending grapevines on distant slopes were calling to their fellows, passing along the news. Herders stared past their charges with glory-glazed eyes, imagining themselves riding off to the land of the Astures in the company of heroes. Children crouching close to hearthfires were told tales of other raids, of splendid red bulls taken by wily stratagems, of glossy-coated cows seized in distant meadows during the days when the entire life of the tribe had revolved around its cattle.

The admiring eyes so recently turned toward Amergin now turned again, toward Éremón.

The warriors had no sooner dispersed to their various families to begin preparing for the raid than a crowd of freemen and craftsmen—and warriors' daughters—began gathering around Éremón, basking in the heat of his confidence.

Taya, daughter of Lugaid, stood among them, and Éremón cut through the pack to join her.

Amergin had been about to go to his house and try out some phrases on Clarsah, but he stopped in his tracks when he saw Éremón and Taya together. Much too close together, oblivious to all around them.

Taya had soft blue eyes that tilted slightly downward at the outer corners, giving her an expression of docility Éremón found extremely appealing. His wife Odba was anything but docile. Taya had a soft voice; Odba's was as strident as a crow's. Taya was shorter than most Gaelician women, many of whom, like Odba, could look level into a man's eyes. With Taya, Éremón felt even bigger than he was; bigger than Milesios, bigger than anyone.

Amergin the bard saw the two of them together as if they stood in a darkling cloud of disharmony. He felt a sudden impulse to grab Taya by the arm and jerk her out of danger.

Éremón's wife Odba was a proud and demanding woman, jealous of her status and of her sons' share of the Milesian clanholdings. She was the daughter of the chieftain of a major

104

tribe, the Artabrians, and her rank was the equivalent of that
of the Míl's own sons. And everyone who knew Odba had
heard her say, too many times, that she did not intend to
share anything she had with a woman of lower rank than her
own, knowing that would mean she would never have to share
at all. Éremón was unlikely to find another tribal chieftain's daughter to marry.

Besides, from their first meeting, Odba and Taya had
experienced that incompatibility of spirits which sometimes
results from enmity in another world. Their mutual dislike
had ripened to hearty hatred in a few short seasons.

Friendship was a necessity between women who shared a
man.

Odba would make a very nasty enemy if she thought Taya
had taken an interest in her husband.

Éremón was stroking his mustache and talking to Taya as if
the two of them were quite alone. And she was listening with
the same shining admiration she once gave to Amergin's
stories. The bard felt a twinge of jealousy he had not expected. He had Scéna Dullsaine, after all . . .

Éremón looked up and saw his brother advancing upon him
with a determined glint in his eye. "Will you compose a saga
of our cattle raid, bard?" he asked pleasantly, continuing to
finger the virile mustache Taya had already complimented.

"If it becomes important to the tribe I will," Amergin
said. "But in the meantime, Éremón, think on this . . . you
have a wife waiting for you in your house. She will be
anxious to hear the news of your planned adventure."

Éremón grinned, too filled with future triumph to let anything upset him. "Ai, you have eyes for little Taya yourself,
do you? It's too bad . . . how can you expect a woman to
choose a bard over a warrior?"

Taya looked from one man to the other. So similar and yet
so different. Seen together, they provided a startling contrast:
massive heavy-boned Éremón with his red-gold hair and bluff,
hearty manner, and Amergin the bard, intense as a flame,
lean and quiet and filled with an inner strength she could not
help feeling as she stood so close to him.

Taya's eyes flicked from one man to the other and Éremón
saw that betraying glance. This was his season for winning;
he would not turn loose of anything this season.

He put a big hand in the small of Taya's back and propelled her several steps away from the bard, interposing his

body between Amergin and the woman. "Do you mean to challenge me for her?" he asked his brother. The question was not an angry one, a dispute about a woman was commonplace and rarely allowed to harm a friendship between clansmen, between brothers. But the very tautness of his face and set of his jaw told Amergin Éremón would fight this out if necessary. Personal business; no druid authority here.

The bard looked past Éremón to Taya. She was a free person, the decision should be hers. And she was not right for him at all; this simmering quarrel was unnecessary.

Something in the bard stepped back and something in Taya, who had no druid vision, saw. "Éremón," she said firmly and without hesitancy.

The warrior grinned. He pounded Amergin's arm with a brotherly fist. "That settles it, doesn't it?"

Amergin nodded. But still he felt the trouble hanging in the air like seamist, and he wanted to warn them. To warn them both. "Odba . . ." he began.

Éremón laughed. "Leave Odba to me," he said. There was a hard undertone to his voice that Amergin had never heard before as he added, "And leave Taya to me, too, Amergin."

I was a fool to push in where I was not invited, Amergin told himself. A bard is supposed to observe, to remember. Now Éremón will think I want Taya and be suspicious of me. I move further away from my brothers every day, it seems.

He shook his head ruefully. At least there was Scéna Dullsaine, still occupying the guesting house with the others of Ferdinón's party. Scéna Dullsaine would provide balm for his loneliness.

As he thought of Scéna, a rising wind blew off the sea.

"Yes?" Amergin said aloud, as a man responds to a call. But there was only the green wind, the north wind. Yet its power was enough to wipe Scéna from his thoughts and draw him to the edge of the cliffs, restless, gazing outward.

Increasingly drunk with excitement, Éremón returned at last to his home to tell his three young sons about the raid and let them see their sire in his new role as leader. Moving out of the Míl's shadow.

He walked with a jaunty stride toward the round stone house built for him by the freemen when he first took Odba as wife. But pleasure began to seep out of him as soon as he passed through the doorway. His boys were already asleep. A low fire burned on the hearth in the center of the room, but

Odba had no tasty meal waiting for him. No fresh bread scented the air. His wife's hand did not occasionally drop heated stones into a pot of rich broth to keep it simmering.

"Where have you been all day?" Odba demanded to know before he could get his cloak unpinned. The day had been too hot for a cloak but all the warriors had worn them, flaunting the colors of their clans. While Éremón struggled with his bronze brooch Odba's tirade galloped on.

"I expected you here by midday when I had a perfectly good baked fish for you, but someone said you were meeting with the clan-chiefs. I expected you at sundown but you didn't come then either; I suppose you were in the hall with your drunken friends, straining wine through your mustache and fondling the serving women. Anything to avoid me. You even traveled many nights away into hostile territory just so you wouldn't have to be with me, didn't you? Why do you treat me like this, Éremón? What have I done to deserve it? My father is chief of the Artabri and a courageous warlord with many trophies to his credit. If he even suspected the way you insult me . . ."

She was a handsome woman once, Éremón reminded himself, biting down on his patience. Must have been.

But now whenever he thought of Odba all he heard was that voice droning on and on. He had long since quit listening.

In the early seasons of their marriage Éremón had tried to encourage Odba to be more thrifty with her tongue. His amusement with feminine chatter quickly faded, and he suggested, "You should learn to use words as sparingly as Scotta does. She says only what needs to be said, and she says it but once. Scotta is everything a wife should be." Lost in admiration of his mother, Éremón had not noticed the expression on his wife's face.

Odba subsequently babbled to the other women at the wellcurb, "Éremón thinks I talk too much and I suppose I do, but you know me, that's how I am . . ." She giggled as a woman does when displaying some special grace, and the monologue flowed on and on. Potential friends dwindled to mere acquaintances who found other things to do when they caught sight of her, rather than waste a good part of the day standing in the hot sun listening to Odba.

"Éremón's wife is always pregnant . . . with words," Éber Finn once commented in the hall, making everyone laugh.

Now Éremón stared morosely into the emptied cooking pot. Only traces of gruel remained from his sons' meal. He scraped the metal sides of the pot with a forefinger and sucked it in silent anger. Then he made the rounds of the sleeping boxes, rumpling each bright, tousled head, admiring each round, boyish face. When he found himself close enough to the door he simply walked out, swept from the house on the continuing torrent of Odba's complaints.

Only when he was gone did his wife close her mouth. She sat down slowly beside the hearth and looked for a long time at the empty doorway, then buried her face in her hands.

"He heard nothing I said tonight. As usual," she whispered to herself, longing to hear some sympathetic voice even if it was only her own. "And perhaps it doesn't matter anymore. When did we have anything to say to each other that was worth hearing?"

Éremón stalked past the homes of clansmen surely enjoying a more felicitous family life than he. A woman's laughter, warm and easy, rippled past him. He turned to glimpse a cousin of his in an open doorway, silhouetted against the hearthfire behind him as he lifted a child high in play. The man's wife pressed against his shoulder, her arm around his waist.

Éremón shook his head and went on.

He walked blindly, unaware that he approached the gateway of the stronghold. When he got there he found Amergin ahead of him, staring outward toward the sea, no doubt musing on whatever smokeswirled things druids dream about.

"Ai, Amergin!" Éremón called, suddenly very happy to see his brother. Amergin's face was dim in the starlight, the mouth only slightly shaped with the gravest of smiles, but Éremón hurried up to him anyway, a man always confident of a welcome.

"I hope you're not holding this afternoon against me," the warrior said.

Amergin lifted one black eyebrow into a peak. "Because you warned me off Taya? Should I be angry about that?"

"Just for a moment . . . from the expression on your face . . . I thought you might be."

"I wasn't the one who seemed angry," Amergin said in a low voice.

"Ai, it's all forgotten then." Éremón did not enjoy verbal explorations into emotional territory; emotions were intangi-

108

bles, uncertain ground for a warrior. "I'm glad to find you here, Amergin," he said, happily changing the subject. "Are you going to the druid groves tomorrow, by any chance?"

"I am."

"Good. Then perhaps we can drive over together. That is, ah, not my favorite place to go alone, and I have to request a diviner to take the auguries for this cattle raid of mine. I want to be absolutely certain we depart on the best-omened day, because every aspect of this venture must gleam and shine."

He seemed almost too anxious, and it was not Érémon's way to be anxious. A cattle raid, like any other undertaking, should be done in proper alignment with the Earth Mother and the Sky Born, but such routine arrangements hardly merited the tension Amergin sensed in his brother.

"Why is this cattle raid so important?" Amergin wanted to know. "Two tens of cows, or three tens, perhaps . . ."

"We need to have something go well for us, and we need it badly," Érémon said in an urgent voice.

"You're right about that," the bard agreed. "I'm just a little surprised to see such a mirror of Milesios so eager to venture into the spirits' domain. The Míl himself has not made many visits to the groves in past seasons."

"I am not the Míl," Érémon reminded him. "Actually, I have no more affinity for the invisible world than Milesios does, but I think this cattle raid can be very important for us and I want to be certain everything is done well. The support of the druids . . ."

"Colptha is a druid, too," Amergin remarked. "He'll be going to the groves tomorrow."

Érémon laughed. "I was right, you are still annoyed about Taya. But thank you, no—I have no intention of going anywhere with Colptha. I'm not that desperate for company. Colptha and I are fire and water; he makes me steam and I make him sputter. Donn is the only one who can get along with him, and that's just because Donn is too slow-tongued to argue with him."

"Come with me, then," the bard said. "But you have to ride in my chariot."

Érémon shook his head. "My horses are faster."

"I've ridden with you before," Amergin remarked dryly. "I handle the reins, or you go without me."

The warrior chuckled. "If you insist. But I agree with Ír, you never know when to use your whip."

"Speaking of Ír—is he going on the raid?"

"I could hardly refuse to take one of my own brothers, could I? Besides, since you recited that chant of yours he's seemed, ah, easier in his mind. He'll never be tranquil, I suppose, but at least you can draw a breath in his vicinity without setting him off." Éremón's speech slowed as an idea occurred to him. "You could come too, Amergin," he said with a reluctance his brother sensed rather than heard. "You could bring your harp."

That was it. The bardic gift to control Ír, that was what Éremón wanted—not Amergin's company. Yet for just a moment his heart had leaped and he almost said yes, his imagination catching fire. To ride with the heroes! To be one of their company, exuberant, indomitable, the brain floating free while the skills of the body seized and shaped adventure . . .

"Are you requesting a bard to accompany your war party?" Amergin asked carefully.

Éremón pulled back. That phrase—war party—what did the druid know? What had he guessed? Nothing must spoil the plan, he dare not disclose it prematurely when someone might still object, some cautious old hen like Donn might tell Milesios and ruin it all! "I do not request a bard," Éremón said aloud. "When was a bard required to attend a cattle raid? Do bards crawl through brush in the dead of night? No. They walk upright in the front lines of formal battle. So there is no place for you, Amergin, unless you want to come and keep an eye on our brother." He said the last so grudgingly he knew Amergin must refuse; pride insisted.

The bard peered through the darkness at the warrior, seeing. Seeing a roil of plans and worries, and the bright hot gleam of Éremón's ambition. He did not see actual untruth, but he glimpsed evasion, and frowned. "I have many duties to keep me here," he told Éremón, while one level of his mind thought of Scéna Dullsaine. "Unless you think you cannot control Ír yourself . . ."

"Of course I can!" Éremón flared. "I could have stopped his foolishness the other night in the hall if we were allowed to carry weapons in. Stay here and tend to bard's business, Amergin. But . . . ah . . . you will go with me to the groves in the morning, won't you?" The bluff heartiness faded from his voice.

Amergin felt a flicker of amusement, which he wisely kept

to himself. Éremón was the first to laugh at Éremón, but he would never laugh at his own unadmitted fears. And mightier warriors than Éremón had been known to shudder when they stepped into the shadow of the trees.

◇ **10** ◇

T HE TWO MEN LEFT the Míl's stronghold next sunrise in Amergin's chariot, an elegant wickerwork construction mounted on iron axles and set with leather panels. Dyed plumes fluttered from bronze bosses on the front and sides. The wheels were ornamented with strips of beaten brass and the spokes were painted crimson.

A bard could accept no less, and the great chariotmakers of the tribe were honored every fourth season at a festival of their own, recognition of the all-important art of the Celtic craftsman.

Éremón watched Amergin's handling of the reins with a critical eye. The bard was a relaxed charioteer. He preferred to let his horses jog along at a trot so he could enjoy the countryside. Éremón tapped his fingers on the crossbar but Amergin refused to be hurried. "Feast your eyes instead of your belly," he advised. "It strengthens your spirit. If you gallop everywhere you see nothing."

Éremón snorted. Druid talk. Land is land; what is there to see unless those hills conceal an enemy, or that meadow offers better pasture and is worth trying to capture?

The sacred groves lay some distance from the headland and from any major roadways, serving to discourage casual visitors. Some druid practices were not meant for the eyes of the uninitiated, and a sense of mystery heightened the respect and awe accorded the order, as its members understood very well.

The groves were frequented by druids from all the Celtic tribes in the area, the Gaelicians and their neighbors alike. The members of the order met together to interact with the spirit world in a commonality of interest not always shared by their various tribes. Even when there was war, druids convened in peace.

Amergin enjoyed the drive to the sacred groves in any season, but the Mother's summer face was especially beautiful. Estuaries dotted with the thick green of oaks and laurels swept down to secluded beaches glittering with white sand. Sinking gently to meet the sea, the last wind-beaten ridges of the great northern mountain range died away as they neared the Gaelician coast. Between eroded hills lay deep, undulating river valleys where grapevines flourished, and in summer these valleys blossomed with roses, perfuming the air.

The road to the groves turned inland, crossing open, rolling ridges of grass and scrub. The granite-strewn land was as implacable as her sister, the ocean, but even so she possessed beauty, and Amergin leaned from his chariot to admire sulfur-colored butterflies flitting over hummocks brilliant with saxifrage, or lizards with jeweled eyes who shaped their sinuous bodies into ancient patterns as they warmed themselves on the scattered boulders.

"Whip up those horses, will you?" Éremón grumbled. "The sun is cooking my skull."

"Soon you'll have more than enough shade, I promise you," the bard replied.

A belt of pines greeted them, a slender company of kindred beings. Many generations stood together compatibly, shoulder to shoulder above a forest floor covered only with eons of pine needles and moss.

As they entered the wood, the trail they were following seemed to disappear altogether. Amergin threaded his way deftly among the trees though Éremón could see no landmarks. He was not aware, as the druid was, that each tree had its own face and character, as distinctive as that of an individual man.

The trees closed in, shutting out warmth and light.

Éremón planted his feet wide apart and gripped the rim of the chariot.

The pines gave way to a dense stand of hardwoods dominated by ancient oaks. In colder lands, when starvation threatened, the ancestors of Amergin and Éremón had survived by eating a paste made of pounded acorns shaped into cakes and cooked over fires of oak deadwood. They had snuggled into drifts of oak leaves for warmth; they had healed themselves with an elixir made from the Oak's Child, the mistletoe, the

112

parasitic growth that could shrivel away the parasitic tumors capable of killing a man.

Father Oak. Protector.

Amergin reined the horses to a halt and tied them to a tree, beckoning Éremón to follow him on foot into the depths of the forest. They had not gone far when Éremón had the distinct sensation of being watched and glanced anxiously over his shoulder, but saw no one. Only the trees. He put his hand on the hilt of his sword but Amergin said, without even turning around, "Your weapons are of no use to you here."

They crossed a sun-dappled clearing and approached a wall of trees crowded together as if to conceal something at their center. Amergin held out his arms and called a greeting to the oaks, then turned to Éremón. "Come," he said formally, "the trees bid you welcome."

Wishing this were over, Éremón followed the druid into the heart of the sacred grove.

A mighty canopy of leaves spread overhead, separating man from the sun. A deep carpet of leaves lay underfoot, separating man from the Earth Mother. Within the sacred grove all was darkness and silence. No bird sang. The world slowed, stopped. Time was not. Old blood stained old wood, smeared on the bark in ceremonies of solemn savagery.

This was the *nemeton*, the place of sanctuary.

The place of sacrifice.

Within the circle of oaks were gathered the druids, guardians of the grove.

Amergin did not have to tell his brother to bow down. Éremón dropped to his knees because he could no longer stand, and bent to press his forehead against the ground. The trees and the druids watched, locked with him in the moment of awe.

The dry brown smell of dead leaves was dusty in his nostrils. He became aware of Amergin kneeling beside him, and was surprised to find that he longed to remain there indefinitely, crouched against the earth, absorbed in tribute to powers beyond his comprehension. He felt at once humble and exalted, insignificant and immense.

Here among the trees beat the heart of the Celtic world and those known as druids embodied the cumulative memory of their people; contained the collective wisdom of all the generations that had gone before, back to the dim beginnings of their very species. Some haunting trace of an ancient, abandoned way of life lingered here; a memory expressed in startled dreams of falling from high places; an awe in the presence of leaves springing to life; a devotion to the blossoming trees and the implicit promise of fruit and seed. Of sustenance. Something beyond words and deeper than reason welled up, commanding reverence of trees. Of trees!

Eaters of fruit, planters of seed, children of the trees.

Amergin stood up, drawing Éremón with him. "You feel the presence," the bard said softly. The warrior nodded, not trusting himself to speak.

Éremón looked around at the druids in their hooded cloaks, marked with the various colors and symbols of their gifts, but he did not recognize Colptha among them. The cloaks granted a degree of anonymity and it was almost too dim in the grove to make out individual faces. The quality of light was curious, a watery green too dark for day and too bright for evening, distorting shapes and blurring time. Éremón felt he had already been in the grove for a long time; he had somehow grown weary here, yet was it not still morning in the world beyond the trees?

A fist squeezed his heart and his breath rasped in his throat.

Amergin, standing beside him, felt and sympathized with his brother's discomfort, though he would not embarrass Éremón by acknowledging it. The bard realized the sacred grove was not an easy place to be for a man who liked to keep solid earth under his feet.

Amergin addressed the chief druid, Irial, on his brother's behalf. "Éremón, son of the Míl, comes to petition for a diviner."

Irial stepped forward, looking fixedly at Éremón. The chief druid was tall and gaunt, with eyes buried deep in cavernous sockets. His skull showed plainly through his skin. The soaring spirit within him was temporarily caught by a mesh of deep lines crisscrossing his face, but time's net could not hold him. Youth burned through the mask of age and Éremón felt the druid's gaze like a blow to his person.

The old women claimed that Irial had lived in this grove since the first members of their tribe came over the mountains from Gaulish territory. On his body the chief druid wore no metal but gold; he ate nothing but the produce of trees. His voice was like the rubbing together of two branches.

"You seek knowledge," he said to Éremón, "and he who requests guidance may find it here." He raised the wooden

114

staff he carried and even the trees fell silent, stilling their rustling leaves. "You want to know if good omens attend your venture. You want to know the best time for departing, for traveling a distance. But what is time? What is distance?

"Such concepts exist only in your own head, Éremón. They are not real. Time and distance have no true meaning and no power over you, except that which you give them. They are part of the illusory surface of existence, reflecting light but having no substance. Reality lies underneath, moving in and around and through the world you think you see, as well as above and below it and in other worlds you have not even guessed.

"If you were to open yourself totally and let awareness flow through you without restriction, you would be part of all, existing everytime and everywhere. As long as you limit yourself to one body and one day, you are trapped in a very small shell."

Éremón strained to understand the druid's words, teased by their challenge. Irial spoke in spirals and interlaces, paths of ideas doubling back on themselves; spoke of the material world as being translucent and yielding as water. Something else lay underneath . . . perceived reality was merely a gilding over a sterner truth . . .

Amorphous thoughts flashed through the warrior's mind. He snatched at them but could not capture them; they were like a horde of horseflies, stinging him, maddening him.

He shook his head to clear it and grabbed Amergin's arm. "What does Irial mean? Will he take the auguries for us, or not? He *has* to; we can't go off on something like this without the cooperation of the spirits!"

At that moment a latecomer hurried into the grove, pushing his way through the assembled druids. He strode up to Éremón and threw back the hood of his cloak, revealing Colptha the sacrificer, flushed and perspiring. His yellow hair clung in dank strands to his temples. "I will divine for you, Éremón," he announced.

Irial cleared his throat. "The assignment of diviners is my responsibility," he said coldly.

But Colptha refused to be intimidated. "This man is from my own clan, sired by my sire. And what is more, I have been given a message from the spirits already, one that must be heard!"

Irial's eyes flashed pale fire in their deep hollows. "You

sound like a young bird in the nest clamoring for more than its share of attention, Colptha. Beware that the rain does not fall in your gaping beak and drown you."

Colptha had never before stood up to the chief druid, but this occasion was so exceptional that the very ambition which had kept him obsequious now forced him to defiance.

Donn had come to him the evening before with furrows of worry plowed deep in his brow. "Everyone is terribly excited about this cattle raid of Éremón's. He has planned the whole thing without consulting the rest of us at all. He should at least have discussed it with me, I'm the eldest. My opinions and suggestions should have been sought, Colptha."

The sacrificer asked, "Do you want to lead the raid yourself, is that it?"

Donn hesitated. "I just want the respect my rank entitles me to. I'm afraid Éremón's slighting of me is a bad omen."

"Ah, it is omens you're concerned about."

Donn nodded. "There seem to be so many bad ones lately. No tin for trade, Ír's moon sickness . . . and now Éremón stepping in and taking charge just as if I didn't exist at all . . . I tried to talk to the other warriors but they wouldn't listen to me. They don't want words of caution, they heed Éremón because he says what they want to hear."

"What do you expect me to do about it? I'm a sacrificer, not a brehon to arbitrate disputes."

"You are a druid," Donn said in an urgent voice, "and yours is the wisdom. Do whatever it is you do to examine the omens for me, Colptha, and do it privately, just to set my mind at ease. I will give you a good gift. I just want to be certain we're not making a mistake, when everything we do lately seems to go against us."

Something warm had come to life in Colptha's eyes. "Yes," he echoed. "Mine is the wisdom. And I applaud your good judgment in seeking me out. Go to your house now and I will prepare a small sacrifice this very night. I will examine the entrails and if I see any bad portents we will know. If you hear nothing from me by moonrise, sleep peacefully in the knowledge that all is well."

Colptha had prepared the promised sacrifice and studied the entrails meticulously, searching for signs. Yet familiar configurations eluded him. He poked among the organs and intestines with increasing anxiety, muttering to himself, finding nothing useful, and growing angrier with every heartbeat.

Conmael, who had served as his acolyte, crept away and curled up to sleep in a dark corner, abandoning his duties as bedwarmer that night. The sacrificer frightened him.

Colptha tried a second sacrifice and then a third, but all he saw was a bloodied muddle that became more indecipherable the longer he poked at it. Yet for once one of his own brothers had called upon him; he must not fail!

At last he fell unwillingly into an exhausted sleep, plagued by dreams. One came sharper than the rest, vivid not only with color but with sound and scent, more real than reality. Colptha's breathing grew very slow and shallow. A watcher might have thought him dead.

In his dream, Colptha saw himself walking across the Milesian clanhold, watching his own feet. The ground was as dry and gray as ashes, and as he walked it began to open in fissures like huge gaping mouths. Terrible groans issued from those mouths. Parched voices screamed for moisture.

And there was no rain. Had been little rain for many seasons.

Drought was not so deadly to people who depended on the tin trade for sustenance, but when that trade was gone, if they went back to counting their wealth in cattle . . .

Too many cattle. In his dream, Colptha saw an immense herd bearing down upon him, tossing a forest of horns and bellowing for grass. And he knew with a shock of truly druidic prescience that this was the herd Éremón meant to bring back from the land of the Astures. More cattle than any of them had seen in their lifetimes. More cattle than their land could hope to support.

He heard the dry earth scream aloud in pain.

Colptha came suddenly awake, drenched with sweat and shaking with fever. He clung to his bedcovering in terror. This was no small manipulation, no clever trick, but a great and awesome *vision* direct from the spirit world. A gift to him, at last! And surely equal in size to—no, excelling, Amergin's talent.

He was desperately frightened. He had tried so long and so hard to convince everyone, including himself, of his abilities and superiority, that this stunning proof was almost more than he could bear. He thought the spirits must surely be crowded around his bed, watching him. He could almost see feral eyes gleaming in the dark. He lay flattened by the weight of revelation and responsibility, listening to the drumbeat of his own heart.

At last, when every bone in his body was aching with tension, Colptha became aware of morning. Conmael lay sleeping on the far side of the room, oblivious; spared terror.

Colptha dragged himself out of his house and stood shivering in the dawn. He should offer a sacrifice of thanksgiving, that much was certain. Perhaps repetition of the familiar performance would ease him into the day.

One must always give thanks for a communication from the spirits; it is the Law.

Working quietly so as not to rouse Conmael, he cleansed himself and went to the pen behind the house for a young she-goat. He led her out and held her to face the rising sun, his knife slicing across her throat so skillfully she had no time for a bleat of surprise.

And as the goat died, Colptha became aware of a very sensual pleasure somehow connected with the act of sacrifice.

The feel of vulnerable living flesh beneath his hands had always given him a sense of power; the life fleeing a dying body had always given him a sense of his own immortality. But this morning, still shaken by the horror of his dream, his spirit sought a counterbalance for fear and turned toward ecstasy.

Warm blood ran over his hands, its heat driving the numbness of lingering shock from his fingers. The rich coppery smell made his nostrils dilate; he felt his groin heat, expanding as he himself had been expanded. Colptha, dreamer of dreams, seer of visions! He cowered on the earth and took pleasure in abasing himself before the invisible forces of the spirit world. Groveling. Denying himself no shred of terror or joy. Then he laved his hands in the goat's blood and smeared it across his face, tilting his head back and grinning at the sky.

It was the most rapturous moment of Colptha's life.

He so lost himself that he barely made it to the nemeton in time for the rituals of the day.

Now he stood before Irial and cried urgently, "I demand the right to speak, and the right to divine for my brother! I have been extraordinarily honored by the spirits with a mighty dream of prophecy!"

One of the other diviners, a man famed for his prophetic dreams, uttered a stifled exclamation of shock.

118

"What are you saying?" Irial challenged Colptha. "You ignore my authority and appoint yourself diviner in this instance?"

Colptha was rigid with urgency. He must make them understand and give him his chance. "My dream empowers me to . . ." he began, but Irial's rage overrode him.

"I have always known your ambition, Colptha," the chief druid told him in a voice that crackled like starfire splitting a tree. "I could smell it in the air around you, pungent as bowel fumes. But I am surprised that you forget yourself in this manner. Step back into the ranks and allow me to select a diviner according to the ancient rules."

White-faced, Colptha stood his ground. "I demand to be heard," he insisted.

Irial's anger exploded. "You *demand?* Who are you to *demand* anything of me?"

"You don't understand about my dream . . ."

"I understand perfectly!" Irial contradicted him. "Never in all my nights have I known one of the order to reach his greedy fingers for another man's gift, and I am appalled, Colptha. Does the rain ever attempt to do the work of the sun? You defy not only my authority, but nature itself! The talent you have is in interpreting the entrails, yet now you claim a gift of prophetic dreaming in a blatant attempt to increase your own prestige. I will not allow it! You are a sacrificer, Colptha, or have you forgotten? Have you added the great weakness of a failing memory to your other crimes?" The chief druid's voice dripped the vinegar of sarcasm.

Irial thrust his face very close to Colptha's and cried, "Who are you, Colptha? Tell me: *who are you?*" The terrible power of command rang through his words, and even from the depths of his reckless passion Colptha was forced to respond.

"I am Colptha the sacrificer," he intoned in a hollow voice. *"Nothing matters but the fire and the blood."*

"Yes. For you, the fire and the blood! Not the dreams, nor the sticks of prophecy. The druid gift is given that one may make a specific contribution to his tribe, Colptha—not gobble up undeserved attention like a glutton eating too much fat meat. You must be punished for your presumption.

"This is my decision. From this moment forward you are invisible in the nemeton for the duration of this moon. We can neither see nor hear you here, and you are prohibited

119

from taking any part in the rituals. The druid Colptha does not exist in the groves until the moon changes."

An interdiction barring a druid from the rituals was a savage punishment, shocking those who heard it. Avoiding meeting their eyes, Colptha drew his hood over his head and arranged it to cover his face so none would see him. But in the darkness he seethed with rage. They rejected his gift and refused to give him the hearing he deserved; very well. Let them make their mistake and suffer for it. Then they would be sorry. Then they would remember he had tried to give a warning, and had been silenced.

Let them all look out for themselves from now on—and he would do likewise.

Turning his back on Colptha's hooded figure, Irial announced, "Éremón, I select the diviner Corisios to throw the ogham croabh for you, the staves and furrows of wisdom. From the sacred sticks he will tell you the pattern of the future."

The ritual of divination began. The druids moved around the grove, fitting themselves into the design for summoning. They began to chant words in the secret language, softly at first but then with rising volume, as if they called across vast distances. The trees creaked in unison, joining the chorus. Robed figures swayed like saplings and saplings swayed with them in perfect harmony.

Éremón stood, chilled, in dense shade. This was not like battle, with formal rules of conduct he understood. This was a swirling and a mystery. He sensed great brooding presences gazing at him down endless vistas.

A breeze moved through the trees. The druids sang to her and she to them, and when the moment felt right, Corisios threw the small branches carved with the runes of wisdom into the lap of the wind. She played with them briefly, arranging various designs, then flung them to earth in a lattice pattern.

The round-shouldered druid known as Corisios crouched over the sticks.

Corisios was a quiet man, held within himself, devoted to the groves. The tensions Colptha had brought into the nemeton vibrated through him, making concentration difficult. He was not satisfied with the way the ogham croabh had fallen; their meaning was not as clear as it should have been. He thought of rethrowing them, but when he glanced up he saw Irial

120

watching him intently, silently demanding that he prophesy with confidence. Colptha's disruption must be counterbalanced. To throw the sticks again would mean uncertainty, and there must be no uncertainty.

Éremón merely sought to know the most propitious day for launching a cattle raid, after all—this was not a matter of great urgency. So Corisios interpreted what he saw in the sticks, thankful that some few things were apparent. "Three nights distant is the next full moon," he said, "and I see much motion. Good omens for departures, for undertakings."

"And will we meet with success?" Éremón asked eagerly.

Corisios looked again. "Yes . . . I see many cattle."

"Ai!" Éremón breathed with satisfaction. His voice indicated that he had the information he sought and Corisios, relieved, looked up again.

By accident he met the intense blue gaze of the bard Amergin.

Corisios crouched over the sticks, very still, his hand hovering above them and his eyes locked with Amergin's. Perhaps from the bard and perhaps from the sticks some current flowed into him like the undertow of the sea, and he shuddered.

The voice of true prophecy came to him then. He said, in a thready whisper, "Over the curling waves of the sea, the curling manes of the horses. Leather cuts through mist. The Sword of Light sleeps but is not dead; it might yet awaken . . ."

His voice died away but he remained hunkered on his heels, looking through manbody and treetrunk into realms only druids saw.

They waited, scarcely breathing. Even Éremón recognized the unmistakable voice of the spirits.

Then the vision faded and Corisios groped among the sticks, seeking to recall the future. It faded from him and he settled down onto the leaves in exhaustion.

"What was that all about?" Éremón wanted to know.

Corisios moaned and held his hands to his throbbing forehead. When he spoke he looked not at Éremón, but Amergin. "Across the sea, with strangers . . ." He sighed and shook his head. The vision was gone.

Irial stepped forward. "Diviners sometimes catch glimpses of other places, other times, for they open themselves and are not limited to here and now. Obviously the last words of Corisios do not apply to anyone here, for we are not going across the sea with strangers.

121

"You have the best time for your departure, Éremón, and the assurance of cattle. The spirits give you this. Go, now. Do nothing mean-spirited; be an honor to your people."

Éremón responded in the time-honored way. "All things as the spirits will."

Éremón was more relieved than he would care to admit when he and the bard were at last in Amergin's chariot again, driving toward their clanhold. It would take the sunlight a while to bake the chill from his bones . . . or make him forget the peculiarity of Corisios' prophecy.

"What do you suppose the diviner meant about the leather cutting through mist?" he wondered aloud. "And the Sword of Light—that had a positively menacing sound, didn't it?"

Amergin looked thoughtfully at the trotting haunches of his horses. The whole incident in the nemeton seemed confused and portentous. Forces were gathering; he could feel but not see them.

"Colptha made an absolute fool of himself today," Éremón said with some satisfaction. "I wonder what prompted that outburst?"

"I was wondering that myself."

"Could he have had a dream of true prophecy after all?"

"I suppose it is possible," Amergin replied. "Sometimes a gift is late in manifesting itself, though it's rare for a person to have talents in two separate areas of the invisible world."

"Does Colptha really have talent as a sacrificer?"

The bard's lips twitched. "He's worked very hard to give that impression."

"Can Irial be fooled?" Éremón wondered.

Amergin's eyes were brooding and dark. "Any man can be fooled. Only the spirits see truly, and they do not always share that ability with us."

They rode in silence for a time, listening to the rhythm of hoofbeats. Then Éremón brightened. "Ai, Amergin! Look there; we're approaching the clanhold of Ítos. I might stop here and pay a visit . . ."

Amergin flicked his whip at the horses, urging them from trot to gallop. "Didn't you say a while back that you needed to get home and start preparing for the raid?"

"Mmm, I suppose I did. My harness needs repair, and I want to be certain the warriors accompanying me are all, ah, suitably equipped for the occasion. Besides"—he chuckled, not distracted by Amergin's evasion—"Taya will still be there when I get around to her!"

With great difficulty, Amergin clamped his teeth on his misgivings and said nothing more. Éremón would listen to a bard but would resent personal advice from a brother, and it was no part of bardic responsibility to interfere between a man and his women.

They arrived at their clanhold to be immediately immersed in people; clamoring people, demanding people. Éremón's warriors wanted to discuss plans and chariots and be told of good omens; Amergin was requested to preside over several rituals, including the relighting of a hearthfire and the first using of a new loom, both of which required bardic invocations.

Life seemed to be movng at a quickened tempo.

Blood even coursed through the body more quickly, driven by excitement. Hot blood. Eager blood.

As Amergin stepped from his chariot he paused and gazed northward, out along the headland. Through the open gateway he could catch the shimmer of the distant sea. He stood silent, briefly lost to those around him. Just listening, with his head slightly cocked and an intense, thoughtful expression on his rough-hewn face. Listening for something . . . longing . . .

When the day's obligations were fulfilled the bard went looking for Scéna Dullsaine.

◇ **11** ◇

SHINANN SAT ON THE OUTFLUNG ARM of a gnarled old apple tree, swinging her feet through space. The world around her was softened by mist, the horizons were blurred and shifting.

Days were growing shorter again. The tree knew it. The long nights of winter were not a good time for a woman to be alone.

You need not be alone, she reminded herself. You have only to hold out your hand to any prince of the Children of Light and he would grasp it gladly.

She thought of them one by one, seeing each face in turn. Dismissing them with regret, one by one.

Unconceived children burned in her belly.

"What are you thinking?" asked a warm voice below her.

She glanced down and saw Eriu standing beside the apple tree. Beyond her, rolling meadows repeated the contours of distant mountains as rounded as the great queen's bosom. The fertile land lay sweetly in lambent light, fragrant with hay, pungent with cattle, a-hum with bees, starred with sparks from the bronze-smith's mallet, patterned by the weavings of the ash-framed loom. Serene and fruitful land, ripe, opening herself in welcome as she always had.

Inevitably, she would be coveted.

Cuill had said as much that morning at the final day of the Being Together. "We are finding more signs of intrusion into our private precincts," he told the others, "and we are reminded of this island's long history of conflict. The Fir Bolg envy us and long to take back what they once thought was theirs. For that matter, invaders could come again from other lands, for since the first days of the sea rovers this island has been famed in places beyond the curve of the earth."

"What have we to fear?" asked a confident voice. "We have stout bronze weapons as well as more subtle arts that can render an enemy impotent. And if all else fails, we always have the Sword of Light and the Invincible Spear."

Fodla, wife of Cet, shuddered at the mention of those names. "We put the Earthkillers away," she reminded the others. "We buried them in the earth forever."

"Forever?" her husband said in a voice as sharp as a plowshare. "Perhaps it was presumptuous to say 'forever.' We meant it at the time because the responsibility for what we had done weighed heavily upon our people. But if there were serious danger now . . ."

Cian interrupted. "*If* is a slippery word. How can we be certain, on the evidence of border skirmishes and some bad dreams that may or may not be prophetic?"

A man rose to speak; a man with the oldest face and the youngest eyes among them. All fell silent to listen to Tuan, Keeper of the Legend.

"Dreams always have meaning," he said. "Everything that exists is interlocked with everything else; our teachers taught us this. There is a connection between each particle of your body and every star in the sky, between each thought

124

and dream and every event. We are composed of spirit and matter, and that is all that exists in the universe. Spirit and matter, forever in conflict. We did not force an end to conflict just by burying our weapons.

"You speak of dreams, and who can deny that, on Ierne, dreams are truth? Remember our history and how it is entangled with the sacred island, and with dreaming."

They knew the story as they knew their loved ones' faces, but they never tired of hearing it. They were the story; an eternal, urgent tale.

"Tell us, Tuan," someone said.

He made himself comfortable and the story unfolded once again. "Many generations ago, far to the east, on that vast body of land then called the broadlands, our ancestors were born. Fair-skinned people with a hunger in them, they flowed across the earth, always searching, following the sun. In time, the mountains and valleys of the broadlands separated them into smaller units of people known as tribes, and these tribes went in many different directions.

"Some remained landfolk and some took to the sea. Some were captured and enslaved; others continued searching, drawn by legends of a paradise in the far west, a land of inexhaustible game where heroes could fight and die and rise refreshed.

"Ships from the broadlands sailed west and found a large island, fog-shrouded, with cliffs white as a swan's breast. The broadlanders settled there and many intermarried with an older native folk, the dark ones who called themselves Pretani.

"But on that island, Albion, there were whispered tales of an island yet farther west, luring the brave who were still restless and unsatisfied. And so it was they found this place, this warm and beautiful island, these timbered hills and green lakelands. A band of colonizers arrived under the leadership of one remembered as Nemed the Fair. The hunters found more deer and boar than they had ever dreamed; the fishermen found more leaping salmon than they had ever imagined.

"But sea rovers roamed the coastlines, savage marauders who appeared without warning in huge ships with painted sails. They came to plunder the island, caring nothing for it. And they were as savage as they were greedy.

"Nemed's children fought them on the cliffs and at the river mouths, they fought them for generations, while the sea rovers, whom they called Fomorians, ravaged their settlements and took their young people as slaves to distant lands.

In time the dreams of Nemed's children died a bloodsoaked death, for they could not prevail against their enemies.

"Some of them retreated to the broadlands. Others fled northward, entrusting themselves in their little boats to the Sea of the Dead, for their mood at being dispossessed was so bleak they thought it better to freeze and die in the waters of constant winter than to live without seeing this island again.

"The sea took pity on them. They were cast up on an unfamiliar shore and found by another band of exiles, the few survivors of a longheaded elder race whose homeland was also lost to them."

The Dananns murmured among themselves, eyes closed in reverence at the memories Tuan's words evoked.

"The old ones who rescued our forefathers were enfeebled and tired of their flesh," Tuan continued, "but when they saw how brightly the flame of life burned in us they taught us what they remembered of the wisdom of their own people.

"From them, our forefathers learned lessons that made the cleverest among them seem like an ignorant child. They learned of the antiquity of knowledge that had already been acquired and then lost and acquired again many times. People had made wondrous discoveries, only to destroy what they had built and had to begin again. Our forefathers were horrified by this, but not as heartsick as their teachers, who grieved for their own civilization and its destruction.

"Life, they taught, was not a straightforward march toward a given goal; it was a series of advances and fallings back, a cruel circle someone must break before the advances could become permanent. They were wise, those old ones, but they had paid a fearful price for their wisdom.

"They told of cities that had risen and long since fallen to dust; of races that once sailed strange ships across unguessed seas; of implements made by the hand of man to harness forces locked within the earth itself. They spoke of what men had once known and then forgotten concerning the nature of the universe and the power controlling it.

"Our forefathers listened in awe, but they did not disbelieve. On this very island they had seen the remains of enormous stone constructions built by another longheaded race they referred to as the Partalonians; complexes designed for purposes they could not guess, with all traces of the builders gone. They described such places as tombs, and their teachers laughed at their ignorance. They told us the past was forgotten when its symbols were destroyed, and subsequent generations did not know what to look for, so they mistook what they saw. What they thought were tombs were wombs for the renewal of life.

"The teachers taught our people all they could, including such arts and sciences as they remembered, but this was only a pitiful remnant of what had been lost, they said. And our forefathers vowed they would build on that wisdom and fulfill the potential the elder race had not realized for itself.

"We would become what they had not. Children of Light, people of the goddess Danu. And as our minds opened we would begin to give birth to new generations whose minds opened still further, like our Shinann." He caught her eye and smiled and Shinann smiled back at him. A luminous woman, devoid of opacity; a promise to the future.

"Go on," someone urged.

"We were taught there are a few extraordinary places on this earth which predispose people to hope, or especially challenge that hope. Men tend to be ambivalent about such places precisely because their otherness is frightening and fascinating. We were taught that this island where we now stand must surely, according to the measurements of the ancients, be one of those places, a sacred center above the heart of the goddess. Ierne. Our land.

"So when the last of our teachers was gone, we came back. The patriarch Dagda led us, he who had been trained in the sciences that guaranteed unfailing harvests. Manannan of the Waves used the sea charts of our teacher to guide our boats. Nuada the Warrior rode in the largest vessel, accompanying the Sword of Light, whose red beam he had been trained to control. Lugh Longhand was in charge of the Irresistible Spear that flashed fire and roared aloud. Breas the Beautiful brought the Stone of Fal, from one of the destroyed cities of our teachers. With them came a host of others whose names are carved in our memories. The descendants of Nemed were coming home to stay."

"Home!" the audience shouted. "We will never be driven out again!"

Tuan's voice rolled on. "They were met and resisted by those who had never left the island, including distant kin who seemed little more than savages to Dagda and his people after all they had experienced. New waves of invaders had come from the broadlands and from the Belgi tribes on Albion, calling themselves by such names as Uliti and Velabri and Robogdi, though they were all branches of one tree. The same tree which produced the Nemedians. Yet in their ignorance they did not see this, and they warred incessantly with one another and meant to do the same with us.

"This island was called Ierne for the strongest of these tribes, the Iverni who held the south. They were infuriated when we referred to them collectively—and perhaps patronizingly—as Fir Bolg, men of the Belgi. Each petty tribe wanted to be thought unique and superior.

"The Fir Bolg fought us as savagely as they knew how, and fought well, for they were descendants of the same mighty warrior race that sired us. We met them with good stout bronze, but also with the terrible weapons known as Earthkillers, which we had learned to use during our long exile. The Fir Bolg accused us of evil magic because they could not understand the sciences that killed them."

"Moy Tura," someone whispered. "The plains ran red; the ravens feasted at Moy Tura."

Tuan's face was somber. "Yes, Moy Tura. And our testing was not over when the Fir Bolg crept away in defeat, for we must still face the sea pirates, the Fomorians, and so terrify them that they would never come again to our island.

"Balor, commander of the Fomorians, met us at the second battle of Moy Tura. He came carrying aloft a great red ruby and claiming it was an eye of death, which could wither and scorch us; perhaps he had gotten the idea from talking with the Fir Bolg, who had made a garbled legend of the Earthkillers.

"But dark Balor was mèt by our Nuada, wielding the Sword of Light. The red beam of its blade sliced through the mountains even as the Irresistible Spear rained fire on the forests. Even the birds of the air were silenced by the terrible forces unleashed on the plains of Moy Tura. The sea pirates saw us as more terrible than they and sailed away in panic, to challenge us no more.

"But in winning, we nearly lost ourselves. Remember? Our teachers had taught us that wisdom branched into two roads, two kinds of science. One would develop the forces locked within our minds; the other direction led to the constant refinement of tools and weapons, increasing reliance on matter rather than spirit. In choosing the second road we had almost followed our teachers to disaster. We had become infatuated with our fearful weapons for their own sake, until

128

we frightened even ourselves and our dream was corrupted into a horror.

"Though it took all the strength we possessed—and the arguments continue to this day—we buried the Sword of Light and the Invisible Spear in the earth they would scar no more, and walked away from them. We returned to our earlier, sweeter dream of cherishing the land and raising our children to a bright future. When Shinann's generation began to be born, we considered them as proof that we had made the right choice. We had begun to grow as a people, developing powers of the mind that could eventually make weapons useless and unnecessary."

"Eventually," Cet interrupted. "When there are enough of us like Shinann to have some real effect. In the meantime, what happens if we are invaded again? If the Fig Bolg are beginning to lose their awe of us, might the Fomorians not also forget—and return? We must do whatever is necessary to avoid being dispossessed again, Tuan. Whatever is necessary!"

The Dananns looked at one another. A cold greater than the cold of the Sea of the Dead seeped into the marrow of their bones.

Shinann could not bear it. She fled the gathering and took refuge in the arms of an old friend of hers, a sane and solid tree on the plain below the Gathering Place.

Eriu found her there.

Burbling to itself, prancing and skipping over stones it had patiently rounded to give itself a comfortable bed, a tiny stream ran almost beneath the roots of the apple tree. For all its life the tree had drunk from that stream. The stream reflected the tree's blossoms, carried away its dead leaves, grew moss in the shade it provided. The stream and the tree had an intimate relationship in which each helped shape the reality of the other, the roots reaching down into the streambed, the water traveling through the tree on its way back to the sky.

Sitting on her branch, Shinann participated in that friendship as much as a human could. Tree, water, earth, sky, person. The roughly scored gray bark felt the press of her cheek; the branch knew the weight of her body. From this security, Shinann looked down at Eriu and spoke from the heart, seeking reassurance.

"We will not be driven out," the great queen promised. The strength of stone underlaid her mellifluous voice.

Shinann swung her feet. She felt life coursing through her body, hot and strong, as she reminded Eriu she had not yet taken a mate and borne children. With some vast amorphous threat hanging over them, it might be better that she had not, she suggested.

But Eriu disagreed. "Do not deny yourself the pleasure of pairing, Shinann. You have already waited too long, I think, rejecting too many men just because they did not live up to some image in your own mind. You have been perverse, if I may say so; you have ignored your obligation to bear children and help our tribe grow. And you must not use the excuse of an uncertain future, either!

"The future is always uncertain, but that very difficulty makes life strong. Look down, to the roots of this tree. See the split rock on either side? When the tree was a tiny seedling, some flood deposited the rock on top of it but the tree kept reaching upward toward the sun, eventually breaking through the stone. Life, Shinann."

Shinann looked down at the split boulder, one half on either side of the tree trunk. Then she looked at Eriu's face in the leaf-dappled light. The tracks of time were visible on that face but the wide eyes held an unassailable serenity. Whatever lay in the future, Eriu had borne her children. She had opened her body to Greine and life had sprung from that union.

Shinann was shaken by a burst of envy so deep it was almost like hatred, shaming her.

Eriu and Greine had been together for so long they were perfectly attuned to one another. One could start to express a thought and the other finish it, yet the listener was unaware of a change in voices. Shinann thought of their relationship as a broad river in which they could safely afford brief, furious arguments, secure in the knowledge that occasional eddies of turbulence could never deflect their joined progress.

Eriu held out her arms, offering an embrace, but Shinann did not accept, though part of her longed for motherly comfort. But comfort was not what she needed. Shinann wanted to summon the indomitable small child within herself, the little new creature who had never imagined fear or pain and so had neither in its world. She sat pressed against the tree trunk, listening to the sap running through its veins as she summoned whatever courage lay latent within herself.

But because she was Shinann she could not be still for

130

long, any more than she could sustain fear or sorrow. They flowed through her and out of her and she let them go. She dropped lightly to the earth and stood smiling at Eriu, her eyes reflecting trees and sky. And then she began to run.

To run across the brown fertile soil, run through heather and gorse, run past meadowsweet and broom and royal ferns, run beneath silvery birches and across rock-riven moorland, run until she was sparkling and laughing and brimming with life.

Run and run and run, Shinann.

Amergin lay in Scéna's arms and wondered why he did not feel peaceful. He was physically satisfied, yes, but . . .

But.

They had been together in the Míl's guesting house, tactfully deserted by the rest of Ferdinón's party. Scéna and Amergin were entwined on a pallet stuffed with straw and feathers, piled with soft calfskins, scented with flower petals. The most luxurious amenities a clan had to offer must furnish its guest house. But luxury was not enough, either.

Restless, restless. The bard threw the calfskin robe back from his body and went to stand at the door, listening to the sounds beyond the snug stone shelter.

Scéna stretched languidly and yawned. "What do you hear?"

"The north wind."

She snuggled deeper under the soft robes. "That's one thing I dislike about your clanhold. The wind is always blowing here, it makes me uncomfortable. My ears get tired of it."

"I like the wind," Amergin said absently. "Scéna . . . what sort of things do you dream about?"

"I never dream," she said, punching the pallet to make it more comfortable. "I sleep very soundly."

"I mean, what do you imagine when you look toward the future? How do you want your life to be?"

"Just the way it is," she told him. "Though with children coming, soon; I want many children. I'm built for it, don't you agree? Here, come back beside me." She patted the pallet invitingly.

The north wind swirled around the guesting house, murmuring. Amergin looked longingly toward the pallet and the

131

woman who lay there, but he did not move away from the door.

Scéna pouted charmingly. "Is it the cattle raid you're dreaming of, Amergin? Are you as eager for it as the rest of them?"

"I'm not going. Éremón has not formally requested a bard. He did hint that I could go along to help control Ír, but that's not enough reason for a bard to leave his clan for so many nights. A cattle raid is not a war; they won't need me to whip up their courage for them."

"You could go anyway if you want to. You're the Míl's son."

Amergin considered this. "Yes. But . . . would you go somewhere you weren't wanted, Scéna?"

She gave him a long-lidded glance. "I'm always wanted," she informed him, rocking her shoulders slightly. Reminding him. When he did not respond as he should have she began to be exasperated with him. "You are too serious, Amergin," she chided him. "We are here for pleasuremaking, to see if we suit one another. I like a man to be merry."

He came to her then, threading his way across the room through the tumbled piles of her clanspeople's possessions, finding a path between rolled-up pallets and past a tripod of shields leaning against each other. He sat on his heels beside Scéna's pallet. His face was intent with his need to communicate. "I was a merry boy, Scéna," he told her. "I don't know where it all went. Once, things seemed so easy . . . then I grew and studied and the seasons passed, and the more I learned the less I knew. The more I saw the less I understood. I began reaching out to something beyond here and now, beyond even the druid order, perhaps. But I have no name for it, just a restlessness that seizes me and shakes me as a hound shakes a rabbit in its jaws. Whatever I do never seems to be enough for me.

"I thought I would be content once I composed a poem like the one I recited for Ír in the Heroes' Hall, but no sooner was that poem alive than I began dreaming of creating another one, bigger, more powerful. I always seem to be reaching . . ."

His words faded into the shadows of the room. He saw no comprehension in her dappled eyes.

"Amergin, everything you need is right here," she told him. She opened her arms wide and drew him into them, yet

132

his spirit went roving on, even while the bard briefly escaped himself in creamthick and tangible flesh.

Lush and languid Scéna Dullsaine.

When at last she fell asleep beside him Amergin closed his eyes, too, but they opened again at once and stayed open. He stared up at the underside of the thatch. He listened to his heart beating. He listened to the woman beside him snoring very faintly, her lips parted.

At last he disentangled himself from her without disturbing her at all, and softfooted out of the guesting house.

The bard stalked across his clanhold, uncertain of any particular direction, only of the need for motion. The Heroes' Hall rose in front of him in the gathering dusk. Soon the warriors' families would be gathering for an evening's feasting; soon the freemen would be bringing up the Hellene amphorae filled with wine from the souterrains beneath the walls.

Amergin walked faster.

Enough wine, drunk quickly enough, could blur sharp edges of dissatisfaction and dull the most relentless restlessness—for a time. Wine could become a place rather than a beverage, a cushioned compartment a man could sink into and let the world go on without him.

For a while.

And if the morning brought a churning stomach and a pounding head, so much the better, Amergin thought to himself. At least you knew where you were with pain.

Amergin drank one bowl and then a second. As he reached for the third, Scéna's face with its lovely, uncomprehending eyes began to fade from his inner vision. To his surprise he found himself seeing Taya instead. Seeing Éremón stalk her like a deer and bring her down, delivering her to the jealous anger of Odba. And then his brain skittered on to offer him a vivid image of Colptha in the nemeton, arguing recklessly against the inarguable authority of the chief druid.

Amergin set his wine bowl down, hard.

What was that all about? he asked himself, feeling a knot of anxiety tighten in his belly. In spite of the wine, he was certain that a serious disharmony had been committed in the sacred groves. A wrongness in the place of sanctuary.

The fourth bowl of wine was the sweetest of all. The bard cradled it in his hands and let the fumes flow up his nostrils, but they were not sufficient to dissolve all thought into mere sensation, freeing him.

Others saw Amergin as preoccupied and self-contained. Only the man himself knew how much of his bardic dignity was a deliberate façade, constantly under assault and patiently repatched. Amergin simultaneously sought refuge within his profession and peered over its walls worrying about others, unable to keep the objective distance from them that would have given him emotional freedom to concentrate on his composing.

The sensitivity of the bard was a two-edged sword.

Over the rim of his wine bowl, Amergin saw Colptha the sacrificer enter the hall. The boy Conmael trod on his heels, looking anxious. Conmael always seemed to look anxious these days.

Amergin watched Colptha sweep through the hall, walking with a rigidly defiant back and meeting no man's eyes.

Long ago, Amergin had seen that Colptha was sacrificing more than animals and birds in the nemeton; he was sacrificing his own fierce pride. No, not sacrificing it—just holding it in abeyance, forcing himself to be obedient and obsequious as he worked himself up through the order, every word and action calculated to better his position no matter how much it rankled inwardly.

Yet this morning in the nemeton Colptha had thrown it all away.

Amergin gazed broodingly across the hall at his brother. Stay out of it, he warned himself. Let Colptha choke on his own bile, he has it coming.

But something was very wrong. And he could not stand outside and watch.

He drained another bowl of wine and found himself on his feet and approaching Colptha's compartment.

He bowed formally, druid to druid, though the motion made him momentarily dizzy. "Colptha," he said.

The sacrificer glanced up. "Ah, so you can see me. In the groves, of course, you could not. You all turned your backs on me there." His tone was cold and very bitter. "I'm glad to know I'm visible now," he went on. He turned toward Conmael. "Observe, boy. My brother the bard can not only compose poetry to de-arm a madman and set a whole tribe shouting his praises, he can also make the invisible visible again! Is that not a great gift? Who could hope to be more talented than that?''

Sarcasm was an art Conmael did not yet understand. A puzzled frown corrugated his freckled forehead. Amergin noticed that the boy was dressed in a tunic cut down from one of Colptha's, and a silver torc formerly worn by the sacrificer encircled Conmael's neck.

Colptha, following the direction of Amergin's gaze, said, ''I've made this lad my foster son. I didn't realize what a difference a child would make in my life until he came to me. I intend to make him very proud of me, Amergin. See the way he looks at me now? That is what it means to have a son—though you wouldn't know, of course. Perhaps Conmael will even develop into a sacrificer and do me double honor.''

''Welcome to the clan of Milesios,'' Amergin told the boy—and immediately began worrying about him as well. Colptha seemed an unfortunate choice for a foster father. ''Be good to him, Colptha,'' he advised his brother.

''I'll be as good to him as you are to that harp of yours,'' the sacrificer snapped. ''Did you want something of me, Amergin? Is there a reason why you stand there blocking my view?''

''Today, in the nemeton,'' Amergin began, but Colptha stiffened immediately.

''That was no business of yours, bard,'' he said.

I am not up to this, Amergin warned himself, trying to throw off the effects of the wine. The fuzziness he had sought for his thinking had made him more vulnerable than ever. I will not do that again! he vowed silently, fighting dizziness. ''Did you really have a prophetic dream, Colptha?'' he managed to ask. ''When Irial gave in to his temper, did he silence you too soon?''

Conmael piped up in a boyish treble. ''The great sacrificer is singularly favored by the spirits. They tell him things they confide to no one else. When the words of a bard are forgotten, the words of Colptha will be honored in the tribe!'' He spoke in the careful singsong of memorization while Colptha's thin fingers stroked his arm; back and forth, back and forth.

Amergin was chilled by the sight. ''I swear by the wind, Colptha! What are you doing to that boy?''

''He loves me, bard. But you wouldn't understand that. You understand nothing. Just go away and leave us alone— but remember this. The day will come when you will listen

135

eagerly for the smallest word from me, acknowledging that I have a greater gift than any of you. I have been chosen."

Amergin narrowed his eyes, trying to really see Colptha. Trying to force the druid vision, to peer through misdirection into truth. But his head was swimming. He could see nothing but what Colptha would let him see: smugness and arrogance. And he was too well trained a bard to mistake those for truth.

He caught hold of his spirit with a firm hand and stood straight, giving the sacrificer one brief nod. "Beware of anointing yourself, Colptha," he said in a cold voice. Then he turned and left the hall.

"You see?" Colptha commented to Conmael. "Amergin turns his back on me. My brothers have always thought they were superior to me. But it will not always be so. My season is coming. Go around the hall, boy, and talk to the other attendants, whisper to the craftsmen beyond the walls, chat with the women at the well-curb. I am sworn to silence for now but you are not. Tell the tribe that Amergin himself suggested I might have had a true vision, but when I tried to issue a warning I was silenced."

"What kind of warning?" Conmael asked.

"Never mind. We don't want to discourage the cattle raiders from going, because unless they do go there will be no proof that I was right. It seems the tribe must suffer before it learns to appreciate me."

His feral smile frightened Conmael.

At that moment a commotion at the doorway announced other arrivals. Ítos and his sons burst into the Heroes' Hall, shouting for wine and already intoxicated with excitement over the cattle raid. They brought their ranking women with them, but the old clan-chief's granddaughter did not qualify for a place in the women's balcony so she remained outside, talking with friends.

Éremón saw her there as he came striding up and halved the distance between them in a single bound. "How do you like my new woman?" he shouted cheerfully to his companions as he caught Taya in one brawny arm and gave her a mighty squeeze.

The other men laughed and made appropriate suggestions.

Odba, hurrying to the hall to take her own place, saw the incident and stopped in her tracks, her lips white with fury.

◇ 12 ◇

THE OTHER GAELICIANS hurrying to the hall also saw; Éremón's arm around Taya, Lugaid's daughter looking up into the warrior's face with the intimate glance a woman gives a man whose body she knows.

"It looks as if Odba will be sharing her house after all," Díl remarked audibly to Donn as they passed and entered the hall. "Éremón will surely ask her to accept a second wife."

Odba planted her hands on her hips and glared at her husband, who was bathing in the admiration in Taya's eyes. The clan was amused at Odba's expense; she could feel it. Her anger burst into flame.

She turned her back on the hall and set off in search of an ally.

Éremón and Taya lingered outside the hall together though voices were raised inside calling Éremón's name. Taya was blossoming in his presence. She could almost feel her hips rounding, her breasts expanding. A flock of birds seemed to be packed inside her gown, beating their wings within her. In Éremón's eyes she saw herself reflected as a desirable woman, and in his touch she felt his unspoken need for softness, for yielding, for all the gentle feminine qualities needed to balance the masculinity of a warrior.

Because the essence of Taya's spirit was generosity, she gave herself with a whole heart to Éremón and never looked back.

When Éremón at last entered the Heroes' Hall, Taya, waiting outside, heard the roar of welcome he was given. She smiled to herself, shyly sharing in his honor already. Then a stern voice shattered the spell.

"Taya, I must speak with you before this goes any further." Scotta stood beside her, and the Míl's wife was scowling.

"I would warn you, before you encourage Éremón any more, that his wife Odba just came running to me, very

137

upset. She has chosen to be insulted by Éremón's interest in you; I gather you and she do not much like each other. She is my son's wife and the mother of his children, and as such she has great rank in our clan, so I listened to her.

"The Míl himself suggested Odba as wife for Éremón seasons ago," Scotta went on, while Taya waited dreamily beside her, enjoying the sound of Éremón's name. "Of all the sons of Milesios, Éremón is most like his father, and the Míl wanted him to have the choicest of women. By marrying Odba Éremón formed a valuable alliance for us with her tribe, the Artabrians, and Odba brought us many sheep as her marriage portion.

"She says that she will go back to her tribe and take her sons and her sheep with her if Éremón tries to force her to accept you in his house."

Taya gasped. "Does she mean it?"

"She has the right, the Law supports her. A first wife's position is unassailable, Taya. Under our Law, a man can take a second wife only if the first proves barren or gives him permission to do so. And Odba is not barren; she has borne three healthy sons."

"We have not even spoken of marriage," Taya said in her soft voice. Scotta had to strain to hear it—unlike Odba's voice, which was all too loud.

"I know my sons," Scotta said. "Éremón is very much like his father; not satisfied with partial conquests, he must possess totally. I have expected him to start thinking of a second wife since Odba first began complaining that he was avoiding her bed, but it's unfortunate his eye has fallen on you, Taya. You must discourage him."

Taya planted her feet apart and took a deep breath. "Why must I? Éremón is the man I choose; no man has ever wanted me as much as he does. He's already told me so."

The diffidence of immaturity seemed to be melting from her, heartbeat by heartbeat, as Taya spoke, so that even Scotta could see what attracted Éremón. Lugaid's daughter was becoming a most appealing woman.

"Listen to me!" Scotta ordered her. "I raised most of my children to adulthood because I was as tough as boiled leather with them. I did not give in to their whims and notions; I knew what was best for them and insisted they obey me." She thought it best not to mention Amergin in this context, however. "You are not good for Éremón, Taya; you will only

138

cause trouble. I will not allow such leaf-spring foolishness to cost me grandsons and our clan sheep!"

"I can't believe Odba would go that far."

"She might not have to," Scotta said. "As she just reminded me she has another option. If Éremón continues to avoid her and leave her womb empty while he enjoys you—which is what he apparently intends—Odba can go to the brehons and ask for a judgment, blaming you for her loss. She can demand that your clan pay an eric in reparation for the children being denied her. It would be a large eric, I warn you; every other animal in the clanhold of Ítos might barely suffice to pay it. A warrior's sons, a chieftain's grandsons, born or unborn, command a high honor price."

Taya recoiled with shock. "My family already has little, such an eric would impoverish them! Would you let her do this? Ítos is uncle to Milesios!"

"But the sons of Milesios are my first concern," Scotta replied, "not his distant relatives who head clans of their own. Every family must control its members or make reparation for any damage they may do to other clans of the tribe; that is the Law. If Ítos is warned that your willfulness could cost his people most of their livestock, he will set a guard over you and keep you prisoner in your own clanhold. A disgrace to your family, a woman without freedom."

"Why do you say these things to me? Why don't you tell Éremón?"

Scotta smiled a small, conspiratorial smile. "Such matters are better handled among women. If I confronted Éremón I would just harden him in his determination to have you. But if you yourself reject him . . ." Odba, suspecting the same thing, had chosen her ally wisely. Scotta had long experience in handling the more delicate tribal matters, particularly since Milesios became less and less interested in anything but himself.

A mottled red flush stained Taya's cheeks. "You bring too much against me," she protested. "I don't know what to do. I must think."

"Think of your clan and your tribe," Scotta advised her. "Make them your overriding consideration as I have always done. Remember, Taya—I expect you to behave sensibly, even if Éremón does not!"

She gave the young woman one last level stare and then hurried to join the crowd gathering in the hall.

139

Taya wandered dejectedly around the Milesian stronghold until she found an open doorway and a friendly fire. She sat down in misery to wait for her father and Ítos to return from the hall and lead their clan homeward.

Meanwhile, Amergin sat in the cool shadows of his house and cradled Clarsah. There had been no formal request for a bard in the Heroes' Hall tonight; this was Éremón's night, and in the excitement of the upcoming cattle raid Amergin had been free to seek the solitude of his house and try to work on his epic history of the Celtic tribes. Sooner or later Milesios would need him, or someone else would raise a cry for a story about the cattle raiding days of old, but until that time came Amergin and the harp were alone together, trying to put all other considerations aside.

Amergin gripped the harp with fierce passion, searching for the freedom of singleminded absorption. His fingers reached for sounds that could be ridden like memory, transporting him backward through time to watch the long lines of wagons snaking out of the forests of Gaul, following the warriors south.

Concentrate!

Beads of sweat materialized at the edge of his hairline and coursed downward, tiny rivulets following the creases of his face as his ancestors had followed the watercourses.

Concentrate. Summon images of the warriors and their bold women . . . their families . . . Colptha's feral face suddenly flickered across his thoughts and Amergin clearly saw the look of hunger in his eyes and the boy squirming in his grasp.

The bard shook his head, trying to force the distracting image away. Concentrate on re-creating the warriors and their women. He closed his eyes to force all vision inward, to the memories buried in the immortal spirit. "Help me, Clarsah," he whispered. "Bring the women to life . . ."

His touch on the strings was fever hot. An unfamiliar melody rippled, then faded. Ribbons of rainbows shimmered the silence.

The bard's druid discipline dissolved in a rush and he surrendered to the music his fingers drew from the strings of the harp.

Amergin held Clarsah tenderly on his lap, keeping his eyes closed in a harper's voluntary blindness while the instrument sang his emotions back to him; sang purely in the darkness

140

that was a harper's refuge, where sight could not distract and only sound had texture. The harp's voice vibrated through Amergin's arms, his thighs, every fiber of his being. His bones were her sounding board, resonating not with an epic of heroes, but with a song of tenderness and desire.

This was private music. Clarsah sang but part of it; the rest existed only inside the bard's mind, where notes of such clarity rang that he despaired of ever transforming them into external sound.

Music! Music to lift and carry a man, fitting itself to his most secret rhythms. Surrender was a voluptuous ecstasy, a melting into sensuality where man and music became indivisible, a joyous losing of himself Amergin had never experienced with another human being, even Scéna Dullsaine.

Clarsah knew his secrets; he had whispered them to her over many a long night. Behind his closed eyes he imagined his body shifting shape, dissolving itself into the frame of the harp. The druids told of a time when the founders of their order had merged with the trees in a marriage both spiritual and physical. If Amergin lost himself in his harp, some might claim she had taken his soul.

But they would be mistaken, he thought; Clarsah *was* his soul.

His dark head bent over her and her voice thrummed through his veins. She sang to him now, or perhaps he chanted to her, of growing desire, of passion tightly reined but never subdued, of lust and longing, wildness and war and sweet return to some heart's-home.

His door was ajar and the voice of the harp carried.

Éremón heard it, even over the clamor in the Heroes' Hall. He paused and lifted his great golden head, sniffing the air as a hound sniffs the wind. "Taya," he said to himself with sudden determination.

Taya heard the music, too, and rose from the hearth where she sat, not even bothering to say farewell to her friend. She crossed the compound to stand near the Heroes' Hall, where he must surely see her when he left. See her and understand that she waited for him.

Scéna, hearing, smiled a secret smile.

Milesios had left the hall early. "Éremón has done all the proper things, he's even paid his respects to the spirits and had the auguries taken. There's nothing further I need to do,

141

so I'm going to bed," the Míl told his wife. "You can stay here as long as you like."

She really wanted to linger; Donn was telling an interminable story colored by his dry wit and everyone was laughing or interrupting with tales of their own. Scotta would have enjoyed reminiscing about her own youthful adventures, but . . .

She sighed and stood up. The clan-chief Ferdinón watched her leave the hall, thinking—not for the first time—what a splendid woman she was. She strode with a straightforward thrust of pelvis, a swing of thigh and lift of knee like a young warrior in training. Although two graying wings like the horns of Cernunnos cut through her dark hair, Scotta still exuded vitality.

Ferdinón quietly left his compartment and followed her outside. They were just clear of the portal when the sound of the harp poured over them.

Scotta stopped in midstride. Amergin was not playing the customary cadence of saga or invocation. The liquid melody of the harp seemed to come straight from the soul of a summer night, heated and perfumed, irresistible.

Then it changed. The rhythm altered and took on an undertone of demand: growing, seeking, swelling . . .

An image flashed through Scotta's mind. She saw the titanic mating of horses, a stallion rearing over a mare's rounded haunches with his teeth bared to seize and hold her neck, his mighty organ plunging . . .

Scotta shuddered and swayed. A strong hand grabbed her shoulder, holding her upright. Milesios? She leaned toward him, compelled by the music.

"Scotta? Are you all right?"

Startled, she caught herself just before their bodies touched. The voice she heard was not that of the Míl; she recognized the faint lisp for which Ferdinón was famed throughout the tribe. He was peering intently into her face in the moonlight. "Are you ill, woman? You looked troubled, so I followed you out."

Her heart thudded under her gown. "I'm all right," she replied, trying to keep her voice level while that music went on and on . . . "I've never felt better. I was just listening to Amergin playing his harp."

Ferdinón nodded. "He has a remarkable gift. I've never heard such music before; it makes me feel very . . . male." He grinned, his white teeth flashing.

Scotta looked up at him—not very far up, for she was almost as tall as he—and admired the boulders of his cheekbones. Everything about the man bespoke strength. Even the slight peculiarity of his speech did not diminish, but enhanced, his appeal. Bold, dashing Ferdinón.

She reined in her giddy spirit with a firm hand. "I must go now, the Míl expects me."

"The Míl has never seemed to appreciate the bard as much as the rest of us do," Ferdinón commented shrewdly. "Perhaps we should listen to the music together for a while, you and I."

There was a long moment when Scotta felt herself teetering on the brink of a cliff, looking out over the breakers far below. It took a mighty effort to draw herself back, but she was Scotta.

"I have time for no one but Milesios," she said firmly, dismissing Ferdinón. She strode away with her shoulders straight and her jaw clamped against surrender in any form.

Amergin's song—like the eyes of Ferdinón—followed her a long way.

On the morning the cattle raiders set out for the territory of the Astures, a large crowd converged on the Míl's clanhold to see the heroes depart. Each clan was sending its foremost warriors on the raid; each warrior was jealously eyeing the others, determined to bring back the best bull and maybe a pregnant cow or two for his own family.

The party was equipped with ornamented iron-bladed swords and iron-headed casting-spears, the number of the latter determined by the owner's rank in his clan and tribe. Some also carried leather slings and pouches of river stones, a very ancient device. Every raider carried a bristle of daggers in his belt in case of close combat. Éremón had checked each man's equipment the day before, filling in from his own supply where a warrior was lacking, expressing good-natured envy over weapons or horses better than his own.

Éremón's brimming confidence made each man in his company feel taller, wider, more certain of success.

He was critical only of Éber Finn—but the brothers were always critical of each other and everyone expected it. "You can't take a dress cloak and two calfskin robes in your chariot and leave yourself enough room to plant your feet when we

143

cross broken ground, Éber," Éremón had complained. "This is a raiding party, we don't need to be burdened with a lot of fancy trappings."

Éber gave him a haughty stare. "There's nothing fancy here. Just the absolute minimum I require."

"Hunh," retorted Éremón. "All a warrior really needs is a sword."

The sons of Milesios and the heads of the various clans would be driving chariots, as befitted their rank. Lesser warriors had a few riding horses but were generally afoot. This was not a handicap, however, for they were thoroughly trained in running and famed for their endurance. They were not only an essential element of declared war, backing up the charioteers or intimidating the opposite side with sheer numbers while champions decided the issue; foot warriors were also very important to a cattle raid, where success depended upon stealth.

At Éremón's specific request, Irial himself would offer a sunrise invocation to the spirits. "Everything must be done to insure the success of this venture," Éremón had explained with great urgency to the chief druid. *"Everything."*

So the crowd gathered to share the excitement of a heroic adventure, dear to every Celtic heart. Not only Gaelicians would be spectators to the start of the event, however; Age-Nor of Tyre was also present, having come to renegotiate part of his trading arrangement with Milesios. He paused on his way, fascinated by the exotic spectacle spread out before him.

Young men of the tribe who had not yet achieved warrior status were in charge of the horses and were hurrying to the headland with the best of the tribe's collection. They took this assignment very seriously and made a great show of controlling their beasts, bragging to one another about the fierceness of this or that animal, secretly encouraging much rearing and pawing.

Horses were, for the most part, outside Age-Nor's experience. Tyre and other eastern Phoenician cities had a climate that did not agree with the animals, and most human transportation was by foot or in a litter carried by slaves. Donkeys and oxen delivered goods, camels arrived with caravans, and only an occasional Hellene prince clattered into town on a warhorse, causing a stir.

Age-Nor edged closer to a young Gaelician horseboy who was holding the lead rope of a flaxen-maned chestnut mare.

"Do you keep these animals in . . . ah . . . stables?" he inquired out of curiosity.

The boy grinned. His red hair matched his mare's coat, and there was a gap between his front teeth. "They usually run free on the clanholdings," he said. "We catch them as needed for training."

"But who looks after them when they are loose?"

The grin widened. "The stallions look after them," the Gaelician replied. "When two herds meet they have a war, and the champion gallops away with the other stallion's mares."

The boy loved watching the wild horses; his love gleamed in his eyes and animated his voice. He knew that when the stallions grew old, their positions were challenged by colts of four or five summers. An old stallion would fight back with all the wiliness of experience, but eventually his worn teeth and slower reflexes would fail him. The patriarch would rise bravely, one last time, on his hind legs, towering above the mares he had once fought for and won for himself, then those tired legs would crumple and he would fall heavily, at the mercy of the other horse.

But the victor did not kill the vanquished. He left the old stallion's broken spirit to do that for him. A few mares might also remain with the deposed monarch out of loyalty, but his days were numbered after that final, inevitable defeat.

Mountain wolves were a constant threat on the rim of the herd. No healthy horse feared them, but the predators were cunning and intelligent, culling out the old and ill, quick to take advantage of weakness. The horseboy was reminded of an amazing sight he had once witnessed and related it to Age-Nor.

"Last summer," he said, "I saw with my own eyes a wolf who crawled into a pool of river mud and wallowed in it. When he was coated with wet mud, he went slinking on his belly toward a mare with a young foal. The mare spread her legs apart—like this!—and lowered her head with bared teeth, but the wolf was too smart. He crept as close as he could and then stood up and shook himself, very hard. The mare jerked her head up to keep from having mud spattered in her eyes, and in that moment the wolf darted past her and seized the baby horse by the throat. Meanwhile, other members of the wolf pack kept the stallion diverted so he could not come to his mare's aid. Once the foal was down, the pack darted in to drive the mother away, and all was soon over."

Age-Nor listened to this tale with fascinated repulsion. What a brutal existence the barbarians knew! Yet . . . was it any more brutal than ships with bronze battering rams, or the cutthroat competition of commerce?

A billow of dust announced the arrival of Éremón, racing his team at full gallop, the whip cracking over them. He wheeled them in a tight circle so his chariot rode precariously on one wheel, then jerked the horses back on their haunches to complete his performance with a rearing halt in front of the assembled crowd.

Odba edged forward to get her husband's attention and saw his eyes find Taya instead. She thought, for a fleeting instant, of hurling herself beneath his horses; then he would have to look at her. Instead she turned and shouldered her way back through the crowd, looking for Scotta. She would renew her complaints; she would not tolerate this constant indignity.

This constant pain.

Scotta, however, was not in the cluster of admirers surrounding Éremón. She stood apart, watching as the clan-chief Ferdinón arrived from his holding to the south. Ferdinón handled his horses skillfully, controlling them with shouted commands as he treated the spectators to a superb display of spear-tossing, the shaft spinning around his head and then wheeling up into the air. Up and up it went, turning and turning, at last falling neatly back into Ferdinón's grip as the chariot moved beneath it.

"Look at that," breathed Díl, standing close to Scotta. "How well Ferdinón carries his seasons, though his sons have sons of their own."

"He does indeed," Scotta agreed.

The tone of her admiring voice made Díl glance sideways at her. "Have you ever . . . ?"

Scotta stiffened. "Milesios is so much man no woman need seek pleasure elsewhere," she said firmly. She turned away and busied herself talking with Ír's wife, but from time to time she turned her head in such a way that Ferdinón was within range of her eyes.

The gathering charioteers jostled for position. Éber Finn, driving as brilliantly as ever, caught his mother's attention and threw her a fond salute, then cut in front of Éremón and Ír, stealing the attention of all eyes. Donn found himself in a contest with Gosten, both men hauling at their reins and losing their tempers as their horses balked and reared.

"Give ground, give ground I say!" cried Gosten.

"I never give ground, I am the Míl's son!" Donn roared back, going for his whip.

The chief druid, watching the eastern sky, raised his staff. The crowd quieted, listening with bowed heads in the sunrise hush as Irial called upon the omnipresent spirit of life, upon the lights in the heaven above, Brother Sun and Sister Moon, and the Earth Mother beneath their feet.

An acolyte stepped forward carrying a shallow bronze bowl. The reek of the dark liquid in the bowl made the horses flare their nostrils and roll their eyes.

"I pour this ox's blood into the lap of the Mother," Irial intoned. "This sacrifice was made in her honor, to ask that still more life be granted us: new breeding stock to enrich the herds of the tribe." A fresh wind rose, in response and acceptance.

Colptha, in disgrace, had not been permitted to conduct the sacrifice. He had had to watch while another slaughtered the ox and fed its flesh to the sacred fire. He had watched in white-hot anger, his jaws clamped shut on the warning he could have given. Let them suffer.

Amergin stood to one side, lost in the chanting. There were numinous occasions when a man felt himself linked with the totality of existence; moments such as this, more intoxicating than wine, without the throbbing head to follow.

When the ceremony was completed, attention turned back to the warriors. Ír had been waiting, fuming with anger because Éber had briefly outshone him. Drawing attention to himself with a mighty bellow, he whipped up his team and urged them to their top speed as he vaulted over the front of his chariot onto its tongue. He ran nimbly along the pole between the racing horses, then whirled around and leaped back into his cart without losing his balance or causing his team to falter.

A great shout of admiration rang in his ears.

Two trumpeters stepped forward, bronze war trumpets at their lips, and blared the signal for action.

Even Age-Nor felt a thrill at the sound, a thrill at the spectacle and pageantry, the bravado of the heroes and the eerie solemnity of the invocation. Before he could throw off the spell, he looked up and saw Éremón's chariot bearing down on him.

Catching sight of the little Tyrian with mouth agape had

given Éremón an idea for a stunt to surpass even that of Ír's run along the chariot pole.

He leaned over the rim of his chariot, scooped Age-Nor up and dragged him into the cart. Holding the horrified merchant firmly in place with one brawny arm, he yelled, "This is what it is to be a *man*, Sea Trader! I will show you things you cannot do in wooden ships!" He wrapped his reins around the hand of the arm pinioning Age-Nor, and with the other hand he whipped his team until the chariot leaped forward, leaving Age-Nor's stomach behind. White clotted foam from the horses' mouths flew backward, spattering the men. Age-Nor clung to the rim with desperation. This was it, this was how his death would find him. His mouth filled with bile.

Éremón's laugh boomed out, crashing against his ears.

Éremón raced his chariot in a wide circle, herding his followers together. He roared at them and they roared back at him exuberantly. Without checking his team, he headed for the cliffs above the sea, his defiant back daring the others to follow him. He made straight for the path that twisted downward toward the beach.

Until they reached the very edge of the cliff Age-Nor could not see this trail. He was certain by now that all Keltoi were demented and homicidal, and Gaelicians were the worst. This particular brute was going to launch himself out onto empty air and plunge them both to their deaths.

But they did not fall. They hurtled downward, the chariot swaying sickeningly as Éremón fought to keep his team under control. Behind them came the thunder of other horses. Éber, not to be outdone, was in full pursuit, followed by Ír and Gosten and the bravest of the others.

Age-Nor was not aware that he screamed.

Éremón's chariot wheels churned in sand. Age-Nor, expecting to be smashed dead, opened his eyes to find himself on level ground once more, splashing through the surf. This stretch of beach was out of sight of the harbor where his ships waited, but at least he was close to the sea again. If he was flung from the chariot here his gods might take pity on him and cushion his fall.

Might. Probably not. The sea gods were not known for their pity.

Éremón fought the team to a shuddering standstill and watched the other charioteers come racing to join him. Age-Nor staggered from the chariot, his knees collapsing under him. He sagged onto the pebble-strewn sand and vomited in misery, while Éremón looked down at him and laughed.

I would like to have you on the deck of a ship during a storm, Age-Nor said silently to the warrior. We would see who laughed then.

The warriors who had followed Éremón to the beach were laughing and yelling, each claiming to be the boldest driver. Their horses were barely controllable, as excited as their masters. Brego cried, brandishing his sword, "I would follow you anywhere, Éremón!"

Ír, not to be outdone, had drawn his own sword and was chanting a war song. Suddenly he shrieked and ran headlong into the foaming surf, slashing at the waves with his weapon and yelling incoherently. While his startled companions looked on he battled the ocean itself, holding up his shield to repulse its watery counterattack.

"You would swallow me?" he screamed. "You would swallow *me*, the son of Milesios?" He ran back to his chariot and snatched up his assortment of casting-spears, hurling them one after another at the incoming breakers.

"You'll lose your spears, you fool!" Donn shouted from the cliff above, but Ír was beyond listening. The ecstasy of battle consumed him. The sea was his chosen opponent, the most awesome possible adversary, and he threw himself into the assault with a joyous frenzy. The uncontrolled energy of man faced the untamed power of the ocean, screaming defiance.

The spectators who had quickly massed along the cliff watched in astonishment as Ír redoubled his attack, dashing about in thigh-deep seafoam, slicing the tops off waves, yelling demands for surrender.

Amergin, standing among them, threw his spirit into the void between himself and his brother and felt what Ír was feeling, opening himself to the intensity of his brother's emotion. To the surprise of those around him, the bard began to chuckle.

He could not help it. Ír—wild, absurd, incredible Ír—was having a wonderful time. He was fighting gloriously with no expectation of victory, for victory was not even necessary. All he required was the total commitment of self and the pure joy of doing.

"You are magnificent!" the bard yelled down to him. His brother could no more have heard Amergin than he had heard Donn, yet the spectators saw him pause and glance upward, one hand lifted briefly as in a salute. Then he plunged back into the sea.

A contagion seized the other warriors on the beach. First Éber, then Gosten and Brego and Éremón ran into the surf as Ír had done, and soon the whole company was floundering about with water dripping from their mustaches as they slashed the waves with their swords and yelled, screamed, laughed.

Age-Nor watched the entire incomprehensible performance with disbelief. They were worse than mad, these Keltoi barbarians. They were so huge and fair and bursting with life their very existence was a threat to smaller, weaker men. They should be driven off the edge of the world.

Watching from the cliffs, Scotta sighed to herself. "Children," she said in a bemused voice.

Another voice hissed in her ear. "My husband plays in the sea and wastes his strength on the waves," Odba complained in a tone that savored misery. "Yet he has nothing to spare for me. You said you would help me, Scotta. You said."

The excitement gradually spent itself and a somewhat subdued group came up the pathway from the beach, their sides aching with laughter and their sword arms tired from swinging. After a time spent regrouping and collecting the horse riders and foot warriors they got under way at last, cheered on by kin and celsine. When they were only a speck in the distance the Gaelicians went to their Míl's stronghold to spend the rest of the day in feasting.

Age-Nor gladly turned his back on them all and returned to the harbor, where he told Bomilcar, "The sooner our repairs are completed the better I will feel. There is madness here, and I will not be forced one step farther into Keltoi territory. When we leave here, we go back to Tyre."

"Even so, we cannot leave before autumn," Bomilcar told him. "Two ships are having to be virtually rebuilt; it is a wonder they got this far. But perhaps we will get lucky with that wool you arranged for, there is always the possibility we may return with it during a time of wool shortage, I suppose."

"We will do the best we can," Age-Nor said, his shoulders slumping. "It is all any of us can do." He retired to his bed and was not seen the rest of the day, preferring to lie in a tight ball with eyes shut and his blanket over his head, hiding him from the vision of the gods who were so obviously angry with him.

Or perhaps—just maybe—there was yet a deal to be made with the gods!

◇ 13 ◇

AMERGIN ACCOMPANIED HIS TRIBESFOLK to the Heroes' Hall, but behind his eyes he was still watching the chariots on the plain and the battle in the sea. Not observing as a bard, but watching with longing as a man. If he could have flung Clarsah from him and taken up the reins of a war cart on that thrilling day he would have done so. He would have yelled and cracked the whip and run daringly along the wagon tongue, challenging the best of them.

Would have felt totally alive, an integral part of the tribe rather than a creature shaped in a different mold, set apart.

He held Clarsah in his arms but in his heart he was unfaithful to her.

He had no sooner taken his seat in the hall when a motion at the doorway attracted his attention. He looked up in time to see Taya accompany Lugaid to the portal, then turn away.

Amergin thought of going outside to speak to her, but what was there to say? She had chosen Éremón, and this very night he would be with Scéna Dullsaine once more before she returned to her clanhold, anticipating his arrival on some future day with gifts to offer Ferdinón. Whatever might have happened between Taya and himself—and in truth he must admit something might have happened—that opportunity was past now. No man of honor would hunt a quarry his brother wanted for himself.

Quarry. Friend. Partner. Dream. What was the word for woman? Preoccupied, he did not notice Odba slip from the hall and follow Taya.

The bard sat brooding on the mystery of himself.

Was the inner language of his spirit so complex that it involved a whole range of feelings no one else experienced, and therefore had not created words to describe? A Hellene trader had once told him that the Celtic mother-tongue was among the most difficult spoken anywhere, with shadings of

151

meaning no other language possessed. Was such a language a remnant of an older time, when gods walked among men and the spirit world more visibly touched the world of the living? Had there been a language necessary then for concepts now lost?

These were questions for a druid, of no importance to anyone else at all.

Amergin listened, with a kind of detached wonder, to the conversations around him. Life seemed simple to other men. First came survival, the basic necessities of food and shelter, and then the overlay of secondary human desires. The interlaced passions of love and hate and lust and ambition were always just beneath the surface, but few articulated them. Only the druids perceived them as tangible.

Watching the warriors, so comfortably certain of their place in the fabric of existence, Amergin felt as if he had blundered into a society of strangers. It was rare that one of the warriors even entered his dreams.

The complexity of those dreams, which he remembered in detail for many nights afterward, seemed to deny the outward simplicity of existence. His dreams were filled with symbols and images that reached intimately into his soul and touched him where no human ever had. Not the prophetic dreams of a diviner, they comprised a private inner landscape containing himself alone. A winter landscape, beautiful but cold and empty, lying hidden below the blaze of Iberian summer.

Like an extra eye that could render a man a monster, Amergin's gift allowed him to see the many layers of his people and the world around them simultaneously, aware of both the dream and the reality and never entirely free of either.

He had memorized the sagas of great-bodied heroes and magnificent women who lived courageously in an ancient world shaped as much by their own actions as by the power of external forces. Nature flowed through them; instinct served for thought. Mortals were conscious in those long ago days of many things no longer perceived, and something had been lost along the way for which Amergin yearned with every fiber of his being.

He yearned for vanished forests whose birds and beasts might become, in the blink of any eye, fighting men and seductive women, their flesh responding to a different reality. In the land of the epics, heroes were not so much individuals as part of a compelling interlocked totality. Everything could be shaped and reshaped as though still in the flux of creation, and man himself took part in the shaping, no longer a helpless creature struggling to appease greater forces but one with the motive power, creator and creation, predator and prey, immortally linked.

What death could last, what fire could burn, what wound could bleed?

Sitting on his bench, forgetting Taya, Amergin dreamed of lost eons.

When Taya turned away from the Heroes' Hall she meant to go no farther than the gateway in the stronghold's outer embankment. From that vantage point she could look along the road Éremón had taken and still see his dust cloud rising. She was so preoccupied she did not hear footsteps behind her until Odba grabbed her shoulder and spun her around.

"What do you think you're doing?" Éremón's wife demanded to know. "Are you planning to follow him? Has he arranged to draw rein in some valley beyond my vision and wait for you?"

Taya, startled, drew back, but the other woman clung to her like burrs in a horse's tail. Pain and rage often wear the same face; Taya could not decipher Odba's expression, but it frightened her.

"We have no agreement to meet anywhere," she protested.

"Haven't you? Do you think me a fool? The whole clan knows he has started looking at you. And more, I think. Last night—*last night*—when a warrior should be with his family on the eve of departure, filling their eyes with the sight of him, Éremón never came home at all. One of his brothers—and how *that* lot stick together!—tried to tell me he was with the other cattle raiders, getting them ready. But I don't believe it; I think he was with you. With a rankless daughter from an unpropertied clan, while Odba of the Artabrians waited alone in his house!

"He insults me, Taya, turning to someone like you when he could have me. Have you put sorcerer's herbs in his wine to turn him away from me? I wouldn't put it past a darkheaded woman like you. All you darkheaded women tangle your fingers in a man so he can never get free of you!"

"I mean you no harm," Taya protested, still trying to back

153

away. But Odba was past listening. She had someone to blame for Éremón's defection; she was not going to turn loose now.

"Did Scotta speak to you?"

Taya nodded. "She did. But I could not believe you would take such actions just to prevent your husband having a second wife. Many men have second wives, Odba, it's no insult . . ."

"I'll decide what is an insult!" Odba yelled at her. "Do you know how long it's been since I last conceived? Since Éremón and I took pleasure together?"

"I have nothing to do with that. I give you my word," Taya added urgently, offering the most sacred vow a Celt could give.

Odba scoffed at her. "What is the word of Lugaid's daughter to me?"

Taya was suddenly angry. Gentleness, reasonableness, honesty—they accomplished nothing with this person. "Lugaid is a Gaelician and his word is sacred. Perhaps your own Artabrian sire would not understand that!"

"You insult my *father?!*" shrieked Odba, livid with rage. Unable to contain herself any longer she leaped at Taya and began pummeling her rival with her fists.

Taya raised her arms in a futile effort to defend herself, but she was no warrior. Odba landed a blow for every time she had seen Éremón's attention wander; for every night she had lain alone, aching for his touch; for every morning she had looked at her children and feared her belly would never again swell with new life.

"You deliberately make me look bad to my husband!" she yelled at Taya, catching a lock of dark brown hair and giving it a vicious yank. "You never ask him for anything, do you? You never expect anything of him and you never complain. Oh, yes, I know what you are doing! Éremón can go to you anytime he pleases and you'll just simper and spread your legs. You've done everything you could to turn him against me!"

Taya tried desperately to get away. She started running but Odba caught her and jerked her down on a dung heap near the wall. She fell headlong into the stinking ordure with her legs doubled under her, slipped and scrambled to her feet and ran again, but Odba was always at her heels, yelling and striking out.

At last Taya fell and could not get up and Odba swarmed all over her.

The commotion brought people running from various parts of the stronghold, forming a laughing circle around the battling women. The men were excited and amused, and quickly made wagers as to the outcome. Odba was the heavy favorite. It was obvious she was both stronger and more agile, whereas Taya's gentle nature was a definite handicap.

The women, who had long since tired of hearing Odba's endless complaints, sided with Taya.

Scotta broke them up at last, straddling the floundering pair and pulling them apart. Odba hit her husband's mother one blow to the chest before she realized who it was. Without hesitation, Scotta hammered her in return with a fist to the side of the head that made Odba's eyes cross.

Scotta stood up, breathing hard. "Get up, both of you," she commanded. "Odba, go to your children. And as for you, Taya . . ." She paused, watching the younger woman lift herself painfully onto her hands and knees and stop there. "Are you badly hurt?"

"My . . . side . . . ." Taya gasped.

Scotta crouched down and pulled Taya's torn gown out of the way, revealing a bruise already purpling on white flesh. "She hit you a good blow," Scotta commented with professional admiration. "I'll say one thing for Odba, she was properly trained. Are you satisfied now that you've brought this on yourself?"

Taya did not answer. Her battered face was beginning to swell and there was a taste of blood in her mouth where a tooth had cut the inside of her lip.

Scotta sighed. "Someone will have to look after you, I suppose. We can't let you go back to Ítos' clanhold looking like this. I always seem to be doing things for someone else, never myself . . ." Her voice trailed away and she shrugged. "Come on, then, we'll fix some compresses for you and you will rest awhile in the hall. But then you are going to leave the Míl's clanhold and not return, for I cannot allow this continual disharmony. You go home, or I may go to the brehons myself."

Over the sound of Taya's hard breathing Scotta could hear the watching crowd beginning to argue among themselves as to who was in the right. Sides were quickly taken, the clan of Ítos on one and the clan of Milesios on the other.

155

The old chieftain was not there to hear it but even if he had been Scotta had terrible doubts as to whether he would do anything. Here was yet one more problem she must deal with herself.

"I'll go home," Taya said in a subdued voice.

Odba headed for her own house in a glow of righteous satisfaction. But after a few steps she winced and hesitated, putting one hand to her belly and the other to her head. Scotta's blow had left her ears ringing and there was a sore place in her belly where Taya must have landed a knee. She glanced around for sympathy but the group nearest her had chosen Taya's side, and rewarded Odba with only stony stares.

Odba bit her lip and squared her shoulders. With an impassive face, she strode on to her dwelling and pulled the summer's wattling door shut behind her.

A small figure materialized from the shadows. Her youngest son, Lagneh, came to her and wrapped his arms around her hips. "Why were you and that woman hitting each other?" the child inquired.

"She wants something that she has no right to," Odba told him.

Lagneh clenched his little jaw and wrinkled his forehead into a child's approximation of a scowl. "I will get my father's sword and kill her if you want me to," he offered.

Odba suppressed a smile. "The sword you have is not Éremón's, but a gift my own father sent to my sons. He seems to care more for us than . . ."

"Than what?"

"Nothing." But in her head, she finished the thought: than your father does, who has taken to avoiding our house and running off into other territories whenever he can manufacture an excuse to do so.

"Is that woman a thief?" Lagneh wanted to know. "Is she our enemy?"

"Yes, she is!" Odba agreed, then tried to bite back the words. Looking closely at her son's trusting face, she remembered that one must always tell a child the truth; it is the Law. "No, she is not the enemy. She is one of our own tribe."

"What does she want that she doesn't deserve?"

"She . . . ah . . . admires Éremón too much," Odba replied.

The child was obviously puzzled, but his reaction was

instantaneous. "Everyone admires Éremón because someday he will be the champion of the whole tribe. And I will, too, as soon as I'm old enough. Then I will take the biggest sword in the whole world and cut off all your enemies' heads!" He struck what he believed to be a wonderfully heroic pose with his sturdy legs braced wide apart. His round little belly protruded in front and his round little bottom stuck out behind. Downy yellow curls framed a belligerent baby face.

Odba dropped to her knees and gathered him into her arms, burying her lips in the soft angle where his neck met his shoulders. The child's hair smelled of wind and sunshine.

Lagneh felt his mother's shoulders tremble. That small sign of parental vulnerability alarmed him. He inflated his chest as far as he could so Odba would realize he was a warrior, capable of protecting her. "It's all right, mother," he assured her in his deepest voice.

He sounded so much like her own father, just for a moment, that she drew back and looked at him in surprise. Firm muscles were beginning to develop beneath the surface of his glossy, childish skin.

My beautiful son, she thought. If I had a hundred like you . . . She gripped him so tightly he wriggled in protest and she quickly released him.

Lagneh backed away, watching her suspiciously. "Are you crying?"

Odba swallowed very hard. "No," she said.

The chariots of the warriors wheeled across the land. The horsemen rode beside them, shouting back and forth, already shaping stories to describe the adventure just beginning. Éremón, in the lead, threw back his golden head and laughed.

The high hot Iberian sun beamed down on them, burnishing the day. When they closed their eyes redness filtered through their lids. They felt radiant with the sun's own power on that glorious morning. They were heroes. Brave, indomitable. Sturdy bones overlaid with mighty muscles. They could feel their strength in their shoulders; they could hold up the sky.

This was their time. Soon they would put to use the cunning of their wits, the keenness of their eyes, the stealth in their feet. Soon they would have a challenge to measure themselves by, and who could ask for anything more?

Or it might end in blood and pain and a mouthful of trampled grass, with some Asturian sentry's knife between the shoulder blades.

But what could that matter to the immortal spirit within? How could the mere threat of death be considered when the chariots were flying and the horses were galloping and the men were running with full lungs and great pumping hearts? When the body sang its paean of strength and the spirit burned like a flame? There was no intoxication to equal such a moment.

The momentum of it carried them until after midday, when the legs of the runners grew shaky and sweat streamed down the sides of the horses. They slowed their pace then, but the drumbeat of inner excitement continued, and when one man met the eyes of another a single gleaming thought leaped between them.

The road east to the territory of the Astures was a trading highway, well-worn and clearly marked. Generations of feet and hooves had trampled it and in the dry season it was hard enough to lame a horse. Éber Finn kept his chariot off the road, seeking out softer footing wherever possible, and watching his brother to see if Éremón had the same idea. But Éremón's mind was filled with the raid to come and he let his team take the easiest way, trotting on the unyielding roadway surface. Most of his warriors followed his lead without thought.

Éber smiled to himself. Let Éremón wear out his horses' legs! If one of his beasts pulled up lame, it would be Éber who returned to the Míl's stronghold in the lead.

As they moved into the mountains the nights became sharper, more star-freckled, and the days possessed a glittering clarity. The cool, damp weather, which had deserted the seacoast for the last several summers, had moved up here instead, creating an abundance of green luxuriance. The Gaelicians climbed steadily upward through lush woodlands of oak and beech, chestnut, ash, and birch; they followed tumbling streams through deep, rocky gorges opening onto broad montane meadows belly-deep in grass.

"I wish Amergin had come with us," Éber remarked. "He could have turned all this into a poem."

"Bards don't go on cattle raids," Soorgeh said. Fierce Soorgeh, with the sun glinting on his war jewelry. "Only formal battles, declared wars, rank a bard in attendance."

158

Éber sighed. "It's been a long time since the last good war."

Éremón grinned, savoring his surprise. "Wait until we camp for the night," he teased. "I have news for you."

The word quickly passed from man to man. Horse warriors yelled at one another above the clatter of hooves and the clank of metal; foot warriors strained the horsemen's dust through their mustaches and spat out a repeated version of Éremón's promise to the men behind them.

Camp was set up early that night.

Éremón addressed the eager crowd gathered around him. "I have not brought all our best warriors into the territory of the Astures for a simple cattle raid," he said, and saw the sudden gleam in their watching eyes. "Raids have always been conducted at night, with men slinking through the darkness like animals in hopes of snatching a fertile cow or a breeding bull and driving it through more darkness to a predetermined spot where horsemen waited. If sentries caught the foot warriors there was fighting, but horses were often injured driving the small collection of cattle away in the night."

His men nodded to one another in agreement. He had described the time-honored tradition by which generations of Celtic tribes replenished their breeding stock at one another's expense. Sometimes the outraged former owners came after their animals, but more often not. Few were reckless enough to venture deep into another tribe's territory and make open war for two or three tens of cows, when their losses could be replaced through a similar snatch-and-grab operation at some future time, when another tribe grew careless.

So it had always been, but now Éremón faced his companions and asked, "Why should we come a long way just to crawl through the dark on our bellies? Why should we settle for a few cows, when we might win them all?"

They stared at him, not quite comprehending.

"If we declared war on the Astures and won, we would be entitled to take whatever we wanted of them!" Éremón declared. "Milesios has discouraged us declaring war on our neighbors of late . . ."

"Because he's getting old and tired and has lost his taste for it," Ferdinón whispered to Étan.

" . . . but the Míl has put me in charge of this party of warriors," Éremón went on, "and I say we have enough

159

valorous men here for a full battle. And to drive home all the booty we care to claim!"

They yelled with delight.

"This is the obvious answer to our problems," Éremón continued. "We don't need to trade with the Sea People to support our clans. We will support them in the future as we did generations ago, with a herd of cattle so vast a man may eat beef every day and trade hides and worked leather for anything else he may want. We will be cattle lords again, as we once were. We will protect and provide!"

"Éremón, leader of the Gaelicians!" screamed Brego, waving his sword.

Éremón grinned at them. He was mightily pleased with himself.

The entire plan, from conception to its anticipated spectacular conclusion, had been his, first glimpsed in the Heroes' Hall the night Amergin dazzled everyone with his poem. Éremón had felt impelled to do something of equal splendor, some achievement that would put bardic brilliance in the shade. He had told no one, so that all the credit would be his own, and he had rewarded himself every night since by lying in the dark and imagining the expression on the Míl's face when all those cattle arrived.

After this, who could question his right to someday take over the rank and honors of Milesios himself?

His warriors were screaming and cheering. At that moment they would have followed him through a wall of fire. The possibility of defeat was never considered. Éremón's confidence forbade it.

Even Éber Finn was impressed. "Think of all those cows!" he murmured, as if with love.

They hurried on with renewed excitement, deeper into Asturian territory.

Soon Éremón led the group off the trade road to follow deer trails and streambeds instead, so their approach would be concealed from casual eyes by the contours of the land. The terrain was rugged and broken and the horses had to be led most of the time, but it never occurred to the Gaelician clan-chiefs to leave their chariots behind and venture into another tribe's land afoot, like untitled warriors or even worse, traders.

The Asturians had long relied on this custom, thinking it

160

prevented a warlord from leading an army too deeply into their mountainous homeland.

The Asturians reckoned without the resourcefulness of Éremón.

Along the way he showed his men nicks he had previously slashed in trees, indicating gaps where a chariot might pass and narrow trails with footing safe enough for horses. In the most difficult terrain he ordered the teams unharnessed and had men pull the chariots, straining upward, while other men lifted and guided the wheels.

"Anything is possible," Éremón said to Donn as they stood together watching one such maneuver. "Once a man realizes that, all he has to do is find the way he knows must exist."

With every step they took Éremón could feel the growing desire in his men for battle. For yelling hitting raging *warfare!* He longed for it himself with a happy lust that defined life and made it worth living. There were too many tensions coiled in him, demanding release. He could hardly recall the last time he had slashed a sword across an enemy body, or felt that good solid thud run up his arm when his blow was deflected by an opponent's shield, and the eyes looking at him from above that shield contained the possibility of his own death.

There was a moment to spice a man's life!

Beauty, for Éremón, was the brilliance of a battle morning, when light flashed on spear points and brave men faced each other across a field where ravens would soon feed. Music was the voice of the war drum, the bodhran, pounding like the beat of a heart. Happiness was the intense bonding of warrior with warrior, one iron bar of courage running through them all, lifting them above the pre-dawn fears they had shared in silence. A man felt such total exhilaration at no other time in his life. The small meannesses of everyday living niggled joy away, losing it in problems and illnesses and the voice of a complaining woman. But manhood could be regained on those splendid mornings when battle was in the offing, and men loved one another with the sweet desperation of comrades who may soon be parted forever.

"We will offer the Asturians war for their cattle," he told his followers. "War in the daylight, and the winner gets everything. We will make that a new truth for our tribe. We do not take unfair advantage, we do not kill from cover, and

161

we do not run. Let the bards put that in their songs! We win in one bold stroke or not at all!''

"We disdain petty theft; we are heroes!'' men told one another, already flushed with admiration of themselves.

In silvery mountain dawnlight, the Gaelician warriors massed above a deep valley where the Asturian herd spread like a lake of honey, golden and opulent.

At the sight of them, Éber Finn could hardly contain himself. "They are everything you promised, Éremón, and more! Fat meat for the pot, oxen for the yoke, and soft calfskins to sleep under. And look at those horses! They make ours look stubby and moth-chewed. Their tails drag the ground! Let's go get them, Éremón!''

"Let's go win them in battle,'' his brother replied.

Étan crowded forward. "I see no one down there but a few herders and some crude huts. Will you go as the representative of the Míl and offer to meet the Asturian champion in single combat?''

Éremón gritted his teeth and resisted the temptation. ("If I put you on a horse of mine it is not for the purpose of having you elope with the horse.'') He waved his arm in a grand gesture that included all his eager followers. "Of course not,'' he assured them. "We will all go down and fight together as an army, so every man gets a chance to swing his sword and take his trophies.''

"A war against herders?'' Donn asked.

Éremón scowled at him. "We will give them ample warning to summon their warriors,'' he said. "You, Brego; come with me and we will drive our chariots into the valley and ask to see their leader. The battle must be arranged at once.''

The Asturians were astonished to see a pair of war chariots racing across their peaceful meadow, and horrified to learn that war had come to them. The herders were frightened, but did not dare let the Gaelicians know their vulnerability, so they told Éremón and Brego they had "any number of warriors'' hidden in the hills.

Éremón smiled magnanimously. "Take your horns and summon your warriors, then,'' he ordered. "We will wait for them.''

He and Brego drove back onto the ridge where the other Gaelicians were gathered. "It's all right,'' Éremón assured Donn. "They have enough fighting men available to give us a rousing good battle!''

◇ **14** ◇

SHINANN of the Túatha Dé Danann was seized with longing to visit the region of her birth, the sweet stretch of Ierne from its heartland to its western cliffs. Without telling anyone—and giving them a chance to argue with her about it—she set off to find and follow her favorite rivercourse, meandering across the land and enjoying its beauties.

She began the journey on a morning drenched with sunlight, when the countryside blossomed with polychrome radiance and the whole space between earth and sky was filled with birdsong.

Goddess weather.

As her travels led her south and west, however, the light changed. The bottomless blue sky solidified, trapping the earth beneath an inverted silver bowl. There might be rain. There was often rain. Shinann, avoiding settlements and signs of Fir Bolg habitation, felt no need to look for shelter, however. She loved to experience the flow of moisture back and forth between earth and sky, keeping one green and the other cloud-foamed. She could walk as happily through showers as others walked in sunshine, with her face upturned and her eyes sparkling with delight.

But no rain fell. The river began to take on a dull metallic sheen, as if its vitality were deadened. The full-throated blackbirds in the hedgerows gradually fell silent; the thrushes in the treetops seemed to lose interest in their elaborate songs. At last even the ducks cruising the broad river floated passively, indifferent and subdued.

Shinann headed for the broad, island-dotted estuary where the river met the sea. Water fowl assured her she was nearing the ocean. River ducks were joined by wading birds on stilted legs, running through the shallows with frantic energy. Redshanks and turnstones competed briskly for the occasional tiny green crab to be found dying in some stagnant backwater. Gulls, heralds of the sea, swooped and screamed.

Shinann noticed a red-throated waterbird paddling just clear of the channel current. As she watched, he discovered some tidbit beneath the surface, ducked his head and simply disappeared, leaving not a ripple behind him.

She waited. After a time so long that she thought he must surely have drowned, the diver reappeared some distance away, gulping down his meal, and resumed his cruise.

On the far bank was a tumble of stone ruins. Shinann shaded her eyes with her hand so she could see the place more clearly. It might be some abandoned stronghold built by the Iverni or the Gangani as a defense against marauding Fomorians, or it might be still older, one of the stone constructions aligned with sun and stars by the ancient race of Partalon. The scholars of the Dananns would know, for they studied such ruins, hoarding knowledge as the squirrels hoarded acorns against their instinctual awareness of approaching winter.

But the crude stone building on Shinann's river had little in common with the great complex on the eastern river near the Gathering Place, where, in corbelled chambers covered by immense, layered mounds and surrounded by standing stones, the wisest of the Dananns reached backward with their minds, striving to reclaim the lost sciences of the builders. They studied the symbols of force and flow carved into the stones; they measured the chambers and alignments and marveled at the precision of the elder race. That center of summoned cosmic power was millennia old yet still vibrated with the energies once channeled through it; energies so compelling that Shinann's sister, Boann, had taken up permanent residence nearby. The eastern river was now called Boann, the White Cow, in her honor.

Shinann was not attracted to the eastern half of the island. The cold sea yawning toward Albion repelled her. She loved the west. The retreating gold of the setting sun beckoned to her as it had to so many, promising the ultimate dreams of inexhaustible resources and certain immortality.

Born on the island that had given birth to many fables, Shinann knew the reality. There was rain and cold and ice, bellies could hollow with hunger, pain could ravage, everything must die.

Yet Ierne was a special place; she knew that, too. Here visible and invisible worlds overlaid one another, interlocked

164

in a balanced geometry of possibilities, such as that recently discovered in the great chambers on Boann's river. Here still existed the cohesive force linking man to his beginnings and giving him access to his divinity—a bond corrupted and shattered elsewhere.

Many places might be called holy, but Ierne was sacred to the power man himself worshiped.

Shinann dawdled at the end of her journey, scenting the pungence of decaying seaweed, enjoying the atmosphere of the marshy lowlands where river died and became sea.

A movement caught her attention and she glanced back toward the supposedly abandoned stone buildings on the distant shore. A figure emerged from the ruins, and then another. She was too far away to make out details, but her sharp eyes recognized the gleam of a stray sunbeam on a bronze shield.

Warriors.

She was alone and unguarded, a merry woman who rambled as she liked, unwilling to let fears imprison her. ("Be careful," Greine was always cautioning her. "Shinann, don't be so reckless.") But life flowed on and she must flow with it, she would not be restrained.

She was a long way from the home territory of the Dananns, for she was a born wanderer. This area was held by . . . yes, she could tell from the choppy way they moved, apparent even at such a distance. Fir Bolg. Iverni, probably.

Since that crushing defeat at Moy Tura, a few Fir Bolg tribes had begun to revere the Dananns as something close to gods, but the Iverni did not. They had been the most determined of the Danann's enemies, refusing to yield the foreigners one basketload of earth until they were forced, and the old injuries still rankled.

Shinann was a woman alone in the territory of her enemies.

They had seen her. Three more emerged from the old fort and gestured toward her, shouting in hostile voices that carried across the unusually quiet water. They dragged a leather boat from behind a tumbled wall and launched it out onto the river, yelling with excitement at having spotted a solitary female, undefended. Women were in short supply in their tribe this season; childbirth had taken a heavy toll.

As they drew nearer, Shinann could make out the details of the four oarsmen and the one crouched in the prow, the probable leader. He wore a leather helmet pulled down over his hair. Even the most ignorant person knows enough to protect the brain inside the skull, Shinann thought to herself.

These were sturdy, muscular men, dressed in coarse tunics colored with vegetable dyes. And housing vermin, apparently—one of the rowers missed his stroke to scratch frantically at his belly. The leader swore at him. They were rowing hard, battling the current, but even so they did not stir up enough wind to lift the otter fur capes on their shoulders.

A nubile woman . . . the leader looked toward Shinann and licked his lips, then stiffened, staring incredulously. She wore the clothing of the sorcerers' race and she stood facing them as if she had nothing whatsoever to fear.

As a precaution, the leader drew his sword in the cramped confines of the boat and held it up so she could see it. Be still, that gleaming bronze commanded. Be still and accept your fate, for you are one and we are many.

Shinann had only a simple dagger in the scabbard attached to her girdle, but she did not reach for it. The leader grinned and shouted something coarse to his oarsmen, promising them turns with her, perhaps.

The oarsmen redoubled their efforts to reach the woman, who did not react in any expected way but stood her ground, looking at them as calmly as if . . . she bent down and scooped up something from among the reeds. Mud? The substance sparkled in her hands, as some sands sparkled . . .

When the boat was very near the bank she threw the sand at them.

The men in the small vessel closed their eyes instinctively. Even the leader lifted his forearm in front of his face, then jerked it aside and whirled to yell in fury at his companions, feeling them flinch and rock the wickerwork shell of the boat.

When he turned back the woman was gone.

Only a stand of silver reeds remained where she had been. A fitful breeze rippled among them, making them sway.

The Iverni beached their boat and clambered onto the bank, shoving one another. No one wanted to go first. They approached the stand of reeds with their weapons in their hands, moving with catfooted caution. Their leader cried, "She must be here somewhere. She probably crouches under the water, holding her breath. Feel with your sword, there, there! Poke your spear in there, hurry! Force her to come out!"

They were warriors, and went everywhere armed, but their weapons could not lead them to Shinann.

They followed orders and found nothing; felt no yielding flesh answer the thrust of their blades. They covered the entire area, growing bolder, beating the reeds to pieces.

"She has to be here!" the baffled Iverni captain insisted. "I saw her. We all saw her. I could almost put my hands on her . . ."

At last they had to give up. When they could not drive her out they had gone wild, stabbing and slashing, ready to kill what they could not possess, but all they had accomplished was to dull their blades on the stalks of the reeds. One man had lost a good spearhead in the mud, putting him into a daylong sulk.

Their leader finally called off the search and they stood on the bank looking at one another, panting, frustrated.

There was a ripple of faraway, mocking laughter. Each man thought it was in his own head and did not mention it to his fellows, fearing ridicule.

They waded nervously back into the water to launch their boat. The river swirled around their legs, playing with them. A soft rain began to fall.

Éremón watched magnanimously as the Asturian herders did what they could to prepare themselves for battle. They gathered all the weapons they possessed and armed themselves additionally with rocks and clubs and fury, ready to fight for every aged cow, every unweaned calf, every pace of earth. Their horns sounded again and again, reverberating through the mountains as they summoned reinforcements from the scattered clusters of habitation along nearby streams or tucked within the steep, narrow valleys. By midmorning a sizable force was assembled on the mountain meadow, a band at least equal in manpower to Éremón's party of selected warriors.

But the Asturians were stockmen; there had been too many seasons of peace in the mountains and their originally fierce fighting blood had cooled. They could not bring it to the boil as quickly as necessary; yet they tried. They tried splendidly.

When they signaled readiness, Éremón extended his arm in the classic gesture for a charge and the Gaelicians poured down into the valley.

The Asturians had drawn themselves into a semblance of a battle line and waited with gritted teeth, their backs to their precious herd. After the grunting, screaming impact of the

167

first charge, Éremón saw an opening and drove his team at an angle through the Asturian line, headed for a holding pen containing a dozen magnificent horses. "Those are mine!" he yelled at the men who tried to follow him. "Turn back, I will capture them alone!"

Three Asturian men defended the penned horses. One of the herders, feeling his bowels loosen when he heard the Gaelician battle-cry, had paused to answer the call of nature and now came to meet Éremón with a peculiar hobbling gait because he was still trying to pull his breeches up and get them fastened. Asturian horsemen wore leggings and breeks, both necessary for their profession and their climate.

Éremón hauled his team back on its haunches and leaped from the chariot. He did not mind that there were three of them and only one of him; he considered that a fair match, for he knew his own strength. He ran grinning to meet them, his feet unable to carry him as fast as his eagerness. The Asturians, armed with pikes and knives, tried to head him off before he got to the horse pen.

Éremón planted his feet wide apart and waited for them. He gripped the hilt of his sword in both hands, whispering endearments to his weapon as Amergin whispered to Clarsah, and when the first man came within range he executed a mighty swing that turned the iron sword into a silver blur. It slashed open the belly of the Asturian and left the man on his knees in blood-drenched grass, trying hopelessly to poke his intestines back inside himself.

The second herder, a thinking man, tried to circle behind Éremón and get a grip on him so his companion could deliver a knife blow to the body. Éremón amused himself by pretending not to notice until the Asturian was directly behind him, then he suddenly whirled and cut the man's head from his shoulders, jumping aside from experience to avoid the sudden fountain of blood.

The remaining Asturian learned quickly. A deadly perimeter surrounded Éremón, circumscribed by the swing of his sword. But a pike was longer than a sword's reach and the Asturian suspected his opponent was not as familiar with a pike as with iron blades.

The herder cocked his arm and balanced the wooden pole like a spear, then rotated it neatly and slammed the end of it across Éremón's throat with deadly accuracy.

The world was blotted out by shock. Éremón staggered but

168

somehow kept his feet under him, reminding himself in some dim, fogged corner of his brain that if he went down he was a dead man. He could smell the horses in the nearby pen; he could hear the cries of his warriors and the answers of the Asturians, the lowing of frightened cattle, the voice of the drum and the trumpet.

This was the moment he had waited for, when the choice was made between life and death and only his physical ability and determination controlled the outcome. Feeling indomitable, he fought off the effects of the pike's blow, holding the pain in abeyance to be suffered in the future, after he had gone through the pike-swinger and claimed his horses.

He did not try to breathe. He clamped his jaws shut and ran forward with the sword cleaving the air in front of him. The Asturian, astonished that the big blond man had absorbed such a blow and not fallen, had not prepared a defense. He stood gaping as Éremón cut him down.

Éremón got as far as the horse pen, and actually had his fingers on the rope fastening the gate before pain overcame him. He gasped and the gulp of air seared all the way down his throat, tearing him with claws of agony. He doubled over and his fingernails dug deep grooves in the gatepost.

Donn was at his side. "Are you all right, Éremón? Answer me. Éremón?" The man tugged at him and Éremón found enough strength to glare in return and strike out, pushing his brother away. What sort of fool demanded a man talk with a crushed throat? I'll kill him as soon as I feel better, Éremón told himself.

The pain ebbed enough for him to realize the battle was continuing at white heat, and without him. He would not waste his energy throttling a brother; he must get back to the war. He could not talk or yell to lead a charge, but his arms were working and he still had his sword. Leaning on Donn's shoulder, he made his way to his chariot and took up the reins.

The jolting of the war cart nauseated him. Lights flashed in his eyes. Something like gray grains of barley fractured his vision, coming between him and the daylight. Still he flapped the reins and urged his horses on. When he reached the area of most intense fighting, he stepped gingerly from his cart and drew a careful breath, fighting the pain back as if it were a human enemy. He shook his fist at it. He dared it to drag him down.

Then he drew his sword and plunged back into the battle.

The herd had become a secondary issue. Daylong, the tides of war swept back and forth across the valley, leaving some men dead or dying and others exalted by courage and daring. Ír fought like a god, dodging and pirouetting among his foes as joyously as if he performed at one of the festival dances. Donn, feet braced and face intent, made up in perseverance what he lacked in brilliance, and never took a step backward. Lugaid, son of Ítos and father of Taya, took a savage knife cut in the shoulder but refused to let that mar his pleasure in the first real war in many seasons.

They are all heroes, Éremón thought, looking across his company. I have taken the petty sport of cattle raiding and turned it into a great battle, shaped by the traditions of war. Whoever wins wins glory and whoever dies dies gloriously.

My name will be sung by the bards for this, he thought. They will say of Éremón that he never did anything small.

In midafternoon he came across an injured Asturian lying at the edge of the meadow, still alive and conscious but clutching his throat. Éremón stooped over him and pulled his hands away. The man had been clubbed, or perhaps hit across the windpipe with the flat of a sword. He was gasping for air and flinching from the pain of breathing.

Éremón squatted down beside him and helped him sit up. With gestures, he indicated that a similar fate had befallen him. The Asturian nodded in dumb misery. Then, shaking his head to clear it, he leaned over and vomited on Éremón's feet.

One of the Gaelicians came running up with sword in hand, but Éremón motioned him back. He pantomimed the word for water and sent the fellow off at a trot, soon returning with a cracked and leaking wooden cup. Éremón held it to the lips of the wounded Asturian and waited patiently while he drank.

When the man was able to draw a full breath, Éremón helped him stand up. Together they hunted in the grass for the Asturian's dagger and the oval wooden shield he had brought to battle. When they finally found it, the shield was split down the center.

The Asturian kicked it in disgust. He was breathing more easily now and his eyes were bright. He gave Éremón a hard look and muttered something almost intelligible.

Éremón threw his own shield aside and, leaving his sword thrust through his belt, attacked the Asturian only with his

170

dagger. The two fought grimly until at last one fell, mortally wounded.

From nearby came the harsh voices of the carrion birds, arriving to clear the battlefield.

The hot days of summer seemed longer to Odba than they had ever been before, yet strangely, the nights were still longer. In Éremón's absence she tried to occupy herself by planning for his return, piling up towers of good intentions. She would cook only the best food for him and season it just the way he liked it. She would make a new winter cloak for him from the choice wool of her flock. She would ration her words and be honey-tongued and uncritical. She could be at least as compliant and inviting as Lugaid's dark daughter!

Most of the time she believed she could do all this, but occasionally she fell into periods of despair when she knew she could not so violate her inner nature. She could never be gentle and deferential.

She could not resist saying cruel things about Taya within the hearing of others, including those who were fond of Lugaid's daughter or had kinsmen of their own in the clan of Ítos. Women she had thought were her friends began to avoid her. Others took her side and argued the point hotly, more for the sake of exercising their tongues than because anyone truly loved Odba.

Odba's antipathy toward Taya began to tug at deepset loyalties within the clan of the Míl, causing growing dissension. Scotta heard it and was troubled. Milesios, if he heard, said nothing.

Some said, "Taya was born into a clan with little property, and she makes a greedy grab to join a richer clan."

Others said, "Odba is perfectly within her rights to refuse to share her man, their house, their pots and tools and jewelry, their herds and share of the clanholding. If my husband treated me as indifferently as Éremón treats Odba, I would deny him the pleasure of a second wife, too."

But no one really wanted to talk with Odba herself about the situation. Her endless carping got on everyone's nerves, and the clan of Milesios avoided her just as Éremón did.

She pretended not to notice—or care. She spent her time with her sons, recalling the happier days of her own childhood on the banks of the Duero river.

"Have I told you about the homeland of the Artabrians?" she would ask when the day's main meal was eaten and too much daylight remained before the forgetfulness of sleep. "Moomneh, Legneh, come over here and sit by me. Lagneh, quit scraping that pot and join us. Now, where was I? Ah, yes, yesterday we were talking about my father, the chief of the tribe. A much more prepossessing man than Milesios, as I remember him. He always had time for his children, sons and daughters alike. And I was his favorite; everyone knew it and envied me. He gave me my own little bronze stove to fill with red-hot pebbles and carry from place to place, so I would always be warm in the winter."

"Where did he get such a stove?" Moomneh wondered.

"From the Hellenes. Our territory is farther south, nearer the Hellene settlement, and we have much commerce with them. We have adopted quite a few of their styles, in fact. My people—I mean, the Artabrians—eat but one small meal a day, because the Hellene physicians believe an empty stomach is better for a man than a distended one."

Lagneh scowled, disagreeing, and cast a wistful glance toward the cooking pot, where some delicious remnants of the meal lingered.

Odba went on, "Instead of heating water in cauldrons for bathing and washing with animal fat strained through wood ashes, the Artabrians adhere to the Hellene custom of washing in cold water to firm the skin."

Legneh, lifting the corner of a scab on his knee and peering under it, asked, "How can they get clean without fat-soap?"

"They use oils for cleansing the skin, in the Hellene fashion."

"Ai, oil and cold water! No wonder the Greeks are so slippery," Moomneh quipped. His brothers chortled with laughter. "I'm mightily thankful we are Gaelician and not Artabrian," he added.

How could I take them back to my birthplace? Odba asked herself. They are of this clan and this tribe, through and through.

And how can I stay here and hold my head up if Éremón openly neglects me? I am a great chieftain's daughter.

She stared into the shadows and saw nothing but darkness. "We are what we are," Odba said aloud, bleakly.

*   *   *

172

A clenched fist pounded on his doorpost, summoning Amergin from solitude. He set Clarsah aside carefully and went to the door, trying to hold together the shreds of his thoughts.

A handful of Gaelicians stood outside. Several elders, bent with the weight of seasons—one an old woman, respected for her wit and wisdom—led the group. Behind them waited Brego's youngest brother in his clan colors, a highly respected artisan wearing a sea-blue cloak and jewelry of his own making, the chief herder, and the senior stonemason of the Milesian clan.

Amergin offered a formal greeting to this representative lot and welcomed them into his home, growing more curious by the moment. They seated themselves and accepted his wine as easily as the formal compliments a host always paid to guests, but it was obvious they had come on a serious mission.

The old woman, whose name was Airtri, squinted at the bard from between gummy eyelids. "A bard composes satires," she began in the formal way.

Amergin nodded acknowledgment. "It is so."

"The follies of the powerful must be attacked with ridicule for the good of the tribe," Airtri continued. "Mockery destroys prestige; it is the most certain denunciation."

"That is true," Amergin agreed again, noting the carefully surreptitious glances being exchanged among his guests. They were not happy about this occasion, whatever its cause. But their sense of responsibility had brought them to the bard's house and held them nailed to their benches.

Airtri drew a deep breath and pushed a scraggle of gray hair away from her forehead. She was so old there was no gender left in her face, only wisdom. Amergin had seen that happen before, among some women in the druid order; healers who had all but outlived their own bodies and were little more than spirits burning bright through thinworn flesh.

"Our tribe has no chief bard to shame a foolish chieftain," Airtri said, "and while that is so, the tribe lacks protection against the mistakes of its head."

Amergin understood their discomfort now. He faced them gravely, betraying no hint of his own inner feelings as they enunciated the recent failings of Milesios. Chief among their complaints was his serious breach of hospitality in the matter of the Phoenician Age-Nor.

"Excitement over the traders and the cattle raid has kept our clanspeople from thinking too much about the events of the night of the banquet," Airtri went on, "but some of us who are less excitable than others have pondered over these things, and believe that Milesios must be called to accounting for his failure as a host. A most important guest was almost killed beneath his roof. The reputation of the entire tribe is endangered. Who will willingly come to trade with us now?"

Amergin saw no need to mention the fact that there was hardly anything to trade. Airtri was right, Milesios had failed in one of his foremost obligations.

"We have come to formally request a satire of you, Amergin," the old woman said slowly. "You are a son of the Míl, but above that you are a bard, and you will remember your first obligation even if the chieftain forgets his. You can compose a satire that will make Milesios squirm on his bench. Mockery and ridicule are terrible weapons, and we ask you to use them to force our leader to step aside, if he can no longer fulfill his duties." She sat up as straight as her age-knotted joints would allow. "We ask you to function as a chief bard would, for all of us."

Amergin knew what they were offering him. If he stepped into the hollow where no strong voice now spoke, the tribe would demand he be named chief bard by acclamation and the rest of the bardagh would surely agree.

And had not Milesios earned condemnation? He grew weaker day by day, passing on responsibilities that were his alone. Perhaps the time had come . . .

"I will think on it," he told them. "Leave me now."

When they were gone, Amergin sat on an oak bench with his long legs stretched toward the hearthfire and his empty hands lying open in his lap. Clarsah could not help him with this.

His gaze fell on an arm-ring wrapped around his wrist, a handsome Celtic design interweaving gold, bronze, and copper with the fluid sinuosity of ongoing life.

Gold for Brego's young brother the warrior, Amergin mused, his eyes following the twisting design. Strong bronze for the herder, patient and resolute; bright copper for the skilled artisan, glowing with his zest for life.

Just a small assortment of people, not even a clan-chief among them, but their individual voices woven together became part of the complete voice of the tribe and must be heard. That was the Law.

174

The Law, which interwove all the disparate natures of the Celts into one people, individually splendid, individually unique.

Amergin gazed at the metal on his arm, simple in its complexity and strong in its grace, and thought of the elaborately interlocked lives of his tribe.

Their needs.

His destiny. Twisted and shaped in the invisible world.

"Chief bard," he said to himself in the silence.

"Milesios," he said, his eyes brooding and dark.

◇ **15** ◇

THE GRAINY GRAY LIGHT of dawn found Amergin still sitting in front of his hearth, though his head was slumped forward on his breast and only dead coals remained of the fire. The bard awoke with a start, shivering, and found himself in a stiff, sore body that resented any effort to stand up.

But he must stand. Yet another caller was outside his door, and Irial's commanding voice would not be ignored.

Amergin fumbled at his belt for his comb-bag but could not find it. He ran long fingers through his thick black hair, trying to shape it into something other than a wild mane as he hurried—painfully—to bid Irial welcome.

The chief druid scanned Amergin's face. The bard looked older than he had the day before, his eyes sunk into hollows above his strong cheekbones. "I understand a request has been made for your talents," Irial said bluntly.

Irial knew everything—or almost everything—that happened in the tribe, sometimes even before it happened. The old women said the moving air told him. "What are you going to do?" he asked Amergin.

"Did you come to offer me advice?"

"I am a samodhi, not a bard. I have just come to hear your decision because it affects all of us. You have a powerful gift, Amergin; you proved that with the chant for Ír. If you compose an equally strong satire upon Milesios, he will have to acknowledge the need for a younger and more energetic chieftain to lead the people. The power of the word is equal to the power of the sword, and not to be used lightly.''

"Or—perhaps—greater than the power of the sword," Amergin said softly. "Therefore I respect it, and I will not use it to cut off the tribe's head before a stronger head is ready to take its place." In some cold clear crystal compartment of his mind he felt the sudden freedom of dispassion and, surprisingly, he smiled.

"I spent this past night looking at Milesios," he told Irial.

"The Míl was here?"

"Only in my thoughts. But I saw him as clearly as I see you now—not as my sire or the head of my clan and tribe, but as an aging man. I *saw* . . . and there is no better word for it . . . the importance of his growing old. The function that serves in the tribe.

"Irial, bodies wear out to remind us they are temporary, and force us to spend more thought on our spirits. That is what Milesios does now—he examines the spirit within himself and works to strengthen it. In time he will take up the reins again because he has never ceased to be himself, the wise champion, and all Gaelicians will be better for having him on the bronze bench. The essential metal of Milesios still holds the tribe together and must not be lightly cast aside."

Irial stroked his chin. His voice was like dry leaves whispering down onto autumn earth. "You do not think the Míl's preoccupation with his sick body deserves mockery?"

"His body is his battlefield," Amergin replied. "The spirits have given us all an instinct for self-preservation, which is a struggle toward life rather than a rejection of death. The Míl obeys the law of the invisible world to concentrate on existence. I will not compose a satire to bring down scorn on that portion of Milesios which is mortal, simply because of its own mortality. Nor will I condemn his spirit, which is obeying the calendar of its seasons. I see no weakness in his spirit."

Irial dropped his eyelids to hood his thoughts from Amergin's too-perceptive eyes. "This is your decision, then? Even though we all know Milesios has never ranked you high among his sons? Even though a brilliant display of wit and sarcasm might result in your bearing the title of chief bard?"

Amergin's lips were tight over his teeth as he replied, "If I

176

cost my people something of value, the title would not be worth having."

"Is that easy to say?" Irial wanted to know.

Amergin looked him straight in the eye. "No."

"But it is truth," the chief druid acknowledged. He almost smiled; a faint cracking of frozen flesh across weathered cheeks. "Stir up your fire and heat some water, Amergin," he ordered. "When you have refreshed yourself, come to the groves. I leave you now to summon a convocation of bardagh, and before the sun rises again the Gaelicians will once more have the services of a chief bard."

He strode crisply across the room and out the door. Amergin stared after him, unable to think of a single word.

The ceremony itself was brief. The attending bardagh seemed to be in total agreement. There was none among them who could compose a chant to equal the one that had freed Age-Nor from Ír, and there was also none among them who did not respect Amergin's courage in standing outside himself and trying to see through to truth, at whatever cost.

"You spoke to me of law," old Irial reminded him, gently placing one hand on the harp in her case for the first and only time. "And for the bard, truth is the law."

Amergin closed his eyes, and even in the crushing shade of the nemeton he felt the sun briefly shine on him, warming him to the marrow of his bones.

By the time that day died with the dying of the sun, and a new day was being conceived in the darkness, crowds of Gaelicians had made their way to the stronghold of Milesios to congratulate Amergin. The bard was dazed by the volume of good wishes poured over him and the growing pile of honor gifts at his door. On the top of the pile his tribeswomen placed a magnificent cloak of six colors, woven seasons ago and still marked by the folds where it had lain in a dark chest, waiting. The wool glowed with the luster only the finest fleeces possessed. Its body bore a bold checkered pattern of red and bright blue, and the cloak's wide border showed these same colors as a background for an elaborate knotwork design of yellow and green, white and purple.

Tyrian purple.

Amergin picked up the cloak and turned it over slowly in his hands, feeling the weight of its many folds. Wondering what future generations of Gaelicians would use in place of Tyrian purple dye.

177

The bard felt the wind of change on his back and it was a cold wind, a threatening wind. He hastily slung the cloak around his shoulders and welcomed its warmth.

When he went to the Heroes' Hall, Milesios stood up to greet him and gestured him to sit on the chief bard's bench, shaped to the form of dead Nial's bones. If Milesios knew the request that had been made of Amergin he never mentioned it—nor did Amergin expect it.

He sat in the chief bard's place and tried to feel different. A desire so unexpectedly realized should have shape and color and taste, should be something you could wrap around yourself and stroke with delight.

"Chief bard," he whispered to Clarsah.

But he did not seem to himself to be any different. He had climbed a mountain, yet the view was very much the same as it had been from halfway up.

"There must be something beyond *this*," he told Clarsah, feeling a creeping alarm.

The patriarch Ítos approached Amergin during a moment when the attention of the others in the hall was focused on the arrival of the cooked meats. Taya's grandsire had lived so many seasons that his smile was a baby's toothless grimace, but his eyes were still sharp and filled with merry malice.

"One might hope that the new chief bard will offer bride gifts for Lugaid's daughter," Ítos suggested.

"She is looking in a different direction," Amergin told him.

"She is looking toward trouble. But . . ." He curled one shoulder up into a shrug. "It's a pity. You have the appearance of a man who will sire many sons, and surely some of them will be bards. It would be good to have a great bard born to my clan. It would be good to know that harp of yours would someday grace our clanhall."

Amergin sat still, listening politely. Ítos did not have a talker's reputation, and yet the bard could almost see the speech he intended to make forming itself on his tongue.

"It is customary to bring a gift of honor to the new chief bard," Ítos went on, "but my family is very poor. As you know. If you will not take our Taya, still we must give you something . . ." He broke off abruptly, peering at Amergin with such intensity the bard felt the old man lay hands on his soul. "Tell me: where did that poem come from that you chanted to Ír in the Heroes' Hall?" he demanded to know.

"It was filled with riddles, and though I have thought on it ever since, some of it riddles me still."

"The poem was intended to be meaningful only to Ír, for whom it was intended," Amergin replied. "And some of it was just for myself," truth forced him to add.

"Ah, you are mistaken," Ítos told him. "Every phrase you uttered sank into someone's heart like a well-cast spear. For me, the phrase was 'the lure from beyond world's end.' Those words haunt me. I cannot sleep another night without an explanation of them, and a white-haired clan-chief needs his sleep, Amergin."

"I told you there were aspects of the chant meant only for me."

Ítos shook his head. "No, bard. Let me tell you a story, and then perhaps you will understand that no poet exists in emptiness. This story will be all the gift I have to offer you, and I trust you will not ridicule me afterward for my poverty, but I think no finer offering will be made to you this season."

Ítos positioned his frail body directly in front of the bard's bench, screening his face and his words so that no one else could share them. Amergin was chief bard now, no one would intrude on what was obviously intended to be a private moment with the head of a clan.

Ítos said, "I was quite a warrior in my youth—not so terrible as Milesios, son of my brother, would become, but still I was respected. It happened that as a boy I had . . . a vision, you might call it, and warriors are not given to visions. A man who claimed to have them might be asked to give up the battlefield and go into the sacred groves, which would not have suited me at all. So it has been many, many seasons since I told anyone what I am about to relate to you.

"When I was a young lad, the fourth son of the great champion Bréoghan, the harbor out there was always bustling with traffic. Merchants coming in, merchants going out. The masts of trading vessels formed a dark forest rising from the water. There were fewer people here then, and fewer clanholds, but I remember us living very well. Even the grass was greener, and the cattle seem to have been fatter—but that may be only an old man's recollection.

"We boys contested with one another to sight new fleets arriving. My father built that watchtower which still stands on the headland, and I climbed to its top one winter evening expecting to see a fleet of ships making for the harbor before

179

dark. But there were no galleys to be seen, nothing but a strange white mist that appeared out of nowhere and hovered over the water. The weak light of the winter sun was trapped in it as in a net, Amergin, and then the mist lifted all at once and I saw an island floating on the northern horizon, where no island was. I saw it as clearly as I see you now. More clearly, even, for my eyes then were young and keen.

"The land was lush and very green, greener than our own fields. I could see every detail of it, as if I were a bird flying overhead and looking down. I knew then that I was experiencing some very powerful magic but I wasn't afraid, I was only enthralled by the richness of the land I saw. It had eastern mountains like granite domes, and a lake-studded central plain; a rugged coastline on the west with many bays and inlets, and the estuary of a broad river that flowed through the heart of the island. I witnessed a land of honey and harvests, timber and ores. I even heard larks sing in its meadows, Amergin. I swear on my honor, I heard them!

"I ran home to tell my clan and Bréoghan did not believe me. My brothers laughed at me and accused me of stealing wine. The old women mumbled about sending me to the druid groves.

"Only the Phoenician traders in the harbor acted as if they believed me. When I described the details of the island I had envisioned, they told me I had the longest eyes in the world, for I had seen a place they called Ierne. They claimed the rivers of Ierne glittered with gold, and copper was mined in its hills; but they told me they no longer visited Ierne because of some battle they had lost there.

"They may have merely been teasing a gullible boy, as I realized even then, for the Sea People had a cruel streak in them. But they seemed uneasy when they spoke of the place, and I had never seen them fearful before.

"That, combined with the reactions of my family, served to seal my lips ever after on the subject of Ierne. But secretly I dreamed about it sometimes, trying to imagine going there, knowing such a journey was impossible. A journey to a vision? I grew older, busier, and in time I began to forget—until I heard your poem. Then it all came back to me in a rush, that green island wreathed in mist, with a beauty that could stop your heart. Floating like a jewel in the sea to the north.''

"North, across the sea," Amergin murmured, feeling a shiver run up his spine. "Beyond the ninth wave."

"Ai, all such magical places lie beyond the ninth wave, for as everyone knows there are only nine waves and beyond them is the unknown.

"When you chanted in the Heroes' Hall I saw Ierne again, the lure from beyond world's end. I felt it all through me, singing! And I came back to my house and could not sleep for wondering. Was it reality or dream? Did the Phoenicians speak of an actual island, or merely take pleasure in tormenting me? Is there such a place out there? From the way you spoke . . . *do you know, bard?*"

Amergin sat still, humbled by the revealed power of the poem to ignite even an old man's fires.

He reached out and put a strong, sure hand on the patriarch's withered and rope-veined one. "I cannot tell you, Ítos," he said gently. "But I think it must be real; at least for you and me."

"Perhaps that has to be sufficient," Ítos sighed, remembered youth slowly fading from his face. "Some can live on dreams. Others must have bread and meat. Old men need bread, and teeth to chew their meat. I wore out some secret part of myself dreaming about a place called Ierne, and to no purpose. Now I am done with it, Amergin . . . but easier in my head for having passed it on to you."

He turned away, suddenly weary, to seek his compartment and his solitary thoughts.

The new chief bard sat on his bench of honor and gazed out over the Heroes' Hall, but he was not seeing smoked stone walls and brawny blond braggarts and colorfully attired women with flashing eyes. Abruptly he stood up and, without even a word to Milesios, left the hall in great bounding strides.

His people stared after the tall figure in the billowing cloak but no one challenged him; no one called him back. The office of chief bard was beyond challenge.

As soon as he got outside Amergin drew one deep breath and then another, trying to slow his hammering heart. He felt as if he had run at top speed for half a day. He felt as if the air around him were too thin to breathe.

The north wind came singing to him, sweet and green, sea-salted. For a moment Amergin thought his heart would burst with a wrenching and nameless desire, and he turned his back on the wind and stood gripping the harp with such anguish that Clarsah hummed a protest.

A man could stand only so much longing. The feeling of being an alien in the wrong place amid the wrong people was suddenly too painful to be borne.

By the next sunrise he was in his chariot, driving to the clanhold of Ferdinón. For once he did not spare the whip and his horses galloped gorgeously, clawing great tufts of earth from the Mother. Amergin did not notice. As he drove he occasionally glanced over his shoulder, toward the sea.

Scéna Dullsaine was with the other women of her family, dyeing wool. When she heard someone call the bard's name she gladly turned her back on the noxious odors of the dye pits and went to meet him, walking with the stately gait for which she was much admired.

"Amergin!" She held out her hands to him, weaponless and beautifully workstained.

The bard leaped from his chariot and caught her hands in one lithe motion, holding her so hard with his sinewy harper's fingers that she felt a tiny, delicious thrill of danger. She gave a flattered laugh and glanced over her shoulder to be sure the other women were watching.

They were. They saw the bard in a vivid six-colored cloak— six colors? The rumors were true, then: Amergin was the new chief of bardagh! They saw Scéna pressing close against him, and the tender way his arm encircled her, drawing her toward Ferdinón's guesting house. Drawing her with a desperate urgency.

The other women smiled and winked at each other. "Who can long resist our Scéna?" they asked. "I knew he would come for her soon," a red-cheeked cousin of Scéna's remarked. "He has had a long drive from the stronghold on the headland; it is a full day at the gallop, and those horses are badly blown. Send for a boy to care for them."

"I'll go," said a younger girl, broad-boned and soft of feature. "Though I'd rather go into the guest house with Scéna and be a mouse in their straw!"

The laughter of the women rang out like hearty bronze bells signaling festival.

Ferdinón's guest house was small but fragrantly floored with herb-scented rushes, and pallets stuffed with feathers were piled beside the door. Wordless—for there was nothing words could do for him at this moment, it seemed—Amergin

182

pushed Scéna down onto the entire pile and threw himself on top of her.

"I'm not fighting you, Amergin," she laughed, wriggling beneath him. "When did I ever? You needn't be so rough."

But he had to be. The restraint of gentleness had become a torment to him.

Scéna's skin was plump and glossy with health. The contours of her body were as skillfully shaped as Clarsah's frame. "I was beginning to wonder if you had forgotten me," she whispered as he pulled her gown aside and searched between her willing thighs for an opening in which to lose himself.

The night labored and a new day was born. Long after sunrise, Scéna Dullsaine emerged from her father's guest house, wearing a satisfied smile that the other women caught and passed around among themselves.

The bard followed her out, bowing his head to avoid bumping the door lintel. Ferdinón's clansfolk, watching with interest, smiled at this. "All the sons of Milesios are very tall," a freckle-faced tanner remarked to his cousin. "This clan will soon be getting bigger."

The other man laughed. They hurried to join the crowd gathering around the visiting bard, requesting just one story, chant, poem, song . . . a gift he did not deny them.

But then he called for his chariot, which was freshly supplied with a new team to replace the one he had exhausted in his hard drive to Ferdinón's clanhold. "I have to go," he explained to the hands outstretched to hold him back. "I am needed by my own clan and by clans that have no bard at all. But I promise you I will see to it that my compositions are taught to the poet of your family."

When his chariot was ready, Amergin and Scéna Dullsaine stood alone together to say their farewells. To please him, she had dressed in a gown dyed with saffron and bordered with a pattern of crimson; her hair was twisted up with pins of ivory gilded by time. Her speckled eyes were dreamy and practical by turns.

Scéna Dullsaine had no doubts about the future.

"Now that you are chief bard you must not wander like a blown leaf," she chided him. "You need a woman in the poet's house, and children to inherit your talent. You will bring bride gifts to Ferdinón and . . . will you build a special new wall around your house to keep the wind away? I don't like that sound, Amergin; I don't want that mournful wailing to make our babies cry."

"I must always be able to hear the wind," he told her, frowning.

"I can make you forget the wind," she said, then realized he was not listening. He was busy putting the harp in her case and fastening the thongs. His calloused fingers, whose touch the woman remembered all too vividly, handled the harp with the grace of love.

Scéna Dullsaine flung back her proud head. "I can even make you forget the harp, bard," she boasted, sure of her power.

He whirled on her unexpectedly. "Can you? *Would you?*" His gaze was so direct and piercing she shrank back, uncertain what answer he demanded. Then she forced herself to smile, she arched her spine and lifted her chin. "I can make you forget everything but me."

There were haggard lines in Amergin's face and she thought he looked tired, as if the weight of his new responsibilities sat heavily upon him. She would help. She would smooth those lines from his face, she could . . .

He stepped into the chariot and picked up the reins. "I need to remember, not forget," he said, and there was a finality in his voice she chose not to hear. She stepped forward quickly and put one hand on the harness as if she would hold his team back through her own physical strength.

Amergin leaned toward her. "I have a destination I never seem to reach, Scéna," he tried to explain to her. "There is a voice that calls me, and I don't want any other voice to override it. Not ever."

She looked at him blankly. "I don't understand a word you're saying. Give the horses back to the horseboy, Amergin, and come into the house again with me, just for a little while. A little while. We will talk if you want, but there are things much better than words. Come with me . . ."

She reached for him but he was gone. With one flick of the reins he moved the horses away, and as they began to trot north, toward the headland, he turned and waved to her.

Scéna. Scéna Dullsaine. All that comfortable warmth, that fleshly ease, that patterned life. She would fight at his side against his restlessness, Amergin knew; enveloping him with her being, shielding him from the green wind as Itos' maturity had once cut him off from his vision of Ierne. No wise

184

warrior would turn his back on a partner like Scéna Dullsaine, but Amergin did.

He waved farewell to her and stood tall in his chariot, bracing himself against its swaying, resolutely turning his face to the north.

Her clanspeople crowded around Scéna. "Will he be back for you? Will you take part in the marriage rituals next leaf-spring? Ai, Scéna—the chief bard!"

"Yes," she assured them in her haughtiest tone. "The chief bard. But in the meantime . . . perhaps I should get busy sampling some of the men I haven't yet enjoyed. If I marry into the Míl's clan I may be expected to adopt that fashion of theirs for wifely fidelity and be as one-manned as Scotta."

Her voice told them she did not find the prospect pleasing. Her voice told them she was already considering other possibilities. Scéna Dullsaine knew how to protect her vulnerability.

◇ **16** ◇

THE JOURNEY BACK to his clanhold took longer than the journey away. Amergin stopped at each holding he passed, so that he took morning bread with one clan and midday broth with another, while a third family gave him the meat and fish of sundown. In this way he spent two easy days, welcomed wherever he went and treated to the best each clan had to offer—a debt he amply repaid.

He recited the timeless hero-sagas, he moved back and forth with fluid grace between poem and story and song, gifting his people with images of magnificence.

Bard.

And there were moments when he was almost content, as he had briefly been content in Scéna's arms. But when he stepped into his chariot again and lifted the reins, he felt restlessness flow through him like a river that will not be turned aside, rushing onward, carrying him . . . somewhere.

185

There were moments when he was angry with Ítos for having given a name to his dream. Like the completion he had thought to feel when he was named chief bard, Ierne was surely an illusion incapable of realization. Yet if it was unreal, what gave it the ability to summon such vivid passion within him?

There *must* be something tangible out there beyond the ninth wave. Forever beyond his reach. Heartbreakingly denied to horse warriors, land people. For the trackless waves were as impenetrable to the Gaelicians as the spaces between the stars.

When he reached the Míl's clanhold, Amergin learned there had been no word from the cattle raiders. "That's a good sign," Milesios remarked. "If they had encountered trouble, someone would have come back here by now. We will wait. My son Éremón will have a triumph and bring back a handsome collection of cattle."

Milesios spoke often, and proudly, of his son Éremón.

Amergin threw himself into his work with all the energy he possessed. There were minor repairs to be made on Clarsah, recitations of genealogies to be given, the next generation of hopeful bardagh clamoring for teaching. His epic to be finished. The bard seemed to be everywhere at once, always moving, his rich voice ringing.

Perhaps only Scotta noticed how often he found time to be alone, wandering out along the headland or down to the beach. She shook her head in silent puzzlement. Amergin would always be a mystery to her. A bard is like no one else, she thought.

On one of these rambles, Amergin encountered Age-Nor the Phoenician—another of the spiritually dispossessed. The two men looked at each other as they had the evening Age-Nor's ships made their way past the headland, to less-than-secure harbor.

The day was late, the shadows were long and blue. Amergin felt tired and he saw maroon shadows like thin pouches filled with red wine sagging below the merchant's eyes. On an impulse, Amergin issued an invitation.

"Come to my house with me, Age-Nor," he offered. "You said we would talk again, but you avoid my clanhold— for reasons I understand," he added, smiling a little.

Age-Nor did not smile, though his black eyes glittered.

186

"You and I, sweet singer . . ." he began, but he did not finish the thought.

Amergin saw the loneliness in the man and it touched him deeply. With a poet's empathy, he understood how isolated Age-Nor must feel, not only set apart from his fellows by the fact of his wealth and position, but also trapped in a disappointing trade situation at what must seem the end of the world to him. If the Gaelicians were unhappy over the trade, how bitter would Age-Nor be, who had come for a wealth of tin?

"You can safely come to my house," Amergin offered. "I promise no one will attack you, and I always have a little store of wine to offer guests. You should not leave our land without some small experience of our true hospitality."

He could not make up for the harm done to this man; he had no intention of trying to fill the empty space Milesios had left. But he must do something.

Age-Nor surprised himself by agreeing, but even as he said the words his quick mercantile mind was at work, probing for an opportunity, seeking an advantage.

Amergin did not make the mistake of offering Age-Nor a ride in his chariot, rightly sensing that the man from Tyre had no taste left for chariot rides. Instead they walked together the long way, and Amergin shortened his stride to suit his companion's shorter legs. Nevertheless, by the time they reached the poet's house—amid the startled stares of the clanspeople within the stronghold—Age-Nor was panting and badly out of wind. He sank down onto the bench outside Amergin's door and mopped at his soaked forehead with the hem of one sleeve.

When he caught his breath, he looked up at the tall man waiting patiently beside him. "This bench of yours is a nice idea, sweet singer," he commented. "How gracious of you to provide a seat where visitors may await you in the comfort of the sunshine."

"That's a fasting-bench," Amergin had to tell him. "If I do someone an injustice that person can come and sit on this bench and starve himself at my doorway until I redress his grievance. Every household has such a seat."

Age-Nor recoiled. "What a shocking custom! Why would anyone do anything so foolish as to willingly starve?"

"It's a powerful form of pressure. If I let a person starve to death at my doorstep I am disgraced forever. My tribe will have nothing further to do with me; they will avert their eyes when I pass. The bards will drop my name from the genealogies and I will be as nothing to all future generations.''

Age-Nor stood up quickly. ''What a peculiar people you are!'' He threw a nervous glance at the bench.

Amergin lifted one black eyebrow. ''Don't worry, I have let no one starve there. Come inside now and I think you will be more comfortable.''

This was Age-Nor's first—and surely only—visit inside a private house of one of the Keltik tribes, and he looked around curiously. He was accustomed to airy seaside villas, painted and plastered and windowed. By comparison the Gaelician dwelling was very dark, its walls smoke-stained, the mighty timbers supporting its lofty thatched roof advancing from the shadows like the hulking prow of a hidden ship. A banked fire glowed on a stone hearth, where a large bronze cauldron of water squatted in the ashes.

''Would you care to wash?'' Amergin offered politely, gesturing toward the cauldron.

Age-Nor eyed the contrivance, surprised that these barbarians had such a passion for bathing. The first thing he had been offered on the night of his arrival was washing water. ''I think not,'' he replied, carefully arranging his features in an amiable expression. ''Let us just sit and talk, sweet singer.''

''Certainly.'' Amergin directed Age-Nor toward the oak benches arranged on three sides of his hearth. The Tyrian had no sooner sat down than a raucous noise nearby startled him to his feet again. ''What was that!?''

''A housemate of mine,'' Amergin said with a smile. Looking around the room, Age-Nor saw an elaborately carved and painted wooden box at one end, which doubtless served Amergin as a bedstead. A similar arrangement opposite the hearth seemed to house domestic poultry. ''Even a bard,'' Amergin explained, ''likes to keep a few birds to furnish him with eggs and feathers, as well as eating the insects that fall from the thatch.''

Age-Nor carefully wiped off the oak bench with the hem of his robe before sitting down again. As Amergin went to get wine, he studied the interior more thoroughly. Iron fire dogs and bronze hearth tools were hammered into fanciful but harmonious shapes, beautifully crafted. Woolen rugs dyed with vivid colors hung from the walls. Bands of copper and white metal were inlaid in the carved timbers supporting the roof.

In fact, every suitable surface was decorated in the curvilinear style Age-Nor had come to recognize as unique to the Keltoi. He found it both gorgeous and disturbing, an art form rich with animal figures that seemed to change shape even as he watched them, becoming instead part of some abstract symmetrical pattern hinting obscurely at deeper meanings. Keltik designs were neither simple nor primitive, but the reflection of an elaborate culture, refined and clever, full of paradoxes, witty and melancholy, rational and irrational, stylized yet somehow as spontaneous and energetic as the flowering of life itself.

Amergin returned with more of the sweet Gaelician wine that had given Age-Nor such a headache the last time he drank it. The Tyrian pretended to touch his lips to the bowl, then set it aside. "Now, sweet singer, we must discuss that payment I still owe you."

"I explained before, you owe me nothing."

"Ah, yes. Because you are a druid. And just what is a druid? I cannot make out if they are priests or judges or physicians."

Teaching was one of Amergin's passions, and this merchant was blank sand, ignorant and smooth. The bard smiled engagingly and his eyes sparkled as he began to explain. "There are two divisions in the order of druids, you see, because even gifted people are not given the same sorts of gifts. One division is the bardagh, the other our priesthood, the diviners. Both begin with the same course of study, but testers watch them and separate those with more mystical talents from those with gifts of hand and ear and tongue. The latter become bardagh, eventually concentrating on poetry, history, oratory, music. The bardagh are a merry band for the most part, Age-Nor. To be in the company of students in the groves is like being at the heart of a blooming flower, surrounded with bright colors."

Age-Nor squinted his eyes, unconsciously raising the wine bowl to his lips again. "Bardagh—bard. Is that you?"

"I'm coming to that; the explanation must seem a little complicated to an outsider."

"Everything you people do seems unnecessarily complicated," remarked the Tyrian, whose world appeared hopelessly complex to Amergin.

"Perhaps—to you. But surely even on your ship you have many diverse talents and divisions. As do we; among the bardagh, for example, those who demonstrate a gift only for music become citharadagh, or instrumental musicians. Others with neat, sharp-edged minds memorize all the poetry defining the Law and become brehons, and a mastery of both music and poetic forms confers the title of bard, which I carry."

He is proud of it, Age-Nor noted, watching him. As proud as a king of his crown. Yet in Tyre, such an accomplishment would be considered a minor asset, not to be compared with the making of money! "And what of your priesthood?" he said aloud, reminded of them by the thought of money.

"Our diviners are students of the natural sciences," Amergin explained.

"Sciences? You talk like a Greek."

Amergin lowered his eyelids with contempt. "The Hellenes think wisdom can be held captive in pictures scratched on wax or dyed on parchment. But such words are easily altered, Age-Nor, once they are written down. Wax melts, parchment burns, dyes can be painted over. The sciences should be carved directly onto the mind with memory, as the druids do."

"You commit everything to memory?" Age-Nor asked, not believing; thinking of the tablets of accounts that governed his life, and the trunks of charts and maps every ship captain owned.

"Memory is a muscle that can be strengthened," Amergin assured him. "All druids must do it, including diviners. We have four degrees of diviner, including those who interpret dreams, those who observe the currents of air through the trees, and those who interpret the entrails of sacrifice. Druids who become samodhii have the longest course of study, for they must understand all the relationships between the Earth Mother and the Sky Born so they can bring their people into harmony with the forces of existence."

Age-Nor was having difficulty following Amergin's words, but he thought he grasped their essence. "You druids are attempting to manipulate the gods," he said. "I tell you from experience that it cannot be done. Life is very cruel and brief, and the mace in the hand of Baal swoops down like a vulture in his fingers."

Amergin looked at the man with pity. "You speak of gods

men have made out of the terrors in their own minds. It is true, there are many sacred spirits; yet they are but parts of one power. *Life* is sacred, Tyrian; life in all its manifestations. We revere some of those manifestations by the names of men and women who represent them to us, such as Taranis the thunderer, voice of storms, or Epona the horse goddess. Or dark Cernunnos, lord of the animals. But they are merely different faces of the one great spirit, life.''

Age-Nor pursed his lips. ''I cannot understand such a preoccupation with life when it is death we must worry about. Death is the weapon the gods hurl at us for their own amusement. Not your simple nature gods, but the real ones, with hideous faces and insatiable appetites. You do not understand how life really is.''

''You do not understand *what* life really is,'' Amergin replied sadly.

The two men locked eyes in the quiet room. Only the fire on the hearth spoke—she whom Amergin knew as the goddess Tena—chuckling quietly to herself.

''Bard,'' Age-Nor said at last. ''So you are only a poet.''

''Only?'' Amergin's black brows came together like stormclouds. ''Bards are the voice of their tribe, the heart of courage and hope! A bard who wails of too much tragedy weakens his people and can make tragedy reality. Bards must call for vigilance when vigilance is needed, and for glory when glory is attainable.

''Bards go in the front line of a formal battle, urging the heroes to valor and sometimes arbitrating the outcome as a brehon would, because brehons do not attend wars. Bards are respected by both sides and exempt from actual combat, since to kill a bard would be to kill part of the tribe's history, all that wealth contained within his memory.''

Age-Nor frowned at him, puzzled by the importance of such things. He had been sipping his wine unaware and now suddenly discovered himself with an empty bowl containing a mess of dregs. With a mental shrug, he held it out for his host to refill; the damage was already done. ''What difference would it make if the past is forgotten?'' he wanted to know, thinking of Hanno and Himilco. ''Sometimes it only causes trouble.''

''The past is the root upon which we grow,'' Amergin told him. ''Destroy that root and the whole plant withers. It is . . . it is like the sea-route that will take you home, Age-Nor. We

191

have to know where we came from if we are ever to find our way back."

Age-Nor smiled broadly for the first time. "Ah, yes, the way home," he said with heartfelt longing. His words were slurring slightly; his tongue seemed to take up too much room in his mouth.

"Do you know what a long way my home is from here, sweet singer?" the Tyrian inquired, "or how much I have suffered to reach this misbegotten place? From the time I determined to attempt a voyage to the far western trade routes, through the Pillars of Herakles, everything has gone against me.

"And such a daring enterprise demanded great courage from the beginning, for it meant running the Carthaginian blockade, which controls the ocean-river and all this western coastline. The freighters of Carthage affix bronze battering rams to their prows and travel with consorts of armed warships to discourage competition. Furthermore, for years they have spread tales of sea monsters in the ocean-river, of pools of floating weed that suffocate men and ships, of endless calms and unexplained nightfalls in midday, of bubbling mud flats and malevolent whirlpools. Such stories have had a decidedly chilling effect on the merchants of Tyre and Sidon and Berytus, I assure you. Once, we from the eastern cities frequently sailed as far west as the Pillars and even beyond. My forefathers searched for islands off the northwest coast of Libya reputed to possess vegetable dyes with properties to rival Tyrian murex. Demand for the royal purple dye was increasing everywhere; such a new discovery would have tripled our fortunes overnight.

"Then Carthage claimed dominance and beat us back. It is a pitiful tale, not worth telling. Carthage claimed everything and we had to watch, feeding on our own discontent. Carthage seethed with raw vitality, an energy long since exhausted in ancient and urbane Tyre or golden Berytus or Sidon of the soft-thighed women. In the east, the influence of the Persians has smoothed away rough edges and taught patience and manipulation in place of brute effort. But in Carthage a man finds it easy to believe great fortunes still await the bold and determined, fortunes to be won with one dazzling triumph.

"How I thirsted for that triumph, sweet singer! *You* cannot possibly imagine the hunger that seizes a man's guts and twists them until nothing else is important. A lifetime spent in commerce had made me a relatively wealthy man among the merchant princes of Tyre, but I had never achieved that honor which occasionally is hurled like a javelin from the heavens by gods bestowing gifts on a favored mortal. A man who enjoyed such success could stand in the prow of his ship and watch other merchants dip their flags to him in passing, the ultimate tribute of my profession.

"So I determined to make the attempt. Though I am not a bold adventurer by nature, and I admit it freely—my ambition has always been held in check by a dark undercurrent, a premonition of catastrophe. Anticipating the worst, I have missed opportunities more reckless men seized to their advantage.

"But when I learned of the treasure awaiting someone brave enough to run the Carthaginian blockade, I sweated my fears out through my pores like blood and began attempting to win the good favor of the gods. I spent a fortune for sacrifices. I emptied my purse again and again to pay spies for the exact Carthaginian sailing dates and sea charts. I learned the name, price, and weaknesses of every harbormaster along my route, particularly those who might have Tyrian sympathies or harbor a grudge against Carthage. I poured my seed into a hundred temple prostitutes, begging intercession with the gods.

"In short, I made every conceivable preparation, and yet it was not enough. The gods knew all along that I hid fear in my heart and they scorned me for it; I know that now.

"The voyage was ill-starred from the beginning. I left Tyre loaded with cedar and cypress, which usually sells well in Egypt, a land short of timber. But when I reached Egypt those thieves with painted eyes told me the Persians had a stranglehold on their economy and construction had slowed almost to a halt. They paid me a laughable price for my lumber and said I should be grateful they gave me that much, on the strength of an old friendship.

"With the profits from the timber I meant to buy linen and medicaments and jewelry, particularly Persian ivories—but there was little ivory for sale at that time, and what there was I now found I could not afford. The Persians twice-thwarted me, but that is how Persians are. They kiss each other on the mouth and carry daggers in their sleeves; they send emissaries with rich diplomatic gifts to the court of the king of Tyre while simultaneously robbing other caravans headed in the same direction. They are silken and vicious . . . though not as savage as the Assyrians; at least one can say that for them.''

Amergin was listening, spellbound, to this recital, this description of an exotic world beyond his imagining, where great merchant fleets crisscrossed distant seas as easily as oxcarts traveled Gaelician roadways.

"We sailed on," Age-Nor continued, "but things got no better. At each port of call I faced some new disappointment, though I had made every effort to cater to the requirements of my trading partners. But the Sidonian carpets in my holds were found to be gnawed by rats, and could not be sold for a price sufficient to buy the bronze braziers I needed for my next port. Again and again, I was unable to turn over a cargo for the expected profit. Always excuses . . . 'The Persians did this, the Athenians did that, we have made a new arrangement with a merchant from Carthage . . .' "

Age-Nor sighed deeply. "How Melqart, god of Tyre, must have laughed over my misfortunes. I could actually feel the pleasure he took from my pain, but he did not relent. We were in the same sea-lane as a sulfur-laden freighter west of Sardinia when a god-bolt from the heavens struck the freighter and it exploded, almost taking my ships with it. My beautiful galleys with two banks of oars and striped sails of crimson and purple! The sky blazed a hideous orange color, though it was the middle of the night, and the stink was enough to mummify a camel. Murex dye factories smell abominably, but it is the stench of prosperity and no one in Tyre resents it. Burning sulfur carries the odor of death and decay, the bowels of angry gods, and I shall never get that smell out of my nostrils.

"I should have turned back then, but I was still stubborn. I was too afraid to admit I was afraid. We went on to Cartagena, that raw colonial outpost where a hundred tribes come together in a babble no one can understand. And then, watching every moment for Carthaginian merchantmen, we made a run for it through the Pillars of Herakles at the one time when no ships from Carthage were expected in that region.''

The swarthy little man shuddered, like someone recalling a too-recent nightmare. "The Pillars of Herakles,'' he repeated in a whisper. "I had offered splendid sacrifices in the temples of Cartagena to buy safe passage, but we were pounded by the inflowing tide and my ships were battered and beaten.

One broke up altogether on the rock called Mount Calpa when the fists of the gods pounded the sea. A single survivor out of all that crew was pulled from the water, a shipwright from my home city, one Sakkar by name. And my fine ship was no more than debris to be washed ashore.

"The captain of my flagship, a wise and sour man called Bomilcar, advised me to throw the rescued shipwright back overboard because he had a broken shoulder and would be of no further use to us. I should have; then the gods would have seen my strength of character. But instead I took pity on him, perhaps because I would pity anyone who had been in that raging sea. So I kept him with me and the gods laughed at me, biding their time.

"We finally found a sheltered harbor where we were able to effect some repairs on our boats, but there the sailors—and my trusted captains!—nearly mutinied. To my astonishment, the crippled shipwright stood by me, and began calmly caulking planks and reinforcing damaged timbers as if he had no question but that we would sail on. Seeing his spirit, the others were ashamed of themselves and fell in beside him, and so we got the ships seaworthy again and moved on along the coast to Tartessos.

"But there, what small generosity the gods had shown me vanished altogether, though I ordered sacrificial altars set up on the beaches and recounted the names of all the infants I had purchased to fill Melqart's hungry maw in the past. Yet when I took my goods inland, expecting mountains of copper and rivers of tin and a culture of wealth and antiquity sufficient to impress even an Egyptian, only more disappointment awaited me.

"What I found was a decayed world sunk to an almost primitive state, with cold-eyed tribal chieftains and no copper, no tin at all. The Carthaginians had long since stripped Tartessos and moved on, leaving only crumbs for me. The costly decorated ostrich eggs I had imported from Libya to tempt the Tartessian chieftains were openly sneered at; even the poorest of them had better collections than I had brought. There was nothing for me there, sweet singer. Nothing. Only impoverishment and ruin.

"A sort of madness seized me then. I set sail again, moving north up the coast of Iberia, finding harbors wherever I could and trying desperately to arrange enough trade to recover some of my losses. I could not allow myself to turn for home with nothing to show for my brave deed but battered ships and empty holds.

"I got this far, sweet singer. This far and no farther, for the heart has gone out of me." He tugged in anguish at his neat black beard. "Even I must admit I have failed to break the monopoly of Carthage on the ocean-river. There are only two choices now, since I failed to find tin here—I can go back to Tyre and spend the rest of my miserable life making small commercial arrangements, rebuilding my fortune one stack of coins at a time. Or I can go on northward, as the Carthaginians have done. Until they catch me and sink me. The only reason they have not already done that, I think, is because Carthage is on the verge of renewing her sporadic warfare with the Hellene city-states, and such diversions tend to interfere with the real business of life. Trade.

"I could go on, as I say. But I will not. No. I have gotten crosswise with the gods. I will head home for Tyre, and if I encounter the ships of Carthage on the way, so be it. It might be better to die a clean death on the open sea than to die a slow death in the markets, watching good merchandise trampled underfoot by bloodsuckers with no appreciation for value."

The little man was one abject slump of despair, and Amergin's heart went out to him. He reached out in a gesture of instinctive sympathy, but Age-Nor shrank back from the barbarian hand, mistrust leaping in his eyes. The Hellenes had a saying about them that was permanently painted across Age-Nor's mind in letters of fire. "The entire barbarian world reeks of blood."

He had nearly been killed in the Míl's hall; he was not willing to have another Gaelician put hands on him now, no matter how sympathetic the man's face seemed to be.

But there was a bond between them and a debt to be settled. The time had come for that. The thought of at last turning homeward demanded it. The gods had shown their contempt for Age-Nor of Tyre, but he would show them he was a clever man after all, a man capable of subtle stratagems even in the most dire situations.

"As I say, I have determined to turn back for Tyre," Age-Nor told the bard, "rather than go on, as I might have done. But before I leave I have a debt to pay to you."

"Please, no," Amergin objected. "I have explained . . ."

The Tyrian shook his head; this time he was adamant. "A life must be exchanged for a life, or Melqart will take great delight in striking me down where I stand. That is how it is, that is how it always must be. And so I have decided to gift you with a bodyservant, a living man who will do your bidding but eat very little, I assure you.''

"I want no servant, Age-Nor. The Celtic tribes do not keep slaves, as we would not want to be slaves ourselves.''

"The man I am thinking of has an injured shoulder but he could serve you as cupbearer,'' Age-Nor went on, undaunted.

"Cupbearers are a Hellene affectation. I tell you again, I have no need of the man.''

Age-Nor's smile was more calculated than drunken. He had seen that quick sympathy in the bard's eyes when he mentioned an injured shoulder. "But he has need of you, sweet singer. It is Sakkar I give you, he who helped me after our ships were damaged in the Pillars. I kept him with me, partly out of gratitude, which is always a weakness, but also because I thought we might need his services, crippled though he is, if we went all the way to Albion and Ierne. Now I have decided that is out of the question, but . . .''

Amergin did not hear the rest. He was staring at Age-Nor with a gaze as piercingly blue as Mediterranean waters.

"Ierne,'' the bard said in a voice hushed with wonder.

◇ **17** ◇

"IERNE?'' Age-Nor repeated. He leaned forward eagerly and then pulled back, trying to look casual. "You have already heard of Ierne?'' He saw the advantage now; saw it and grabbed it.

"Only recently,'' Amergin told him. "And in a very strange way.''

"Strange things happen in this backwater of the world,'' Age-Nor commented, not meaning it as flattery. "As it happens, Ierne—and Albion, the other of the Pretanic Islands— partly inspire my choice of a gift for you. I have become very aware of the awkwardness of your situation here, sweet singer.

Your tribe is poor and getting poorer, and eventually poor people can revolt against even the strongest leaders; it happens all the time in the larger world, I assure you. And I think you and your chieftain would not want this to happen. You need something to offer to your tribe. You Keltoi have developed a great taste for merchandise from my part of the world, but now that traders will no longer come to your harbor here, what can you offer your people?" Age-Nor was speaking slowly; thinking fast.

"Ierne, as you may or may not know, is practically awash with gold. And copper ore. And there is tin on Albion, so the two islands have endless ores for bronzemaking. They are really not such a great voyage from here, for hardy men like yourselves in well-designed ships . . ."

"We are not sea people," Amergin pointed out.

"No, that is obvious. But my Sakkar is a good shipwright, and your race, whatever its many shortcomings, possesses most remarkable craftsmen. Under Sakkar's supervision they could no doubt build you a boat capable of transporting gold, for it does not take much gold ore to be worth a fortune. If you had just a little gold to offer you would have merchant fleets in your harbor again soon enough."

Age-Nor seemed too eager, and in spite of the seduction of Ierne's name, Amergin's druid intuition warned him to pull back; be cautious. These were traders, and honor was not in them.

"If the Sea People want gold, why do they not go themselves to the islands you name, and get it?"

"You must understand, such a voyage is a very great distance for us. I have been at sea for many, many days myself, and my ships are battered, as you know. It is just too much to go farther and then hope to return to Tyre. But you, sweet singer, are already on the very edge of the world. Ierne lies just a little farther. You could learn the necessary techniques easily and make the voyage, for there is hardly anything between you and the Pretanic Islands but that large bay north of you along the Gaulish coast. It would be such an easy matter . . . if you had Sakkar . . ." He checked himself, seeing suspicion in Amergin's eyes.

"That is just a small suggestion, of course; the kind of idea a merchant would have. It might mean nothing to you at all. I really only hoped you would take Sakkar off my hands, save his life, and allow me to cancel my debt to you. Surely you can find some use for him; he is thoroughly obedient.''

Amergin was having difficulties pulling his thoughts from Ierne. ''This island with the gold,'' he said, ''would not its natives resist us and try to defend their treasures?''

Age-Nor waved his hand airily. ''There are tribes on Albion, but Ierne is scarcely populated at all. Everyone knows that,'' he added, larding his words with contempt so Amergin would be embarrassed to question them.

''Let me tell you about Sakkar,'' he went on quickly, now that the bait had been dropped in the water. ''I said you could save his life, and I think you are a man who would consider that important. He is terrified of returning to Tyre because he got into some very serious trouble there. I do not know what; I signed a contract for a certain number of shipwrights and he was among the lot. One does not question contractors dealing in men about the backgrounds of their wares, only about their skills.

''As it happens I now owe this Sakkar a favor. He stood by me when he was needed, so I do not want to return him to whatever doom awaits him. The Tyrian authorities can be . . . ah, very severe. If you will accept him he will be safe here with you, and of course you are free to use him as you will.''

Age-Nor smiled with such perfect innocence it could only be the result of long practice.

As soon as the Tyrian returned to the harbor he ordered Sakkar to be bathed and dressed in new clothing, readied for his delivery to Amergin. Then he settled himself in the small private cabin in the stern of his flagship and sent for Bomilcar.

The ship's captain was dubious. ''You gave away an expensive shipwright to barbarians who have no use for him?''

Age-Nor's black eyes twinkled. ''I have made a very clever trading arrangement with the gods. I gave a life for a life, as they require, and made the sweet singer feel he was doing a great kindness in taking Sakkar. These Keltoi put a preposterous value on individual human life, though conversely they seem to have no fear of death. Mad, all of them.

''At any rate, I told the one called Amergin, who is some sort of noble or priest or something, just enough about Ierne to whet his appetite. I used the word *gold* several times. And even if I had not, I saw a most peculiar look in his eyes—that lust for far horizons one sometimes sees in men who set out across the sea because they must, not because they intend to make a profit. That sweet singer is a dreamer of dreams, and I think he will not long be able to resist the lure I have thrown out.

"He and his savage companions will get Sakkar to build them a boat, sooner or later, and they will brave the wrath of Asherat-Yam. I will pray to the Lady of the Sea this very afternoon and explain that they are to be my sacrifice to her, in place of myself and my own ships. If she is impressed with my cleverness perhaps she will at last relent in her tormenting of me and allow us to get back to Tyre alive after all.

"Is that not an elegant arrangement?"

Bomilcar barked a short, hard laugh. "I call it a mean trick. And a very smart one—particularly if it works."

"Something has to work," Age-Nor muttered. "My head is bloody from the blows the gods have rained upon it and I just want to get home. Pass me that wine, will you?"

Later that same day, Sakkar was delivered to Amergin with the ceremony appropriate to an ambassadorial offering. He was newly scrubbed with salt water, his black beard was trimmed, his prematurely balding pate was shiny with almond oil. He wore a swathe of bleached linen wrapped around his body, one wide section of fabric drawn between his legs and looped through a girdle of knotted cord. He had no jewelry and brought no personal property, Amergin noticed.

Sakkar's misshapen shoulder was a disturbing disharmony. The broken bone had been allowed to heal in ignorance, rather than properly guided. But there was intelligence in the man's face, and a resilient if wary spirit peeped out of his eyes.

The bard liked him on sight.

"I hardly know what to do with you," Amergin said, addressing Sakkar as if he were a houseguest instead of a possession. "Your Age-Nor urged you on me as a shipwright, and though the idea is one to dream about, it is hardly practical for us." His bardic commitment was to the truth; must be to the truth, no matter how much his heart might dream otherwise. Amergin knew with certainty that Age-Nor's gift was an attempt at manipulation, for the Tyrian could not hide his nature from a druid's eyes. Yet the temptation lay there all too fortuitously, burning inside him, challenging his will and his wisdom. Impractical. Not possible.

Unforgettable.

With a mighty effort he strove to push it aside.

To Sakkar, he explained aloud, "You must understand that among my people, slavery is not the custom. Attendants serve the warrior class willingly in return for sharing what we have, but they are from the class of freemen, you see." Sakkar did not see. He made no reply, just stared at the bard. "We occasionally take women captives after battle, of course," Amergin went on, driven by the druidic necessity to teach, "but their situation is merely that of a loss of family status and we treat them well; we keep them in our houses and raise their children as part of our tribe. Relationship and service among us are different from what you may have experienced elsewhere, and I do not want you to be uncomfortable . . ." Amergin broke off, aware of the Phoenician's blank, uncomprehending expression. The man looked like an ox patiently expecting the yoke.

Sakkar stood stiffly, with desperate dignity, trying to convince himself this might be better than the torture and death awaiting him inevitably had he returned to Tyre. A loved woman's dying moans . . . a dark alley . . . a rich man's purse . . . escape on a doomed ship and now this.

"I do not . . . talk your talk," he said haltingly.

"Ai! Of course, how thoughtless of me to go rattling on like an empty wagon," Amergin apologized at once. "Words are my life, I will teach you . . . but not so many words as to make you a nuisance," he added for his own benefit. He glanced around his house. "You'll need a pallet. Caicher owes me a gift for a praise song I composed for his father's father; I'll suggest that some soft calfskins and a pillow filled with feathers would please me. But what work can we find for you, Sakkar?"

The Phoenician waited. He had nothing else to do.

Amergin returned to his composing. The great festival of summer's dying drew near and he felt a growing urgency to complete his epic as the sun receded and the possibilities of the season diminished.

Yet—and this was a question he sometimes asked himself in the still of the night, listening to the unfamiliar rhythm of

Sakkar's breathing as the man slept on his new pallet—was the poem capable of completion? Was the history of his tribe a finished saga, or did he have only the prelude to tell?

And sometimes he did not work on the poem at all, but lay in his bedbox dreaming of an island of meadows and forest, lakes and mountains; a green dream of misty beauty he related only to Clarsah.

The nights ran past. Soon the cattle raiders must return with their walking treasure, a fertile new cow or strong young bull for every clanholding. Their arrival would coincide with the lighting of the festival fires on hilltop and headland, marking the turn of the seasons. The warriors would surely come home in time for the dancing.

Anticipating the festival dances made every Gaelician heart beat faster.

First word of the returning warriors was carried by an excited horse herder who raced into the Míl's stronghold, yelling, "They're here, they're home! There's a great cloud of dust coming this way; Éremón's bringing all the cattle in the world with him!"

His estimate was a Celtic exaggeration, but the herd was indeed enormous. It blanketed the roadway and overflowed across the fields, knocking down the small stone walls piled up by freemen to keep one man's field of beans or kale separate from another's. The herd trampled earth into sun-baked brick and drowned it beneath a sea of tossing horns and bawling voices, of animals briefly mounting one another in excitement, of men yelling and horses whinnying and motion, action, life.

Wild with delight, the Gaelicians rushed to welcome their heroes home.

"Éremón!" Odba cried as she burst from her house, her sons at her heels. She ran across the compound and through the gate in the wall, shading her eyes with her hands so she could pick Éremón out of the approaching crowd. But she did not see him.

Chariot warriors and horse riders flowed around her, calling to their families and trying to offer boasts to somehow exceed the awesome herd behind them. Even foot warriors began to arrive, but Odba could not locate Éremón anywhere amid the dust and the noise and the seething panorama of livestock.

Donn drove up, hollow-eyed and disheveled, his horses

sharp-hipped from the journey. "Where is my husband?" Odba demanded to know. "I thought he would be leading you."

Donn glanced back the way he had come. "I don't see him right now," he said vaguely. "But he'll be along . . . Ai, there's Díl! Look, wife, come see what I brought you!" Odba noticed then that the heads of enemies slain in battle hung from the rim of Donn's chariot; trophies not usually taken in a mere cattle raid. "Preserve these for me in cedar oil," Donn ordered Díl. "They will make a display to impress my sons' sons, someday."

Having said this, Donn beamed happily down at the female children clustering around his chariot, and the whole family swept away together, leaving Odba on the road, husbandless.

Éber Finn drove by, looking distracted. When he halted his chariot Odba could see that it was all but filled with the doubled-up form of an injured calf, bedded on Éber's best cloak. He eased out of the chariot and lifted the little animal with a gentle solicitude no battlefield opponent would have recognized in the man. Éber carefully straightened the knobbly legs and guided the calf forward until he caught the eye of a healer, whom he hastily summoned.

"Take care of this little beast," he ordered. "It was badly torn in an accident and has lost much blood, but been very brave." He dropped a stroking hand on the calf's forehead and the shape of his mouth was sweet and soft as a woman's.

Éremón's wife, watching, burned with envy of that calf, recipient of the kindness that lay interlocked with courage in Celtic hearts.

Éremón isn't coming back to me, Odba thought. I have finally driven him away and he stayed in the land of the Astures. Or he stopped at the clanholding of Ítos to be with that milk-mouthed Taya, and Donn wouldn't tell me. Those men hold together like twigs in a duck's nest.

Or he's dead, she thought last, hardly daring allow herself the thought at all. There are limits to pain, and she could not accept the permanent loss of Éremón, for all her temporary anger.

Her boys tugged at her. "Where is he, where is our father?"

"We'll find him," she promised them, setting her mouth in a grim line. She began shoving her way against the tide of cheering, excited people, the women laughing and crying, the children yelling, the old ones babbling of their own days of adventure.

And then she saw Éremón leading his chariot team, both of whom were limping slightly. He was accompanied by a small herd of wavymaned horses guarded by several foot warriors, and he was alive.

He had come home!

"Look, just look!" cried Moomneh, running past her, not to greet Éremón but to get closer to the Asturian horses. Shining bays and dapple grays and mares like polished onyx, with long rippling manes covering their necks and shoulders in waves of glossy silk. Moomneh, his heart in his eyes, called only the most casual word of greeting to his father before he laid hands on the nearest mare and began crooning to her.

Odba experienced an unusual attack of shyness. Éremón looked tired and there were dark circles under his eyes. When he saw her, he nodded but did not come toward her. She forced herself to go to him, step by step, feeling humiliated at having to do it all.

They both wondered what she would say.

"You look as if you've been to a war," she remarked at last.

"I have." Proudly. His voice was very hoarse and roughened, deeper than she remembered. "We charged in our full strength and they met us head to head. We fought from sunrise to sunset, and drank wine with the survivors that night. We claimed their herd as spoils of war and brought it home."

"I don't understand . . ."

"We fought honorably in the daylight and we won, woman! Is your skull too thick to understand that? We won everything. The pride of the Gaelicians is increased by ten tens, and it was my doing, Odba. Mine!"

She fell back before the flame in his eyes.

Like a cupbearer, she followed in his wake as he made his way to the stronghold on the headland. Éremón's sons capered around his chariot, begging for rides.

"Let me just stand in it and hold the reins!" Moomneh pleaded. "I know I could drive your horses if I had the reins in my hands."

"My horses lamed themselves on the rocks," Éremón cautioned. "If I let you drive, you must stay at the walk."

204

The boy agreed with breathless excitement. Éremón followed him into the chariot and stood behind him as Moomneh triumphantly guided the war cart home. A warrior's son, with the towering figure of his hero at his shoulder, mighty arms folded, radiating pride.

The night was given to feasting, and the heroes stayed in the hall until dawn. Their women went to empty beds and did not complain; even Odba did not complain.

The next day, the druid measurers accompanied the clan-chiefs on their inspection of the herd. Milesios walked heavily, keeping Éremón beside him, and when no one was looking he leaned on his son's shoulder.

"So many cattle," the Míl said rather vaguely, gazing at the sea of animals, some of whom were already bawling their discontent. Instead of lush mountain meadowland they could find only dry saltgrass and yellow furze to eat, and they pawed the earth and looked around in bewilderment. Their captors did not notice; they were too busy congratulating themselves and arguing over who would get what.

"I claim all the white cows!" Éber Finn cried, ready for an argument.

"White cows are beloved of the Mother and you already have enough of her favor," Étan said immediately. Gosten agreed with him and fists were doubled.

"Mine should be the first choosing because this was my victory," Éremón croaked, trying to make his ruined voice rise above the general noise.

Colptha the sacrificer stood to one side, listening. He heard the unending rivalry, felt the pull and tug this way and that, sensed the fault lines where a solid mass could be split asunder. Dissension between his brothers gave him pleasure. The more petty their behavior, the more noble he seemed in his own eyes. They could not gang up against him when they were at war with each other.

Colptha walked among the warriors, saying softly, "You are right, Éremón, you should have the pick of the herd."

And, elsewhere, "Éber, you deserve the choice cattle and the best breeding stock, for there is no doubt you have a gift with animals."

He did not, however, say anything to Ír. Ír was a dry pine log capable of exploding dangerously, and better left alone.

"Those cattle should be yours, Éremón."

205

"Stand up for yourself and claim what you want, Donn."

"Take the best breeding animals, Éber."

The squabbling provided a morning's entertainment. Amergin brought Clarsah, safe from dust in her leather satchel, to the new herd. The voices of the cattle could penetrate leather, could sink into the wooden frame and brass strings and come out again at some future time when the bard sang the song of this victory, the praise song of its heroes.

Standing on the perimeter of the herd, Amergin looked to the east and thought with envy of the sights the warriors must have seen on their journey. Then he looked north, toward the ninth wave, and felt that same irresistible impulse that had once led his ancestors out of the forests and riverlands of Gaul.

It is time to move on, a voice whispered to him, surprising him. Perhaps it came from the harp in the pungent darkness of her leather case.

Perhaps it came from the wind, blowing across the headland.

But there is no need to go anywhere, he thought. Éremón and his warriors have made us cattle lords again; we will be greatly respected by the other tribes and the celsine will court our favor in return for calves and oxen. Even Milesios has forgotten that his son declared a war without his permission, and joins in the praise being lavished upon Éremón. The hard times are over for now.

Are they? whispered the wind from the sea.

Amergin went back to his house and his composing.

Meanwhile, Éremón was explaining—for the seventh or eighth time, and enlarging the tale with each telling—how he had won the Asturian cattle. Milesios had wearied and gone to seek the cool shadows of the Heroes' Hall, but an admiring crowd still surrounded the warrior, urging him on.

"We took most of their best cattle and horses," Éremón said, "but we left them a few breeding animals. Heroes do not crush honorable opponents. And I gave them something in return: my word in the name of all Gaelicians that for three generations we will not attack them again. That will give them adequate time to restore their herds and they accepted the arrangement as a fair treaty. We parted friends." He grinned. "We can almost count the Asturians as allies now, in fact," he added, knowing full well that new tribal alliances were usually credited to the chieftain. But this alliance was

Éremón's alone, an earnest against the day when he would sit on the bronze-sheathed bench in the Heroes' Hall.

He wished Taya were there to hear him. Looking around, he saw many female faces among the admiring crowd, but no sign of the dark-haired woman with the level eyebrows. He began asking questions, and he did not like the answers he was given.

When Amergin reached his house he found Sakkar lounging on the fasting-bench, letting the sun's heat comfort his aching shoulder.

The bard gave him a long and thoughtful look. "Is it true you can build an entire ship?" he asked at last.

Sakkar's head bobbed. "Not with this hurt," he explained. "But I could tell how. Ship for ocean-river, go anywhere." Under Amergin's tutelage, his Gaelician vocabulary was improving. "You want ship? Be trader?"

The bard's lips smiled but his eyes did not. "No . . . I just wondered if it was really possible." He sat down companionably beside Sakkar and took Clarsah from her case.

The Phoenician eyed the harp with interest. It vaguely resembled the portable lyres used in his homeland, but was finer and more skillfully made than any musical instrument he had ever seen. There were so many strings, gleaming like gold, and so many curves and carvings, giving the harp a form akin to that of a living creature. And though Sakkar did not yet understand many Gaelician words, he understood the harp perfectly.

He closed his eyes in contentment he had never expected to feel again and braced his back against the sun-warmed granite wall of the bard's house.

A shadow fell across the two men.

Amergin came back from the far place where he and Clarsah had been together and saw Éremón standing over him, wearing a most truculent expression.

"Where is Taya?" the warrior demanded to know.

"She stays in her own clanholding now," Amergin replied.

"I have heard people speak of you and her in one breath; did you quarrel with her? Did you drive her away?"

"Of course not, Éremón! Who could quarrel with Taya? As soon shake a spear at the rain." Amergin would not mention Odba. Éremón would find out for himself, and soon enough.

207

"I expected her to be here to welcome me when I returned," Éremón said. "Is she being hidden away from me?"

"Did you think she was for your private use?" Amergin retorted, trying to hold on to his rising temper.

"Scotta has never shared the bed of another man," Éremón reminded his brother, "and thus she honors Milesios above all other men. I expect the same of my women."

"Odba is the only woman you have any claim to."

"Odba?" Éremón looked as if he had forgotten the name.

"She is your one wife."

"I mean to correct that as soon as possible. I have let her get away with her nonsense far too long. A spoiled woman is worse than a spoiled horse; she won't pull her weight at all. I think Lugaid's daughter will suit me much better."

"Don't be in such a hurry about it," Amergin advised him.

The warrior's eyebrows shot up. "Why? Do you tardily intend to make an offer for her? I warn you, it won't do any good. She was mine before I left, and she is much more mine now. No woman can resist a hero, bard!"

Riding high on the crest of confidence, Éremón turned his back on Amergin and strode away toward the Heroes' Hall.

As he walked, he thought of his last conversation with Lugaid's daughter—the way she listened to him, silently and with shining eyes, as if his words were the most important things in the world. Her admiration was so obvious that the need to boast had melted away and he found himself telling her things he had never told anyone before, things about himself even he had not realized until he tried to articulate them for Taya. Old wounds dating back to his early childhood were exposed, soothed, and laid to rest. The desperate bravado of his youth was transformed into heroic valor; the rough camaraderie he enjoyed with his fellow warriors made Taya smile instead of frown, as Odba did. "How fortunate you are to have so many good friends," she had said.

"My wife resents them."

"She does? Why? I think it's important for a man to have friends—I know I hate being alone. I'm glad you're the sort of person who needs people, Éremón." She had smiled at him and he felt like a god.

The time had come to claim her.

Éremón entered the Heroes' Hall with a full wind in his sails. Though it hurt his throat to speak loudly, he announced, "I have decided to have a second wife, now that our clanhold contains so many fine animals. Where are Ítos and Lugaid? I have gifts to offer them for . . ."

His mother's hand closed tightly on his arm. "No, Éremón," Scotta said.

He looked at her in astonishment. "What do you mean, no?"

"I mean you are not to ask for Taya as a wife. There is bad air between her and Odba, and Odba has made a number of threats. Ítos keeps Taya in his clanhold now to avoid any more trouble, and I ask you to help me preserve harmony in the tribe by forgetting about her. Perhaps some day next season, when Odba's head has cooled, you can find someone she will accept . . ."

"No!" Éremón jerked away from his mother and crossed the hall in long strides until he stood in front of the chieftain's bench. The Míl jerked upright to stare at his son, who was red-faced and obviously angry. "What's this all about, Milesios?" Éremón rasped. "You explain it to me!"

The Míl blinked and looked toward his wife. "Scotta . . . ? Is there some problem . . . ?"

She hurried to stand beside him. "I didn't bother you with it because you were busy with so many other matters," she said in a loud voice for public consumption. "This is a little thing, really; a quarrel between women."

"It is not a little thing to me!" Éremón shouted.

Éremón's anger battered Milesios, making him feel very tired. "Explain what this is about, wife," he said wearily.

In a measured voice that allowed itself no partisanship, Scotta told of Odba's complaints. Éremón neglected her, she had not conceived for seasons, and Éremón had recently shown interest in a woman Odba considered to be of insultingly lower rank than her own. If Éremón did not forget Taya and return to her Odba would sue for a huge eric, and if Éremón insisted on bringing Taya into his house anyway, Odba would take her children and her personal property—including all those sheep—back to the Artabrians.

Éremón's face turned crimson. "She can't do that!" he bellowed, shredding his damaged voice.

"Is there a brehon in the hall?" Scotta inquired.

Findbar, senior judge in the order of druids, stepped forward. "My knowledge is yours to command," he said formally.

"Tell my son the Law in this matter."

Findbar spoke directly to Éremón. "If your wife leaves you

209

of her own choice, or if you set her aside for any reason other than a failure of mothering, she can take her children with her. None of them is yet trained to bear arms; they are still mother-age."

"But they belong with me, they are my sons too!"

"Perhaps. Yet what man can be certain he is the sire? We can be sure of motherhood, however, and for that reason the Law supports the woman in these situations. Her connection to the child was witnessed at birth and is unmistakable. As for the eric, if Odba conceives no more children and can prove to us that you turn from her to Lugaid's daughter . . ."

"Bed Odba at once, and often," one of the gathering crowd suggested with a bawdy laugh.

"I want nothing further to do with a woman so mean-spirited she attacks me behind my back like this, running and crying to Scotta!"

"Can you accuse her of being a poor mother?" Findbar's calm voice inquired.

Éremón hesitated. But his Celtic tongue would not frame an untruth; dishonor would be even worse than giving Odba the credit she had earned. "No," he said reluctantly. "She bears healthy children and takes good care of them. But that does not make her a satisfactory wife to *me!*"

Scotta was losing her temper. "Do you mean you don't care if you cost Taya's clan half those wonderful new cattle they're all so excited about? Or our clan the use of a herd of fine sheep? Or me the sight of my grandsons? Are your own desires more important to you than the tribe?"

"You women stick together to thwart me," Éremón complained. "Milesios, have you no say in this? Will you let your wife do all your talking?"

The Míl's eyes brightened dangerously.

"I will not embrace Odba again and none of you can force me to do it!" Éremón cried, letting his anger gallop out of control.

Milesios got to his feet and glared at his son with a remnant of his famed ferocity. "I am ashamed of your words," he said. "I forbid you to cost my uncle's clan an eric, or to drive Odba away. I will not have it said that Milesios can no longer hold his clan together!"

"But . . ." Éremón clenched his fists and waved them in the air, seeking something to strike. "But . . . !"

"I have told you how it is to be!" Milesios commanded

with all a chieftain's authority. "Let us hear no more about this!"

Éremón shook his head from side to side like a baffled bear. For the first time in his life, he found himself in a situation with no foreseeable victory. Coming like a counter-punch after his triumph, frustration shocked him.

"I have promised myself I would have Taya as a wife," he said in a choking voice, turning his head so Milesios did not hear him. "I will find a way . . ."

◇ **18** ◇

THE MÍLS ELDEST SON was whistling to himself as he supervised the construction of a wattle fence for pro-tecting the clan's new Asturian horses—the pick of which was still hotly contested between Éremón and Éber Finn. Donn had no great desire for the animals himself, but he was routinely called upon for such tasks. Whatever he did was accomplished with painstaking thoroughness, as every-one knew. Now he directed the freemen doing the actual labor with sharp eyes that missed no smallest detail. Donn might have been a fine craftsman if he had not been born into the warrior class.

The wattle pens were built in sections the length of a tall man, with axe and billhook used for cutting the upright staves and an iron mallet and spike for setting the holes. Flexible branches, split and shaped with an adze, were woven among the uprights to form a sturdy panel that was then bound to other panels until a wall of the desired length was produced. Some stockmen put their fences together carelessly, seduced by the ease of manufacture into thinking the task was an unimportant one, easily redone if the fence did not hold. But that was not Donn's style.

By alternately bullying and cajoling the freemen, he was building a pen smoother than the walls of a noble's house, so carefully woven that no loose ends stuck out to rip a lock of

211

wavy mane or heavy tail from one of the magnificent Asturian horses.

Donn suspected that life was, in total, unmanageable, but he believed it could be controlled in small segments, if one took everything step by step. A neat straight fence was control. Speaking slowly so that others must wait for your words was control.

He did not really long for the acclaim Éremón enjoyed as a leader of warriors, though he was jealous of his standing as favorite son of the Míl. Donn's inmost ambitions reached no further than a cheerful, tidy existence with a cheerful, tidy woman and a houseful of children. Some sons at last, if the spirits were willing.

Donn did not lust for larger challenges.

Colptha found him just then, standing to one side and quietly enjoying the perfection of his pen.

"Donn, I have something to tell you right now," the sacrificer said. Colptha always contrived to sound urgent, as if the rising of the sun depended upon his words.

"Wait a moment, will you? I think I better shake that panel one more time and be sure it will hold up against crowding horses."

"Forget the pen; your people need you."

Donn stopped short and stared at him. "Me?"

"Éremón behaved very badly just now in the Heroes' Hall; he showed Milesios that he may not be longheaded enough to become chieftain one day. There are those of us who have already suspected this; I feel safe in admitting as much to you, now. In spite of this recent showy venture of Éremón's, I tell you the time will come when the tribe looks elsewhere for a leader. I just want you to know that I believe the bronze bench should rightly go to the chieftain's eldest son, Donn. You have long been denied the respect that should be yours, while louder men claimed all the glory. No chief of a lesser clan should lead the tribe—nor Éremón, either. I will support you for that honor when the time comes, my brother."

Donn was staring at him. "Chief of the tribe? Me?" He was obviously taken aback.

"Your Díl would be very pleased, would she not? And all those daughters of yours—think how hotly they would be sought as wives. It is every man's ambition to marry a chieftain's daughter."

Donn stood squarely, feet planted on solid earth, and thought

212

his way step by step along the path Colptha was leading him. "I have never dreamed of chiefdom," he said uncertainly.

"Heed my words, Donn," the sacrificer said. "I was given a great gift that has been neither recognized nor appreciated because the rest of the tribe is as shortsighted as Éremón. You are the only one of my brothers to respect my wisdom; you are the only one capable of making that wisdom available to all the tribe in the future. We could do so much together, you and I. Allies as well as brothers. Allies . . ." Colptha's head moved rhythmically from side to side; his words became a deliberate chant. Éremón would have laughed at him. Éber Finn would have walked away. But Donn, who did not like to be rude, watched. As Conmael had watched, allowing Colptha to perfect his technique.

"If you become chieftain, you will remember that I was your first supporter. Your brother, your friend. Brothers and friends help each other, Donn. I help you, you help me, that is a balance, and the spirits always demand balance." He held Donn's eyes with an intense, fixed gaze.

Donn found himself nodding in agreement. "Yes . . . a balance."

"Very good. Remember, I help you and *you help me*," the sacrificer repeated. "You will remember. You will remember."

"I will remember," Donn murmured.

Colptha returned to his house and Conmael, walking with the elastic gait of a man buoyed by his own cleverness.

The wheel of the seasons was turning; Milesios was obviously fading and must soon die. In time Irial would also undertake his transition, and a new chief druid would command authority in the groves. Would be respected, admired, listened to without question.

Unlike Milesios, Irial would name his own successor; there would be no election. The spirits always spoke unequivocally through the chief druid.

When the Míl was dead, Donn could replace him if the right pressures were skillfully applied. Donn, the most malleable of Colptha's brothers and the one least capable of resisting him.

Irial's wiry health assured Colptha of enough seasons to win his way back into the chief druid's good graces before Irial himself made his transition, and when the time was right, Colptha would call in his debt. When Irial felt death approaching and prepared to name his successor, Colptha would send Donn, chief of the tribe, to him. Irial, for all his arrogance, was not above political pressure, Colptha felt sure. He had his weak spots, every man did. There were dark stains on every spirit and rotten places in every heart.

Colptha knew. He would find them, and he and Donn would work on them together. Colptha would be named Irial's successor.

"For the good of the tribe," the sacrificer whispered to himself, almost believing it.

The time of festival arrived. Great fires were ignited at sunset all up and down the coast and on the high ground inland, sending a signal from clanhold to clanhold. It was time for the gathering of the clans.

The lighting of the great fires, which announced festival or attack or the inauguration of a chieftain, was always a thrilling occasion, whatever its cause. The moment when the torch was put to the carefully constructed timber pyre was pure magic, and the gasp of the spectators when the next fire down the coast blazed in response was an expression of sheer exultation.

Amergin, observing, mused on the power man had acquired over space. By building a signal fire he had brought a faraway point nearer, expanded his own horizon, extended his reach. Looking from blaze to blaze, a man could encompass formidable distances in a series of instantaneous visual strides. Space and time were transmuted, perception altered.

"Faraway" was only three signal fires distant.

At sunrise the Gaelicians gathered to take part in the ceremonies marking the death and birth of the seasons. And when the more serious rituals were over, they turned their faces to the sun and danced.

The dancing was the affirmation of life, when tall men and lusty women moved together to the primitive surge of their blood, telling with graceful hands and quick feet and flashing eyes the ancient stories of love and war and pastoral life. To the beat of the drums and the wailing of the pipes they celebrated the fertile marriage of earth and sun.

The dancing men took the initiative while the women at first kept their eyes lowered, watching their partners' feet—

though those demürely hidden female eyes danced with mirth. The men set the figures and the women followed, circling among a multiplicity of patterns without breaking the all-important rhythm that controlled life.

Every large family had its particular dance demonstrating some favorite episode from their history. On festival days a bard might recite the story while the clan danced behind him, acting out the tale to the shouted approval of other families, who were waiting their own time as the center of attention. There was the Dance of Wheels and the Dance of Ribbons, the Arch Dance and the magnificent and dangerous Dance of Swords, the presentation of the Míl's own family. Iron swords, honed for the occasion, flashed in the hot sun as muscular bodies pressed against their rounded points and flirted along their sharpened cutting edges. "Olaha! Olaha!" the spectators cried in admiration.

Dancing was life.

And if the famed Celtic moodiness came upon them, if the weather was bad or the fisher tribes had small catches, if the meat was maggoted and the grape harvest meager—then, too, the people came together and danced. And somehow, by the time the sun sank like a yellow cheese into the western sea to mark the birth of a new day according to tradition, everyone felt better.

Sakkar came to watch the dancing. Age-Nor, busy with preparations for departure, did not. The Tyrian merchant had seen enough of Gaelician customs.

Éremón had just offered a sacrifice of a white bullock in thanksgiving for the unprecedented success of his recent venture. Colptha had watched with jealous eyes as another sacrificer asked the animal's acquiescence, then cut its throat and chanted the invocations. Almost immediately the drums signaled the start of the dancing.

Díl wore a red sash for the occasion and teased her husband Donn about his serious expression. Éber's women came in a group, chattering happily among themselves, complimenting each other on their appearance. Scotta moved with a powerful, stamping rhythm, tossing her head. Ír ignored the traditional patterns, following music no one else heard.

The chief bard stood in a place of honor with Clarsah slung from his shoulder. The women crowded around him. "Join us, Amergin!" "Come, shape the pattern with me." "Ai, Amergin, the dance will not be complete without you."

215

They tugged and pleaded and at last he bowed his dark head and stepped forward. An eager citharadagh held out his hands for Clarsah, warned to be very careful with her by one look from the bard.

When Amergin joined the Dance of the Swords the spectators held their breaths to watch him. Long, lean-hipped, graceful as flame, he scorched them with the passion of his dancing. In the heat of the day he had laid his tunic aside, stripping to the brief kilt preferred in summer weather. The warriors boasted their fearlessness against the sharpened edges, but it was the bard who threw himself among the swords most recklessly. His sweat-polished torso bowed over the blades as if he meant to cut himself in two. A sword spun in his grasp and raked along his body; he flung himself into the air in flawless imitation of a man receiving a fatal slashing and then whipped back to represent the victor, brandishing the weapon triumphantly, stamping his feet in exultation.

"Olaha, Amergin!" his tribesmen screamed.

Taya stood with the clan of Ítos, waiting their turn to dance. Though she avoided any contact with the clan of Milesios, no one expected her to deny herself participation in the festivals and the rituals. To do so would isolate her from the spirit of life. She stood buried behind a wall of her clanspeople, trying to catch a glimpse of Éremón.

But when she saw Amergin dancing, she stared like all the others. Who could think of anyone else while Amergin gathered all the passion of his race into his body and flung it back for everyone to see?

When the dance ended, Amergin reclaimed Clarsah and made his way to a trestle table where basins of water for hot faces waited beside even more welcome wine.

Scéna Dullsaine threaded her way through the crowd and appeared at the bard's elbow. "Here, Amergin, let me wipe the sweat from your eyes," she said, offering him a folded cloth and a dazzling smile. Other women were thronging around him too, their bodies pressing against his, warming themselves with his heat.

Scéna warned them away with a glare, but these were Gaelician women, not easily intimidated. One stamped her feet; another favored Scéna with a long-lidded look bordering on defiance.

"We have been expecting to see you again in our clanhold," Scéna said meaningfully to Amergin.

A small stray breeze blew in from the sea to the north, gently blotting the moisture from his forehead. A scent of green wind curled around him.

"Expecting me?" he said to Scéna in a distracted fashion. "What for?"

She drew in her breath sharply. "I don't remember," she answered in her frostiest voice. Turning sharply, she stalked through the crowd in search of the first interested eyes, the first available and receptive man. The sun, and the blood of Scéna Dullsaine, were hot.

Amergin looked after her for a moment in genuine bafflement, then regretted too late the words she had mistaken as insult. The tangle of women seemed oppressive to him. As gracefully as he could he separated himself from them, protesting that he needed to go off someplace and prepare himself to recite later at the bardic competition.

As soon as he was out of reach of the women he felt some part of his being yearning back toward them. Yearning for completion—the completion he found in nothing and no one. Family, friends, work . . . he took Clarsah from his shoulder and carried her in front of him almost like a shield, holding on to the one thing he had.

A small stand of wind-warped pines clustered together at the edge of the festival ground. The druid in Amergin headed for trees, as so often before. He was halfway there when he caught sight of Taya drifting in the same direction, glancing back over her shoulder occasionally as if in wistful hope of seeing one certain face.

"Taya?"

"Amergin! You startled me." Her cheeks were rosy. "I was hoping . . ."

"To see Éremón," he finished for her.

She dropped her eyes. "To see Éremón without Odba. I was watching him during the dancing, but then I lost sight of him in the crowd and I don't know where he's gone."

"I think he went with Caicher and Brego to limber his muscles for the spear-casting competition."

"Oh."

That one short word sounded so disconsolate Amergin had to offer what comfort he could. "Come and sit with me in the shade while I tune my harp," he suggested. "It would be better for both of you if you and Éremón don't meet here."

The floor of the pine grove was carpeted with needles. The

217

two Gaelicians made comfortable seats for themselves, backs propped against tree trunks. Amergin glanced at Taya out of the corner of his eye. She seemed almost frail compared to the opulence of Scéna Dullsaine, and now that her brief blush had faded he saw how very pale she was. Skin normally milk-white was almost bluish, as if too much water had been added.

"Are you well?" he couldn't help asking her as he took the harp from its case.

Taya shrugged. "Well enough. I eat. I work. I salt meat and bake bread and card wool, I sandscrub cauldrons and help care for other women's children. And . . . how is Éremón, Amergin? Is he angry with me for some reason? I thought he would try to see me since he got back, but he hasn't."

"Do you want him to?"

"Yes. No. I don't know. All of you are right, it would only make trouble." With her fingernails, Taya clawed an amber bead of resin from the trunk of the pine tree. The sticky substance formed a ball as she rolled it between her fingers and she frowned down into it, looking for answers. But Taya was not a druid diviner; the tree had no messages for her.

"What am I to do, Amergin?" she wondered aloud. "I feel like I'm just hanging on a peg, waiting, and I'm not even certain what I'm waiting for."

The bard barked a short laugh without humor. "I understand exactly what you mean."

Taya dropped her resin ball and gave him a searching look. "It's possible to be discontented though you have strong walls around you and plenty to eat, isn't it?" she asked him. "And it's even possible to feel lonely in the heart of a crowd."

Scéna Dullsaine would never have made such a perceptive remark, Amergin suddenly realized. She would never come out of herself that far. And the Taya he had seen as a child would not have said such things, either. When had she shapechanged from a tagalong girl into a wise woman?

"It isn't my nature to push myself forward, Amergin," Taya went on. "I always preferred for someone else to be the center of attention. I am a born audience, I suppose, which is why I always sought you out—before the sun rose in my sky and I recognized it as Éremón."

Even in quiet Taya the Celtic gift for poetry bloomed, like

218

violets in deep shade. Amergin felt a rush of tenderness toward her. Her simple revealing of herself was a precious gift of trust. Looking down into her round and wistful face, Amergin found himself seeing Taya in a way he had never seen a woman before. Within her undeniably female body he recognized a friend beyond gender or guile, a friend who became from that moment infinitely dear to him.

"Éremón is a lucky man," he said.

The sharp eyes of Colptha the sacrificer had seen Taya walk with the bard toward the pine grove. He ran his tongue over his thin lips, sensing another opportunity for demonstrating Éremón's excessive rashness to the tribe. To all the assembled tribe.

He hurried to the site of the spear-casting competition and tugged impatiently at Éremón's arm, ruining his shot. The warrior spun around with a cocked fist to hit him, only barely restraining himself in time. What living man would strike a druid?

"Get out of here, sacrificer," he warned through gritted teeth.

"You look hot, brother," Colptha responded as if the warning meant nothing. "You should seek shade—in that pine grove over there, for instance; the one where Amergin has taken Taya. It's dark and quite secluded."

Éremón glared at him. "What are you trying to do?"

"Look out for your welfare, nothing more. You appear to be overheated, Éremón."

The warrior was indeed overheated. He crossed the distance to the pine grove in bounding strides, and Colptha watched him go, smiling. Éremón needed to learn how it felt to lose to someone else; he had won too much too easily.

In their youth Colptha had suffered too many humiliating defeats at Éremón's hands.

The warrior burst into the pine grove like a runaway bull. "What are you doing here with Taya?" he demanded of Amergin.

"Tuning my harp," Amergin replied.

"Tuning my woman!"

"She is my friend," Amergin said, savoring the term. "We were talking together."

"A woman can be your friend when she fights at your side

219

in battle," Éremón told him, "but on soft pine needles she's something very different. Get out of here and leave us alone."

Amergin stood up slowly, unfolding his lanky length until he could look straight into Éremón's eyes. "I go where I want, when I want, and on no man's orders," he said in a measured voice. "If one of us must leave here, it will have to be you, since I claimed this spot first. And Taya is a free woman, she can stay with whomever she chooses."

Éremón's eyes sparkled with blue flames. He doubled his huge fists and swelled his chest, but Amergin did not move back by a hair's thickness. Indeed, he seemed almost to lean forward, ready and able to land a blow that would rock Éremón onto his heels.

Taya, staring at them both with the secret thrill of a woman who sees men fighting over her, thought to herself with surprise, The bard is more man than the warrior!

And then her clear, practical woman's mind told her, And I am enough for Éremón, but could never be enough for Amergin.

She stepped forward and put one small hand on the warrior's brawny chest. "I will go with you wherever you wish, Éremón," she said contentedly.

Éremón flashed his brother a look of triumph before he took Taya's hand and guided her away.

Colptha in the distance, watching, marked the direction they took and then went looking for Odba.

The most deserted part of the clanhold that latesummer day was the chariot shed, where the war carts of the Míl and his sons were stored beneath the golden gloom of a thatched roof. The painted leather coverings and curving grace of the wickerwork designs glowed through the shadows. There must be beauty to offset the brutality of the sword: art and style to balance the pain and the screaming.

Éremón saw only Taya's loveliness, however, a charm doubly desirable to him since he thought he had just wrested it from one of his own brothers. Taya could feel jealousy fueling his fires, but womanly wisdom prevented her telling him how unnecessary that jealousy was; how totally she belonged to him. Far better to bask silently in the delight of his desire as he flattered and fondled her, murmuring into her hair, pulling her clothing aside, making her feel more beautiful than any woman could possibly be . . .

An outraged shriek knifed through the heated air.

Holding Taya tightly against him, Éremón rolled over and

half-rose to face Odba, who advanced upon them white-faced and furious.

"I was told you were here together but I didn't want to believe it!" Odba cried.

Taya burrowed into Éremón's chest. With unusual tenderness, the warrior cupped her head protectively with one big hand as he scowled at his wife, meeting assault with assault. "What are you doing here? And who are you, to shout at *me?*"

"I'm defending my territory!"

Tucked safely in Éremón's arms, Taya began to feel almost audacious, catching bravado from the hot flesh pressed against her own. "You're defending this whole row of chariots against big savage me, Odba?" she laughed.

"I'll wipe that smug smirk off your face!" the other woman threatened, advancing upon her. But whatever Odba intended was never completed, for the voice of the Míl thundered through the chariot shed.

"I thought I had put an end to this! Why does the problem keep coming back to disturb me like undigested shellfish?"

The trio turned to face him. Milesios stood with Scotta at his side and a crowd at his back, alerted and excited by Colptha's casual mention of "a terrible fight between Odba and Taya in the chariot shed." Colptha had given the pot just enough time to come to the simmer; now it was boiling, and there would be many witnesses.

Lugaid shoved through to Milesios. "Your son lured my daughter in here," he claimed. "My family should not have to pay for trouble he causes!" He did not like bringing such a charge against his good friend and recent leader, but Odba's threatened eric was very much on his mind.

Éremón pointed to his wife. "This woman is to blame for everything, I tell you. If she is barren, it is because she has such an unpleasant nature I can no longer stand to be with her. Even when I embrace her she buzzes constantly in my ear, complaining, finding fault, telling me how much better she was treated among the Artabrians. Odba herself has driven me away from her to Taya, who is a woman grown and has a right to accept any man she chooses."

Milesios shook his head at his son. "Why all this fuss over a woman, Éremón? I would have expected it of Éber Finn, perhaps, but not of you."

There was not enough room in the shed for both the chariots and the principals in the argument, much less for all the eager spectators. Somehow the people swirled outside and the crowd grew still larger as old Ítos came forward, walking with the caution of a brittleboned whitebeard.

He addressed Milesios as the head of one clan to another. "Mindful of your wishes, we have done what we could to keep Lugaid's daughter away from your son Éremón. We have behaved with honor. Is Éremón now trying to force a situation whereby your clan takes away all our new cattle after supposedly helping us win them? Such unheard-of treachery is sufficient reason for clan-war, Milesios!"

The summer air frosted. Clan-war. A man did not say those words lightly. The tearing asunder of clan-war could lead to the disintegration of a whole tribe, weakening it beyond repair and laying it open to conquest by outsiders. Better flood, better famine, than the war of clan against clan.

Long after, Éremón would think to ask, "Where did Ítos and Lugaid get such terrible ideas about me? Have I not always been the most honorable of men? What could possibly have suggested such treachery to them?" But too much time had passed before he asked that question, and no one could tell him the answer.

Scotta, standing at her husband's shoulder throughout the confrontation, was invoking the spirits in desperate silence. Let him be the man he was just once more, she whispered inwardly. Please!

The Míl lifted his grizzled head and gazed at Ítos with the implacability of ten generations of warriors in his eyes; the authority of ten generations of nobles in his bearing. "There will be no clan-war," he said. His voice was granite. "Findbar, step forward and hear me, that my words may be witnessed by a brehon. Odba will have no further cause to threaten the clan of Ítos with an eric, because as long as he lives in my clanhold, Éremón will never put his hands on the woman Taya again. I pledge my own honor price on it, the full value of the chieftain of the Gaelicians."

Thank you, Scotta whispered in gratitude to the silent ones who always heard.

Éremón was stunned. The full weight of the Law and his own sire's honor had been invoked against him. Rather than surrender a chieftain's honor price, which would totally im-

222

poverish them, his clan would form a fence of living bodies if necessary to keep him apart from Taya. The prosperity and prestige of his entire family was pledged against him.

"Scotta!" Éremón cried out as a man cries his mother's name when there are no other answers.

The wife of the Míl stood straight and tall. "I would cut you down with my own sword if you tried to dishonor the word of Milesios, or to set yourself against the Law that protects us all. How can I teach my children to respect the Law if I do not uphold it myself?"

There was a startled silence. No one present could remember hearing a woman threaten to destroy her own child in such a fashion. Éremón gritted his teeth, swallowing pain.

His arms slowly fell away from Taya. His face slowly turned toward Odba. "Come, wife," Éremón said huskily. "Let us go back to the festival."

Odba had dressed that morning in her very best robes and arranged her hair in yet another clever style. She had perfumed her skin with the last drops of an imported oil she had long been hoarding. She had made herself as beautiful as possible, but Éremón was looking through her as if she had ceased to exist.

A woman in the crowd remarked, "If I were Odba, I would just take my pleasure with another man. The Law allows a woman that if her husband doesn't satisfy her."

Díl responded, "Scotta accepts no man but Milesios, and her sons constantly extol her to their wives as a model of female perfection. So we have adopted the custom as well. I suspect Éremón would never forgive Odba if she attempted to do otherwise."

"Look at his face. I don't think he'll ever forgive her anyway."

The diversion was over; the people drifted away, eager for bread and wine and more dancing, anxious to hear the first recital of the bardic competition. There was obviously no more juice to be drained from Éremón's troubles.

Scotta was the last to leave—except for Taya. The Míl's wife lingered at the doorway of the chariot shed when Taya went back inside to arrange her disordered clothing in private dignity.

"I am sorry it has come to this, Taya," Scotta said. "I have always been fond of you, personally—I remember when

223

you used to come to our clanhold as a little girl to listen openmouthed to Amergin's storytelling. You were always such a pleasant child; surely more pleasant than Odba has ever been."

"It's all right, Scotta," Taya replied. A disheveled woman in a sea of slanting gilded light aswim with dust motes. She lifted her arms slowly, her thoughts elsewhere, and began repinning her tumbled hair.

"There must be no clan-war," Scotta went on, "nor can we afford to damage the alliance with the Artabrians now that we have all those new cattle to protect. Surely you understand . . ."

Taya favored her with a serene gaze. "Of course," she replied. Her mouth looked soft and bruised. And triumphant.

"I really think you should take a husband," Scotta advised, wanting to leave her with something. "Consider some other man . . ."

"Would you?" Taya asked.

Scotta took a deep breath. "I must get back to the festival," she said.

Éremón stalked beside Odba, feeling the full weight of the Law like a boulder on his shoulders. Since a time recalled only by druids, the Law had protected the hotblooded Celtic tribes from themselves. Composed from the wise pronouncements of respected chieftains and the endless debates of generations of brehons, and guided by the wisdom of the spirits, the Law was sacred. As sacred as the oak, the stones, the harp.

The Law.

"But there has to be a way," Éremón promised himself. He had sighted along his spear and seen his quarry waiting, a trophy he now desired above all others. He would never relinquish her.

"Dance!" screamed a voice. "Dance, dance, dance with me!"

A man whirled into the heart of the crowd; a tall and beautiful man, radiant as sunrise, flawlessly formed and splendidly jeweled. Oblivious to the tensions of the group he danced right through them and seized Odba's hands, carrying her away with him.

"Ír!" someone breathed in astonishment.

The tension shattered like glass. There was startled laughter followed by great deep guffaws from the belly as a sudden

224

wildness seized the Gaelicians, one after another, drawing them in Ír's wake as leaves are drawn after a windswirl. They threw themselves into the pattern of a new and wonderful dance because they could not help themselves; because dancing was a tremendous release amounting to compulsion.

"Dance!" Ír commanded, and they did. The pipes sang and the drums thudded like happy feet and the people danced.

The pattern gripped and held them, color and motion and gaiety snatched from the fiery heart of the sun; life, life, life! Odba surrendered to it thankfully, truly lovely now, her cheeks flushed and her eyes bright. Against his will even Éremón was pulled into the maelstrom, shoved and pushed and guided until his anger ebbed away and he stamped and turned with his head thrown back and a grin beaming through his mustache.

Lugaid danced, and Díl; Scotta and Donn and Scéna and Brego, Findbar the brehon and Éber Finn. Éber Finn, weaving his way among the women, his hands reaching for lushness.

All this arguing over Taya had stimulated his interest in the woman. His wives were an amiable band, they would not object to an addition to their number. More ways to divide the work, more companions to share a laugh or a gossip.

He was surprised that he had not noticed Taya's charms before. He watched for her in the pattern of the dance, and when he saw a dark curly head coming toward him Éber prepared his best smile.

On the beaten earth of the headland the Gaelicians danced out the newest, oldest dance of all, as the male spirit of fire penetrated the female spirit of earth, and the Mother, in a constant state of labor, brought forth life.

And when the exhausted dancers sank down onto the Mother herself, sweating and panting and still smiling, enmity at least temporarily forgotten, the bards gathered for the great competition of oratory.

Every clan's ambition was to have its own bard, but the complex array of gifts necessary for a true bard were seldom bestowed on one man. Still, among the numerous families of the Gaelicians there were enough poets to assure a fine spectacle; solemn, lofty, intensely meaningful to all present. Bards from areas many nights distant made the long journey just to attend this most prestigious of competitions and try to win honor for their clans.

One by one, they now stepped forward to recite the epics

225

and satires and eulogies for which they were famed. Each was rewarded with a gold ring from the arm of a clan-chief or a bullock presented by his retinue, and in the case of an exceptional performance a whole stack of honor gifts was piled at the bard's feet.

Amergin, chief of his profession, was last to recite. He stood on the platform of honor, a tall man with closed eyes, holding a magnificent harp of polished wood and famed power. As the Gaelicians listened, he began to bring to life for them their own history, the saga of their days. The poetic epic he had been so diligently preparing.

Clarsah accompanied him, her voice now lyrical, now a thundering chant, now a soft rain on the tombs of men and women long and never dead. The poetic history flowed like the heartsblood of the people; wild as Ír, diligent as Donn, celebrating the pastoral life beloved of Éber and the battles that were Éremón's joy. Strong solid Scotta; gentle yielding Taya; Milesios, gruff and wise. Even Colptha's dark thread wound through the music, an undertone of shadowed mystery. The people, marching and seeking, laughing and weeping and brimming with a zest for life, poets and takers of heads, indomitable in battle but obedient to the Law.

Celts.

The listening crowd looked at each other with shining eyes, sharing the joy of an exceptional event. None of them doubted they were hearing the greatest saga ever composed by a bard. The sparkle of the harp combined with Amergin's alliterative phrasing to summon ancient days, touch and sound and emotion spun together to re-create reality and essence . . .

Then Amergin's voice fell silent. The sound of the harp faded to nothingness. The spell was broken, too soon, too abruptly!

The crowd began to murmur with disappointment and confusion.

Amergin, stricken, opened his eyes. "It is not finished," he whispered in a voice so clear it carried like a shout. "The poem is not finished, and I do not know the ending."

With great and terrible dignity, the bard stepped down from the platform of honor. He walked slowly through the crowd and they fell back to let him pass. His head was high, his eyes unseeing. Clarsah rode silently on his shoulder. No one spoke to him, for who would willingly offend a bard?

226

When he was gone, whispers filled the space he had occupied. His tribespeople crowded together, seeking explanations. "What does this mean? Is the chief bard ill? Is this a bad omen?"

The unexpected end of the competition left everyone anxious and baffled. A winner must surely be announced, that was the tradition. But who? Amergin's song had promised to be an incomparable triumph, yet he himself had rejected it. The clan-chiefs, the elders, the brehons, everyone who held any degree of authority gathered together and argued and reasoned and in the end nothing was decided.

The great festival came to a close in the smoldering ashes of its fire and a fresh salt wind blew in from the north, from the sea.

◇ **19** ◇

I N A RAGE of incompletion the bard stalked the headland. Sometimes the harp rode his shoulder, suspended by her thong; more often she languished in her gilded satchel while Amergin endured his misery alone.

Sakkar was distraught. He had come to love the bard's house as much for its atmosphere as for its comforts. Beneath Amergin's roof Sakkar had felt both respected and unthreatened for the first time in his life, and he had begun to relax, a condition a poor Tyrian seaman could not have imagined before. He tried to comfort Amergin and restore the lost harmony.

"Master, you must not take this so hard. It is only a poem . . ."

Amergin groaned. "Only a poem. You don't understand, Sakkar. What you call a poem was a . . . a ship to carry my ancestors, my ambitions, the best part of me. And it is lost in a fog and may never reach shore. I have failed myself and those who entrusted me with the task of composition."

Sometimes, for a few moments only, Amergin allowed

himself to wonder if Clarsah had betrayed him. She had only sung an accompaniment, she had not inspired or led him in the epic. Always before she had given him help when he needed it, but at the crucial peak of his career she had taken a secondary role and left the entire burden of creation to him.

The betrayal—if it was a betrayal—was almost more painful than his inability to finish the poem.

"When was I unfaithful to you, Clarsah?" he whispered once in the night. "When did I betray you to cause such cruel retaliation?"

And then he remembered. The sunbathed plain and the chariots circling, the hot high lust for adventure gripping him . . . the agonized wish to be just one of the warriors, a bard no longer . . .

The season turned and the first autumnal winds blew, heralds from ice-tinged Marimarusa, sea of the dead.

Something vicious gnawed the bard's groin. The need to create or procreate, he did not know which. They were the same. Tormented, he prowled the cliffs and stared at the sea.

The interdiction against Colptha had passed with the change of moons and the sacrificer took part in the rituals once more, but with a new distance between himself and the others. Colptha carried himself with the unmistakable air of a man who has suffered a great injustice.

The immense new herd of the Gaelicians was apportioned among the clanholds to gnaw parched grass and prickly furze, seeking a nourishment that no longer existed.

Miners from neighboring tribes fought to wrest a few last scoops of tin ore from the grudging earth, then set their implements aside and went home to their clans, barring the doors.

The wind shrieked and blew. The season threatened to be more bitter than any in bardic memory, grimly cold and grimly dry. There was no fecund moisture left in the land that was once so productive, the Mother who had been so moistly fertile.

The repaired Phoenician vessels were at last declared seaworthy, loaded with a cargo of sheep's wool—second grade, as Age-Nor complained to Bomilcar—Celtic crafts and salted beef, and prepared to go back the way they had come, racing against the weather.

The Míl's clan lined the headland to view the sailing. The finality of the traders' departure was not such a tragedy now that countless cows grazed in Gaelician clanholds, but still there were those who felt a tug of sadness as the great galleys hoisted their sails and the shouted commands to their crews rang across the water.

Sakkar had accompanied Amergin to see the sight, which he viewed with mixed feelings. Now he was truly cut off from his past, the former shipwright thought—but what of his future?

Amergin thought he recognized the figure of Age-Nor in the prow of the foremost galley and lifted his arm in farewell, but instead of returning the gesture, Age-Nor turned away, almost as if he was embarrassed.

"That's strange," Amergin remarked aloud. "I thought the Tyrian and I had developed a friendly relationship, of sorts."

Sakkar tightened his cloak and began rubbing his shoulder, which ached constantly in the cooling weather. "I do not think the commander was anxious to make friends. He just wanted to get back to Tyre. He was . . . what is the word? . . . disappointed in this voyage, and afraid of Carthage."

"Don't you miss Tyre, yourself?" the bard inquired.

Sakkar responded with a gap-toothed grimace. Unlike the Gaelicians, the Sea People had bad teeth. Too much soft food, the druids said. "I miss my city," Sakkar admitted. "Sometimes. I had a woman there. Young. Big with my child. She got sick, legs swelled, urine stank. She cried. I made good enough wages, but the herbalists took it all. Then the priests said I must offer sacrifices or the gods would kill her. I had no coins to buy sacrifices. So I robbed a man. A rich, important man. Someone saw me, and told, for a price." He related the pitiful tale in the flat voice of fatalism, all emotion long since expunged.

"My woman died anyway. The king's agents were looking for me. To punish me. Ccchhh." He made a graphic noise and drew his finger across his throat. "I escaped with Commander Age-Nor's fleet. If I went back, they would still kill me."

"That's unjust," Amergin protested. "Your wife was sick . . . why didn't you appeal to the brehons?"

"We have no brehons. We have a king of the city, and a government."

"This government you speak of is your tribal council, your eldest and wisest?"

Sakkar laughed hollowly. "Oh, no. Government is men appointed by the king because they will do whatever he says. Rats who eat crumbs from his table. Our law is anything the king desires, and if we object his agents can imprison us, torture us, kill us."

Amergin shook his head. "How can such deeds be used to enforce law? The spirit cannot be imprisoned and never dies; the body dies anyway, so a threat to kill it means absolutely nothing. Your king is a fool, Sakkar; especially if he thinks one man can be wise enough to make all the laws for everyone else."

"How is law enforced among your people?"

"We keep it ourselves to avoid dishonor, for a man's honor is his most valuable possession. The prestige of the clan is its final wealth that can be neither stolen nor bartered away—which reminds me: why didn't someone of your clan, your family, help you when your woman was so sick? One of our clans would be seriously disgraced for neglecting to help a member in trouble."

"I have no family," Sakkar answered. "I was born in an alley and grew up on the docks, hiding from slavers and snatching food from refuse heaps. If I ever had a mother, she threw me away when I was born."

Amergin had never been so shocked in his life. The Phoenicians described the Mideast as the hub of the earth, compared to which the Celtic tribes lived in brutish outlands. But now Amergin, looking through Sakkar's eyes, saw the "civilized" world as a composite of savageries where degradation was taken for granted and brutality was an accepted mode of conduct within one's own family. No wonder the wise men inveighed against the contamination of cities!

The wool of the sheep came in thicker than it had been within anyone's memory. The women measured it with their finger joints and began hastily weaving additional warm cloaks and blankets against the coming winter.

The convocation of brehons met at the next change of the moon, and Éremón appeared before them as was his right to protest his situation and air his grievances. When it was over, he encountered Amergin outside the stronghold gate.

"What happened?" the bard inquired.

"I wasted my valuable wind. The brehons found that Odba

230

had fulfilled her obligations as wife under the Law and therefore was within her rights in denying me another wife. The Míl's order forbidding me from visiting Taya stands, and as long as I obey Odba has agreed to forget about the eric and about returning to the Artabrians." Éremón spat out every word as if it had a bad taste in his mouth.

"It seems the fairest decision under the circumstances," Amergin commented.

"I wasn't seeking a *fair* decision. I wanted one that would let me have Taya and all else that is mine!" Then in spite of himself, Éremón chuckled. "I want it all, you know."

"You always have," Amergin agreed.

"And I still mean to have it." Éremón pounded one great fist against the open palm of his other hand, like a war drum.

"Let it go, Éremón," Amergin advised his brother.

"And let Odba win? Let her smile in her sleep for the rest of her life, knowing she has thwarted me and somehow gotten my own mother to stand with her? No! May the spirits defend me from the terrible power of women!"

The winter grew colder and darker. The hipbones of the cattle stood out like the timbers of burned cottages. In addition to the sparse and desiccated grass, they chewed the soil itself in search of nourishment. The Gaelicians slaughtered and salted as much beef as they could, until they ran out of salt and had to begin the laborious process of making more by evaporating seawater. They traded cattle to celsine for raw materials and to more distant tribes as well, but the drought was uniform across the western part of the peninsula and no one had grass for cattle; no one was seeking larger herds in that bitter season.

They had thought themselves wealthy; now they saw themselves as worse off than before.

Milesios was growing weaker every day. Scotta fought a solitary battle to keep anyone from guessing how little remained of the old champion. When he could no longer lead—or appear to lead—there would be a struggle among the factions eager for his chiefdom, and such a struggle could not come at a worse time. The other clan-chiefs were openly eyeing the bronze-sheathed bench in the Heroes' Hall, and the Míl's own sons were arguing continually with one another as if goaded by some invisible force. The tightly woven fabric of the clan seemed to be fraying, and Scotta was very worried.

Éremón took his son Moomneh to the calf pens to select a

young bullock for the boy to train. As Milesios had once said to him, Éremón told his son, "Livestock are good teachers. You will be a warrior like me, so you will need to develop strength and endurance. You will acquire them from the ox you are going to train."

Each boy, before reaching manhood, must put some brawny headstrong calf into a miniature yoke and train it, leading the animal around until it grew accustomed to the gear. By the time the ox reached maturity the habit of obedience was so firmly established the animal never thought to rebel. The boy who trained it, having matured also in its company, felt a physical bond with the powerful creature, and in addition had had to acquire as much patience and self-discipline as a young Celt could be expected to accept.

Éremón watched proudly as Moomneh selected the largest of the newly castrated calves, a bony creature with a broad beige forehead and sprouting horns. "Try him, boy!" Éremón urged. "Try him now." Everything he felt about himself he saw, at that moment, in the child.

Moomneh flung his arms around the calf's neck and wrestled it to earth to establish an early superiority, then sat on its neck as he was instructed and stroked the animal, crooning to it.

"He has my way with animals," Éber remarked unexpectedly at Éremón's shoulder.

"I sired him!" Éremón shot back.

"Oh, I wasn't disputing that. Your Odba has never drawn my eye. I thought your taste in women rather dull, in fact, until I got to know Taya better."

"You leave her alone!"

"Only one woman lives in your house," Éber Finn said, "and her name is Odba, not Taya. You have no rights where Lugaid's daughter is concerned."

"I tell you, Taya will be mine somewhere," Éremón vowed in a voice that rasped and crackled. "If not in my house, then in another one. If not in this *world*, then in another one. I will have her!"

Winter deepened. The herds ravaged the land, turning the denuded earth to beaten clay and roiling dust. The starving cattle lowed incessantly, dreaming of vanished green meadows. The weakest died, and Colptha the sacrificer watched and waited.

And then, too late to save the grass, the weather turned.

One storm after another roared in off the ocean and the northern bay, smashing against the headland, hurling a spray of white foam back at the glowering sky. Rain came in torrents. At times it seemed to fall in a solid mass rather than individual drops. The howling wind blew it in horizontal lines, driving in through open doorways and seeking out cracks in walls and gaps in thatch.

Overgrazed fields, their grass roots destroyed, became glutinous seas of mud. Floods roared along watercourses, catching hapless livestock and sending their bloated bodies swirling downstream, drowned and useless.

The world was sodden. The horses' hooves rotted as they stood, keeping the druids busy preparing poultices for the horseboys to apply. Food left in the pot overnight grew a green fur. Stone walls oozed dampness no hearthfire could dispel.

And still it rained. Still the wind howled.

When the drowned land could tolerate no more the ice storms began.

Colptha glowed with vindication. "The Earth Mother is furious with us for asking too much of her when she was in a weakened condition. I tried to issue a warning, but I was silenced."

Deputations from the various clans and tribes visited the sacred groves almost daily, bringing gifts of propitiation to offer to the Mother. And many among them looked at Colptha the sacrificer with new respect.

He made certain Irial noticed this, of course. And in private, he commented to Conmael, "The spirits are all on my side, you see? Everything is being arranged for my ultimate benefit. Now I have a little task for you to do . . ."

Conmael circulated among the clans, and when he found a receptive ear he said, "Éremón did more harm than good, bringing all those cattle. His judgment is flawed; he wouldn't make a good chief of the tribe, would he?"

Meanwhile, Colptha never missed an opportunity to comment on the steadiness and reliability of Donn. "Milesios has always paid more attention to Éremón, I realize, but that's because Donn is steady and reliable and needs no watching. Donn is oak; what a fine chieftain he would make."

Éber Finn complained to Ír as the two were checking on their clan's livestock, "Have you heard this talk about making Donn the Míl's successor? Why Donn, answer me that?

He has no ambition and he certainly lacks flair. I've never seen him lead a battle, though he's an able enough follower. If some of the people are turning against Éremón, why shouldn't they turn to me? I'm as good as he is in every way, and I wasn't responsible for this plague of cattle.'' Éber ran an appraising eye over the herd. "But you will notice, Ír,'' he could not resist adding, "my share of the clan's cattle doesn't appear as starveling as the rest of them.''

Ír, who saw no such thing, had noticed something else.

Across the field from the two brothers, young Moomneh appeared with his little ox in tow. To test the calf's obedience the boy intended to lead it right through the herd, insisting that it follow him without pausing to graze or socialize. But the sight of so many of its own kind excited the calf. It tugged against its lead rope and braced its feet, determined to stay with the herd.

Moomneh pulled. The calf pulled back. This was the classic moment when a boy must learn to use his wits instead of his strength, for the animal was already stronger than the human. But Moomneh felt only a stubborn determination to force the issue. He tugged violently and yelled. The calf lowered its head and shook its nubbined horns. Moomneh yelled louder and hit it on the shoulder with the lead rope.

A few paces away, Éber Finn's old black bull raised his head and watched. He did not know the boy who stood with his back turned toward him, nor did he know the young ox. He only knew he disliked the sight of that flailing rope, and the yelling was heating his sluggish blood. He was hungry and he was in a bad temper.

He dropped his head and pawed the earth; once, slowly, and then once more, cutting deeper into the sticky mud.

Moomneh lashed his calf again and it bawled in protest.

The bull took a step backward and moved his head from side to side, slicing the air with gleaming horns.

"Look out!'' Ír cried, too late.

The bull charged.

Now Éber saw the boy and bull, but before his mind had time to order a reaction Ír was off and running. He sped over the mud as if it were a hardpacked race course, his golden hair streaming behind him. As he ran he stripped his red cloak from his shoulders and began waving it to draw the bull's attention. But the animal, with the singlemindedness of its species, saw only Moomneh and the swinging rope.

Moomneh recognized his danger and abandoned the ox calf, running for his life as the hot breath of the bull scorched his neck. The huge animal caught his boyish body between its horns, fortunately not impaling him, and butted him with such force he flew through the air to fall unconscious amid the furze.

The bull skidded to a halt and shook its head to clear its rage-reddened vision. It spotted the form of its enemy lying helpless and still. With a bellow of anger the bull prepared to charge again, to grind the boy into the earth with its horns and trample him beneath its hooves.

Ír raced through the herd, spooking them, so the entire mass was soon a chaos of milling, bawling animals, unstable and dangerous. But Ír did not care. He cared only about the boy.

He reached the bull just as the animal prepared to charge again. Ír ran in front of it, flapping his cloak in the bull's face. The bull threw its head up, startled. "Hiya!" the man shouted, waving the cloak. "Hiya! Chase me, horned one. Chase me!" He deliberately turned his back on the bull and ran.

With a bellow that shook the earth the furious animal came after him, following the red cloak.

"You'll be killed!" Éber cried to his brother, but it was no use.

Tallest of the Míl's sons, Ír of the long legs had always been the best runner in the tribe. Now he sped like a swallow before the bull, intoxicated by his own daring. Intoxicated by his flirtation with a painful and ugly death. The danger made him faster; he felt invincible.

He was totally free, he could do anything. The spirits had taken control of him, moving his limbs for him and turning the mud to solid earth beneath his feet.

He dodged to one side and swirled his cloak through the air, making a broad red target for the bull. Drawn to the motion, the bull brandished its horns and charged blindly, head lowered and eyes closed to protect them. Ír sidestepped neatly and let his cloak slide over the bull's shoulders as it passed by him.

Éber could not believe his eyes. "Mad," he commented to no one in particular, shaking his head. And then he screamed, "Don't hurt my bull, Ír!" for he saw Ír draw his sword from his belt. "We should never have let Ír wear his sword in the clanholding,'' Éber muttered, knowing no warrior would willingly step beyond his house without the symbol of his rank on his hip.

When the bull realized its attack had met only empty air it slowed and stopped, turning with eyes open now to relocate its tormentor.

Ír grinned and waved the cloak.

The bull lowered its head, closed its eyes, and charged.

Ír, invincible, waited until the animal was one pace away from him and then stepped back, staying so close that the horns almost grazed his belly. As the bull's lowered neck passed in front of him he plunged his sword straight down into it.

Momentum carried the animal a few steps farther, but it was already dead. It crumpled slowly to earth, a mountain of flesh emptied of its animating spirit.

Ír laughed. He lifted both arms above his head and capered around his fallen enemy, swirling his red cloak in violent patterns and laughing; laughing.

The herd, nearing hysteria by now, wheeled and ran.

"By the wind!" Éber swore desperately, not knowing which way to go. Ír, heedless of everything around him, was dancing his victory dance at the heart of a roiling herd of crazed cattle, while the crumpled form of Moomneh lay in the bushes, waiting for the first running hoof to crush the life from his skull.

◇ **20** ◇

AMERGIN'S RESTLESS FEET would not submit to standing in a chariot. They insisted on movement, and so, with Clarsah on his shoulder, he paced the clanholding, trying to work out the tangle inside himself and reestablish harmony with his harp.

But still he could not force the ending of the epic to take

236

shape. The pattern of his people seemed open-ended, an unresolved design.

The day was cold and raw and he had wandered some distance from the stronghold, paying little attention to the direction his feet chose. Movement caught his attention and he glanced southward in time to see a herd of cattle circling restlessly, a man running through its center—and, at the herd's edge, a boy being struck by a charging bull.

Amergin began to run, too.

He was too far away to do anything, but he heard Éber's howl of anger at seeing his best bull mortally wounded, and the bard watched in horror as the cattle took fright and bolted.

The fallen boy must be directly in their path, yet Ír seemed oblivious to anything but his otherworldly jubilation.

Amergin was fast, but he knew the voice of Clarsah could travel faster. He unslung her from his shoulder and laid his palm against the strings, demanding her magic more urgently than ever before.

She sang out in reply.

The great harps knew three kinds of enchantments. There was merry music that no feet could resist, filling hearts with laughter. There was mourning music, summoning all the sadness of the living into their eyes to be cried away at once, so they could turn away from the tombs and get on with their lives. And there was sleeping music, the soporific capable of making armies yawn, and stretch, and sink to the earth, their swords forgotten at their sides.

Amergin held Clarsah and played the sleeping music.

The sound seemed lost in the rumble of the running herd, but the ears of animals are keener than those of humans, and their spirits are more sensitive to vibrations. Even in their fright the cattle heard the harp and felt invisible hands laid on their heads, soothing them. They circled, slowed, and then walked, milling about rather than stampeding headlong.

Éber reached Moomneh before Amergin could. He hardly knew where to grieve—over his fallen nephew or his dead bull. He solved the problem by swearing at Ír.

"You weakskulled mooncalf!" he cried, shaking his fist at his brother. "You didn't even take time to propitiate his spirit first, you just struck him down and set it loose to wander. Perhaps to come back and demand justice from me! You had no right, it wasn't necessary, I could have handled him myself if you weren't so . . ."

Ír was aware that Éber was mouthing words at him but he did not want to listen. Words would bring him back to earth and lock him in a place and a time, and he wanted to prolong the feeling of floating free, untouchable.

The bard came trotting up, panting. "He doesn't hear you," he said to Éber. "Where's the boy?"

Éber looked at Amergin with growing awe. "You stopped the cattle," he said incredulously. "You stopped a stampede with your music!"

"Never mind that, help me find the boy."

Abashed, Éber led the way to a slender form crumpled in an icebrittle clump of yellow furze. Moomneh's pale face was scored with scratches and he was breathing shallowly, but as the two men bent over him he opened his eyes.

In a flash Amergin was cradling him in his arms, feeling his body with the fingers of a druid, sensitive to any disharmony of broken bone or ruptured organ.

"He's all right, I think," Amergin told Éber. "The wind's knocked out of him and he's had a fright, but he'll go home to Éremón's house and scrape the leavings from the cooking pot."

Éber, relieved, went over to his bull. "This is a bad omen," he remarked. "The best of the bulls, the chief bull, is dead. The strength of the herd is cut down."

Moomneh opened his eyes again and smiled up at the bard. "Ai, Amergin," he said softly. "Did you see me with the bull?"

"I saw you. How do you feel? Can you stand up?"

"I think so." Leaning on Amergin's arm, Moomneh got to his feet and dusted himself off. He glanced once at the ruin of Éber's bull and quickly looked away. "My ox wandered off," he said, with a tragic outthrust of his lower lip.

"We'll catch him," Amergin promised.

Moomneh drew a deep breath, savoring the crisp air. The day seemed marvelously beautiful to him, as it does to survivors. "How clean and sparkling everything is!" he commented.

"Enjoy it while you can," a morose Éber muttered. "As you get older you'll see the wear and tear. Look, Ír, see what you've done," he called to his brother, but Ír was still lost in his own reality.

"Ír. Ír!" Amergin's voice was sharp, piercing the rosy fog in which Ír floated. "You saved a child's life," the bard said. "I'm proud of you."

He extended his hand and Ír took it, like a trusting child himself. Amergin took hold of Moomneh with his other hand and led the two of them, the bemused adult and the shaken child, in the direction of the stronghold, leaving Éber alone to mourn his bull.

After they had gone a few paces Ír roused himself enough to look over his shoulder. The dead bull opened its eye and stared at him. That mean little eye, memorizing his face and form against some future encounter.

There is my enemy, Ír thought suddenly. He shuddered with fear. The bull, the horned one. Now I know his face.

A celebration was held that night in the Heroes' Hall in honor of Ír and Amergin jointly. Scotta, proud mother of heroes, stood behind the Míl's bench and beamed on everyone. Colptha lounged in his compartment, begrudging Amergin the admiration showered upon him.

"Amergin is very quick to take credit," Colptha said out of the side of his mouth to Conmael. "Do you really think he stopped a maddened herd with just the sound of his harp? I never thought his gift was that great, actually. And I still don't. I supect in the dust and confusion, Éber mistook what he saw. Don't you agree?"

Conmael had learned among other things the rhetorical nature of the questions the sacrificer put to him, so he contented himself with chewing and drinking and did not try to reply. There were times when he thought of himself as a mirror of polished copper Colptha held up in which to admire his own cleverness.

Lately Conmael had made a new friend. A boy fostered into the clan of the ruling chieftain would not normally spend his spare time with a laborer of another race entirely, but Sakkar the Phoenician was not just a laborer. Even Sakkar found it hard to explain his status in the community.

"I'm a gift," he said when he and Conmael happened to find themselves sheltering from a storm beneath the same roof one morning. "I was a life exchanged for a life."

"But you're not a slave?"

"I am not treated like a slave. Your bard talks to me the same way he talks to everyone else. He shares his food with me in equal portions and does not even keep the choice morsels for himself. I do not understand him—but I like him."

"My foster father is Colptha the druid," Conmael volunteered. "He lets me eat from his table, and he talks to me. But I don't think it's quite the same."

"What is a foster father?"

"Among Celtic tribes, a child from one clan is often sent to another to be raised. It strengthens ties between the clans and helps hold the tribe together."

"Families are very important to you," Sakkar remarked.

"Isn't your family important to you?" Conmael asked, puzzled by some hidden sadness in the little man's voice.

"The bard is all the family I have now," Sakkar replied.

Conmael offered Sakkar a freckle-faced, understanding smile. He, too, felt isolated from parents and siblings, for Colptha kept him apart from everyone else as much as possible, and he had not visited Gosten's clanholding for several cycles of the moon.

There was more than a generation's difference in age between Conmael and Sakkar, as well as an inequality of rank and a total physical dissimilarity, yet their spirits had a common ground.

Sakkar's dark eyes twinkled in response.

Thereafter, whenever Colptha was not watching him Conmael invented errands to carry him near the bard's house. Once he had been beneath Amergin's roof he realized how different the atmosphere was from that of Colptha's dwelling, where the very air seemed brittle with ambition and anger. Even when Amergin was not present, echoes of music seemed to cling to his stone walls. The fire on the hearth sang happily to itself; the birds in their boxes clucked in harmony. Conmael discovered as Sakkar had that the bard's home was a pleasant refuge.

Conmael also discovered a passion for sea lore, and soon had Sakkar teaching him sailors' terminology and showing him how to tie knots. When the bard came home from a day's rambles the three sat on the oaken benches with their feet warming at the hearth, and Amergin recited or played Clarsah while the other two listened and drowsed, thoroughly at home.

The worst part of Conmael's day was twilight, when he must scurry back to Colptha with some excuse.

Now, in the Heroes' Hall, Conmael's mind had wandered

off to consider the intricacies of rudders, Sakkar's most recent lesson. Conmael was growing fast now, elongating and becoming gangly, and his jaw had a tendency to sag when he daydreamed.

Colptha noticed.

He jabbed the boy with a sharp elbow. "Sit up and pay attention, you disgrace me! Here comes the chief druid, bow to him, show him how my son honors the great Irial. He will speak and you will listen, so sit tall and look attentive."

As Colptha whispered to him, Conmael felt a familiar dark shadow blot out the remembered brightness of the bard's house. "Listen," Colptha's insidious voice commanded. "Listen, listen."

The chief druid, his shoulders at last stooping beneath the weight of untold seasons, stepped to the center of the hall. He walked with the deliberate delicacy of a man whose feet hurt.

"Heroes bring honor to their people," Irial proclaimed. "Ír, son of Milesios, enhances the prestige of his clan, and Amergin enhances the order of druids." It was obvious from the tone of the chief druid's voice which achievement he found more important. He continued, "Through Amergin we are reminded of the powers of the invisible world, the force of words and music. What we see is only a thin skin and our eyes deceive us; what we do not see is more potent. Amergin understands.

"I am an old man. No, do not shake your heads, good friends, for I am more aware of the seasons than any of you. Ours is the class which counts and measures, and I have counted the moons of my life, both the bright faces and the dark."

Something in his words alerted Milesios, who twisted around to look into his face as Irial stood beside him. He saw skin cracked like dry mud, and a fast-fading light.

"Soon I will shed this outgrown body," Irial affirmed. "A new chief druid must be named before then. Today an old bull died and tonight a new young bull stands guard over his cows. Such a sign from the spirits cannot be ignored.

"It is my obligation to leave the future of the order in good hands, and so this night, even in the darkness that has never been dark to me, I will go to the nemeton. There, alone, I will invoke the spirits and ask their guidance in the naming of my successor, while I still have the strength to be wise."

A hush fell over the hall.

Colptha drew a long suck of air through his teeth. "He's going to choose Amergin," the sacrificer whispered angrily to Conmael. "No matter what he says now about consulting the spirits he's going to name a member of the bardagh to succeed him, instead of a diviner!" Colptha's teeth grated together audibly.

"Have you had a vision?" Conmael wondered.

"I don't need any vision to know what will happen now. Didn't you hear how Irial smeared fat on Amergin's name? The bard has always been his favorite, only the trees know why, and that business with the cattle today just confirmed him in his intention to place Amergin over us. Idiocy! *I* should be chief druid, Conmael. The Mother spoke to *me!*"

Colptha was experiencing a strange sensation, one that had come to him before, but never so vividly as now. He seemed to be a watcher sitting inside his own skull, peering out through the sacrificer's eyes with sardonic amusement. A wolf stalking through a flock of sheep aware, and singular in his awareness.

A flooding certainty of his own gifts and cleverness rose in Colptha, seducing him with its implications of power.

Fools, he thought, looking at the assembled Gaelicians. (The silent watcher in his head, watching.) Trained to recognize the larger pattern, which included these lives but was not limited to them; a pattern that an aware individual might manipulate to his own advantage.

Was a gift such as Colptha's a mandate, demanding by its very singularity to be used?

How sweet it was to think so. Why else would the spirits have been so generous? He, Colptha the sacrificer, was equipped to shape the pattern of the future according to his own special wisdom for the good of his people. Controlling them with his skill, his subtle temptations; enlarging the uses of blood sacrifice . . .

His druid training rose up in him, silent voices crying out in revulsion against the vision the watcher painted within Colptha's vaulted skull.

"No!" Colptha said under his breath.

Conmael glanced at him nervously.

The balance within Colptha shifted ever so slightly. The symmetry was destroyed. He took strength from the fear he saw in the boy's eyes and it was not a healthy strength.

"Yes," he said to himself, a little louder. "Yes."

Conmael wedged himself into a corner of the compartment, wishing he were a druid so he could melt into the wood and become one with it, beyond Colptha's reach.

Irial left the Heroes' Hall, pacing with stately tread, bowed with his responsibilities. All eyes followed him. It was as if the great black bull lay dead in the center of the hall, his death the hub of some mighty, unseen wheel, irrevocably turning.

When the chief druid had gone the celebration resumed, though with a sense of impending change the more sensitive in the hall could not ignore. Colptha waited until the clamor rose to its usual level and then, with an impatient gesture to Conmael to follow him, he left the hall and went to seek the darkness.

Amergin sat on his bench and held Clarsah in his lap to share in his honor. The triumph was really hers, he thought. Once again inspiration had come from and through the harp, and the man had only been her instrument.

He was forgiven, then.

He stroked her polished frame, thinking of his poem. Irial had said he understood about the invisible world and the power of words . . . perhaps if he reshaped his epic to make Clarsah the symbol of his people, she would be willing to take part in the creative process again and help him complete his work. He thought, briefly and shockingly, of Age-Nor bartering with his gods, but dismissed the idea from his brain.

The harp as symbol for the people . . .

Amergin stared into shifting shadows.

Symbols.

The outward representation of the inner essence. Even human flesh, Amergin saw with druid vision, had little importance save to symbolize something of immortal value contained within it.

All matter was symbol, then. All that appeared solid was, in truth, ephemeral. How could a man judge one of those fleeting images—a tree, a bull, a person—to be more precious or more perfect than another?

He stared in astonishment at the perfection of the shared spirit of life in every living thing.

Éremón had seen it in Taya, and claimed her, but had been

blind to the same quality in Odba, allowing his blindness to make her ugly. Why?

The riddle of existence twisted on and on, and Amergin pursued it down the pathways of his mind.

Others, meanwhile, pursued different visions.

When Corisios arrived at the sacred grove shortly after dawn he found the chief druid. The diviner was concentrating on the daily tribute to the trees and so at first he did not notice a huddled form beneath one of the oaks. A shaft of sunlight, piercing through the leaves, brought it to his attention. He could not believe he was seeing a man. The object was so insignificant in appearance, a mere heap of discarded . . .

"Irial!" Corisios cried, running forward.

He quickly summoned the few other trained samodhii and, though they examined Irial's body thoroughly, they could not determine the specific cause of death. Yet the chief druid did not look as serene as a man should after willingly surrendering to old age in this sacred sanctuary. His mouth was twisted, his lips drawn back from his teeth, and his blackened tongue protruded slightly. His fingers were hooked into claws as if he fought something. Yet there was no blood, no wound. He might almost have been smothered by the mound of drifted leaves that pillowed his head.

Ollach, the sandy-haired senior samodhi, now that Irial was dead, ran his healer's fingers over Irial's body again and again, frowning as he did so. "I feel more than death here," he said at last. "There is a residue of . . . surprise. And anger. I felt it when I first touched his skin; it almost burned my fingers in spite of the cold."

Druids were arriving like streams of water hurrying to form a pool. The wind carried word of Irial's death beyond the boundaries of Gaelician territory to their neighboring Celtic tribes, sighing over the hills, creeping into hidden valleys, curling around tombs, summoning. The members of the order, whatever their tribe, were informed by a deep unease of spirit and began traveling by foot or chariot or oxcart to the sacred groves.

"Irial is dead," Ollach informed them. "Dead before his appointed night, we think."

"Do you mean . . . he was killed?" Findbar the brehon

244

asked, unable to imagine such a thing but chilled by an almost malignant atmosphere lingering in the grove.

Ollach bowed his head. "If so, this is the most severe disharmony of my lifetime, for Irial was slain here in the nemeton, and the repercussions will be beyond our ability to measure."

"Perhaps you are mistaken," someone said hopefully.

"Only the Earth Mother knows for certain, and the trees, who saw."

Amergin spoke. "Corisios, you are of the trees. Throw the staves and furrows of wisdom and read them; tell us who did this deed and why."

Corisios prepared his particular ritual of divination and threw the ogham croabh. But for the second time in recent experience he could not read them clearly; their meaning was blurred by vibrations still emanating from the place and the deed. He forced himself as he had never forced himself before. For Irial, he thought. Help me, Irial. He threw the sticks again and the message on their carved faces this time was as clear to him as the lines on his palm. "I see a man and . . . a small man?" he said aloud. "Darkness. Not one, but many dangers . . . *the water drags you down!*" he shrieked suddenly.

"What does that mean?" Ollach demanded to know. Colptha stood just behind him, his white face stiff with tension.

Corisios fought his way back to the solid world through a dizzying haze. He felt very tired. "Someone was angry; someone else was terrified."

"Ai! Irial was killed, then!"

"The matter is already beyond our reach, we are not meant to intervene," Corisios said, recalling the pattern of the sticks. "The crime, if crime it was, was so terrible no living man is capable of judging it. The retribution, if retribution is needed, must be so terrible no living man is capable of it. Irial himself is many lives past the seeking of vengeance and we must allow him to go on; his spirit does not wish to be held here because fear and anger are kept alive. Balance will be restored in the invisible world; that is what the ogham croabh promises."

No search for the killer; no honor price paid. Acceptance came hard, even for druids, but they bowed to the authority of the invisible world.

Yet each man felt an unseen presence at his back. Not that of the benign Irial, but a hideous haunting that defiled the sanctuary. A sickening realization moved through them. Only those who were druids would dare visit the sacred groves at night, so a druid must have raised his hand against Irial and struck him down in some fashion.

The shame was too great to reveal to any outside the order. If Irial wished the murder unrevenged in this world, it would be so; by common consent the druids would let it be assumed that Irial had died of an excess of seasons. But in the days to come the members of the order would look at one another with suspicion, feeling its poison permeate their rituals and their holy place.

In death, the chief druid commanded even more ritual than he had in life. As a son of the trees, he would not be entombed. His body was to be burned on a funeral pyre constructed of only sacred woods, and his ashes would be entrusted to the keeping of the wind.

Milesios was stunned by the occurrence. "I thought I would die first," he told Scotta, over and over again. "I thought the omen of the bull was meant for me, in fact. And I don't understand this—it wasn't like Irial to leave before he had all in readiness and a successor named."

"No, it wasn't," Scotta agreed. She was at least glad to see Milesios taking an interest. "But now you can forget about your own transition and get on with living, because whatever sacrifice was required has already been made."

Milesios, uncertain, went off by himself to think. He found it an effort to get his rusty mental equipment polished and usable again; living was obviously harder than dying. But the confusion the tribe felt as a result of the chief druid's death demanded that at least one strong hand remain to guide them, as Scotta was quick to remind him. Besides, the pains in his belly seemed to have diminished a trifle. And was it his imagination or was the ache in his joints also lessened? He certainly did not seem as nauseated as he had recently.

He ate a little broth from the pot and it stayed down. He took a flesh-fork from its hook and ripped a tiny morsel of meat from a shin bone in the cauldron and chewed the food slowly, surprised to find it tasted good.

Perhaps not good, but not bad, either. He was able to swallow it and eat more.

That night he did not fall at once into exhausted slumber but sat beside the hearth talking about the tribe's business with Scotta as they had done in so many past seasons.

"Irial's pyre will be lit at the next sunrise," Milesios said, "and I think we can expect representatives from every tribe in the region. It's amazing how fast news travels along the druid chain. There will be a big crowd and they will all come through our clanholdings, where they cannot help noticing our scrawny cattle. They will perceive us as impoverished . . . and *weak*. We have a serious problem there, Scotta. I should have done something about it sooner."

Scotta squeezed her hands together in her lap. Irial, she thought. From the next world, Irial has arranged with the spirits to send my husband back to me. Her throat burned with gratitude.

When the first light bleached the eastern sky the next morning, the crowd gathered to offer final honor to the most famous of chief druids. Champions and chieftains arrayed in mantles of mourning stood respectfully beside their chariots, their heads lower than that of the body waiting on the funeral pyre.

As the dead man was a druid, there would be no funeral gifts. Irial would go forward to his new life, whatever and wherever that might be, enriched not by manmade artifacts but with the immeasurably more valuable wisdom accrued in the life just concluded; a treasury only druids could transport through the transition called death. "Druids can remember between lives," was an axiom every mother taught her children. "All others are allowed to forget."

The great bard Amergin stood beside Irial's funeral pyre and recited the genealogy of the deceased, calling upon the spirits of his ancestors to be witness to the respect he had earned in this life. "He was a man of long head and keen eyes," Amergin sang in his eulogy, "a man who made himself see clearly even those things that are most painful to see. Irial could look through smoke and see flame; could look through clouds and see stars. Irial's special vision extended past the painted surfaces to the inner truth."

When the eulogy was completed Amergin stepped aside so the torchbearers could set the pyre ablaze. Its light carried far out over the sea, a rival for the rising sun.

As Milesios returned to his stronghold with the sound of Amergin's eulogy still ringing in his ears, he seemed to see with freshly opened eyes himself, as if the bard's words had somehow cleared his own vision. He was astonished at the number of people who crowded the area. So many children had been born in the long fat seasons of the Míl's lifetime; so many mouths to be fed.

His ears seemed to hear with restored vigor, catching snatches of conversations he formerly ignored. "Éremón is to blame," one clan-chief was saying to another, "for the destruction of our pastures. Éremón has turned the Mother against us."

"Are you blind?" Milesios demanded to know, rounding on the speaker. "The cattle who are destroying your fields are also going into your children's bellies to keep them from starving to death! If Éremón and his heroes had not brought back all that livestock from the land of the Astures, what would your clansmen eat? Food bought from traders with tin we no longer possess?"

The men shrank from their chieftain's anger. "I never personally blamed Éremón," the second one protested. "I just know that some are saying . . ."

"What 'some'? Where do these rumors start?" the Míl demanded to know.

The man waved his hand. "On the wind."

"Then consign them to the wind, don't pass them on." Milesios stalked away, glowering. Hearing an attack against any of his sons, the part of himself destined for the future, angered him. There were obviously divisions in the tribe, dangerous and growing.

Milesios had made an inward choice, without conscious volition, to retreat to some shadowy area where the world and its problems seemed unreal to him and the unwinnable challenge of aging could be sidestepped by sinking into illness instead. In this marginal area of misdirection he had been occupied and shielded—but life had refused to make it so easy for him, for the grizzled warrior. As always, life had continued on its own path and now he found himself awake once more and very far behind.

Within a few nights of Irial's death the Milesian clan was aware that their patriarch was taking a much more active interest in daily business. Amergin was one of the first to notice, and he felt a sense of relief when he thought of the savage, slashing satire he might have composed, bringing down a chieftain before his time. His vision of the strength remaining in Milesios had been accurate then; true guidance from the invisible world.

Colptha thought otherwise. He told Conmael, "Milesios is a used-up hulk with only one sputtering spark left in him.

Such sparks flare up but they die soon, as he must. He must! And then the tribe will need a new leader.''

"Donn?"

"Of course, Donn! And the sooner the better. Now that Irial is gone the entire order of druids must choose his successor among themselves, since Irial left him unnamed. They are uncertain and keep putting it off, but they cannot delay forever. If I can forestall them until Milesios—who would never use his influence in my behalf—is gone, I can see to it that Donn is chief of the tribe. And he will support me in turn as new chief druid.''

"How can you be sure?"

"Ah, Conmael; I have my ways. You, of all people, know that I have my ways. I was given gifts necessary to help me achieve power because my tribe needs me in these hard days.''

The sacrificer's eyes blazed with such passionate conviction that Conmael almost believed him; almost believed Colptha was unselfishly dedicated to the good of his people, in the druid tradition. Colptha's vision of his own destiny was compelling.

But that certainty was not a blanket Conmael could extend to cover and comfort himself. When he was not in Colptha's company he could see that he was nothing more than a tool, less important to Colptha than his sacrificial knife. The boy had allowed the druid to manipulate him—at first only in small ways, too petty to be refused—until obedience had become a habit and then a compulsion, forced on him by the sacrificer's whispered commands and irresistible eyes.

Now Conmael was helpless, knowing he had lost the precious ability to say no. Lost the one word that was the key to freedom.

His nights were spent in feverish wakefulness, holding himself rigid to keep from tossing and attracting Colptha's attention. His days were worse.

When he could bear it no longer, he wrapped himself in his warmest cloak and went to see his friend Sakkar, hoping to talk out the poison chewing his belly. He found the Phoenician building a new door for Amergin's house. Even in his own misery, Conmael noticed an improvement in the shipwright's damaged shoulder. The samodhii had driven probes through the skin, applied poultices and braces, and now Sakkar carried himself almost normally, though one arm was not yet as strong as the other.

Sakkar waved at Conmael with his good arm and beckoned the boy into the warmth of the bard's house. "My master is not here," he said, "but I welcome you in his name." Sakkar had learned Gaelician formalities and he enjoyed using them.

Conmael hesitated. "Sakkar," he began abruptly, "have you seen men killed? Have you ever . . . helped kill anyone? For what you believed at the time was a good reason?"

"Shipwrights are not warriors."

"I don't mean in a war."

Sakkar had a polite way of averting his eyes to avoid enlarging another person's embarrassment. "At sea, of course, one sees deaths frequently. And I . . . attacked a man once, though not at sea. If he had struggled I might have killed him."

Two red spots, like the hectic touch of fever, burned on Conmael's cheeks. "Would you have regretted it afterward?"

Sakkar considered. "I cannot say. At the time, nothing seemed as important as getting that man's purse. Later . . ."

"Yes," Conmael said miserably. "Later." Turning his back on warmth and shelter, he walked away, heading into the north wind.

Milesios called a meeting of the clan-chiefs and the council of elders. There were no female clan-chiefs at the moment, but many of the elders were women and Scotta took a place among them, radiating silent pride over her restored husband. When Ferdinón strode into the hall she scarcely glanced at him. His mustache seemed skimpy compared to the great drooping ornament of silver-gilt on the Míl's lip. Ferdinón's lisp sounded ineffectual contrasted with the Míl's deep voice.

"I have become aware," Milesios began, "of efforts behind my back to maneuver this or that person closer to the chieftain's bench, to take my place if I should fail. I hear you muttering but you need not try to deny it. I remind you that I am not yet in my tomb, and I tell you this: I will oppose, even beyond death, any man who tries to elevate himself by discrediting one of my sons!"

Donn squirmed in his compartment. He was uncomfortably aware that factions had formed and pressures were being applied. Only the day before he had said to Díl, "I'm really flattered, but I'm not so certain I want to lead the tribe, wife.

Such a complicated undertaking, so many considerations . . . all I ever truly wanted was to . . ."

"To stand as high in the Míl's affections as Éremón," Díl finished for him. "Ai, Donn." She had sighed and beckoned to him to put his head in her comfortable lap.

Now Milesios was continuing, "Some of you blame Éremón for our misfortunes. I agree that he is rash and hasty" (he cast a reproving glance at the ruddy warrior son he had thought most like himself), "but our problem is not just one of too many cattle. Our problem is too many people for the land to support."

"There can never be too many people!" a clan-chief cried out. "People are strength!"

An old woman rose from her seat among the elders. "In cities, where slave labor supports free folk, people are strength," she agreed, "but we have no desire for cities. We depend on the Earth Mother, and the druid Colptha says we have asked too much of her without repaying her by sufficient sacrifices. He reminds us that maintaining a good relationship with the Mother is the profession of druids."

"Providing for the tribe is the profession of *warriors,*" Ferdinón proclaimed. "If we have too many people and not enough land the answer is simple. We declare war on the nearest tribe with grassland and move into their territory. What about the Asturians?"

"I made a treaty with them not to invade for three generations," Éremón pointed out.

Milesios gave his son a cold look. That unauthorized arrangement had increased Éremón's prestige at the time, but in retrospect it seemed shortsighted. Éremón was too fond of making grand gestures.

"What about the land of the Artabrians?" Éber Finn suggested, unable to resist a dig at Éremón.

"We have an alliance there too," the warrior sighed.

"Or the Celtiberians, inland?"

"The drought also destroyed their grasslands. And they are very well armed."

No one had a solution. The discussion disintegrated into a free-for-all, one Gaelician after another making a suggestion only to have the flaw in it pointed out by someone else. When this day began with the last sunset no one had worried about overpopulation on exhausted land; now the problem sat in their center like a squamous toad, polluting the very air they breathed.

The meeting lasted until even the strongest men yawned constantly, but nothing was decided. The participants at last went home to worry beside their own hearthfires.

"Now I'm certain I have no desire to be chieftain," Donn confided to Díl over a late supper. "How can a man think clearly when everyone's yelling at him? But Milesios seems strong again; he's solved problems before and surely he'll find an answer for this one."

"It isn't one problem, but many," Díl said. "Nothing left to lure the Sea People; mud and flood and starving cattle; dissension among both men and women. And now the Míl says the trouble is too many people . . ."

"The trouble is my dinner," Donn muttered darkly, poking at his food with distaste. "Boiled beef. Oxbone broth. Calves' tongues in vinegar. Isn't there a stewed eel around here anywhere? Or a roasted seabird, anything? I'll eat cormorant eggs if you have them."

"We have to eat the cattle," Díl said firmly. "The Mother is pained by their starving cries."

"I swear by the moon! Once Milesios solves this problem for us I will never eat any more beef as long as I live!"

Éremón had become adept at finding ways to avoid his own house. After the meeting broke up in the Heroes' Hall he wandered to Amergin's house, peering around the doorpost as if he just happened to be passing by.

"Are you doing anything?" he asked innocently.

"Unfortunately, no," the bard replied. "Is the meeting over? I left early; they didn't seem to be getting anywhere, but now I don't seem to be accomplishing anything either. Come in and sit by the fire if you like. There's only driftwood on the hearth, but it burns warm and Sakkar and I have some wine you can share."

Éremón needed no more urging. He sprawled onto a bench and wiggled his cold toes closer to the hearth while he discussed the proceedings in the hall with Amergin.

"There has been some talk against you," Amergin told him. "I've heard it, but I paid no attention. There is always talk of one kind or another, most of it no more than blown air."

"It's more than talk," Éremón said. "At first I thought

252

Donn was actively trying to discredit me, but now I'm not so sure. Disloyalty just isn't like him.''

"No, it isn't. Who among us is guileful enough to try to turn us against each other?" He asked as a man does who has already decided on the answer.

Understanding dawned slowly in Éremón's eyes. "Colptha!"

"Yes."

"But why? I have no great fondness for him; the only one who will tolerate him is Donn and Donn will put up with anybody. But why would Colptha want to hurt me?"

"I can't answer that, but I feel certain he has found a way to further his own ambition by doing so. Colptha never did anything for anyone except himself; you can be certain this ploy to have Donn elected chieftain is not for love of Donn.''

The men stared at the fire in silence for a time. Éremón stretched his legs farther and sighed. "I wish I could think of some dazzling answer to our problems. Then I would be back in the Míl's good favor again; he's still angry with me, I can feel it. If I were his certain favorite again this move to support Donn would fade away and Colptha would be thwarted in whatever it is he's trying to do. As I have been thwarted lately," he added sourly.

"We do have problems," Amergin said, "but it is wrong to wish to solve them just to hurt someone else. When did you start hitting at your brothers in real anger, Éremón?"

When Éremón did not answer, Amergin turned his thoughts to the flames, watching islands of light appear in a crimson sea. A piece of wood collapsed in a shower of sparks and a brief golden forest bloomed above the coals. Sakkar moved closer to the hearth, stretching out his hands to warm them.

Calloused hands.

Shipwright's hands.

Amergin heard his own voice speaking as if from very far away, surprising all three of them.

"We could build ships and sail to a fertile new land," the bard said. "We could go to Ierne."

◇ **21** ◇

ERNE.

Amergin said the name aloud and the world as it existed within his familiar stone walls shrank; swelled, spun, spiraled outward in pulsating waves of radiance. Was concentrated in one breathless word symbolizing a universe of dreams.

The blood beneath Amergin's skin prickled and boiled.

"Ierne," he said.

And saw with wonder how the pattern had been formed, the great spirit of life catching the seemingly unrelated threads of Ítos and Ierne and Age-Nor and Sakkar and Éremón—and Amergin's aching, restless hunger—and weaving them all together, forcing this moment with irresistible purpose.

Ierne. The bard's mouth was dry as sand. The impossible had become possible because he said the word. Because he pulled it out of his own heart and gut and held it up for all to see.

Ierne. Green island of green wind, really out there, somewhere; waiting. Waiting for the bard to reach out and grasp it and claim it; promised to him in a thousand lonely nights and dreaming days.

He clamped himself around it with all his strength, willing myth into reality.

"We could go to Ierne," said Amergin.

His words went through Éremón like the blade of a dagger. "Ierne? Where's that?" the warrior demanded to know.

When Amergin answered, the passion throbbing in his clear voice captivated his listeners. He spoke of Ierne as other men speak of battle victories and women and strong sons. He spoke as a man speaks of limitless possibilities. "I will tell you the story old Ítos told me," he began, and Éremón and Sakkar leaned forward like small children, tense with anticipation.

He recounted Ítos' vision exactly as it had been given to

him, ever mindful of passing on another man's truth. And then he bent and shaped words with his bardic gift until he re-created the far homeland of his dreams, bringing to life the rounded hills and fern-shadowed glens, streams roiling with fish, meadows rolling with flowers. He gave them his truth for Ierne as it had built in silence within him long before he heard the name. As it had built in silence within him because it simply had to be there.

Éremón's fierce blue eyes glazed with pleasure as he listened. Even the most aggressive warrior honors the power of the poet; it is the Law. Even Sakkar, who had thought himself marvelously content where he was, began longing for the shores of Ierne as the bard's words constructed them.

"How do we get there?" Éremón asked eagerly.

Amergin's vision, which had been fixed on Ierne, suddenly wheeled within him and he had a vivid flashing memory of Age-Nor's face, with its guile and manipulation clearly drawn.

Though he had been fascinated when Age-Nor told him of Ierne, the bard had also felt a growing, uncomfortable suspicion: the cunning Tyrian would do nothing without selfish purpose. The druid had seen deeply into the merchant, and knew him.

Still . . . Age-Nor was gone, and whatever he hoped to gain could scarcely be realized now. Ierne, however, was still out there, beyond the ninth wave, waiting.

"Sakkar knows how to build the kind of ships that could carry us there," Amergin said.

Éremón's head swiveled and he fixed Sakkar with a look of commanding interest. "Is that true?"

"The bard always speaks truth!" Sakkar replied, surprised to hear him scold a warrior as if they were equals. But this was a night of surprises, and Sakkar's newfound audacity was not the least of them. "I am a trained shipwright," he went on to explain. "I know how each plank must be laid and every joint caulked. I can design ships; I have built enough of them. And . . ." He jumped up and ran to a carved chest Amergin had given him to store his growing assortment of personal possessions, gifts given him by Milesians for whom he had been doing small jobs of woodworking as his shoulder mended.

He returned carrying a tightly rolled sct of sea charts, wrapped in oilskins. "Commander Age-Nor gave me these as a parting present," he told the two Gaelicians as he carefully

255

removed the charts from their packaging. "I thought it was most peculiar at the time, for what master gives presents to a bondsman he is disposing of? But he said he had no further use for them and was most insistent that I take them. These maps show the waters from here to the Pretanic Islands."

Amergin's suspicion flared again. "Was most insistent?" Had Age-Nor baited a trap and even left them maps leading to it?

But to what purpose? And even if that were so, what difference did it make, balanced against the radiant possibility of reaching Ierne?

Still he hesitated for one more heartbeat, imagining time were as fluid as Irial had taught; imagining he could move backward and unsay the words, keep Ierne for himself alone, glowing in his heart, uninvaded, unsullied, unproven.

Then he grabbed the charts from Sakkar's hands and spread them out on the floor in the firelight. Two dark heads and one golden one bent over them. Ierne. Real, and on maps!

"Look at this, Éremón," Amergin said. "I have no knowledge of sea charts, but isn't this the shape of our own coast? It seems to me we could sail right along the edge of the land for most of the way to . . . what is this, here, Sakkar?"

The shipwright squinted. "The Pretanic Islands. And yes, there are only two serious stretches of open sea if you follow the route along the rim of this vast bay to the north of us."

"If you follow?" Éremón laughed. "You mean, if *we* follow! You will be building the ships for us and going with us, Sakkar; we have no one else who knows the sea."

Beneath his olive skin, Sakkar's blood receded from his face. The enormity of the idea began to seep into the marrow of his bones. These men were talking as if he, alone, could take them to Ierne. *Would* take them to Ierne!

"Master, I . . . you cannot mean this seriously . . ." Sakkar held out his hands to Amergin. "The dangers are enormous, particularly for landmen. It takes years to learn to sail ships, you would have to . . ."

"Nonsense," snorted Éremón. "We can do anything anyone else has ever been able to do, and probably do it better. You won't discourage us that easily. And if you can design the vessels and supervise the construction, we have plenty of trained craftsmen who can build ships for us. The samodhii seem to be healing your shoulder, I can see that from here, so I expect you could do some hard labor yourself in time." He turned toward his brother. "Think of it, Amergin! Ore and timberland and deep green pastures, you said." His voice thickened with desire.

Truth demanded the bard remind his brother, "Age-Nor said something about a small population of natives . . ."

"Natives! We don't have any agreements with them, do we? No fosterings or intermarriages, no alliances to honor? So what are the natives of Ierne to us? We are mighty warriors, they will stand no chance against us." His enthusiasm was galloping faster and faster, like a runaway horse. "A fertile new land and a fresh start, Amergin." His eyes gleamed hotly as the most persuasive reason of all occurred to him. "Milesios has sworn me to keep my hands off Taya *as long as I live in his clanhold,* but if I led the expedition to Ierne I would have a clanhold of my own! Milesios is too old to make such a journey, but I . . . Yes! My own clanhold with my own new house and my own new woman in it!"

Amergin chuckled in spite of himself. Given the seed of an idea Éremón could grow the whole tree instantly and taste the juice from its fruit running down his throat. His headlong recklessness was necessary; it would propel them northward against all odds.

And the bard must go northward. For him as for Éremón, the future now existed as reality. "You're not talking about an expedition, but a colony," he said aloud. "We'll colonize Ierne!"

"Yes! Taking many of our tribe to a fertile new land is the answer to so many of our problems. It's the answer we've all been searching for, and we must go to Milesios right away and tell him of it. If I give Ierne to the tribe, who can deny me the chiefdom there?"

Amergin stood up abruptly, a muscle knotting in his jaw. "Ierne isn't *yours* to offer," he said, his voice hardened with controlled anger. He already saw the ugly shape of the rivalry that would build between himself and the warrior and knew it was the price to be paid for Ierne.

Part of the price.

"Of course, of course," Éremón laughed with great good humor. "I'll give you full credit, don't worry. But let's go see Milesios right now." He too was on his feet, hurrying toward the door.

The bard's long strides caught up with him and carried Amergin out before him.

257

* * *

Milesios had already fallen asleep. He lay with mouth agape, snoring an old man's snores. Scotta was reluctant to disturb him but Amergin and Éremón were insistent.

"Your sons say they must talk with you, now!" she yelled in her husband's ear. "They say it is urgent."

Milesios dragged himself back from some sodden swamp, some deep dank pit he had to crawl out of, hand over hand, until at last he opened his eyes and saw his sons watching him.

At first he did not recognize them.

Scotta brought the seven-colored cloak of chiefdom and wrapped it around his shoulders, talking briskly to him all the while until he could fix his attention on her words and understand. Then he looked beyond her to Éremón and Amergin, and nodded a greeting. "This had better be very important," he warned, yawning.

They told him, Éremón rushing in first with a torrent of words. The Míl hitched his cloak around his body and tried to make sense of what Éremón was saying, but at last he silenced the warrior with an impatient gesture. "You tell me, Amergin," he commanded. "You're not hoarse and you don't babble."

Amergin obeyed. Several times Éremón tried to interrupt him but the bard raised his voice to its full thundering power and overrode him. Not this time, brother, he thought. You will not grab what is mine.

He described Ierne for Milesios as he had described the island for Éremón and Sakkar, with all the music implicit in language. The words forced the dream to fill the room, glowing; the land he had whispered of only to Clarsah. His land, the bard's land.

Ierne.

Milesios heard him through, then said, "I have heard of Ierne before. Traders talked of it still, when I was very young, though I have not heard it mentioned for many seasons now.

"You have given me much to think about. When I lay down to sleep a while ago the future was like an enemy who had all the weapons, but it seems more promising now. Go away and let me think on this."

Shortly after midday the citharadagh pipers summoned a

second meeting of clan-chiefs, elders, and the sons of the Míl. Before the moon had changed the news was spread throughout Gaelician territory. For the first time in generations the tribe would be on the move again, not in wagons and chariots but in *ships*, daring the dark sea. An adventure beyond all imagining.

"And it is my idea," Éremón insisted on telling everyone; already remembering it that way.

"I did not expect the need to arise within my lifetime," Milesios told his followers, "but our tribe has become a great river that must fork or wash away all before it. We will therefore send half the tribe to seek out new land on Ierne, a force large enough to assure conquest and colonization of a sparsely peopled island. The remainder of our tribe will stay here, where the Mother has adequate strength to support their reduced number."

The Gaelicians heard this pronouncement with a variety of emotions. "Who will go? Who will stay?" was on everyone's lips. The idea of a sea voyage into the unknown terrified many who did not dare say so aloud because they were more frightened of the ridicule of their fellows. What Celt could admit to cowardice?

"Who will stay? Who must go? How long before we have to decide?"

Ierne.

"Timber and ores, it is said. Gold in the streams and rivers, flowing like water no doubt. We can run huge herds on the limitless grass . . ." enthused the eager.

"Who says the grass is limitless?" asked the more prudent.

"The bard," Éremón answered, suddenly remembering Amergin's involvement in all this, though remembering it as a lesser role than his own. "Get the bard to tell you about Ierne."

They came to Amergin with uncertainty carved into the lines of their faces, and he gathered them in a circle around him while he sang of lush lakelands and silver-reeded rivers. And they left him reassured, already adopting Ierne as a dream of their own.

It was too large a dream to realize without help, Amergin understood. The energy, the skills, the courage of many people would be needed if any one of them was to reach Ierne; it was not a vision he could hug to his breast in solitude any longer. So he looked deep into each man and woman and

259

found the secret longings hidden there, then clothed them in words and brought them to life, embodied in Ierne.

And the Gaelicians clamored for the unknown island.

"Who will go? Who must stay? How soon can we depart?"

"We will choose the clans by lot when the time comes," Milesios decreed. "The druids will tell us when the auspices are best."

"But there is still no chief druid," the clan-chief Caicher complained. "How can we look to them for guidance?"

"Sakkar says it will take a long time to train craftsmen and assemble materials, and longer still to build the ships," Milesios replied. "By the time we are ready to select the clans, there will undoubtedly be a new chief druid."

Undoubtedly Colptha, the sacrificer promised himself. Someone who knows the true faces of the spirit world; someone who knows that the stones of sacrifice thirst for blood to drink. "I should be chief of the order right now," he raged to Conmael. "This is the opportunity I was born for."

But the druids were in no hurry to name Irial's successor. They were watching one another out of the corners of their eyes and more than one of them performed certain rituals in secret, petitioning the spirits to divulge the name of Irial's killer.

The answer was no. No informative visions were forthcoming. Human vengeance was not requested.

And though the entire order had been made well aware of Colptha's qualifications ("I was the only one to be warned of the disaster of the cattle!"), still no one proposed his name as the next chief druid.

The sacrificer redoubled his efforts to promote an increasingly reluctant Donn as the Míl's own successor, until even Milesios lashed out at him, "I am not dead yet, druid! Keep to the spirits and leave tribal affairs to me."

Tribal affairs had grown both more challenging and more complex, and Milesios was—secretly—unsure of his own strength to deal with the coming adventure. Éremón must constantly be watched and reined in, and the Míl had come to see Amergin as an unexpected ally, particularly when new waves of hesitation swept over the tribe.

"There is no question but that we must follow where the pattern has led us, and send many of our people to Ierne," the chieftain told Amergin. "They lean forward like horses awaiting the start of a chariot race, but then they fall back and

260

leave slack in their breastplates. This is a great thing we are asking of them, a march across the trackless sea, and as the time grows nearer they may cling more and more resolutely to the Earth Mother.

"I have heard the power in your words, bard, and I know that you and only you can unclench the Gaelicians from this land and send them outward. I bid you do it."

This was the closest that Amergin would ever come to approval and commendation from Milesios, and he knew it; he stood with bowed head for a moment, absorbing it, trying to make it be enough.

With Clarsah in his hands he drove and strode across the entire territory, singing of Ierne, reciting poetry that did not, perhaps, have basis in any reality except his own heart's truth—but it was enough.

Where Amergin passed, voices were raised in a continual, swelling roar: Ierne, they cried.

Ierne!

A drumbeat across the land. A signal fire from high ground to high ground, diminishing distance.

Another voice still sang to Amergin on the wind, in his few private moments, but now he could answer—I am coming.

But there were nights when the bravery inspired by the bard's poetry dwindled into bravado, and then faded away altogether, to be replaced by the inevitable uncertainty and fear.

Amergin was as susceptible to it as anyone else. More than once he lay in his bed in the darkness and was chilled by reality. No one in all the Gaelician territory had ever sailed to the Pretanic Islands; even Sakkar had not made the voyage himself, all his information came from others who claimed to have done so, and from maps and charts that could be badly drawn or totally spurious. The act of faith required to believe in such a possibility was almost beyond imagining, itself.

Yet they were imagining it. They were preparing to attempt it. In boats that might not be seaworthy—how could anyone know, until lives were risked on the water? Would they be attacked by the Sea People once they ventured off solid earth? Would the ocean last, or become a waterfall cascading off the rim of the world and plunging them all into some terrible dark gulf from which no one ever returned?

Terror quivered in the night, when their stock of courage was lowest.

The Gaelicians lay in the darkness and thought these things, or whispered them softly to husband or wife on the pillow. Hearts raced, hands clutched at each other, desperate for reality and certainty.

But in the morning, when the soft green wind summoned Amergin again, he got up and slung Clarsah from his shoulder and set out to sing to his people of Ierne, refusing to let fear overcome his dream. And the phrases he shaped rang through the land, their beauty more compelling than the fear a Celt would not admit aloud, in daylight.

It might all be a trick; it might all be an illusion. But all life was an illusion and death and rebirth were certain anyway. So one might as well reach out to the dream, and dare.

As he had fought his shyness and self-doubt, Amergin now fought back his anxieties and reached hungrily for Ierne.

His brothers were also scorched by the mounting fever of excitement. Éber Finn no longer planned to contest with Éremón for the Míl's bench and belt and Gaelician clanholdings; the familiar honors of his homeland seemed shabby in comparison to the riches Amergin had furnished to his imagination.

While the bard told of Ierne in the Heroes' Hall, Éber sat in his compartment, but only his body was present. His unfocused eyes gazed through granite walls to a place all his own, the Heroes' Hall of Éber Finn on the island of Ierne.

On Ierne, his door would be stouter than the Míl's, and carved from some massive oak that fed its roots in earth laced with gold. Bright coverings would hang from his walls and his roof pillars would be inlaid with pure copper. Great hounds would lounge at his feet, lifting their heads with negligent grace to lick his fingers. His father's hounds were old and surly and crawling with vermin, but there would be no vermin on his island; in his hall.

His women would wear gold taken from his own earth and fashioned by craftsmen sworn to him, not perverted by Hellene influences. Scotta would have new jewelry from his hand; a broad gold lunula to wear around her neck like a polished moon, the gift of her loving son. His cattle would grow sleek on grasslands reputed to stay green even in winter. There would be enough timber to build houses; warm dwellings not chilled by damp stone walls. Éber leaned back and closed his eyes, smiling.

In his adjacent compartment Éremón dreamed similar dreams, their shape subtly changed by the pattern of his own personality. He, too, saw himself as a chieftain in a mighty hall—but his hall was less luxurious than Éber's. It was a gathering place for warriors, with shields hung on its walls, and a dark-haired, submissive woman tended its hearth.

Éremón's children would learn new traditions that he himself would establish. There would be more hospitality offered to one's friends for the sheer pleasure of it, and no female voice would complain when the heroes stayed up all night together, drinking wine and celebrating life. Exuberant wars would give every man the opportunity to measure himself against another and grow stronger—with Éremón the strongest among them. "I will be the leap over Milesios," he promised himself, not realizing he spoke aloud.

But Amergin heard him in passing and stopped by his stall. "What did you say?"

Éremón imagined his brother superimposed over a battlefield ringing with the brazen voice of trumpets. "I said Ierne will be sword land," he replied, with trumpets still in his voice. "Hero land! No strong man will fret away with boredom there. We will hunt the boar and the stag for days without end, and we will set a new style for courage. My people will be splendid in battle and generous in victory, Amergin; we will grow stronger sons than ever and our daughters will be as charming as Taya. Everything will be perfect on Ierne."

"Sword land," the bard said in a cool voice. "Is that all you think about?"

"I am a man! My purpose is to acquire for my tribe, to protect them and add to their prestige."

"You share the same purpose we all have, Éremón. We exist to praise the great spirit of life and find beauty in all its manifestations."

"That's druid talk. You find beauty in poetry; I find it in swords and chariots. And who's to say your choice is better than mine? Don't frown at me like that, Amergin. Hear this: I promise you we will have plenty of poetry on Ierne. Great warriors always need bards to immortalize their victories, and you will have an honored place in my hall." He spoke easily, giving away nothing that mattered. In his enthusiasm Éremón overlooked the quick angry glitter in Amergin's eyes.

He did not miss seeing Éber Finn, however, who had left his compartment and was now swaggering around the hall in a new mantle dyed with five colors and bordered with Celtic

263

knotwork. He paraded in front of the women's balcony, stroking his mustache and exchanging outrageous flattery with a handful of females at once. All seemed to be having a wonderful time.

Éremón heard an echo of Colptha's apparently casual remark the day before: "Éber Finn drives often to the clanhold of Ítos. Perhaps he's thinking of yet another wife."

Éremón turned quickly to Amergin. "There used to be talk about you and Lugaid's daughter. Do you ever visit her?"

Amergin kept his face carefully closed. "I wasn't aware you had relinquished your claim on her. Besides, I am far too busy right now to go hunting women."

"Ai!" Éremón grinned, relaxing a little. "You, at least, still honor my claim to Taya, then. I'm glad to know that of you, Amergin. Very glad."

"The honor of a bard is at least as great as that of a warrior," Amergin said with a sarcasm that flew unnoticed past Éremón, whose mind was already galloping down a new path.

He said eagerly, leaning forward to fix Amergin's attention, "I need you to do something for me. Something a man can ask only of a trusted clansman. You have a polished and persuasive tongue; I have only a ruin of a voice and the clumsy words men speak to one another on a battlefield. Will you go for me to Taya and assure her that I still mean to have her as my wife? Tell her there is a way for us, I can make it happen, but she must wait for me. She must accept no other offer in the meantime."

He shot a meaningful glance toward Éber Finn, who had lured one of Étan's sisters into hanging halfway over the balcony railing and was addressing fulsome compliments to her throat and bosom. The woman's delighted laughter rang through the hall and Éremón scowled.

Amergin hoisted Clarsah onto his shoulder. "I don't want to get involved with you and your women," he said.

"Please, Amergin," replied Éremón, who never pleaded with anyone, for anything. "You're my brother, who else can I ask?"

Only a fool would put himself in such a position, Amergin thought. But we need each other now, if we are to reach Ierne. I must not allow a breach to develop between us.

"Brother?" Éremón repeated hopefully.

*   *   *

Dawn found Amergin at the clanhold of Ítos. Taya met him outside Lugaid's house and the bard thought he detected a new dignity in her, a measure of inner strength that lowered her voice and lifted her round little chin. Amid the bright thunder of the Gaelicians, Taya was a cool and shadowed serenity.

And a friend, dearer than a bedmate. He did not want to see her hurt.

"Since Éremón is forbidden to see you he has asked me to speak for him," Amergin explained. "One reason for his great eagerness to go to Ierne is because he means to take you with him as his wife. He wants to be certain you are aware of this and will wait for him." A nice, formal little speech, perfectly fulfilling Éremón's requirements. While he said it, Amergin kept his eyes on the horizon and away from Taya's face.

"I thought the clans for Ierne would be decided by lot," she said. "How can Éremón be so certain of going?"

"As long as Milesios is head of the tribe, if his sons want to be on the ships to Ierne, I assure you they will be."

Taya drew a deep, slow breath. With one hand, she rubbed the fabric of her blue woolen tunic, a warm winter overgarment covering the customary long gown. "Is Ierne cold in the winter?" she wondered aloud. "We sail north—does that mean we will need heavier clothes than these?"

Her words surprised him. "You'll wait for Éremón?"

"Did you think I wouldn't?"

"I never thought of you as . . . as adventurous," he said lamely.

Taya laughed. "I'm not. When other girls went to the training ground I hid so they couldn't find me, then played house quite happily with little toys the craftsmen made me. But if Éremón wants me in Ierne, I will go."

The day was raw and bitter. Clouds pregnant with sleet were gathering over the headland. Amergin felt suddenly desolate, reserving this warm and generous woman for someone who already had a wife to tend his hearthfires and children to remember his name.

It was not in him to betray a brother, but neither was it in him to omit a warning to a friend. Honor allowed both, he thought. Choosing his words carefully among all the possible disloyalties, he said, "Be certain you know what you're doing, Taya. Éremón is a hunter by nature and inclination."

"You're trying to tell me the chase is more important to him than the capture? I know that already, Amergin."

"Then why . . ." he began, and stopped.

She gave him an opaque look. "Even a druid can never know all a woman's secrets," she said. "There comes a time when a woman must reach out or start to shrink away. When I reached, Éremón took my hand. It's as simple as that."

"Nothing is ever that simple," Amergin replied, looking into himself.

Taya studied his face. Deep lines were etched in it like crevices in stone, framing a guarded expression the bard never seemed to set aside. "Ai, Amergin," she said, tracing the peak of his eyebrow with one finger, daring to touch the sacred head of another human because she was now desired and claimed, sure of her place, a person of status. "You worry about me so I will worry about you," she told the bard. "Who will warm your bed and tend your hearth when we get to Éremón's island?"

"It isn't Éremón's island!" he cried. The sudden passion in his voice made her hand fall from his face as if his skin were on fire. "If Ierne belongs to anyone," Amergin proclaimed, "she is mine. *Bard land*, not sword land. Éremón has you, but the harp will claim Ierne!"

Taya was staring at him with shock and sympathy. "Ai, Amergin, you care too much," she said. "But it is in our blood, I think."

The bard's blue eyes were very dark behind the coarse hedge of their black lashes. "Yes," he replied, his voice little more than a whisper. "It is in our blood."

When he returned to the Míl's clanhold Éremón came running to meet his chariot. "What did Taya say? Will she wait for me?"

Amergin busied himself with unharnessing the team, waving away a horseboy who hurried to help. "She'll wait," he said in clipped syllables. "Lugaid is hungry for bride gifts, but Taya gave her word she will refuse every man until we are ready to go to Ierne. And as you suggested, she will never mention you in her refusals."

"Why give Odba cause to be suspicious of anything?" Éremón remarked. "I'm planning this campaign carefully,

Amergin, and I'm glad I can count on you. I've always been a remarkably good judge of men."

"I hope you appreciate Taya."

"Of course I do."

"You appreciated Odba until you got used to her," Amergin reminded his brother.

"That's different. I know what a choice find Taya is." A sly expression, quite unfamiliar to Éremón's face, flitted briefly across it, almost as if Colptha peeped for a moment through his eyes. "Tell me, Amergin—man to man. Are you certain you didn't allow yourself the pleasure of . . . ah . . . touching Taya, while you were alone with her? I could hardly blame you . . ."

"Your trust has become a very fragile thread," the bard said in a voice as deep and cold as the earth. "One moment you call me brother, the next moment you doubt me. We were not raised like that, Éremón. What's happened to you?"

"I . . . I honestly don't know," Éremón replied, sounding perplexed.

Amergin turned his back on his brother and began reharnessing his team in a silence so heavy it pushed his brother away. The warrior mumbled thanks or farewell or some other trivial comment and went off to find more congenial companions, leaving the bard alone.

How easy it would be, Amergin thought, to get into his chariot and drive to Ferdinón's clanhold. That had been his first intention when he began reharnessing the team. Scéna would forgive him his neglect; he could see her being as firm with him as a mother hound to a wandering puppy, pawing and licking him into the shape she thought proper. She would accept his fever and cool it in her flesh, giving him a brief relief from the forces that drove him. Silencing the voices that called him on the wind.

But he would awake, he knew, to inevitable disappointment, with the taste of ashes in his mouth.

He could go to her anyway; he was in the chariot now, the reins in his hands, wheeling the horses toward the gate of the stronghold. He could go to Scéna with bride gifts and set out on the sea with a woman of his own at his side, like his warrior brothers. What did it matter if the pattern of her thinking did not fit the pattern of his? Scéna Dullsaine was full-bodied and fertile; she could survive a sea voyage and bear strong children on Ierne. Perhaps one of them would be a gentle, dreamy boy with the poet's gift . . .

He did not take the road toward Ferdinón's clanhold as soon as he got out of the gate. Instead, stalling for time in his own mind, Amergin drove out along the headland as he so often did, gazing toward the sea. Imagining a verdant island over the rim of the world, floating in a nimbus of light.

His land. His dream. Not that of Ítos, nor of Éremón, either; not a land of sword and spear, but bard land, filled with poetry and music, with time for learning and time for the laughter that surely lurked somewhere inside himself, waiting for release.

Bard land, gracious and prosperous. Bard land, where people would bloom like flowers . . . the poet's fancy rambled on, and the horses picked their way along the edge of the cliff unguided.

A peculiar sound made them prick their ears and swerve from the path. Amergin caught at the reins, listening. It came again—a moan, perhaps? A groan of pain? He could not be sure. He halted the team and listened carefully.

A very human sound of anguish floated up to him from the beach below the cliffs.

Amergin sprang from his chariot and peered over the edge of the cliff. The day was older than he had realized, already shading into the ice-blue light of a winter evening. He would not have gone to Scéna so late in the day anyway, such a long drive . . .

And then Scéna vanished from his thoughts altogether. He saw a pale figure sprawled on the rocks below, moving with the convulsive jerking motions of an injured animal. But it was no animal.

Amergin flung himself over the edge and slithered and slid down the cliff face, not bothering to search out a safe pathway. He reached a narrow strip of beach studded by irregular boulders. A boy lay draped across one of these boulders, his arms awkwardly bent, his head lolling. He made one more effort to rise and then fell back, groaning. Amergin scrambled over the rocks to reach him.

"Conmael, is that you?" He crouched beside the boy and saw that the blood which had run from mouth and nose was crusty, dry. He had been here a long time, then. The increasingly bitter cold of approaching evening had roused him at last, setting him amoan with agony. Amergin swept wet hair back from the youth's pallid face. The breakers crashing against the shore would soon come high enough to carry his body away altogether.

Conmael shuddered and opened his eyes. A wet glisten of fresh blood threaded out the corner of his mouth and down his jaw.

"I'll get you to the stronghold and summon healers," Amergin promised, but when he tried to lift the boy Conmael shrieked with such anguish the bard almost dropped him. He set Conmael down as carefully as he could and crouched beside him, wondering what to do.

The mist of pain cleared briefly and Conmael recognized Amergin bending over him. He lifted one hand as if to point upward and tried to say something, but his words were lost in a great choking sob. His eyes closed and his head bobbled loosely on his neck.

"No!" Amergin cried. "This is no way to die, lad; listen to me! Open your eyes!" Then he looked from Conmael to the cliff above, following the boy's aborted gesture. From the headland a person would have to be hurled far outward to strike the rocks at the edge of the surf. Such a fall could not be accidental.

"Were you thrown, Conmael?" Amergin asked, and thought he detected a faint negative shake of the head. Perhaps. Perhaps not. "Did you jump?" he asked next. But Conmael was forever beyond answering.

Amergin had to carry the uninhabited body far down the beach before he found a way to get back up the cliff with his burden. When he reached the top his chariot was gone. In his excitement he had forgotten to tether the horses and they had already returned to the stronghold, anxious to be unharnessed and fed.

The bard had a long and lonely walk through the twilight, carrying ruined youth in his arms.

◇ **22** ◇

COLPTHA MOURNED THE DEATH of his foster son with extravagant ceremony, filling the tomb with funeral gifts and bestowing still more on Gosten's clan, until he far exceeded the dead boy's honor price. But then for a time he failed to attend rituals in the nemeton; he neglected to come to the Heroes' Hall for feasts.

"Is it possible our brother grieves?" Éber Finn asked Amergin. "I would not have thought him capable of it."

"I suspect we do not know just what Colptha is capable of," Amergin replied carefully. "But I mean to find out. He is part of us."

Gosten was upset about the loss of his son. "I cannot imagine him just jumping off a cliff!" he said to anyone who would listen.

"Perhaps he was clumsy, and fell," someone suggested.

"Perhaps he was moon sick, like Ír, and thought he could fly," said another.

"Do you believe that, Amergin?" Gosten wanted to know.

"No," the bard replied.

Only Sakkar offered a clue about Conmael's death, but it was a small one, an obscure signpost buried in the boy's own character and marked only by a curious turn of phrase; a clue found in words by a bard who paid very close attention to words.

"Conmael was unhappy, no matter what the sacrificer claims," Sakkar told Amergin. "Several times he started to talk to me about it and then drew back. Once he said he had brought a dishonor on himself he would not outlive in nine lives."

"What dishonor could a half-grown boy commit?"

Sakkar studied his fingernails. "I do not know. It was his private grief. But he reminded me of a trapped animal, like the ones vendors sell in cages in Tyre to be used as sacrifices. Some of those caged animals are human."

Amergin shuddered. "You knew Conmael," he said.

"Yes, master."

"How many times must I remind you that I am not your master? None of my tribe acknowledges another as master; we each contain the same share of the great spirit. But to get back to Conmael—would he have killed himself for any reason, do you think?"

Sakkar picked up a small wooden ship, a careful replica of a Phoenician forty-oared galley. "I began this to give your carpenters a pattern," he explained, "because teaching meant for the hands enters most easily through the eyes. Conmael watched me for a time, then begged to be taught how to do it. He proved more skilled than I at putting together all these little pieces and he was so proud of his accomplishment. But it is not yet finished, as you can see.

"As a craftsman myself, I know this: Conmael would not have deliberately leaped out of life before the project was completed."

"Leaped out of life . . . ." Amergin mused. "Yes. He had no abrasions from rolling down the slope. Only his bones were injured, broken to pieces in the sack of his skin. And I found him lying almost two spear lengths beyond the over-hang of the cliff. Yet you are right, he would not have sought transition before this little ship was finished, for I can see for myself the love and care he was putting into it."

"When the galley was finished we planned to make a prototype of the smaller boats, which will be much more numerous. Hide-covered boats I am designing myself, some-what based on a variety of Egyptian vessel. There is much more leather in this territory than timber. Conmael would have worked on those, too," Sakkar said sadly. "I was counting on him."

"We must all rely on one another if we are to get to Ierne," Amergin said. "A man alone could not make it, I think. It is a task for a tribe."

A tribe, thought Sakkar the shipwright. A whole tribe working together, looking out for each other. And I am . . . almost . . . part of it. A tribe with no masters.

Having committed themselves to the course, the Gaelicians labored unstintingly. While Amergin worked on his epic and puzzled over the death of Conmael, both warriors and freemen were scouring the region for timber and enlarging their tanning pits to treat countless hides. Soon the stench of curing leather hung on the cold winter air like a nauseating pall.

At the Imbolc festival that celebrated the lactating of the ewes Milesios requested the druid measurers to take a head count of the tribe, but put off having the clans draw lots to determine who would go, in spite of constant pressure to do so. He told Scotta, "As long as the outcome is not certain, every man expects to have a place in a boat and therefore works on the boats to his best ability. There are always a few feckless ones who might grow careless if they did not expect to profit personally from their labors."

"Everyone will benefit," Scotta said. "Those who stay behind will have twice as much land and most of the adult livestock, for Éber Finn has pointed out we must take only the youngest, smallest animals in order to save room. Calves and colts, lambs, weanlings."

"We, Scotta?" Milesios laughed.

"Of course we're going! Do you intend to miss this opportunity now that you're yourself again? As for me, I must go with my children because they will never do anything properly if left to themselves."

She radiated the blazing energy that pulsed through the entire tribe. Excitement was a leaping flame and the Gaelicians were consumed by it; hot and hungry.

Only Milesios held back, but he did not want the others to see this. As quickly as his vigor returned it had begun to ebb away again, leaving him feeling older and wearier than ever. He had set so much in motion, but now, contemplating it, he was horrified at the thought of having to take part.

He just wanted to lie down and go to sleep.

And then one morning he did not get up at all.

Scotta rose as usual in the half-light before dawn to awaken the fire and bring some of yesterday's bread from the bakehouse for the morning's meal. She bustled around in the quiet, enjoying a sense of being the only person in a private universe. Milesios lay with his back toward her, not even snoring for a change. Nothing disturbed the silence except the clucks and rustlings of the domestic fowl in their boxes.

Too much silence.

Just before the fire found its voice and began to crackle Scotta cocked her head, listening intently. She heard the wind beyond the door and a herder calling to his wife, but nothing else.

No sound from Milesios at all.

She felt a strange disinclination to approach him. The distance between her hearth and his bedbox was a journey across worlds. Twice she started toward him; twice she stopped. She deliberately struck an iron flesh fork against a copper pot and made the metal clang but her husband neither twitched nor snorted.

I am being foolish, she said to herself. I will get back into bed beside him and pull the covers over my head, and after a little more sleep we will awake together as we have for so many seasons.

She took her nerve in both hands and got into the bed, willing the future to be as she expected it. She was a brave woman, but never so brave as at this moment. She settled herself in the nest she had left, a nest now chill because the Míl's body had not kept it warm. She turned her back to his, not touching, and lay there with wide eyes, staring across the room.

I am asleep. I will wake up soon.

The wind blew harder and she heard a cart go rumbling by, close to her door. The clan was awake and at work.

The chief and his wife must be awake, too.

She got up very slowly and reached behind herself to touch the Míl's shoulder. She did not look around at him. His skin felt unfamiliar to her fingers.

There was no life in it.

Scotta dropped her head and closed her eyes, her hand still on him.

"You have gone down your new road without me after all," she said at last into the terrible silence.

She sat and Milesios lay beside her. Her heart beat, her lungs expanded and emptied, and his did not. A large spider emerged from the thatch and made its way down the roof pillar, crawling purposefully toward some spiderish goal. The motion caught Scotta's eye and she watched as if there were nothing else in the world to see. Nothing else in the world to do.

She had outlived and helped bury the Míl's other women; she had raised children for him and honored him and always considered herself the indispensable half of a team. Now there was no team. One horse alone does not pull a chariot.

"This is the pit at the bottom of my life," she said aloud to the spider. "Nothing will ever be worse than this."

273

Some part of her brain took comfort from the words.

Éber, coming to get his mother to settle some petty dispute between his women, found the Míl and his wife together in their silence. Éber stripped off his cloak and wrapped it and his arms around Scotta, who was trembling. But her eyes were dry.

"He must have a splendid tomb," was all she said. "He was the champion."

Sleet drummed on the roof; beads from a broken string.

Winter was death's season.

The tomb of Milesios was indeed fitting for a chieftain and a champion. His untenanted body was placed on a bronze bed made in the form of a high-backed bench, supported by eight metal figures of women balanced acrobatically over functional wheels of iron and bronze. The smiths of the Gaelicians outdid themselves in their final, elegant tribute to a great man.

And as the tomb was about to be sealed, Éremón caught one last glimpse of his father looking almost as he had in life, the splendid belt of the champion fastened around his waist for all eternity. "Now we will never contest for it," Éremón said regretfully.

Éber Finn frowned at him. "That belt belongs with the Míl; it was his highest honor."

"Would you not like to have fought me for it?"

Éber considered the question gravely. "No," he said at last.

"That was a mistake," Colptha said to him under his breath. "You could have defeated Éremón; you could have had that belt for yourself."

Colptha in his misery longed to see unhappiness on every other face as well. He did indeed grieve for Conmael; his nightmares were haunted with images of Conmael smashed on the rocks. The bloody rocks. The thirsty Earth Mother, drinking, taking at last the sacrifice she had cried for with her open and gaping mouth.

Now he saw the true meaning of that earlier vision. It was not rain the Mother demanded.

He had tried, once, to warn his people, and they had turned their backs on him and refused to listen. Irial had forced him to keep silent. But Irial could not silence him now, now that

274

he truly understood. Now that the Earth Mother had truly revealed herself to him alone by taking Conmael from him in even exchange for the gift of divine wisdom.

His people had underestimated him. Very well. What others thought and felt did not matter to him anymore, because there was no one left alive who mattered to him. Colptha saw himself as alone in the world and with terrible bravado, he laughed. Coldly, darkly, inside himself, the sacrificer laughed.

He no longer had Conmael to send through the tribe, carrying rumors and dropping hints, so he redoubled his own efforts to encourage the election of Donn as chief of the tribe before the druids finally selected their own leader. And to give himself a little added pleasure he also redoubled his efforts to set his brothers against each other. Just for the satisfaction of it.

If Colptha must be alone, let every man feel alone.

Colptha's partisanship had become open and obvious and Donn resented it. He felt he was being pushed and said so to Éremón. "I don't want you to think I'm trying to crowd you out," he explained. "As oldest, I will be clan-chief after Scotta and that's all the responsibility I want. Truly. If any of the Míl's sons should lead the tribe that man is you . . ."

"What about me?" Éber Finn demanded, thrusting himself into the conversation. He had become intensely aware that Éremón's following seemed larger and more vociferous than his own. Colptha never failed to point that out to him. "We are cattle lords again," Éber said, "and I have the most talent with animals. I should be chief of the tribe!"

Donn looked from one to the other. His brothers were almost as alike as two calves born in one sac; big and brawny and high-colored. A strong rivalry had always existed between them, but never as palpably as now. It was as if a new element had been added, an underlying meanness turning mirror images against each other.

Maybe things really will be better on Ierne, Donn thought hopefully. Where there is enough for all.

Ierne.

The elders and clan representatives met and argued long over the council fires. The brehons arbitrated the inevitable quarrels late into the night. When the sun rose, Éremón, gritty-eyed, returned to his house and fell across his bed.

"Is it over?" Odba asked eagerly.

"It's over. Ferdinón is chief of the Gaelicians."

Odba's jaw dropped. "How could that happen?"

"My supporters wanted me, Éber's friends yelled for him, there was a strong vote for Donn and a slightly lesser one for Gosten. No one could agree. In the end we were all so tired we had to make a choice, any choice. Ferdinón is popular with almost everybody and has a clanhold of sons to speak for his virility, so we elected him and came home to bed. I hope we're not all enemies in the morning."

He sank at once into an exhausted sleep, leaving Odba staring at him with her hands on her hips.

Colptha the sacrificer was sick with anger. Ferdinón, of all people! Ferdinón owed Colptha no debts and was singularly resistant to persuasion. Furthermore, like his predecessor, he had no desire to take part in druid affairs. The sun would forget to rise before Ferdinón would use his new influence on Colptha's behalf.

Colptha dug his nails into the palms of his hands in impotent fury. But he was not impotent. He was a druid, chosen and favored by the spirits. This was a riddle they were posing him, a test to make him stronger.

The other sons of Milesios were experiencing other anxieties. With the Míl dead, they could no longer be assured of places among the colonizers. Now they were just another clan instead of privileged members of the chieftain's family.

"It's your fault," Éremón accused Éber. "If you hadn't insisted on arguing so much I would have been chosen at the start and the leadership would have remained in our line."

"I had a right to be heard!" Éber told him. "And I would have made a better leader than you; ask Colptha. He told me so himself." He gestured toward the sacrificer, who was just entering the hall.

Colptha came to Éber's beckoning, but he was in a dark mood indeed and would not give anyone else fat meat to eat while he had to suck on bones. "Now that it no longer matters," he said, "I tell you both that I don't think either one of you could have taken the Míl's place. Perhaps you'd better wait until we get to Ierne and fight over that, since fighting is the only real talent you have. You are small-headed, both of you."

Donn stepped between them before either Éremón or Éber committed the grave offense of striking a druid. "Why quarrel over something that's already decided?" Donn wanted to know.

"Donn the conciliator," Colptha sneered. He need not court Donn's favor now; he could show his contempt for such a boring, stolid fellow. "Who would you put on the chieftain's bench, Donn? Surely not yourself; that was obvious from the way you refused to fight for it. Maybe you would have chosen Ír, just to avoid having trouble with him. You lack the manhood to fight for anything, Donn. That's why you sire only daughters."

Donn was too astonished to reply.

At the next ritual gathering of the druids Ollach said, "Ten nights from the first new moon of Oester, the patterns of earth and sky will be in a powerful conjunction. If each of us with the power of divination goes off alone, away from the unsettling atmosphere still lingering in the grove, perhaps the spirits will speak to us and guide our choice."

The druids agreed. They were as tense as men are when a great responsibility hangs over them, and the earnest desire to make the right choice burned in every face.

No eyes burned more brightly than those of Colptha the sacrificer. Now was his time; now!

Meanwhile, strange skeletons were being assembled in sheltered coves. Wooden frames propped and braced on the sand resembled huge beached sea-animals, imbued with a half-life of expectation instead of the stench of decay. When the weather permitted the boatbuilders to work Amergin came almost daily with Clarsah, to sing the merry music for them and speed their hands.

The other Gaelicians crowded to the scene as well, to admire the construction of the few timbered galleys and exclaim over the cleverness of the more numerous hide boats.

Ribs and framework for these grew under the boatbuilders' hands, waiting for the sewn hides that would form the outer shell. The tanned hides were painstakingly stretched and fitted, then all seams were thoroughly greased with fat to serve as waterproofing. Sakkar did much worrying about the masts and sails for the hide boats, finally deciding on hardwood masts with thin leather sails for sturdiness.

"Much of the voyage will be into the wind and against the tide," he explained to his crew. "We will need sails that will not tear but are light enough to be taken down easily when they start to work against us. At that time every man in the boat must take to the oars."

The masts were rigged with shrouds and forestays and the

hulls were reinforced with a timber stem, keel, and deadwood. Oars were fitted and shaped, then patiently smoothed so they would not tear the hands with splinters. Sakkar took groups of men out, a few at a time, and instructed them in sail management and the techniques of rowing.

The Phoenician was enjoying the project. He was beginning to feel like a captain, or perhaps even a commander, with so many aspects of the voyage under his supervision. He started to swagger a bit when he walked.

"That Sakkar thinks he's a Gaelician now," the women commented to each other, watching him with a certain fond amusement. Everyone liked the industrious little man. "He wears a saffron tunic like a freeman these days, and since the samodhii healed his shoulder he has a rather harmonious form."

"He's an interesting enough man for a woman who doesn't want much," another commented. "He's little—but those dark eyes are most exotic, don't you agree? I suppose he might welcome a pleasant chat with a woman from time to time; he must be rather lonely here."

"You're just curious to know if Phoenicians are made like other men!"

Sakkar knew they were watching him and assumed some of their giggling was about him, but he did not mind. He did more than copy the Celtic way of walking; he shaved off his beard and grew as full a mustache as he could, and with Amergin's permission he had begun wearing bits of jewelry the bard did not care for. As chief bard of the tribe, Amergin received more gifts in return for his services than he would ever use.

And sometimes in the night Sakkar thought of Conmael, or of his dead wife and child, and buried his face in his hands and allowed himself a few tears. He had learned that Celts did not scorn tears as being unmanly.

He had also found them to be openhanded and tolerant. Their social classes were sharply delineated yet divided without prejudice. Though he was considered a laborer, he had the same rights under Celtic law as a member of the warrior aristocracy. He also had an honor price, a set figure indicating his worth to the community. As Findbar the brehon explained it to him, Sakkar the shipwright was worth six cows, a most respectable sum.

"If someone killed you they would have to pay an eric to

the Milesian clan of six cows, since I suppose you are to be considered a member of the Míl's family now," Findbar said.

Sakkar, who had grown up as a wharf rat on the docks of Tyre, had never expected to have a tangible value, a rock of pride on which to stand. From time to time he murmured to himself as he worked, "Six cows." And smiled beneath his growing mustache.

He felt increasingly at home in the Gaelician world now that his boatbuilding operation had become a full-scale industry. Familiar noise and bustle shaped his days.

Countless shallow pans of seawater sat in the sun, their moisture evaporating to leave a residue of salt for meat preservation. There was much meat to be preserved. The sacrificers were kept busy propitiating the spirits of cattle to be slaughtered, explaining to the gaunt animals the need for leather hides to cover the hide boats. The cattle must not be allowed to resent their deaths, but must acquiesce to them as part of the endless circle of survival.

As soon as the hides were removed they were rushed to lime pits to soften the hair, which was then scraped off by children Sakkar had trained to use special double-handled scrapers. Next the hides went into the tanning pits, holes dug in the earth and filled with a dark-brown, creamy-foamed mixture of oak bark and water. They would soak for a long time in this brew, the sickly sweet smell pervading the atmosphere until no one bothered to comment on it anymore.

The strongest men and women hauled the soaked hides from the pits and worked wool grease into them by hand. Now the stench could not be ignored, and the grease-rubbers wrapped cloths around their faces to turn back the worst of it.

The druids assembled on the appointed day. The diviners came one by one from their various solitudes, where they had gone to await the guidance of the spirits. Some had new wisdom in their eyes. Some had only the disappointment a man must endure from time to time. One looked desperate.

They gathered to chant beneath the great trees and whisper the great names, connecting themselves with the forces of creation and letting the power of life flow through them.

They recited in turn whatever experiences had been given them. The stories they told were complex and obscure, yet each man who had received a vision found an arrow in it, and the arrows all pointed in the same direction.

Colptha listened incredulously. He had lain in a cold, dank

cave, shivering more from passion than chill, and used the considerable strength of his mind to try to force the pattern to fit his desire. He had concentrated so intently on this he would not have heard the true voices of the spirits if they had spoken to him.

Others had heard them, however. "It is clear to us that Ollach is best prepared to lead the order," Corisios said, speaking for his fellows. "The samodhii have seen it in the stars, the dreamers have dreamed it beside the tombs. We have heard one man's vision of a sun-dappled meadow and Ollach is still dappled with freckles, like a child. Another discovered a mighty river flowing across the heavens and Ollach lives on the banks of a river of the same configuration. A third dreamed of seven trees with seven branches, and Ollach is the seventh son of a seventh son, a powerful symbol in itself. The pieces of the riddle have been parceled out among us for interpretation and we fit them together as Ollach, the samodhi."

"What about me?" Colptha protested. "I was given a special warning from the Earth Mother herself, about the cattle!"

"Your vision was clouded," Corisios told him. "The cattle tore up the land and went hungry, but leaf-spring has come and the grass is returning. And we find we need every cow we have to furnish hides for the boats. Amergin and his Phoenician shipwright have turned a calamity into an opportunity."

Ollach said, "I have often thought that Irial, if he had lived, would have named the bard his successor. Perhaps he would still be the best choice . . ."

"No!" Colptha cried. "Anyone but . . . I mean, the spirits have made their decision and it is you, Ollach. We accept with grace." The sacrificer's mouth flooded with acid as he said those words. To have worked so hard and dared so much, then see the prize fall into other hands, was a crushing blow. But at least the hands were not those of Amergin.

Ollach bowed his head in true humility. "I accept the will of the spirits," he said.

The ritual of ordination must be held in the same place where the former chief druid had left his life; that is the Law. Ollach would lie prostrate at the foot of the oak and endure the trials of flame and water and earth, giving the spirits every chance to strike him down if he was not their true choice.

Colptha had one small comfort. At least he would not have to lie naked and vulnerable where Irial's body had lain.

Meanwhile the work on the boats continued. Teaching a shipwright's skills to so many landmen was not an easy task, and Sakkar was having to discover depths of patience within himself he had not known he possessed. It was soon obvious the boats would not be ready in time to sail on the next summer tide, which meant they would have to wait another year before launching. Sakkar knew enough about the waters to the north to realize the voyage could be made only in spring or summer. The terrible autumnal storms along the Gaulish coast would turn Phoenician galleys back; what chance would hide boats have against such weather?

He went to the Heroes' Hall to explain this to Ferdinón. Sakkar was dressed in a fresh tunic and a cloak of scarlet wool. His mustache was dark and flat instead of golden and heavy, but at least he had one. Every man in the hall was taller than he but he stood erect and looked Ferdinón straight in the eye, as no Tyrian shipwright would have dared to look at the king of Tyre.

He might have been mistaken for a short, dark Gaelician if it had not been for his beaked nose.

Ferdinón was distressed over his news. "Next leaf-spring, you say? The people will be in desperate shape by then, I'm afraid. They have been unusually patient already, and they want to go now. They need to go now, Sakkar!"

"It is not possible. We have enough tall hardwood for the frames and keels of four big galleys, which we will plank with pine, but the work cannot be rushed. And there are many hide boats still to be completed if you want vessels for half the tribe. But we can start training crews in the boats we have; it will make the voyage seem that much closer."

Ferdinón agreed; he had no choice. But he dreaded having to tell his tribesmen that the season of departure was pushed back, over the horizon and out of sight. The tribe's good will was worn thin, eroded by bad weather and starving cattle.

In her new and permanent seat in the women's balcony, Scéna Dullsaine murmured to Díl, "Now Amergin will have yet another excuse to put off asking for me. He is balkier than a bull calf about choosing a wife to take to Ierne."

"None of us is that certain of going to Ierne anymore," Díl

281

reminded her. "Since Milesios died, his sons stand no closer to the ships than anyone else. Uncertainty is a sword over our heads."

"I detest uncertainty," Scéna replied. "I prefer to make my own decisions without waiting on someone else's whim. I am a Celt, after all. My life is my own." She tossed her head and let her bold eyes roam over the warriors assembled in the Heroes' Hall.

"Since Ferdinón and his closest clansmen came here to occupy the tribal stronghold and lead the Gaelicians, I have done nothing but stumble over Milesians," Scéna went on. "We are all crowded in here together like too many sheep in a pen. If I were to go to some man's house as his wife, at least I would have more room." She saw Caicher's brother looking at her and looked back, arching her spine a little, making promises with her eyes. "I am tired of waiting for Amergin," she told Díl frankly. "The bard is wrapped up in words like a man in a winter cloak. All that thinking, all those ideas . . . they get in the way. He has a world of his own with no place for me in it, and that harp guards the gate to his stronghold.

"I like a man who laughs louder than the bard does, and laughs more often. I like a man who takes life as it comes to him instead of expecting something of it."

"So—will you marry someone else at the next festival of Bealtaine?" Díl inquired.

Scéna shrugged. "I will do as I please," was all she would say.

The season of warmth and light had come at last; the season of birth and growth. Oester wore her brightest face and it seemed that all wives—except Odba—had prayers for fertility answered.

The need for new land had never been more apparent.

The chief bard was frequently summoned to the sides of women in labor, to prepare a harmonious atmosphere for the infant's arrival. Poetry should be the first sound new ears hear; that is the Law.

He stood beside Un's young wife when she bore her latest child and watched its emerging face. In the baby's wizened, toothless countenance the bard glimpsed both past and future; the ancient visage the spirit had worn at the end of its last life and the equally old face it would show the world on some distant day of transition. For a brief moment, Amergin thought he saw the spirit itself in that enduring, changeless mask of wisdom, wrinkled and bright-eyed, a joyous gnome indifferent to flesh yet lusty for each new stage of existence.

As Amergin watched, the intelligence within the infant began to discover once more what it felt like to be new, to be young. The tiny mouth opened and sucked in air to inflate the minuscule lungs. A cry, hardly more than a squeak, emerged, and almost immediately the flesh began to plump out, the wrinkles to soften and fade. Soon the child would resemble every other baby, a little lump of pink clay waiting to be sculpted. It was only at the far extremes of birth and age that the face of the spirit within could sometimes be seen, arriving from or launching out on the voyage between lives.

Amergin bowed his head before the recurring miracle and stroked Clarsah, who sang a welcome to the child.

Amergin's thoughts flickered backward to another child, one who had left this life too early, with the best part of it yet before him. In his memory he found a clear picture of Conmael's broken body on the beach.

When he left Un's clanholding he drove thoughtfully back to the headland. Everywhere he looked he saw new shoots of heartbreakingly tender green; grass and bud and leaf, springing into life. Living, growing beings, certain of their place on the wheel of the seasons, sure of their destiny of flowering and fulfillment.

Amergin wandered to the far side of the headland, to a spot he had not visited since Conmael's death. He looked northward, expecting the green wind on such a verdant day, but the air was very still and the sun beat down hotly. He saw a shady niche a little way down the cliff face and eased himself down into it, bracing his back comfortably against the vertical earth and gazing out at the sea. Ierne.

"Amergin? Is that you down there?"

He looked up to see Colptha peering down at him from the edge of the cliff. "Finding you here is a sign from the spirits," the sacrificer said. "They always guide me, you know. *Always.*" His eyes had a hectic gleam. "Since you and I are both here, and I see you have your harp—play a eulogy for my foster son, bard. I will give you a fine gift for it."

"You did not request a eulogy from me during his funeral ritual."

"That was a hard day for me. I . . . I do not think I could have borne to listen. But compose one now, will you? The boy deserves it, Amergin."

The bard looked up at Colptha, then down to the deadly rocks. "Yes," he agreed. "Conmael surely deserves it."

Easing Clarsah from her case, he closed his eyes and sang. The eulogy came easily, a celebration of Conmael's youth and energy, his open, trusting nature, his obedience and nimble fingers and once-bright spirit. The poem was not one of the classic compositions a bard would create to commemorate a deified hero, but there was a sweetness to it like the curve of the dead boy's mouth. A mournful, tender music, occasionally dappled with merriment like freckles on a Celtic face.

When Clarsah hummed the last note and Amergin looked up, he saw that Colptha was crying.

◇ **23** ◇

SLINGING THE HARP over his shoulder by her carrying-thong, Amergin scrambled up to join Colptha. The sacrificer was definitely weeping. Bitter tears welled up and spilled onto his cheeks. He glared angrily at Amergin, as if ashamed to be seen with his emotion.

"You honor Conmael by crying for him," Amergin assured Colptha.

"You didn't think I could cry, did you?"

"Oh, yes, I remember your crying. You frequently did it when one of us defeated you in a contest. But you didn't mourn your loss at the Míl's tomb and I didn't expect to see you grieve over losing Conmael."

"You have a low opinion of me, don't you?" Colptha's flow of tears dried up but his expression remained angry.

"I am constantly revising my opinion of you," Amergin told him. "If you truly mourn Conmael . . ."

"If!" Colptha flung back his head so a strand of lank

yellow hair lifted briefly like a cock's comb. "You can't begin to understand how I felt about that boy, Amergin. You can't imagine how I suffer when I see his empty stool, or the bowl he drank his wine from. His cloaks still hang on pegs in my house. He admired me. That may be a little thing to the great bard, but it meant a lot to me, I assure you. There were times when we talked late into the night, or he laughed at some little jest of mine . . ." The sacrificer's tone lost its customary cutting edge. For a moment his eyes were gentle with memories summoned from deep inside himself by the bardic gift. With words and music Amergin had reached into Colptha's inner darkness and plucked out all the beauty that remained there; wrenching it loose, painfully. Raw. Bleeding . . .

The terrible gift of the bard.

Tenderness dissolved in fury. "You wouldn't understand!" Colptha raged at Amergin. "You can't love anything but that harp!"

Amergin took the verbal blow without flinching, but the watchful sacrificer saw something flicker in the bard's eyes and marked it down. That momentary expression revealed a sore point, a weakness to be exploited. A way to cause pain to balance the pain that continually ate at Colptha.

Amergin's eulogy had released the pain, and with it came pouring all the hatred dammed up behind it. Colptha stepped closer to his brother. The sacrificer's lean body quivered with intensity, seeming to swell like a pustule about to break open and spill its poison on the clean wind. "Don't look at me like that, as if you're trying to understand me!" Colptha shrieked. "You could never understand me, any of you. The sons of the great Champion, strutting around, so sure of yourselves. He bragged about every one of you at some time or the other. About all his sons—but me. Éremón and Éber Finn, his sword and spear. That's what he called them. And the rest of you named me the Swordsman behind my back, and laughed. Did you think I didn't know that? I knew, all right. Even then I had druid ears, I knew I was ridiculed for my weakness and my lack of grace. As if muscle and bone really mattered!

"And Ír—physical perfection. I hated to be seen anywhere near him because he made me look positively deformed by comparison. Donn, that mushmouthed appeaser, was not only the eldest but could do anything he set his hand to, and do it well. It might take him a while, but when he finished a task it was correctly done and he was respected for it. No one laughed at Donn.

"And you, Amergin—you most of all. You think you see some kinship between us? You try with cruel flattery to spread your mantle of honor so it includes me? The great bard Amergin! Men fear your curses and offer high prices for your praise songs. How does it feel, Amergin, to have people staring at you with admiration wherever you go?"

Colptha seemed to envision a personage so unlike Amergin's own view of himself that the bard could only shake his head. "Would you have me apologize for my talent, Colptha? Would it make you feel better if I admitted to you that the gift is more the harp's than mine?" He paused, stunned by the naked emotion he saw on his brother's face and in every line of his crouching body. "You actually hate me, don't you?" Amergin whispered.

"Yes!" the sacrificer hissed. His hands curved into clawed talons and he half-lifted them as if to strike. To rend, to tear . . . The admission was a relief. And it was safe; Amergin never informed on a clansman, he would never repeat this conversation to his own brother's discredit. "Yes, I despise you, Amergin! For the sake of all those more deserving of honors, I despise you. In the name of all those who want to be great but never will, I despise you!"

Amergin was sickened. "Listen to yourself, Colptha! Have you forgotten the lessons we learned as boys in the sacred groves? Whatever talent one person has is not his property alone. All spirits are part of One, you know that. And of each other. So my gift is to your credit as much as it is to mine; I'm only the instrument through which one particular art is expressed. Poetry flows through me but it originates in the wellspring of creation that is the source of us all. When you strike out at someone else's achievement you are attacking your own share of a great gift."

"There is no gift the equal of mine," Colptha said in a flat voice. "And you have no share in it. None! The spirits gave me a vision but you all rejected it, so I have no further obligation to share with any of you."

"What are you talking about?" The fanatic light in Colptha's eyes made Amergin uneasy. They were standing very near the edge of the cliff where Conmael had died, and the sea was crashing below, beating against the rocks.

"I shared what I had with Conmael," Colptha went on,

seemingly unable to halt the flow of his words. "But even he finally rejected me." He followed the direction of Amergin's glance; down, down.

There were dried stains on Colptha's sallow cheeks, tear tracks left from his grief. Looking at them, Amergin felt the last knot of the puzzle dissolve. "Yes, Conmael rejected you," the bard said aloud. "But he didn't deliberately kill himself. And you didn't kill him." The druid's eye saw, unclouded.

Colptha was startled. "Did you think I did? Do you think that little of me, Amergin?"

"I thought it was a distinct possibility. You would have killed anyone who threatened to expose your viciousness."

"Expose me? How?"

"Conmael was carrying a burden too heavy for him, but he was too young to have done anything very terrible—unless he helped you in some way. And what awful thing could you have done that would drive a child to despair?" Amergin very carefully stepped away from the cliff edge before he went on. "You killed Irial, Colptha. When I realized you were capable of doing that, I thought you could also have killed your little assistant to protect your secret. But Sakkar said 'he leaped out, leaped out of life,' and you are not strong enough to have flung that boy as far out as he fell.

"Conmael really did leap out of life, I believe. But not on purpose. He was upset and desperate, but he was also young and resilient and had an incentive to stay in this life. I think Conmael struck the rocks so far out because he *ran* off this cliff, Colptha. Running in blind panic, as deer sometimes run right into a pack of hounds. I think he finally could not bear his burden any longer and just ran from you heedlessly, as fast as he could. He probably didn't even realize he was at the edge of the cliff until there was no ground beneath him. But he struck the rocks free, no longer enslaved by you.

"Conmael died nobly, in full possession of himself as a Celt should be, and I am proud to have sung his eulogy."

Coptha had stared open-mouthed at the bard throughout Amergin's accusation. But he made no attempt to deny it, not to another druid who could see what lay beneath the surface. He merely said, "Are you prepared to formally accuse me of murdering Irial?"

"I have no proof, and the brehons would insist on proof, even from a fellow druid. Besides, the spirits have taken the

287

matter into the invisible world and will redress the balance there. It's out of our hands.''

''Then why make these accusations against me now? To lord it over me once more, Amergin? How typical of a son of the Míl!''

''I told you all this to warn you off. There is something terrible eating at you, Colptha, something that deforms not the body but the spirit.'' Amergin looked over the sacrificer's shoulder, facing into the green wind. ''I don't want you going to Ierne to infect a new land with your hatreds.''

Colptha's eyes lit with icy fire. ''What makes you think you can stop me? I have as much right as any of you. I should even go as chief druid, if the tribe of Ollach stays here.''

''Never!''

''Ai, but you would not raise your hand against a brother to stop me, would you? You can accuse me of murder, Amergin, but the passion to kill is not in you, so you have no real weapon against me. I think if any of us goes to Ierne, I will.''

His thin lips curled with cruel amusement. ''If you want to stop someone, why don't you stop Éremón? With him out of the way you might at last stand a chance at that ripe little Taya. Ai! Yes! You felt that spear, didn't you? You are vulnerable, bard.''

The sacrificer spun on his heel and walked away. Amergin stared after him. Colptha had gone only a few steps before he turned and indulged in one final attack.

''All you have is your poetry, bard. No woman, no weapon, no real power. I am the one the spirits love and reward, the one who should lead our people on Ierne. I was *chosen*, Amergin, and you cannot stop me now. No one can!''

The green wind moaned around Amergin, playing a mournful note on the harp in his numbed hand.

''I *have* to lead the expedition to Ierne,'' Éremón was fuming to his good friend Brego. ''With Milesios gone I'm the obvious choice; it was my idea in the first place.'' Honesty tapped him on the shoulder. ''I mean I was one of the first to suggest it,'' he amended.

''The clan of Milesios may have to stay here,'' Brego reminded him. ''It all depends on the drawing of lots.''

''They should have been drawn yesterday; then at least

we'd know. I hate this waiting!'' Éremón cried in frustration, downing his fifth bowl of wine that afternoon.

Afternoon, evening, morning, and the wheel of the seasons turned. Oak fires consecrated the solstices. The remaining cattle sought what nourishment they could from the partially recovered land, but they were still very thin. The spirit of the Gaelicians was wearing thin as well, as they threw all their resources behind the twin efforts of survival and preparing the ships.

Colptha found it increasingly easy—and amusing—to stir up quarrels between men balanced on the ragged edge of their nerves. A whisper here, a repetitive murmur there, and soon no man would trust another. They would have no one left to trust but the spirits, and Colptha the druid would speak for the spirits.

On Ierne.

Amergin the bard moved among his people, heartening, encouraging, his active eye seeing their fears and weaknesses and his bardic gift singing them into strengths. He worked like a man obsessed to hold on to the dream; to keep it from being lost in the daily tatters of their lives.

He seemed too busy for women; too busy for Scéna Dullsaine, though there were times when he managed to go alone to the headland and lose himself in the songs of the north wind.

The second winter set in, more savage than its predecessor. Wind howled. Sleet slashed. Ferdinón heard the tragic story of an outlying clan that had been forced to eat its seed bull and now was without either cattle or future. Food was rushed to them from the stores within the stronghold, but those stores were dwindling. The new chieftain could not possibly feed his entire tribe.

''Things will be all right once we set sail for Ierne,'' the Gaelicians told one another grimly.

Éremón sought to cling to the same consolation. As long as Ierne was on his horizon, however distant, he found he could even view Odba with a certain degree of tolerance. He spent more time in his house, letting her chatter at him. Hostility lessened between them and Odba began humming to herself as she bent over the cooking pots.

Amergin could not resist asking about her; worrying about her.

''Odba isn't such an awful woman,'' Éremón told him. ''I

could be quite comfortable with her if she'd be reasonable about Taya. You'd think she would welcome having another woman to share the work." Éremón heaved a great sigh. "It's a pity, Amergin. I'm used to Odba, I like the way she makes my clothes, I even like the way her food tastes when she isn't angry with me. These past nights, I have begun to remember how it was when she first came into my house."

"I think your eye is wandering again," Amergin commented.

That night Odba looked up from her chores to see her husband watching her with a pleasant expression on his face, and she offered him half a smile in return.

Éremón was suddenly reminded how long it had been since he embraced a woman. He patted his knee. "Come here," he said.

The boys were asleep. The fire burned low on the hearth.

After a moment's hesitation, Odba settled into Éremón's arms and nestled her cheek into the curve of his neck in a way he had almost forgotten. His hands wandered over her body and she made a small purring noise in her throat, wriggling to fit more closely against him.

When they woke together the next morning, Odba turned her head and gave Éremón a long-lidded, languorous glance, then twisted to stretch voluptuously. Every part of her body felt well used and contented.

Everything will be all right now, she thought. Éremón will be a husband to me; he realizes at last what an excellent wife I am.

Her cheeks dimpled as she recalled the pleasures of the night. And this would be the first of many such times; from now on she would be doubly careful to do everything as Éremón wished it, keeping him as pleased as he looked this morning. Her wonderful Éremón . . . all any woman could wish for . . .

There was just one fly in the milk. Her enemy, though defeated, was not discredited. It was important that Taya have no strength left.

"I hope my womb will swell with a new son, or perhaps a girl this time," she murmured to Éremón as she stroked his shoulder. "I only have one small worry. What if Lugaid's spiteful daughter has put a curse on my womb to keep it barren? She is mean, Éremón; I've always seen it in her, and I ask you to protect me."

Éremón cried a savage oath and flung himself from the

bed. When Odba fixed the sunset meal he still had not returned.

He had spent a long and bitter day at the harbor, feeling all the old angers against his wife boiling up again. He watched the boatbuilders work, urging them to greater speed, and even saw old Ítos among them, toothless and shaky but so consumed with excitement that he came every day to help.

"Ierne is burning the life out of him," Donn remarked. "No one thinks he could survive the journey even if his clan is chosen, but he thinks of nothing else."

"My wife accuses Taya of dispensing curses," Éremón replied, "but I think Ierne is the source of sorcery, reaching across the water and drawing us all." He gazed moodily at the vessels spread along the beach. Éber Finn claimed the boats were as beautiful as seabirds, but Éremón was not looking for beauty. The fine curved sheer and long lifting bows that would enable them to rise and ride over rough seas meant nothing to him. He just wanted to see them launched and himself in one. Waiting in rows on the sand they reminded him of so many braces of coursing hounds, eager to be off and running.

In spite of the winter seas, Sakkar began urging all the able-bodied Gaelicians to familiarize themselves with oars and sail, taking advantage of the shelter offered by the headland to protect them from the worst of the storms that annually assailed the vast bay to the north. Though adventure raced the blood when it lay in the future, it became all too real and immediate when a landman was forced to step into a seagoing vessel for the first time and entrust himself to the heaving bosom of the water. More than one brawny warrior kept a tight grip on his sword while boarding, though none repeated Ír's now-legendary attack on the waves.

Scotta presented herself for instruction on the same day as Éber Finn. She strode onto the beach dressed in plain tunic and leggings like a man and headed boldly for the nearest hide boat. Éber had been hiding a certain hesitancy himself, but when Scotta waded into the surf to help launch the boat he could hardly hang back.

When the boat met the sea it leaped onto the outgoing tide like a living creature. At Sakkar's signal, the neophyte crew clambered over the sides gracelessly. Sakkar, who was obviously enjoying himself, got them seated on the cross bracing that served for benches and demonstrated the proper technique for rowing.

Éber took a place just behind his mother. "Scotta," he said in a low voice as he leaned forward, "are you certain you want to do this?"

"And why shouldn't I?" she answered crisply. She already felt the rhythm of the waves beneath the thin shell of the boat and was eager to match her oar strokes to them, to propel this intriguing new vehicle forward. "I drove a chariot in my youth," she told her son over her shoulder. "I was very good at it long before I ever thought of you."

Éber felt like a child again, sternly reproved. "There's not much juice left in your paps," he said with unaccustomed harshness to her, "and this is going to be a long journey. I see no need for you to man an oar."

"There's more juice in my paps right now than there will ever be in yours!" Scotta snapped at him. "I carried you once and I can carry you again. Look out there, you've already let your oar come out of the water."

Sakkar was delighted with the hide boats. Under oar or sail they rose with extraordinary liveliness to meet and surmount the waves. Suggestions made to him by Gaelician craftsmen had been incorporated into the final design, and Sakkar was quick to recognize the ingenuity of the Celtic mind. He appreciated these improvements more as time passed. The boats surrendered with docility to strong wind or rough tide, allowing themselves to be carried like leaves on the water until the sea calmed and they could resume their desired course. They were light enough to be easily beached and dragged beyond the tide line so they required no moorings, making them much easier to handle than the cumbersome galleys. They were, in short, a shipwright's triumph.

Sakkar was a happy man. For the first time in his life he gloried in freedom and was exalted by a sense of his own worth. The craftsman was honored among these people, his skills considered a talent like those of a bard or a healer, perhaps not so mysterious but equally necessary to the welfare of the tribe. And Sakkar was often greeted with, "Ai, craftsman!"

He began to feel very Gaelician.

Ferdinón was impressed by Scotta's display in the hide boat. He had long coveted all of the Míl's treasures, the bronze bench and the clanholding now shared by his sons—

but most of all, Ferdinón had envied Milesios his wife. His widow, who was surely too vital to remain long without a man. She not only had the vigor of a much younger person, but in moments of uncertainty the new chief of the tribe found himself relying on her more and more.

Perhaps it would be a bad idea to allow the Milesians to go to Ierne, even though their departure would mean he could take over their clanholdiṅgs and add them to his own—if he stayed. And he had secretly already determined to stay. Ferdinón had hungered too long for the bronze bench and the granite Heroes' Hall of Milesios ever to want to leave them.

He spoke to his other wives about adding to their number. "Wnat makes you think Scotta would be willing to be the newest wife, bound by custom to the hardest work?" they asked him. "The loss in rank, even if she were willing to accept it, would shame a chieftain's widow, Ferdinón."

He knew they were right. Still, whenever Ferdinón sat on his bench in the Heroes' Hall, he found himself looking for Scotta's bold face and dauntless eyes.

The winter deepened and the wind moaned. Boatbuilding dragged to a halt.

Eremón stood in the doorway of his house, gazing out at the cruel face of the Mother as she imprisoned him beneath his roof. Punishing him for all those cattle. Frustration burned in him like the burning tumors the samodhii shrank with a decoction of mistletoe. But that healing potion worked on the flesh only; it could not cure an ailment of the spirit.

Ierne had come to represent everything he wanted and was being denied. At first he had expected the boats would be quickly built and they would all be there by now, he and Taya together at last. But a pattern of delay had begun and then expanded itself with willful maliciousness. Now this long winter without progress must be endured, while Odba nagged at him about her latest obsession and renewed her threats to go to the brehons if she did not conceive.

In desperation he bedded her repeatedly, until the act took on a juiceless joylessness and he feared she would rob him of his very manhood. But she must be placated to avoid having her bring charges against Taya; everything must be held together somehow, until the boats were ready.

In the Heroes' Hall, Amergin sympathized with him. "There are times I wish I could dive into the sea and swim to Ierne," the bard said with a laugh. "If I were a little more like Ír I might try it."

"There are times I want to throttle my wife and send her back to her father on a litter, with her scrawny sheep trailing after her corpse," Éremón responded, not laughing.

"Then we would have a war we can ill afford right now when we need all our strength to get ready for the voyage," Donn commented, stepping into the conversation. "Try to be sensible, Éremón."

"There's no satisfaction in being sensible," Éremón complained. He doubled his fist and pounded the wall, skinning knuckles already permanently disfigured from similar assaults on unyielding surfaces. "I want to *do* something."

When he awoke the following morning Éremón discovered a rash on his hands and the thong broke as he tried to lace up his warm leggings and there was mold in the bread and his head was stopped up and his accumulating anger made him so careless he cut himself on the jaw with his obsidian razor and for a blinding moment he hoped he would just bleed to death and be done with it.

But the spirits would not countenance it. No. That was not the heroes' way. After transition he would look back and hate himself for being so weak, seeking such a petty escape.

He stood in the doorway and bleakly stared at the equally bleak land, trying to wait in stillness in the private recesses of his being, riding above the inactivity and frustration. For once he envied Amergin, who at least had that poetic history of his to keep him busy. Though Éremón did not understand busyness confined to the inside of one's own head, at least he could see it did not depend on the weather.

He must hold himself together, not letting anything destroy his strength of purpose. He must continue to be a caring friend and resolute leader, building up his support against the time when they sailed for Ierne. He would endure, holding it all within and losing nothing, not one precious drop of his fine fire and fury, until leaf-spring.

A chariot just leaving the stronghold caught his attention. "Colptha again," he said aloud to no one because he was hungry for the sound of a voice that was not Odba's. "Almost every day now the sacrificer drives off in the direction of the chief druid's clanhold. What's he doing with Ollach?"

Amergin was wondering the same thing. One chill morning shortly after Imbolc he returned from a professional visit to the clan of Caicher and encountered the sacrificer on a converging road—one that led only to the chief druid's small dwelling. It could hardly be called a house. Upon being named head of the order Ollach had moved into a tiny hut no bigger than a bedbox. To balance the opulence of a tribal chieftain, chief druids traditionally practiced a severe austerity. Ollach had given away his jewelry and his household goods on the day of his inauguration, keeping only one iron cooking pot and a beechwood walking stick generations old. The simplicity of these possessions shouted of the wealth and prestige Ollach now commanded in the invisible world.

Amergin noticed that Colptha had removed all ornamentation from his chariot and harness and was wearing a very plain cloak himself. And looking very pleased.

"Your shadow continually darkens Ollach's doorway," the bard said; not bothering with a greeting. "Why?"

Colptha glanced enviously over his shoulder toward Ollach's mean little, magnificent little hut. "Ollach has learned to value my opinions and I have found him . . . a receptive audience," he replied.

The bard's knuckles were white on the reins. "What are you up to now?"

"Working for the good of the tribe, of course. Assuring that they have the best leadership from the invisible world—once we get to Ierne. I have spent considerable time with Ollach lately, demonstrating . . . my gifts. He was a little uncertain, a little humbled by the honor that had befallen him. He did not . . . resist my support." Colptha's thin lips curved into something that would have been a smile on a different man. "Ollach agrees that I am the logical choice for chief druid on Ierne if my clan goes there and his does not."

Colptha was amused by Amergin's appalled expression. "The honors I have always deserved will come to me at last," he said complacently. "To replace what I lost . . . in Conmael. Warmth. Life. Don't you understand, bard? We made a grave mistake in neglecting our responsibilities to the Mother here, but when I am chief druid on Ierne I will see that that mistake is not repeated. We will win the Mother's favor with constant sacrifices. Warm and living." His voice sank to a lascivious purr. "The altars will run red on Ierne," the sacrificer crooned.

Shock held Amergin rooted to his chariot. Colptha's face, transfigured by naked lust, no longer seemed human to him, but the face of some implacable enemy against which he must struggle to the death . . . or surrender Ierne to Colptha's bloody vision. But what weapons could he fight with? How could one druid attack another?

While he struggled for answers, Colptha looked beyond him and bared his teeth in a feral grin. "The spirits send an omen to show me they approve," he said with overweening confidence. "Look over your shoulder, bard, at that orange light in the sky. It is a signal fire on the headland. The ships must be almost ready, for Ferdinón is summoning the clans to draw lots!"

◇ **24** ◇

FERDINÓN WAITED through one bright face and one dark face of the Moon Sister in order to give clan-chiefs from the farthest reaches of Gaelician territory time to reach his stronghold. The druid measurers had reported the entire tribe to contain more than forty hundreds, the clans ranging in size from a handful of people huddled in a remote valley to sprawling communities like that of the Milesians. Such a clan might contain tens of tens itself, and as Milesios had said, the tribe was growing.

Their territory was not.

People began arriving. Clan-chiefs in their chariots, bronze bedecked and haughty, accompanied by warriors on horseback carrying trophies from battles long since won but never forgotten. Even women in ox-drawn carts, children in their arms, eager to see their future decided.

The guest house was filled to overflowing and the Gaelicians camped in the lee of the walls and under wagons, too heated with excitement to feel the lingering chill of the departing winter.

A huge copper bowl was set up in front of the Heroes' Hall. Ferdinón's craftsmen had spent days painting an assortment of sea-rounded stones, some in brilliant but solid colors, others with elaborate designs. The significance of their work was understood by the painters, and they took great care to give the stones the beauty their importance demanded.

The copper bowl, gleaming from an energetic sandscrubbing, stood on a carved wooden platform, and after Ollach delivered the sunrise invocation the clan-chiefs lined up before it. Ferdinón had spread his seven-colored cloak over the bowl with only one edge turned back so a person might reach beneath it into darkness. Mindful of the forms of hospitality, Ferdinón invited the clans who had come the longest distance to draw first—a ploy that left the final stones for his own family, Ítos, and the Milesians.

The first stone drawn from the bowl was dark red with a bright blue interlace painted around its circumference.

A cheer went up. The happy clan-chief held his trophy aloft and his wives came running to him, elbowing through the crowd with a parade of children in their wake. They had raised many sons and daughters for this man and every one wanted to congratulate him. They joined in an impromptu dance that slowed down the proceeding, to the annoyance of all those still waiting their turn.

The sun moved in the sky and the line moved forward. Scotta would draw for her clan, so she was in no hurry to wait in a line; she preferred to stand to one side, watching the people. Wondering if the Míl, wherever he was, was watching too.

"Do you hope to go, or hope to stay?" a lisping voice inquired behind her.

She turned to face Ferdinón. "My sons are eager for Ierne, and my place is with my clan."

The chieftain gave her a searching look. "Suppose I told you I want you to stay here? As my wife, and more importantly, as my advisor. You were invaluable to Milesios, everyone knew that, and you would be invaluable to me; I would even buy a slave from the Hellenes to do the chores that would otherwise be assigned to you as newest wife in my house. I want you with me, Scotta."

She met his eyes unflinchingly. "You mean to stay here?"

"I do."

"And if I say no to your offer? You are a shrewd man, Ferdinón; I often said so to my husband. Am I correct in assuming you know what stones lie in the very bottom of the bowl, and you could manipulate them to keep my whole clan here with you? Obviously you know how to get a blank one for yourself.''

He did not answer her, but his eyes sparkled with delight at her cleverness.

The drawing went on.

When the head of Ollach's clan stepped forward, Colptha watched as tensely as the chief druid himself. The man reached into the bowl, winked over his shoulder at his followers, wiggled his fingers among the stones to add to the suspense, and at last drew out a plain blue pebble. He turned it over and over, seeking ornamentation, but there was none. He shuffled away from the bowl and his women wailed in disappointment. When Ollach stepped forward to comfort his clan-chief, Colptha turned so none could see the light of triumph in his eyes.

Clan by clan the decision was made. These to the boats, those to stay behind and reclaim the pastures, tend the remaining herds. Those who stayed would be assured of sustenance, if not the level of luxury they had enjoyed in the old days of trade with the Sea People. Those who went could be certain of nothing but adventure and a dream besung by the bard.

They were Celts, and that was enough.

When only three clans remained, old Ítos slid his skinny arm into the bowl. Veins bulged in his forehead. He licked his lips and hesitated, caught between two worlds. Then he gulped and picked out a stone.

A stone the color of wild mustard, with an ocher serpentine balanced between its two halves.

Lugaid and his clansmen shouted for joy. Ítos just stood holding the large pebble while a light dawned on his face to rival the sun. He turned his head slowly, looking not for his own sons and grandsons but for Amergin. When his eyes met those of the bard he lifted the stone above his head and cried, ''Ierne!'' Then he crumpled and fell as if a spear had gone through his heart.

He was dead by the time anyone could reach him.

The Gaelicians gasped. ''Ierne killed him,'' someone said in a shocked voice. Instinctively the people drew back, unwilling to be too close to the dead man until some druid interpreted this startling omen.

Ollach hurried forward and bent over Ítos. Looking into the old man's faded blue eyes, the samodhi watched life recede down a spiraling tunnel. The Gaelicians huddled together in silence, allowing the departing spirit room, and waited.

Ollach stood up and faced them. "With his last breath Ítos directed us to Ierne," the chief druid said. "This is a most potent sign, for the spirit of a strong man precedes us, easing our way." He turned toward Ferdinón. "Have them finish the drawing."

"But what of Ítos?" Lugaid wanted to know, pointing to his father's body.

"Ítos is no longer here. Let his spirit's empty house lie where he left it until the more important task is completed."

They recognized the druid wisdom in his voice, that certain knowledge which comes only from the invisible world; the awareness of and adherence to a pattern larger than the life of ears and eyes.

Ferdinón and Scotta came forward to draw for the last remaining clans. Ítos lay directly in their path. Scotta crouched down beside him and pressed the back of her hand gently against his withered cheek in a final salute. Then she rose and with straight back and high head she stepped over the body and marched to the bowl.

Her hair had turned iron gray since the Míl's death and she had taken to wearing the short tunic of a warrior all the time, claiming it was less hampering than a long skirt. Her calf muscles flexed as she walked away from Ferdinón.

Mother of warriors, he thought. Can I afford to let such a lioness leave me?

Only a few stones remained in the bowl, and he knew which ones. Knew them by their feel, had held and studied them and turned them over and over in his hands, memorizing them.

He joined Scotta beside the bowl and turned to face the assembled crowd. "As chief of the tribe, I have chosen for myself and my clan to stay here," he said. "I will therefore forfeit my turn at the bowl and Scotta, daughter of Faronn, will draw for the Milesian clan." Leave it to the spirits to decide, he thought. If I am meant to have her, they will see to it; they have already given me the bronze bench.

"No, Ferdinón," Scotta said. "You draw for me."

They stared at each other. "It is your right," he insisted, but she shook her head.

"You are chief of the tribe now, Ferdinón, which means the responsibility for all of us is yours," Scotta reminded him. "Draw for us, and we will accept the stone you choose. We will trust you."

The full weight of chiefdom descended on Ferdinón's broad shoulders then, as Scotta knew it would. At the Míl's side she had learned many lessons, and this was one she must pass on to his successor.

Ferdinón looked at her for a long, unblinking time, examining every strong plane of her face and trying to see her spirit. But she let him see only his own obligation, burdening him with her trust. If he failed, he would not be fit to lead the Gaelicians.

Ferdinón reached into the bowl and lifted out the first stone his fingers touched without making any effort to feel it surreptitiously. He held up a round green stone with a spiral design covering most of its surface, then gravely extended it to Scotta.

There was a flicker of genuine regret on her face as she took it. "You are a man, Ferdinón," she told him.

Éremón and Éber Finn crowded forward, jostling each other. Ír was close behind them, smiling a bright hot smile. Donn leaned forward, tense in spite of himself. Colptha licked his thin lips and his hands curved into predatory claws, waiting. And on the edge of the crowd Amergin the bard stood tall and silent, with Clarsah on his shoulder.

Scéna rose on tiptoe, seeking his eyes. The two of them gazed—and it was a yearning gaze, neither could deny it—at each other across the heaving sea of excited people. Her people . . . his people . . . her pattern . . . his pattern . . .

Once again, and for the last time, they moved in unison. Simultaneously, Scéna Dullsaine and Amergin the bard looked away from each other, toward their different futures.

Scotta raised her arm high above her head. "The clan of Milesios goes to Ierne!" she cried. She glanced once at Ferdinón, letting her eyes run approvingly down his body to pay him a final compliment. "And I go with them," she added. "What sons have ever outgrown their mother?"

She turned toward the tall dark man on the edge of the crowd. "Sing to us of Ierne, Amergin!" she called. And the bard lifted the harp.

Eriu of the Túatha De Danann walked through her kingdom. In her heart the hawthorn was already blooming; in her heart the newly hatched cygnets already nestled beneath the swan, peeping with bright eyes through her breast feathers. Winter—an easy winter this year, wet but gentled by the warm green river that flows through the ocean—was fading before the strengthening sun. The season of birth was approaching.

And the season of anxiety.

"The Fir Bolg are growing older," Cet had reported just the day before, dividing his worries by sharing them with Greine and Cuill and their queens. "One of the women saw a band of warriors beyond the hazel grove."

"Not *my* hazel grove!" Cuill protested, angered at an invasion of his favorite place.

"Perhaps they were only following a stag," Greine suggested.

"They were wearing full battle dress," Cet told him. "They were deliberately coming as close as they dared to jab at us and see if we would hit back. They dare the Sword of Light."

"Fighting, quarreling, threatening the land," sighed Eriu, shaking her head at them. "Perhaps the time has come to consider Unbodying and put ourselves forever beyond war. Where else do our studies lead us?"

"We are not ready!" shouted several voices at once, alarmed by her words.

Eriu the ardent walked barefoot through the fields of Ierne. Under the high arch of her foot she felt the living land. Living. Great sentient goddess, capable of adapting the conditions of existence for her many life forms. Goddess with her vital organs at the core, her renewable parts on the surface in a constant state of change, of birth and death and evolution. Sometimes of change forced against the will of one part, for the good of the whole.

Eriu came to a pond lying in the lap of the hills, a mirror for the sky. The surface of the pond was as smooth as a sheet of polished metal. No leaf floated on the motionless water, no insect skimmed over it. The fish that lurked on the bottom lay unmoving in their green gloom so that no ripple betrayed their presence. She knew they were there by feel only, the small vital energy of their minds touching hers with delicate nibbles. Shinann would have felt them more keenly.

Eriu sat on the bank, wrapping her arms around her knees like a young girl, and experienced the land.

The pond was fringed with willows giving way on the east

301

to a stand of sapling birch trees. A breeze moved across the hills, but the growth sheltering the pool kept its surface undisturbed. Perhaps nothing could disturb it; perhaps it was frozen forever, the door to the past barred, the window to the future sealed, sky and clouds trapped in their own reflections for all the eons. On Ierne, perhaps nothing changed. Beauty was held captive by serenity and the land cherished them both.

With a movement so slow it might not have been movement at all Eriu tipped her head back and looked up at the sky. Clouds sailed there like huge white galleys under invisible power. She watched them until her eyes burned, then she looked down at the water and saw the sky reflected there, the clouds less white, more menacingly piled atop one another. Clouds before a storm.

Something moved in, or over, the pond. Some small thing—a first raindrop, a windblown seed—broke the unbearable tension of the surface and the ripples spread out in concentric circles, shattering the polished image until nothing could be seen but motion and change.

Eriu bowed her head on her knees.

Time, the druids taught, was as amorphous as fog. Now it shrank overnight from an endless wasteland to become a rapidly closing door. The Gaelicians must scurry through quickly, gathering up their possessions in a desperate rush. Sakkar was adamant about an early departure; something about storms on northern waters later in the season. So herds must be divided and the youngest, lightest animals selected for the voyage, which meant not only searching the livestock pens in the clanholds but driving in the stock allowed to run wild in the hills and valleys. The similar selection or rejection of property—what to take and what to leave behind, and with whom—was a worry that consumed the women, making them as tired and irritable as their men. A number of fights were waged for reasons other than the pure joy of combat.

Clans disappointed in the outcome of the drawing tried to prove their nobility by being excessively magnanimous, overburdening the colonists with more than they could ever carry. Findmall, son of Ferdinón, insisted on giving Soorgeh his best chariot, enough salted meat for three winters, and ten splendidly carved ox yokes.

"We're only taking calves," Soorgeh protested. "They won't wear heavy yokes for several seasons after we reach Ierne, and those things will take up unnecessary room in the boat."

"They are a gift to a good friend and a great warrior," Findmall protested, aggrieved. "I will never see you again; would you reject this last small gesture? Your wives can sit on the yokes, it isn't much to ask. Or do you already scorn the craftsmanship of your native land?"

"I'll take them," Soorgeh said with a sigh. Ten ox yokes in his boat would mean the women would have to leave some of their own boxes and chests behind, and there would surely be trouble over that.

While Sakkar was overseeing the last details at the harbor, Amergin took time to say good-bye to his house. A few nights remained before the actual departure, but Amergin thought it best to have his farewells behind him by then so he could concentrate on seeing and remembering every aspect of the adventure.

There was the climax of his epic, he thought; the story he could not tell because it had not yet happened.

He sat alone beneath his roof and looked at the familiar smoked walls. The birds in their carved boxes. His firedogs, alive with motion frozen in iron. His bedbox piled with soft calfskins, and the platform of honor beside it for Clarsah.

Benches worn to the shape of his buttocks.

Why, the bard asked himself in the silence, did I never really appreciate how beautiful and comfortable this house is until now? Will I be able to build another as good on Ierne?

Are we making a mistake?

He said it again, aloud, but Clarsah did not answer him. "Some things are hard to know, even for a druid. My instincts were right about Colptha, but when I try to look ahead to the voyage and Ierne they become entangled in seawind and daydreams and I cannot be certain . . . Never mind the signs and portents. If we wanted to stay here I suspect we could find plenty of omens telling us we should remain where we are."

He cradled the harp in his arms. What would so many days on the open sea do to a fragile being of wood and wire? He had always sheltered and protected her; now he would take her onto the ocean, perhaps drown her in it with himself, swallowed by dark waves. Singing songs for whatever lives at the bottom of the sea.

But he would take her, no matter what lay in store. As Colptha had so rightly pointed out, Amergin carried no weapon save for the harp. The gift of poetry, pitted against Colptha's rampant hatred in a green land none of them had yet seen, except in their secret dreams.

Amergin held Clarsah against himself and rested his cheek on her wooden frame. Cold, hard, lifeless wood.

If Éremón were out of the way, Colptha had said . . .

"No!" the bard cried aloud. "No, sacrificer! I will fight you with all the strength I have!"

The bard's voice echoed hollowly in the silence of his house. The birds in their boxes, disturbed, admonished him with clucking reproof.

And then, when everyone agreed that no one was ready, the season of departure arrived.

Corisios threw the staves and furrows of wisdom, Colptha examined the entrails of sacrifice, the samodhii consulted the patterns of the stars. Ferdinón and Éremón consulted with Sakkar about boats and tides and currents, Éber Finn and the herders consulted with their livestock.

And Ollach appointed Colptha the sacrificer to be chief druid when the colonists reached Ierne.

Amergin stood in rigid silence in the nemeton as Colptha's name was chanted to the trees and the watching spirits. The bard saw fire leap in the sacrificer's eyes.

There seemed to be a smell of blood on the wind.

Four nights later the Moon Sister would show her full face to the Earth Mother and they would lock invisible hands across emptiness, tugging at each other. At this most auspicious time for journeying, the fleet of colonization would set sail.

With departure set for the next day, Éremón chose full-moon night for an act of courage even the bravest man might postpone as long as he could. Odba was packing cheese and dried fruit for their journey, and he stood behind her stooped back so he need not see her face as he said, "Taya, daughter of Lugaid, will sail with us in my ship and she will live in my house when we get to Ierne."

Odba did not move. She did not even straighten up and whirl around to yell at him. The posture of her bent back was eloquent enough. "I am your wife," she said in a muffled voice. "Your only wife; the only woman entitled to live in your house."

"You will still be my wife on Ierne. My *senior* wife."

"Why didn't you tell me about this sooner?" she asked, straightening very slowly, still not turning to face him.

"I thought it better to wait for the right time."

"And the last moment is the right time? When there is no opportunity left for me to do anything about it?"

Answering questions was a defensive position, and Éremón scorned being on the defensive. "Are you threatening to refuse to come with me if Taya does?"

"The boats sail tomorrow! I can hardly petition the brehons now, they will not convene again for . . . but yes. Yes! I can refuse to go." In her anger she had swallowed his suggestion.

Éremón appeared to consider this for the first time. "I suppose you could. I'll be leaving a lot of property behind me, of course, everything that won't fit in the ship. Sheep, cattle, household goods, tools, even some jewelry, I think. And you would have my share of the clanhold land, of course. As long as you occupy it Ferdinón cannot claim that parcel. You would be a wealthy woman, Odba."

"You mean you would leave your sons wealthy," she said bitterly, refusing to allow him the smallest credit for generosity.

This was the worst moment for Éremón. "I do not leave my sons at all," he told her. "They're going on the ship with me. Scotta has been training them and even the smallest can now manage a weapon and must be considered a man, independent of his mother."

In the silence he could hear insects move through the thatch of his roof.

Odba's face had convulsed with so many emotions during the seasons of their marriage he thought he knew them all, but the one she wore now as she slowly looked toward him was unique. She looked dead.

"Did you hear me, Odba?"

She nodded, but made no sound. She forced him to fill the silence by defending his position after all, and he resented it. He should have expected a woman like Odba to fight unfairly. "My sons will be needed on Ierne, the place has some natives and we expect to fight for the island. My sons belong with their clan, not left behind and cut off from their chance for glory."

"Glory," Odba said with a sniff. "What is glory to me? I

305

never sought it, I only wanted to be your wife and raise children for you. They should be with me and I with them, wherever they go. After all, your mother goes with you."

"Scotta understands the need for glory," Éremón said. "Besides, who could stop her?" Then he realized he must strike now and decisively, before Odba's mind was made up; he must use his knowledge of the woman against her if he was to win. He reminded himself that she had already fought unfairly—this was her fault, she forced him to it.

He grabbed her more roughly than a man should ever grab a chieftain's daughter and shook her as he had wanted to shake her so many times before. "If you want to be with my sons you shall," he told her. "You will come with us and live in my house with Taya and me, and even if you are barren you can help her when her babies start to come. You can guide them into this life, you can . . ."

"How dare you?" she shrieked at him, losing all control. "You expect me to be a midwife to that . . . to that . . . she's put a curse on you all right, and on me as well! I would rather go to my tomb this very night than ever have to see her again, or have to watch my sons share their inheritance with hers! Go to Ierne. Take my children and turn them into replicas of yourself. But don't expect me to submit to any further humiliation at the hands of Lugaid's daughter. You can both sink to the bottom of the sea while I stay here wealthy and happily free of both of you!"

She abandoned her chores from that moment and lay down on the bed, pulling a calfskin robe over her head. The three boys, confused and upset by this particular quarrel, clustered around Éremón demanding an explanation.

"Your mother has decided not to undertake the voyage to Ierne," he told them. "Many women are reluctant, as you know. But you are going with me anyway, and I will take you boar hunting when we get there . . . and let you drive my chariot."

The boys looked uncertainly toward their mother, but the silent mound beneath the calfskin had withdrawn from all of them.

Dawn. A cool, clear dawn, with strands of coral cloud parting like old wool to allow the sun to rise through them. The livestock were penned and hobbled, parcels and chests and sacks were piled on the beaches, long and emotional good-byes had been said and must not be endured a second time.

The Gaels were leaving Iberia.

With prodigious effort, they had built and readied a fleet for the migration. Four tens of hide boats, holding a maximum of ten oarsmen to a side, would carry not only their crewmen but wives and children and penned young animals. The four wooden galleys were reserved for the largest clans, and of these, the Milesians occupied two. The children of the Míl as well as the occupants of his clanhold, nobles and freemen alike, had loaded their livestock and possessions and war carts aboard until the two big ships were crammed from bow to stern.

Éremón, who had campaigned hard to assert his right to be leader of the expedition, had examined the timber vessels beforehand and claimed the choicest for himself. He had chafed at Sakkar's prohibition against bringing more than one team of grown horses per chariot, and the limitation of only one chariot to a warrior—but Éber Finn, who had many fine horses, complained more. Sakkar was amused that they had no concept of a flagship, but hung their shields along the bows and thought that adequate identification.

When Donn had been assigned the second galley, Colptha had muttered to Éber Finn, "Éremón and Donn between them will squeeze you out if you let them."

"Scotta is clan-chief; she made the decision."

"You see? Already they are trying to separate you from her, now that she has the Míl's authority. They are jealous of you because you have the closest bond with Scotta, Éber. Watch them, watch them closely."

Éber Finn scowled and worried, and began watching his brothers.

As luggage piled up along the beach, Díl grew concerned. "Can we get everything in that ship?" she asked Donn. "I'm afraid I will be so squeezed I cannot breathe."

Donn smiled and patted her arm. "Breathe when we get to Ierne," he told her.

Scotta, clan-chief of the Milesians, had intended to sail in Éremón's galley, but Éber came to her at the last moment and made such a fuss about having her in Donn's galley that she relented. "I go with Donn and I want you with us, where we can take care of you," Éber said urgently.

307

Scotta accepted, but in her head she changed the order of his words around to better define the situation as she saw it.

Ír and Amergin would make the journey in Éremón's ship, and Sakkar as well, with the priceless sea charts. Two tiers of oarsmen were required for each of the big ships, and warriors and freemen alike took their places as crew. Only the druids were exempt from labor.

Amergin was relieved when Scotta told Colptha he must go in Donn's ship. "Though I would prefer she told him he could not go at all," the bard whispered to Clarsah.

Ollach delivered the sunrise invocation on the morning of departure, though for once even the chief druid had difficulty quieting the huge crowd. Then, as the baggage and livestock were taken aboard, Findbar the brehon began reciting the rights and entitlements of the various classes of the tribe, so that they would remember the Law in their new land and not let it be pulled out of shape.

Even the wind hushed to listen as Findbar recited, from perfect memory, the prerequisites for being a cattle lord. "Each of you who sets foot on the new land is to claim land for himself and his livestock in the amount of at least twenty-seven cumals. Build the best house you can, for a man's dwelling is the exterior skin he fashions to represent himself and must speak nobly for him. Select your building materials for strength and beauty, and use only the most skilled craftsmen, rewarding them generously according to their ability.

"Each noble must equip his dwelling with one bronze ceremonial cauldron with a spit and handles, a vat in which a measure of grain liquor can be brewed, an iron cauldron for common use, enough iron cups and mugs and kneading troughs that you will never have to borrow, a washing trough and washing ewer, rush-cutting knives, ropes, an adze, an auger, a saw, shears, an axe, a whetstone, and a bill-hook of the best quality, all wrapped in oiled hides, a spear for butchering cattle, three lamps for every circle, a plow for the earth, a bucket for milk and a bucket for grain liquor, three leather sacks for grain, salt, and charcoal, a cloak chest for every member of your household, a washing kettle for guests."

Changing his voice one tone to indicate a change in rank, Findbar began enumerating the allowance for those one step lower in status than cattle lords. "You may own a barn, a shed, a kiln, one share of a mill, a pigsty, a calf-fold, a sheep-fold, twenty cows, six oxen, twenty sheep, two brood sows, one horse with an enameled bridle, four changes of clothes for each member of your household . . ."

His voice went on and on, specifying property, until even Éremón's voice was not so hoarse. Meanwhile, other brehons recited the Law as it applied to beekeeping, to fabric dyeing, to every aspect of Celtic life, demanding that the people remember and continue to be guided by the ancient wisdoms.

Sakkar observed this seemingly endless recital with amazement. Whatever he had once thought these people were, it was obvious they were something else. Something ancient and complex and irresistibly beautiful to him, a way of life in which both individuality and responsibility for each other were simultaneously emphasized, and a person's freedom and dignity considered the natural birthright of men and women alike.

The archaic world just approaching its peak in the Celtic tribes was already too far in the past for the average Phoenician mind to grasp. Sakkar was intelligent enough to realize that his own culture was a chasm, separating him from these people and their Law—their Law that held them balanced between savage flesh and soaring spirit, at one with themselves and their environment, controlled by the demands of honor and prestige and freed by their awareness of their own immortality.

Cities, and ships, and the calculated cruelties the Hellenes called civilization had, Sakkar thought, deformed man more than a broken shoulder ever could.

Perhaps he would never truly be one of them, but Sakkar would go wherever these people led, go by choice and with love, for whatever they were was the kernel of his own small personal dream.

And if the Lady of the Sea swallowed them all, at least he would die in good and chosen company.

Having lost the services of a wife, Éremón was forced to complete his personal preparations for departure by himself. But he had gotten everything together somehow and he and his sons were on the beach long before sunrise on departure day, shivering with anticipation rather than cold.

The wind off the sea sang a song of passage.

Loading the boats was a tedious process. Éremón led his best team of chariot horses aboard with cloths tied over their eyes to keep them docile. Éber Finn made a big display of loading his team without blindfolds. "My animals are too well trained to think of disobeying," he yelled across the water so Éremón could hear him.

Ír could hardly be lured on board. He splashed wildly in the surf, to his watching wife's despair, and after he got on he got off again a dozen times, running onto the beach to say farewell to someone or just to admire the spectacle from some new vantage point. No one could manage him until Amergin boarded with Clarsah, but when the bard began to sing Ír settled himself to listen and did not leave the ship again.

Some of the others, even stalwart Brego and valiant Soorgeh, eyed the rolling surf with a fixity of expression usually seen only on the evening before battle, when a man must seek in strange places to find his courage. Once they were on their own vessels they watched the shore, or the horizon—anything but the sea.

At Éremón's direction, the clans had been divided among the boats so that even if some were lost, other members of that family might survive. This had been Scotta's idea, one she suggested to Éremón to enhance his own reputation for wise leadership. But Éremón did not like to think ideas could come from women, even warrior women, so Scotta mentioned it casually as something Milesios had once suggested, then dropped the subject.

When Éremón announced the plan everyone applauded its cleverness.

"Children," Scotta snorted to Díl as they made themselves comfortable on Donn's ship. "You might tell them six times how to do a thing, step by step, expecting the clear reasonableness of it to be sufficient inducement. But one's children never understand. They never simply swallow what you hand them. They close their ears and think of something else when a parent speaks, and then, when an idea finally breaks through the resistant murk of their minds they believe it to be their own discovery and are mightily pleased with themselves for having had a new thought."

Scotta knew how to handle her children.

The vessels were loaded; the captains went ashore one last time to make certain nothing was being left behind. Now Éremón brought his sons to the water's edge, following him in an obedient row like golden-crested ducklings. Moomneh had grown tall for his age, with a line of masculine jaw jutting through the boyish roundness of his face. Legneh was stocky and deep-chested, possessed of a strength he had not yet fully realized. And bringing up the rear was young Lag-neh, the only one who looked back over his shoulder to catch a glimpse of his mother. Lagneh of the chubby cheeks and irrepressibly curly hair; Lagneh, with his toes turned in.

"Come ahead, men!" Éremón yelled hoarsely, spreading the compliment over them like honey. "We need you in the ship!"

Odba could not bear to stand with the other spectators. She edged away from the crowd and waited alone, dressed in a new gown and all the jewelry Éremón had left beind. It weighed her down, embracing her flesh with cold metal.

She saw Lagneh look back, searching for her face, excitement and apprehension warring in his blue eyes.

Éremón's blue eyes. Éremón striding forward eagerly, fearless and magnificent, lost to her because of her own unbending pride.

There was still time. If she called his name, if she ran . . .

A female figure detached itself from the throng saying farewell to the clan of Ítos and hurried toward Éremón. Lugaid yelled in sudden anger but the woman did not turn around and go back to him. She continued forward, struggling under the weight of her belongings. As she neared the timber galleys she called Éremón's name and he stopped for her, ran to her, helped her collect the things she had dropped along the beach in her hurry.

Taya boarded Éremón's ship with him, his sons looking at her with surprise and a degree of hostility.

In deaf and dumb isolation, Odba watched the fleet set sail without her.

◇ **25** ◇

THERE MUST BE no hesitation now. Summoning all the courage of their ancestors, the Gaels turned their faces toward Ierne and stepped off the edge of their world. Floating on faith, driven by dreams, the fleet went out with the tide. The sea heaved and swelled and carried them, and the coastline of their birthland shrank and disappeared.

The sons of the Míl led the way, riding triumphantly in the big wooden galleys and keeping their eyes fixed on the far horizon. Held in the Celtic thrall of excessive emotion, they laughed and shouted and wept by turns, freely.

It was not long, of course, before some of the Gaels turned green and developed a passionate interest in leaning over the side. Even the children were not immune to surging stomachs, but they soon made a contest of their ailment, seeing who could spew vomit farthest.

Amergin found a place for himself amidships, where Clarsah was relatively safe from seaspray thanks to a screen of leather erected to shield perishable goods. Amergin was not allowed to man the oars. His contribution was of the mind and spirit and must be kept separate, but he saw how gladly the warriors applied themselves to the new challenge. They urged one another on and laughed as blisters arose on their hands, and in a great rush of release they forgot the enmities that had strangely developed among them during the last few seasons.

The great leather sails stood square and clean and the wind leaned into them, so the oarsmen could relax. "It will rarely be this easy," Sakkar warned Éremón. "If the charts are right, most of the time we will have to forgo the sails and row against the current. The oars are our only true friends in these waters."

Oars might be more necessary, but Amergin preferred the beauty of the sails. Artisans had painted them with symbols of meaning for the people on the various vessels; Éremón's main sail depicted a sword and, as an acknowledgment of Amergin's role in the venture, a representation of a harp.

At Éber Finn's insistence Donn had had a stylized Celtic version of a Libyan lion painted on his sail, primarily because he could think of no showy symbol of his own.

"I don't care what design you put on the sail," Colptha had said. "But paint the background red. The color of life." Donn could not summon the will to resist, and thereafter those on his galley often found themselves bathed in a peculiar red glow when light was reflected from the crimson sail.

Amergin disliked looking across the water and seeing that bloody hue stain his brothers' ship. Turning his back on it, he held up Clarsah to Éremón's sail instead so she could hear the wind singing across its surface. That sound must be incorporated into his epic when the time came.

The poem was coming to life in him again. It had lain quiescent in a fluid darkness, its bright colors dimmed while the bard was torn between distractions. Amergin had been constantly, painfully aware of it, and sometimes he had feared it would die for lack of nourishment while he spent his energies fretting over Taya and Éremón, Conmael and Colptha . . .

But on board ship the sharp wind sang into the sails and the poem began to grow again. Or perhaps . . . it was not a poem. It was all of language shaped into a song, words sufficing for music. It was a brand-new thing that had never been before.

Amergin had originally intended the history of his race to be contained in the traditional forms, constructed from symbol to symbol to a chanted accompaniment, as was the Celtic custom. But the epic growing within him was its own self, struggling to be free of narrow traditional boundaries. New forms were implicit in its existence; new concepts for man and his relation to the world around him were constantly being suggested to Amergin by the very experience he was undergoing.

Gaul and Iberia, ocean and Ierne, all were shaping the people. Their past was formed but their future would form them, shaped by the dreams that men create.

The men that dreams create.

He had not been able to tell the story of his race so long as it existed only in the past, like bones in a tomb. The epic of the Celts must include the new land they were seeking and the new people they were becoming, led by the longing of a bard.

A song of possibilities.

Perhaps it came from his heart; perhaps it came from his head. He felt it as a physical presence within his skull, squirming when he tried to get a grip on it and force it into shape. He clamped down with all his concentration, hammering and molding like a smith at his forge. The poem was a living thing and would not be forced. It shifted shape and he pursued it, oblivious to everything else.

"I said, 'Sing us a song of Ierne!' " Éremón was shouting at him. "When you describe our destination the oarsmen seem to row harder!"

So Amergin turned his back to the wind and sang of Ierne as he dreamed her, sweet and fruitful and wise, separated from the struggle for existence and endless warfare of the known world by a band of broad sea. He sang of ruddy-cheeked Gaelic children who would be less obsessed by the sword than by the beauty with which Ierne showered them. He sang of bards and craftsmen and healers, fat golden cattle and thatched cottages and close-knit clans.

Beneath the red sail of Donn's galley Colptha stood listening, catching snatches of Amergin's words across the water. "The bard is a fool," he said contemptuously to Donn. "He dismisses the power of the blade because it does not interest him, but I tell you that life everywhere depends on the spilling of blood. Nothing else is as important. Our people suffered greatly because they put their trust in traders and did not placate the Earth Mother with sufficient sacrifices."

"We observed the druid rituals," Donn replied, insulted. "Sacrifice is only one part of them, a lesser one than you imply."

"Wrong! Irial taught that, but he was wrong! The tin failed and the floods came because we did not woo the Mother with enough blood. She is a savage goddess and I alone understand her."

Donn went to the first tier of oarsmen and commented to his brother, Éber, who was taking his turn at the oars, "Since Conmael died all Colptha seems to think about is blood sacrifice. It gives me the itch, listening to him."

"Maybe he's right. All those years of trade made us fat and complacent and we didn't pay as much attention to the rituals as we once did. When we get to Ierne, I for one intend to have a big healthy herd, and if that means offering more sacrifices I'll gladly send for Colptha."

Donn's wiry eyebrows tangled into a frown. "Does Colptha ever stand behind you and just . . . whisper? In a strange way?"

Éber Finn thought for a moment. "Yes, now that you mention it. He has a most insidious voice. He doesn't seem to be saying anything much but I can't help listening."

"Maybe we shouldn't," Donn said thoughtfully. "We should all think for ourselves."

Éber laughed, not unkindly. "If I thought as ponderously and slowly as you do I'd be dead before I finished."

Donn chuckled with him, accustomed to the teasing of brothers. Loving brothers.

The sea was kind, at first. Sometimes the vessels wallowed windless in long slow swells and the oarsmen sweated and

314

grunted, but then a light breeze would spring up and give them a heartening push. And even when the prevailing wind was against them, which was much of the time, Sakkar's ships and boats proved well-designed and managed to make steady progress. But the journey had begun with deceptive ease that Sakkar, after a lifetime at sea, heartily mistrusted. He said as much to Éremón, who was not interested in gloomy predictions.

As they reached the edge of Gaulish territory and turned north to follow the rim of the great gulf to the land of the Fir Morca, the first real trouble began.

Éremón was standing in the prow of his ship, enjoying the sensation of being propelled over immeasurable watery distances. World, world, the world, he thought, gazing toward the far horizon. We used to speak of the world as if we knew what it was, yet we rarely went farther than ten nights from home.

Out there lies the world, and this endless water is the roadway to it. I did not realize. On the sea we could go anywhere, take whatever we need . . .

In the blinking of an eye the sky turned dark and the wind changed; changed with a vengeance, hitting the boats broadside and pummeling them savagely. The water became as dark as the sky, and Éremón saw white crests curl across the choppy waves, whipped by the lash of the wind like the manes of white horses.

Corisios' voice echoed in his mind, magnified by memory. "Over the curling waves of the sea, the manes of the horses . . ."

Sakkar was yelling, trying to prepare the crew for the fast-approaching squall and hoping the other captains would remember to watch and copy the tactics of the lead ship.

Waves raked the hide boats, an occasional outsize rogue rising to reflect its green light on the pallid faces of the people within.

Éremón's galley rolled into a deep wave-trough and water poured over the side, drenching everything. The bard's feet slipped out from under him and he fell across the harp. Clarsah cried out with discordant affront. Amergin's eyes and mouth filled with salt water as warm as blood, hissing with foam.

"Head into the wind! Head into the wind!" Sakkar was screaming, but in the excitement he forgot his recent Celtic fluency and issued furious orders in Phoenician. His babble fell on uncomprehending ears.

The timber galleys were having difficulties but the hide boats seemed to bob atop the water jauntily, driven before the wind but remaining afloat. Their crews gave up fighting the sea and concentrated on bailing it out of their boats.

When they realized their galleys were floundering, the other captains looked toward Éremón's ship for guidance. They saw Sakkar waving his arms and heard him shouting, but though the wind carried his words toward them the words themselves were no more than gibberish.

The Milesians, grim-faced, the powerful muscles of their shoulders and backs bulging with effort, were bent over their oars, committed to a losing battle. Donn's galley rolled heavily to one side and one of Éber's chariot horses, tethered amidships, broke loose and went scrambling and sliding across the deck, his hooves battering the planking.

The ship heeled up again, higher than before, and it seemed half the sea came splashing over the side. When it went hissing back the panicked horse went with it.

Éber Finn screamed like a man who has lost a leg in battle.

Díl crouched in the stern, her youngest daughter clutched to her bosom. Éber's wives were taking turns at the oars and his stronger sons were helping them, but Díl had no inclination to join in. She was certain that if she moved one step in any direction the whole ship would turn over.

Donn, in spite of the desperation of the moment, looked for his wife and caught her eye. He looked as competent and solid as always, and Díl managed to force her icy lips to send him a brave little smile. Somehow that made them both feel better. Maybe they would all survive this.

Maybe.

Amergin had gotten to his feet again and wedged Clarsah between two coils of rope, where she should be safe if not dry. He waded a deck awash with seawater to yell in Sakkar's ear, "You're giving orders in Phoenician! No one can understand you!"

Sakkar looked stricken. "I should be sacrificed," he said, rolling his eyes skyward.

"We all will be if you don't tell us what to do!"

In the Gaelician dialect now, and at the top of his lungs, Sakkar cried, "Into the wind, head into the wind," and ran down the deck issuing more detailed instructions to the various crewmen. Slowly, Éremón's ship came around. Donn observed the maneuver and gave his crew similar orders and the other galleys followed their example. By the time the squall began to subside, the ships were under control again.

There was no heart for proceeding farther that day. They made for the nearest beach to wait until the hide boats could regain their course and catch up. Only then could casualties be determined.

As they went ashore, a sense of jubilation seized the Gaels. They felt they had met the worst the sea had to offer and had survived it. Ír was running his hands through his drenched hair and laughing gleefully.

Sakkar hated having to tell them this was just a squall; the sea was capable of much more violent behavior.

The druids counted the boats as they straggled in. It was well into the next morning before the last one appeared, having searched a long way up the coast while its anxious crew feared the whole expedition, except themselves, had been lost. Their joyful cries upon finding their tribesmen rang back from the wooded shore.

They were well into the territory of the Gauls now. Sakkar disliked spending time ashore. He was ever mindful of the storms sure to come later in the season. "If you think that was bad," he told Éremón, "you should know it was nothing compared to what we will run into if we don't reach Ierne by summer."

Ír laughed. "We're not afraid. You build good boats, Phoenician; they can ride out anything."

"No ship has ever been built that can ride out anything," Sakkar tried to tell him, but Ír was in no mood to listen. He had never enjoyed himself so much and was already looking forward eagerly to the next storm.

In spite of Sakkar's urging, Éber argued that they spend a few nights ashore, trading with the Gauls for food and water and, he hoped, a replacement chariot horse. He was distraught over his loss.

"We brought only one team apiece and now mine is ruined," he complained to Scotta. "I will be ashamed before my brothers."

"Let him get another horse," Scotta advised Éremón. "I cannot listen to that all the way to Ierne."

A trading party made its way inland but soon returned empty handed. Éremón explained, "The Gauls are there, all

317

right; there's a big tribe just beyond that forestland. But they were very suspicious of us. They've seen too many Sea People in these waters, they don't trust anyone in a ship anymore.

"And they have no interest in trade these days. The whole tribe is singing the praises of a mighty chieftain named Brennus who has marched east with an army to attack the city of the Romans. They have taken warriors with them from all over the territory."

"Why are the Gauls attacking the Romans?" Scotta wondered.

"Who are the Romans?" others asked.

Sakkar, who knew, did not volunteer a comment. Even the Hellenes had begun to look nervously northward, toward the rising power of the Romans.

"I learned very little about them," Éremón replied. "They are an arrogant people who seem to have intruded themselves in some dispute between the Etruscans and a Celtic tribe in that region, and they gravely insulted the Celts. Honor must be defended and our distant kinsmen marched to do so. Soon the Celtic tribes along the borders of the land these Romans claim found themselves at war with the Romans. The men of Rome seem to have a warped sense of justice, and even went so far as to insist that their concept of the Law superseded our own.

"War has run through Gaulish territory like brushfire, for of course the chieftains could not allow such ideas voice in their own lands. Brennus has drawn enthusiastic followers from many tribes and seems to have attacked, or intends to attack, the city of the Romans itself."

"It sounds like a lovely war," he added wistfully.

"We have our own adventure awaiting us," Amergin reminded them.

Taya put her hand on Éremón's arm and tugged, and at last his thoughts came back to her. "Yes," he said slowly. "Yes! We go on to Ierne and the Gauls must settle their own quarrels. They should teach those Romans about brehons."

They put out to sea again, in search of their particular destiny.

The encounter with the Gauls made Sakkar fearful of too much land involvement. When the last boat cleared the shore, he suggested to Éremón that the time had come to stop beaching the vessels each night. Too much daylight was being wasted in the maneuver, not to mention the danger of encountering even more hostile tribes along the shore.

"There are numerous reasons for sleeping aboard ship," Sakkar explained. "The timber galleys have anchors and the hide boats can be lashed to one another so they do not drift away. It will be much better; we will reach Ierne sooner. We have enough supplies now, we really do not need to put ashore until the land my chart calls that of the Fir Morca, just before we cross the open sea."

So they slept that night on the bosom of the waves. Amergin lay with his head on his folded cloak as the stars above him wheeled by in their silver chariots. The sea rocked him to her own rhythms. He held Clarsah and let his fingers stroke her as they pleased, his mind disengaged from the process, only peripherally wondering if he would be able to get brass wire for harpstrings on Ierne.

The music floated out across the water. Taya, lying curled against Éremón with her head on his shoulder, felt the voice of the harp pluck at the fibers of her spirit. The pain of beauty was almost unbearable—the harp, the stars, the sea.

"Listen, Éremón!" she whispered.

But the warrior was asleep.

She had no one to talk to, and that was the worst of it. Odba woke up in the morning and looked at the carved chests— hers, the ornate bronzeware—hers, the sheep and cattle beyond the house—all hers. And none of it meant anything.

Her sons' belongings were not in those chests; her husband did not use the bronze utensils. The sheep and cattle truly belonged to the herders who tended them and knew their spirits more intimately than she ever would. All Odba had was the echoing silence.

She could not keep her eyes from straying to Éremón's left-behinds, the small arrangements with which he had once added comfort to his life. A full wineskin suspended by a thong near his bed, because he often awakened at night with a dry throat. A three-legged stool he propped his foot on while massaging a battle-damaged knee. A little alabaster box, forgotten in the final confusion, containing Éremón's favorite polishing compound. On rainy days he liked to sit by the hearth, burnishing his weapons and jewelry, while the boys

319

clustered around him, begging to be allowed to polish the bronze bosses on his horse harness.

Just a little thing, an imported box of paste . . .

I don't have to sit here with my hands folded, Odba told herself. I am a daughter of the Artabri, I can go back to my tribe. I can accept another husband.

But how would she explain to a new man the loss of her former one? Who would want a woman another abandoned? Who would believe she was simply too fearful to make the voyage? Everyone who knew Odba knew she was not a timid woman.

She must get outside, under the sky, and talk to someone other than herself. Anyplace was better than the house that was now hers. All hers. Hers alone.

She almost bolted from the house, and the first person she met was Scéna Dullsaine.

Odba greeted Ferdinón's favorite daughter as a kindred spirit. Had not Amergin sailed off and left her behind? But when she said something of the sort aloud, Scéna rewarded her with an arrogant look and a patronizing voice. "No man leaves me," she said coolly. "I had no intention of crowding myself into an uncomfortable, smelly boat, and drowning in cold water for the sake of a man who had begun to bore me anyway. It was my decision to stay here and live as I like, on familiar ground."

"I live as I like, also," Odba's pride forced her to reply. The whine had gone out of her voice when hope had gone. Complaint was a form of pressure, and now she had no one to pressure.

Scéna put her hands on her ample hips and faced Odba sternly, as she contradicted the woman. "You're miserable and you know it. Look at you. Your eyes are as red as raw meat. I asssure you you won't feel any better until you admit you feel bad."

"What good would it do, Scéna?" Odba said. "What good does anything do? I would have drunk the muddy water from Éremón's footprints, yet I drove him away. I can see that now, but it makes no sense to me."

Scéna waggled her shoulders. "Life makes no sense, but we enjoy it anyway, perhaps for that very reason."

"I have nothing left to enjoy." Odba felt so beaten she could not even savor her misery. "Tell me, Scéna, what hurts most—regret for something you've done, or regret for something you didn't do?"

"Those are druid questions. I never think about such things."

"I think about a lot of things I never concerned myself with before. What else have I to do? I have even wondered if I should have jumped into the water and tried to swim after them . . . perhaps Éremón would have taken pity on me and had me pulled into a boat."

"Why bother to swim at all?" Scéna asked idly. "If you want to be in a boat, take one of those we already have."

"What do you mean?"

"Ferdinón had Sakkar leave two hide boats behind to trade to the fisher tribe. They are in perfect shape and quite seaworthy, I should think."

Odba's rounded shoulders straightened perceptibly. A light came into her eyes which Scéna did not like. "Boats," she murmured.

"Don't think mad thoughts!" Scéna warned her, too late. "Leave such glorious foolishness to the Milesians."

"Glory," Odba said in the same faraway tone. "Éremón would be mightily impressed if I followed him all the way to Ierne. Even Scotta never earned such glory as I would have then."

"Even Scotta would never have done such a thing!"

Odba shook her head. "She might have, in her youth. You don't know her as I do; you haven't had her virtues and victories endlessly rammed down your throat."

"Such talk is idle chatter and you know it, Odba. You couldn't sail to Ierne by yourself, and you haven't a crew."

Odba's eyes narrowed to slits, seeing visions. The very bones of her face seemed to be rearranging themselves into a new and gallant set, shapechanging like a druid to take on needed qualities. "Many men were disappointed when their clans weren't able to go," she said thoughtfully. "Surely I could find enough strong arms to man one boat for Ierne, if Ferdinón would give his permission."

Scéna felt herself being drawn into the spirit of the adventure. "He just might," she told the other woman. "I know he was upset when he found one part of the Milesian clanhold was still claimed by a clanmember. He might give you a boat and men gladly enough if you were willing to abandon your property to him." Then caution overtook her. "But the dangers, Odba! You could die out there and no one would know. The sea could swallow you and no one would mourn you."

Odba shrugged. "You threaten me with very small discomforts compared to the misery of sitting in an empty house watching an empty doorway." The idea had come to her in a rush and she embraced it without hesitation, knowing she dare not pause to consider. She was a chieftain's daughter, and as fearless as her husband. Her sons.

Little Lagneh, who had looked back at her.

"Will you go with me to talk to Ferdinón?" she asked Scéna.

"I wouldn't miss it," the other woman assured her.

Odba felt as if she were walking into a shifting wind. Between one heartbeat and the next everything had changed for her, and no matter what happened in the future, she had taken charge of her life again; she would not be moved about and discarded at the whim of others.

When she told Ferdinón of her intention he proved more generous than she had hoped. He offered her all the men who were willing to go, until she had filled one boat, and all the supplies the party would need to take. Glowing with pleasure at his windfall of the last Milesian holdings, Ferdinón even promised, "In honor of you and the other colonists, we will make a monument of Breoghan's watchtower from which Ítos first saw the vision of Ierne. That way we will never forget any of you," he assured Odba, picturing Scotta in his mind.

As they left the Heroes' Hall, Odba turned almost shyly to Scéna Dullsaine. "Will you go with me?" she invited. "Amergin might be glad to see you."

Scéna laughed. "Oh, no. I never chew my meat twice. But you can do something for me, if you will. Should you meet the bard again, will you tell him I had the chance to come and refused? Tell him I could think of no sufficient inducement. Put it just that way, Odba—no sufficient inducement."

Scéna's laugh was deep and throaty, without malice, and she threw her head back to let it ring out merrily. Odba joined in, feeling she had just returned to life.

As Odba was making her hurried preparations, the fleet of the Gaels continued northward, following the coast as she soon would. Familiarity with the sea was making them bolder. They sailed farther out from shore in hopes of picking up

322

good winds, and they saw sights their landmen's eyes had never seen before.

When the sails were filled with wind a man could relax from rowing and enjoy the sea. Ír liked those moments best. Separated from past and future, isolated by time and space rather than inward alienation, he felt curiously freed of self as well. Amergin sat comfortably on a coil of rope with the harp on his lap and Ír called out suggestions for music, letting the sound sing through him and merge with the creaking of the sail, the smell of wet wood, the warm sun beating on his naked shoulders.

Ír turned to look at his wife and the cluster of his children, two sturdy boys and a comely girl who would bring many bride gifts one day. Children. Odd small creatures. Would one of them turn on him eventually and become his enemy?

One of his boys was pointing and yelling and Ír turned to follow the direction of his gesture; then the grown man's jaw dropped and he half-rose, staring.

"A god," he whispered in awe.

Amergin had seen it, too, and felt his body's unconscious worship as the hair lifted on his scalp like a small forest surging toward the sun. He set Clarsah aside without even thinking of her. Who could think of anything but the gigantic being that rose effortlessly from the sea, ascending into sunlight as if it could make its home in any element it chose?

The creature was enormous; the Gaels had no basis for comparison, for no land animal could rival it. Even Sakkar, who had heard of such things before, could only shake his head and stare. Staring was all any of them could do.

Ír's god erupted from the waves in a great fountain of flesh, slowly, with splendid majesty, describing a curve of pure grace with its immense body. It seemed to hang in the air beside Éremón's galley. Ír saw its eye—the eye of a god!—brilliant with intelligence and some dark and secret mirth, looking at him.

But he was not frightened as he had been frightened by the gaze of the dead bull. He felt no malice in this being, only a sense of kinship. Here was life larger than life.

Within the tabernacle of the god's body a huge heart thundered.

Then the great mottled head, gleaming with strange phosphorescence, dove back toward the sea. The body arced, following, and a fluked tail lifted above the water, leaving the watchers with its imprint burned into their minds.

"What was it?" Éremón wondered, unable to believe his eyes.

"We have seen a god," Ír told him with finality.

"A whale," Sakkar said. His mouth was dry and his palms were wet. "A kind of sea monster. I have heard of such creatures beyond the Pillars, but the commander Age-Nor said those were stories to frighten children and we should ignore them."

"That was no monster, that was a *god!*" Ír insisted.

Amergin was inclined to agree with him.

The bard recovered Clarsah, regretting belatedly that he had not held her up to share the experience. He found a place for himself and the harp behind a stack of crates, where no one would bother them and he could think. The whale—the god—was too large and too important to be dismissed from his mind until he had considered all it might symbolize.

Considered, with awe, the gradations of existence, the truly infinite number of possibilities for rapture or horror represented by the incalculable number of beings nurturing sparks from the great spirit.

A god had leaped out of the ocean gulf, confronting Amergin with the unsuspected, and he felt his mind spinning away down limitless vistas.

Life, the all-encompassing and most sacred spirit, was a tremendous ongoing explosion, its particles filling the void between worlds, animating not only tribes and trees and cattle but Ír's god and the stars in the sky and creatures monumental and minute whose existence Amergin had never before considered.

And if he could interpenetrate that terrible, beautiful oneness that contained both Clarsah and the sea god, he could distill it all into poetry, as the whale had created poetry for his eyes with its vibrant flesh.

The flame of the word at the heart of creation.

In a world of such transcendent wonder, what might not await them on Ierne?

26

THE BEING TOGETHER of the Túatha Dé Danann was held under difficult circumstances that season. A flare-up of hostility was reported from various parts of the island, one Fir Bolg tribe threatening another as well as skirmishing with Dananns along the fringes of Danann territory.

"There will be war soon if we do not discourage them," Cet of the Plow warned the others. "War again on the sacred island. Our Fir Bolg cousins are an aggressive people who have not yet outgrown their need for conflict; they snatch things from one another like two babies in a box. They have forgotten that we could shrivel them where they stand and put an end to all their savagery."

Eriu scowled at him. "How can you accuse the Fir Bolg of being savage in one breath, and threaten to turn the Earthkillers against them in the next as if that were not the ultimate savagery?"

"The Fir Bolg take great pleasure in war," Cet said with condescension. "We do not; we fight only to defend ourselves. That makes all the difference."

"Beware how you cry for war, no matter what the excuse," warned Fodla the wise. "When there is keening on the night wind in the camps of the Iverni and the Velabri, there will be wailing likewise in the halls of the Túatha Dé Danann. The pain we bring to others we cannot escape ourselves."

"We have become too sensitive, perhaps," Cuill suggested. "That is a weakness."

Fodla contradicted him. "Being able to feel the pain of others is a strength. It gives us incentive to avoid causing pain."

"Rather than endure this increasing hostility, we should intimidate the Fir Bolg into peacefulness by bringing back the weapons that scared war out of them once," said Cet. "We

325

can remind them of the days when the red beam of the Sword of Light sliced the tops off mountains and the barking thunder of the Irresistible Spear rained fire on the forests.''

"Reminding them would not be enough," a Danann commented. "They would have to see for themselves. Their bards have failed to keep the past sufficiently alive in their memories."

Eriu insisted, "We must not use the Earthkillers again! The earth is sacred!"

"If we take up the Sword of Light, can we resist using it?" wondered Tuan, Keeper of the Legend.

"For three generations we have limited ourselves to good stout bronze weapons and fought what battles we had to fight in the style of our ancestors," brave Banba said. "Clean fighting, eye to eye. When a man can kill at no greater distance than he can hurl a javelin he has to bear the responsibility of his actions, for their consequences are all too visible to him. Let us forget this talk of Earthkillers and continue to trust our bronze."

"Unless we start to lose," Greine interjected somberly. "Everything changes when you start to lose."

"I am sick of this talk of winning and losing," said Eriu. "Why do we need such words at all?"

"Ask Shinann," said Fodla with a laugh, breaking the tension. "They may not even be in her vocabulary."

Odba sat in the bottom of her boat and watched the ridges of muscle clench and unclench on the sweating backs of her oarsmen. Turning her back on them, she squatted over the communal pot and tried to ignore the cramping of her bowels. The heaving surface of the sea had thrown off all the woman's natural rhythms, but she refused to surrender to her discomfort. Her body would not tyrannize her; her will would override it.

So Odba thought, in the first hard grip of determination.

"Try sitting on the edge of the boat and letting that cold sea slap your backside," one of the oarsmen suggested with a laugh. "I did that, and the shock made everything let go!"

Odba pursed her lips and did not bother to answer.

"Don't tease her; she's a brave woman," a Gael said to the rower who had first spoken.

"I thought a laugh would make her feel better."

"Getting to Ierne is what will make her feel better. And the rest of us, too. Here, mind your oar, I'm not going to pull my stroke and yours, too!"

By following the coastline they were assured of taking the same route the fleet was following, and they expected to find someone along the way who would have sighted such a large expedition and could give them further guidance if necessary. Odba had to be within sight of the other boats before they set out across the open sea, and to this end she insisted they row until the last light died and begin again before dawn. Had her crew not been well-rewarded by Ferdinón, they might have resented her pushing them so.

Two full days and two brief nights had elapsed before Odba's momentum began to fail her. In the light of the third dawn she looked at the seemingly fragile boat, dwarfed by the immense gulf of water, and cold seeped into the hollow of her bones. Sickening cold compounded from the unknown and anger at her own brashness.

There was no mercy to be expected from the sea, who never asked mercy for herself.

Ír, meanwhile, dreamed over his oars at the forefront of the fleet. He thought of the great body soaring up from the sea, and the eye, seeking him out.

The god had spoken to him.

When it dived back into the water, the creature had sent up a silvery spray, fine as mist, prismatic in the sun. A rainbow trapped in its moist exhalation had marked the god's return to the deep. The wind had blown the spray in a cloud that bathed Ír from head to foot like a benediction.

He had stood entranced, the image of the god enshrined in a rainbow cloud forever burned into his brain.

Nothing would be the same for him again. A cloak of serenity enveloped him, and secure in its peace he was able to look back at himself and realize how frenzied he had been.

Envied all his life for his face and form, Ír had struggled from the beginning to live up to that surface splendor. Had tried desperately, knowing deep inside that he could never be as strong, nor as beautiful, nor as heroic as his appearance proclaimed; fearing that others would discover how short the reality fell of the image.

He had exhausted himself trying. His only standard of

measurement was excess. Bigger, louder; more keen, more diligent, more belligerent, more playful; laugh louder, run faster, fight harder; sing, dance, fear . . . life had become a wild scramble against impossible odds. No matter what he did, it was not enough, and Milesios was always watching, pitting him against his brothers, demanding still more of him. At last he had surrendered to the emotions seething inside him because there was no solid ground for him to stand on.

But the dead bull knew. It had opened its dead eye and looked at him and known everything. It recognized him hiding behind his wall of madness, so he had not escaped after all. For one stark, terrible moment the dead bull looked at him and Ír knew it could destroy him at any time, for he had no defenses against the darkness it represented.

Then the sea god appeared. If the eye of the bull watched, so did the eye of the sea god—larger, wiser, benevolent. Balanced between the opposing forces, Ír unhesitatingly put his trust in the greater strength of the giant from the sea, larger than any bull. His personal champion.

From now on, he would be like the god. He would re-form himself in the god's image. He would float serenely on the vast lap of the Sea Mother, moving with the slow, ponderous rhythms of giantism. He would, on occasion, leap upward into rainbows, transfigured by prisms of polychrome light, revealing his true nature in blinding beauty.

Yes.

His true nature. His new harmony of inner and outer beauty.

He saw Amergin looking at him. "Why are you frowning at me, bard?"

"You don't seem to be yourself today," Amergin replied with caution. One must always sort out words before presenting them to Ír. But Amergin did not avoid his brother as others did; he sought him out as the tongue seeks the aching tooth, offering comfort warily.

He stood beside the oarsmen's bench and looked down at Ír's sun-bronzed shoulders. The galleys boasted two levels of rowers, and men manning oars had found they were more comfortable if naked. Those on the open upper deck quickly sunburned, their fair skin red and angrily blistered, keeping their women busy applying unguents and melted fat. Only Ír toasted to a glowing, golden brown without a trace of red. Looking at him, Amergin thought of his brother's beauty as a promise, an assurance that a master craftsman molded human flesh.

Ír tilted his head back and wiped the sweat from his forehead with his forearm. His eyes were clear and lucid, and when he spoke his voice was pitched to a normal conversational level. "I am more myself than I have been since I first lifted a sword," he told the bard. "I wish I could share my feelings now with you, Amergin."

"Try."

Ír shook his head. "This was meant for me alone, I'm sorry. If it had been intended for you, the god would have spoken to you. But he knew I needed him more."

"The god . . . the sea creature?"

"Yes. Sakkar calls it a sea monster, isn't that funny? I thought Phoenicians were supposed to be so clever, yet he could look at something like that and mistake it for a giant fish."

"I suspect the wisdom of the Sea People has some limitations," Amergin remarked drily. "They put too many things—ships, trade, cities—between themselves and the spirits. They think constantly of such matters and never pause to listen to the voices from the invisible world. Is that what you heard, the voice of the god?"

Ír tried then to recapture the flavor of his experience for his brother, but found it as ephemeral as blown spume from the sounding whale. "He didn't speak in a voice like ours, Amergin, but he . . . he bathed my spirit. And after he was gone, I just *knew*. I knew he had taken away the demons haunting me and carried them down into the sea with him. I feel calm now. I feel like a grown man, sitting at an oar, on a ship sailing to Ierne. That may seem like a little thing to you, but to me it is a wonder."

Amergin looked at him closely. "No, I wouldn't say it is a little thing, whatever you experienced. I envy you, Ír."

A suddenly guarded expression peeped from Ír's face. "You envy me? Why?"

"Because you have something that is intensely important to you. Éremón has Taya, Colptha has his ambition, and you have the sea god."

"You have the harp," Ír suggested after a moment's thought. He would have been incapable of such vision a few days earlier.

"No, the harp has me. That's different."

"Ai, Amergin," his brother said softly, putting out one calloused hand and touching the bard's arm with roughened, kind fingers.

The fleet sailed on and the weather held. They followed the Gaulish coast until it turned toward the setting sun and became the territory of the Fir Morca. They encountered numerous fishermen in these waters, and one minor clan-chief after another came out in boats fashioned from single tree trunks, standing in challenging postures in the prow and questioning the Gaels' intentions.

The Fir Morcans were of shorter stature than the Gaels, generally dark-haired and often dark-eyed as well; nonetheless they were unmistakably Celts. Part of his epic, thought Amergin, observing them. Their clothing, their arts, their manner stamped them as surely as their passionate pride. Whatever the source of the Celtic river, this darkly brilliant current was part of it.

The Gaelic leaders went ashore and sat around strange hearthfires, explaining the purpose of their voyage and offering trinkets from their dwindling supply in exchange for fresh water and assurance they would not be attacked at sea.

"That's ridiculous," Colptha snorted to Éber Finn. "What could fisher tribes do against us? They would be mad to attack trained warriors."

Donn explained, "They're defending their own territory, and that makes people twice as strong. It's better not to antagonize them."

Colptha remarked in a sarcastic undertone, clearly audible to all present, "Donn seems to think he has acquired the wisdom of a chieftain. It's a pity he didn't want responsibility earlier."

"I've never avoided responsibility!" Donn protested, stung by the injustice of the comment.

"If you had made more effort, you could have caught Éber Finn's horse for him before it went overboard," Colptha said to him. "Even from Éremón's ship we all saw you; you were the nearest man to it." The sacrificer was gratified by the angry glare Éber turned on Donn.

By the time they reached Ierne, Colptha promised himself, he would see to it that they were such a splintered clan only the voice of the spirits would have any real authority over them.

His voice.

Éber confronted Éremón. "You're dipping into our personal property to give gifts to the Fir Morcans, Colptha tells me. You're a poor leader, giving away too much for too little."

"The Fir Morcans know the waters from here to the Pretanic Islands," Éremón explained, "and Sakkar says we will need them as guides across the open sea. They ask a high price because they want to leave their families prosperous in case they don't return."

"And I want to be still prosperous when we get to Ierne!" Éber cried. *"If* we get to Ierne."

"We'll get there," Éremón assured him.

"Commander Éremón is always confident," Sakkar remarked to Amergin. "I find that unsettling, somehow."

Amergin grinned. "So do I," he confided. But he saw that Éremón's determined optimism and boundless exuberance were an integral part of the whole, belonging in the epic of the Gaels. The bard watched Éremón working shoulder to shoulder with his men, challenging them, daring them, asking after their families, helping them patch broken equipment or giving to them from his own stores. Éremón, whose Celtic pride was so unshakable he could humble himself to crouch in the slosh and rubbish among the lower tier of oarsmen and gladly mend a broken sandal for one of the rowers.

Éremón was a large part of the epic.

And so were the hardwood keels and frames and the pine plankings of the ships, always smelling of rank seawater. So was the stench, after a few days at sea, of urine and animal dung, and the sweet-copper odor of blood when an animal was slaughtered for meat—always with its head turned to the direction of desired wind by Colptha's order, so its sacrifice would have a doubly beneficial result.

And to balance foulness was the great blue gulf they skirted, dazzling white beaches, fresh sharp wind, and glimpses of green farmland and woodland. So many things contributed their essence to the epic, demanding inclusion—the flock of migrating birds that accompanied the fleet for one entire day, snatching at scraps of food the children flung to them. The sun lying in silvery crescents on the waveslopes; the crescent moon tipping and spilling out stars. The sea god . . .

Amergin would not describe these things in minute detail for they were not important to the exterior eye. What must be sent on to future generations was the anxiety and exultation of

331

departure, the menace and generosity of the sea, the deep thudding rhythm of the oars, which a man felt to the pit of his belly, the hair rising on the scalp when the god surfaced. A great poem must speak to the soul, summoning responses beyond the reach of eyes and ears.

Amergin struggled at his lonely task, feeling, as he had so many times before, the inadequacy of words to capture the spectrum of emotion. If only there were a more direct way, a more vivid form of communication . . . he bent over Clarsah, wrestling with phrases, striving to transcend human limitations.

Anyone could say, "I saw a sea monster, this long and this wide." A bard must say, "I was in the presence of a god, and this is how it felt. Share."

A lookout reported to Éremón, "Several times yesterday we caught sight of what appears to be a hide boat, following us at a distance. But it never comes closer. Should we send someone back to see who it is and what they intend?"

"If they were part of this fleet, they would hurry to join us before we enter the open sea," Éremón said. "They are probably fisher folk following a school of fish that happens to be coming our way. Don't bother them, they'll fall behind soon enough."

"Now that we've sighted them, don't try to get too close," Odba ordered her exhausted oarsmen. Recently, in desperation, they had begun trying to use the sail again, for their terror of being left behind when the fleet set out across open water was greater than their terror of overturning or being blown off course.

One of the men said to Odba, "I still think it would be better to join them immediately. We're taking a chance, hanging back like this."

She narrowed her mouth to a stubborn line they had all come to know. "Éremón would put me ashore," she said. "But once we've crossed the open sea he cannot send me back, for even Scotta has never proved herself as I will. Besides, as long as we keep them in sight we'll be all right."

The crew went back to their task, numbed by the succession of days.

On a hazy morning ripped by the cries of seagulls the Gaels finished applying an additional coat of grease to their hide boats and set out across the sea from the last tip of Fir Morca.

The timber ships led the way and the small vessels clustered in their wake like goslings out for a first swim.

Nothing seemed to exist between them and the rim of the world but bleak and hostile waters.

◇ **27** ◇

ACROSS THE DEEP SEA, driven as much by the words of a bard as by wind or oars, the Gaels advanced toward Ierne.

The Túatha Dé Danann tossed in their sleep, dreaming. When they awoke they ordered sentries into the hills, and compared their nocturnal visions of danger.

The tribes of Fir Bolg, interpreting this activity as an escalation of hostilities, honed their weapons and chanted war songs. This time the Dananns would not win, they promised one another with the sour taste of defeat summoned from old memories to energize them.

On board the ships of the Gaels a new tension gripped the voyagers as soon as they left the last wave-lashed stone finger of Fir Morcan territory behind and faced a landless horizon. Their ties with the Earth Mother were severed and they were now committed to the unknown. They summoned fortitude in ways as various as their individual natures and crossed, with oar and sail, the trackless water. Éremón, his face scoured clean of frustration by seawind, gazed eagerly ahead the whole way. The two Fir Morcan guides he had acquired rode in the Milesian vessels and offered advice as to winds and tides, and their visible confidence gave confidence to the Gaels.

They reached the southern tip of Albion, a region so beaten by wind and wave that Taya felt pity for the Earth Mother there, with her eroded stony face hoary with moss. They moored in a rocky cove and Éremón led a landing party ashore to a precipitous headland inhabited by surly tin miners. They took on fresh water—paying exorbitant prices for it—a little food and a number of bird eggs, and were soon ready to be under way again.

The last and widest stretch of open sea they had to cross was rough water, even in early summer. Sakkar disliked its looks, and he saw that the Fir Morcans eyed it apprehensively. They had asked to be left ashore in Albion, in fact, and only the blade of Éremón's sword was persuading them to stay with the voyage to its conclusion.

"Wise men no longer visit Ierne," they had muttered through clenched teeth.

"Why not?" Éremón demanded to know.

They would not meet his eyes or answer him. To discuss dark powers was to bring them down on one's own head.

"We're going to Ierne," Éremón said firmly. "The sons of the Míl fear nothing."

The fleet sailed boldly into the waters future generations would call the Celtic Sea in their honor, and though the waves rolled and a cold wind played around their masts, they made the crossing safely. The Gaels were toughened now; even the rough water did not sicken them, and their tiredness fell away as they advanced.

The lookouts were craning their necks and straining their eyes, but it was Amergin who first sighted Ierne floating between sea and sky, disappearing beyond wave troughs only to reappear, beckoning . . . its green wind caressing his face . . .

He whispered the name, softly for himself alone, and then he cried it aloud. "Ierne!"

Joy leaped like flame from boat to boat.

The Gaels advanced upon the land as a man advances upon his sleeping bride, taking stock of her charms. And from that first glimpse Amergin loved her.

Loved the misty green reaches of her, loved the sounding sea against the rounded shoulders of the bouldered shore, loved the rainbows and the rain. Loved enough to live and die for her, struggling to retain a fingerhold of soil, a tuft of grass. Meadowgrass and brookbabble, sweet high moment when happiness flowed like wine through the starved tissues of his body, and rapture was the land . . . the land . . . the lush gentle hills and embracing harbors waiting to welcome them . . . the pearlescent play of light and shadow over more shades of green than they had ever seen before . . . the piping of a songbird, a ribbon of audible silver . . .

334

So many days of rough water and hostile shores, and now Ierne was opening her lap and beckoning them home.

The Danann sentries brought word of a fleet of ships off the southern coast, large enough to be carrying an invasion force. "They are cruising along the shore looking for the best landing sites and planning to seize the island," they reported.

"Stop the invaders!" cried many voices. "Turn them back before they set one foot on our sacred island!"

"We do not occupy this land alone," Banba reminded the others. "There are not only the Fir Bolg tribes as well, but even little clusters of forgotten people from forgotten ages, hiding away in forgotten folds of the hills. If the invaders come ashore they will break their spears against those warriors first, and we may not need to get involved at all."

"But what if they form an alliance with the Fir Bolg?"

Greine snorted. "Even we have not been able to win the friendship of the more belligerent Fir Bolg tribes. Warriors like the Iverni will resist these invaders quite fiercely, I feel certain."

"And if they are defeated . . . what then?" asked Cuill of the Hazel. "I say we should attack the foreigners immediately ourselves, before they get the advantage. Take no chances, bring out the Sword of Light."

"Not the Earthkillers!" cried Eriu in a voice of desperation. "I beg you to remember the land is *sacred!*"

"Does she speak for you?" a Danann asked Greine.

"Eriu speaks for herself," he replied, "but she is a wise woman and I listen to wisdom. We have more than one means at our disposal to repel this attack of invaders; we will try other things first."

Eriu threw him a grateful look.

"That does not mean you have won," he told her reluctantly. "It only means we have forestalled, perhaps, making that final decision."

The fleet of the Gaels approached a sheltered harbor almost cut off from the sea by a great finger of land. To the south, firm sand and shingle fringed a wide bay. To the north, mud flats gave off a pervasive aroma of fertility and swarmed with so many waterfowl the hunters' hands itched for their slings and casting-spears.

"This is the best place we have seen to land and establish a settlement," Éremón decided. He had a piper send the signal from ship to boat and the voyagers responded with glad cries. The women immediately began pawing through boxes preparatory to landing and the children began pulling favorite animals from their pens to take them ashore.

In their excitement, they did not notice the fog until it rolled over them.

A glittering fog, a multihued fog filled with light instead of grayness. Sparkling, shimmering, blinding.

The welcoming harbor disappeared.

The Gaels found themselves trapped in an otherworld where the wind died suddenly and the only sound was the lapping of the waves. Waves of dark water; unimaginably deep water. Water without land.

Odba, in her hide boat, had glimpsed them in the distance and driven her crewmen to extraordinary efforts to stay within sight of them. The spirits had been good, allowing her to catch up with the fleet and hold them on her horizon across the open sea. Her relief at the proximity of her tribesmen was so great she had not even glanced at the land beyond them. She had been brave through so much adversity, but the advent of hope broke her and she began to cry.

Then the mist rolled over her boat.

"We should have joined the fleet the first time we saw them!" her crew wailed. "Now we are lost! The sea will swallow us!"

When he was not playing Clarsah, Amergin kept the harp in her case with a piece of bread to absorb as much dampness as possible, but in this wilderness of fog she was needed. Whatever happened here, she was part of it; this was her fate, too. The responsibility was hers as well as his.

When he took her from the satchel and plucked her strings she answered him in her new sea-voice, tarnished but beautiful.

The bard had often played to the thrust of the oars, leading the rhythm as the captains had cith_aradagh play the war drums to set the beat for rowing. But that insistent thunder was inappropriate in this situation. They were locked in a shrunken universe with horizons stretching no farther than the ships' bows. Melancholy music seemed better suited to their circumstance.

The bard raised his voice in a eulogy for a warrior who had not died in battle but wasted away with a disease the druids

336

could not cure, while his wife bathed his face with her tear-wet hair. The fleet floated ghostlike through the mist and the haunting music drifted in its wake. Like a disembodied hand it reached across the water to the hide boat where Odba and her men drifted, despairing.

"Listen!" Odba commanded, sitting straighter and wiping her eyes. "Do you hear?"

Her crewmen exchanged glances, listening. Fog distorted sound.

"That's Amergin's harp!" Odba exulted. "He is telling us where they are, which way to row. Whatever happens from now on, you must *follow the harp!*"

The mist shifted and shimmered, laying streaks of scarlet across the waves. The coastal winds wavered and shifted, pushing the fleet of the Gaels ahead of it. Éremón dared not order his men to row for he had no idea where they were and was afraid they would strike the rocks. He stood with one hand on the mast of his ship and his other arm around Taya.

"Is this kind of fog common in these waters?" Donn asked the darkly handsome Fir Morcan who had been assigned to his ship.

The man's eyes were opaque with fear. "I do not know. We told you before, wise men never come to Ierne now."

The fleet clustered together, held by the web of Amergin's music and driven by a strange wind. Time passed but they had no way of judging it for they could see neither sun nor stars, just luminous mist. Days might have passed; nights might have fallen and lifted; they could scarcely make out the nearest boats and frequently called out to one another, fearful of being separated while the bard stopped to rest or take a little food.

No one noticed Odba's boat slip in thankfully among the others.

Then the mist dissolved as suddenly as it had come in a dazzle of late-afternoon sun, and they found themselves drifting along a fretted coastline of cliffs and bays and brilliantly blue water, reminding Sakkar of parts of the Mediterranean. He searched among his charts but could not identify their location, and the Fir Morcan was no help.

Donn, squinting toward the sun, remarked, "I am certain we are somewhere on the west side of Ierne; the south and west, I should think. And . . . Ai! Look there! That must be the mouth of a large river, see how the water changes color?

337

And there's a bay ahead, sheltered and sandy-beached. We are safe. We are here!''

Indeed, they were. As they sailed into the western bay grebes and puffins and kingfishers greeted them, and they caught sight of enormous schools of fish in the clear water beside their vessels. A shout of relief passed from boat to boat, revealing fear the Gaels had not dared admit to themselves until it was over.

This time there was no hesitation at all. People leaped overboard before the boats could be beached, leaving property and livestock behind, desperate to feel the Earth Mother beneath their feet again. Éremón made no effort to hold them back. He was over the side, too, splashing through the surf and shouting hoarsely.

Amergin the bard passed him, running like a deer.

"I'm the leader!" Éremón yelled at him, but Amergin never looked around. Éremón heard both Donn and Éber behind him and redoubled his efforts to catch up with the bard, furious to think Amergin's might be the first Gaelic foot on Ierne.

Ír was running, too, his strong legs pumping and his laughter ringing. Donn and Lugaid were just behind him, and Colptha called out to them, "See how a madman surpasses you!"

Lugaid turned an angry red and swore under his breath. This was no time to have a fight among the clans, Donn thought. Trying to placate him, Donn cried, "It isn't right that a son of the Míl should reach shore before a son of Ítos—this was his dream, first."

"It's *my* dream," Éremón shouted over his shoulder to them. "Close your yapping mouth, Donn!"

The Gaels were overboard en masse now, fighting one another to get to land and claim one pace of it for themselves. And Amergin the bard, lean and inspired, outraced all of them. His was the first foot to touch the shore, and he held Clarsah high above his head and cried with all the power in his lungs, *"Bard land!"*

He was speechless with happiness, but as long as he had Clarsah he was not without poetry. As the Gaels came streaming past him he began to sing a tribute to their new home, a joyous song of a fish-full sea and a fruit-full land.

Éremón caught up with him, scowling at being beaten. But the magic of the harp was so strong his scowl soon collapsed into a merry grin. The contest was won, after all; the outcome could not be reversed. But Taya was his, and would be for all of her life. "I'm going back for my wife," he told the bard. "And my sons."

Odba and her crew landed with the others, and she watched wistfully as her men went splashing to join old friends. Some instinct warned her to hang around the edges and make herself as invisible as if the mist still cloaked her. This was not the time to call attention to her presence. They were so newly arrived, so unsettled, and Éremón was involved with many different things at once. He would be short-tempered at having something else unexpected happen, no matter how thrilled he might be by her exploit. Better to wait for the right time; better to wait until Taya was not standing so close to Éremón.

She glimpsed her sons in the distance, strolling among the older warriors, and lost herself in a crowd of freemen so they would not see her and tell Éremón. Waiting would be hard, but not so hard as waiting in a cold house Éremón had deserted.

The Gaels camped that night on the beach, many of them using the overturned hide boats for shelter. Some tried to think, before they fell asleep, of Iberia; tried to fix images of their homeland in their minds so they would never forget. But the magic of Ierne stole over them as they slept and they dreamed of her instead.

Amergin lay on his back amid pebbles and shells and stared up at the sky, memorizing the pattern of the stars as seen from Ierne.

From Ierne, he thought. I am actually seeing the stars from Ierne.

He turned over and laid his hand flat on the earth, as if on a woman's body.

The moon dripped light. It flowed down the flanks of mountains and pooled in valleys tapestried with purple and white heather. Stars dangled from the fingertips of holly and mountain ash, an openhanded treasure offered to anyone with eyes to see. Air was liquid, a benign moisture bathing the skin and comforting the lungs.

Even the livestock were quiet, gentled and eased and hushed.

The Gaels awoke in the morning to a delicate rain that fell briefly and then vanished, scarcely dampening them. The sun came out and gorse and arbutus sparkled, spanned by silver cobwebs.

"I want to take a party farther inland at once and explore the surrounding area," Éremón announced. "We need to determine just how 'scarcely populated' Ierne is, and if there are natives in any number I want to locate their strongholds and assess their strength. We will set up a temporary settlement here for the noncombatant women and children and the livestock, and leave a sizable armed force to guard them . . . you, Éber, you can be in charge of that."

Éber Finn flushed crimson. "You would leave me here with the women while you go pick chunks of gold out of rivers? Colptha was right about you, Éremón!"

Scotta quickly interceded between them. "You should both go if you want to—all the sons of the Míl should go, and set their feet on this land they have claimed for us."

"Wise woman," Éremón commended her. "I will go, then—with my brothers and clansmen and warriors of the clans of Brego, Lugaid, Un, Étan, Caicher, and Soorgeh. That will give us one army of warriors and leave a second here in case of trouble. Scotta, perhaps you would like to take charge of the women and . . ."

"I'm going with you," Scotta said firmly.

She was gaunt and gray, her face webbed with lines. Mother of warriors. Her gaze was level and commanding.

"We won't need . . ." Éremón began, but she cut him off with one slashing phrase. "I am going!" she said.

Donn and Éber Finn ducked their heads to hide their grins in their mustaches. Ír beamed on his mother from his newfound serenity, at last removed from the need to compete with lesser beings.

"Come, then," Éremón agreed, admitting defeat. Over her shoulder he saw a handful of other women running to get their own weapons, following Scotta's example.

While the freemen went to work digging a defensive bank and erecting an earthen wall—and complaining about the shortage of tall timber on this otherwise well-supplied coast—Éremón organized his army. Éber Finn was still grumbling about his chariot horse. "Take my team, since my ship's wallowing cost you yours," Donn offered. "I don't mind marching afoot."

Donn's generosity seemed to Amergin a good omen; perhaps their brotherhood would grow closer in this new land. What could help becoming more beautiful on Ierne? He went to Donn and insisted Donn drive the poet's chariot. "I'm not

340

trying to match your gesture," he assured his older brother. "I just realized that I really want to walk on the surface of this new earth."

Donn smiled, pleased, and accepted the reins of Amergin's team.

They left the settlement as soon as it had been made defensible. The sons of Milesios, together with Brego and Soorgeh, drove in the front line of the chariots. Scotta took a turn riding with each of them, though she could find no foot room in Éber Finn's overloaded vehicle, and the time she spent with Colptha was no longer than politeness demanded.

The body of warriors followed behind, walking shoulder to shoulder, armed and ready for anything. Invaders in a strange land.

Though he had no chariot to offer Scotta a ride in, Amergin was glad he had given up the cart. As a druid, he was of the earth and the earth was of him, a fact he seemed to appreciate most fully once he touched the soil of Ierne. He had formed the habit of going barefoot when he lost his best sandals and now he thought he would never imprison his feet again. Through their naked soles he felt the naked earth; the wonder of her. As alive as he, interlocked with all the life she supported, she recognized his touch.

Wondering, bemused, the bard walked barefoot on Ierne, thinking of the land. Listening to her through his skin.

Earth Mother. Great sentient entity, capable of nurturing or punishing, even beyond a druid's understanding. Too complex to be manipulated with rituals and sacrifices as the order understood ritual and sacrifice. The druid concept of interaction with nature was wise as far as it went, but their understanding was no more than a small child's version of the adult world—the druids were looking no higher than the knees, Amergin thought, smiling to himself. There was more—and here, on this unique island, they might learn it. All this Ierne taught him as Amergin walked across her flesh, yielding and resilient and welcoming.

They began to catch sight of stone walls protecting fields, and empty fishermen's huts. "There are people here, all right," Éremón warned his men. "Don't be fooled by the empty look of those dwellings—they may have gathered somewhere else to form an army to resist us." Then he laughed. His croaking bark bore little resemblance to the merry bellow he had possessed before his injury, but it brought answering

341

grins to the faces of the army accompanying him. "We will see some action, ai? And it doesn't matter how many there are—we are the sons of the Míl, we can't be defeated!"

They caught sight of the ruins of a stone ring-fort. "This coast has seen battles before," Éremón commented. "It's a good thing we left Sakkar behind, Amergin. He would have been out of his depth here."

Sakkar had actually been disappointed over being left behind with the bulk of the tribe. Part of him was frightened by the possibility of battle; part of him was growing increasingly eager to share the adventures of the warriors. Amergin had cheered him by promising, "We'll get Scotta to teach you to handle weapons when there is more time. Right now Éremón wants us to travel light, fully prepared for war."

Éber Finn could never travel light, even on a war party. He could hardly shift foot in his chariot without stepping on his piled necessaries, items as indispensable as a calfskin bench cushion and his carved box of hair pastes and a set of obsidian razors with inlaid ivory handles. As well as all his weaponry.

Amergin carried only a change of clothing and Clarsah. He had discovered, with no great surprise, that sometime during the voyage he had lost his kidskin comb-bag and silver comb.

"If anyone wanted to follow us they could make a trail of your lost possessions," Éremón teased him.

Inland was mountain country, and their line of march was upward. They soon found themselves facing a dark and daunting peak with no pathway for the chariots. Even while they were debating about the best way to continue, they were attacked.

Roughly dressed demons with unkempt hair and bronze weapons came pouring over the nearest ridge, screaming horribly. Their onslaught was so sudden and savage the Gaels were taken by surprise. The enemy behaved with a total disregard for the conventions of war, Éremón noticed to his disgust, for they used a sneak attack and did not even send out a champion with an offer to resolve the matter by single combat. They just fell upon the Gaels with impartial butchery, howling all the while.

Each warrior was fighting for survival. There was no time to form a battle line, no time to test the effectiveness of intimidating gestures and threats. Just war; sudden, total, devoid of style and beauty.

But when the screaming savages saw Amergin with his harp they went around him instead of attacking him.

"They must be a Celtic tribe," he told Clarsah in surprise. "They know and honor a bard."

The attackers did not differentiate between male and female warriors, however. They attacked Scotta and the few other women in the party as eagerly as they attacked the men, yelling for blood and brandishing their nicked bronze swordblades. Scotta thought with swift contempt how inferior their weapons were, but it was the only thought she had time for before they closed in on her.

Scotta had been trained in a hard school; the paralysis of fear had been beaten out of her long ago. Many seasons had passed since she fought in a real war, but the old skills had not been forgotten; they pulsed like blood just beneath the surface of her skin. With fierce joy she pulled her sword from her belt and swung it, the iron blue blade slicing through foreign air.

Scotta's Gaelic sword slammed into that of the nearest native and the man reeled back in astonishment as his own blade broke.

"Take the blow of Milesios!" Scotta cried, exulting.

But these men, Ivernians born and raised in the mountains, were younger than Scotta, and their reflexes were swifter. Even as she cried her victory aloud another man darted in under her guard and thrust a triangular-headed spear at her ribs. She felt the stab of pain but disregarded it as a trained warrior should, twisting away from the weapon before it could reach her lungs.

Hot blood poured down her side.

She heard her sons' voices amid the din and clatter of sword and shield, the neighing of horses, the rush of bodies. Someone was attacking her sons . . .

There was pain like heat in her shoulder, and blood again—she could smell it. A third blow struck her and for an awful moment she feared her bladder would fail her, disgracing her on the battlefield. She used to instruct her young students: "Eat nothing after sundown and empty yourself before sunrise. I don't want good warriors to stumble on the slime shocked out of you when battle begins."

Scotta ground her teeth through her lower lip, concentrating on that sensation until it overrode other pain and she could continue fighting. She was soaked with sweat and her legs felt shaky, but she was still on her feet. She lunged toward the nearest Iverni warrior and saw him dance away, mocking her slowness.

Then she heard the harp. Heard the resonant voice of the bard, of her beloved son, even above the roar of battle. Heard him exhorting the Gaelic heroes to greater valor, and thought, I must say the words I have never said to him. I want him to know . . .

A man in otterskins stepped up behind her and tore her head from her shoulders with his bronze sword.

◇ **28** ◇

IN BATTLE there is no time for mourning. Amergin saw Scotta fall, saw the swordswing that killed her, and their eyes met briefly across her body. Ír brought down her attacker with a single mighty blow that left the man weltering in a puddle of his own intestines, and the Gaels fought on until the battle was won.

Then they gathered up their dead. Brego's younger brother, Soorgeh's oldest son. Brave warriors and beautiful Fas, a clan-chief's wife. Scotta, clan-chief to the Milesians.

Éremón could not speak. He tried two or three times to say something in his hoarse, ruined voice, but at last he just turned his head away from Scotta's body and gazed up at the mountain, the terrible mountain where she died.

Éber Finn knelt beside her and cradled her body in his arms, for once indifferent to the blood that ruined his fine tunic. He was trying with desperate tenderness to find some way to rejoin head to neck so she would be herself again. The rain of his tears bathed her face.

Donn slammed his doubled fist against his open palm in an incessant, impotent rhythm, and Ír, who bore a wound of his own where a forearm was laid open to the bone, sat down and put Scotta's feet in his lap as if in attendance on a queen.

Scotta's druid sons prepared her funeral where she fell. "She is the first sacrifice to Ierne," Colptha said.

Amergin hated him. "She was a warrior, not a sacrifice."

"She was my mother!" Éber wailed. "And she has taken my childhood with her. Now we can never go back."

The death of Milesios had not been totally unexpected; even Scotta's valiant efforts had not concealed his failing health from his sons. But nothing had prepared them for her dying. Scotta had always been a stone wall, enduring and invincible, in a world where death came easily to old and young alike and was as much a part of living as birth. More, for death is another form of birth and always precedes life. That is the Law.

Yet Scotta had gone suddenly and without warning, leaving the Milesians deserted in a strange land with only a ruined body to bury.

The others were almost as shocked by her death. "I can't believe she is gone," Lugaid said repeatedly. Forgetting their recent differences, he stood at Éremón's shoulder during the entombment, his thick-jowled face somber with sorrow. "We all had to live up to Scotta," he said to Éremón. "She is a great loss to us."

Éremón, silent, closed his eyes.

Amergin and Colptha together set the final guardian stone at the mouth of the tomb, and with the knife of sacrifice Colptha cut squares of sod to fit over the tomb, Ierne's soft cloak covering the harsh stone. The bard sang the eulogy for his mother, and the Gaels stood around him with bowed heads as a soft rain fell. When the eulogy was over, Amergin unfastened one brass wire from Clarsah's frame and left it beside Scotta's tomb. He could not spare it, and so he gave it.

Scotta's death reduced Éber Finn to tears, but it turned Éremón grim. The laughter went out of him and his eyes were the blue of his iron sword-blade.

"Shall we go back and tell the others what has happened?" someone asked him—foolishly.

"We don't need any help, if that's what you mean. We are the Milesians. We will go on from here and find every one of that miserable tribe, whatever it was, and take their heads. They will pay Scotta's honor price in blood."

Colptha's eyes gleamed. "Yes, Éremón," he murmured.

The army of invasion moved on, north and east. They were

345

now a war party in truth and the battle trumpets talked to each other up and down the line.

No one had bothered to gather and bury the natives the Gaels had slain, and no one came forward to request a eulogy for them. Yet Amergin could not forget they had recognized a bard as sacred and had not attacked him. It was something to think about as he and the others advanced over the hills and followed the banks of moss-girdled streams.

Celtic people. Already here . . . for how long? How many of their own kind had they buried, as Scotta was buried? How many of their spirits remained on Ierne after the flesh died? This land, every pace of it, every lungful of air, felt like home to him as his birthland never had, and in spite of his anger over Scotta's death he could not deny a growing feeling of kinship with this land and all its life. Scotta's spirit was here somewhere now, here forever, linking him to Ierne . . .

For the first time since her death he was suddenly flooded with an awareness of her. He stopped and watched the warriors go marching on without him, unaware, leaving him to druids' business.

A sense of Scotta surrounded Amergin like light. More than light; her love was a vivid presence bypassing his five senses and communicating directly, spirit to spirit.

He stepped blindly forward, smiling, not needing to look where he was going. Nothing here would hurt him. He stood on a rolling meadow that stretched to a wooded range of foothills and felt Scotta all around and through him. His eyes burned with gratitude. "Mother," he whispered. He removed the harp case from his shoulder and set it aside, thinking of other things.

Links of a chain. Roads leading not only across space but through time, shining roads invisible to human eyes but as solid as the stone ribs of the earth. Roads connecting ages and people . . . all those whose kindred spirits were of one ancient family, drawing them together with longing for their own kind. Their own connection with the earth.

Throughout his life kindred spirits had haunted him with a sweet, wild language of their own, dearer to him than the tongue of the Gaels; turning his feet from their intended path with an irresistible summons, the communication of his true family, his heart's people.

And now the dreams and images and splintered shards of memory suddenly came together for him on Ierne, and he

346

knew they were more than ephemera. They were signposts, weathered but still recognizable; hints of home. A shade of light, a windblown scent, a certain combination of sounds that had always been enough to summon him, alert as a hunting hound, quivering and eager . . .

Ierne.

Light ran through him like blood.

He realized his eyes were closed and he opened them and found he was not alone.

They formed a semicircle around him, their faces no higher than his heart, all watching him with identical grave expressions. Their skin was as pale, their coloring as fair as the fairest of the Gaels, but this was not his tribe. These people were like none he had seen before.

A woman stepped forward. She was as light and insubstantial as the glassware of the Phoenicians, yet as solid as the earth. He had no standard by which to judge her age, though instinct told him she was no longer young. Looking at her, he experienced the peculiar sensation of sinking into and through her as if her flesh offered no resistance to him. Sunlight and mist, absorbing him.

He shook his head to clear it, refusing to be alarmed. Was this the secret that frightened the Fir Morcans, this strange . . .

"Magic," he said aloud.

"There is no magic," she said in words he knew, though her enunciation was exotic.

"You speak our tongue?" he asked in surprise.

"You speak ours," she corrected him. The language as she spoke it was almost too soft to follow, its sibilance unlike the rolling Iberian Celtic.

He began to think she was beautiful, and fright leaped in him. "Are you trying to put a spell on me?"

The whole group of them laughed like a chiming of bells. "I told you there is no magic," the woman said. "There are many realities, however, and what you see is one. Surely you understand that; your harp and your style proclaim you a bard."

He made a mighty effort to behave as if everything were normal. "I am Amergin, son of the Míl," he said with formal dignity. Then, because such a name could mean nothing to her, he added, "I am a prince of the Gael."

"I am Banba," she told him, fixing him with abnormally large gray eyes. "I am a queen of the Túatha Dé Danann."

This was a most difficult conversation. These people were

obviously the ruling class of Ierne, as far above the savages in the mountains as the stars were above a torch. Éremón and the clan-chiefs should be conducting this important first meeting, discussing terms of battle or surrender. They were an invasion party, after all, and one lone bard was not an appropriate negotiator; no invocations were required here, no satires . . . there was not yet a dispute to arbitrate . . . He fumbled with the fastenings of Clarsah's satchel, seeking an ally.

"Why have you come here?" Banba asked.

Poetry would not help him. Her question was terribly direct and must be answered in kind. "Of necessity," he said to her. "Our clans grew larger and our clanholds could not."

"You have come to stay," Banba replied. It was not a question.

"We cannot go back," he told her, thinking of Scotta.

"How many of you are there? How many valleys will satisfy you?"

"It is our intention to claim the whole island for our tribe," Amergin told her.

She looked at him as an adult looks at a child while explaining the obvious. "But there are other tribes here before you. It is the hope of my own people that they will all learn, eventually, to exist and prosper together like a reunited family. If you would join that family, tell us what you truly require."

From the stores of druid memory, Amergin heard Éremón's voice saying very clearly, *I want it all.*

"I cannot speak for everyone," Amergin said to Banba, carefully sifting his words.

The Danann queen looked at him speculatively, then turned and beckoned a younger woman to come and stand beside her, facing him.

The first thing Amergin noticed was the way she walked. She sprang up from the arches of her feet as if earth had no power to hold her down.

"This is Shinann," Banba told the bard.

"She is of your tribe?" He could not stop looking at Shinann; would never be ready to stop looking at Shinann. He did not even hear Banba's affirmation. He was too busy listening to a ripple of laughter running through his own mind . . . from outside it . . . The girl . . . woman? . . . Shinann had pale hair worn in a shining ribbon around her head, with one rebel lock falling across her eyes. Enormous eyes. Skin

348

so white it glowed as if lit from within. A narrow, pointed chin, like the cat faces on Éber's Egyptian pottery. A thistle-down body filled with laughter that overran it and flooded his own, driving out all the melancholy . . .

In a melting rush, the long winter of Amergin the bard was over.

If Shinann spoke to him—and she must have spoken, because he understood her perfectly—her words had no more weight than swansdown on summer air. Yet he quickly learned she was glad of his coming; that she was bright and sparkling and deep and wise; that her playful surface overlaid a sensitive spirit, a feeling for poetry and music as intense as his own. His own fiery tenderness, met and matched.

She tilted her head and gave him a quick shy merry glance, looked away, then back to him sidelong, beguiling him. Banba was still talking but he could not listen, he just wanted to continue his conversation with Shinann and go on smiling at her. With her. Now that he knew how good a smile felt when it went all the way to his toes.

Banba addressed him by name, forcing his attention. "Amergin, our Shinann tells me there is no harm in you. Are you representative of your tribe?"

He was not aware Shinann had spoken to Banba. His eyes, he thought, had never left her face.

He tried to answer truthfully. "I doubt if I am." Shinann had a dimple in her chin. "My tribe is . . . we are . . ." he was struggling with concepts that no longer interested him . . . "we are cattle lords and warriors."

"And we are the Children of Light," Banba responded cryptically.

"This is your land?" Amergin asked, watching Shinann toss the hair out of her eyes. Her eyes, her eyes.

"We are this land," Banba replied. She too was looking at Shinann. Then she turned to her companions. "Shinann reminds us that we are in Iverni territory and have a distance to travel yet before sundown," Banba said.

Amergin was baffled. "She spoke to you just now?" He had been watching Shinann intently and her lips had not moved, except to smile at him.

There were lines in Banba's face, he realized now as he turned to her for an explanation. She must be even older than he thought. But Shinann . . .

"It is difficult to explain Shinann in words," the Danann

349

queen told him. "She is extraordinarily gifted; her whole generation is exceptional, in fact. Words are no longer necessary for them and so they do not speak."

"She is *mute?* That can't be possible, I was just . . ."

"You do not understand," Banba interrupted. "It is to be expected. Shinann has no voice, that is true, but she communicates very clearly. Tell me, bard—when you dream, do you not dream in images? Pictures in your mind?"

"Yes."

"That is how Shinann talks. Her dreaming mind, if you can accept that term, speaks into the dreaming mind of another person, conveying the feel or touch or sound or emotion she wishes to communicate. Such symbols are more powerful than mere words.

"You see, Amergin, words have limits, but for Shinann there are no limits. Whatever she wishes us to know she gives to us directly, and there are no misunderstandings such as speaking people suffer."

Without words, Amergin thought, dazed. Incredulous. Dismayed.

Words were the heart and soul of a bard.

The silent laughter of Shinann rippled like sunlit water through his mind.

One of the other Dananns spoke, a man no taller than the women and similarly dressed, but with a strong masculine face and laugh lines around his eyes. "If Shinann causes you to see rain, hear rain, feel rain, smell rain, and to watch it drop on a parched flower and revive the blossom, then she has told you more about rain than you can say in ten thousand words. Shinann gives you the truth of rain."

A bard must always tell the truth; that is the Law.

In Amergin's mind there was a sudden clasping of hands reaching across space and grasping each other firmly, flesh to known flesh. Her skin was soft and warm and her fingers trusting . . . He gasped aloud and Shinann winked at him.

"If you have such power as this," the bard said in awe, "what terrible forces might you turn against an enemy?"

"He is perceptive," a Danann commented.

Banba said, "You are assuming that knowledge comes first, and is followed by powers of destruction. You have it backward, Gael, for that is not the necessary sequence. A weapon designed for destroying living bodies is not the ultimate achievement of man."

Some sort of argument had erupted behind her. The Dananns were gesticulating and whispering angrily among themselves.

Banba frowned, "We must go now," she said abruptly. "For those of us who lack Shinann's abilities, unanimity of thought is difficult and agreement sometimes impossible."

Shinann made a slight gesture, scarcely more than a lifted brow, and Banba looked at her intently. "Ah, yes, of course," the queen said. "A gift of some sort would be appropriate, a token exchanged between friends. If you personally are as noble as our Shinann thinks you are."

"I will gladly offer whatever I have," Amergin replied without hesitation.

The Danann queen held out her hand to him. "Very well, bard; I ask this. Whatever happens when your invaders meet . . . my people, let my name be on this island forevermore."

Shinann's huge eyes were watching him. Not forcing, not pleading, merely watching and smiling and filled with light.

"Banba," Amergin said.

"Banba," the queen agreed.

The bard raised his voice to its full poetic timbre. "Let Banba be a name for this land forevermore!" he cried.

The Dananns sighed and smiled and nodded and began to drift away as silently as they had come, disappearing behind outcroppings of stone; wandering into woodlands.

Shinann was last to go—Banba had to call twice to her, and the second time there was a sharp sound in the queen's voice. Shinann looked back over her shoulder to Amergin and he stepped toward her, but his foot brushed against the forgotten harp in her case and knocked her aside. Clarsah cried out.

With a pang of guilt he bent down to her and lifted the case to his shoulder, quickly refastening the thongs that held it there. The familiar task took less than a moment, but it was enough.

When he looked up, Shinann was gone.

The bard ran like a footracer, pounding over the beaten grass along the track of the warriors. He caught up with them two hills beyond and ran into their midst panting and disheveled, startling everyone.

"I saw them, I was just talking to them!" he cried to the throng of Gaelicians clustering around him.

Éremón parted the ranks with his chariot. "You talked to whom?"

"The ruling tribe of Ierne. They were . . . ."

"How can you be so certain they were the ruling tribe? And how could you talk to them? What is their language?"

"You would be certain, too, if you'd seen them," Amergin assured him. "As for language, they speak a strange variation of our mothertongue. At least some of them do. But others . . . a woman . . ."

"A woman!" hooted Éber Finn. "The bard is one of us after all!" The other men laughed with him, even Éremón, though the leader quickly returned the conversation to more serious business. "Tell me everything you learned about these foreigners," he demanded.

"We are the foreigners here," Amergin said.

Éremón stared at him. "What did you say to them, Amergin?"

Amergin struggled to remember the exact conversation. It seemed to have been on so many different levels he could only snatch at fragments. "I promised to call this island by the name of the Danann queen," he said at random.

Colptha crowded closer. His thin lips were drawn tight against his teeth. "The bard tries to undercut you, Éremón. He's already giving concessions on his own; he has a very inflated idea of his importance."

Éremón's eyes flickered. "I am the leader here, Amergin," he said sternly. "If we encounter these people you speak of again, I expect you to remember that. And you, Colptha . . . don't crowd against my chariot, you're scraping my wheel hub with your own and making my horses nervous. Get back there, all of you. We have to go on, there's plenty of daylight left and I want to know a lot more about this place."

The battle trumpets screamed.

They saw more signs of habitation that day, but no natives came out to meet them. "Perhaps word of our iron weapons travels ahead of us," Brego suggested. "I can feel eyes on the back of my neck from time to time, but after we gave that first group such a battering their kin may be reluctant to face us with bronze. Bronze!" He snorted, patting his own good iron blade.

They camped that night in a flower-fragrant valley surrounding a star-filled lake. Ír came to sit by Amergin's campfire. "Tell me about the people you met, bard," he requested. "Tell me about the woman."

Amergin tried, but Shinann was inexplicable, with or without words. "Ai, Amergin," his brother said. "It has come to you at last, I think."

352

"What do you mean?"

"The sea god, remember? You envied me the thing I had found."

"The Túatha Dé Danann are not gods," Amergin told him. "They are people like us—perhaps less like us than the Gaulish tribes or the Fir Morcans, but kin to us still, I believe. Yet if Éremón intends to war on them, he is making a terrible mistake. They have powers Éremón cannot imagine."

"You won't frighten him off so easily. You just said they are people like us. That's all Éremón needs to know. He and Éber and Gosten and Brego and Lugaid and Soorgeh—they're all alike, they will attack your Danamns without hesitation and Colptha will use their blood as a sacrifice to this new land." He stopped at the horror on Amergin's face. "We are warriors," Ir reminded his brother. "And Colptha is right to that extent—blood is the life that must always be given back to the Mother."

"No!" Amergin cried, seeing Shinann's face in his mind. "I cannot allow it!"

"You're a bard. One of your chief duties is to inspire men for battle, not to weaken their resolve. You are bound by the Law, Amergin."

The army of invasion moved across the land in rippling waves as the shadows of clouds drifted across the hills and meadows. They traveled north and east, guided by the contours of the island, along meandering rivercourses that carved lush valleys through the central plain. As they advanced they realized this was not a new land they had reached but a very old one, long settled, its fields cleared and woodlands many times cut, its roads packed by the travel of centuries.

Farmsteads dotted the landscape, set in fields rich with grain. Kine—fine fat cattle—were everywhere, ripe for the taking. When the natives at last began coming out to fight they came armed with belligerence and bronze and were easily defeated by the superior iron of the Gaels, who found even the largest Fir Bolg tribe was little more than a small clustering of clans.

But for generations these tribes had defended their land against invaders from the sea, the cruel Fomorians and then the mystifying Danamns. Now they saw the advancing Gaels as yet one more enemy who must be fought to the death, generally ignoring the Celtic traditions of intimidation and the battle of single champions. Only two champions came out to meet the Gaels, and Éremón cut them both down, laughing as he did so.

The army marched on. Fighting, killing, winning. Again, and again, and again. The losses they suffered were not sufficient to stop them; to stop Éremón, who refused to be stopped.

They began to see, first in scattered glimpsings and then in startling profusion, a vast web of stone monuments dotting the land. The Fir Bolg avoided such sites. Cairns and dolmens and huge monolithic slabs challenged the sky, perhaps commemorating unimaginable events and unnamable heroes. Stone circles and arrangements aligned with the Sky Born spoke of forces beyond the understanding of warriors or pastoralists. The Gaels advanced step by step into some ancient network of power, which hummed with awareness not only of the latest invaders but of other beings, elder gods.

Roads. Lakes. Canals . . . the island of Ierne had been tamed and encouraged millennia ago to bloom and bear as if the gods themselves had shaped its topography. Surely all this was not natural, yet how had it been done, and by whom? For whose ease and advantage? Certainly not the simple natives they encountered.

The sons of the Míl moved through the homeland of cultures older than anything they had ever encountered and felt like children wondering at the accomplishments of adults. Yet they did not see the adults; only more of those tribes the Dananns called Fir Bolg, muscular fair-skinned farmers who came running from wickerwork cottages and wooden huts, from the ruins of stone hill-forts and from dark glens. The Fir Bolg hurried to defend the pastureland, the river gold, the timber and copper and warm wet climate, the otter and deer and stoat and badger and hare and boar. They fought with valor and violence and the Gaels cut them down with iron, cleansed themselves of the spattered blood and clotted locks of hair, and marched on.

"You say you met the ruling tribe, and it is obvious these fur-mantled savages we meet are not the people you describe," Colptha said to Amergin. "So . . . where are your nobles, these Dananns as you call them? Or did you imagine them, bard? Have you become as moon sick as Ír?"

"Ír isn't as mad as you think," Amergin replied.

Colptha laughed. "Madmen defend each other."

But the Dananns were there; Amergin knew it. He felt

them in a way he could explain to no one, so he kept their presence a secret in the bubble of his consciousness and waited, occupying himself with memorizing the history of the inexorable advance of the iron-bladed Gaels across Ierne.

Some nights after Amergin had first encountered them the people of the goddess Danu appeared again, and this time everyone saw them.

The Gaels were traversing a region of low wooded hills and brown bogland that Éber was criticizing for not offering as much pasturage as the country to the south. The farther north they came, in fact, the more he resented each step, until Éremón felt compelled to defend the new territory's virtues.

"There are more defensible positions here," he told his brother, "and it would be easy to lure an enemy into one of those bogs and trap them there."

"It would be easy for some of my cattle to wander into one of those bogs and die there," Éber growled. "I can't see why we didn't . . . ." He stopped and stared. The others followed the direction of his gaze.

A group was assembled on a low hill just ahead of them, amid a circle of standing stones. A group of short-statured, fair-haired people who turned almost as one and looked down at the approaching Gaels with neither curiosity nor hostility, merely an air of patient waiting.

"Túatha Dé Danann," Amergin said softly.

Éremón drove next to him. "I believed you all along," he said. "But I don't remember your saying they were so little—they're no taller than Sakkar the Phoenician. Will they attack us?"

"No. And I would advise you not to attack them."

After a few long heartbeats, the Dananns came forward to meet the Gaels.

Once more a woman led them. At first Amergin thought she was Banba, magically transported so as to be here ahead of the invaders. But Banba had said there was no magic . . . and closer scrutiny told him the woman was not Banba, just very like her.

She announced herself. "I am Fodla, a queen of the Túatha Dé Danann."

"I am Éremón, leader of this army!" the warrior shouted hoarsely, jerking his reins to make his chariot team rear and prance. But the Danann woman did not seem to be impressed. She watched him with the same expression adults use watching the antics of silly children.

Amergin, meanwhile, was searching the crowd behind her for one particular face filled with light and laughter, but he did not find it.

"I have come to claim this land for my tribe," Éremón told Fodla. "Do you speak for your people? Will you surrender to me or offer me battle?"

"Do you consider that an honorable request?" Fodla asked him.

Éremón's eyes bugged. "I am famous for my honor!"

"Honor is a virtue of varying degrees," Fodla remarked.

"Beware, Éremón," Colptha hissed to his brother. "These are deceitful people. Their spirits stain the air around them."

Amergin saw no stain. To him it seemed that the atmosphere around the Dananns was exceptionally bright, as in the first moment of sunshine after a rain.

Fodla looked toward him. "I am but one of the queens," she said. "I do not speak for all my people, but I will direct you to those who can, if you are determined to try to capture this entire island."

"Losers *try*," Éremón said with contempt. "Winners *do*. I will capture this island, for no man can exceed my strength."

Fodla bent down and scooped up a handful of soft dirt. The loam trickled slowly through her fingers, scenting the air with its pungence. "This is strength," she said. "A man is nourished in his mother's womb as his mother is nourished by the food she eats, the crops and game taken from the land, the source of all strength. Each bite of grain or flesh or fruit goes to build bone and muscle, so the land becomes part of the person.

"In return, we must treat the earth with honor. The man who breaks her surface with a plow must know the texture of the soil between his fingers and love its scent in his nostrils, must feel himself part of the earth's process of nurturing life; life she nourishes in her own dark womb, feeding on sun and rain."

"Yes!" cried Éber, moved in spite of himself, and one of the Dananns simultaneously cried "Yes!" as well. The two men exchanged startled glances across the distance between them.

"There is a fragile link between man and the land that supports him," Fodla continued, "and if that link is damaged disaster will follow. A man who hires another to farm his fields while he stays far away in the city" (The Gaels lifted

356

their eyebrows at one another. What could this woman on this remote island know of cities?) "such a man has broken the umbilical cord that sustained his ancestors. He will grow weak, and the generations after him still weaker. Every person cannot be a herder or a plowman, but every man and woman and child must know and revere the earth as the source of his physical continuity."

Éremón was following this speech with difficulty, half afraid the woman was using it to distract him from some sort of rear attack. He kept glancing around, his eyes searching different horizons, and he held his hand on his sword hilt.

"Éremón!" Fodla called to him. "You have come here to take whatever you want from this land; you think you can strip the metal from the earth and the timber from the hills with impunity, but I remind you of this: you must ask, first, and give thanks afterward. You must bind up any wounds you give the earth and you must feed her to replace what you take from her. Every gift she gives, every tree, every stalk of grain, costs her. Only if you repay your debts will she continue to provide."

"This is a race of Celts and druids," Amergin murmured.

Colptha nodded in agreement, then froze in midmotion, angered to find himself acknowledging a spiritual kinship with the enemy.

"Hear me, men of the Gael!" Fodla cried, raising her voice and lifting her slender white arms. She had come to stand just next to Éremón's chariot, and she held one uplifted hand to him, opening it slowly. The palm was almost empty, but he caught a whiff of the departed soil, sweet and alive. A clean smell; an immortal fragrance.

"This is a goddess!" Fodla proclaimed. "Break your connection with her and you will drift out into the dark and lonely spaces, a child with no home and no parent."

"We have no intention of damaging the Earth Mother," Colptha told her sternly.

Fodla turned a shrewd gaze upon him. "We have made the same oath," she said. "But some of us forget. Some of us are willing to destroy the very thing we revere, in the name of keeping it." She sounded angry and an angry buzz from the other Dananns greeted her words.

"What's all this about?" Éremón whispered to Éber. "Are they fighting among themselves?"

"If so, we can use it," Colptha said.

"My spear is ready," Brego interjected.

"Spears!" Fodla laughed. "You will not need your spears against us. See, our hands are empty. I will direct you to our Gathering Place where you can confer with the nobles of our tribe and come to whatever arrangement you will, but I ask one thing in return."

"What is it?" Éremón was instantly suspicious.

"A small thing, no more than a favor you have already done for my sister."

"You would have us give your name to this island," Amergin said.

Fodla smiled. She spoke directly to Amergin then, as if the other Gaels had ceased to exist for her. "Remember that I wanted the land protected and was willing to sacrifice much for her sake," the queen said. "Here, take this. It is as close as you can come to embracing a goddess."

She walked to the bard and from the residue in her hand she dropped one tiny clod of brown earth onto Amergin's outstretched palm. He was too awed to close his fingers over it.

"Follow the road to the east," Fodla then instructed them, "until you come to the next river. You will find a ford above the riverbend and . . ." The Gaels listened intently to her directions as she explained the way to the Gathering Place, but Amergin stood apart from the warriors with his head bowed, holding the flesh of Ierne in his hand.

The other Dananns heard the directions wise Fodla gave the invaders, and smiled among themselves. She sent them along a route that would indeed take them to the Gathering Place, but first led them right into the heart of the most militant Fir Bolg encampment. The Dananns were amused. Fodla might scold them for wanting to use the Sword and Spear, but at least she had enough of the blood of her warrior ancestors to direct an enemy into mortal danger without a moment's hesitation.

The Children of Light stood aside and let the army of the Gael march past them, a river of bright colors and clanking metal and creaking leather.

When the river had gone, the Dananns remained.

◇ **29** ◇

WHEN THE GAELS CAMPED for the night, fat dripping from the haunches of freshly hunted venison sputtered in the cooking fires, and plump salmon caught in a nearby river added to the feast. Everyone ate hungrily except Colptha, who had other things on his mind.

"I like nothing about those ugly little Dananns and I trust them even less," the sacrificer told Éremón.

His brother was mildy surprised. Picking the last sweet morsel off a salmon spine he replied, "Do you really think they're ugly?"

"Of course, don't you? Big eyes like scared animals and bodies too slender for strength—what good are they? And did you notice how the one called Fodla kept trying to impress us? Irial used to do that; he spoke down to the other druids from some superior pinnacle of knowledge in an effort to make the rest of us feel small, but it never worked with me. You should have struck Fodla down where she stood, her and the rest of them, and had fewer Dananns to worry about in the future."

"I would have disgraced myself forever, killing people during one of their rituals!" Éremón protested.

"What difference would it make? They're not *our* people. You're as slow as Donn when it comes to taking advantage of a situation. I'm warning you, kill them before they can harm you; strike when the enemy least expects it. Haven't we already had proof that the savages of Ierne do not honor the conventions of battle as we do?" The flames of the cooking fire were reflected in the sacrificer's eyes, setting them darkly aglow.

"A couple of the other tribes we've met here have sent champions to stand against us, in the Celtic way," Éremón reminded him.

Colptha's thin lips twitched. "That doesn't mean anyone

359

on Ierne has respect for formal conduct in warfare. There is a very real threat of tricks and treachery, Éremón; I'm warning you, and you know I speak for the spirits when I tell you to attack your enemies before they attack you . . ."

"Get away from me, Colptha!" Éremón lashed out. "You're no battle expert; I am. And I'm tired of having you buzz in my ear like a biting fly."

But the fly had left a germ to grow and fester in the recesses of Éremón's mind.

Late the next day, the advance guard reported a native settlement in a valley ahead. "A large encampment of warriors with a full retinue," the scouts asserted. "The greenwood they used to build a palisade is dried and warped, so they've been there for several seasons."

"Is it a Danann camp?" Amergin asked.

"No, we could tell that much, though we don't know enough about the other tribes here to identify the various ones. These men wear otter fur cloaks, and . . ."

"Like the people who killed Scotta!" Éber cried, instantly inflamed.

"Restore the balance," Colptha urged. "Spill their blood in exactly the same style they spilled hers."

"We will go and offer them battle," Éremón began, but Colptha outyelled his hoarse voice. "They did not *offer* you battle when they attacked us in the mountains! Treat them the same way now! Attack without warning and feed them to the ravens!"

"When did you get to be a battle leader?" Éremón demanded to know.

"When Ollach named me chief druid I was given the responsibility of advising you according to the dictates of the spirits," Colptha reminded him, invoking the power of the invisible world. "I tell you the spirits demand a sacrifice in kind, in the name of Scotta."

"I do not believe Colptha speaks for the spirits, but from his own thirst for vengeance," Amergin tried to tell Éremón, but the warrior was hearing too many voices from too many directions and losing patience with all of them. The warriors were beating the earth with the hafts of their spears and pounding their fists against their shields; Colptha was calling for revenge; the temptation to pay a debt in kind was flooding through him . . .

"Very well," he said. "It is almost twilight. By the time

360

we reach them darkness will have fallen. We will watch and wait, and when their fires die down we will fall on them as they fell on Scotta and the others.''

Colptha has infected even Éremón; indomitable Éremón, Amergin thought with mingled grief and anger.

The bard refused to march in the front rank of an unprovoked attack under cover of darkness. But Éremón was too agitated to be shamed out of his decision. Colptha kept dancing around him, praising the wisdom of his leadership, until at last Éremón snarled at Amergin and came close to openly insulting him.

Colptha is hungry for blood, Amergin told Clarsah. That's what this is about. There will be much more blood this way than in an honorable daylight battle.

He was right.

The Fir Bolg were sunk into that deepest sleep which comes soon after a man closes his eyes, and is hardest to shake off. Groggy and confused, they fought the attackers who poured through a breach in their palisade as best they could, but the element of surprise was too much for them and the iron weapons of the Gaels were too terrible. In the end they were defeated and in the uncertainty of darkness almost all were slaughtered—including a number of women and children who had been unseen and unreported by the scouts.

Colptha had a surfeit of blood now.

The dawn was gray and the scene depressing. Battle fever had cooled and the Gaels wandered through the camp, averting their eyes from the sight of dead noncombatants. This was a shameful thing and they knew it.

Éremón was in a terrible mood.

Within its palisade, the Fir Bolg encampment was a village of wickerwork huts with hides for doors and only the most casual mud daubing to keep out the elements.

"These things wouldn't last two seasons on the coast we came from," Lugaid remarked, kicking at a flimsy wall and watching its daubing shatter into powder.

"The Mother wears a more temperate face here," Éber Finn pointed out. "This may be all the protection one needs."

Lugaid shook his head. "We've seen fur-bearing animals with good pelts. I think it's reasonable to expect some cold winters, even for you, Éber. Unless you sleep under all your women at once!''

The ripple of laughter following his jest only partially

relieved the mood of the warriors, and did not help Éremón at all.

His disappointment in himself was enormous. He had made such a point of honor, the prestige of Milesios, the nobility of the Champion's son. He had paraded himself in it, like Éber Finn swaggering around in that motheaten lion's pelt he treasured. Then with one reckless act he destroyed the reputation he had worked so hard to build. Not only had he been guilty of a night attack, after deliberately eschewing such unfair forms of battle; he had been responsible for the slaughter of women and children, knee-high tots who now lay weltering in their own blood while shocked Gaels looked the other way and tried to forget the night's madness. Few of them had actually struck mothers and children, but the responsibility of each man who had passed on to his leader. The head, the chief of the expedition, the warlord.

Éremón. Furious, sullen Éremón, hating himself for the ultimate betrayal of oneself, a betrayal he had never expected.

He could not deal with it. He could not redress the wrong by swinging a sword or striking with a fist, and he knew no other way to fight back; he had no other weapons.

He stalked through the ruined encampment with his shoulders hunched, like a man in pain.

Étan called to him, "We've got one of them alive at least—their leader, it seems. He was away spying on the Dananns and just got back to find his stronghold destroyed. What do you want to do with him?"

"Hold him!" cried Éremón. "I'm coming!"

Like the Dananns, the Fir Bolg chieftain spoke an approximation of the Celtic mother-tongue, but in his case the words were belligerently inflected and spat in Éremón's face. His hair was matted and needed washing, his face was streaked with paint apparently meant to denote status within his tribe, and his clothing was caked with mud, though made of good leather and fine wool in addition to the ubiquitous otterskin cape.

The leader of the Fir Bolg had long bones and fiercely blue eyes.

"Are there any more of your kind hiding out there?" Éremón demanded of him.

"What is your name and tribe?" Donn interjected, not willing to be left out.

The man swung a speculative glance in his direction. "Who asks?"

"Donn, clan-chief of the Milesians since the death of Scotta, and a prince of the Gael."

Their captive chewed this over. "Clan-chief. Prince." He tugged at his bound arms, testing the ropes. "I am Eochaid," he said grudgingly. "I should not be alive. My people are dead."

"You won't have to live much longer," Soorgeh promised him cheerfully. "Just give us some information about the Dananns and we'll give you back your sword. You can seek your death on it."

Eochaid spat an oyster-gray globule of phlegm directly between Soorgeh's feet. "Kill me yourself," he snarled.

Aside from his name, Eochaid gave the Gaels no information. When Éremón tried to question him about the Dananns he drew into himself like a turtle and seemed almost fearful.

"I can't understand why he should be afraid of the Dananns," Éremón said.

"Everyone who has seen them seems to have a different impression of them," commented Donn. "Colptha thinks they are hideous, Amergin thinks they are beautiful—perhaps to these savages they appear as monsters. Sorcerers of some kind who practice unfamiliar rites of magic."

"There is no magic," Amergin spoke up. "Only another kind of reality, and we misunderstand its nature."

Éremón refused to allow his men to take heads or any other form of trophy. "This was not an honorable victory," he said. Éber, who had his eye on some handsome bronze cooking vessels, was angry and showed it. And Colptha took his side, agreeing and encouraging him.

Of them all, Éber Finn seemed to Colptha to be the most open to influence now. Éber Finn was weakened by his jealousy of Éremón's authority; he could be maneuvered and manipulated. He, rather than stolid and conciliatory Donn, could become a flexible tool, a war leader controlled by the invisible power of the sacrificer . . .

When Éber Finn complained too loudly Éremón responded irritably, "Would you take trophies from adversaries who did not have a chance to meet you in open combat? What glory is there in that?

"And furthermore, I've decided not to kill the native leader after all. I'll keep Eochaid alive as a pet until he dies of old age. I like him, we have much in common."

"You're a fool!" Colptha burst out. "He's very dangerous; give him to me as a sacrifice and I'll cut his throat . . ."

Éremón favored his brother with an icy look. "I will give
you no gifts, Colptha. You have done me no service."

In the darkest part of the night, Colptha crept soundlessly
to the side of the bound Fir Bolg chieftain and cut his ropes.

At first light Éremón found his captive gone and his own
son Legneh, who had stood the late watch, badly hurt. Eochaid
had clubbed Legneh down as he made his escape.

Colptha was smug. "I warned Éremón, you all heard me.
When will you start listening to me?"

"Now," Caicher vowed openly. Several others agreed,
though none of the Míl's sons joined them. Not yet.

Éremón would not go on to the Gathering Place until his
son was sufficiently recovered from his wounds, but Éber
Finn wanted to resume the march immediately. Another argument flared between the brothers, and Colptha was pleased.

Legneh had a fever and in the night he called Odba's name
again and again, as Éber Finn sometimes called for Scotta in
his own sleep.

"Your mother is at the other end of the world," Éremón
gently reminded the hurt boy, "but I'm here. Everything will
be all right. I'm here, Legneh, on Ierne with you."

And so was Odba, though neither of them yet knew it.

She had fashioned a shelter from the overturned hide boat that
had brought her across the sea, and was waiting with the
other Gaels for the return of the war party. She had tried to be
as unobtrusive as possible but it was only a short time before
everyone was aware of her presence.

Donn's wife Díl reported it to Taya. "What are you going
to do?" she asked eagerly, trying to imagine herself in the
same situation.

Taya shook her head. "I don't know. I can hardly believe
it's possible!"

"She's here, I assure you. I saw her myself when I went to
get one of our calves that had wandered off to eat seaweed. I
even spoke with her, Taya. She said Ferdinón let her have a
boat and she followed us all the way; she had some terrible
experiences. Isn't it incredible?"

Taya felt as if all the blood in her body had run down into
her belly and congealed there. "Éremón will never send her

away now," she said in a faint voice. "He will think she is
. . . magnificent. And I suppose she is. She has won after all,
Díl."

"Nonsense," Díl said briskly. "This is a new land, things
will not necessarily be arranged according to the old ways.
Éremón may not be bound to the old marriage here; the
brehons will have to decide."

"The brehons brought the Law with us," Taya said. "It is
carved in our minds; we cannot escape it. And Odba knows
how to invoke the Law."

Díl folded her calloused and blistered hands—they were
not aristocrats living in luxury here, but pioneers, and everyone had to do hard labor—and glared at the younger woman.
"This won't do, Taya. If you want Éremón you're going to
fight for him, because we come from a race of fighters. Don't
just sit there gawping at me, get up. On your feet! Stiffen
your spine! That's better. Don't let awe of Odba shrivel you
away; she's a woman just like you and not one curl better.

"When Éremón comes back you're going to meet him
wearing your best finery and mine, with paint on your face
and perfumed oil on your skin. We'll borrow some from
Éber's women—they always have it." Díl, who had cowered
in the ship during the storm, was finding it was easier to
exhort someone else to be brave than to be brave oneself.

Odba's son Legneh was learning about courage his own way.
Though the side of his face was still purple and one eye was
closed, and his ear rang where Eochaid had slammed a rock
against it, he told Éremón he was feeling fine and ready to go on.

"That's my son!" Éremón crowed, slapping him on the
back. Legneh managed to resist wincing, and grinned.

"At dawn we march on to the Danann stronghold to win
Ierne!" Éremón announced joyfully to his army of invasion.

Chariot wheels cut through soft turf; mossy meadows were
trampled to mud; broken branches marked the storm of the
Gaels through a gentle woodland. Noise and clatter, bravado
and boasting. And amid it all the chief bard walked in silence, with his thoughts and his harp for company.

They crossed a well-watered plain dotted by shale hills.
The trail the Gaels followed, like all others in the area,
converged on one particular rise, some ancient mountain
worn to just a soft lifting of the land.

365

As the warriors moved up the gentle incline toward what must be the Danann Gathering Place, Amergin turned and looked back along the way they had come, as far as the mountains embracing the wide central plain of Ierne. It was a regal view; a location from which kings would survey their holdings.

An earthwork bank of exceptional depth and height marked this as a royal fortification. Seen from its summit, the hill was actually a ridge, not high but with a sweeping vista. From this point, human vision embraced and possessed the land in every direction.

Éremón, thinking similar thoughts, halted his chariot and stretched his arms as wide as they would reach.

The Gaels came clambering up the slope, weapons ready, eyes darting from side to side. This was the stronghold of the Danann aristocracy, yet they were surprised that no armed guards ran forward to challenge them and no palisades crowned the great earthwork embankment. The only manmade structures on the entire hill were simple, timbered halls, open to light and air, and a large grass-covered mound in the style of a burial cairn.

The columned halls were not built to a design the Gaels knew. Amergin strode closer for a better look, admiring the grace and airiness of the structures. Then he saw one single large stone slab, set off by itself like a monument on a hill otherwise free of standing stones, and turned in that direction.

The stone was aware of his presence.

The Stone of Fal was centered over one of the holy places of the earth. Man had not sanctified this spot; it was a focus of power long before the advent of humankind, and the force it both contained and summoned was not created for the specific use of men.

This was a holy place—but not a temple of worship. The animals, never having lost sight of their creator, needed no place set aside for veneration. Sanctified structures were a human requirement, the peculiar invention of a species that had lost hold of the creator's hand somewhere along the way, in some frightening darkness, and was forever trying to regain that steadying touch. So humans built temples and erected altars, but the Stone of Fal was neither.

The long granitic slab waited and watched in splendid solitude, unconcerned with the desperate seeking hungers of mankind.

The force of the stone reached out to summon Amergin, who approached it barefoot across earth beaten free of grass by generations of feet. The closer he got to the stone the slower he walked. When he stood in front of it he had the peculiar impression that it was humming, deep inside itself, though the bard heard no sound. But some vibration too subtle for human ears transmitted itself to Clarsah and the harp on her shoulder thong hummed, too.

Amergin stretched out a cautious hand and touched the surface of the stone. Instantly he was no longer alone, but enveloped by multitudes. A congregation of selves, his own inexplicably among them, responded with a flooding transmittal of such raw energy that the bard jerked his hand away and stood dazed, staring at the gray rock.

Someone laughed without malice. "The stone from Falias has spoken to you," a pleasant voice commented, and Amergin turned to see a group advancing toward him from one of the timbered halls. A group of Dananns, led by a grizzled man with singularly bright eyes. It was this man who had spoken.

"I am Greine, Son of the Sun," he introduced himself politely. "And I see you have already met the Stone of Fal." He laughed again and the sound spread around him in a warm ripple, including the dozen or so men who stood with him and an equal number of Danann women just emerging from the hall.

Before Amergin could respond Éremón came bounding into the middle of the scene, his hair bristling with lime paste, his jewelry clanking. "I am the leader of this army," he announced in his crackling, ruined voice. "I am called Éremón!"

"Son of Milesios and prince of the Gael," Greine added.

Éremón was visibly startled. "How did you know that?"

Greine lifted pale eyebrows. "Was it supposed to be a secret?"

Éremón was disconcerted. These were physically inconsequential people, the tallest a head shorter than he and all of them slender, but there was something slippery about them. Something odd, which might be more dangerous than he had first thought. Their actions and responses were very unpredictable, and Éremón was not a man who liked surprises from others.

A fresh wind was blowing; there was always a breeze on this hill. It sang unimpeded through the columns of the Danann halls. It flowed between the strings of Amergin's harp.

Two men stepped forward to stand shoulder to shoulder with Greine. "These are my fellow kings," he announced. "Cuill of the Hazel, son of Cermat, and Cet of the Plow, husband of my wife's sister Fodla."

Donn was thinking, These are not savages but people of form and tradition like ourselves, knowing enough to introduce themselves by style and family.

From the way the Dananns glittered, Éber Finn was wondering if their clothing was woven with gold threads in it.

Éremón said aloud, "We have come to claim all this island for our tribe, which has great need of new and fertile land. In accordance with our custom, we offer you the choice of battle or surrender." He drew himself to his full height, inflated his chest to its maximum breadth, and waited.

Greine looked at him as mildly as if he had only commented on the weather.

A woman came forward now, followed by several younger people who seemed to be of Shinann's age, though Amergin did not see her face among theirs. The woman who joined Greine bore a striking resemblance to the first two queens the Gaels had met, but the indomitable courage of Banba was softened in her face and the timeless wisdom of Fodla was replaced by an ardor that set her eyes aglow when Greine turned and smiled at her.

"This is my wife, the queen Eriu," the Danann king announced proudly.

Éremón spoke out of the corner of his mouth to the men behind him: "We must behave very correctly here, princes to princes. Let me do all the talking."

Amergin put his hand on his brother's arm. "Listen to me first, Éremón." The ruddy warrior inclined his head to listen, but kept his eyes fixed on the Dananns who waited politely, obviously accepting the need for a conference among princes.

"When I met the first group of Dananns, their queen spoke as if they would be willing to share this land with us without bloodshed," Amergin told his brother. "And in our long march across the island, they have never appeared with weapons or raised their hands against us. There may be no need either to humiliate them by demanding a surrender, or to involve ourselves in a battle with them. I do not think we *should* war with them, Éremón—various things they have said and done lead me to believe that would be a mistake. Perhaps . . ."

Éremón cut him off with a hasty gesture. "How can we be honored as conquerors if they don't surrender? You don't appreciate the prestige of the warlord, Amergin. And what's wrong with battle? How else can we prove we are superior and entitled to this island?" Once more overthrowing the traditions he generally espoused by choosing to be deaf to the warning of a bard, he turned back toward the waiting Dananns and raised his voice to its full hoarse volume.

"We have come many days and nights across the sea to reach Ierne," he began, intending to restate his demands in lofty terms to impress and intimidate the Dananns. But Eriu spoke into one of the gaps left by his rasping voice.

"In the name of my people I bid you welcome to this land," she said in tones so pure each word was a polished jewel, and her listeners leaned forward eagerly to grasp them. "May your descendants live here forevermore." She extended her hands, palms up, and smiled.

"She's going to give us Ierne without a murmur!" Donn said in delight. "What an astonishingly gracious gesture."

"You smallskulled fool," Colptha hissed in his ear. "You are more gullible than a puppy; you would have made a pathetic chieftain. A real leader would be able to see that her words are no more than a clever trick to throw us off guard. But chieftains sire *sons*, don't they, my poor brother?"

A red blaze was ignited within Donn's brain. When Colptha had lost interest in him and begun hovering at Éber Finn's shoulder, Donn had felt relief. The mantle of chiefdom was not for him. But the sacrificer's voice had a terrible power beyond its spoken words; it wormed into a man's mind and twisted his thoughts, reminding him of forgotten injustices, rubbing scabs off old wounds. Defenseless against its goading, Donn struck out wildly, not even bothering to choose his direction.

"You can't fool us with false welcomes!" he yelled at Eriu. "We give you no thanks! Our own strength and our own spirits brought us here and will deliver Ierne to us!" His face was crimson with anger; Díl would not have recognized her amiable Donn in that moment.

In the twinkling of an eye, the warmth was gone from Eriu's voice. She had not expected an insulting response. Until Donn shouted at her, Eriu still hoped that these new invaders could somehow be won to terms of accommodation—

369

Shinann had certainly reported as much after meeting the one called Amergin.

But perhaps Amergin was not representative of his tribe. Perhaps the sturdy tousled warrior, yelling and red-faced, was the best these newcomers had to offer, and the strange blue-bladed swords they carried were the only language they understood.

We will be both mourners and mourned, she thought with a wrenching sadness. "Thank whom you will," she told Donn coldly, "but now I tell you this: neither you nor your children will have joy of this island!"

Greine was also scowling at the insult offered his wife. He had hoped she was right and war might be avoided, but now he thought not. All that really remained to be chosen was the strategy and . . . the weapons.

Éremón, too, felt war in the air he breathed. But for him there had never been a choice; this was what he came for, and he was ready. More than ready. He balanced on the balls of his feet and put his hand on his sword-hilt. "I repeat my offer to you," he told Greine, ignoring the woman. "Surrender or battle. Our druids"—he cast a quick glance at Amergin—"tell us you are the dominant tribe on the island and therefore you can surrender it to us if you choose. Or you can fight. We have consistently defeated your under-tribes in battle and are anxious to match our skills against yours, if that is your wish."

There had been a chance, just for one long moment. Amergin had known it the moment he saw Eriu's face. There was no need to slaughter these people, these beautiful and remarkable people . . . Shinann . . . I will fight the fighting! the bard swore to himself in silence. If I just have time alone with Éremón, away from the others pushing at him, I can talk sense to him. But I need *time*.

As far as Éremón was concerned, time had run out and the longed-for confrontation with its attendant opportunity for glory had arrived. He grinned with anticipation, awaiting Greine's answer.

The Danann king drew a deep breath. "If we should choose battle, will you put up a champion to stand against a champion of ours?" he asked.

Éremón started to answer in the affirmative but then he heard muttering behind him and hesitated. He had brought his warriors a long way and built up their expectations as well as

370

their confidence. Every one of them was primed and ready to fight for Ierne; to fight not just poorly equipped savages, but these nobles, who would be more prestigious opponents and provide more valuable trophies.

"My warriors are all champions," Éremón told Greine, "and so I can hardly pick one above the others. We will all fight."

They laughed and shouted behind him, delighted with him; the brotherhood of warriors.

"I would like to confer with my own counselors, Prince Éremón," Greine said. "Will you allow me that privilege?"

"Of course." Éremón was pleased to see that things had returned to the formal atmosphere he had originally intended. When the bards sang afterward of the winning of Ierne, they would be able to say that Éremón, son of Milesios, had conducted himself with the greatest nobility at all times; had observed the ancient and honorable formal Celtic conventions preceding warfare.

He looked around for the Danann elders, but saw only a crowd of young people surrounding Greine. Men and women with but twenty or so winters behind them; big-eyed, bright-faced men and women encircling the king, touching him, looking from him to Éremón and back again. Yet never appearing to open their mouths.

Amergin was watching them too, but he could not find Shinann among them. She was not here, then . . . he did not know whether to be glad or sorry.

Greine dismissed his young friends with a gentle gesture and turned toward Éremón, taking one carefully measured pace forward. "Prince Éremón," he said, "you have come upon us with a full military force but without first sending emissaries to warn us. You allow us no time to prepare—and as you can see, this is not a war party you address here. We have the same mother-tongue, so we would have expected you to be an honorable people, as we are. From Éremón, son of Milesios, we expected heroic behavior; yet now you come like a thief in the night to rob us when we are least ready."

Éremón clenched his fists in astonishment. He felt he was standing unarmed before these soft-handed, indoor-pale people and they were judging him. They were shaming him! They not only knew his pedigree and called his sire by name but were aware of the value he placed on personal honor and had turned that as a weapon against him.

371

How? How did they know?

One of the silent young Dananns stared fixedly at Éremón and the Gael had a brief, painfully vivid image of the slaughtered Fir Bolg children in their encampment. Éremón's cheeks burned red with humiliation. The Danann smiled.

Colptha crowded close to Éremón. "Be careful," the sacrificer whispered. "They're trying to trick you; you don't know how to fight people like this."

"I know how to fight anybody!" Éremón grated. He would not let Colptha lead him again like a yoked bullock to some even larger humiliation.

"Will you withdraw and give us time to prepare for battle?" Greine asked politely.

"How long would you need?"

"At least nine days," Greine replied. "We would have to summon our fighting force from various parts of our territory. But as you said, we are the dominant tribe in this land. We will give you our word that during that time no hand of ours will be raised against you, and we will do what we can to safeguard you from attack by the Fir Bolg, the other tribes here, who are . . . sometimes . . . obedient to us."

Éremón was trying to think but his ears were filled with a strange and distracting humming. The sun was too bright, perhaps; something was too bright, glaring in his brain . . . his thoughts jittered and jangled and he needed to think clearly. "Nine days seems a long time," he began tentatively, then paused, trying to figure out just how long it would reasonably take the Dananns to summon an army. But mists were swirling in his mind. The responsibility he had sought so avidly now seemed too great to bear alone; he did not want to make any more mistakes . . .

"I, too, would like to confer with my counselors," he told Greine. "My druids . . ." and at once Colptha was edging closer to him with hungry eyes.

No. Not Colptha. Fighting off the humming in his ears, Éremón gestured toward a tall, dark Gael who had carried a splendid harp with him onto the Danann hill. A harp he now held in his hands as his companions held their weapons.

"This is the great bard Amergin," Éremón said. "We brought no brehon with us, but as a druid Amergin is trained in clear thought and the Law. Will you accept his judgment in this matter of the number of days to be allowed you?"

"Amergin!" Eriu acknowledged the bard with a sudden

smile like the rising of the sun. She told Éremón, "Among our people bards are highly revered and their word considered the equivalent of gold. We will gladly accept your bard as arbiter here." She glanced past the invaders to the gray stone that watched. "Our elements would kill him on the spot if he mis-spoke," she added.

Her voice was honey but her words were as chilling as wind off the Sea of the Dead. The Gaels felt their hackles rise. Those standing nearest the Stone of Fal hurriedly moved away.

Éremón turned to Amergin, to his brother who had never let him down in all the fog of shifting loyalties. "Render your judgment, bard."

Donn had angered the Dananns by his refusal to conciliate their queen, but Amergin would not make that mistake—not when the precious gift of time had just been handed to him. Bowing to Eriu, he intoned, "Let your name be on this island forevermore, great lady. Eriu."

Their eyes held and locked.

Amergin ran his fingers over Clarsah's strings, summoning silence. "This is my decision," he announced. "We will give our adversaries adequate time to meet us in battle as equals, fully prepared, so that those who win Eriu's land will truly deserve her. We will return to our ships in the south and retire . . . beyond the ninth wave," he thought with sudden inspiration as the wind blowing through the halls of the Dananns blew across Clarsah's strings, making music to lift his voice. "When we come ashore again, we will meet the Túatha Dé Danann at once and the battle will be joined."

"You give them too much!" yelped Colptha in outrage, but Éremón's strident voice cried, "We accept! Let this noble agreement become part of the history of our people, remembered in the name of Éremón, son of the Míl."

"In the histories of both our tribes, so let your name be remembered," Greine murmured in agreement.

Éremón was delighted with the decision. His trust in Amergin had not been misplaced. He would not only be long remembered as having made a very magnanimous gesture, but he now had the opportunity to get back to the ships and collect the rest of his warriors, Gosten and the other brave clanchiefs, and be certain of having enough men to defeat any size force the Dananns were able to raise.

The small, frail Túatha Dé Danann. He looked at them with pity, rulers of a land where all the weapons were bronze.

Éremón asked Greine, "Is there a battlefield where we can agree to meet, where the land gives no advantage to either side? We are chariot warriors; we do not fight our best in mud or on hillsides. If we give you so much time to prepare surely you will give us something in return."

Greine nodded. "The plain beyond these hills is perfect for your purpose, and you can land your fleet in the rivermouth not far distant. You will come to the battlefield fresh. We will meet you there, the winner will claim Ierne and the loser will withdraw."

"We can't withdraw!" Caicher gasped in dismay. "Where would we go?"

"We won't lose, you sheep-fart," Éremón growled at him. "All the advantage is on our side now, thanks to Amergin."

"Fools," Colptha swore angrily. "Fools! Amergin gives the Dananns the advantage, he hobbles you with your own honor. Who knows what kind of army they can raise in so much time?"

But the agreement was sealed. The Gaels camped that night below the ridge known as the Gathering Place and the Dananns retired into their columned halls. Neither group spent a restful night.

Colptha was furious. He protested the day's events to anyone who would listen. And he found men who would listen; there are always men who are dissatisfied. From the moment he saw them, he had known the Túatha Dé Danann as his enemies; had felt a visceral revulsion to them. He was convinced they had somehow manipulated Éremón today and Amergin had helped them. Quivering with self-righteousness, he set out through the camp to persuade others to his view.

He paused at last beside the smoldering campfire of Éber Finn. "Your brother is failing as a leader," Colptha said openly. "You are a better warrior than he and less foolhardy. Many of the men are dissatisfied with today's proceedings and unhappy about having to march back to the ships with nothing resolved. Why don't you offer them an alternative? You could storm the hill tonight and kill the Danann nobles as they sleep, effectively beheading their forces. And you could claim their gold, I saw you looking at it. You deserve . . ."

Iron fingers clamped on Colptha's shoulder and spun him around to face a furious Amergin. "Are you trying to start a rebellion?" the bard cried so half the camp could hear.

Colptha squirmed in his grip. "How dare you lay hands on me!"

A muscle knotted in Amergin's jaw. "I'll do more than that, sacrificer. I'll break you like a dry branch if you keep on playing your ugly games here. I heard you just now, trying to get Éber to sneak up that hill and murder the Dananns as they slept. That's your style, isn't it?"

"You wouldn't like that at all, would you?" Colptha shot back. "Those puny people have somehow seduced you, Amergin; that's the real explanation for that insane judgment of yours about the nine waves. From the day we first set foot on this accursed place you have belonged to it and not to us. I've seen it, we've all seen it. You have changed so much I hardly recognize you anymore."

There was an unfortunate seed of truth in Colptha's distorted accusation. Each word hit Amergin like a polished stone. He could not strike a fellow druid for telling even a partial truth.

But he could attack Colptha man to man, as anyone would attack another who was threatening to despoil something he loved. He forgot he was a druid. He forgot that he and Colptha owed allegiance to the same clan. He surrendered to the passion boiling up in him and it felt wonderful, it felt . . .

"Stop it, you're killing him!" Men were trying to pinion his arms, though they were all but helpless against his inspired strength. Voices shouted to him dimly, across vast distances. His fists were pounding Colptha's face and the sacrificer was shrieking and trying to protect himself with ineffectual swats and kicks . . .

The Gaels at last pulled the bard off Colptha, but it took six strong men to do it. "Can't any of you see what Colptha is trying to do?" the bard panted.

"Do you want to make a formal accusation against me?" Colptha countered, wiping blood and spittle from his chin. "When we get back to the ships you can petition a brehon; I would welcome it."

"So you think you can twist the brehons to your purposes as well," Amergin accused him. "Is there no limit to your pride and your greed, sacrificer? You anger everyone and yet you make that very anger work for you; you feed on it as ravens feed on battlefield blood . . ."

"Keep him away from me!" Colptha yelled, seeing the bard struggling to break free of the men holding him. "Remember I am the chief druid here, and I say this bard has forfeited his rank by his attack on me. As soon as I have the opportunity to consult with the spirits he may well be expelled from the order of druids.''

Amergin's eyes blazed. "Do that and you set me free! What little protection you still have from me, Colptha, exists because we are both druids, but if I am no longer one of the order I will beat you to death with my bare hands, I promise it!"

He had scored a victory; Colptha bit his lip and made no further threat.

They retired to separate areas of the encampment, a camp fractured by arguments. Some took sides with Amergin and some agreed with Colptha; some defended Éremón and others called for Éber as leader. Colptha sulked beside the campfire and nursed his wounds. "Amergin will be sacrificed," he promised himself. "On Ierne I will silence the voice of the bard forever. Then only my voice will be heard."

The camp of the Gaels roiled with disagreements, and the Dananns on the heights had their own differences.

"Your ploy gained us a little time but nothing more," Cuill told Greine. "The Gaels return to their ships—but what happens when they come ashore again?"

"*If* they come ashore again," Greine corrected him.

"You think our weather sciences will be sufficient to stop a people so relentless they have come all the way across the sea?"

"If they land and give battle, we will fight them," Greine promised.

"With bronze weapons? I got a good look at those blades they carry. Will that strange blue metal not hew through our swords and axes as it has cut through the Fir Bolg clans?"

"When you concentrate on weapons, you become blind to other possibilities," Eriu spoke up. "Did you not recognize the intelligence on the face of the Gaelic bard? We can still reason with these people, I think—if we can find a way to set aside our own anger and mistrust as well as theirs. Perhaps with the help of Shinann and the other young people we can make the Gaels see our dream for Ierne and be willing to take part in it.

"They are wonderfully energetic, the invaders. Together, our children and theirs might go further toward achieving our goals for this island than we ever could alone—clearing more plains, putting sun and wind and water to work for us, turning this into a safe and prosperous homeland for all the tribes of our people.

"When our ancestors first came here they found the remnants of a vanished culture that had constructed great chambers and circles of stones, hinting at some marvelous network of power utilizing the forces of earth and stars. We have studied, and rediscovered, much of that ancient knowledge. By combining that with the lessons taught us during our long exile, and the strength and energy of these Gaels, what might we not accomplish?

"And think of what we could give in return! We could teach Amergin and his people to develop the full range of their minds, opening doors for them that they do not even dream exist. And they could learn, as we have, to cherish one another instead of hurting each other . . ."

"They are intelligent, I grant you that," Cet interrupted. "But they are still little more than savages by our standards. And did not one of them cause even you to lose your temper, Eriu? That is a dangerous sign. I cannot imagine a partnership such as you envision. Men who come hungry for battle and conquest are not interested in education."

"But some of them have gentle faces," Eriu insisted. "Some have dreamer's eyes."

"I am afraid you are the dreamer," Greine told his wife fondly. Sadly. "If the Gaels manage to come ashore again, there is no doubt we will have to fight them. All that remains is to choose our weapons."

◇ **30** ◇

THE ARMY OF THE GAELS retraced its route across Ierne, headed for reinforcements and the ninth wave. They encountered some scattered groups of Fir Bolg but fought only easy skirmishes with them. The people of the Fir Bolg were not a problem.

The problem was within their own ranks, and Éremón was deeply troubled. Tight as they seemed in the face of oncoming battle, the bonds of brotherhood could be broken, and with them the strength of the Gaels as well. And the friendships he had cherished all his life; no small treasure. Éremón and his companions had drunk much wine together over the seasons, their conversation growing more incoherent with each bowl though they understood one another perfectly, reaching new heights of inebriated comprehension where every jest was funnier and each spoken truth more profound than the one before. On such occasions one man saw into another's soul, forgiving the flaws of friend and brother because they were part of himself.

Now that bond was being threatened, was in danger of disappearing in the deep wet grass and sinking out of sight in the peaty brown bogs. Each night more men seemed to sit around Éber Finn's campfire and fewer around Éremón's.

But facing a mutual enemy would unite them all again; at least Éremón could count on that much. He looked forward to the battle with the Dananns more than he had ever anticipated any battle in his life.

Then Amergin began trying to dissuade him from that very cleansing warfare.

The gift of time was precious and the army was moving fast. Amergin took his chariot back from Donn—who seemed to have lost much of his easygoing good humor, and returned the cart with a scowl—so he could drive beside Éremón and talk to him as they traveled.

"The Túatha Dé Danann are not like other tribes we have encountered," Amergin tried to explain.

"No, they are not," Éremón agreed. "They are totally different; they do not belong here."

"They are not as different as you think," Amergin argued. "And I am convinced they would share the land with us if we approached them properly."

"I don't want to share Ierne," Éremón said.

"What we *want* is not so important as finding some workable arrangement we can devise together, Éremón. Once we make enemies of these people we will have to go on fighting and fighting them, for I do not think they will bend the knee and accept subjugation. Nor will they be driven out. We would have to kill them all . . ."

(Shinann. Shinann.)

"What's wrong with that?" Éremón asked him, flicking his whip at his team. "Then there will be more for us."

"We can stop anywhere along the way and send word back to the Gathering Place," Amergin urged desperately. He was driving a chariot; he did not have his harp in his hands, adding her persuasions. "We could tell them we want to have further discussions . . ."

"Back off, bard!" demanded Colptha, wheeling his own chariot in close to Éremón's other side. "What do you know of leadership? You have given Éremón bad advice once; are you trying to give him more? He'll learn soon enough what you've done to him."

The tension between the two crackled louder than Éremón's whip. "Leave me alone, both of you!" he shouted at last. "I don't want to consider any more restricting alliances, bard," he added.

Amergin tried again; again and again, but each time he attempted to speak to Éremón alone Colptha somehow knew it and thrust himself between them, fraying Éremón's damaged temper still further. The sacrificer did not actually accuse Amergin of betraying the Gaels, but he hinted it, as he hinted that Taya would be more glad to see Amergin returning than Éremón.

He hinted and he whispered the breadth of Ierne, and even though Éremón tried to close his ears against him, some of Colptha's insinuations got through.

There were weak places in every man; Colptha knew.

"Fight the Dananns and kill them; kill them all, they are our mortal enemies," Colptha chanted to receptive ears. "Feed the Mother their blood so we will prosper in this new land."

Éremón, who was hungry for battle, could not help hearing.

Amergin fought his solitary fight with increasing desperation but the time he had won was not enough, and it ran out when they reached the coast where they had left the ships.

Merdith the herder, acting as sentry at the easternmost outpost, was the first of the colonists to hear the approaching call of the trumpets; the beat of the war drums. With a glad yell he deserted his station and ran to greet the heroes.

When Donn saw Díl hurrying toward him with her arms open he forgot everything else and raced happily home. Éber Finn whirled his chariot into the settlement and was immediately smothered by his eager wives, crowding around him and touching him to make certain he was in good working order.

Éremón stepped down from his own chariot and searched the excited, welcoming crowd for Taya's face—but he saw Odba first.

He stared in utter disbelief. Young Moomneh ran past him, yelling with joy.

Taya came up to Éremón then, walking almost fearfully, her eyes fixed on the warrior's face. "Explain this to me!" he ordered her, with no other word of greeting. Whatever was between them was held in abeyance as Odba once more dominated their horizon.

"She followed us all the way in a boat Ferdinón gave her," Taya explained. She looked at her rival with awe she could not disguise. "Odba did an incredible deed, an impossible deed, Éremón. I want to hate her for it, but how can I? When I start to get angry with her I find myself imagining what it must have been like, out there on the empty sea in one lonely boat, without the comfort of the tribe around her. I couldn't have done it; I don't know anyone else who could, either. Only Scotta, maybe."

Éremón's harsh face softened perceptibly. "You have a generous heart, Taya," he told her. He walked away from his chariot and stood between the two women, looking from one to the other. Both were as finely dressed and beautifully groomed as possible. Both forced themselves to watch him with impassive faces, waiting for his next words.

Taya had resolved that somehow she would display a nobility like Odba's. She must never let Éremón know of the nights she had argued with herself, longing to push the other woman into the sea or split her head with an axe, longing to scream and wail because the brightest of all dreams was tarnished. She had won a hard victory over herself during those long and lonely nights, and now she stood with no trace of them showing and waited. As Odba waited, equally proud.

The need to be in control was as much a part of Éremón's character as his roaring energy and his need for action. When the ships sailed for Ierne he had thought he at last held all the reins in his hands. But everything was coming apart and he could not understand why. He was no longer sure of his allies . . . his eye fell on Amergin.

"What am I to do, bard?" he asked.

Amergin did not welcome the question. He saw with wry amusement that even Colptha wanted no part of this responsibility, and was making himself as invisible as possible among the crowd.

Taya also turned toward Amergin. Her eyes were wide and lovely (though not as lovely as the eyes of Shinann). Her face was well known and long dear (though not as dear as the face of Shinann).

"There are brehons present," Amergin told Éremón. "This is a matter for a trained judge."

"You rendered a judgment for me in the Danann stronghold," Éremón replied, "and I will trust you for another now." He remembered all too well how the brehons had decided the matter before. Avoiding their suddenly angry eyes now, he told Amergin, "As leader of this colony I request you to make a new judgment that will stand *here*, on *Ierne*."

Bard land, Amergin thought to himself.

He paced forward solemnly until he stood as Éremón did, equidistant from Taya and Odba. He took a deep breath and silently invoked the spirits to give him wisdom. "The daughter of Lugaid is the woman you chose to be your first wife on Ierne," the bard said to Éremón. "But the woman called Odba is the mother of your sons, and for that reason her rank is inarguable. It is therefore my belief that they should be accorded equal honor separately. I say you should provide for them with two houses, each built and furnished in accordance with the Law to accommodate the wife of a chieftain."

The brehons murmured among themselves until Findbar spoke up, anxious to have their opinion at least represented here lest a new tradition pull everything out of shape. But he could not deny the wisdom of Amergin's statement. "According to the Law," he intoned, "there is no specific prohibition against such an arrangement." He was surprised by this himself, and his surprise sounded in his voice.

Éremón's ruddy face split with a grin. "Then I will build two fine houses!" he cried. "Ierne is rich enough to provide a man with two homes of equal luxury; Taya will live in one and Odba in the other."

Findbar turned to Taya. "Do you agree to this?"

How could she not? "Whatever Éremón wants, I want," she said.

"And you, Odba—is this arrangement acceptable to you?"

Odba hesitated before answering. She might have hoped for more—but she had been left with much less, in Iberia.

381

And there was always the chance she would be able to win Éremón away from Taya entirely, now that she had proved herself so dramatically. "I accept," she said.

Findbar breathed a sigh of relief. "Then the arrangement suggested by Amergin the bard will become the Law *in this one instance only,*" he said, stressing the last phrase carefully. Already his mind was conceiving the possible problems that could arise if this exception were allowed to become the rule.

Colptha was having similar thoughts. He said to Éber Finn, "Now Éremón will demand to receive twice as much of everything, while you will have only one roof for your women. If he is allowed two separate households, what's to keep him from expanding to three, or four? He will grow in every direction, overrunning you. You should have taken control of the leadership long ago; you should have stopped him."

Éber Finn scowled. "He's my brother," he said, but his eyes were angry beneath their ruddy brows.

Calling the clan-chiefs together, Éremón explained his agreement with the Túatha Dé Danann. Some praised his generosity and cleverness; others had reservations. "We will have to sail around this island for days to get to that rivermouth you spoke of," someone said. "Entrusting ourselves to the sea again. You should have fought the Dananns when you met them and resolved the matter then."

"He wanted to give them every advantage," Colptha said with a sneer. "*Amergin* wanted to give them every advantage."

Éremón would not let himself be pushed into a corner where he had to defend his position. He had all his warriors together again and that was enough; he would listen to no further arguments. Asserting his authority and daring anyone to openly challenge it, he ordered the settlement dismantled and the Gaels back into the boats.

Éremón managed to keep so busy supervising the operation that he did not have to spend time with either Taya or Odba. He was in no mood to deal with woman-problems.

As soon as they could gather their belongings together and reclaim ships' rope and sails and oars from more recent domestic uses, the Gaels began trying to drag their livestock on board the vessels. But the animals were even less enthused over the prospect than the people. The scene became a grim and chaotic nightmare of horses neighing, calves bawling, sheep bleating, men cursing, and women threatening heedless children with dire and dreadful punishments.

Éremón's popularity as a leader was sinking fast.

Once they finally got aboard and under way, however, the voyage was surprisingly uneventful, though many endured it in a sullen silence. The Gaels were propelled by obliging winds and currents around the lower end of Ierne and up the east coast until they at last stood off shore at the appointed landing site. Everyone felt a sense of relief as ephemeral as the slanting silver sunlight . . . which suddenly disappeared behind dark clouds.

The fleet was exactly nine waves from shore when the storm rolled down on them.

Wind wailed from every direction, panicking the livestock and threatening to dismast the ships. The galleys of the Milesians were side by side. Colptha's triumphant, vindicated scream rang across the water to Éremón. "Now you see that you have been betrayed! Amergin has betrayed us all to the sorcery of the Túatha Dé Danann!"

Amergin had no time to defend himself against the charge; no one had time for anything but to grab the nearest handhold and hang on desperately as cliff after cliff of water rose up in front of the ships, yearned over them, and crashed down across their decks.

The galleys tried to turn into the wind but it was no use, for the wind was omnidirectional, a monster with no head or tail, only a whirling and a roaring and a smashing of wood and ripping of leather.

Amergin managed to knot his belt through Clarsah's frame so they would not be separated, then looked up to see the remarkable vision of a dark green sea hanging *above* him, hissing like a nest of serpents.

Then it fell with a roar.

In a sea that would be known for its storms, the one that attacked the Gaels was exceptional for its ferocity. Even the hide boats could not ride it out. The waves came too fast and too high, swamping many of them. Their crews gave up any pretense of rowing and devoted themselves to bailing with grim desperation, but in spite of their efforts, first one boat and then another disappeared beneath the waves. Their passing was marked by a spoor of floating debris and occasional bobbing heads or thrashing arms.

Amergin, coughing and sputtering from the last wave to

break over the galley, scrambled on the slippery deck, looking for a rope to throw the nearest survivors in the water. The ship rolled and a wave even larger than its predecessor reared over him and thundered down, sweeping the bard overboard.

Meanwhile, on his own galley, Donn was shaking his fist at the shore in anger. "The land denies us!" he screamed above the shriek of the wind. "We have come so far and endured so much and still the land denies us! Éremón is right; I myself will put this island under sword and spear!" Suddenly he lusted for the leadership as he never had before; lusted to be the first man ashore, brandishing his weapons.

For a moment it seemed as if the wind drew back, but it was not retreating. It concentrated itself into a giant fist that slammed full force against Donn's wooden ship and crimson sail with willful deliberation.

The vessel spun like a leaf on the surface of a river. It heeled over dangerously, righted itself too slowly, and heeled over again. The wind caught it with one savage shoulder and finished its destruction. Men and women leaped from the sinking galley in terror as the storm raged around them.

Cold water revived the bard. Clarsah . . . he felt her against his body and began swimming instinctively, trying to get the two of them to some sort of safety. He looked for Donn's ship and saw with horror that it was sinking fast, stern first. Éremón's galley, still afloat, was not that far away, but Amergin had never spent much time learning to swim and the violent water was hampering his efforts. He clenched his teeth and attacked the waves in earnest, fighting for his life.

Something struck him in the water and he clutched at it without thinking, clawing at a broken section of decking that was floating by with Colptha sprawled atop it.

"Get away!" Colptha yelled at him. "This raft is mine!"

Amergin tightened his grip on the splintery wood. "It will hold both of us," he called back before a wave broke over his head, making him cough and sputter.

Colptha's glittering eyes stared down at him. "I say it will never hold you, bard. You will die in the sea as you deserve, a sacrifice I gladly offer her!" He put both hands on top of Amergin's head and violently shoved him under.

The salt water seared into Amergin's nasal passages and flooded his brain with red agony. Some confused instinct urged him to lift Clarsah up even if he was drowning, and he tore her loose from his belt and tried to raise her above the water. He somehow broke free of Colptha's grip and followed the harp into breathable air. "You tried to kill me!" he gasped at the sacrificer, who was grabbing for him again.

"I *will* kill you," Colptha assured him, seizing him by the hair.

The bard struck back with all his strength, with the only weapon he had.

Clarsah hit the side of Colptha's head with a ringing blow.

For a heartbeat of time which had no limit and no definition Amergin stared up into his brother's face and knew he had killed him. The awareness of death in Colptha's eyes was transmitted directly to Amergin, like the handclasping he had felt with Shinann. In this moment the two men were similarly locked together, druids, brothers, one to live and the other to die, the action irreversible. Amergin and Colptha stared at each other in the raging sea and there were no barriers at all between them anymore.

Then the sacrificer shrieked and rolled over on the broken planking, clutching at his head while blood spurted between his fingers. He writhed in pain, unbalancing the raft just as a massive wave hit it. The section of timber tilted precariously, then rolled over and plunged Colptha beneath itself into the sea.

He heard, in one shocked and disbelieving compartment of his mind, the voice of Corisios prophesying, *"The water drags you down."*

Mortally injured, Colptha fought blindly in a darkness beyond comprehension. He could not tell which direction was down, or up; he could not find light and air. He thrashed in fury, hating. Hating those who might yet live while he struggled and died, defeated by Amergin . . .

His last coherent thought was that Amergin should not have Ierne. He would find a way to reach back, to have them all at each other's throats again, to make the land run red with . . . to deny them their dreams as he was denied . . .

Down and down, baffled and raging and unforgiving, into the darkness. His fierce pride hurled ahead of him like a spear, leading the way to . . .

From Éremón's ship, Ír had seen Donn's galley go down, though he was not aware Amergin was also in the water. A great cry was wrung from him as Donn's galley overturned. He immediately abandoned his place by the mast and leaped up onto the ship's rail. "No!" his wife screamed, but Ír dived off without once looking back. He arced up and out with astonishing grace before slicing cleanly down into the sea.

He dropped like a stone into nightblack turbulence, but no fear accompanied him. The moment he left the galley he had merged with the sea god and this was his element; nothing could hurt him here. He twisted back toward the surface, and as soon as his head broke water he began swimming with strong, confident strokes toward the nearest floundering Gael.

Éremón had his hands full fighting to keep his own ship afloat, but the oarsmen yelled the news to him as Ír plucked the first survivor from the sea and thrust his sodden form into the nearest hide boat. "By the wind!" Éremón swore. "Throw him a rope, somebody, and get him back here before he drowns himself!"

But Ír had no intention of returning to the ship. When huge waves folded over him he submitted serenely, holding his breath, and found without surprise that he bobbed to the surface again unharmed. Only terror could have dragged him down, but the sea god had taken all his fears away. He was actually smiling as he struck out for the next victim struggling nearby—Díl, Donn's wife, who was making a valiant effort to keep both herself and one of Éber's children afloat.

Éber Finn had leaped off the far side of the sinking galley in time to avoid being sucked under by it, but when he surfaced the first thing his eyes fixed upon was Éremón's ship, some distance away. Still afloat. Once again, the spirits are favoring Éremón over the others, he could almost hear Colptha saying. Éber deliberately turned his back on Éremón's galley and swam toward a hide boat instead.

The wind screamed and howled.

Amergin, clutching the harp, was having a hard time trying to reach Éremón's ship because he could spare only one hand for swimming. But he would not turn loose of Clarsah; he could not even imagine turning loose of Clarsah. Sakkar, who had just missed him, looked overboard in time to spot his dark head against a crest of foam and ordered a rope thrown to him immediately.

Willing arms pulled the bard from the sea.

"It's Amergin!" Taya gasped. Heedless of her own safety she made her way across the slippery deck toward him, ignoring the angry look Éremón gave her. But Sakkar reached the bard first.

"Take the harp," Amergin said breathlessly to Sakkar,

even before his body was pulled over the railing into the ship. "Take Clarsah!" In his anxiety to get her safely aboard in case he somehow fell back into the sea, he did not even notice he had spoken her secret name aloud.

Sakkar accepted the instrument with reverence, touched by Amergin's trust. Taya shoved past him and wrapped her own cloak around the bard as soon as he was safely lying in the bottom of the ship. His lips were blue and his teeth were chattering, and she lay down against him and pressed her warm body to his, begging him to be all right. "Dear friend," she whispered to him. "My dear, dear friend."

Éremón could not go to them, there were too many orders to be issued at once and too many strong hands needed—but he saw Taya with her arms around the bard.

As soon as Amergin caught his breath he made himself sit up and gently but firmly pushed her away. "I'm all right," he assured her. "Truly. But I . . . my harp! Where is my harp!"

Sakkar hurried forward, holding the instrument so Amergin could see it. "Clarsah," the shipwright murmured as the bard reached thankfully for her.

Amergin gave him a startled look. He had not heard that name spoken aloud since it had been whispered into his ear by Nial on his deathbed.

The storm had blown many of the vessels out to sea, but some of the hide boats not only managed to stay afloat but to take aboard survivors. In time, not only Díl and Éber Finn but a number of other Milesians were saved in this fashion, several of them by Ír. "Where is Donn?" Díl cried to him as he swam to the boat where she crouched shivering and helped yet another half-drowned child over the side.

"I haven't found him yet," Ír gasped. His face was very pale and suddenly Díl forgot her own worry to reach for him. "Come aboard now," she pleaded. "You look exhausted."

Ír laughed. "I've never felt better!" he boasted. "I'll look for Donn right now and bring him to you." Before she could stop him he had relinquished his hold on the side of the boat and plunged back into the waves. The last Díl saw of him, before the dark water closed over his head, was a fearless smile and a merry wink.

The sea seemed to have no control over its own rage and drove Éremón's galley into the shallows of the broad rivermouth. It grounded there, listing badly to one side.

Those aboard saw other survivors making their way toward shore, while farther out the storm continued to rage and it was obvious the fleet was being torn apart. Black javelins of rain assaulted them.

"How will we ever find the others?" Taya moaned.

Sakkar stood beside her, bone-weary and discouraged. "It looks as if many of the boats have been blown toward the south," he said. "They will come ashore once they pass beyond the storm."

Érémon nodded. "Those who survive will find us soon enough. What we must worry about now are the vessels we can still see, for the storm is likely to sink them all. How long can such a wind last?" He stared at the black boiling clouds overhead.

Amergin followed his gaze. The clouds looked like black sheep, like stampeding cattle . . .

"Perhaps the Fir Morcans were right," Sakkar said in misery. "There are terrible legends about this land; seamen whisper them along the docks. I have brought my friends to their doom . . ."

"No!" cried Amergin. "You have brought us to Ierne, and there is no evil here. I feel this island's nature as I feel the limbs of my body, and there is no fault in the land."

My hand struck Colptha. *My* harp.

Anguish lay waiting to seize him by the throat.

The bard was buffeted by the tireless storm and tortured by the cries of his tribesmen as they fought the waves for their lives. Something tore loose in him then, wrenched raw and bleeding from the depths of the man, all his pent-up desire bursting forth as he turned toward the denied shores of Ierne. The beautiful, unattainable dream of Ierne.

With a heartrending cry of longing he lifted the harp. *"Now,* Clarsah!" he commanded.

One hand held the harp with compelling strength as the other struck boldly across her strings, but he did not know what power he summoned. Did not know until he felt it come flooding through him as it had that night in the Heroes' Hall. Prickling his skin, burning and freezing him simultaneously, filling him with the rising thundering certainty of the words. *The words!*

He drew in a great deep breath of wind and rain and raised his voice to its fullest volume, calling out to the spirit of the

388

watching land as if he and Ierne were alone together and nothing else existed.

For he must win her body and soul, or live and die alone.

And the invocation he had waited all his life to utter rose to fill earth and sky, challenging the storm itself.

> I invoke the land of Eriu!
> Well-traveled be her fertile sea,
> Fertile be her fruit-strewn mountains,
> Fruit-strewn be her showery woods,
> Showery be her river of waterfalls,
> Waterfalls tumbling into deep pools,
> Deep pools filling hilltop wells.

> Welling from broadlands come the Milesians!
> Sons of the Míl, assaulted by storm,
> Stormclouds lifting, bright crowd landing,
> Land of the lady, cunning and fair,
> Fair be Ierne, lofty and fertile,
> Fertile for Éremón, Éber, and Ír,
> I invoke the land of Eriu!

The screaming wind caught its breath in a pause; shuddered; fell silent. The waves flattened into ripples, frothcrowned. The soft green island opened her lap and waited, guarded no longer. Surrendered to the irresistible passion of the bard.

The Gaels moaned in awe.

As quickly as it had blown up the storm was gone, leaving a morass of floating debris and disaster. A misty sun broke through shredding clouds, bathing the scene in radiance. The stunned survivors stared at one another wordlessly.

Amergin was exhausted. He left the wrecked galley and splashed to the shore, where he flung himself face down on gritty mud, feeling sharp pebbles dig into his body but not caring. He could care about nothing; his brain felt numb. He thought he still heard the roar of the storm in his ears, and in the dark behind his eyelids he saw Colptha's face staring at him just before the waves swallowed him.

He heard Éremón's voice above him but was too tired to roll over and look up. "How many are lost?" he asked dully.

"It's too soon to tell. We're going to assemble the surviving clan-chiefs and get a measurer to take a head count. No one's seen Donn. Or Ír."

"Colptha's dead," Amergin told the sand and the pebbles.

Éremón squatted beside him. "What did you say? Are you sure? It was so hard to tell anything . . ."

"I'm sure," Amergin said. "I killed him."

Silence battered him. He turned his head sideways and looked at Éremón. "Did you hear me?"

"Yes, you just told me you killed Colptha. Have you anything more to say?" Éremón looked like an old man, with a gray skin and a ragged whisper of a voice that did not sound surprised.

Amergin closed his eyes again. "No."

Steps crunched away; others approached. "Amergin?" It was Sakkar's voice. If Amergin had not been so tired he would have been surprised to notice that Sakkar no longer referred to him as "master."

"I'm all right, Sakkar," the bard said. He sighed and sat up. The world would not wait, could not be held at bay forever beyond closed eyelids.

"We need all the help we can get to save as much as possible," Sakkar suggested, knowing one did not demand labor of a druid.

Amergin dragged himself to his feet. He flexed the muscles of his arms, taut-fibered as new rope, and decided he was still functional. "Show me where to start," he said.

Once the last gasping survivor was dragged ashore, the druids began counting the dead. Éremón sent scouts along the coast in both directions, searching for wreckage, but when the final totals were in they knew many of the Gaels were lost forever.

"It could have been worse," Sakkar said to Amergin. "If you had not stopped the storm most of the tribe would have been drowned."

"You are a kind man, Sakkar," Amergin said gratefully. "You always look away when someone steps awkwardly, don't you?"

Kindness eased some of the pain, but wherever Amergin looked he saw gaps where there should have been faces. Caicher's wife and Gosten's brother and Brego. Tribespeople and clanspeople. Colptha . . .

He could not stop thinking about Colptha, no matter how deep he waded into the sea or how much sodden property he hauled ashore. Had there been a moment when he realized the deadly force with which he was swinging the harp and tried to lessen it?

Or to double it?

He should be able to remember.

He did not want to remember.

But when he gripped the frame of Clarsah, he had a clear and perfect vision of that moment when power and rage had filled the harp and she had leaped at the sacrificer's head as if she were an inspired weapon. The bard could not stop her, he could only hold her so she would not be lost in the sea afterward.

"There's no sign of Ír anywhere," the scouts reported. "Those who saw him during the storm thought surely he would survive, because he was swimming so strongly, so sure of himself. But he has not come ashore either alive or dead."

Amergin thought of the great whale leaping up, gleaming in the sunlight. "Ír won't come back to us anymore," he said.

Amergin approached Éremón with an offer. "I will sing all the eulogies myself, and none of the families are to give me gifts for them."

Éremón's face was deeply set in rigid lines and stony planes. "You will eulogize the chief druid?"

"Of course."

"I heard him; we all heard him. At the last moment he accused you of betraying us."

Taya stepped quickly between the two men. "The bard's invocation to the land turned the storm aside and *saved* us!"

"Storms blow out on their own. Amergin may have had nothing to do with it."

"If you think that, then you must accept that the storm could develop on its own as well and hold him equally innocent there. He did not betray us, Éremón; Amergin is incapable of betrayal."

It was almost as if Colptha stood at Éremón's shoulder, urging him to listen for certain subtleties of voice and mistakes of mannerism. "Taya speaks of Amergin and betrayal in the same breath," Colptha would have said. Éremón could hear him.

But Amergin was the ranking druid now, and one of the only three surviving sons of the Míl. Éremón built a wall colder and more implacable than anger between himself and the bard, and from that day on he treated Amergin with rigid formality and no trace of affection.

Éber Finn, who had lost a perfectly good wife and several

healthy children in the storm, did not share Éremón's attitude. His losses had begun with Scotta, cutting deeply through his shell of self-interest, and the etching of grief upon his spirit had left grooves now beginning to fill with empathy for others.

Éber caught sight of Amergin walking, head down, amid the splintered planks and debris washed ashore after the storm. Something in the hunch of the bard's shoulders was painful to see.

Éber fell into step beside his brother. "Éremón is not as angry with you as he appears," he offered. "He insisted on being the leader and now he feels responsible for the loss of so many tribesmen, so he wants someone else to help him carry the blame, that's all. He'll quit blaming you as soon as we go into battle and he has something to distract him."

"He thinks I betrayed him; betrayed us all."

"I don't believe that for a moment," Éber said loyally.

"I am grateful to you for that," Amergin told him. "I rendered the judgment at the Gathering Place as fairly as I knew how, answering the requirements of both honor and practicality. I give you my word as bard I did not weight the scales.

"But . . . am I deceiving myself, Éber? I see a great beauty in the Túatha Dé Danann and I admit I do not want that destroyed. I want part of what the Dananns are for ourselves. We *need* it, Éber; all my intuition tells me this. I am convinced that if we took a calm and reasoned view of our . . . our separate realities, we could find a way to live together on this island and benefit from the arrangement. All of us.

"The Túatha Dé Danann refer to Ierne as sacred, and I believe I have always been guided toward this place for some special reason. As I was guided toward the harp and away from the sword."

His dark head bowed, his voice sank to a resonant whisper. "And if I have been misguided, then nothing I have done in my entire life is right."

Éber squinted at him, trying to understand. The bard's words sang as deep and true as if the harp supported them—yet he was not playing the harp. Éber Finn shook his head. "I think you need a wife, brother," he advised.

There were many bodies and the summer was warm. Éremón ordered mass graves dug with only a few tombs for ranking

Gaels. Colptha's body washed ashore on a strand to the south; Donn was found in the surf, battered and broken but looking surprisingly placid.

As several of the men carried his corpse to dry land, Díl tore free of the restraining grip of her daughters and ran into the sea that had killed her husband. She was wailing and tearing her hair from her scalp with frantic hands. Her foot stepped off an unsuspected shelf and she disappeared suddenly, without even time to call for help.

They went after her but it was too late. Her drowned body was eventually recovered and she was eulogized and buried as befitted the wife of a major clan-chief. Éremón himself put the first sod on her tomb.

"Donn would have done this for me," he said aloud, "if he was burying Odba."

The eyes of Taya and Odba met across Díl's tomb. Taya winced, hearing her husband still name Odba as his wife. Odba kept her face carefully impassive. She would not allow herself the cheap victory of smirking; Scotta would not have smirked.

Bearers brought Colptha's body on a plank, rather than the shield they would have used to carry a warrior. He was not damaged as Donn had been, there was only one great gaping wound on his skull. His hands were clenched into fists and his eyes had fed the fish.

"What eulogy will you sing for your brother, bard?" Éremón asked through clenched teeth as he looked down at that dead face. He had not thought the loss of the sacrificer could be so painful to him. It was a severed connection, an amputation he could not afford.

Amergin forced himself to look at Colptha, too. His eyes lingered on the wound, accepting responsibility for it, and grief seeped through him. "I will sing of him that he longed to be a great swordsman, and he offended no man by accident," Amergin said, searching among truthful possibilities. "And that, more than any other son of the Míl, Colptha could not bear to lose."

When the funeral rituals were finally completed and the transition of the immortal spirits to their new existences was assured, the demands of the living took over. With a sense of relief, Éremón announced, "We have a land to win. I summon all warriors to join me for an assessment of strength and weapons. When we leave this place we will go to meet and destroy the Túatha Dé Danann and decorate our new houses with their heads!''

More than ever, Éremón meant Ierne to be sword land. A voice in his head whispered that the blood of the dead cried out for vengeance.

◇ **31** ◇

LOOKOUTS BROUGHT THE NEWS to the Gathering Place. ''Nothing stops the invaders,'' they reported. ''Their vessels blackened the surface of the sea and the storm battered and sank many of them, but still they made landfall and many survived. Their bard is credited with doing magic. Their warriors are massing to do battle.''

Greine turned to his wife. ''You see? They are as inexorable as the change of seasons. Now we have no choices left.''

''We have one,'' she reminded him.

The three Danann queens were assembled with their husbands and the nobility. Shinann sat near them with her back against a wooden column, dreaming as if this were any other pleasant day in Goddess weather when the bees hummed and the milk was sweet in the pitchers.

''Would you have us give up life as we know it?'' Greine asked angrily. Life burned strongly in him; you could feel its heat if you stood too close.

Once Eriu had thought they had put all arguments behind them, laying aside the wounding weapons of words and becoming gentle with one another. But peace was slipping away from them. ''I do not suggest we give up life, merely take on a new form of life,'' she said.

''How can we know what to expect from this change you urge on us?'' Cet asked. His tone was surly; he did not want to be convinced.

''Have you forgotten what our teachers taught us of the great whales?'' Eriu asked him. ''Once they, too, lived on land in a brutal, savage world, where the only rule was kill or be killed. But they grew into wisdom and moved into the sea. In order to survive, they learned to adapt themselves to a new environment. They found a way of life that did not include ceaseless aggression. Now, in their new innocence, they can no longer even conceive of fear, but dwell in serene communities, cherishing each other and enjoying every moment of life to the utmost, while improving the reach of their own vast mental powers.

"We cannot emulate them and go into the sea, for we do not have the luxury of endless generations in which to alter our bodies so drastically. So we must leave flesh behind; we must become Unbodied, joining the host of spirits already inhabiting this sacred island.

"If you are afraid, think of the trees. We are to trees as the Unbodied are to us. Trees cannot see us as we know sight, yet they are aware of us through the ways we act upon them. So we are aware of the ways the invisible world acts upon us, and I feel certain we will be in good company there. We will continue to exist as individuals, and aware, but we will enter a realm where sword and spear cannot displace us."

"This is foolish speculation!" Cian snorted. "How do we know we can do it at all? Not one of us has actually become Unbodied; your noble experiment might give us no more than an exotic form of death. More than our bodies might be destroyed, for such forces as you mean to harness could burn our spirits to cinders as well."

Eriu's eyes blazed. "If we continue to war our spirits will shrivel and die anyway! And if we do use the terrible weapons, if we put them into the hands of our children and they somehow make them work, they will butcher the sacred earth. We will become worse than extinct; we will have become monsters."

Greine watched her in the mellow afternoon light, thinking how beautiful she was. How dear every seam and line of her face, every flaw and imperfection of her body. Could such a body be left behind like a worn-out garment while it was still loving and capable of being loved? Could they give up the only life they knew without a struggle?

His voice held firm. "You have had your say and I will have mine. We will meet the Gaels on the battle plain and fight in the flesh for this land—and kill for it too, if we must. We have done so before. But"—his eyes met the large, lambent eyes of his wife—"we will go to battle with only bronze weapons in our hands, and *so long as there is a chance we might win* we will leave the Sword of Light and the Irresistible Spear where they are."

Shinann leaped to her feet and ran to stand in front of him. Her eyes were glittering and her face was white with intensity. "We will kill all who stand against us, if we must," Greine said to her as gently as he could. "Perhaps even your bard, Shinann, though I would be sorry to do it. As long as his strength is in his poetry we will spare him, for the poet is sacred, but if he has a weapon in his hand we must strike him as a warrior."

"And what if the battle goes against us?" Cet cried, unwilling to leave the question unanswered. "What then?"

Eriu met her husband's eyes and the battle raged between them.

While the Túatha Dé Danann argued, the Gaels prepared for the final conflict.

The chosen battlefield was the fertile plain beyond the Gathering Place, a rolling land which, as the Dananns had promised, gave no advantage to either side, though the terrain was well-suited to chariot warfare.

"Our adversaries have made a fair choice," Éremón admitted as he surveyed the battleground from a distance.

"They are sorcerers who cursed us with a magical storm," snarled Soorgeh, who had lost many of his clan to the waves.

Éber gestured toward Amergin. "If they are sorcerers," he said, "at least we have a druid of equal power who can break their enchantments."

Amergin was surprised to hear the ring of brotherly affection in Éber's voice. When did that happen, and how? the bard wondered. He smiled back warmly in thanks, no longer guarding himself from the vulnerability of caring. Reaching out.

Éremón stood with his broad back to Amergin, not looking at the bard as he announced, "We will send an emissary to the Dananns and offer them battle at sunrise."

"I will go," Amergin offered, but Éremón pretended not to hear. "Soorgeh will be our emissary," the warrior said loudly.

I did not have to reach out to Shinann, Amergin thought. She came in, to me. His brooding eyes swept over the green meadows where soon her kin and his must die. He saw only waving grass and the shadows of scudding clouds, but his bones and blood knew Shinann was out there somewhere. Close enough to be in danger.

Éremón insisted that only those needed for battle would go to the battlefield; noncombatants would stay at a safe distance, informed of the progress of the fighting by runners under the direction of Merdith the herder. He did not like the idea of having Taya within reach of the Dananns.

To his vast surprise, when he went to tell her good-bye he found Odba with her.

The look on his face made both women smile.

"You fight at dawn?" Odba asked in a calm voice.

"Have you seen the Danann army? Is it terrible?" Taya's words ran over one another's heels in their anxiety.

Odba had sent Éremón into battle before. She knew the fears a woman must keep silently locked within, to avoid weakening her warrior at a crucial moment. Now she put one arm around Taya's shoulders. "He will be splendid in combat and return victorious," she said firmly. As firmly as Scotta would have spoken the same words.

Glancing sideways, she caught the look of admiration Éremón gave her.

"They are frail, small people," Éremón told both women. "The strongest they have to send against us is less than our weakest warrior."

"You see?" Odba gave Taya's hand a gentle pat that made Éremón's eyes sting oddly. He turned his head aside and busied himself with preparing his weapons and instructing his eager sons.

Legneh's injuries had healed and he was more fit than ever, anxious to prove himself. Moomneh and even young Lagneh had broadened and filled out this summer, shapechanging into fighting men with the glint of courage in their eyes. They would need all their courage for the coming battle, Éremón suspected but did not say aloud.

Frail, small people . . . he had his secret doubts.

Assembling the warriors, he looked over the sea of their heads, the hair stiffened with lime paste to resemble the manes of war horses, and he was proud of them. At least for the duration of battle they would be a brotherhood again.

"We will march on the Dananns in the style of the Gauls," he announced, "for that seems to have a paralyzing effect on the enemy. We will be naked and in a state of excitation. The Dananns try to trick our minds, so we will trick theirs. Let

397

them see how much we lust for battle and they will know we are not to be denied! They will begin fighting expecting to lose, and so they shall!''

The heroes yelled and stamped and beat on their shields. Their voices were a thunder rolling across Ierne.

"How splendid he is, and how good," Taya murmured, standing with the other women who had gathered to see their men march away. "I can always find a smile in Éremón's eyes," she went on. "Like sunshine is Éremón. Have you noticed that?''

Odba stood beside her, shading her own eyes with her hand. "No, I hadn't noticed that," she said.

Sakkar came to Amergin carrying a sword and wearing lime paste to stiffen his black hair and cover the small bald spot on top. "Éremón will let me fight with the warriors," he told the bard, no longer seeking permission for anything. "So many men were lost during the storm he is glad to have me now. The clan-chief Soorgeh himself has been showing me how to wield the sword.''

Amergin did not allow himself to smile but he could not keep his eyes from twinkling. "Have you mastered it yet?" he asked this fierce little new warrior.

"No. But practice will help." Sakkar's shoulders were almost level now, the deformity gone, and his formerly bony chest was laced with muscle. Once he had been humble and obedient, pathetically appreciative of kindness. Now he exuded confidence and stood with his feet firmly planted on the earth, sure of his place. "I will fight for our people!" he boasted in a ringing voice. And then, a little less stridently, "I will make you proud of me, bard.''

"I've always been proud of you," Amergin told him, "and glad to share my meat and roof with you.''

"Éremón says if I survive this battle I will have warrior status and be able to build a house of my own," Sakkar said, unable to keep the excitement out of his voice. He reminded Amergin of a child who has been promised a treat so wonderful he can hardly believe it exists. "To win that, I am prepared to go naked into battle and feed the Dananns my sword. But . . . but . . .'' He hesitated and began to fidget.

"But what?"

Sakkar would not meet Amergin's eyes. A dull red flush moved upward from his neck, staining his olive skin. He said in a voice almost too low to hear, "But I do not think I can manage an erection just to intimidate the enemy."

Amergin laughed for the first time in many nights. "Don't worry, you won't be the only one!" he assured his friend.

No night had ever been so long. The army of the Gaels marched to the very edge of the battlefield and camped there, awaiting the dawn. Amergin sat beside a small fire with only Clarsah for company, mentally running over the battle exhortations he would sing on the next day, and studying the pattern of the Sky Born, wondering if he would be alive to see them the next night.

Wondering if Shinann was looking at them, too. He knew instinctively that she was a woman who often looked at the stars. Scéna had once said, "Amergin, they're so cold, like angry eyes watching us."

But Shinann would not think of stars that way.

He did not feel lonely. He could not feel lonely as long as he and Shinann were in the same world, sharing existence.

He dared not think of the possible outcome of the battle.

Éremón and Éber, Soorgeh and Gosten and Étan and Caicher slept beside the wheels of their chariots and dreamed warriors' dreams, while Sakkar tossed restlessly and tried to feel like a Gael.

The gods of Tyre were probably laughing heartlessly over the peculiar destiny of one insignificant shipwright, he told himself. At least the gods of the Gaels were kinder. He still did not understand just who or what they were—trees, rivers, the dead?—but he had a deep conviction they laughed with man and not at him. And sometimes they wept, as the Gaels themselves wept.

There was very little Phoenician left in Sakkar, formerly of Tyre.

The night passed, one slow heartbeat at a time. A brief shower sprinkled the earth and a wolf howled on a distant hillock. Men snorted and farted and muttered in their sleep, already at war.

In a slower rhythm than any man could perceive, the infinite womb of the universe continued its expansion, contraction, expansion, the sacred throes of creation sending great dim echoes of ever-recurring birth across the eons.

Transfixed in a fleeting flash of light on the rim of eternity, the Danaans waited in their own encampment, dreaming their own dreams.

*   *   *

The sun rose on an island incandescent with courage.

Before first light, Éremón sent scouts to bring back a report on the strength of the opposition. They returned at the run. "The Dananns have indeed put together a large force," they reported. "They are already stirring about, preparing to come to meet us."

"Do they have as many warriors as we do?" Éber wanted to know.

"We are evenly matched," one of the scouts said. "If what we saw were warriors."

"But you just said they have an army. Make sense, man, or is your head deformed?"

The sturdy, auburn-haired Gael fingered his flowing mustache in embarrassment. "I guess it's an army; I don't know what else to call it. You'll have to see for yourself when the sun rises."

Soft fog lay over the land, then faded gently away at the first flare of sunrise. The Gaels were on their feet and ready, with their weapons in their hands, as the Túatha Dé Danann approached the appointed battleground.

They ghosted over the hills and across the plain, aware of themselves and each other, of the limitations of space and the vast perspective of geologic time, aware of the final and inevitable moment of evolutionary change when there is no turning back.

Creatures throughout the millennia had passed through that doorway unwittingly, but this time the choice, if it was made, would be with the full knowledge of its consequences. The arguments had been long and bitter, with Eriu and her followers arguing on one side for the sanctity of life and land, and the old warrior blood on the other side, singing for victory.

But they had all known from the beginning what the outcome must finally be.

The Gaels had drawn themselves up into their traditional battle formation, the broad line of frontal attack. The heroes in their chariots were foremost, accompanied by the bardagh, who paced in solemn dignity amid the panoply of gleaming metal and painted and plumed war carts. The warriors were naked, as Éremón had ordered, and they wore all their jewelry. An army that glittered with metal and glistened with muscle.

Looking along the front line, Éremón grinned. Who could stand against such magnificence? He was glad there would be no single combat between champions, though he would have been honored to represent his people. It was better this way; more beautiful and splendid this way. An army.

"Remember this, bard!" he shouted hoarsely, his first direct speech to Amergin in days. "Commemorate every step we take and every thrust of the sword, for this will be the legend by which our children's children know us!"

Amergin, wearing tunic and short cloak, carried no weapon but the harp on his shoulder. He gazed toward the host across the waiting grass, searching for the faces of the enemy.

The enemy. Forms molded by the same craftsman who shaped the Gaels, though the Dananns were lighter and not so tall. Yet among them Amergin felt he recognized friends unseen for many ages. For many lives. Faces softened by the blur of time, but faces he knew.

Not The Enemy.

We *must* not slaughter these people for the sake of this island, he said in his head. To cut and hack them would be to desecrate a poem. To amputate some irreplaceable part of ourselves.

He unslung his weapon from his shoulder.

He held Clarsah against his heart and words shaped themselves in his mouth with the immense and undeniable power of his gift; the power to grip listeners in one mighty hand and hold them transfixed while his words drove down into the inner reaches of their souls.

The words. The power. He strummed Clarsah commandingly.

Turning his back on the oncoming Dananns, he cried out to his own tribesmen, "Stop where you are! There is no need for bloodshed! This land desires no sacrifice of blood; her gifts are of the heart and the mind and she offers them freely. Here we can acquire knowledge even druids do not have. The Túatha Dé Danann can *help* us . . ."

They could not hear him. The bard could hold listeners in the palm of his hand but the Gaels could not listen in the tramping of feet and the hoarse shouts of rage and the beating of the drums and the thunder of the hooves and the cacophony of war cries. They saw the bard and assumed he was performing his traditional role, exhorting them to valor. They even thought they heard his song.

But they did not. Deaf to all but the trumpets and war drums, the Gaels charged forward.

401

Then, clear as a shout in silence, a response filled Amergin's mind. Light shattered. He knew beyond doubt that his words had been not only heard, but answered.

Yet who heard? And what was the answer?

He felt coolness above him like the shade of a mighty tree. He sensed the surrounding comfort of friends, as if he sat beneath that tree with beloved companions. But these were not pictures his mind painted for him, for he knew its images as he knew the roof of his mouth and these were not his thoughts. If he imagined a tree it would be smaller, the leaves duller and the trunk a different shape . . . in the shadowed recesses of his awareness he felt loving arms around his shoulders and knew himself to be surrounded by people more dear to him than blood, tender and compassionate, wise and full of laughter, the family he had longed to be part of for all his days.

The trumpets screamed and the war drums pounded and the images were gone, but their golden light remained within Amergin the bard.

He turned back, to watch the advance of the Túatha Dé Danann.

The Gaelic war chiefs rubbed their eyes as they got a good look at the army approaching them. If army it was.

The Túatha Dé Danann were not marching forward, nor charging at the run, bellowing with fury and holding up their weapons. They . . . capered. They flowed. They rippled and shimmered across the flower-starred meadows of late summer. They poured in a tide of luminous grace, colored banners streaming, unfamiliar music lilting with a gaiety totally inappropriate to war. The Dananns, not only men but women and youngsters as well, skipped and pirouetted toward the Gaels, as joyous as a crowd on festival day.

"They come to battle dancing, with flowers in their hair!" Éber gasped in disbelief.

The Gaels, disconcerted, screamed their most ferocious battle cries and charged forward with weapons upraised, but the lust to kill wilted on many of the warriors at the sight of the Dananns, dancing.

Greine, leading the Túatha Dé Danann, had studied the force arrayed against him and felt his heart sink. He had underestimated the Gaelic invasion force; theirs was an awesome army, well-supplied with the strange unbreakable blue blades. Against them he had brought people armed only with bronze swords and battle-axes concealed in their swirling clothing as they danced. Bronze weapons, and the subtle arts of the mind.

But the Earthkillers lay waiting. He had only to give the signal. When he knew his back was to the wall and the terrible new warriors were about to roll over Ierne, he could . . .

Shinann and the other young men and women crowded around him, demanding access to his thoughts. Following the direction of their gaze he saw the bard stop and turn to defy the inexorable march of his own people.

A green wind sang across Ierne. It caught the bard's voice and carried it away from the competition of battle trumpet and war drum, to be heard by the waiting Túatha Dé Danann.

In the beauty of Amergin's words, Greine glimpsed the essence of the invaders and knew they were not the enemy after all. Just branches of the same tree, drawn here by fate or circumstance or . . . the power of the sacred island.

And all the decisions were irrevocably made.

Éremón was trying to assess the force arrayed against him right up to the moment of initial impact, though they defied his understanding. They were a people rather than an army—perhaps the entire people of the Túatha Dé Danann. And they hurried toward him as if they were heading for someplace on the other side of the Gaels; a desirable, festival destination.

His eyes singled out a woman in the front line of the Dananns and he watched her incredulously, for she seemed the most unlikely of warriors, a slight ripple among the more substantial wave of her people, a fragile almost-child coming to do battle with armed and hardened warriors.

As she drew nearer, Éremón saw that she was neither as slender nor as childish as he had thought. Her body had a supple maturity, a fluid undulation of movement far different from the coltish prancings of a child. She frolicked toward him, fragile and fruitful and fresh, child and woman, curving and gliding, holding his eyes like light glinting on water. She came breasting through the heather, skirting a bog, bubbling up into the sunlight, growing as she advanced, filling out and rounding into richness, maturing into dignity. Éremón had never seen anything to compare with her, the changeableness of her.

She looked into his face and laughed and his sword arm was too numb to lift.

The banners flew and the music piped and skirled and the

young woman came straight toward him. A riverrun of a woman, lightly armed and armored, her bright face wreathed in smiles, her pale hair floating free on her shoulders, her bare feet skipping through puddles of ooze and weed. She came in the front line of the Túatha Dé Danann, the attack force, and her brothers and sisters came with her.

Off to one side Éremón heard Amergin cry something that sounded like "Shi-*nahn!*" in an agonized voice.

The Gaels gripped their iron swords and hefted their shields as this army that was not, could not possibly be, an army, advanced upon them. They tried to imagine the battle such people would offer. Would the Dananns yell and break into a charge, gloriously wild with battle-joy? Would there be a fierce coming-together of body and weapon, an impact sexual in its thrust and satisfying in its concussion?

How could there be the intense cathartic of warrior frenzy when the opponents came dancing with flowers in their hair?

The two armies met at the center of the plain.

Amergin was trying desperately to make his way through the melee to Shinann, but she had vanished from his sight almost at once. Éber was slashing his team with a whip and racing them at an angle across the front of the Gaelic line in an effort to put himself in front of Éremón at the heart of the battle. And whatever link had frozen Éremón's sword arm was severed as the leader of the Gaels howled in rage and attacked his own brother even before he struck the first of the Dananns. "You won't get my place!" Éremón roared at Éber Finn.

They struggled, wheel to wheel and hub to hub, for a few desperate heartbeats, then Éremón's horses triumphed and he pushed ahead, leaving an angry Éber to suffer second place and a faceful of spattered mud.

The Dananns swirled among them in a blaze of color and a fragrance of flowers. Up close, it could be seen that they had weapons in their hands; short bronze swords and heavy-headed battle-axes appeared mysteriously from the folds of their clothing. Colored capes were flung back to reveal shields buckled to Danann arms. They had come to war, and war had come to them.

Possessed by a tumultuous energy, Éremón hacked his way into his opponents as if he were clearing a forest. But they did not meet his weapons; it was like fighting fog. He found it difficult to catch and kill adversaries who shifted from space to space with ease, too agile, too darting. They would not stand and give battle toe-to-toe as honest warriors should, but flowed among the Gaels striking a blow here, suffering a slash there, refusing to lock one body against another in the total embrace of life and death.

For a time it seemed there was no battle at all. The Dananns were not killing anyone and the Gaels could not catch and kill them.

But Éremón's warriors had come a great distance and there was a grimness in them. Slowly, inexorably, they pinned their opponents down and forced them to fight. They pitted their brawn and battletraining against wiry quicksilver strength and found themselves almost evenly matched, to their vast surprise—but when iron met bronze there was no contest.

Cries of pain rang across the summer meadows.

Amergin was searching frantically for Shinann. He saw a Danann woman with a familiar face—Banba!—lift her shield just as Caicher swung his boar-headed sword, and the brave queen fell with a groan that echoed through Amergin's bones. He saw Cet of the Plow run toward Éremón, and the Gael whirled and with one swift swordslash severed his neck and spine.

But Amergin did not see Shinann anywhere.

Cuill of the Hazel took a terrible wound in the belly and fell. Fodla, unbound hair streaming, ran toward him and Étan cut her down.

The Son of the Sun held his shield close to his body and stayed on his feet though others were falling all around him. He caught sight of Eriu advancing through the melee, wearing an expression of unshakable serenity. Feeling his eyes upon her, she turned and met them. And smiled.

For one brief moment the two of them were young again, and alone together.

The leader of the Gaels was only three paces from him, hacking his latest opponent. Greine felt the hot red anger of old days and old wars as the instinct for self-preservation rose up in him, unwilling to surrender bodies that had served so long and so well. He must strike a blow, for he was a *man* . . . He ran forward on swift silent feet and raised his sword above Éremón's unguarded back.

Amergin saw. There was no point in shouting a warning that would never be heard in the din of battle. An abandoned weapon lay bloodsmeared on the grass—a bronze-bladed sword, not Gaelic—and Amergin bent and seized it and ran forward with the grace of the born warrior.

The sword plunged into Greine's body. The tough muscles resisted at first, then yielded almost gladly. Amergin felt the Danann king's death shudder run up the blade and into his arm, and he saw the large eyes glaze even as they turned toward him in surprise.

This will be still worse than killing Colptha, Amergin thought, not understanding his own thought, as he stepped backward and let the weight of the falling body pull itself off the sword blade.

The Son of the Sun lay dying at Amergin's feet. Clarsah hung from the bard's shoulder thong, for a sword was in his hands now. And tears were in his eyes, though no one noticed.

Éremón was not even aware his brother had saved his life. He finished his kill and moved happily on to the next one, caught up in the rhythm of thrust and slash and counter.

Amergin stood in a space briefly emptied of war and looked down at his fallen foe.

Men do not die neatly in battle. They sprawl and twist, their convulsing bodies forming ugly patterns representative of violence. Broken and tossed aside they lie in ruin, stripped of all but the terrible dignity of death.

That was the worst of it, Amergin said to himself. The impossible postures of the slain bodies.

He gazed at the man he had dealt a mortal blow; a brother forever joined to him now, not by life, but by death. He felt an awful tenderness, a fullness of awe, as a woman is full with child. Something akin to love invaded him, mingled with grief. And alien shame.

He had taken from this cooling meat the most sacred of all properties, life, and yet he had not added one heartbeat from Greine's span of seasons to his own. All he had done was diminish their common existence.

He looked at the finely modeled curve of the dying man's lips, a beauty even the grotesquerie of pain could not destroy, and thought how he would have admired just such a mouth on a friend of his. How many good conversations, how much easy laughter, he might have shared with that intelligent face!

Cooling meat.

32 ◇

E RIU DID NOT SEE Greine fall, but she felt it. She was surrounded by Gaelic warriors and fighting for her own life, but that fight lost its meaning the moment Greine went down. She uttered a deep moan and whirled faster than eye could follow, ducking under a warrior's lifted arm before his reflexes could complete the blow aimed at her. She ran heedlessly past knots of fighters until she reached the place where her husband lay, and ignoring those around him, she flung herself down beside him and lifted his head and shoulders onto her lap.

Warriors circled them, but none would strike her in such a moment.

Amergin watched, stricken with pain, as she bent forward and pressed her lips against Greine's bloodless cheek. She whispered to him and he slowly opened his eyes.

Sakkar came running from somewhere and jostled Amergin's arm as he stood on tiptoe, trying to get a good look. "It is the queen," he said. "And the king of the Dananns. Who . . . ?"

The look Amergin gave him made Sakkar swallow the rest of his question.

Greine struggled to see his wife through shifting textures of light. "Eriu?"

"I am here."

A spasm of pain twisted his face and he fought to keep his eyes open, unwilling to lose sight of her while he still had eyes to see. "Eriu?"

"Do not try to talk. Save your strength."

"There is none left to save. How goes the battle?"

She said nothing but her face told him everything and he sighed aloud. "We have come to the fork in the road, then. And we will go your way, my brave queen. I did not give the order. I . . . did not . . ." He fought for breath. "The Sword . . . and the . . ." He gagged, tried to raise himself clear of her lap, and spat out a gobbet of black blood.

Amergin made some inadvertent gesture of pity which caught the dying man's attention. Greine turned his head, peering through grayness toward the bard. He wanted to speak to Amergin but realized there were few words left to him, and each one was precious. "Eriu?" he murmured.

She bent lower to hear him. "Eriu . . . when the morning comes, this will only be a dream. We will have the music of flowers blooming and the laughter of the sun in the valleys . . . we will dance on the wind . . ." His voice faded.

She bent lower, her face eclipsing his, and called out to him with the urgency of a mighty promise, *"In the morning, Greine!"*

When she raised her head, all the sorrows of the world were etched in the lines of her face. And Greine, Son of the Sun, lay dead.

She eased him from her lap and straightened his body into a graceful position. She arranged the folds of his clothing; she combed his sweat-dampened hair with her fingers. Then she stood up joint by joint, like an old woman, and looked down at the fearful wound in his side from which blood still seeped. She turned in a slow circle, scorching the spectators with her eyes. Even the most audacious warrior stepped back.

"Who did this?" she asked. Her voice sounded hollow, a cry from a deep cave. "What cursed iron sword brought my husband down?"

Amergin, bound by bardic truth, stepped forward and held out the weapon he still gripped, forgotten until this moment, in nerveless fingers. "It is not an iron sword, but one of your own forging," he told Eriu, holding up the bronze blade so she could see it with her husband's blood still on it.

She stared at the sword, recognizing, with a shock, the fancy inlay of brass wire worked into it by some Danann craftsman who had needed a bit of sparkle to make a weapon beautiful; the fragment of brass she had thought safely buried and forgotten. Perhaps the soft rain of Ierne had uncovered it again.

Eriu looked up and met Amergin's eyes. Because she loved all life, because she must mother and nurture any living creature in pain, she came to him and laid the palm of her hand flat on his chest. Looking up a long, long way, into his sorrowing face, she said, "I exonerate you of this, bard."

He could have borne anything but her forgiveness. He turned away from her and flung the sword as far as he could, hating it as he had never hated anything.

One step at a time, with straight back and bowed head, Eriu the queen walked away and left her husband's body lying on the meadowgrass. The ranks of the Gaels parted in respect to let her pass through, and more than one brave warrior turned his face aside because he was frightened of meeting her eyes.

Elsewhere on the plain the fighting continued. Eriu walked without hesitation toward the nearest conflict, holding up neither shield nor weapon, striding among the warriors as if she did not see them. She went through the heart of the battle unscathed, but at last Soorgeh, having just defeated a Danann after a fierce struggle, turned and saw another coming right at him and struck her down.

Amergin did not see it happen, for which he was grateful, afterwards. He had decided he and Clarsah had no place on this battleground. He only wanted to find Shinann and go far away, to some leafy glade where they could not hear the grunts and screams.

Sakkar came trotting after him, wiping a bloodied sword. "Where are you going, Amergin? Are you singing no more?"

"No," the bard said. Then, less abruptly, "I'm looking for a woman, Sakkar; small and very fair."

"A Danann, then? That describes them all. What do you want with her?"

"Everything," Amergin told him.

Druid talk—Sakkar had been among the Gaels long enough to recognize it. There was no point in going farther, so he drew a resolute breath and turned back toward the battle. He was still giddy with the residue of conquered fear and drunk with the rising exhilaration of one who has survived against great odds. He felt tall and golden, one of the company of heroes.

Amergin stalked the battleground, searching for the one face that mattered. He came upon a Danann with a slight wound who had withdrawn from the fighting and was sitting huddled on a stone outcropping, staunching the flow of blood from his shoulder with a wad of fabric torn from his clothing.

"Have you seen the woman called Shinann?" the bard asked.

"I suppose she was killed," the man replied, watching the speed with which the cloth absorbed the blood. "You are killing all of us, are you not?"

"Of course not!" Amergin cried, horrified. "We will spare anyone who surrenders their weapons; that is our tradition."

The shoulder seemed to have stopped bleeding. When the

Danann pulled the cloth away Amergin could see a deep and vicious slash cutting across the muscle. Blood should still be welling, he thought.

The injured man said bitterly, "We never took *up* our weapons; that was our mistake."

"What do you mean by that?"

The Danann did not answer him, merely clapped his hand over his wound and sat staring in misery at the battlefield.

The war raged from sunrise to sunset. The Dananns fought on when all their leaders were slain and it was obvious they were badly outnumbered, until the light began to fade over a plain littered with corpses. Then the survivors began slowly sheathing their blades, one by one, and turning aside from further conflict by silent but mutual agreement.

There was no need to fight on. The fate of Ierne was decided.

Éremón, bloodsmeared and begrimed, ordered his warriors to gather up their dead and prepare for a victory celebration.

Considering the scope of the battle, there were surprisingly few dead Gaels. In the long white summer twilight their bodies were gathered and carried off the field together with the wounded, and runners were sent to summon their kin.

Magnanimous in victory, Éremón spoke again. "We have never faced a braver foe, and so we will go ourselves and gather up the Danann bodies with respect, for they heaped their clans with honor this day. Only a mighty champion could have defeated them," he said with a grin. "Each warrior may claim the trophies he is entitled to, with full ceremony, and then we will present the bodies of their dead heroes to the remaining representatives of the Túatha Dé Danann. We will carry them on our own shields and in our chariots, for they deserve no less."

This announcement was greeted with a few weary cheers.

Amergin accompanied the warriors back to the battleground. Death was already in his heart; he expected to see the crumpled body of Shinann somewhere in the waving grass. When he found her dead, Ierne would be dead for him.

The sun had set but the sky was still filled with light. A mist hung suspended in the crowns of distant trees. Insects hummed in trampled grass. Deep grooves left by chariot wheels crisscrossed soft earth. Battered bronze weapons lay forever abandoned.

And there were no Danann bodies. None.

The Gaels halted abruptly.

"Their whole tribe fought and died here today!" Éber Finn protested, refusing to believe his eyes. "There weren't enough left alive to carry off even tens of bodies—so where are they?" He shook an angry fist at his brother, who stood as slackjawed and staring as everyone else.

With a visible effort, Éremón recovered from his astonishment enough to rasp out an order. "Find the Dananns! Spread out and search the entire region and do not rest or stop until you bring the survivors back to me, do you hear me? There must be enough of the ruling tribe left alive to surrender this island to its conquerors! That is the *Law!*"

No bodies. No trophy heads. A tangle of ruined bronze weapons and not even very much blood. The Gaels had to fight off shock, man by man, before they could set out to scour the area, searching farther than any Danann could possibly have fled.

But they found nothing. Hunting throughout that haunted night and several boneweary days, they located only trees and watercourses and a complex of great grassy mounds ringed by standing stones and overgrown with vines and bushes. But there were no Danann villages anywhere; no Danann buildings at all except for the deserted halls of the Gathering Place, where the wind sang a lonely song.

Finally his men were forced to report to Éremón that the Túatha Dé Danann, alive or dead, had vanished as totally as if they had never existed. They had slipped through a veil of tilted twilight and taken his final victory with them.

◇ **33** ◇

TWELVE GAELIC CLAN-CHIEFS still lived. In the frustrating aftermath of the battle, fracture lines between the clans broke wide open as quarrels and grievances held in abeyance for the sake of winning came flooding to the surface. The dissension Éremón feared burst out with a vengeance.

411

Men who had long thought Éber Finn might make the better leader blamed Éremón for letting the Dananns escape. No one had fully realized the flames of anger that Colptha's constant efforts had fed and fanned until the Gaels no longer faced a common enemy—but without that enemy they turned on each other, snarling. Slashing.

It was as if Colptha still stalked among them. Amergin could almost feel him there, refusing to be left out, taking credit for slaughter and claiming the slain as his sacrifices. Subtle, vicious, turning again and again and moving among them. Refusing to die, accepting neither sunlight nor shadow . . .

The sacrificer, beckoning.

Doubter and doubt, the soul of mistrust, his song a paean to the beauty of rage.

The sacrificer.

The earth trembled beneath the feet of the conquerors. In spite of the constant arguments that now seemed to erupt over nothing, the Gaelic leaders began trying to force some degree of organization onto their followers so they could move inland and begin setting up permanent settlements. The seasons of Ierne were, as yet, unfamiliar, but the slanting light heralded the approach of leaf-fall and the women were anxious to have walls up and roofs thatched and hearthfires lighted.

Odba and Taya found themselves working side by side, packing Éremón's domestic belongings. Women from those clans supporting Éber Finn glared at them.

"When we are settled, there will undoubtedly be an outcry to elect a chieftain for the entire tribe," Odba remarked. "Once that fruit would have fallen into Éremón's lap, but now I'm not so sure."

"He will need all our support," Taya agreed.

Odba glanced sideways at her. *Our*, Taya had said. And Taya was taking the hardest jobs upon herself without discussion, gently deferring to Odba on all major decisions.

"Here, that box is too heavy for you to lift alone," Odba heard herself saying crisply. "Let me take the other end of it."

Amergin, passing by, overheard and smiled.

Odba glanced up at him, remembering a message she had not yet had the opportunity to deliver. "I forgot to tell you, Amergin," she said. "Scéna Dullsaine asked me to say . . ."

"Who?" Amergin raised one dark eyebrow.

Odba wanted to laugh. What would Scéna say if she knew the bard had mislaid her memory? "Scéna Dullsaine—Ferdinón's daughter. She asked me to tell you specifically that she could have come with me, but she could think of *no sufficient inducement.*" Odba emphasized the last three words so strongly Amergin could not mistake their message.

He chuckled and Taya laughed outright. Odba laughed with them, feeling the cleansing power of laughter pour over her; wash her clean of bitterness, as soft rain washed the green land.

Things were different, here on Ierne.

Amergin noticed how tired Odba looked, however; how deep a sadness dwelled in her eyes. He waited until she was out of the earshot of others and then asked her, "Are you content here, Odba? You deserve to be happy and I want it for you; you more than earned it, with your courage."

"Éremón was impressed," she told the bard. "Wonderfully impressed; I have that much. Now he treats me with unfailing honor. He calls me his wife in front of others, he compares me favorably to Scotta so everyone will hear. I have all that." She tilted her head back and looked up at a soft scudding of gray clouds moving across the sky. "It is as if I stepped into her empty shoes. He treats me exactly as he did her . . . and at night he wraps his cloak around himself and Taya, whom he has never confused with his mother."

Amergin's heart turned with pity. "Under the Law," he reminded her, "you could seek pleasure with another man."

Odba barked a short, sharp laugh. "Look at me. Look closely! Does the sight of me fill your eyes sweetly, bard? Ai! My poor breasts are flat leather bags that droop on my chest. My skin is like harness leather. I have acquired, rightly or wrongly, a reputation for being barren; dried fruit. Who would want me?"

"Men never stopped admiring Scotta and following her with their eyes," Amergin said. "She was so strong . . ."

"Why do I keep having her name thrown at me?" Odba wailed unexpectedly. She turned and ran away from Amergin, gracelessly, with flapping elbows.

The Gaels continued to argue among themselves. Findbar and several of the other brehons had drowned in the great storm, and the tribesmen began coming to Amergin for arbitration, citing his judgment at the Gathering Place as precedent. Once he would have found some polite way to avoid the responsibility, but on Ierne he seemed to feel responsible for everything. He no longer stood to one side and held himself safe.

Only Éremón never came to him for advice. Éremón never spoke to him at all unless it was absolutely necessary, and Amergin nursed the loss in his heart, in silence.

The length of the nights reminded the bard it would soon be time for the festival of the great fire, which must be a double celebration this season to commemorate also the conquest of Ierne. Since their defeat of the Dananns, the Gaels had not seen even one of the Fir Bolg, and scouts reported that the natives had dismantled their settlements and taken themselves to remote areas.

"No one remains willing to fight us for Ierne," the warriors boasted to one another—those who were speaking to one another.

"The savages fear confrontation with us now that we've proved our power," Éremón boasted to Taya. "They were terrified of the Dananns and we beat the Dananns, so they may never trouble us again." He did not sound totally happy about this. He was a warrior, and the end to warring was a threat to him.

The Gaels decided to remain camped near the rivermouth until after the great festival, for the location was rich in fish and game. This was the place where they had finally and forever come ashore; they felt safe here. But they also knew they could not all stay. Each clan must find its own clanhold; Ierne must be portioned out among them.

Before the festival, Éremón took Taya in his chariot to view the scene of his triumph over the Túatha Dé Danann. He found himself often revisiting the battlefield, as if he might someday find there some small clue he had overlooked, a trail blazed to show him where they had gone. Their disappearance tormented him.

He was in a bravado mood when he and Taya set out, but as they neared the long green ridge known as the Gathering Place, he began glancing over his shoulder.

"What's the matter?" Taya asked, pressing close to him.

"Nothing," he said. Nothing but a feeling of being watched, though the broad meadows were empty, fog-hushed.

Éremón saw a battleground. Taya, mature and changed, saw a beauty she would not have noticed a few seasons before.

"Let's go up on that hill, Éremón," she pleaded. "See how lovely it is, wreathed in mist!"

Éremón had no desire to return to the Gathering Place. He

414

felt too small up there; the eerie song of the wind made him too uncomfortable. He wanted to stay on the plain, driving in large arcs and describing this or that fight, this mighty sword cut or that clever bit of footwork. But battles did not interest Taya much, and she had grown confident enough to say what she thought.

"I want to see that hill, Éremón," she insisted. "Look, isn't that someone up there?"

He halted his horses and glared up the ridge. Was it possible one of the Dananns had at last emerged from concealment? His heart was racing; his hand reached for his sword hilt.

At the same moment Taya recognized the tall, lean form atop the hill and cried, "It's Amergin! Oh, Éremón, let's go up there with him. I just have to see what it looks like from up there!"

He could not think fast enough to give her a believable argument, so he reluctantly turned his team and drove up the slope.

Amergin and Éremón exchanged the most cursory of greetings, but Taya did not notice. She jumped from the chariot and ran across the smooth green grass that covered the hilltop. "You can't see anything from here," Éremón called to her. "There's nothing but fog and mist out there today."

As if to steal the truth from his words for spite, the lowering clouds lifted then and all Ierne lay spread out before them in green and blue glory.

Taya held her arms wide. "This is the most beautiful place in the world," she said with certainty. The two men stood beside her, Éremón silent and annoyed, Amergin nodding in agreement.

She turned to the bard. "Look over there, Amergin, in that far distance. See those hills? Or are they mountains? That shade of blue changes constantly, it's like magic . . ." She went on and on, pointing out beauties. He looked down at her in amusement, and when she ran out of words she met his eyes in startled silence, seeing the passion smoldering there.

Yet it was Shinann he thought of; Shinnan he saw in those rolling meadows and blue hills. And the look of love he gave Taya went right through her toward another woman, an invisible presence who filled the space around them.

With a woman's instinct Taya knew. She turned abruptly to Éremón and concentrated on him after that with gentle and flattering interest.

415

They wandered amid the deserted halls of the Túatha Dé Danann, among timbered colonnades, past earthwork banks and a great tomb-mound, letting Taya's interest guide them. Amergin drifted off on his own, leaving Éremón and his woman together.

Taya bent suddenly to pluck a tiny flower from the grass and Éremón ambled forward without her—and looked up to find himself facing the Stone of Fal. He stopped with one foot frozen in midair.

The stone hummed.

No human courage would have been sufficient to make Éremón complete his step toward the grim gray stone, but Taya ran right past him, exclaiming, "Is this a monument, Éremón? Does it mark a tomb, or represent a god?"

He tried with all his strength to go forward and stop her, but he could not. To his dismay, he saw Taya actually touch the stone and lay her cheek against it, closing her eyes.

"Amergin!" Éremón bellowed, fighting the enchantment that held him bound. Hearing the stone hum.

Amergin ran toward them. Taya opened her eyes, surprised at Éremón's yell. She smiled at him.

Éremón found he could walk, could run, and he bounded to her side and wrapped his arms around her tightly, being careful not to let them brush against the stone as he did so. He did not want to touch that thing.

Amergin reached them and paused, puzzled.

Taya snuggled against Éremón. "I have never asked you for a bride gift, or anything at all for myself," she said in her soft voice.

Éremón was so relieved to find the incident apparently ended with no harm done that he hugged her all the harder. "No, you never have," he said. "And I would give you anything." He suddenly recalled how many things Odba had demanded, in her time. But Taya was different.

"Then may I claim just one now?" she asked him. "I will never ask for another, you have my word on it."

"Anything you want," Éremón assured her. "Am I not famed for my generosity?"

"Then give me this hill, Éremón. For my own, my own place. In our mother-tongue Tara means the hill of Taya, so let it be known henceforth as Tara, and when I am dead build my tomb here."

Éremón did not know what to make of her peculiar request.

He glanced suspiciously at the stone, but it was as silent as all stones are; so silent he found it hard to believe he had heard it hum.

Amergin was frowning like a man trying to solve a riddle. "I don't think this is the right bride gift for you, Taya," the bard said.

Éremón's bluster returned in a rush. "Of course it is! If my new wife wants land, she shall have land; a hill, a mountain, anything! I can give it all to her!" Now that he thought of it, perhaps this was his ultimate gesture of triumph, for what could be more appropriate than bestowing the sacred precincts of the enemy upon his woman as a bauble?

"This hill is yours," he told Taya, and suddenly he lifted her high above his head and held her there, pinned against the sky of Ierne like a trophy brandished aloft.

When he set her down he accidentally brushed his arm against the Stone of Fal. He jerked away immediately, but for days afterward the arm ached and throbbed as if it had been badly burned.

Amergin watched his brother and Taya whirl away in the warrior's chariot. Éremón was driving fast to impress his woman, and his multicolored cloak billowed out over her wind-flared gown. When Taya tried to turn and wave back up the hill to Amergin, Éremón shouted and lashed the horses so they careened even faster, swaying the cart and making Taya forget everything but holding on.

Inside himself Amergin could imagine Donn's mother-hen voice cautioning, "Be careful with that chariot, Éremón, until we are settled and have time to repair it or build new ones."

Amergin smiled. Now that so many who had been important to him were dead, he had become more fully aware of one of the great responsibilities of being a bard. Donn and all the dead were alive inside him, carried whole and vibrant in his memory to be brought out into the sun again whenever he told of them. As long as he lived, they lived, and when he had passed them on to the next generation of bards they would live again, their selves and their deeds as immortal as their spirits.

Bard.

Strange, how wise a man felt standing on this particular hill! No wonder the Dananns chose to convene here, Amergin thought. The high ground now known as Tara was a place for understandings, for important decisions—perhaps even to inaugurate kings. Something beyond man's comprehension was here, and through the soles of his bare feet Amergin felt the holiness of the earth.

The surviving druids prepared the rituals for the great festival at the close of summer. There would be dances, but there were fewer Gaels to dance. Some young men would do the dance just coming into fashion in Iberia when they left it, commemorating Ír's fight with the bull with a great flaring of red capes and much swirling and cheering. Others would imitate a step they had seen in the Fir Morcan land, linking hands and dancing forward and back like the waves along the beach. Patterns of life forever frozen into the dance. There would be no bardic competition, however. It would take many seasons, perhaps generations, for the tribe to rebuild itself to the point where enough were born with the true bardic gift to have a competition among them.

So no one asked Amergin about his epic. No one reminded him of its incompletion, for they all felt a sense of incompletion now. Nothing would be finished, settled, accomplished, until they spread out across the face of Ierne and claimed their own clanholds. A man could not feel in harmony with the Mother until he had taken his first season's living from her.

Amergin was disappointed that the poem was not demanded of him, for to his own surprise he thought he could have had it ready. Sometime after arriving on Ierne he had opened himself up and quit guarding his vulnerability—perhaps when Shinann walked in and made all barriers irrelevant—and since then the composing had flowed smoothly, the epic building itself inside him without any great effort on his part.

He talked to Shinann sometimes, aloud or silently as the mood took him. Some of his tribesmen whispered about his behavior behind their hands, remembering Ír, but their words did not hurt him. Words had lost their power to hurt him. Only emotions were painful, like Éremón's anger and distrust.

Sometimes when he thought of Shinann Amergin was angry, though never with her.

So he worked on his composition daily, though he was no longer obsessed with poetry. Until he reached Ierne his work had been the only life he had, but that was not true now. He had a life of his own. He was just waiting to find it again.

By the time the ashes of the festival fire were cool, fights had broken out in several areas of the encampment. Soorgeh and Caicher had pummeled each other into insensibility ("A short journey for both'' Donn might have commented, did comment, in bardic darkness), and Éber approached Amergin, asking him to arbitrate the dispute. "You are the ranking druid," Éber reminded his brother unnecessarily. "I hear whispers you will be named as chief druid eventually."

"I do not want it," Amergin told him. "Nor do I want to go on finding myself between you and your men and Éremón and his. The time has obviously come when the island must be apportioned between you, for the longer you stay together the less you seem to agree."

"I've noticed that too," Éber commented, "though I can't really understand it. We didn't always fight over everything the way we do now."

"Oh, you fought," Amergin told him. "But never past sundown. And then you patched each other's cuts and scrapes and had a laugh together."

"What happened to us?" Éber Finn wondered sadly. "We were like knots in a fisherman's net, each of us making the whole fabric stronger as long as we remained connected to each other. Now I feel we are torn apart. Great gaping holes, and weakness . . .''

"You sound like a poet," Amergin told his brother. "How can a man be both poet and warrior?"

Éber considered the question. "I don't know," he said thoughtfully. "But perhaps . . . perhaps I would like to try to be both. When we are permanently settled. Tell us how to divide the land between us, Amergin, so we can build our homes." And then he frowned. "And remember, Éremón gets only two houses, and that is a special exception. He is not to claim more land than me!"

Éremón disliked submitting any question to Amergin for arbitration, but he knew the matter must be settled and no one else seemed willing to take such a responsibility. The other druids still felt uncertain in the new land, groping for connections with an invisible world they had not yet been able to explore and understand.

"Divide Ierne between the clan-chiefs who support me and the misguided ones who adhere to Éber Finn," Éremón told Amergin. "You have to decide; it seems our people will not listen to anyone else."

Amergin drove alone to the hill he now thought of as Tara and spent a long day in solitude, considering the size and shape of the island as he knew it from his own explorations and from such diverse sources as Fir Morcan descriptions and Sakkar's sea charts. He ached to be wise. A judge must be the instrument of justice as a poet was the instrument of poetry, and yet he did not know how to channel such wisdom through himself.

His mind played with words. Instrument. Weapon. He was a bard, armed with the harp, guardian of both the past and the future. On Tara he was acutely aware of the Túatha Dé Danann in the past as well as the Gaels in the future, and he realized that he must be the voice . . . for both of them. For both of them!

He must. Not Clarsah. The gift was his, and *he* was the instrument.

Knowledge came flooding into him as if it rose from the earth through the naked souls of his feet. He stood transfixed, hardly daring to breathe. On Tara.

He saw with dazzling clarity that the gift had been his all along; it required no harp in his hand. He gently unbound Clarsah from his shoulder and set her down as tenderly as ever. He stood erect without her, feeling naked and free.

Free to make the apportionment of the land with confidence and trust in his own inner voice.

He drove back to the Gaelic encampment and announced his decision with no further hesitation.

"The island will be shared, occupied in equal portions by the followers of Éremón and those of Éber Finn. Éremón will take the north and east, since he has already claimed the Danann hill as a gift for his wife. Éber Finn will have the south and west, good cattle land with a climate his women will enjoy."

He spoke with such total conviction that neither Éremón nor Éber Finn raised any objection at all.

"I claim the bard to come with me as ranking druid," Éremón said with obvious reluctance, to keep an edge on prestige.

Amergin agreed. He would have been more comfortable with Éber, but he had last seen Shinann on the plain below Tara and he did not want to settle too far away from that place.

Éremón included the surviving sons of Ír in his band, promising them their own clanholds when they reached manhood. "Ír was in my ship," he said in justification when Éber accused him of trying to shift the balance of warriors more

420

heavily in his favor. "You take Donn's daughters, Éber," he offered.

In addition to Amergin, such noblemen as Gosten and Soorgeh chose to remain with Éremón, while Éber Finn claimed the loyalty of Caicher and Étan, and Taya's father Lugaid, as well as their clans and adherents and several other major families.

"You must choose your own leader," Amergin told Sakkar. "Éremón or Éber Finn, only you can say whom you will follow as a free man."

Sakkar had been considering the question. "Your brother Éremón grows surly and suspicious," he said, "and I miss the way he used to laugh at himself as well as everyone else. Éber Finn seems sunnier now, and he goes to the sunnier region. But Soorgeh stays with Éremón, and Soorgeh has a tall daughter with red hair . . ."

"Soorgeh is a clan-chief," the bard reminded his friend.

"And I am a blooded warrior now," Sakkar responded, "so I can ask for a clan-chief's daughter." Stretching toward independence, he did not even think to ask for Amergin's advice, and the bard was pleased.

"You have come a long way, little shipwright," Amergin said.

Sakkar's dark and twinkling eyes turned solemn. "I have that; a very long way. I have come so far that soon I will have my own holding and count not only the Milesians as allies, but the clan of Soorgeh also. Part of my family, Amergin; *my family!* All of us together!" He flung his arms wide. His face was radiant.

Amergin had never loved Sakkar as much as he did in that moment when the essence of the Celtic spirit shone through a small and swarthy man born on a very different shore. "You have this poet's blessing," Amergin told him. "Build yourself a stronghold and sire a lot of healthy children on that handsome big daughter of Soorgeh's."

"I intend to," Sakkar assured him. "We will need many children if we hope to people this island with Gaels."

Gaels.

Because the greatest of the bards chose to stay with Éremón, Éber insisted on having the most skilled of the surviving citharadagh accompany him to the south. When Éremón objected the two men came close to blows on their last day in camp together. "What are you doing to yourselves?" Amergin cried, hoping to shame them, but Éber stubbornly repeated his demand for perfect equality and Éremón replied with a coarse comment, so in the end they had to be held apart by their followers and the two surviving warrior sons of the Míl parted in permanent anger.

Fortunately for both sides there was much work to be done, and smoldering anger fueled the fires of energy. In order to establish settled clanholdings forests must be cleared, causeways erected across bogs, banks and walls and houses and halls constructed.

Éremón had two houses to build under the watchful eyes of two women and of his sons, who were determined that their mother not be slighted. Taya had a suggestion for her new home. "Build me a chamber open to air and sunlight like the hall of the Danann king on my hill," she asked Éremón. "What did you say that king's name was?"

"Greine. He called himself the Son of the Sun."

Taya smiled delightedly. "How perfect! Build me a Greine hall, then, instead of putting some dark cramped balcony in the hall you build for your clan-chiefs and heroes."

"Build a Greine hall for Odba, too," Lagneh promptly insisted.

"You force me to twice as much labor," Éremón said.

"You have always said you were the strongest of men," his oldest son Moomneh replied, looking him in the eye.

"You are getting a twisty tongue like a druid," Éremón told his son sourly.

Across the land of Ierne, the strongholds of the Gaels rose. In spite of the richness of the land things did not go easily, and the Fir Bolg tribes began to recover their courage and launched limited attacks in areas where they perceived some weakness. But the iron swords and superior skill of the conquerors discouraged them, in time, and their elders began suggesting such expedient arrangements as trade agreements and an exchange of marriageable women.

In the south, Éber Finn stocked his new holding with the animals from Iberia and many fine fat cattle taken from the hapless Fir Bolg tribes. The cattle quickly became his walking gold, his sustenance and measure of wealth, guarded and herded and besung. Ierne proved, indeed, to offer fine pasture to the livestock of the Gaels.

Soorgeh built himself a lofty fort that he called Dun Edair, and that Sakkar visited to offer bride gifts for the tall girl with red hair. Sakkar labored mightily over a stronghold to be known as Delginis, and even Éremón was impressed by the order and elegance of its appointments, and the quality of the craftsmen honored within its walls.

All over Ierne, warriors were erecting earthen banks and supervising the breeding of cattle while their sons were training oxen to the plow, so that by next leaf-spring-out Ierne would be ready to receive their seed.

The chief bard's new house was built in the hills at the southernmost reach of Éremón's territory. Amergin did not spend much time there, however. Even when the rain pelted its hardest he could be found driving his chariot along the roads and byways, as if searching for someone.

◇ **34** ◇

THE WARRIOR CROUCHED LOW, hugging the wall. He was breathing hard and his grip on his casting-spear was white-knuckled. Listening intently, he crept forward on the balls of his feet, expecting an attacker to come around the wall at any moment and fall on him screaming.

When he reached the corner he peered cautiously around it and saw nothing more menacing than a broad lawn of grass sweeping down to the hazel grove, and a line of ducks solemnly parading across the green expanse, headed for the nearby pond.

Moomneh stood up and hurled his spear away with an expression of disgust. Legneh came trotting to join him. "What was it? Did you see anybody—one of the Fir Bolg? One of the Dananns, perhaps?"

"Nobody ever sees the Dananns," Moomneh snorted. "They're all gone, don't you believe that yet? And that noise we heard wasn't an attack by any native tribe, it was just those ducks over there. No enemy." He sighed, flexing his brawny young arms. "Nothing to do."

"We could hunt," Legneh suggested hopefully. "Pick up your spear and get one of those ducks for the pot."

"Odba doesn't feel like cooking it anyway," Moomneh pointed out. "She wouldn't thank us for it."

Legneh looked worried. "She still has fever, then?"

Moomneh nodded. He had grown into a leaner replica of Éremón, and the same energy animated his body even in repose. As the two young men talked he shifted his feet, massaged the bulging thews of his arms, adjusted and readjusted the massive bronze brooch holding his light woolen cloak. "It's a pity the most gifted of the samodhii were lost in that storm at sea," he said. "That's just one of the many things Éremón holds against the Dananns; we are left with no one who understands fevers sufficiently to drive one out of Odba."

"She wouldn't be sick in the first place if she hadn't insisted on acting 'as Scotta would' in Éremón's absence," Legneh grumbled.

"She may be the senior wife, but there was really no need for her to go out in the cold rain to see how Taya was doing."

"It isn't Taya's fault. She's about to have a child and she was right to summon a woman of her clan when she felt uneasy."

"Are you defending her?"

Moomneh shrugged. "She's always been pleasant to all of us. Taya goes out of her way to do nice things for others, to be cheerful and thoughtful. I can't stay mad at her."

Legneh pounded one knotted fist against an open palm. "I need to be mad at *somebody*," he complained. "I'm a warrior with no one to fight."

Moomneh nodded sympathetically. "I understand what you mean. I wish now we'd at least gone hunting with Éremón instead of . . . What's that? Do you hear Odba's bronze bell ringing?"

"Yes, that's her signal. At least now we'll have something to do," said Legneh. He shouldered his spear and the two young men trotted briskly across the stronghold to Odba's dwelling.

Their mother was in her greine-hall, a loftlike balcony open to the sun on the east side. Though the day was warm and dust-motes danced gaily in the golden light within the lime-washed chamber, Odba was wrapped in both blankets and a cloak. Her face was flushed; her blue eyes were too bright.

Her sons jostled each other as they thudded up the wooden

424

steps to her chamber. "I thought Lagneh was with you to-day," the eldest said as soon as he reached her side.

Odba put down the piece of sewing she was working on. "He kept fussing over me and I got tired of it. I sent him off to fish, but now I find I need some strong young arms to help me move this chest—from here to over there . . . I need to have it in the light so I can find my other copper needle, I know it's in the bottom somewhere . . ."

"You shouldn't be doing things like that at all," Moomneh said with a scowl. "Get some freeman's wife to stay up here with you all the time and help you with things. There are several in the compound today."

"I don't like the way the other women look at me," Odba said. "They all know Éremón never spends the night here. They pity me, and I cannot stand to be pitied."

Neither young man commented aloud, but they both remembered the old days, and the way their mother used to be. More things had changed than the color of her now-faded hair. "I'm going to get some women to attend you," Legneh said briskly. "And I give you my word they won't pity you." His square jaw and meaty body put weight behind his promise.

As he disappeared back down the steps, Moomneh sat down on the carved bench beside his mother. She looked at him critically, narrowing her eyes. "You should not wear that lime paste on your hair unless you are going into battle," she said. "It bleaches out all your natural color, and I like the gold. It reminds me of . . ." She did not finish, but looked down fixedly at the sewing in her lap.

"We'll speak to him too, when he returns," Moomneh told her. "How long can he stay in the west country hunting? We'll remind him of his obligations to you."

"Oh please, don't!" Her eyes were sunken but urgent. "I could not bear to be pushed into Éremón's face anymore, it's too humiliating. You know, when Taya began to swell with her child I thought he might come to me for more than just formal visits and polite courtesies; I braided my hair and oiled my skin—I did everything I knew to do. But he didn't come. He listened to those tales of wild boar in the west and put together a hunting party instead. Even Taya could not make him stay, now that he's grown used to having her."

"We stayed," Moomneh reminded his mother. "To protect you and Éremón's holding."

Odba rewarded him with a faint smile. "You hoped there

425

would be some threat to defend us against; I'm almost sorry you were disappointed. It is painful for me to watch my sons moping around because there is so little to do.''

"There is always plenty to do," Moomneh said, trying to reassure her. "We've helped the freemen build and plow and clear land and drain bogs; we don't want for activity. It's just . . ."

"I know. It's just that your father filled you with tales of heroism and gave you a taste of battle glory, and now you cannot forget." She stopped speaking and cocked her head. "I hear the voices of women below," she said. "Legneh has brought me a handful of unwanted female companions, so I suppose I must accept them gracefully. You and he go now; don't think I haven't seen you drumming your fingers impatiently against your thigh! Go and find Lagneh and do some fishing. I'll be all right."

So the two elder sons of Éremón took off with their mother's blessing in search of sport. And the small band of Fir Bolg warriors that had patiently waited in hiding beyond the birch grove saw the last warriors leave the area of Éremón's stronghold.

Encouraging one another, they crept closer to the outer earthwork bank. Fear made them both cautious and devious, but they could not overlook such an opportunity. Even the craftsmen and herders were, for once, all too far away on various duties to be within earshot if the women in Éremón's houses should call. Two rich and undefended houses waited, offering ample opportunity for the Fir Bolg to snatch some treasure and offer an insult, at least, to the conqueror of Ierne.

Éremón's stronghold was in the center of his large clanholding, and he had been diligent about building his wives two equal houses in every respect—except that the wall around Taya's house had both a formal gate in front, in full view of the entire clanhold, and a small wooden gate behind, half-hidden by bushes. Éremón had installed this second gate to give Taya access to a well some paces distant, wherein lived a spirit of sparkling purity. Taya made frequent pilgrimages to that well and felt the water spirit giving added strength to her unborn child.

The little gate was easily smashed by determined shoulders and kicking feet, and a dozen Fir Bolg warriors crept into the compound, looking around nervously. No male voice challenged them; no eyes saw them.

They scurried across the grass and disappeared inside Taya's open doorway.

Odba heard Taya scream. The sound pierced through her like a spear of ice, driving out the fever. "That's Taya voice, but it's too soon for her baby to be coming," Odba said to the other women.

Taya screamed again and Odba stood up, fighting off dizziness. Her sewing slipped unnoticed from her lap to the floor. "Whatever it is, let your sons take care of it," one of her women urged, frightened by the terror in Taya's voice.

"I sent my sons away to do the things men enjoy," Odba said. "If they were close enough to be of any use now, Taya would not have had to scream twice." Clutching at the wall, she made her way down the steps and out her own door. The other women followed, reluctant to be left alone and afraid of what Éremón would say if they let Odba face danger by herself.

When Odba stepped into the outside light she heard small silvery bells ringing—in her ears, in her head?—and bright yellow and blue flashes danced around the edges of her vision. She clenched her teeth and shook her head, but that made matters worse. Ignore it, then.

Beside her door was a rack holding spears and knives for butchery, and she grabbed the nearest spear, nearly dropping it in her weakness. No! She clutched the weapon and broke into a shambling run and the other women followed her.

Out her own gate, across the meadow, and into Taya's compound she ran, pulled by Taya's repeated screams. She was dizzy and nauseated and she went forward unaware of her feet on the earth or the passage of distance. Nothing seemed real to her until she saw that Taya's door was ajar and stepped inside. Then everything was too real.

Taya lay on the floor near the hearth, and a man in the clothing of a Fir Bolg warrior was just lowering himself onto her body, grinning. Taya had her arms crossed protectively over the little mound of her belly but two men held her legs wide apart, pinioning her helplessly on her back. A handful of other men were pawing greedily through Éremón's chests and boxes, spilling his treasures onto the rush-covered floor.

Odba was surprised at the speed with which her thoughts raced. She saw everything in that one quick glance, while time itself seemed to grind to a halt. The man on top of Taya thrust downward so slowly it was almost comical and the other men moved with equal slowness. One still had in his hands the clothing they had just enjoyed tearing from Taya's body, and he was fondling the soft fabric as he waited his turn at her. Fondling it slowly, while Odba's fever-sharpened mind took in every detail of the cloth and his hands and raced on, considering all the possibilities.

She could let them finish, rape Taya and kill the child within her, rob Éremón and have their revenge. She could probably turn and tiptoe out the door without their even seeing her, because they were so preoccupied. She and the women with her could run for their own safety and fear would make them fast.

But Odba felt no fear. She had once summoned such reserves of courage that the residue would be with her all her life. In her long ordeal on the sea animosity had been washed out of her, for there was no room for hatred when all one's energies must be devoted to survival. Now she did not see Taya as a despised rival, but as part of her tribe. And she threw her spear with deadly accuracy.

It sank between the shoulder blades of the man just entering Taya's body. Pleasure and pain swept through him together, but pain triumphed. With a grunt of shocked surprise he collapsed onto the woman beneath him. His fingers twitched in a hopeless effort to reach around to his back and draw out the spear, but in a few moments he was dead, with his eyes and mouth still open in astonishment.

His companions whirled to face the doorway and the white-faced woman swaying there. With wild yells, they leaped toward her.

Éremón's older sons had encountered Lagneh just returning from his fishing expedition with a splendid catch, and the sight of the silvery fish made their mouths water. "Even if Odba doesn't feel like cooking, there are plenty of women in her house now who will be willing to feed us," suggested stocky Legneh. "Let's go back and have a meal before we do any hunting."

They turned back toward their father's stronghold, exchanging rowdy jests, punching one another on the arm, boasting about the quantity of fish they could devour. Then they heard the yelling and began to run.

Three nights later, Éremón and his hunting party returned from the west country, laden with game. The head of a

428

mighty boar, complete with savage curling tusks, decorated the new war chariot of proud Sakkar of the Gaels—who had a charioteer to drive him, however, as a man cannot master too many skills at one time.

As they neared his clanhold Éremón grew uneasy. He was not a sensitive man, but there was something wrong in the very atmosphere of the land. The light was too bleak and the birds were too quiet.

Then he saw Amergin coming out to meet him in a chariot bedecked with mourning plumage.

"What is this?" Éremón demanded to know. He was never happy to see Amergin anywhere near his stronghold. As a druid, the bard claimed no land as his own, for it might be construed as an insult to the Mother if a druid preferred one part of her over another. But he had built a fine house for himself on the farthest reaches of Éremón's holding and that was where the warrior preferred him to stay.

"My presence was required," Amergin said formally. Clarsah rode his shoulder but she would be no help to him now. The words must come from within himself, and he must cushion their wounding as much as possible.

"While you were away," he told Éremón, "the Fir Bolg at last found enough courage to attack your stronghold."

"My sons!" Éremón cried.

"They're all right. They were . . . a little distance away when the attack occurred, but they arrived quickly and fought bravely. There were only a dozen of the enemy and they are all dead."

"The chief bard does not deck himself in mourning colors for a slain enemy," Éremón remarked. "Who else is dead?"

"Step from your chariot and walk a way with me and I will tell you," Amergin said gently. "This is not news to be shouted."

Éremón felt a peculiar numbness creeping over his body. It was bad, very bad, whatever this message was that Amergin brought him. He tossed his reins to one of his men and walked a few paces away with the bard, while the others watched, each imagining his own possibilities for loss and grief.

"The Fir Bolg stormed your house and attacked Taya," Amergin said. "One of them . . ." He saw an insane glitter in Éremón's eyes and quickly put his hand on his brother's arm. "No, not that, he was not able to complete a rape, for Odba heard the screams and came running with a spear in her

429

hand. She killed the man with Taya before his companions could stop her.''

"Taya is all right? Is the infant . . ."

"Taya and her unborn child are alive, Éremón."

The warrior wiped beads of sweat from his forehead. "I thank the great spirit for it," he said. "Well then, that wasn't so bad, Amergin. Why did you startle me like that? Why come with every appearance of bad news? You play a cruel trick, and I will remember it."

Amergin let the bluster beat against him until it died of its own momentum. "You have not asked about your first wife," he said quietly.

Éremón stopped in his tracks. "Where is she?"

"I will take you to her. Her sons are constructing her cairn themselves, and I will officiate at the burial, but it is not to be here. Moomneh and the others thought she would not want to be so close to Taya."

"Odba? Dead?" Éremón said the two words separately, as if they could not have the slightest connection.

"She died of her wounds the next day," Amergin told him.

"Wounds, and fever—it is hard to know which really took her. The attackers struck her but the women with her defended her bravely until your sons arrived, and I do not think she was mortally wounded then. But she was sick with an illness that came upon her after she went out in cold rain to see to Taya in your absence."

"I cannot believe any of this," said Éremón from that numbed place where he stood, staring at the spoils of the chase heaped in his chariot.

When she was forever beyond his reach, Éremón began to discover what a treasure he had had in Odba. He heaped her tomb with gifts; he wept openly for her; he talked incessantly of her virtues. He remembered her as much more beautiful than Taya, who now had a puffy face and a swollen belly and seemed quiet and withdrawn.

He even, with a certain reluctance, invited Amergin to sit by his hearth when the funeral rituals were completed, so that the bard might share in the conversation and contribute his own memories of Odba. Cherished Odba. Admired and flawless Odba. Being surrounded by others who had known her made Odba more vividly alive for Éremón. If his surviving wife did not share his eagerness to recapture her, he did not notice.

430

Clansmen and fellow chieftains crowded into Taya's house, passing wine cups and trying to think of flattering things to say about the dead woman. But Éremón's harsh voice rose above them all. "My first wife was a glorious woman!" he proclaimed, while Taya absentmindedly poked at the hearthfire. She still felt weak and shaky but would not have dared say anything about it; not with Odba's courage held over her head like a torch, calling attention to any possible weaknesses she might have.

"See what strong sons Odba has left for me!" Éremón cried, gesturing toward the young men with a sweeping embrace. "You would expect no less from a woman of courage. Courage right until the end—didn't you tell me, Moomneh, that she never said a word about her pain?"

Moomneh reddened at being singled out to praise Odba. In his hidden heart Éremón's oldest son admired the bard Amergin, who was such a master of words, and he was sorry he could never come close to similar skill. The beauty of words excited him but he thought their grace eluded him, and now he resented being forced to make a speech in front of everyone. He had been taught to boast of his strengths, not expose his weaknesses.

"She didn't complain," he said in a low voice. "She never said anything after we got there, except once she murmured something about braiding her hair."

Éremón shook his head. "You must have misunderstood her. Odba was long past all that sort of women's jabber. She was like our Scotta, I tell you, and had more important things on her mind. You know nothing about other people."

Moomneh turned away, redfaced.

Taya found a moment to speak to him when Éremón was involved elsewhere. "Forgive my husband, Moomneh," she said. "He was not always so hard, so rude. The outcome of the battle with the Dananns has left him with a simmering anger and he takes it out on everyone."

The young man wanted to hate her, as he remembered his mother had once hated her. Surely he remembered that; it had seemed very clear at the time. "My mother would be alive if it were not for you," he made himself say in a cold tone. But Taya's eyes were warm and compassionate, and he did not like himself very much for having said it.

*　　*　　*

Amergin drove home quietly through the starry twilight. Except for Clarsah he was alone, but not lonely. He had not felt truly lonely since first setting foot on Ierne.

He wanted to think about Odba in privacy, to break through to her essence and taste the flavor of her life. To know if it had contained enough meat and honey to make the living of it worthwhile, so he would know the degree of mourning he should feel for her transition.

What larger symbol did the pattern of Odba's life represent? he wondered. All lives were symbols, as important to the totality of existence as the interwoven gold and bronze and copper in his arm ring were important to the totality of the design; important for their uniqueness, their individual contribution.

Odba. Like Colptha, Odba had fought to win—and lost.

Or was it possible to lose? Were *winning* and *losing* irrelevant terms, concepts like "fairness," which had no meaning beyond a narrow human expectation? Invented realities, not deeper truths.

He reined in his horses and stood quietly, musing in a silvered darkness that was not darkness.

The whole of Ierne shimmered and glowed from within.

Like the vanished Túatha Dé Danann.

Amergin, startled, looked around, expecting to see some big-eyed, narrow-chinned face, familiar and dear and no higher than his heart. "Shinann!" he cried out desperately.

His horses snorted and pawed the earth; the earth of Eriu's island, older than old and wiser than wise, slashed and scarred and beautiful—and now forever illumined by a very special glow.

"Children of Light . . ." Amergin whispered softly. No voice answered, and at last he gathered up his reins and drove slowly home.

He refused to have a guard with him, even after the attack on Éremón's stronghold. Amergin was the chief bard, sacrosanct among Celtic peoples. To admit that Ierne was a place where even bards could be slaughtered was to admit that it could not be the realization of his dreams, the poetry hidden in his heart. Only a land for conquest, the sword triumphant over the word.

No, said the bard.

But he had a remorseless enemy and he knew it. Iron blades might thirst for flesh and blood, but Amergin's enemy was elusive and could not be killed by such simple weapons as swords. Their use only nourished him. Only—perhaps—the bardic gift could stand against Colptha's spirit; ideas and dreams and beauty against ignorance and anger and bloodlust. One intangible reality against another.

On Ierne, the night was haunted by many spirits. Faces glimpsed in hawthorn boughs, memories of Scotta and Donn and Ir . . . and Colptha's unsatisfied hunger stalking the land, creating animosities among clansmen and tribesmen.

After the attack that killed Odba, Éremón had vowed, "My warriors and I will drive every Fir Bolg tribe into the far corners of this island or into the cold sea!" But Amergin saw that the Fir Bolg had little heart left for fighting; the attack on Éremón's stronghold was the desperate gesture of a defeated people who no longer dared meet the conquerors in open battle.

So there would not be many splendid and satisfying battles to be fought with the Fir Bolg in the future. And the Túatha Dé Danann were . . . gone . . .

Who was left for Éremón and his warriors to fight?

And fight they must; it was not only bred and trained into them, shaped by many generations of fighting for survival on the broadlands from which they came, but the aggressiveness of their natures had been so amplified by Colptha for the sake of his own ambition that it could no longer be satisfied by simple sports and contests. The rivalry of the Milesians infected all the Gaels now with a keen lust for the heroics of battle, and when there was no one else to fight they would fight each other, less for pleasure than out of an inner compulsion. Brother savaging brother until the very reasons for the quarrels were forgotten and war was not part of life, but life itself.

Hideous! Amergin thought, recoiling from his druid vision. And no one else seemed to see it. Colptha's whispered words lived after him—the *words*, surviving!—fostering jealousy and suspicion. Only other words could defeat them.

And Éremón could not be enlisted in the fight because he could not even understand it; he had become its tool, all his generosity and zest and laughter misdirected.

Éremón's spirit was still too young, perhaps. Only with maturity would it be able to resist something as powerful as Colptha, to judge wisely, to listen and learn. But how many lives must be spent before a spirit matured?

Druid questions, not easily answered by druids. The answers lay beyond druidry, then . . . but where?

Always beyond, Amergin thought, with a sense of irony. Yet I have reached my beyond, and the restlessness that drove me here is gone. All that remains is the struggle against Colptha, and my thoughts of Shinann . . .

Thoughts, not memories. Memories were of the dead.

Sister Moon changed her face and the nights passed. The voice of the pipe wailed across Éremón's clanhold, signaling the birth of a chieftain's child.

Amergin drove his chariot headlong northward, not sparing the whip until he could see the tall tree the young of the clan had erected in front of Taya's house on Bealtaine, decorating it with symbols and ribbons to complete the rituals of marriage. The tree as representative of both nurturer and phallus, source of food and shelter and source of bodylife.

Bodylife had been given to a fresh spirit, and Taya's new son came into the world rump first. His mother shrieked in pain. Samodhii, summoned by the pipes, stood with Amergin at her bedside until the child was finally delivered from an exhausted woman lying in a pool of her own blood. The samodhi who lifted the child to its mother's breast met Amergin's eyes and shook his head. "She is alive for now," the healer said, "but she is badly damaged. We will pack her with poultices and bind her, but this has been a hard birth. Life exacts a high price."

Amergin sang the song of welcome to Éremón's new son, holding up the harp so it was the first object the baby's vague blue eyes encountered.

Éremón was not present for his son's birth. He had taken Gosten and Sakkar and a war party to track down a rumored Fir Bolg encampment several nights distant, though Taya had pleaded with him to stay. He shook her off impatiently. "I do this to protect you and all the other women and children," he told her. "Odba would have understood."

He was two nights away from her before he recalled the look in her eyes at hearing those words, and found himself regretting them; an unusual occurrence for him. But then the trail grew hot and the battle fever rose in him and he forgot Taya.

"Did Éremón leave a name for your son?" the samodhii inquired of the exhausted mother.

Taya's voice was a whisper. "He meant to, I am certain,

434

but he was so anxious to be off . . . Amergin? A child must have a name as soon as he comes into the world, something to know himself by in this life. Will you give one to my son?"

Amergin looked down at the little wrinkled face of the baby, trying to catch a glimpse of the newly housed spirit. He did not see someone he recognized, but he smiled anyway and suggested, "Let the son of Éremón be called Irial, after the old chief druid. That is an honorable name and should be honored in our new homeland."

When Éremón returned he was furious, of course. Furious because his son bore a name Amergin had chosen, and even angrier because the baby had a thick cap of dark hair.

Éremón thoroughly examined the red and mewling infant known as Irial. When the baby was first put into his big hands he rejoiced in the feel of it, for he had always enjoyed the squirming liveliness of children. But then it seemed as if a voice whispered at his shoulder, "Look at that dark hair. Observe the long fingers, the thick eyelashes. Who does the child most resemble?"

Éremón thrust the baby at Taya, who still lay in her bed, too weak to be up and about. "My other children are blond," he said hoarsely. "And their eyes are light blue. These eyes are very dark."

Taya's house bustled with old women, the crowd who always arrives in birthing time to feed the mother brews and broths and praise or condemn the quality of her milk. One of them, the mother of many children, faced Éremón with her hands on her broad hips and reminded him, "All babies have dark blue eyes when they are first born."

"All babies don't have black hair."

"I have dark hair, Éremón," Taya said softly. "Why are you so angry? I thought you would be pleased with our son."

Our son. Éremón glowered at the infant and then swung around to glare at the bard. "And how long have you been here, Amergin?"

"The pipes summoned me when she went into labor."

"And I dismiss you now! Go and stay a distance from my house from now on, and if you are needed for any purpose you will fulfill your obligations outside my door. I am tired of your face."

Amergin stood his ground. "I was hoping you and I could talk together," he said.

"What have we to talk about? You could have talked with

435

Donn, he was a great one for that. But he's dead; dead in a storm nine waves from shore." Spittle sprayed with Érémón's words.

"I was obliged by my profession to give the fairest possible decision for all concerned," Amergin replied. "The Dananns were ill-prepared and you wanted to appear generous. I did what I could to accommodate both sides, to keep the scale in balance."

"Colptha didn't think so!"

"Colptha did everything he could to turn us against one another, so his would be the only voice anyone listened to," Amergin reminded his brother. "Yet he was never trustworthy, Érémón, you know that. Remember the short cuts he used to take in foot races? Remember the day he got Ír to drink a bucketful of water just before they grappled together?"

Érémón's face looked boiled and red with anger, but as the bard's words stirred up old memories a shade of doubt entered his eyes. "Yes . . . ," he said, hesitatingly.

The words. The words are the weapon! "Colptha would sacrifice any of us for his own self-interest," Amergin went on. "Must we still be sacrificed to him in this new land? We all want the same things here—good food and safe shelter and a future for our children . . ."

"Our children!" whispered the insidious voice from the dark recesses of Érémón's spirit. "What children is the bard most concerned about? What dark child claims him as father?"

"Go home, Amergin!" Érémón thundered. "We have nothing to say to each other, and I will not hear our dead brother vilified. Nor do I want to discuss *children* with you."

Amergin drove home sadly, down the great broad avenue Érémón had ordered leveled and weeded through the heart of his clanhold. The wealth of the land spread on every side: the fruited trees, the golden thatch, the glossy young heifers suckling their first calves. The dwellings of the clansmen were timbered and limewashed, mild houses for a kind climate; the soft rain kept everything perpetually clean and green. Ierne was meant to be a happy land; yet the Gaels who had won her at such terrible cost were not happy.

The words were the weapon, but they had to be used carefully. If one wrong word fell into Colptha's grasp he could somehow twist it like a knife and turn it to his advantage.

For one flashing moment Amergin wished that death were a permanent condition instead of merely a veil separating

436

states of living, for he felt Colptha reach back through that veil and exult in doing damage.

One of Éremón's men encountered a member of Étan's clan building a fishing weir within the borders of Éremón's share of the island. He came at the gallop to tell of his discovery, and Éremón ordered a honing of weapons and burnishing of war jewelry.

The chief of the north announced, to a wildly shouting and enthusiastic band of his followers, "We will drive Éber Finn and his clans well back from our borders, and then we will nibble away a bit of their land for ourselves, to give us a margin of safety against future depredations. It is plain he is not to be trusted, so we have the right; it is only fair!"

Amergin was appalled. The day he heard the news from one of Éremón's runners he was on his way to visit Sakkar, and he finished the journey beneath dark clouds that had nothing to do with Ierne's misty skies.

Sakkar's snug fortress was built on a thorn-crowned coastal island reached by a ferryboat of the former shipwright's own design. Sakkar had also discovered a Celtic name that sounded vaguely like his Tyrian one and had begun insisting everyone call him Sétga, a further obscuring of his origins. His friends, and they were many, were happy to oblige him.

Sakkar—Sétga—came out to welcome Amergin personally to his holding, and proudly rowed his guest across choppy wavelets, spangled by brief peepings of sunlight. They climbed a path lined with selected pebbles arranged in a purely Celtic design. Gates carved with knotwork were set in the walls of Delginis and the smell of fresh limewash on wall and building was crisp and clean. Sétga's husky redheaded wife came bustling forward, apple-cheeked, proud to offer heated water for washing and hot cakes from her beehive-shaped oven of stone.

Her husband patted her haunch with a proprietary air. "The samodhii say she may be carrying twins," he confided, winking.

"Clarsah and I have not sung a welcoming song to twins in a long time," Amergin said. "I will look forward to such a good omen eagerly. The Mother is generous to you here, my friend."

They sat beside the hearth, for the wind off the sea was enough to chill anyone's toes. Amergin talked of trivial matters, gradually spiraling inward toward the reason for his gray mood. "There is no need for Éremón's followers to go warring against the clans of Éber Finn," he said. "We have everything here; we need not batter each other over every pathway and fishing weir."

Sétga gazed into his wine bowl. "You are probably right," he said. "But Éremón reminds us that warriors need to keep in practice, and this will be little more than an exercise to strengthen our skills. In case the Dananns return."

"The Dananns were never our enemies."

Sétga cocked a beady black eye at the bard. "We fought them, and some of us died."

"Not many. All the loss seemed to be on their side."

"Sometimes I wonder." Sétga looked out through his open door at gulls against blue sky. "When I first came to your house, bard, I thought I could hear the music you made echoing from your walls, even when you were away. Now, sometimes when I least expect it, I hear sounds like the music the Dananns played when coming to battle. And I think they are all still here somewhere."

His wife joined in the conversation. "There is a path that crosses our island, a path we did not make. We believe it is an old Danann roadway, for each time we have tried to put a wall across it to pen in our livestock, the wall just . . . falls down. Or comes apart, no matter how well it was made." She gave a delicious little shudder, more intrigued than afraid.

Sétga returned to the central problem. "Will you go to Éremón and try to discourage him from this plan to attack Éber?"

"I want to more than anything. But Éremón and I look at each other over shields these days; I fear if I said anything to him right now he would do the opposite thing just to hit out at me. I am hobbled, Sétga, until I find a way to get through to him again."

"I will try speaking to him myself," Sétga volunteered, getting to his feet. Standing straight and proud, with no hint of injury to mar his symmetry. "But expect little from it; you know how hard it is to turn him aside from something once he sets his will on it."

As Amergin drove home, he thought of the twins to come and then took a hard look at the surprising sense of ease, of brotherhood, he had felt in the company of the former Tyrian shipwright.

Perhaps *brotherhood* was a word of power!

He took Clarsah from her case and whispered to her, though he no longer believed she held all the magic. "I must find a way to make Éremón feel kinship with his brothers again," he told the harp. "He has to be reminded of the bonds they share and the importance of keeping those links unbroken."

He who had stood outside the bright circle of brotherhood could appreciate it more than most.

But before Amergin could find the necessary phrases an event occurred that put a halt to Éremón's martial plans—for a time. The pipes sang mournfully on the hills, announcing death.

◇ **35** ◇

THE SAMODHII WERE EMBARRASSED because none of their many skills had been able to save her. Éremón was angry and bitter and frustrated, with no enemy to blame and batter. Odba's sons were saddened more than anyone expected, for in the seasons on Ierne they had come to a grudging respect, and then a fondness, for Taya.

Lagnch had been with her at the well, helping her draw up the sweet water she loved. He had been as quiet as he always was in her presence, reluctant to show his growing affection for the kind, softspoken woman, because he did not want to be accused of disloyalty to Odba. But he had been trying to take the weight of the filled wellbucket on himself to spare her, just as Taya reached out to catch hold of it, insisting on doing her share of the labor. Insisting though everyone knew she was still weak from the hard birth, and her eyes were sunken in dark circles.

She reached wrong; turned too sharply; twisted awkwardly—no one would ever know. She gave one short cry and doubled over with her forearms clamped against her belly. Lagneh dropped the bucket and knelt beside Taya as she lay on the ground, staring up at him.

"Something tore . . . . inside me . . . ." she said breathlessly.

He ripped off his speckled mantle and wrapped it around

her before he ran for help. By the time he returned with Éremón and two craftsmen's wives, Taya's eyes were closed and her clammy skin was cold to the touch.

She died almost at once.

Moomneh went to tell Amergin. He delivered his message while shifting uncomfortably from one foot to the other, awkward in grief. As he spoke, Amergin thought he heard a subtle whisper below his words. A voice like Colptha's seemed to suggest, inside the bard's head, "Éremón could have sent for you sooner; you could have been with Taya for the transition. But he delayed summoning you out of spite."

"No!" Amergin cried aloud, startling Moomneh so badly the young man's words dried and withered in his mouth. Amergin turned from side to side, glaring at the walls, the peg-hung cloaks and shadowy carved chests within his house, expecting to find some relict of Colptha lurking there. He would burn his dwelling to the ground before he would offer malice any shelter! he thought furiously.

Moomneh recovered enough to say, "Éremón bids me remind you that the chief bard must sing the eulogy for a chieftain's wife."

The corners of Amergin's lips twitched. "He must hate asking that of me."

Moomneh understood and smiled faintly. "It did seem difficult for him to say the words."

Bound by her request, Taya's people would entomb her on the grassy hill she had loved, close to the deserted halls of the Túatha Dé Danann. Close to the Stone of Fal. Éremón was doubly unhappy at surrendering her body to this reminder of a race that had somehow triumphed in defeat. He had a deep suspicion that the stone had taken her from him in some way. These were feelings he could have discussed with Amergin the druid—if he had not built so many walls between them.

Everyone who had known Taya seemed to have a suggestion for her eulogy. She was washed toward her next life on an outpouring of love, for her sweetness and generosity had been more widely respected than all of Éremón's boastings.

Amergin listened politely to each suggestion and expressed his gratitude. But when he stood beside Taya's tomb the poem he composed for her was his alone—his and hers, the only act of creation they could share. And the power came to him once more.

The rich, resonant voice of the great bard rang out from the hill of Tara and rolled across the plains of Ierne.

Three great beauties had the daughter of Lugaid.
Her soft low speech, her quiet courage, her steadfast
    devotion.
Three great beauties have the Gael.
The love of learning, the voice of the poets, the
    perfection of craftsmen.
Three slender columns support the world.
The thin haft of the hunter's spear, the narrow stream
    of milk into a pail, the fine thread woven by a skilled
    woman.
Three columns likewise support the Gael.
The generosity of the earth, the good will of the spirits,
    the untorn fabric of the tribe.
Three enemies had Éremón's wife.
The pain of thoughtless words, the ache of separation,
    the brutality of vengeance.
Three enemies have the Gael.
Ears closed to wisdom, eyes indifferent to beauty, hands
    raised against brothers!

Amergin finished the astonishing and unconventional eulogy and stood with head bowed. The throng attending the
ritual saw with surprise that at some time the harp had slipped
from his hand and now stood propped against the mounded
tomb-earth. It was not Clarsah's voice that had sung but
Amergin's own, unaided.

The clans that had come to pay homage to Taya had arrived
in separate groups, each family keeping to itself. But they
did not leave that way. The bard's words were like a hand
stirring water, swirling it in unexpected directions and new
patterns. Men who had been rivals found themselves talking
to each other in friendly voices, commenting on the occasion, the grandeur of the tomb, the loss of such a woman.
And on the eulogy, which was less a praise song than a
challenge.

Amergin's phrases were repeated among them. "The untorn
fabric of the tribe." "Hands raised against brothers."

"Has anyone sent word to Lugaid in the south?" Gosten
asked. "If not, I will arrange a party of my clansmen to make
the journey and tell her father of Taya's death. Perhaps take
him a pair of young heifers and some of our harvest."

Soorgeh spoke up. "Some of my men would probably like

to go with them. Women of my clan are married into the clan of Étan, and their brothers might like to see them.''

''I was a foster son to Caicher,'' said another. ''He was always generous to me, and I would like to see him again in this life.''

The tomb stood on the green hill as a symbol of the separation between lives. Amergin's words still seemed to echo in the soft air, reminding people of the deliberate separations men inflict upon themselves, which may yet be repaired.

They had arrived in separate units, but the clans of Éremón's followers went down the slope together like brothers; like one half of a tribe.

When they were gone, only Éremón and Amergin remained beside the tomb.

''Your words have power, bard,'' Éremón admitted.

''Sometimes. Not always.''

''I should be angry with you; you didn't compose the eulogy I expected for my wife.''

''Are you angry?''

''For reminding me of things I sometimes forget? No, Amergin. You spoke of all those matters which are truly important—except, perhaps, the courage of valorous men. It is strange, but . . . listening to you, I was reminded of so many things. Not about Taya, but about Donn and Ír and Éber Finn. Pleasures we shared as boys, dreams we had in common.''

''And the men who went with Éber?'' Amergin prodded gently. ''They were your friends, too. Tribesmen and brothers. You have laughed with all of them, hunted with them, put your shoulder to their chariot wheels when they were mired in mud. They helped build the boats that brought you here, the followers of Éber Finn. Like you, they are quick, brave, passionate. Like Donn, they take great pride in doing a thing as skillfully and perfectly as possible. Like Ír, they are capable of astonishing beauty and grace. Like Éber Finn, they love the land, cherish their women as you cherished yours, enjoy the sight of fine fat cattle.''

''Yes,'' said Éremón slowly, gazing out across the waving grass, watching patches of purple shadow chase one another over flowered meadows.

The two men were silent for a time. Amergin was just waiting, though he did not know for what; Éremón was wrestling with his thoughts.

"You said Taya was devoted," he remarked at last. "Dark-haired young Irial . . ."

"Your son," Amergin said firmly.

"Yes." Éremón frowned a little. "I wonder why I ever thought anything else?"

A mind that follows the curves of poetry sometimes makes unexpected discoveries. "You loved Taya, Amergin," Éremón said, making himself listen to the eulogy again. "But you did not think of her in the same way I did."

"No. She and the shipwright were my dearest friends."

Éremón's blue eyes kindled with tardy understanding. "As Éber and Caicher and Étan were once among mine . . . And I kept the two of you apart. 'The ache of separation,' you called it."

Amergin watched his brother and saw the play of light and shadow over that known, familiar face. "I miss Éber Finn," Éremón said at last.

"Go to him and tell him so."

"He would be suspicious of my motives now."

"You are a courageous warrior, Éremón," the bard said. "There is a new war for you to fight. Win back the unity of the tribe."

"The column that supports the Gael . . ." Éremón mused aloud.

Amergin faced his brother squarely and drilled into him with a level gaze. "I challenge you to try," the bard said.

"I never *try; I do!*"

"Then do this."

There was silence on the green hill again. After a long time, and without a final word, Éremón mounted his chariot and drove slowly away, head bowed in thought, leaving Amergin alone.

Only then did the bard remember his harp. But he did not reach for Clarsah. He left her waiting on the grass while he gazed across Eriu's island at the curious, lambent, shimmering glow his druid vision was always aware of now, permeating the landscape.

The wind was holding its breath. The patches of shadow on distant fields softened and blurred as if with the advance of evening, though the sun was still high in the sky. One of the bard's tethered chariot horses nickered softly, suggesting it might be time to go home and summon a horseboy to rub their hides with straw, to carry fodder for them.

443

Amergin was reluctant to leave Taya's tomb, though he knew she was no longer there. There were things he still wanted to say to her, incomplete or never-begun conversations with a friend that would have to wait until some other life, perhaps.

A friend. He was diminished without her.

More intensely than ever before, Amergin felt the druid desire to move beyond the walls of flesh imprisoning the spirit. He longed to stretch until he filled the world—this world or another, that of the Gaels or the Dananns, it hardly mattered which. Perhaps they were the same after all. He ached to soar free across time and space, to draw sunlight into the pores of his body as . . .

. . . as Shinann appeared to be doing, coming toward him up the slope of Tara.

Children of Light.

There was a twinkling of thinking and a luminescence of laughter and she ran the rest of the way up to him, holding out her hands.

◇ **36** ◇

AGAINST THE PALMS of her hands, she felt the pebbled flesh rise on his shoulders. Amergin groaned once, so deeply the sound resonated in her bones. A slow, massive shudder moved through them, from him to her or from her to him, there was no distinction now. The convulsion of the flesh was an exultation of the spirit; mind and body and soul perfectly blended.

Shinann threw back her head and laughed and Amergin laughed with her, joyous and complete.

She had brought him to a sun-dappled glade beside a cheerful brook. The water bubbled and murmured to itself and birds in the trees sang an accompaniment for it, but Amergin had no desire to translate the sounds into music for Clarsah. The harp in her case was in his chariot, waiting with

444

the tethered horses. The long golden afternoon had surrendered to an opalescent evening, but the passage of time was unimportant. Time was unimportant.

An image filled the bard's mind: time as a river, and you could step into it or out of it on any curve of the bank you chose. He looked at Shinann, who lay beside him with her cheek pillowed on moss, and she nodded.

"Is it really possible?" he asked.

She nodded again.

Riddles would always tempt the druid. "Is that what happened to the rest of your tribe?" he wanted to know. "Did they use some sorcerer's art to escape us?"

No magic, her face reminded him, suddenly serious. Amergin realized he did not want her to be serious; not now. There would be plenty of time in the future for him to revel in the brilliance of her mind, delighted to have a companion who could both learn and teach, who could follow the twists and turns of his own thoughts. But for now he just wanted to see Shinann's dimples twinkle.

The very dignified chief bard of the Gaels, who had new threads of silver in his black hair, propped himself on one elbow and dug a tickling finger into the ribs of the woman who lay cuddled against him.

Shinann chortled and tried to twist away, but he was relentless, grabbing her and searching out her most ticklish places until tears of helpless laughter welled in her eyes and she began to hiccup. Instantly remorseful, Amergin gathered her into his arms and held her tight against his chest until the spasms subsided.

She lay quiet for a time, her head pillowed over the drumbeat of his heart—and then she attacked him with tickling fingers of her own. They rolled together on the ground like merry children, wrestling and laughing and carefree.

But they were not children. The mood turned deep, and rich; Amergin caught Shinann's fine-boned wrist and drew it to his lips, savoring the taste of her skin. Her very human skin, salty and sweet. Slowly, tenderly, he explored the underside of her arm, following the track of blue veins. His warm mouth moved on across her uncovered skin, tonguing the creases in her flesh until she trembled and closed her eyes. This was still teasing, but a different kind of teasing.

Since time did not exist he had all the time in the world, and he took it.

The horses woke them at last. Night had fallen and Amergin's team had tried to be patient and obedient, but they were tired of standing in harness and tired of gnawing the leaves and bark within their tethered reach. They pawed the earth, they tossed their heads and jingled their bits, and when that did no good they began moving back and forth, making the chariot wheels creak. Finally one of the pair whinnied in exasperation, and Amergin sat up, yawning.

In a moment he was feeling the earth beside him—and she was still there, asleep. Her shoulders were cool to his touch, though her light breath was warm on his anxious hand. He wrapped his cloak around her even before he gently shook her awake, and they lay hugged together for a few heartbeats more before Amergin made himself get up.

Shinann was curled into comfort, but when he rose she did not hesitate to join him, though some stiffened muscles protested and she flinched.

The bard understood. His own bones complained; his joints ached from lying for too long on damp ground. He massaged his lower back with the heels of his hands while Shinann stretched warmth back into her chilled limbs.

"Will you come to my house with me?" Amergin asked her formally, although he hardly felt such a question was necessary between them. "I will gladly offer bride gifts to your family. But . . . where do I take them?"

Shinann put her two small hands on his chest and he could see the pale glimmer of her face in the moonlight filtering into their glade. Then his vision seemed to change, and he was not in the glade any longer. Rather, he was *of* the glade; he was looking down on it from a higher perspective, aware of life flowing through arteries, aware of strength and suppleness and scurryings of insect industry beneath bark. Where he had had arms and fingers, he now sensed branches and twigs, and the susurration of leaves. But he was not the tree; he was *of* the tree.

Then his comprehension of place shifted and he was of the brook, cold and earthbanked, endless motion. And again he was of the stones, compressed by the weight of eons into a density beyond imagining, flickering with memories of ancient fires.

Then he was of a hill. Of a lake. Of the island of Ierne in a way so intimate it should have dissolved his own individuality, but did not. He was not melted into the land but was

446

inhabiting it in its specific parts. He was still Amergin, still himself and aware.

And he knew what had happened to the Túatha Dé Danann. They had not been driven out; they had not surrendered one pace of earth. They were all around him in the night, joined with Ierne forever.

The woman sagged against him, exhausted by the effort of letting him see through her eyes, and share through her mind, the triumphant continuance of her people. Amergin quickly sat down on a fallen tree and took Shinann on his lap while he chafed her cold hands. Hugging her, he whispered tender, senseless, meaningful phrases that tumbled out of him unconstructed, words of praise and promise.

Shinann drew a deep breath and he felt her strength returning.

"The Dananns aren't dead; they still hold their sacred island," the bard whispered, marveling.

Yes.

"You could have . . . you could be with them. Be what they are. Why didn't you?"

In his mind an image of his own face appeared, only more finely modeled, wider of brow, nobler of form. Idealized by her devotion. "You stayed behind for *me?*"

Yes.

"But I was so worried about you! I saw Dananns all around me, bleeding. Dying, I thought. And I couldn't find you. I was desperate, afraid you were dead and lost to me . . ."

She bowed her head in contrition. But her eyes sparkled with the mischief of a child who has played a small joke; just a little prank, hiding behind a tree while everyone searched and worried.

"So you were there all along," Amergin mused, wanting to be angry with her but unable to do so. She was alive and she was Shinann; what else mattered? "Yet I didn't see you until I put my harp aside . . ."

Shinann slipped from his lap and ran to fetch Clarsah in her gilded satchel. She placed the instrument in the bard's hands with a respectful gesture, and indicated she hoped he would play the harp often.

She was too wise a woman to earn the enmity of Clarsah by excluding her.

But there were still questions to be asked. "Are you the only one of the Dananns left alive?" Amergin wanted to know. Then he saw the merry crinkle at the corner of Shinann's eyes and realized his mistake. *All* of the Túatha Dé Danann were alive.

Shinann explained, however, that a few of her people had been unable to accept the Unbodying and were still in hiding, as she had been. Amergin understood. Some of the Gaelicians had gotten out of the boats at the last moment and huddled on shore, waving farewell instead.

He felt the pang of a new concern. If Éremón knew of the other Dananns he would not rest until he had hunted every one of them down with his sword. And he would never accept Shinann; he would never forgive her for the sweet surrender and total conquest her people had denied him.

"I can't take you into my brother's clanholding," Amergin told her. "And as a druid I have no land of my own to offer you."

Laughing, Shinann flung her arms wide.

Amergin laughed too. How easily it came! "Of course, I see. You and I have all of Ierne, don't we? And if I can't take you with me then I will go with you, wherever it is you go."

She put one small hand on his chest and asked a question.

"I won't regret leaving my tribe now," he said, reassuring her. "Éremón is willing to wage peace with Éber; I can leave him to it and have a life of my own. I am only needed for . . ."

The epic poem of his race. Shinann glimpsed its winged form in his mind and addressed it, looking earnestly into his face until the bard's eyes blazed.

"You will help me!" he rejoiced, grabbing her and hugging her. "All that *has* been, has led us here. And all that is here *must* lead us on. You know Ierne's secrets, Shinann, and you understand the flow of life that is the heart of poetry. Tell me. Show me. With your help I can someday tell my people the entire truth of themselves as a bard is meant to do. When the song is complete we will sing it together, Shinann; you and I, and the voice of the Gael will also be the voice of the Túatha Dé Danann. And of the rocks and the rivers and the piled banks of cloud and the silver twilight . . ."

He was being fanciful and he knew it, but the lines of reality had become very blurred. He rocked back and forth with joy and Shinann shimmered in his arms. If they were living a dream or dreaming a life, it was all the same.

* * *

Some nights later, Amergin's horseboy came to Éremón's stronghold. "The bard has not returned his team for my care since he drove them to Taya's entombment," the lad reported. "I am beginning to worry."

When Éremón reached Amergin's house he saw the empty chariot shed and the open gate of the horse pen. The earth of Ierne was soft and easily rutted, and chariot tracks were easier to read than the ogham croabh. These ruts were days old.

Advancing cautiously, with his hand on his sword hilt, Éremón approached the bard's dwelling and eased the door open. Behind him he could hear the horseboy's breathing as the young man tiptoed on his shadow. "Wait out here," he said. "And be watchful."

Éremón went inside. As soon as his eyes adjusted to the dusky light he saw that the house was empty but not untenanted. The bard's belongings hung from pegs and were folded into carved chests, awaiting him. His new collection of domestic fowl had grown hungry and ripped open a sack of grain to feed themselves, and the large bowl of water he kept for them was empty. Éremón filled it, seriously worried now. He could not imagine anything compelling enough to make Amergin forget his responsibilities in such a way. Unless . . .

Unless he had never returned from Tara. Amergin had been the last to leave; it was possible that Fir Bolg, or even Dananns, had waylaid one man alone and taken their revenge on him. It was not only possible, but the more Éremón thought about it, the more likely it seemed.

And just when they had repaired their differences and grown close again! This additional loss was too much to bear. With a groan of anguish the warrior sank onto Amergin's hearth and squatted among cold ashes, pounding one fist against the unyielding floor.

He sent out search parties, leading the largest himself. They scoured the land but could no more find Amergin than they had been able to find the Túatha Dé Danann. In his fury, Éremón put a torch to every Fir Bolg settlement they came across.

And then he heard the whispers behind his back. "Éremón and Amergin were quarreling," one warrior said to another. "Is it possible Éremón has killed his brother and does all this to mislead us?"

Éremón was enraged that such a suspicion could draw breath. He roared denials and saw that some of his men believed him—and others looked at him carefully, out of the corners of their eyes, alerted by his vehement denials to possibilities they might not have considered otherwise.

The seasons changed, and Amergin did not return. Words seemed to travel faster than horses, and ugly rumors reached Éber Finn in the south. He sent a messenger at the gallop to inquire after Amergin, and the man's questions to Éremón were so pointed, so obviously suspicious, that the warrior's temper flared anew.

"How could my own brother believe such a thing of me?" he cried, pain piled upon pain and unforgivable.

There was, as always, much work to be done. The season of leaf-fall brought a spate of flooding, with brooks becoming rivers and springs bursting from their bounds to form lakes where none had been before. Cattle strayed, people fell ill and died or recovered, a hunter was savaged by a wild boar, a child was lost and never returned from darkling woodlands ("The Dananns took it," the old women said), an ice-storm silvered the east coast and chilled Éremón's clanholdings.

An uneasy peace held between Éber Finn and his brother. Ierne was theirs together, and together they ruled her, while trying to build up a sufficient band of followers to be certain of holding the island. With great reluctance both men acceded to intermarriages between Gaelic men and native women, though the day came when Éber Finn complained to Caicher, "Éremón is claiming a larger population for his share of the land than I have." And Éremón grumbled to Gosten, "Éber Finn is letting warriors marry anyone, no matter how low the rank, and is accepting Fir Bolg celsine into his hall."

Amid the subtle shiftings of power, however, the words of the bard were remembered by all who had heard them, and eagerly repeated for those who had not. They were a signpost he had left behind, guiding the way the Gaels must go together in this new land. The love of learning, the voice of the poets, and the perfection of craftsmen were to be revered; the hunter, the herder, and the woman were to have their places of honor; the earth and the spirits were to be wooed and won. And the fabric of the tribe must be held intact.

And then it became obvious to Éremón that the scales had been badly tipped in his brother's favor.

From three ranges of hills in Éber Finn's territory, celsine were bringing out gold and copper in spectacular quantities. Éber Finn could not help flaunting it. He made more than one call on his brother, just for the satisfaction of allowing those who had chosen Éremón's side to see what riches they had cost themselves. Bronze gleamed and clanked; gold glittered. The Fir Bolg who mined the ores had believed themselves to be craftsmen, but they were no match for the Gaelic artisans who forged new tools and weapons and implements in dazzling variety, and decked themselves in so much red gold that even children wore finger rings of the precious metal.

Éremón was infuriated. He had numerous pent-up angers dating back to the frustrating disappearance of the Túatha Dé Danann. Now that Amergin had disappeared as well, in his mind he somehow lumped the two together and found it convenient to blame the absent bard for many things—including the obviously unfair division of land that had given Éber Finn three great ridges of copper and streambeds glittering with nuggets of gold.

He demanded that the region be shared. Éber Finn laughed at him.

Éremón returned to his stronghold and sulked, but not for long. His weapons waited in the shadows and he felt their strength, needing to be used. As his own warrior's skills needed to be used before the passage of seasons rendered them ineffective at last, and he went as Milesios had gone before him.

Sétga came to him, speaking against war. "There is no need to march on your brother," the swarthy little man insisted. "If the two of you will just sit down together and listen to each other . . ."

"You sound like Amergin," Éremón interrupted. "And where is he, now that we need him? Captured or dead, he has abandoned me. Like Scotta, and Odba. Taya, Donn, Ír . . . Colptha . . ." He brooded over his losses, which seemed in his anger to be deliberate defections. He was being left alone while Éber Finn claimed everything worth having. Éber Finn was said to have five wives, all fair and fertile. Or was it six, now?

While Éremón's two fine houses sat wifeless.

There should be women in those houses and gold around the necks of those women, to show that their man was a great chieftain.

Éber Finn had the gold.

The shadows whispered to Éremón and he dismissed Sétga, unwilling to listen to his arguments.

In leaf-spring-out an army marched from Éremón's clanholdings, bound on claiming what they believed to be their fair share. Sétga marched with them, for he was one of them now; but when he thought of warring on other Gaels he got a bitter taste in his mouth and a hollow feeling in his stomach.

The hot blaze of a fine fighting fury scorched across Ierne again, and the cottagers huddled in their homes, letting it burn past them.

Éber Finn was outraged. "Éremón is using some flimsy excuse to try to steal my land!" he cried to his followers. "The division was correct at the time; he was given the part he wanted and he did not complain about it then. He cannot change his mind now!"

He raised his own army of kin and celsine and marched out to meet Éremón. The two brothers came together at a place to be remembered afterward as the Hill of the Oxen. Éber Finn had brought additional oxcarts filled with newly forged weapons in an effort to intimidate his brother, and the beasts waited stolidly with their drivers on a low rise of land, clear of the mud, which could bog them down. Their blank brown eyes watched the battle without comprehension; its outcome would make no difference in the pattern of their lives.

The two halves of the tribe came together with a great shout of anger and a clanging of metal. There was no sport now, no contest to be won or lost, no trinket to be rechallenged for the next day. Éremón and Éber Finn were both deadly serious, and as they advanced toward one another on the battlefield each man had the same thought: I always knew it would come to this, between us. It was as if some third party stood off to the side and told them this, assuring them that their battle was the fulfillment of an irrevocable destiny.

They screamed with rage and flaunted their iron weapons; they paraded their gold and bronze beauty; they slashed their whips and raced their chariots and flung the essence of their lives into the very teeth of death, defying the darkness.

And the green mounds that dotted the earth of Ierne watched them silently, waiting to entomb the loser.

The sounds of battle form a martial music that, once heard, is never forgotten. The wind caught this music and carried it across Ierne until its last dying echoes reached a distant and secluded woodland, where a cottage stood at the edge of a

452

grassy glade. The cottage was a simple dwelling, little more than wickerwork walls and a thatched roof, but there were touches of beauty about the place. Some creative hand had carved the door lintel, a heavy wooden one better suited to a stone construction. A flowering vine had been trained up one corner of the cottage, and stones had been arranged in an artistic pattern to serve as a well-curb for a tiny bubbling spring just a step beyond the doorway.

A man was working outside, taking advantage of the brief sunlight between spring showers. He was tall and lanky, with the sinewy fingers of an artisan, and he enjoyed the homely task of repairing a damaged copper cooking pot. He was stripped to the waist and covered only by a brief kilt like a battle apron, its wool woven into a pattern that had no importance to him now. He might have been any tough but graying cottager, had it not been for the splendor of the gilded harp that leaned beside his cottage door.

The wind touched the harp. She responded with a faint hum, recognizing the old familiar music.

Amergin straightened abruptly. "What was that?" he asked aloud.

A face peered around the cottage doorway. A small and saucy face with a pointed chin and improbably large eyes. She glanced toward Amergin and then looked down at the harp with grave respect; even the most confident woman must never underestimate a rival.

The twinkle in Shinann's eyes died. She went swiftly to Amergin and answered his question, letting him feel from a great distance those last echoes of anger and pain. From among the many interwoven threads of lives on a faraway battlefield she sought to extract the ones of most importance to the bard.

But it was not necessary; his druid awareness told him. "War," he said somberly. "Éremón and Éber Finn attack each other; I know it. I must go to them, Shinann; perhaps there is still time for me to intervene . . ."

He reached out and smoothed back the rebel lock of hair tumbling across her eyes. They smiled at each other in a privacy no war could enter.

Shinann slid her hand across her breasts and down to her rounded belly, where life kindled.

Amergin nodded. "I'll come back. I give my word."

He raised his head and listened intently, thinking he heard

the faintest cry of a battle trumpet. His heart began to race, for what heart would not respond with a leap to that summons?

Realization struck him.

Colptha had not been the only danger to his people. Amergin remembered exulting in the pageantry of the warriors and longing for the breathless excitement of their brotherhood; their momentary and deathless glory. Battle was the forge of heroes, and what Celt would not lust to be one of the heroes?

The bard's blue eyes darkened with the remembered future. "We hear the voice of the trumpet too readily," he told her. "It can even outcall the harp."

He put Clarsah in her leather satchel and harnessed his chariot team. They had been idle too long; they resented the bridle and clenched their jaws to resist the bit.

Amergin struggled with breastplates and cruppers, feeling time to be too terribly real again, caught up in it and helpless to move faster, though he tried. By the time he had driven across hills and fields the battle was over and the druid measurers had come to count the dead.

Trampled and bloodied was the soft earth, and the wind moaned above it. From the distant hills came an eerie shriek too chilling to be human, too tormented to be forgotten; mourning dead men and dead dreams. The survivors who heard it paled and clutched their weapons, with a terrible foreboding that they would hear that cry again. On other days, on other battlefields.

Éber Finn lay on his shield, sightless eyes staring at the soft gray sky.

His men, battered and beaten, were too exhausted to do more than gape at the unexpected appearance of the chief bard driving into their midst. Amergin leaped from his chariot and ran to stand beside his dead brother.

"They have taken all his jewelry from him," the bard murmured, agonized. In all their adult seasons he had never seen Éber Finn without an excess of ornaments. "Who did this?"

"Éremón, with his own hand," someone told him.

Amergin clutched the harp in cold fingers. His voice sounded rusty in his ears as he sang Éber Finn's eulogy. And then he crossed the battlefield and walked with heavy heart among the dead from the other side, mourning friends he would never see again. Gosten, bashed and bloodied. Courageous Soorgeh.

And a small dark man lying face down in the mud.

454

Amergin crouched quickly and turned the body over. He wiped the brown soil from features that were, in death, as Gaelic as any others, and pressed his lips in farewell to the forehead of Sétga the warrior, late of Tyre.

Men crowded around him, asking questions, anxious to know where he had been and what had happened to him. He had not been assaulted by so many spoken words in a long time, and he found the necessity of formulating spoken answers tiresome.

He asked his own question again and again until he got an answer. "Where has Éremón gone?"

Finally Legneh—a boy hardened into a man, with all the softness burned away—said, "He has already driven east toward his stronghold. He took the death of his brother hard."

"He killed him," Amergin said through tight lips.

"He did not want to."

Amergin was shaken with rage. "There is always a choice!" he told his nephew. "In the very moment before the spear is hurled or the sword is swung, there is always a choice."

The harp descending on Colptha's head . . .

The bard's horses were fat and out of condition, but he forced them to their fastest pace and kept them there as long as he could. He slept at night beside his chariot wheels, his empty belly growling because he had no appetite to feed it, and at dawn he was up and harnessing the horses again, driven by fury.

He stalked into Éremón's hall. His brother and a few of the surviving chieftains were already there, but the atmosphere of the place was not as joyous as might be expected after a victory. In the Heroes' Hall of Éremón, few men felt like heroes that day. Their conversation was subdued, embarrassed, and they were drinking too much and too fast.

Éremón sat slumped on his bench—his carved, bronze-sheathed bench. His face had grown florid and heavy, the skin sagging downward toward eventual reclamation by the Earth Mother. His weapons, with the dried blood still on them, lay scattered around his feet like picked bones.

"You aren't dead after all," was his greeting to Amergin. His voice was a hoarse croaking, both apathetic and bitter.

Amergin reached him in three great strides. "What have you done?"

Éremón looked at him and blinked. "Won."

"You've won nothing! You've killed your own brother and a host of others besides, good men Ierne could ill afford to lose."

"If you're talking about your friend Sétga, I can tell you he went as bravely into battle as any of us and died a happy man, having killed many of the enemy . . ."

For once it was the bard who interrupted. "The *enemy!* You have no enemy until you make one. That is the ugliest and most unworthy of all man's creations, built from the angers and suspicions in his own mind.

"And do you really believe Sétga was happy to kill men he had come to feel kinship with? You have never reined yourself in long enough to talk *with* another person and get to know their inner spirit, Éremón. Odba would have lived, if you had understood her. She chose to die of her wounds because you neglected her!" Amergin flung the words in his brother's face and took pleasure in seeing the pain of their impact.

"Will you accuse me of killing Taya, too?" the warrior gasped.

"She did not live quite long enough for you to kill her by abandoning her for the next woman to catch your eye," Amergin retorted, giving in to cruelty to ease his own grief. Even the gentlest person may possess a sharp blade; it is the Law.

"I wouldn't have done that to Taya!"

"She thought you would. And so did I. But none of us ever imagined you could slaughter Éber Finn! That is almost beyond belief, Éremón."

"I'm not the only one who killed a brother!" Éremón shouted back at him. When he first saw Amergin he had been glad, but that warmth had vanished as soon as the bard spoke. Now all Éremón felt was anger. This was yet another turning against him by someone who did not understand.

Éremón's weapon hit its mark, and Amergin's shoulders sagged. "Yes, I sent Colptha to his death," the bard said in a low voice. "So the sons of Milesios have twice-cursed their descendants. But it can stop now, Éremón. *Here.* Hold out the hand of peace to Éber Finn's followers and mourn your dead together. Give your word that such a thing will not happen again. Your word . . ."

"I am not a man of words," Éremón said, letting one hand drop so its fingers brushed the blood-encrusted sword beside him.

456

"You've always prided yourself on your honor."

"I'm still honorable. I have been generous and fair, which is more than you can say for Éber Finn. The eldest son of Ír fought on my side and I've given him all the northernmost portion of Ierne, as a tribute to Ír. Éber Finn's portion I will give freely to his sons. Donn left no sons, nor did Colptha. And as for you, Amergin—if a young man of your family stood before me this day I would give him a portion of Ierne, too, to hold in the name of the Milesian line."

"You have no right to carve up this island with your bloody sword," Amergin replied. His voice was no more than a whisper of fury, but it filled the hall. "I tell you this, Éremón: the poets I sire will never stand with hands outstretched for your favors. Even if I don't succeed in doing it in this lifetime, they will eventually find the words to turn you and your kind aside from the warrior road. My children will celebrate life instead of death, and one day all Ierne will be theirs.

"Bard land. *Bard land!*"

The magnificent voice rose to one last crescendo of power, then Amergin whirled around and strode from the hall. Éremón's men fell back to let him pass. Their leader sprang to his feet and shouted, "Where are you going, Amergin? Where have you been? I demand an answer, I am chieftain here!"

But Amergin never looked back.

They heard him call a greeting to his horses; they heard the team nicker a reply. Then Éremón's men were crowding around their leader, assaulting him with questions he could not answer. "What was that about?" "Is the bard coming back?" "Have you brought a curse upon us?"

"If we've lost the chief bard, we are truly cursed," someone murmured fearfully.

Moomneh spoke up then, trying to sound confident for Éremón's sake. "Amergin will never desert the Gaels," he assured them as his father stared with bleak eyes toward the empty doorway. "The bard's gift and his harp are ours. Besides, he has yet to give us the epic history he promised!"

Like cattle released from a pen, the warriors stampeded toward the doorway then, pushing and shoving. But they were too late. By the time they got outside Amergin was already gone.

The singing wheels of his chariot had whirled him away down a road Éremón could never find, and Clarsah rode the bard's shoulder.

Éremón left the Heroes' Hall. The watching eyes of his men made him uncomfortable. It was as if they expected something of him and he no longer knew what to give them. He went to the house he had built for Taya, now occupied only by young Irial and his attendants. Entering unannounced, Éremón pulled the door closed behind him and dropped the bar with a heavy thud. He went to the hearth and blew on its coals with a leather bellows until the fire blazed up, but its flames did not seem to warm him.

Irial toddled toward him, followed by his nurse, a herder's buxom wife who had raised many children. "Why are you here?" she wanted to know. "The sun has not set and there's no meal ready."

Éremón rubbed his hands together and held them closer to the heatless blaze.

"Are you all right?" the woman asked nervously. "Why did you bar the door?"

"There is a wind rising," Éremón told her. She listened but heard no wind.

Little Irial tugged at the sword in his father's belt, gurgling with approval. His fat baby hands stroked the cold iron.

The warrior looked down at him. "There is a wind rising," Éremón repeated in a hoarse whisper. "And I dread the fading of the light."

AUTHOR'S NOTE

Robert Graves said in *The White Goddess*, "English poetic education should, really, begin not with *The Canterbury Tales*, not with the *Odyssey*, not even with *Genesis*, but with the *Song of Amergin*." The poetry of Amergin, the great bard of the Gaels in the pre-Christian era, has survived in various versions and translations to the present time, making Amergin the oldest known western European poet. The first two bardic chants in this novel are the author's versions of compositions attributed to Amergin. The third, Taya's eulogy, is my own interpretation of a traditional theme.

Recorded history and archaeological evidence combine to provide a detailed picture of the Phoenician civilization of two and a half thousand years ago. Age-Nor, from the city of Tyre in what is now Lebanon, is referred to in mythology as the father of Europa, who gave her name to an entire continent. As described in *Bard*, Age-Nor and his contemporaries are fictional characters, though representative of their people and their era in the Mediterranean. The voyages of Hanno and Himilco are historic fact, however; monumental voyages of discovery.

For Amergin's tribe, the Celts I call Gaelicians, I have taken a linguistic liberty in order to show their progression from Gaul—now France—to the northwestern corner of the Iberian peninsula, an area of Spain still referred to as Galicia. The Gauls are classically called Galli, and the tribe that settled in Spain is known as the Gallaeci. It is this tribe that is shown as becoming the Gaels of Ierne—Ireland.

By referring to Amergin's tribe as Gaelicians, I have short-cut the difficulties that would have been encountered otherwise and would have made *Bard* more complicated for nonscholars of philology. There are a number of problems

459

involved with the terms *Galli, Gallaeci,* and *Gael;* the most important perhaps being that *Gael* comes from the Old Irish *Goidel* and is a version of the Welsh name for the Irish, *Gwyddel. Gall,* deriving from "a Gaul," means "foreigner" in Gaelic and is the Breton name for the French.

Actually, all these names are applicable to one people, a branch of the Celtic race that dominated Europe before the Roman Empire, eventually developing specific cultural and language differences and becoming known as the Irish, the Welsh, the Scots, the Manx, and the Bretons, while leaving haunting traces of their culture in such nations as Spain and France and Austria.

Anthropologists now believe that successive waves of Celtic peoples reached the British Isles; the Gaels were but the latest in a long line of invaders. Some think the Gaels came directly from mainland Europe, while others accept the possibility embodied in the ancient Irish legends that say the Gaels—the "Milesians"—came by way of Spain. To tell Amergin's story I have chosen to use these legends, because what we call myth or folklore often contains the seeds of historical truth. An archaeological miracle occurred in the last century, for example, when Dr. Heinrich Schliemann refused to accept Homer's epics as figments of the poet's imagination and used them as maps, which led to the eventual discovery of the actual ruins of Troy.

The tremendous detail of the oldest Irish legends, in which name after name and deed after deed are reported with an exhaustive thoroughness, indicates a mighty effort to fix historical fact firmly in the memory of a people who kept all their records through oral tradition—and decreed a curse on any man who would attempt to alter the truth.

The structure of this novel is built upon the Irish historical-mythological cycle known as the *Lebor Gabála Érenn* (The Book of the Conquests of Ireland). Taken from bardic histories dating to long before the Christian Era, this work was once believed to be totally mythological, but recent discoveries have indicated it may be rooted, at least to some extent, in truth; a people's re-telling of its past.

By comparing the invasion legends with maps, sea charts, and the work of the great Greek geographers, it can be seen that the story of the Milesians is not only possible but plausible. The Phoenicians had indeed reached the British Isles, establishing a lucrative trade route, and from them the inhabitants of Galicia may well have learned to build ships capable of such a voyage. They had adequate reason, for this was the era when the tin mines of the Iberian peninsula are known to have become depleted.

Only when the Gaels reach the shores of Ierne does straightforward, if speculative, history become charged with the shimmer of magic. For it is impossible to tell of ancient Ireland without telling of the Túatha Dé Danann. They are forever interwoven into the fabric of the land and its people.

Who has not heard of the fairies of Erin, the little people, the ban shee? Some scholars claim they were no more than a pantheon of pagan deities, symbols without substance. Others believe the Dananns represent one of the pre-Gaelic Celtic tribes that invaded Ireland, and I subscribe to this latter view. But no one has been able to account for the powerful grip they have held on Irish art and imagination for over two millennia.

From a variety of sources, both ancient and modern, I formed the hypothesis presented in *Bard*. Like the Dananns themselves, it is filled with mystery, yet there is little in it that is inexplicable in the light of modern scientific knowledge— except the most puzzling mystery of all: what happened to them? This may be the wildest fantasy, and yet . . . every day, science is discovering that the ancient world was more highly developed than we guessed, and that civilization may reach farther backward than we know.

The Celts and the Phoenicians are firmly anchored in time and space and reality. As for the Túatha Dé Danann—make of them what you will.

A SELECTED BIBLIOGRAPHY

Annals of the Four Masters. Dublin: Hodges, Smith & Co., 1854.

Banbury, Philip. *Man and the Sea*. London: Adlard Coles, Ltd., 1975.

Binchy, D. S. *Early Irish Society*. Dublin, 1954.

Bowen, E. G. *Britain and the Western Seaways*. London: Thames & Hudson, 1972.

Carpenter, Rhys. *Beyond the Pillars of Hercules*. New York: Delacorte, 1966.

Casson, L. *Ships and Seamanship in the Ancient World*. Princeton: Princeton University Press, 1971.

Celtic Miscellany, A. New York: Penguin Classics, 1977.

Celts, The. Alexandria, Va.: Time-Life Books, 1974.

Chadwick, Nora. *The Celts*. Gretna, La.: Pelican, 1977.

Collins, Desmond. *Origins of Europe*. New York: Thomas Y. Crowell, 1976.

Cunliffe, Barry. *The Celtic World*. New York: McGraw-Hill, 1979.

Dillon, Myles. *Irish Saga*. Dublin: Mercier, n.d.

————and Nora Chadwick. *The Celtic Realms*. New York: New American Library, 1967.

Dottin, Georges. *The Celts*. Geneva, Switzerland: Minerva Press, 1977.

Driscoll, Robert. *The Celtic Consciousness*. New York: George Braziller, 1981.

Graves, Robert. *The White Goddess*. New York: Farrar, Strauss, & Giroux, 1968.

Greenhill, Basil. *Archaeology of the Boat*. Middletown, Ct.: Wesleyan University Press, 1976.

Hapgood, Charles. *Maps of the Ancient Sea Kings*. Radnor, Pa.: Chilton, 1966.

Harden, Donald. *The Phoenicians*. New York: Praeger, 1962.

Hawkes, Jacquetta. *Atlas of Early Man*. New York: St Martin's, 1976.

Herm, Gerhard. *The Celts*. New York: St. Martin's, 1976.
———. *The Phoenicians*. New York: Morrow, 1975.
Herrmann, Paul. *Conquest by Man*. New York: Harper & Row, 1954.
Herodotus: The Histories. New York: Penguin Classics, 1978.
Hubert, Henri. *Greatness and Decline of the Celts*. New York: Arno, 1980.
Joyce, P. W. *History of Gaelic Ireland*. Dublin: Educational Co. of Ireland, Ltd., 1924.
———. *Social History of Ancient Ireland*. New York and London: Benjamin Blom, 1968.
Keating, Geoffrey. *History of Ireland*. Kansas City, Mo.: Irish Genealogical Foundation, 1857.
Laing, Lloyd. *Celtic Britain*. New York: Scribner's, 1979.
Lebor Gabála Érenn. Dublin: The Irish Texts Society, 1956.
Livermore, Harold, *History of Spain*. New York: Minerva, 1968.
Macalister, R. A. S. *Archaeology of Ireland*. New York: Benjamin Blom, 1972.
———. *Tara*. New York: Scribner's, 1931.
MacCana, Proinsias, *Celtic Mythology*. London: Hamlyn, 1970.
Maclean, L. *History of the Celtic Language*. Edinburgh; Dugald Moore, 1840.
MacNeill, Eoin. *Celtic Ireland* Dublin: Martin Lester, 1921.
Markale, Jean. *Celtic Civilization*. London: Gordon & Cremonesi, 1978.
Moore, Mabel. *Carthage of the Phoenicians*. New York: Dutton, 1905.
Moscati, Sabatino. *The World of the Phoenicians*. London: Weidenfeld, 1968.
Neeson, Eoin. *First Book of Irish Myths and Legends*. Dublin: Mercier, n.d.
O'Rahilly, T. F. *Early Irish History and Mythology*. Dublin: Dublin Institute for Advanced Studies, 1946.
O'Riordain, Sean P. *Tara*. Dundalk, Ireland: Dundalgan Press, 1979.
Piggott, Stuart. *Ancient Europe*. New York: Aldine, 1966.
———. *The Druids*. Gretna, La.: Pelican, 1978.
Powell, T. G. E. *The Celts*. London: Thames & Hudson, 1980.
Power, Patrick. *Sex and Marriage in Ancient Ireland*. Dublin: Mercier, 1976.
Raftery, Joseph. *The Celts*. Dublin: Mercier, 1978.

————. *Prehistoric Ireland*. London: B. T. Batsford, Ltd., 1951.

Rees, Alwyn, and Brinley Rees. *Celtic Heritage*. London: Thames & Hudson, 1961.

Renfrew, Colin. *Before Civilization*. New York: Knopf, 1975.

Ross, Anne. *Pagan Celtic Britain*. London: Routledge & Kegan Paul, 1967.

Sanders, N. K. *The Sea Peoples*. London: Thames & Hudson, 1978.

Sharkey, John. *Celtic Mysteries: The Ancient Religion*. London: Thames & Hudson, 1975.

Sjoestedt, Marie-Louise. *Gods and Heroes of the Celts*. Berkeley, Calif.: Netzahualcoyotl Historical Society, 1982.

Spanuth, Jürgen. *Atlantis of the North*. New York: Van Nostrand, 1980.

Trump, D. H. *Prehistory of the Mediterranean*. New Haven: Yale University Press, 1980.

THE SNOWBLIND MOON
JOHN BYRNE COOKE

"An epic canvas created with sure, masterful strokes. Bravo!"
—John Jakes

"*The Snowblind Moon* is an intensely readable story."
—The Washington Post

"An epic tale . . . lyrically beautiful."
—Los Angeles Times Book Review

HERALDING.....

Avalon to Camelot, a widely praised and handsomely produced illustrated quarterly magazine. Prominent writers and scholars explore the Arthurian legend from the Dark Ages to the present in features and columns including the arts, literature, the quest for the historical Arthur and more. Articles, news, reviews.

- Illustrated quarterly
- 48 pages
- 8½"x 11"
- Ideal gift, card enclosed.

Arthur and Merlin have been my solace on more than one miserable night, and guests through countless dreams. I'll keep subscribing year-to-year and would like to order back issues.

Russell J. Davis   *Rochester, New York*

I am always impressed with how beautiful the A to C issues are. This requires a lot of doing—attention to detail and plenty of professional know-how, which you certainly seem to have.

Isadore Lichstein   *Former editor,* Philadelphia Bulletin World Almanac

You have hit on something here that I can only wish would have existed during my years as an English student and "Arthurian buff." *Finally* a publication I can read "cover to cover."

Tim Fabrizio   *Capistrano Beach, California*